OTHER BO

AN AMERICAN FAMILY IN JAPAN SERIES:
GAIJIN! GAIJIN! FOREIGNER! FOREIGNER!
MoIchido, Once More
Suteindo Garasu: Stained Glass

What Others said about the American Family in Japan Series which was published from 1985-1990:

"A must read for anybody interested in Japanese culture; I couldn't put this book down and finished it in just a few days. It follows an American family who moves to a small Japanese city and teaches English at a local public school. While the writing style is not extraordinary, the palpable daily life experiences of the family are priceless glimpses into one of the most unique cultures on the planet.

I liken the book to reality television - while the production values are not as high as on a show with professional actors, the shows featuring real life people are much more intriguing as they deal with issues apropos to the human experience. As someone who appreciates every last detail about the smallest banalties of foreign culture, I appreciated the care that the author took to record each encounter. The book was written in the early 1980s, and it is quite possible that Japan has changed considerably since.

Nonetheless, it still remains a valuable education about the origins and history of Japanese culture. ***Preston Hunt, Portland, 9/30/02***

In March of 2007 I visited Japan for the first time since I lived there for two years almost twenty years ago. In preparation for the trip I read a number of books. Rather than create a page for each, I will just write a mini-review of some of them on this page.

I very much enjoyed ***Gaijin! Gaijin!*** and the follow up ***Mo Ichido.*** Kenneth Fenter is a good observer and describer of Japan, the Japanese people, and Japanese culture. He can tell a good, detailed story. Anyone who has lived in Japan should enjoy these books. Those going to live in Japan will have much to learn from them before going. In ***Suteindo Grasu, Stained Glass: An American Family in Japan,*** Fenter finishes the story of his adventures in Japan. The book is different than the first two but will still be enjoyed if you read and liked the first two. It will also be of interest, on a stand-alone basis, to those who haven't read the first two if they are planning on doing business in Japan or if they have an interest in Stained Glass. ***2thinkForums (www.2think.org)***

"Dear Ken, I feel I can call you "Ken" since you are near and dear to my heart after reading "Gaijin.." I'm in Japan on a Mombusho post-doctoral fellowship....your story was just what I needed during my Christmas bout with homesickness! I go next to the island of Shikoku and will be somewhat isolated from an inernational community. Your book helped immensely in psychologically preparing for that experience. Marty Turner, Osaka, Japan

For Availability of these books contact:
Arborwood Press
arborwoodpress@aol.com
arborwoodpress.com

The Ruin

A boy's quest to rebuild his self worth
by seeking refuge in the wilderness

By Kenneth Fenter

Author of An American Family in Japan Series

Arborwood Press

Excerpt: Chapter 10 based on "The Night the Vultures Came" by Darrel Fenter from the book Summit Ridge, ©2005, Arborwood Press
Description of Summit Ridge: Chapter 4 based on "Once Upon a Time" by Darrel Fenter from the book Summit Ridge, ©2005 Arborwood Press

The
Ruin
By Kenneth Fenter
ISBN: 978-0-930693-03-09

Library of Congress Control Number: 2010901063

Published by Arborwood Press
1937 SE Arborwood Ave.
Bend, Oregon 97702

Dedication

To my parents Earl and Jewell Fenter who settled on that little half square mile of archaeological and geological paradise called Summit Ridge Colorado. To Darrel, Mark, Betty, and Eva who grew up with me on it.

To my wife Lora, son Phil and daughter Janelle who encouraged me with the project.

Kenneth Fenter

Cast of Characters

East Lake View Grade School at the end of the School year 1954
Grades 1-8, one room
Mrs. Campbell, teacher from 1952-1954
Mr. Johnson, teacher from before 1946 to 1952

Christina Ortega, 7	*First grade*	Miguel's sister
Pitina Rodriguez, 7	*First grade*	Hector's sister
Alicia Guzman, 7	*First grade*	Katia's sister
Cesar Rodriguez, 8	*Second grade*	Hector's brother
Miguel Ortega, 9	*Second grade*	Christina and Porferio's brother
Maria Rodriguez, 9	*Third grade*	Hector's sister
Cecilia Ramirez, 9	*Third grade*	Adolph's sister
Ester Chavez, 9	*Third grade*	Ignacio's sister
Margaret Florez, 9	*Third grade*	Gabriela's sister
Carlos Hernandez, 10	*Fourth grade*	Ana's brother
Carmen Munoz, 10	*Fourth grade*	Felix's sister
Katia Guzman, 10	*Fourth grade*	Alicia's sister
Margaret Rodriguez, 10	*Fourth grade*	Hector's sister
Adolph Ramiriz, 11	*Fifth grade*	Cecilia's brother
Gabriela Florez, 11	*Fifth grade*	Margaret's sister
Hermano Rodriguez, 11	*Fifth grade*	Hector's brother
Felix Munoz, 12	*Sixth grade*	Carmen's brother
Ignacio Chavez, 12	*Sixth grade*	Ester's brother
Ana Hernandez, 13	*Seventh grade*	Carlos' sister
Porferio Ortega, 13	*Seventh grade*	Christina and Miguel's brother
Emilio Rodriguez, 13	*Seventh grade*	Uncle (tio) to the other Rodriguez kids
Hector Rodriguez, 13	*Seventh grade*	Brother to all but Emilio, nephew (sobrimo) of Emilio
Clifton Kelley, 14	*Eighth grade*	East Lake View Grade School
Angelina Martinez, 14	*Eighth grade*	Attends Mesa Verde Grade School

Other Characters

Ed Kelly	*Clifton's Father,*	Farmer on Summit Ridge Colorado
Etta Mae Kelly	*Clifton's Mother,*	Farmwife
Charlie Kelley, 21	*Clifton's brother,*	Army Pfc. stationed in Japan
Raul & Inez Rodriguez	*Hector's parents,*	Mexican family lives down the road a mile southwest of the Kelley farm house
Ignacio Rodriguez	*Hector's Uncle,*	Mountain Shepherd
George Williamson	*Farmer,*	Neighbor on a farm adjoining the east fence line of the Kelley farm
Sheriff Bill Kirkendall	*County Sheriff*	

Four Corners area of Colorado circa 1954

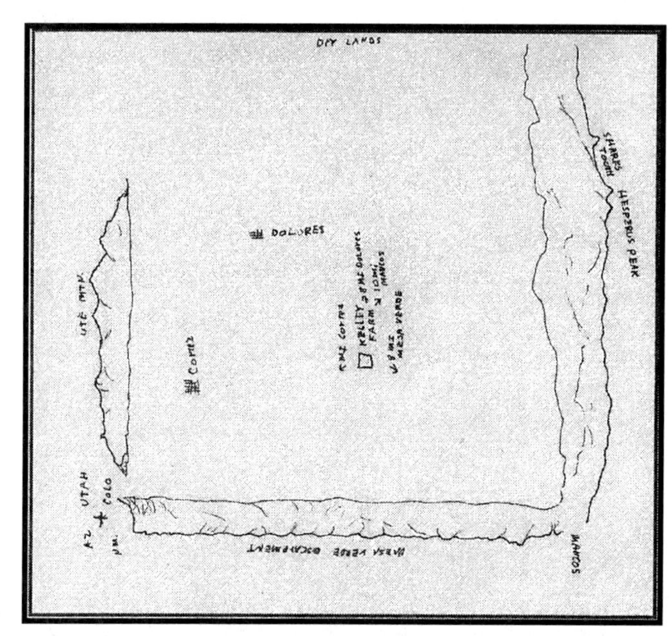

Clifton's Universe, Hesperus, Mesa Verde, Ute Mountain. Scale roughly 40 miles from Ute Mtn. to Hesperus.

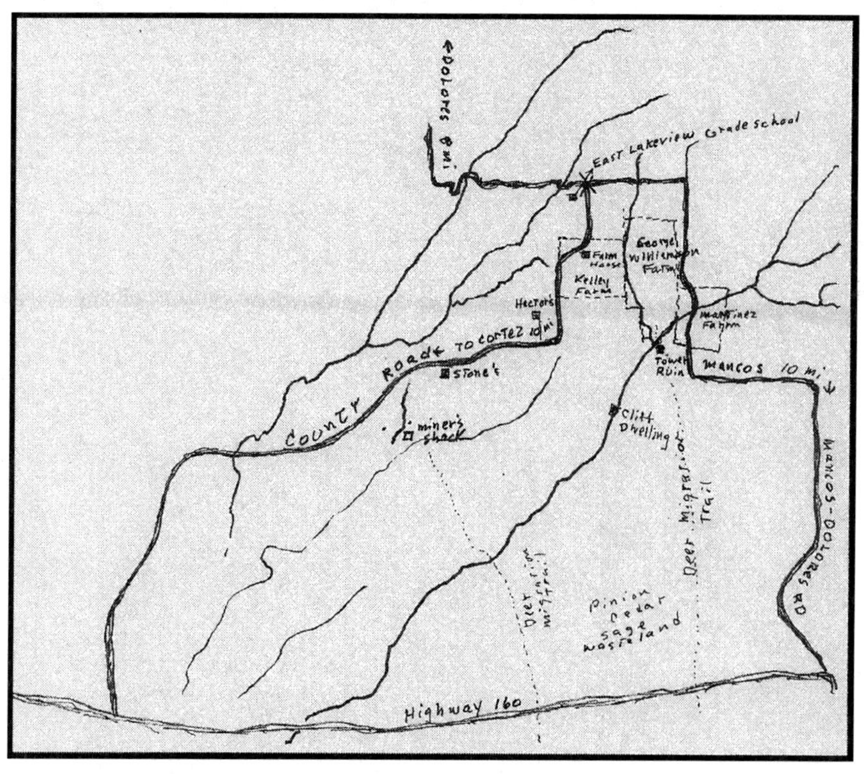

Book I

Monday morning, June 1, 2000, 8:10 a.m.
South High School

Naturalist Joseph Wood Krutch wrote, "Not to have known - as most men have not - either mountain or the desert is not to have known one's self." And "Not to have known one's self is to have known no one."

Based on readings these nine weeks, discussions and your own personal experience, how do you interpret Joseph Krutch's observations?

Mr. Kelley turned from the chalkboard at the sound of a faint musical jingle. Rita quietly grabbed her purse and slipped out the door of the classroom. Hardly anyone paid attention to her as she disappeared.

"I have my car listed in the classifieds. Can I leave my phone on this morning, please, please, please?" She had asked before the bell rang.

How could he refuse the effervescent straight A student with perfect attendance who brought sweetness and light to his first period senior literature class every morning? "If it rings, please quietly take it out to the hall to answer it. OK?"

In the year 2000 very few students in the small western town carried cellular phones. He had no objection to them as long as they were not disruptive.

Mr. Kelley had begun researching cell phones for himself after examining Rita's.

His retirement began at the end of the week. He and Angie were ready to explore. A cellular phone might be useful as they crossed the vast high plateaus and prairies of the American west. The literature was a little vague on how well the cellular phones covered the deserts. He would have to check on that before signing any contracts, he thought.

Mr. Kelley scanned the class as he silently took the roll. Everyone quietly read his or her novel. If eyes were not focused on the pages, the minds behind them were at least at rest, for the moment. He smiled. They were great kids. He still enjoyed working with them and his job, and he had vacillated over the decision to retire. "Retire at the earliest you are eligible," a friend had advised, "while you are still enjoying it."

His classes were popular. He tried to be strict but fair. He had set boundaries between himself and them. They seemed to respect that. He was not their "friend" but their teacher. In an age when many teachers allowed students to address them by first name, to his students he was Mr. Kelley, Kelley, or Kell. They never called him Clifton. Somehow, there was a difference.

He wrote an absent student's name on the form and hung it on the clip outside the door. Rita stood down the hall with her back to him. "We're ready to begin the test Rita."

She did not seem to hear him. Her posture was strange. He started to approach her to see if she was OK, but she turned and waved him off. Her expression showed he should not interrupt her. He went back inside the classroom.

He glanced at the clock. It was time to begin. "Time to put your novels away," he said.

It was the seniors' last week of school. They had come through the door laughing and teasing each other even more animatedly than usual that morning. They were ready to be gone, to embark on the rest of their lives. Redirecting their thoughts that particular Monday morning would have been very difficult but for an established routine in his classes. They began class every day with a few minutes of silent reading in a novel of their choice. He had established the routine the first day of the semester and after a week or two had not had to remind them that it was how the period began in his classes.

Silent reading refocused their thoughts from home and friends. When they opened their novels and became absorbed in their book, the few minutes of silent reading helped them put aside what was going on in their lives.

That morning his seniors faced huge changes in their relationships, summer jobs, travel, vacations, and possibly moving away from home.

Some of his students had arrived that morning on top of the world with bright futures ahead.

Several possibly had hangovers from drugs or alcohol.

One or two had faced a bully or bullies on the bus, or within the walls of their own home.

Some would quietly sit to one side envying the life and advantages others enjoyed.

"Please read the directions on the first page of the booklet I've provided for you. "I have written the essay portion of your test on the board. You have until the end of the period to respond."

Before the likable varsity athlete could open the door, Rita reentered the room, closed the door quietly and slumped against it. The cellular phone slipped from her hand, and she turned and grasped the wastebasket by the door, sick to her stomach.

Mr. Kelley ran toward her from across the room, but before he could reach her Rita turned to the room gasping for breath, "He's killing kids at North High School!" she finally blurted out.

"What? What's going on Rita? Who...?"

"My boy friend Josh. He goes to North. A kid came into the cafeteria a few minutes ago, and he opened fire... with a rifle. He's killing kids, Mr. Kelley! He's killing kids......!"

Students came to their feet and moved closer, straining to hear what

Rita said.

Mr. Kelley's throat constricted. He fought to breathe. After the shootings at Moses Lake, Washington and Paducah, Kentucky in 1996 and '97 and then Springfield, Oregon and Columbine at Littleton, Colorado in 1998 and 1999, the district was on constant alert.

Along with school districts across America, District 23 conducted routine training exercises to prevent or react to shootings, bomb threats, abductions and other intrusions. Columbine had raised the specter of more than one shooter acting together. Now here it was 2000, a year later and the fifth year in a row that a school shooting would be in the news.

Could there be a shooter here at South too? He rushed to the door and locked it.

"Arnie, for their own safety nobody leaves the room!"

"Yes, sir!" Arnie said. He knew the drill. He moved his desk closer to the door. In a lock down, no one entered or left. The school might not be on lock down yet, but he had just put this room on it on his order.

After Thurston in Oregon and Columbine in Colorado, the district had changed classroom doors to solid doors with peepholes giving the teacher a view of anyone approaching from the hallway. Before then doors had glass panels allowing the full view of the classroom from the hallway.

"Jessica, stay here with Rita. Everybody please take a seat, any seat, and listen up. I want you to be as calm as you reasonably can. You heard what Rita said so you know as much as I do, and we have to take it as a rumor, although we have no reason to assume her boyfriend would tell her something like that, if it isn't true. For everyone's safety, no one's to leave this room until I can find out what's going on. All we can do right now is hope they have stopped him, and that he has not hurt anyone seriously. We all have friends over there. Most of all, we have to hope that no one is acting with him right here in our own building!"

"Can't you call the police or something?" Ronny pleaded.

"You can bet the police are already on their way."

An image of a boy sitting in a pile of brush by a country road with a rifle in his hands flashed through his mind.

"If any of you have religious feelings and want to pray either silently or aloud, do that in any manner you've been taught," he said.

He went back to Rita's desk. Color was returning to her cheeks. "You OK?" He asked.

"No! I just tried to call Bobby back, and he didn't answer. My God, Mr. Kelley! What if he's dead too?"

She clutched her stomach and rocked in her seat, tears streaming down her face. Her friend Jessica kneeled next to her trying to console her.

Mr. Kelley picked up the phone on his desk and held his breath as he dialed the principal's extension. The secretary answered. "Mr. Johnson is on another line, May I take a message?"

"Nancy? It's Clifton. Has Brad heard anything about a shooting over at North?"

"He just got the word from the Superintendent. Cliff, it's a nightmare over there. I'm not supposed to talk about it until Brad makes the announcement. We don't want to cause panic. He'll go on the intercom, as soon as he has final instructions from the Super. However, we are, as of now, on lock down.

She hesitated, uncertainly, "Cliff," she whispered, "The shooter is apparently Zack Whitley and Emma didn't come to work this morning. The police are on their way out to Emma's right now." Her voice broke and Cliff could hear her trying to control her breathing.

Nancy had to keep her composure. Cliff knew that she was not supposed to tell anyone yet. "I have to go now, I'm sorry to be the one to break this to you." At that her voice did break.

Nancy, Emma, and Principal Johnson had been at his retirement party the night before at Connie Smith's home.

A stunned Cliff could hardly whisper, "Thank you Nancy...," He hung up, sat down, dropped his head into his hands and sobbed. History was repeating itself. Another teacher's son just like at Springfield. In that situation, he had killed his parents, both Spanish teachers, before going to school. *Please Zack, let Emma be safe.* He thought. He closed his eyes. *Long suppressed images began cascading through his mind of fists bruising his ribs... his eyes streaming tears... running down the gravel road toward home his ruined lunch pail banging against his dirty torn overall leg....*

Several students rushed to his side. He felt comforting arms around his shoulders and hands rubbing his back. He looked up at them through a veil of tears and out across the class.

They don't ask, but they know the information I've received confirmed the truth of Rita's call. It's true! Oh, God! It's true! This isn't some detached incident on television or radio about a place in some other state where they can think, "Oh, too bad, I'm so glad I live in a small town where that can never happen." And it is even worse than they can even imagine. Hold it together now Cliff.

The announcement will come in a moment and the whole school will lose its innocence, Clifton Kelley thought.

The students understood rules prohibited him from saying much, but they knew the announcement would be bad when it came. They wanted him to tell them, but they didn't want to know.

What they don't know is the son of one of their favorite teachers is possibly doing the shooting at North. Is she in danger too? Will she ever be able to stand in front of her classes again and greet them with a cheery, "Bonjour?"

He closed his eyes seeing Emma waving good-bye at Connie's door the night before. "*Bonsoir* Cliff. You and Angelina have a long and happy life in your retirement," she had called to him before turning and walking away. Angelina had called, "*Via Con Dios*" to her in return. *If Emma's son is killing kids at North High School this morning, what did she go home to after the party? Did Zack act normally and secretly sneak off to school with a gun this morning? Or did he kill her the way Kip Kinkel did his parents two years ago?*

Only a few minutes had passed since Rita's cell phone call. Had it been turned off, or if Rita had left it home, at that moment, they would be busily writing their test in blissful ignorance of what was going on across town.

Mr. Kelley's students gravitated into groups. One group gathered in a front corner of the room and settled cross-legged on the floor where they grasped hands, bowed their heads and quietly took turns praying.

Other students somberly consoled each other. A student took a cell phone from his backpack and held it up for Mr. Kelley to see. When his teacher shook his head no, the student put it back without argument.

All were cooperating completely.

The intercom speaker buzzed, "Students and staff, please pardon this interruption. This is Brad Johnson, speaking to you as both Principal and a concerned member of this community. At approximately five minutes after eight A.M. this morning, a student, believed to be acting alone, entered the cafeteria at our sister school, and opened fire with a rifle. An unknown number of students are injured. First emergency response teams are now at the scene or are on the way.

"Police and the Superintendent ask that teachers keep first period classes in your classrooms until further notice. Follow lock down procedures. Lock doors and admit no one except staff, police or district personnel with proper authentication until further notice. On district and police orders, all schools in the district are on strict lock down until it is determined whether this person is acting alone or in conjunction with other individuals.

"You will be kept informed as we receive further information. Keep our colleagues, students and friends at North High School in your prayers. We thank you all for your continuing cooperation."

Clifton noted there was no mention of Zack Whitley's name. That probably also meant that they had no word on the fate of his mother, Emma.

The phone rang on his desk. It was Connie Smith, head of the English department. "Emma is dead," Connie said in a choking whisper. "The police just reported to the school district that when they went out to the Whitley residence, they found Emma. Emma had been dead for several hours. Zack must have killed her last night. Cliff, she must have gone home from our party last night, and he killed her when she walked in," Connie cried.

There was a long silence on the phone. The two teachers sat at their desks only a classroom wall apart, but unable to leave their rooms during the lock down.

"It hurts Cliff. Emma was probably my best friend and one of our best teachers."

"Did you have any idea what was going on with Zack?"

"Emma was becoming more and more worried about him. Zack had trouble with some kids all through middle school. Emma worked with Zack's counselors at the Middle School and High School both, and it was discouraging. More often than not, they blamed Zack more than they blamed the kids who bullied him. She thought things were getting better when he started high school this year. He was on the cross-country team and band and seemed to be fitting in well, and then this spring it started up again and with some of the same kids. Emma started meeting with the school counselors and with a private family counselor and the principal. I think she was even threatening a lawsuit against one of the families. Oh, Cliff how could this happen?"

"Only someone who has been through what Zack has can ever understand why Connie," Cliff said. "Being bullied for a long time tears you down and breaks a person. It causes a person to do desperate things. I didn't realize Zack had to put up with that. I wish I'd known. I may have been able to help him. Now it's too late.

"I thought Emma and I were close enough to talk about matters like that, but I guess away from school, maybe I didn't know her that well after all. I never heard Emma talk about the trouble Zack was having," he said sadly.

"Emma never let her personal life show here at school to either us or to her students. Only the counselors at school and one or two of us who knew how troubled she was with Zack. It was a hard life for her after her husband died. Zack was a handful even without the trouble he was having at school, but you would never know it from the way she handled herself here with her students and the rest of the staff."

Connie paused. Cliff could hear her trying to control her breathing and to make her voice continue. "...I have to notify the rest of the department now. Good-bye Cliff..." she said in barely a whisper.

All eyes turned on Mr. Kelley as he hung up the phone. The students were waiting for further word at North and yet dreading any new information. He did not know how to keep the information about Mrs. Whitley from them.

The intercom speaker buzzed.

Principal Johnson's voice began quietly, caught, paused and began again in a subdued voice. "...Students and staff...I am sad to have to inform you that our beloved...," His voice choked, and he paused for several moments until he could get his emotion under control.

Instinctively Rita began sobbing again. Other students began to clasp hands of students next to them. Some began to pray silently and others began to sob. "...Our beloved Mrs. Whitley was found in her home this morning."

"God No!" Arnie wailed and slumped into his chair. "No, no, no, no...!" He banged the desk and sobbed. Other students began crying. A student, frustrated, threw a book against the chalkboard.

"...Police allege that Zack Whitley, a freshman at North High School, took his mother's life sometime last night before he went to school this morning and opened fire in the cafeteria. Zack was subdued by several students and a teacher a few minutes ago and has been taken into custody by the police..." Again his voice broke.

"At this time there is an unknown number of fatalities there besides Mrs. Whitley. Numerous injured students are being evaluated and transported to trauma centers according to the severity of their wounds..."

Mr. Kelley could only faintly hear the final remarks over his students' grief.

"Teachers, please continue to keep your first period students in your room. A district wide lock down continues until further notice. Thank you for your continuing cooperation," the Principal finished with a whisper.

Social and legal barriers forbade physical contact between teachers and students, just as a legal separation between church and state forbade public prayer in the public schools. However, both barriers became meaningless and were forgotten as the announcement ended.

Mr. Kelley left his desk and the students opened their ranks to enclose him. They embraced him and shared his tears, as he shared theirs. The class as one, including Mr. Kelley, formed a prayer circle, and they bowed their heads and silently prayed for Mrs. Whitley, her son, his victims, and themselves.

He had lost a colleague that he admired. They had loved her as a teacher. Her French classes had waiting lists. A mix of star athletes, debutants, misfits, average and college bound students, all thrived under her warmth, vitality, love of her language and life, and skill as a teacher as they learned the language and culture of the French.

Suddenly, they had lost their teacher and their innocence.

One student finally broke from the group and went to the chalkboard. She slowly erased the test from the board, wiped it carefully from border to border and then in a graceful calligraphy wrote:

Cher Professeur Diadieu

After writing the good-bye, she drew a border of vines and then embellished it with flowers.

Other students soon followed her example; until they covered the board with flowers and comments in French.

Slowly, they drifted to their desks, and began to write notes, poems, memories, and statements about Madame Whitley and her French classes. They had no clear idea about what to do with their art and writings, but they had to express their feelings in a permanent way.

They forgot all about their semester test. Mr. Kelley did not remind them of it, but silently went around the room collecting the booklets except for those booklets, which had become testaments to a departed loved one.

The desk phone rang again. "Cliff, Connie. Brad just called. They are confirming six dead at the scene and eighteen seriously injured and on their way to the hospitals so far. There are also a number of minor injuries that are being transported by school officials or waiting ambulances from further hospitals. Is everything still under control in your area?"

"We're doing as well as can be expected, Connie. The kids are writing notes and messages to Emma. I'm thinking they might tape them to the door or wall down in the language hall when the lock down is over. What do you think?"

"Mine are too," she said. "We're also going to place them out in front of the school. However, they can place their thoughts at her room too."

"I hadn't thought of out front. I'll mention it," Cliff said.

"In my room, the kids have come up with everything on their own. I've been in too much of a daze to think of anything," Connie said. "Any sign of panic?" she asked.

"No. They have been wonderful. They've been keeping me from falling to pieces in here," Cliff said. "Do they think Zack was acting alone?"

"Brad said the police are being cautious. They have found no evidence anyone else is involved. Zack told arresting officers he was alone. He refused to say anything more."

"What about our tests?

"Don't you think we could probably figure out pretty closely what they've earned without a test if we have to?"

"Yea, I think so. Today was our test day. I don't know what kind of plan they'll draw up. I can come up with something. It won't be on the level I was going to ask of them this morning. And I darned sure don't think I'd be able to concentrate on reading them either."

"Yea, me too. At least you're almost done here. I have to come back next fall. I don't know if I'll be able to do that or not."

"I know," he said. "I'm glad I won't have to face it."

Clifton Kelley, retiring Language Arts teacher, watched the students, some with tears running down their faces, bent over heartfelt poetry, sketches and comments to a beloved teacher and friend.

There but for the grace of God go I, thought Clifton. *The last week of school forty-six years ago, at the end of the eighth grade, bullied to the breaking point, beaten and surrounded by screaming students on the playground I fled, and took my rifle in hand. The frame of mind I was in that afternoon, I would have murdered Hector, Emilio and probably any of the rest of them I could.*

Robert Frost wrote, "Two roads diverged in a wood, and I...I took the one less traveled by, And that has made all the difference." I ran from that place in time, but how close I came to taking the same path as you, Zack...

Week One
East Lakeview Grade School
Kelley Farm
Bee Tree and Pueblo Ruin
Martinez Ruin

1

Friday afternoon, May 7, 1954
East Lakeview Grade School

Cliff's big mistake that afternoon was taking the lead down the road. He thought he had the right as the school's eighth grader, although he seldom had the chance to exercise it. However, Hector soon caught up with him and walked alongside, almost friendly. They walked along the side of the gravel road for a minute or two without speaking, and then Cliff turned to Hector. That was when Hector "accidentally" bumped him.

Cliff stumbled over the roadside into the barrow pit and pitched forward onto his knees in the dust, gravel and new nettle growth. He pushed himself up, wiped his gravel scraped palms on his overall legs and brushed the nettle burn on his cheek. He scrambled back up onto the road. "What the heck did you do that for!"

Hector spread his hands and acted surprised, "It was an accident *amigo*. You should watch where you step. You could get hurt stepping off the road like that," he laughed derisively.

Theoretically, Hector was younger than Cliff, but if so, he was maturing faster. His upper lip already supported a pronounced moustache while Cliff hadn't even thought about shaving. The top of Cliff's head came about even with Hector's shoulder and Hector outweighed Cliff's 90 pounds half again.

"You pushed me...," Cliff said angrily. "Just stay away from me!"

"It may be difficult to stay away, because do you know what? My fist is thinking about rearranging your face for you today, just for fun, *Cabron*. What you think about that?"

"I think you'll have to catch me first!" Cliff said and sprinted down the road toward the trail leading into the canyon where Mrs. Campbell said they were going.

"Stay with the rest of us Cliff and Hector!" Mrs. Campbell called in vain, as the two boys began to run.

Little Canyon, or Cash Canyon as it was sometimes called, was the smallest and shortest of the canyons on Summit Ridge starting a quarter of a mile north of the road crossing and ending two miles later where it intersected Big Canyon.

Cliff was fifty yards ahead when he cut off the road onto the trail and ran down it to the bottom of the canyon and the shallow meandering creek.

The trail followed the east bank of the creek that cut its narrow course between banks of silt deposited during high water flash floods during summer thunderstorms, and spring runoff. Occasional pools supported willow and cattail groves joined by a shallow, rippling, transparent ribbon over amber gravel beds sprinkled with glassy quartz.

He glanced over his shoulder to be sure Hector hadn't appeared, and without pausing, leaped off the trail onto an outcropping of rock embedded in the canyon slope. He scrambled behind more rocks and sagebrush, dropped to the ground, and froze facing up the trail. He hid his eyes behind his hands and peeked through his fingers keeping an eye on the trail, ready to flee again if spotted.

This works for a cottontail rabbit when caught in the open. It is practically invisible until it moves. If it works for a rabbit, maybe it'll work for me. At least I have some rocks and sagebrush to hide behind, he thought.

He tried to control his breathing, but his lungs burned from gulping the dry, thin, high altitude air. He gasped for breath then held it as Hector charged past on the trail without pausing. Cliff stayed still as hector disappeared around a bend, and then he relaxed a little but stayed in placed and remained vigilant.

~~~

Mrs. Campbell was surprised that Cliff had decided to lead the pack down the road that afternoon. In her two years at East Lakeview Grade School, Hector and Emilio Rodriguez were the assumptive leaders. Ordinarily Cliff stayed close to her where he was safe from Hector's attention.

Hector was cunning, and she had not actually seen him push Cliff. She was not aware something was happening, until she heard Cliff yelling, as he climbed out of the barrow pit, and she saw him take off down the road.

As a special treat, Mrs. Campbell had promised a field trip on this last Friday afternoon of the school year. *I should have known this would happen. Hector, why couldn't you give it a rest for at least one day? I thought you would all be on your best behavior. I meant it as a treat for us to spend the afternoon in the sunshine after a long winter in the schoolroom.*

Clifton Kelley had been a challenge the past two years. In many respects, he should not have been there. The larger school in the Valley or better yet, at the middle school in town is where he belonged. The teacher and student harassment had beaten him down badly. His self-esteem was very low.

Cliff had several counts against him at East Lakeview Grade School. He was the only eighth grader. He was also the only Anglo. He was the only boy whose parents sent him to school in farmer's overalls, He was thin and didn't like sports, preferring to stay inside reading to playing softball or physical games on the playground. He told her, "he got enough physical exercise in the work at home and the work was less painful."

She wasn't sure if race had anything to do with Hector's harassment. Hector was a playground bully to the other kids too, although his primary focus was on Cliff.

Cliff had told her about Mr. Johnson, the teacher before her who had enforced a total participation in playground activities such as softball and competitive games after third grade. Hector and Emilio had used the
~~~

games as bullying tactics right under Mr. Johnson's nose. She had tried to stop the problem after taking over at the beginning of his seventh grade by making participation in the activities voluntary.

He was a good student and studied well on his own. With his leaning style, he had thrived to her relief. Her hands were full teaching the younger students who came to her in first grade barely able to speak English. She had to plan eight different daily lessons and adjust each to the level of language skill of the various members of each grade. It was a logistics nightmare.

Thankfully, his lesson was the easiest, although in quantity it could have been the most challenging. In some ways it was because she had to gather the resources. Once they were gathered though, he devoured everything she offered to him with little tutoring. Once she gave him directions, usually in written form, he became absorbed in the books supplied by her. He required little attention on her part.

When he finished assignments, he went to the next or read a novel, also supplied by her, either from her own list or from his list.

Hector didn't dare bother him within her sight, but she couldn't be everywhere at once.

It was no secret around school that Cliff hated Hector. He was Hector's target before and after school, if Hector caught him on the road, and during recesses and the lunch break if Cliff strayed far from the schoolhouse or dared participate in any playground game.

Cliff was careful to ask for bathroom breaks during class time to avoid confrontation. Mrs. Campbell refused like requests from Hector until Cliff's return.

~~~

When Cliff's breathing returned to normal, he stood, brushed the dust and pebbles from the front of his overalls, backtracked to the trail, and waited for Mrs. Campbell and the others. He had no sooner joined them than Hector sullenly walked back up the trail.

"Where you been *sobrino*?" Emilio, heckled.

Hector's dad was Emilio's older brother making Emilio Hector's uncle. Emilio was a willing participant most of the time when Hector went after Cliff, but he did not hesitate to ridicule his nephew, given the chance, which made Hector even more determined to get back at Cliff for dodging him.

"Callate! (Shut up!) Hector hissed and flipped Emilio off behind Mrs. Campbell's back.

Together once again, teacher and students continued down the canyon trail. Cliff caught Hector staring at him each time he looked up. Hector raised an eyebrow, or bared his teeth into a threatening smile and punctuated his expressions with a nod of the head or silent snarl.

It definitely was not over.
~~~

Mrs. Campbell threatened both boys to behave with her glare. Her main control over Hector was through his father and over Cliff through her goodwill.

When they reached the deepest part of the canyon, a half mile from the road, the students gathered around her. She began identifying the native plants that grew along the creek, most of which were familiar to the students.

Varieties of wild grass, cattails, asparagus and willows grew on the bank or in the creek. Wildflowers, cactus, lichen, yucca, cedar, piñon pines and sage grew along the canyon slopes.

"I thought this was called tamarack," Cliff interrupted her when she identified a pink flowering shrub as salt cedar.

"Everyone around here calls it that," she agreed. "But technically its name is salt cedar or tamarix. Real 'tamarack' is a very different tree. I think people have just heard 'tamarix' and thought it was 'tamarack' by mistake. It isn't native. Some immigrant imported it because of its pretty lacy pink flowers and because of its nectar. I'll bet those are some of your bees working the blossoms right now. Unfortunately, it has the nasty habit of accumulating salt in its stems and later depositing the salt into the soil around it, which eventually kills off all the other competing plants. Fortunately it doesn't do very well up here at this altitude. It likes the lower, hotter country in the Valley better. It's a serious problem down in McElmo. The asparagus isn't native either, by the way," she added. "It was planted by the farmers in their gardens around here, and some of it was transplanted by birds eating the seeds. The habitat along the creek is ideal. So, we have a good non-native species and an invasive species. Do you know what invasive is?"

"Bad?" Adolph Ramirez guessed.

"It means it could be harmful," but it is kind of a new idea. The agricultural department is just beginning to be concerned about such things. Maybe one of you will become a scientist who will find ways to wipe out invasive species like salt cedar. How about you Adolph?"

They turned over rocks to examine bugs, frogs, salamanders and worms. She explained which caterpillars would soon spin cocoons to become butterflies and which would become moths.

On their own, several students pointed out poison milkweed growing along the creek. They had watched beautiful red and black monarch butterflies visit the plants, lay eggs, which hatched into hungry yellow, white and black banded caterpillars that fed on the milkweeds. After a few weeks of leaf munching, they made green cocoons that hung from partially denuded milkweed branches. The students, many of whom herded sheep or cows in the canyons and along the roadways during the summer knew to keep their charges away from milkweed, because to livestock it was deadly. Birds avoided the butterflies, caterpillars and cocoons, because they were toxic from their milkweed diet.

She explained which of the native plants were edible, which were toxic and which became toxic under certain conditions.

She pointed out which plants would produce edible seed and how they might use them.

Mrs. Campbell dug a dandelion root out of damp soil near the creek, washed it off and offered it to anyone who would try eating it. All hung back. "It's like a carrot, except it's a little bit bitter. Anyone have rabbits?" Cliff held up his hand. "Do you feed it dandelion root?"

"Sometimes."

"Do they eat them?"

"They seem to like them better than carrots," he said.

"That's what I've noticed." She cut the tip off and began chewing the root just as she would a carrot. "Not bad," she said. "I could get use to it. It's filled with all kinds of good vitamins and minerals. I understand people bake it and make coffee substitute out of it."

Following their teacher's example, each student pulled a cattail stalk and peeled back the outer layers of leaf until they held only the pure white succulent core. Again, following her example, all but the most finicky eaters bit off a chunk and chewed.

"Tastes like a cucumber," Adolph said.

"This plant was very important to the original Indians in this area," she said. "The stalk was used for food, just the way we're eating it. They used the leaves for thatch on roofs, wove them into beautiful baskets, and mats. They even broke them down into fiber and wove the fiber into clothing." As she spoke, she split long cattail leaves into narrow bands and braided a wreath which she placed on first grader Margaret Florez' head. Margaret immediately pulled clover blossoms, wove them into the wreath and pranced about like a fairy princess.

"By the way, you might have noticed those clover aren't blooming up around the schoolhouse on top. Down here in the canyon clover is beginning to bloom. Dandelions are blooming, and other weeds and grass are much further along. Do you know why?"

No one ventured a guess.

"The sun shining on the canyon walls reflects off the rocks down onto the canyon bottom. Also the sun hits the north side of the canyon wall more directly in the spring heating the rocks, and that helps warm it up here in the canyon. It creates a mini climate that the Indians could take advantage of. Here in the canyons they grew cotton, gourds, and squash that were hard to grow in the open up on top."

Mrs. Campbell cut a brown cattail seed head, still standing from the summer before, which resembled a wiener already impaled on a roasting stick. She pinched the grey brown covering, and a handful of compacted white cotton-like material containing seed spewed forth. "If you are ever lost in the woods and can find a swampy area where cattails grow, this cattail cotton makes a really good fire starter. The outer layer is so tightly packed it's waterproof. Break it open, and it's ready to use. It's easy to start, and it burns slowly. All it takes is a spark to start it smoldering. Does anyone know how to make a spark?"

"I know," said Alicia.

"How?"

"Use a firefly?"

"Where do you get a firefly?"

"At my grandmother's house in Texas!"

Mrs. Campbell laughed. "That's a good idea. But Alicia do you see any problems with that?"

"You mean besides being stupid?" asked Hector. "Fireflies are a bug!"

"So!" Alicia cried, and began to pucker.

"It's OK Alicia. It's a wonderful idea, except it is a little far away if you are lost in the woods in Colorado is all." She hugged the little girl and patted her on the back warmly. "Who else has an idea?"

"Hit two rocks together?" ventured Maria Rodriguez and looked at her brother daring him to make fun of her for her suggestion.

"No, I got it," said Adolph Ramirez, "You got to rub a rock with a piece of steel. When my dad sharpens his shovel he gets sparks from the grinder!"

"That's right Adolph. The sparks you see when he sharpens his shovel are bits of burning metal. They will also cause a fire. However, you can hardly carry around a grindstone and shovel when you are lost in the woods. All you need is a very hard stone, the harder the better. Around here, that's quartz or flint and any soft iron. A horseshoe will work or a nail. If you strike either a nail or a horseshoe against a hard rock, you'll knock loose tiny flakes of iron. A flake of iron will burn at a very low temperature when exposed to oxygen. If the entire surface is exposed, it gets very hot and becomes a spark. If the clean iron surface is part of a large body of iron the surface oxidizes and turns to rust because the bulk of iron absorbs the heat.

Most of the students looked at her and at each other and then back at her with a blank expression.

"Say what?" Hector said.

Mrs. Campbell looked from face to face. They hadn't understood her very complicated explanation of rapid oxidation. She wasn't sure she understood it either.

"In other words iron burns very rapidly at a very low temperature when it is exposed to oxygen. Air is mostly oxygen. Rust is a sign of iron burning. If you have a tiny piece of freshly scraped iron, small enough that it can't absorb much heat, it will burn up. So strike a nail against a hard stone to break a flake loose. It is clean and tiny. It can't absorb much heat. It flies off toward your bed of cattail cotton. Between the time it falls from the rock and reaches the cotton, it reaches very high temperatures and makes a bright spark. When it hits the cotton, it continues to burn at a much hotter temperature than the cotton burns."

"I understand now," Maria said excitedly. "I think!"

"That's how old muskets fired black powder, with a piece of flint striking iron. The flint flaked off a fragment of iron, which instantly burned and landed in gunpowder," Mrs. Campbell said.

"So, I have a nail. See who can find a piece of quartz, and let's see if we can build a fire with this handful of cattail seeds. How about it?"

The students waded up and down the shallow creek and pools scavenging for sparkling glasslike quartz pebbles. In no time pebbles, containing streaks of quartz filled her palm. Last to return was Hector with a stone the size of her fist with streaks of the hard glassy mineral layered through it.

Mrs. Campbell had Cliff gather a few twigs of sage, juniper and piñon and stack them by a wide spot in the trail while she used a flat stone to widen and smooth the loose dirt into a circle of smooth clear dirt two yards wide. She directed Emilio to assemble sand rocks into a small fire pit in the middle of the cleared space. Then she put the cattail seed cotton in the new fire pit. Finally, she gathered the 23 students around her with the youngest kneeling in front and the older leaning over their shoulders while she kneeled over the fire pit holding Hector's quartz nodule in her left hand a few inches above the fluffy white cottony seeds. She struck the stone with the nail. It was difficult to see the tiny streaks of spark in the bright sunlight, but after a couple of strikes, a thin blue thread of smoke rose from the cotton. She bent forward and blew gently. The smoke grew in volume until suddenly everyone could see a tiny yellow flame.

Cliff handed her leaves of dry grass, which she added as she continued gently to blow on the flame, and then added the sage twigs.

"Ole!" Shouted Hector excitedly.

She added a handful of juniper bark.

"Ole!" Everyone shouted.

She added the final piñon branches.

"Ole!" The students clapped and cheered excitedly and began to jump around.

She had started a fire. They could hardly wait to get home to try it for themselves.

Mrs. Campbell stood, brushed off her knees and returned to the stand of cattails.

She cut another of the last seed heads and broke it apart. "Only a few heads survived the winter storms and birds looking for nesting material. In the summer and fall, this stand and other stands like it are thick with heads. It was at those times that the Indians collected the heads.

"You can stuff pillows or blankets with cattail seed and it feels like goose down. Indians put it inside moccasins and around cradles for additional warmth. The only problem with them is it takes a lot of them."

Mrs. Campbell cut a fresh cattail stalk and peeled the leaves back to the white center shoot. "This tastes good raw, but it's also good in soup, and in sandwiches. You should volunteer to cook some for supper tonight."

"My mother already does," Maria Rodriguez said.

Mrs. Campbell watched the students enjoying the fresh air in the canyon. It was warm. Insect and a few frog sounds intermingled with the pleasant sounds of the children talking and laughing. Many of them had dropped into their first language, Spanish. She did not permit them to speak Spanish in the schoolhouse, but she didn't say anything here. She didn't feel they were being dis-respectful. She was bi-lingual and could understand the conversations around her, so it really didn't matter. In the classroom, the mission was to improve their English to compete well enough to attend high school, if they went on.

Everyone seemed to be enjoying the afternoon including Cliff and Hector. They were finally ignoring each other. Her eye fell on her youngest charge, Alicia who sat near the fire holding her hand and looking a little sad. Mrs. Campbell kneeled beside her.

"Are you sad Alicia?"

Little Alicia timidly held her right hand forward and uncurled her fingers. A spot across the inside of her little finger was red and raw and oozed a clear liquid. "I burned it," she said. "On the stove this morning." The ensuing blister had burst sometime during the day.

"I know just the thing that might help that," Mrs. Campbell said. "Come with me Alicia."

She took the girl by her left hand, led her over to the clump of cattail, and called the students to gather around.

"The Native Americans also used the cattails for medicine." Mrs. Campbell cut another stalk and peeled back the young leaves, carefully exposing a jellylike sap next to the shoot. "This jelly is excellent to treat your burns, sunburns or insect bites. Just spread it on, and if you have a light bandage or band aide cover it. It will heal clean."

Alicia bravely allowed Mrs. Campbell to spread the jelly sap on the burn.

So it went. Mrs. Campbell told them about the medicinal properties of other plants growing along the creek: Sweet clover tea could sooth headaches; willow bark tea was almost as good as taking aspirin.

"If you're lost and hungry enough," she laughed, "some of the grubs, worms, grasshoppers, and ants are good sources of protein. Even maggots can keep you from starving." Mrs. Campbell looked at Cliff as she said this.

Several of the older students giggled, interpreting this glance to mean she was suggesting Cliff might supplement his diet with maggots to gain a little weight to fill out his thin frame. But, he knew she was quoting from his own words.

Mrs. Campbell had not given Cliff credit for fear it would embarrass him, or bring more harassment, but she had learned some of the information she used that afternoon from him. It had come from his Graduation Project titled "Native Culture, Crafts, Plant use, Hunting and Recipes, of the Four Corners area in the Mesa Verde era". He had worked on it through the year and she had just finished grading it.

Cliff beamed with pleasure. He did not need recognition from the students. But, that afternoon she had given his research creditability. She noted from his smile and eye contact that he understood the implication of her using information from it that afternoon. *It's almost as if I have written a textbook. Wow!* He thought.

Emilio and Hector caught big grasshoppers, skewered them on willow shoots and roasted them over the fire then ate them.

"This is so good!" Emilio declared as he crunched down on a charred grasshopper.

To his delight, several of the girls pretended to throw up.

Hector thoughtfully crunched a couple of the big insects, but did not seem as enthusiastic.

The afternoon passed quickly for the students as they ranged over the canyon side with checklists in hand identifying plants, rocks, lizards, snakes, rodents and birdlife.

Too soon, it was time to go back to the confining walls of the tiny one room schoolhouse.

"Thank you Teacher. My finger feel better," Alicia said.

Mrs. Campbell examined her little finger and patted her hair affectionately. "It looks better. When we get back to school, I'll put a band-aid on it. Have your mother put salve on it when you get home, and it should be all better by Monday."

Alicia had come to her in the fall shy, reluctant and unable to speak more than a few words of English. Now she was speaking and reading nearly as well as some of the second graders.

Mrs. Campbell still had not spoken to either Hector or Cliff about their earlier behavior, but she managed to keep herself between them on the return hike to school.

After dismissing the students for the day and weekend, Mrs. Campbell motioned for Cliff to stay behind for a moment. "So what was that all about out there this afternoon Cliff?" She asked quietly.

"Hector pushed me and made me fall into the barrow pit. Then he said he wanted to mess up my face!"

She listened thoughtfully as he repeated Hector's threat.

"He taunts you, but he doesn't follow through on it. His dad would kick him from here to Dove Creek and back if he really hit you. And he knows that!"

"So far... But, why can't he just leave me alone? I can't go out and play or act normally without him roughing me up and pretending it is just part of the game. That's how he has always gotten away with it. I am so tired of it."

"I know. But he will be gone in a week."

"Then it will be someone else?"

"Only if you let it be..."

"I don't remember that just letting it be has worked very well."

"I wasn't here when it all started, Cliff. I've done what I could to keep the peace. He doesn't bother you when I'm right there. He knows I'll go to his father in a moment if I can give an eyewitness to his laying a hand on you. I think he'll forget his threat to you over the weekend. Do you think you can hold it together next week? After next week, you'll be out of here. It'll be different at the high school next year. Hector'll still be here. You'll make friends there. Your mother tells me you haven't had problems with Hector and the other kids in the neighborhood in the summertime. The Hispanic kids will be in the minority at Montezuma County High School. Besides, they are not all like Hector. You'll have so many new experiences. Just try to avoid him for one more week. OK? Can you do that? It will be a great help to me if you can."

"This has been going on since about the fourth grade. I can't avoid him. He's on the road before school, here and after school. He didn't get me today, but he'll try again on Monday. He'll enjoy letting me think about it over the weekend. It's his nature!" Cliff said indignantly.

"When he was a first grader he was as big as I was and each year it just got worse. I should have just tried to beat the tar out of him back then, but my dad wouldn't have me fighting....

"I'll be here Monday, and I'll avoid him just like I always do. I can hardly wait to be out of here and away from him.

"But I will miss working with you, Mrs. Campbell. Thank you for using my project today."

"You are welcome, Cliff. It was such a pleasure reading it. You did a fine job collecting and arranging the articles. I didn't know you could draw. Your illustrations are really coming along. I am making some notations in it and will hand it back to you first thing on Monday. I'm really proud of it."

2
Monday Lunch Hour
East Lakeview Grade School

Hector had not forgotten by Monday morning.

When Cliff arrived at school, Hector and Emilio stood talking by the cistern pump. Kids in all grades played near Hector to be close when the main event occurred. Cliff felt their eyes on him as he entered the safety of the schoolhouse.

Will today be the day I finally call his bluff? What a perfect ending for the school year. Crap! He thought miserably.

As usual, Cliff stayed in the building during first recess. As classes resumed, and the students filed back into the schoolhouse, Cliff avoided their looks, but he could hear their whispers.

The easiest way to avoid confrontation with Hector was to stay cloistered in the schoolhouse. It had worked many times before, in fact, nearly every recess and lunch break for two years.

Hector's powers grew each time Cliff ran away from him or avoided him. He had endured the boy's bullying for much of the time they had been in school together. *Here I am afraid to go outside at all. This is ridiculous. He doesn't even have to lift a hand. All he has to do is utter a threat, and he's a hero. Well, this needs to be the last time!* He thought. *I refuse to hide behind Mrs. Campbell my entire last week of school.*

Mrs. Campbell handed Cliff's project back to him just before lunch. He accepted the heavy album and ran his hand over the cover. He had poured his efforts into the project over the school year. Mrs. Campbell had set aside time in his daily schedule for him to work on it. She had also allowed him to use time between other assignments when they were completed. He had enlisted his mother's help who gladly took him to the public library in Cortez and helped him send letters to the agricultural department at Colorado State University to receive free publications and information. He was anxious for school to be out and summer Sunday afternoons when he would be free to try out some of the things he had learned in his research.

Before Cliff could open the cover and begin reading the notations Mrs. Campbell had written in the album, she dismissed school for lunch.

The younger students grabbed their lunch buckets, raced to the schoolyard and jostled for a position on the playground equipment. Older students congregated in smaller groups laughing and talking as they ate.

All positioned themselves to see the front door of the schoolhouse except Emilio and Hector, who sat to one side of the building on chunks of firewood eating their lunch. Hector talked excitedly about leaving for the mountains the day after school was out. "This time next week, *Tio* Ignacio and I will be eating tortillas around a campfire right about there."

He pointed to a spot just below timberline on the north end of the La Plata Mountains. "It is my first summer helping *Tio* tend the sheep. Man it will be so good." He slapped Emilio on the leg.

"I envy you, *Sobrimo*. Unfortunately, I have to stay home for a while, and then I will have to go to work in the bean fields over by Dove Creek with my old man," Emilio said sadly. He is way too old, and I am too young. I would rather be up in the mountains with you and my brother.

Cliff had not moved from his desk. He studied the cover of his album:

NATIVE CULTURE, CRAFTS, PLANT USE,
HUNTING, AND RECIPES,
OF THE FOUR CORNERS AREA
IN THE MESA VERDE ERA
BY CLIFTON THOMAS KELLEY, ESQ

Cliff smiled at the cover. It had taken many revisions to fit the whole title onto the album cover space. The wording had to be just right to fit the contents.

His lunch pail sat alone on the shelf on the porch. Mrs. Campbell looked up from her desk where she checked papers and ate her lunch. She smiled at Cliff, expecting him to spend the lunch hour examining her notations in his album.

He smiled back. *How can she respect the coward that I am?*

Cliff sighed and put the album inside his desk under the hinged desk-top. He walked to his lunch pail and picked his drinking cup off its peg by the water bucket. The bucket was half-full of fresh cold water. All he had to do was fill his cup from the dipper and go back to his seat. *And hide!*

The low overhanging tin roof shut the noonday completely out of the schoolroom leaving Mrs. Campbell in shadow. He looked back to where she ate her lunch and checked papers. He was on his own. *What did I expect? She would follow me out the door?* He slowly walked the five feet across the vestibule to the front door, opened it, and stepped out into the sunshine.

All talking, laughing, singing and teasing stopped. Suddenly, the only sound he could hear was his heart beating and the sparrows chirping in the cottonwood tree by the front gate.

He looked around. It had been a long time since he had eaten lunch outside.

The silence continued as Cliff walked over to the raised concrete cistern top and sat down.

He was aware of the sudden sound of running feet. Younger and older students alike left what they were doing and raced back toward the building to gather in a semi-circle around the cistern, jostling for a position to view the impending action.

"*Vete a la chingada!* What's he doing out there?" Hector asked.

"He's one crazy *cabron*," Emilio said. "He knows better than to come out here today. Is he really going to challenge you?"

"He won't stay, He'll run as usual. You'll see. The *cobarde.*"

"And if he doesn't?"

"It'll be the first time."

"Hey coyote, yep, yep, yep...." Emilio heckled Cliff, who ignored him.

The cistern was a square submerged concrete tank located about fifteen feet in front and to the right of the schoolhouse front door. It was out of view of any of the schoolhouse windows. The top protruded out of the ground about a foot providing an ideal seating area for kids on sunny days. In the center of the slab, someone had bolted a three-foot tall by six inches by eighteen inches green sheet metal casing. On one side was a crank handle. The individual operating the pump with the right hand faced the front of the pump where a spout delivered water to a bucket or cup. Turning the handle slowly eventually yielded mere splashes of water. Turning the handle steadily produced a near constant stream, which filled the water bucket in a few minutes. Turning the handle too vigorously was not productive, as most of the water spilled on the journey up the chain. The handle turned a large sprocket inside with a continuous chain of cups, which scooped ice-cold water from the concrete lined tank, lifted it and emptied the water into a trough above the spout.

The advantage of the chain pump was that it never needed priming.

Cliff stepped over to the pump, cranked until water flowed from the spout, and filled his cup. He was painfully aware of the jostling crowd of 20 students watching him. The only ones missing from the pack were Hector and Emilio. He sat back down on the front edge of the cistern top facing the semi-circle of students. He opened his lunch box, and took out a peanut butter and jelly sandwich.

He did not look up into their faces. He established eye contact with no one. He ignored them.

The line drew closer and the whispering became louder as the jostling continued.

He pretended they weren't there as he took a bite of his sandwich. He tried to look calm, but he could hear his heart racing.

His throat felt constricted. He felt like throwing up.

He wanted to leap up and run back into the schoolhouse, but it was too late. The encircling students cut off a direct line of escape to the door, but they had left the way clear to the gate. He could be up and out the gate of the schoolyard fence and down the road before anyone could catch him, including Hector.

You might not be tough, but you're fast, a voice prompted him.

I'm fast because I've had plenty of practice! He silently argued back.

Run Cliff, run while you have time, run now before it's too late! The voice inside his head screamed.

It's time to quit running Cliff, if he comes after you, show him he can't get away with it. Give it to him once and for all.

Steady Cliff. You can't run forever! He debated with himself.

Cliff took a bite of the sandwich. He could hardly swallow. He lifted the tin cup to his lips.

The feet in front of him shuffled closer. They nearly bumped against the toe of his shoes.

He drank deeply to wet his increasingly dry mouth.

The debate within his mind continued: *Run.*

No! Stay and stand up to Hector.

Time ran out on him. It was suddenly silent.

Feet separated in front of him, and he stared down at Hector's scuffed shoes. Beside them were Emilio's.

He still did not look up.

"I'm thirsty *Cabron*. Give me some water!" Hector demanded above him.

He will run now, Hector thought.

Cliff didn't react.

Hector had not considered what would happen if Cliff didn't act true to form and scat. Hector waited.

Cliff slowly reached forward with the tin cup and emptied it onto Hector's rough school shoe. "Well shoot, I'm all out. Guess you'll have to get your own!" he sighed.

Hector shook his foot and wiped the wet spot off on his other pant leg.

This isn't supposed to happen, Hector thought. *He's never defied me before. He's always run. Why is he doing this now?*

Still he hesitated.

"You gonna let him talk to you like that and get away with it?" chided Gabriela, a fifth grader.

"Hit him Hector," goaded Hermano, a fifth grader.

"Come on," Emilio said through clenched teeth. "Don't let him get away with it."

He's trying to embarrass me, thought Hector. *Now I have no choice.*

Hector kicked the cup out of Cliff's hand, and then he brought his foot down hard on the lunch pail and kicked it, scattering the contents across the cistern. The mangled metal box landed halfway to the gate.

"Now get out of here before I crush you too, *cobarde!*" hissed Hector.

Now! Time for debate is over, Cliff thought.

Cliff uncoiled from his seemingly relaxed sitting position. He tackled Hector's legs, and they fell together in the dirt at their startled classmates' feet.

Almost before the fight began, Cliff was on his back. Hector sat astride him slapping his face alternately with each hand.

The students scattered shortly then regrouped into a complete circle around the two combatants, their manic screams urging their hero on.

Cliff pulled his feet back under him and pushed up hard throwing

Hector slightly off balance. At the same time, he swung upward with his right then left fists, connecting squarely on Hector's jaw.

That's when he discovered that Hector had just been sparring with him.

Hector's face turned from a smile to a snarl.

Cliff covered his own face to ward off the barrage of blows that followed.

Hector pounded Cliff in the ribs until Cliff moved his arms down to protect himself, and then the fists moved to Cliff's face.

The encouraging circle of kids screamed their approval.

"Hit him!"

"Get him good!"

"Come on, you can do better!"

Mrs. Campbell heard the excited screaming and hurried out the door. Fights were rare on the school ground. She rushed to the tight knot of students and tore her way through to reach the two boys on the ground.

Blood from Cliff's nose covered his face.

Hector sat astride the smaller Cliff systematically pounding him in the face, upper body and ribs.

Mrs. Campbell was strong. She reached behind Hector's back, looped her arms under his armpits and up around his neck forcing his head forward immobilizing him. She dragged Hector backward off Cliff, so the beaten boy could struggle to his feet.

The screaming students were suddenly silent.

"That's it! I quit!" Cliff screamed. "I'm through with this stupid school! I don't care if I don't graduate! I don't care if I never see any of you again! That's what you wanted, wasn't it Hector?"

"This *greaser* should be arrested!" he shouted to Mrs. Campbell.

The students began to shout encouragement to Hector and Emelio.

"You've done quite enough. Now leave him alone!" Mrs. Campbell shouted back and glared them down.

Cliff spat blood as he stormed inside the schoolhouse. He pulled his torn shirt off his back, wiped his face with it and tied the sleeves together to make a pouch. He cleaned out his desk, throwing his only book, writing tablet, album and pencils into it.

On the way out of the schoolyard, he picked up his tin cup and the unusable twisted piece of metal that had been his lunch pail, ran out the gate and down the road toward home.

Mrs. Campbell held on to Hector long enough to keep him from following Cliff.

Farmer Harris, working in the field next to the schoolyard, stopped his tractor when he heard the taunting jeers and stood by the fence watching as Cliff dodged through the gate. He beckoned to Cliff to climb through the fence into his protective custody, but the boy shook his head, and clutching his meager school items wrapped in his tattered shirt, he took off at a steady run down the road toward his home a half mile away.

3
Monday, early afternoon
Kelley Farm

Cliff's mother climbed down from the tractor, and brushed the dust off her long skirt. She removed her gloves and sunbonnet as she walked across the freshly disked garden space toward the house.

She'll be angry with me for coming home in the middle of the day, Cliff thought.

He stepped through the back door and washed his face in the utility room sink. He looked at his face. His eye was beginning to swell and discolor. He had cuts on his face and forehead.

"Why are you home early?" Etta Mae asked. "Are you getting the headache?"

He spun around, and she saw his face. "Yes, I have a headache, but not one of those. I just quit school!" he said bitterly.

She looked at him in horror, "Cliff, what happened to you?" She ran to him and examined his face. His nose was bloody and swollen. His left eye was turning bluish-black and had nearly swollen shut. Grime and blood covered his clothes and arms. Multiple cuts and bruises marked his cheeks and forehead and large round welts on his shirtless chest and ribs were beginning to turn purple and blue.

Cliff's dirt smudged, torn shirt was open on the floor displaying bent remains of his lunch box, smashed cup, assorted school items and Cliff's assignment album.

"Hector went after me at lunch just like he said he would! He threatened me on Friday, and I ran away from him, but today I refused to run. Over and over again, I've tried to tell you guys what Hector's like, and all I get is 'walk away from it,' or 'reason with him.' I've had it! It's the last time he's going to get a chance at me!" Cliff said, fighting back tears. "I'm not going back there this time!"

"I'm so sorry Cliff. I don't blame you. Why didn't you stay in the schoolhouse? Didn't Mrs. Campbell help you?"

Cliff said nothing, but stood looking at her grimly.

Your dad needs to talk to the sheriff and to Raul about this. This can't be allowed to happen. Did you do anything to provoke him?" She asked as she ran a pan of warm water, and pulled antiseptic and bandages from the medicine cabinet.

Cliff exploded. "I went outside to eat my lunch in the sunshine. Do you know how long it has been since I've gone outside at lunchtime? Every day I sit inside cowering so Mrs. Campbell can protect me! I can only go outside if she goes outside!"

"Isn't it her job to be outside to supervise?"

"Why should I have protection from Hector every minute, Mom? I didn't do anything! I told you, he threatened me last Friday, but I got away from him like Dad said I had to. He was waiting for me today."

"Why didn't you say something to your Dad?"

"I did say something. It's like Dad doesn't believe me. Hector's a lot bigger than I am, Mom. I can't beat him in a fair fight! As though he'd fight fair anyway!"

"Exactly what happened today?"

"It was at lunch. I stayed in at recess."

"Why didn't you stay in at lunch today? You say you have been staying in every day for a long time. Why did it make a difference today or the next four days?"

"I just got tired of being afraid of Hector and Emilio. I don't care if Dad gives me a whipping for fighting."

"Cliff, is that what you think? That your dad will whip you for this? That he will whip you on top of this beating. Cliff I'm sorry you feel that way. Your father would never do that!"

"Mom, don't you remember the whipping I got after each time Old Man Johnson whipped me for refusing to play softball or Red Rover at lunchtime? Don't you remember those times? What's the difference? Today I got into a fight. 'Get into a fight, no matter who starts it; you'll have a whipping waiting for you at home too!' How many times have I heard Dad say that?"

"There were circumstances, Cliff! This is not one of those times! Do you think your dad is a monster?"

"I guess I know him better than you do, Mom," Cliff said quietly. Cliff looked at his mom. Etta Mae had endured too. He had listened to his parents' arguments and observed the days of silence between them. He wondered if some of those arguments were because she had interceded on his behalf. *She must be afraid to disagree with him!*

"Cliff be still, and let me clean your eye. Oh, what a mess. I need to take you to the doctor. Your nose might be broken, and your ribs...." She cried as he winced when she touched the bruise on his left side. She cleaned his cuts, applied salve and Mercurochrome and either applied Band-Aids or wrapped tape and gauze around him.

"I can't go to the doctor. You can't afford a big doctor bill just to clean me up. I'm fine. The bruises will go away. Just don't make me go back!" he pleaded.

"But, there's just four more days until you graduate son!" she said. "What are you going to do about that? You may not need that certificate this fall when you register at MCHS, but it would be an achievement. Surely, the sheriff and Mrs. Campbell won't let Hector back in school after what he did to you! I'll go with you to school tomorrow, and if he's there, I'll raise cane, and if that doesn't work, I'll bring you home and personally call the sheriff and see that he gets up here and removes that boy!"

"Thanks mom! However, you can't remove them all. You didn't see the looks on those kids' faces. They all gathered around Hector yelling and encouraging him. They hate me too! Why? I never did anything to any of them!"

"Why don't you go lie down for awhile? You'll feel better if you let the aspirin take effect. Take care of yourself," she said. "If you need anything, I'll be out in the garden."

His mother tried to put her arms around him, but he shook her off and turned away. *Why did I do that? She's always been on my side.* However, when he turned back to her, it was too late.

"Suit yourself," she said wth a hurt tone in her voice.

With tears welling in his eyes, Cliff headed for his room.

Cliff heard the tractor start. *I didn't thank her for fixing me up. Of all the people in my life, she has done the most for me. She feeds me. She listens to my dreams and gives me encouragement. In her own way, she shields me from dad. Why did I blame her along with him? She's on my side, and I wish I knew how to show her that I appreciate it. I'm a failure at school, with my dad, and as a son too,* he thought dejectedly.

He changed from dirty school clothes into work overalls and put on a clean tee-shirt and a denim work shirt. He had to get away from the house to think. *I don't want to be here when Dad gets home from work. Even if I don't get a whipping, Dad will be furious. It would be better if Dad doesn't see my face.*

Cliff had all afternoon before facing his dad, Ed Kelley. He was angry and needed a quiet place away from everyone where he could think. *Dad had left home and was living on his own when he was my age. Maybe I should do that too.*

His mom kept a stack of fresh, clean, brown, burlap "gunnysacks" on the back porch. The sacks served myriad purposes around the farm; hauling potatoes, pinto beans, wheat, corn, barley, oats, skunks and, with adaptation, even fish.

He grabbed the top one off the stack and took it back to his room.

Into it he placed a change of underwear, socks, a fresh tee shirt, a light denim work shirt and a pair of denim overalls. He already had his pocket comb in his back pocket.

He also put in the album that Mrs. Campbell had returned to him that morning. He hadn't even had time to read her comments. *She used some of this stuff on the field trip Friday, so she must have liked it.*

On his way out, he stopped at the kitchen and took a box of matches.

On the utility porch next to the stack of gunnysacks was a floor to ceiling rack of shelves, which at this time of year contained row after row of empty sterilized quart and pint canning jars. Each jar had a brass ring but no lid as a new lid had to be used each year to guarantee a safe seal. On the end of one shelf, a wire basket held one-piece lids from mayonnaise jars that were not suitable for canning pickles or keeping dry goods, but that was about all.

Cliff grabbed a couple of jars and replaced the brass rings with one-piece lids. He filled one with oatmeal cookies from the bottomless cookie jar and the other with a handful of thick, homemade beef jerky sticks.

The box of matches and the two jars went into the gunnysack with the clothing and album.

He exited the house through his dad's tiny office. In the window was the two-frame observation beehive. On the wall behind the door was a rack that held his dad's .30-.30 Winchester lever action saddle rifle, his brother's sleek, bolt action, .22 Remington Sports Master with the peep sight and long barrel, and Cliff's antique, long barrel, single shot, .22 rifle, handed down from his great-grandpa, to his grandpa, to his dad and finally to Cliff.

His dad had promised his two sons .22 rifles for their 13th birthdays. His brother had received the modern seventeen round magazine rifle while Cliff had to settle for the old worn out single shot.

Cliff took the rifle and all the .22 shells he could find; two boxes of an assortment of long rifle, hollow points, shorts and birds hot, all together a little over 50 rounds. Each had a purpose. Long rifle for jackrabbits, shorts for cottontails and prairie dogs, bird shot for robins in the cherry tree. The boxes went into the gunnysack. The loose rounds went into his overall pockets.

He stuffed his new elk hide work gloves into his back pocket.

Cliff carried the gunnysack in his right hand, and the .22 in his left. He didn't look back over his shoulder toward the garden when he left the house. If his mother saw him leave the house, she wouldn't wonder about either the gunnysack or rifle as he usually took both with him when he went to the field. He carried the sack low, so she couldn't see that it wasn't empty. The gunnysack was for young weaned skunks. The .22 was for prairie dogs and gophers. He sold the skunks to a vet in town. Prairie dogs and gophers played havoc with irrigation and wasted precious water, so Ed allowed him to hunt them anytime they were out.

The granary was located within the fenced barnyard only twenty feet or so from the milking barn. It was designed as a twenty-foot diameter round galvanized metal structure with a peaked roof. Similar structures dotted the dry land bean and farming areas.

Most farmers erected them as upright cylinders. When Ed Kelley erected his granary, he set it on a six-foot high concrete block wall with a concrete floor. He had arranged the curved metal sections into the shape of a Quonset hut. He used the roof and floor sheets to close the ends. The finished structure gave him a combination granary and storage shed.

Wooden partitions separated grain, beans and corn. Ed partitioned off the front corner for sacks, supplies, saddle, bridles, ropes and packs.

Cliff was after an old wool Navajo saddle blanket about three feet by five feet in size. A newer fleece-lined pad now hung with the saddle. Cliff folded the Navajo saddle blanket lengthwise, rolled it and placed it into the gunnysack along with the longest coil of rope hanging in the granary.

Cliff left the granary and picked up his shovel at the equipment shed across the lane. He passed through the two gates leading to the fields, turned and looked back at the house and his mother still working down the garden soil on the tractor. She would have it clean and smooth before she quit that afternoon.

A cold chill spread down through him. He had a premonition that he was walking away from the only way of life he had known in his short 14-year lifetime.

It's not too late, go back.

You can't go back.

Yes, you can, you've done nothing wrong. Yet.

You know that you have to get even with those who won't let you alone!

Give it time. They'll go away!

They were not exactly voices, but jumbled thoughts looping through his mind, an endless churning debate. Once they began, he could not make them stop. They had begun at school almost the very second that he had smashed open the gate, stormed out of the schoolyard and onto the road, and worsened as he ran toward home. The thoughts had paused while he was at the house.

They were back.

He closed his eyes trying in vain to make them stop as he walked on down the lane.

4

Monday, early afternoon
Kelley Farm, dog town

The prairie dog town was located in the center of the farm on a quarter acre knoll too high to irrigate. The farmer before Ed Kelley had used the knoll as a haystack lot. Ed had moved the haystack to a new barnyard near the present farmhouse. The small colony of prairie dogs that had lived around the haystack rapidly multiplied in the abandoned hay yard. Eventually, the Kelleys referred to the knoll as Dog Town.

Dog Town knoll was the highest spot on the farm. Early inhabitants of the Ridge had told his dad that it had originally been a much higher mound with exposed walls between the drifted soil and brush. Over the years, various owners of the farm had hauled away stone and given it away to neighbors to use for cellar walls, homes and farm buildings. They had plowed through it and around it and tried to work it down to use as farm land, but had given up trying to break it down to irrigation level. Uniform size stones still lay about. Cliff had cleared away soil on the knoll and uncovered rows of stone outlining tops of walls.

Soil dug out by the prairie dogs and deposited around their holes created mounds, which yielded broken pottery, beads, bone needles and other artifacts giving further evidence that the spot had at one time been the site of many dwellings. Perhaps they were the dwellings of the Indian farmers who had tilled the same fields that Cliff's family now farmed.

Because the knoll was higher than surrounding terrain and the mounds around the prairie dog holes were sometimes a foot or so higher than the soil around them, sentinels could see threats coming from at least a quarter of a mile in every direction, plenty of time to bark warnings. Ed had left the colony alone, as long as the rodents confined their burrows to the knoll. It was a worthless piece of ground, and they caused little harm. Mostly, they consumed vegetation, the weeds and grasses, which grew wild on the knoll and on the ditches surrounding it. They in turn were food for the snakes, foxes, bobcats, badgers, owls and hawks that inhabited the area.

All sign of life above ground ceased in Dog Town as soon as Cliff closed the gate and entered the lane. He was a well-known threat. He had made many visits to the knoll before.

As he neared the knoll, Cliff stepped into the empty irrigation ditch, on the right side of the lane. He crouched down behind new clover that grew along the bank, walked bent over and then crawled until he was even with the east edge of Dog Town. He put the gunnysack down and then sat down in the ditch and stretched his legs out to wait for a prairie dog sentinel to re-appear.

He very slowly re-adjusted the clover and grass to give him a view of the knoll and placed the rifle so that he could shift his aim as needed with very little movement.

Prairie dogs were intelligent little rodents, and Cliff usually enjoyed watching them when he was in a better mood. Their survival rates were high. Killing one with the rifle was a challenge, not only because they were hard to hit, but also because they were so hard to sneak up on. They had a highly organized social system. The sentries were particularly wary, and at any sight or scent of danger, a barked warning sent all inhabitants scurrying for cover where they waited patiently for the all clear signal.

Hunting or observing prairie dogs required patience. Cliff had learned patience, if nothing else.

He got comfortable, adjusted his straw hat to shade his face, broke off a stem of sweet clover to suck on and waited. He checked the placement of the rifle to see if, with only slight movement, he could sight it on all the major mounds on the knoll. He would get only one shot. That was the thing with the single shot. You got one shot. There were no second chances.

Fire, lower the rifle, eject the casing with the bolt, fish in a pocket for another shell, manually insert the shell into the barrel, close the breech with the bolt, pull the spring-loaded firing pin out into the cocked position and raise the rifle to the shoulder into the aiming position, sight and fire.

Comparing his brother's bolt action .22 Remington Sports Master, 17 round magazine to the old single shot was like comparing the new '53 Chevy Corvette to the '31 Model A Ford. Charlie could sight through the peep sight, fire, eject and load another round without lowering the rifle. It was ready to fire another shot. Charlie could get off four or five shots to his one.

Nevertheless, the old single shot was lightweight and accurate. Cliff's eyes were sharp and his hands were steady. For practice, he stood on the front steps of the farmhouse and shot the heads off sunflowers in the garden. In a shooting match, Charlie could power through a box of shells in no time, but in accuracy, Cliff could outshoot Charlie shot for shot every time.

He usually had about fifteen minutes to wait before a sentry poked its head out of a hole to see if the coast was clear.

Cliff gently rubbed his swollen left eye. It had already begun to turn black and blue before he left the house. Now it was nearly swollen shut. He picked at the clot in his nose, and his finger came away bright red. Fortunately, the aspirin had kicked in and his headache had calmed to a dull throb.

Cliff stopped here often on his way to the fields. Waiting for a sentinel to appear forced him to take time to appreciate the natural beauty that surrounded the farm. On the other hand, if he brought a book to the fields, he could read a chapter or two without guilt until he heard the first bark.

His eyes lifted above the knoll to gaze out across the gently sloping western fields of the farm and then out beyond.

He loved the beautiful landscape surrounding the farm. However, for all its beauty the Four Corners region of the United States where Colorado, New Mexico, Arizona and Utah came together shared a harsh environment in which to eke out a living. Temperatures rose into the hundreds in summer. Winters were long and temperatures often dropped to below zero.

Mountains surrounded Cliff's universe on three sides: Ute Mountain to the west, Mesa Verde to the south, and the La Plata Mountains to the east. Deep Lost Canyon defined the northern boundary. If he were to set out early in the morning at a fast walking pace, he could reach any one of those barriers before sundown. The nearest was Lost Canyon.

The Kelley farm was on Summit Ridge. More accurately, it was a plateau on average 7500 feet above sea level and from about six hundred feet higher than the valley below its western edge.

Water drained off the ridge via creeks in the bottom of four canyons draining into either the Dolores River, or the San Juan River, and both flowed into the Colorado River.

Cliff sat with his back against the side of the ditch facing Ute Mountain fifteen miles to the west on the far side of Cortez. He was at a perfect angle to see the full figure of the great sleeping chief. The chief lay with his head to the north at McElmo Canyon, his toes to the south just short of the New Mexico line. The giant lay on his back with arms folded over his chest. His legs and knees were in perfect proportion down to the tall toe monument at the end of the mountain at the little Ute Indian town of

Towaoc.

The altitude of the farm put it level with the mid-point of the main peak of Ute Mountain. In winter clouds hovered over the valley dropping rain or snow on Cortez. Sometimes the clouds hung low enough that the whole of Ute Mountain seemed to float in crystal clear air on a sea of white clouds. At such times, Cliff could pretend to walk across to old Ute Mountain on a blanket of goose down and climb the mountain.

At times, the mountain was as angry and moody as Cliff felt at that very moment. Ominous black clouds would shroud the peak. Continuous lightening flashes would send thunder booming down its slopes and across the valley stirring hopes that the chief was finally rising up to drive the white man from the Indians' lands.

I understand you Old Chief. White men bullied your people just as Hector bullies me. Just as you will someday rise up and drive off your offenders, I will rise up and destroy Hector! He thought bitterly.

The mighty La Plata Mountains stood twenty miles to the east. Spruce and aspen trees covered the not so steep rounded top southern portion. The center peaks soared high above timberline to over 13,000 feet, and most of the year they were covered with a mantel of snow or showed patches of snow and ice in the crevices. To the left of the majestic peaks stood one lone sharp rocky peak, not as tall as its sister's, but shaped much like a giant shark's tooth, which gave it its name.

As the seasons changed, so did the mood of these beautiful mountains. Every year Cliff watched them in the full cycle of fall, winter, spring and summer again. The shadows and highlights changed from day to day as the sun trekked from north to south and back again through the changing seasons.

Spring solstice, March 21, when day and night were the same, the sun rose between the two tallest peaks announcing the approaching spring.

On the summer solstice June 21, the first day of summer, the sun rose to the very north end of the La Plata Range between Hesperus peak and Sharks Tooth. The snow by then would have melted off the lower slopes. Aspen and oak green would replace the white snow. Migrating deer and elk would once again roam the valleys and ridges.

When the fall equinox arrived on September 23, the sun's travel brought it back to between the two peaks. That is when the most vivid changes took place. Spruce trees changed to a deeper green color, and white barked aspen turned from all shades of light green to yellows and shades of orange and gold. The glorious burst of color lasted only a few days before the leaves dropped back to earth. Patches of naked aspen clothed only in their white bark, dotted wide swatches of blue spruce forest. Lower on the slopes the oak brush leaves turned from green into crimson red, and finally they too dropped. Deer and elk herds restlessly began their migration to the foothills. Snow soon again completely covered the high places, putting everything to sleep the winter through.

Winter solstice, the last day of fall and the first day of winter, arrived on December twenty-first. Those four days before Christmas, the sun rose at its most southern position south of the La Plata Range, in a "V" notch caused by Mancos Creek at the very east end of Mesa Verde.

Cliff ignored the pain in his torso and turned to face the south.

Forming the southern edge of the box eight miles due south was Mesa Verde. The fifteen-mile long northern escarpment of Mesa Verde appeared to be a mountain covered with trees and brush. There were no high spectacular peaks above timberline, but still it was an impressive range.

In fact, it was not a mountain range at all, but as the Spanish name "Mesa Verde" implied, a "green table top" with the north edge lifted 2000 feet above the foothills at its feet. The top of the mesa sloped back into New Mexico at such an angle that in the fifteen miles from the edge of the escarpment south to the park headquarters/museum the elevation was lower than at the foot of the escarpment.

This big tableland was creased with deep canyons and caves, and within the caves of the cliffs the ancient ones, the Ancestral Puebloans, had lived some seven hundred or so years before, and had disappeared around 1350 A.D. about the time of a devastating thirty-year drought.

Of the various geographic boundaries to Cliff's world, Mesa Verde was the most mysterious and the most magnetic.

Cliff considered Mesa Verde to be a second home. The Ancient Puebloan Indian culture fascinated his dad, Ed Kelley. Ed had told Cliff that Cliff was the descendent of a full-blooded Choctaw Indian whose tribe lived in the Arkansas region, and that his mother Etta Mae was a descendent of a Comanche great grandmother in the Texas Territory.

Cliff thought his dad was a different man when he took his family up to Mesa Verde. They walked among the ruins or strolled through the Museum many Sunday afternoons. Cliff had visited Mesa Verde so many times that he had memorized some of the speeches the rangers gave at the various ruins. He could anticipate the questions and knew the answers.

When relatives visited from Texas, New Mexico, Oklahoma and Arkansas, Ed arranged to take them to Mesa Verde for the full tour.

By the time Cliff was seven or eight, if for any reason his dad and mom couldn't go with visitors, he volunteered to be their tour guide. Some of the Rangers recognized him, and when they asked if anyone from the audience knew what *metate* or *mano* was, or if anyone knew the significance of the *Sipapu* they gave him the opportunity to show off his knowledge and let him identify corn grinding stones and the ancestral spirit entrance from the underworld.

From the age of eight, he was certain that his future was in some way to involve Mesa Verde or the study of ancient cultures.

A fire lookout stood on one of the higher points of the Mesa Verde range due south of the Kelley farm. This look out was a glass building low to the ground where an attendant watched over hundreds of thousands of acres of timber and give an early warning for forest fires. For about a week around the vernal and autumnal equinox, the sun reflected off its windows and shone into a person's eye if he faced due south. During that week of reflection, Ed taught Cliff that winter was over and spring had arrived or that summer was over and fall had arrived.

Just to the left end of the Mesa, like ghosts in the distance, the giant monuments of Monument Valley were visible in New Mexico, Utah and Arizona.

The northern boundary of Cliff's universe was not visible. That was deep Lost Canyon beginning on the slopes of the La Plata Mountains and ending at the Dolores River at the town of Dolores. Lost Canyon was a mystery close to home. It snaked to within two miles of the schoolhouse and on a quiet day, Cliff could hear the whistle of the Colorado and Southern steam locomotive heading toward Mancos. However, he had never explored that canyon. Fences prohibited access directly from the house on horseback, and it was a little far to walk to and back on a Sunday afternoon. He had heard that, of all the nearby canyons, it had the most cliff dwellings.

5

Monday, early afternoon, 20 minutes later
Kelley Farm, dog town

Cliff drew his eyes back to the knoll and scanned for a lookout. It was time for a lone sand-colored animal to poke its nose out of a burrow and sniff. Cliff heard a sharp bark. An alert prairie dog had appeared atop a mound slightly to the right of the tallest burrow. The ten-inch tall rodent stood on his hind legs with his stubby tail pointed straight out behind him. It looked directly at the spot where Cliff sat in the irrigation ditch. Cliff's straw hat blended with the clover and grass. The only thing out of place was the dull black steel rifle barrel poking through the clover and possibly the faint scent of fresh blood, which continued to ooze from Cliff's nose.

Cliff froze in place. The rodent could relax and give the all clear signal, or it could drop back into its hole and wait for another quarter hour.

The all clear bark finally sounded, and other heads began to pop up from mounds throughout Dog Town.

The sentry continued to stand at alert, turning its head, its eyes constantly shifting, checking in every direction for danger to the town.

The "town" was divided into "wards", each with its own sentry, which was also on alert. Within each ward were social units, "coteries" with its own territory.

On a normal day, Cliff would have spent more time watching the interplay between the inhabitants of the wards and coteries. They obviously had a complex society and communication system to go along with it. When a youngster from one coterie wandered across some invisible territorial line into neighboring coterie, sharp barks or calls rang out as residents challenged the intruder. If it did not leave, one or more resident dogs applied immediate force to drive it away.

He had observed different warning barks from the sentries for different predators. One kind of bark signified a flying threat, another for a crawling predator, still another for an upright threat. He swore that they had a special bark just for him.

It was not so different in Dog Town than on the school playground. The main difference was that Hector had staked out the entire school ground as his territory, and it was his self-designated duty to police it from Cliff when he intruded.

Cliff barely moved the rifle to align with the mound where the sentry stood. He had already loaded the .22 short shell into the single shot rifle, he pulled back on the knurled knob end of the firing pin, until he heard the trigger engage, and he set the safety tab.

A metal bump was welded a half inch forward of the pull knob on the firing pin shaft. The safety was a slotted sleeve that rotated a quarter of a turn around the firing pin shaft between the bolt and the firing pin pull knob. The bump moved back and forth in the sleeve slot. A rounded three eights inch wide tab extended three eights inch from the sleeve. To set the safety, he flipped the tab to the left, blocking the pin from traveling forward to strike the rim of the shell. Moving the tab to the right allowed the pin to spring forward when he pulled the trigger.

Before he could remove a shell after cocking the firing pin, he had to set the pin in the safety position, pull the trigger, then holding the pin between thumb and second finger, flip the safety off with the first finger, and slowly lower the pin.

The knurled edge, with its diamond crosshatching, helped keep a grip on the thin round knob. If the firing pin knob slipped, the shell would fire, just as if he had pulled the trigger.

He sighted on the sentry that had given the all clear when danger was still present. It should take the blame for announcing to the colony that all was safe. At Cliff's slight movement the sandy-brown rodent turned and stared directly at Cliff. One bark and all life in the colony would vanish.

He had no reason to kill the prairie dog. It had done nothing to him. It was protecting its town and its family. It had failed just as his dad, Ed Kelley, had failed, and just as the school board had failed. However, at least the prairie dog had tried.

Cliff started to lower the .22, but suddenly he saw not the animal's, but Hector's face. His piercing black eyes mocked him. His lips seemed to mouth the hated word that he so often called Cliff, *"Cabron."* Cliff didn't know the exact meaning of the word, but by context, he was pretty sure he knew its intent.

He flipped the safety and squeezed the trigger. The rifle spoke, and the prairie dog leaped into the air simultaneously. Cliff seldom missed. The animal fell back into the hole and disappeared. Although Cliff couldn't see the victim, he knew it was dead.

Suddenly, it was silent on the knoll. All sign of life had disappeared. All was silent on the Kelley farm. Moments before, magpies and crows called to each other; meadowlarks, bluebirds and sparrows sang and chattered. Now all was silent.

The silence frightened him, and a cold chill shook his body as he rose from the dry ditch. For an instant, it felt as though he had actually killed Hector, not a prairie dog. In the last moment before he pulled the trigger, the rage toward Hector had boiled over like a teakettle that had been simmering on the stove all day.

He felt the weight of years of torment, from the hands of Hector, promoted by Hector's heckling, or Hector's manipulation. While he sat in a ditch stalking rodents and licking his cuts and bruises, Hector still strutted like a crowing rooster among his admiring relatives and friends, manipulating everyone and setting an example for the rest of the kids.

Could I actually end it all just like that? Pow?

Cliff picked up the sack and looked back at the house. He did not hear the tractor running anymore. His mother must have gone back to the house. He looked south to the timber where he had been heading before he had stopped at Dog Town.

In that direction, he had discovered a place in the canyon, the only place he knew, where he could hunker down. It was a safe place to hide, but he had unfinished business.

He looked across the alfalfa field to the county road. *Hector, Emilio and the others will be coming down that road soon. I can cross the field, step through the fence into the woods and wait for them. See how loud they laugh when Hector hits the ground with a bullet in his head! Maybe that's what I should do. End this finally. I'll show him who's a Cabron!*

The debate began in his head.

Get out of here now before it is too late!

You stood up to him. It's over!

It'll never be over!

Go!

Kill Him!

He dropped the sack and the shovel back into the ditch. Carrying only the rifle, he skirted the knoll, and walked in a near trance to the northeast across the alfalfa field to the woods west of the house and climbed over the fence.

He came out on the other side of the woods on the south side of the county road.

The road, because of a draw, cut off the northwest corner of the farm from the rest of the one half mile square, 160-acre farm. A draw, draining from east to west, began at a ridge roughly two-thirds the distance to the eastern corner of the farm. That ridge traversed the farm from the north fence line south to the southern fence line and conveniently carried a major irrigation ditch that supplied water to roughly one-half the farm. At the southern fence line, it turned to the west and continued to the west fence line that paralleled the county road. On the southern side, the ridge leveled out to a gently sloping half-mile wide timbered shelf that drained into Martinez Canyon.

Cliff couldn't see the draw from where he stood because of the trees on the other side of the county road.

The draw sloped gradually to the west, and the Kelley fence line ran roughly down the lowest point of it, until it intersected the county road running north and south. Ordinarily, in this situation, a county road would have made a 90 degree turn to the western corner of a farm before continuing south, but within a few hundred yards, the draw began to narrow and deepen, until by the time it reached the western corner, it would have to cross the beginning of a small canyon. The county had taken the easiest route, which was to cut off about eight acres of trees, and wetland. The concession to the landowner was to build an underpass so that livestock had a free passage from one side of the road to the other.

The owner before Ed had built an earthen dam across the draw just inside the western fence line. At some point, a flash flood had washed a channel through the middle of it, leaving a standing pool several hundred feet long behind the remaining part of the failed dam, choked with cattails, waterweeds and frogs.

In an effort to let the sunshine melt snow and ice off the road, county crews had cut a forty-foot strip of trees on the south side of the road inside the Kelley fence line. Then they had bulldozed the trees and brush into large piles. Over the years, the piles of piñon and cedar were still a source of firewood for the Kelley family as well as the schoolhouse stove. Several heaps of dead trees and limbs still remained.

Cliff positioned himself behind a tangle of trunks and branches and settled in to wait until Hector and the rest of the kids came laughing and chattering down the road.

He tried several positions trying to get comfortable yet stay hidden and at the same time improving his view of the road.

His left eye had swollen completely shut now. It didn't matter. He aimed with his right eye anyway. However, the temporary loss of vision in his left eye interfered with his depth perception, and he couldn't see clearly even as close away as the corner where the road turned to the north.

He would have to wait until they were almost even with him to see well enough to aim.

Cliff's heart beat rapidly as he replayed the fight that morning. What bothered him almost as much as the beating itself was the way the rest of the kids encouraged Hector. Their ferocity and hatred were frightening. *What did I ever do to them? They acted as though they wanted to get in there and get in a few licks themselves. I always wanted to be their friends. I think I could have been, without Hector there.*

The loudest encouragement came from Emilio. That was no surprise. He's a coward by himself. When we are by ourselves, we talk and laugh together almost like friends. However, when Hector enters the picture, Emilio struts around just like him.

I should take down Hector and Emilio both.

Even though the sunshine was warm, Cliff felt cold. He closed his still functioning right eye for a moment while he waited. Like a dam breaking, vivid images flooded the space behind his eyes. He saw himself *sitting in the fifth grade row in the one room school. The stern thin faced teacher, Mr. Johnson, in his starched white shirt, checking his pocket watch, tapping on his desk with the oak mallet announcing, "Recess. Fifteen minutes. Take your restroom break. Today it's group games, mandatory participation. Dismissed."*

"Mandatory participation." Mr. Johnson's favorite rule. All students must participate. No exceptions! No sideline sitters. Refusing to participate is insubordination. The penalty for insubordination is a whipping. Weapon of choice: hard twist rope hanging in plain view by the front door.

Exempt first-third grade students run to the newly erected playground equipment to fight over the swings, slide, and the teeter-totter; while teacher appointed fourth grade captains, Hector and Emilio, chose sides for a quick game of "Red Rover, Red Rover." Emilio finally chooses lone fifth grader Cliff. The next time they play the game Hector will choose Cliff. It all seems prearranged.

Is this how it all began? Mr. Johnson gave them the power in the beginning, and they ran with it. The few older students at that time were not aggressive enough to want to be team leaders and were happy to follow their younger cousins.

The action played out like Saturday afternoon serials in Cliff's head, short choppy episodes in grainy black and white.

Teams lining up, linking arms, moving to form two lines ten feet apart. The captains summoning students back and forth. The summoned raising their arms above their heads and breaking through linked hands with their stomachs or chests all in good fun. Breakors bring breakees back to their side. Those who can't break through must join the unbroken line. The winning team has the most remaining players when time is up.

Inevitably, Cliff hears Emilio's call, "Red Rover, Red Rover, let Hector come over."

Hector smiles. Next time when Cliff is on his side, he will call Emilio over. It is the same every time they play the game.

In their games if a big kid roughs up one of the younger kids, it is probably a family member and there are consequences at home if someone gets hurt. It is a game and not to be carried too far.

The only odd person out is Cliff. All rules are suspended when it comes to him. For some perverse reason, Mr. Johnson turns a blind eye to Hector and Emilio's game. He always conveniently calls an end to recess and goes inside the building just at that point in the game and the teacher misses the action.

Hector looks over at Cliff, prances out of line, stretches, leaps forward, sprints between the teams to Cliff's position. He pivots, raises his arms then, against the rules, brings his hands together making a double fist. It's the same old routine. Emilio does the same thing when he is called over.

Cliff struggles to break free of hands on either side of him, but realizes those hands are now tightly gripping his wrists. Hector is targeting the arm held by the strongest classmate.

Hector shouts a guttural, "Huuhhhh" as he brings his clenched double fist down onto Cliff's forearm with bruising force. Pain shoots through Cliff's arm and wrist. His teammate turns loose an instant later. Laughter erupts as the two lines break and the students run for the building, leaving Cliff holding his arm with tears streaming down his face.

It is a scene repeated, with some variation, time after time. When Cliff complains to the teacher, Mr. Johnson quips, *"You've got to learn to get along out there. It's just a game. You've got to learn to be a team player."*

In the fall and spring, the game is softball, and Mr. Johnson is both pitcher and umpire. There are just enough older students to play a game of workup.

"Strike two," Pitcher-umpire Mr. Johnson calls. Emilio taps home plate, spits in his palms, grips the bat, and takes his stance. Mr. Johnson winds up. Emilio hits a hard line drive between first and second.

Hector scoops up the ball ten feet from first base. He can easily run it to the base and make the out.

Cliff guards first base. Like all the other players, he has no mitt. Only Mr. Johnson has a mitt. Cliff dreads the throw to come. From ten feet a gentle toss will be enough to put Emilio out. His hands and thumbs are swollen and ache from earlier hard throws by Hector, a condition that starts each spring after the first few games.

Cliff wonders why they call it a softball. It's twice the size of a baseball and pitched underhand, but it's as hard as a baseball when it strikes the hand, thumb, face, ribs or any other part of the anatomy. Because of its weight, additional surface area and mass, it does even more damage than a baseball.

Hector's lip curls. He watches as Emilio races toward first, and at the last minute unleashes the hard softball with all the power he has. The softball spins across the short space like a bullet straight into Cliff's bare hands, thumbs bending back, stretching, straining, spraining. Which is the lesser of two evils, catch the hard thrown ball and damage his hands further or be hit in the body by the ball? Cliff tenses causing more pain to ribs already bruised from hard thrown balls from Hector's hand. Cliff's hands close around the ball and hold on. He chokes back a scream and steps on the base making the out.

He throws the ball down and stalks off the field.

"Game's not over Mr. Kelley!"

"Game's over for me! It's not a game anymore!"

"You play when I say so."

"My hands won't take it anymore! I don't have a mitt like you do. You and he both know he doesn't need to throw the ball that hard at that distance."

Hector laughs...

"Either get back to your base or bring me the rope. You know the rules young man!"

"Get the rope yourself!"

"Emilio! Bring me the rope!"

"Yes, sir!" Emilio gleefully races to the schoolhouse and returns a moment later with the hard twist rope.

Mr. Johnson grabs Cliff by the arm and swings the inch thick rope hard against the back of Cliff's legs. Through clenched teeth the teacher utters, "... participate with the rest of the students... never talk back to me...!"

Cliff doesn't reply and wills himself not to cry. He wants the teacher to confine him to his desk in the schoolhouse for the rest of the day without recess. It will be a reward, not a punishment. He's willing to take another whipping from Mr. Johnson the next day if that is what it takes to let the swelling in his thumbs to go down... He chooses the lesser of two evils...Mr. Johnson's rope or suffering at the hands of Hector. Either way, Hector has won.

More images...shifting to the playground side of the schoolhouse. "Annie Over," Carmen calling from the side of the stucco schoolhouse facing the road. Kids on Cliff's side scattering beneath the eves of the tin roof waiting for a first glimpse of the softball, just then appearing over the roof ridge and rolling toward Porferio's waiting hands. Porferio and team making a mad dash around the end of the building, half going left, half to the right, arriving on the other side too late to tag anyone.

"Annie Over," Porferio calls, launching the ball over the rooftop, team and ball disappearing simultaneously on the way to the other side of the schoolhouse.

The goal: catch the ball, run it around the building, tag a member of the opposing team by touching him/her with the ball. The ball can be thrown to another member of the team to make the tag, but cannot be thrown at a member of the opposing team, before they leave the area from which the ball was launched. The catcher must either run with the ball or return it over the roof. It can only be run if caught.

Cliff reaches the safe zone.

Hector waits for him.

He should not be here. He should have run the ball if he caught it. The rest of the team would not have run if he had not caught it. They ran to the other side of the building. He should be with his team. He has the ball. If he doesn't run with it, he must throw it back over the roof according to the rules.

Too late, Cliff realizes Hector will ignore the rules. Again. It is an ambush.

Hector draws back and throws with full force the length of the school building.

Cliff dodges but feels indescribable pain as the ball connects with his already bruised rib cage.

Each scene in his mind becomes progressively painful as he advances through sixth grade. He is caught between Hector, Mr. Johnson and his dad's unwitting support of Mr. Johnson's disciplinary control of his students, a control that is geared toward deportment toward the teacher within the classroom.

He gives up telling his folks when they examine his thumbs and palms. He can barely move them. The thumbs aren't broken. They think he is exaggerating and making excuses. They don't interfere. He almost cries when he milks the cows or holds a pencil.

When he gets a whipping at school for refusing to participate, the hardest part is receiving the same punishment when he gets home. He must hand his dad the hated "insubordination," notes and watch his expression change from concern to rage. He waits as his dad returns with the razor strop. One lash, two lashes, three lashes…"

"Because of my hands Dad…!"

"Insubordination! Questioning the teacher's authority isn't acceptable!"

"No extenuating circumstances permitted."

Who was worse, Mr. Johnson or Dad? Dad was supposed to be my first line of defense wasn't he? Maybe I should take the .22 to him too!

The last day of sixth grade Mr. Johnson announces that he will not be back the next year. It is the happiest day of his life. Blessed relief at last!

Seventh and eighth grades were better during the school day under the protection of Mrs. Campbell, so Hector moved it to the road after school. In his mind, Cliff relives facing a gauntlet stretching across the road.

The kids standing, hands linked, bigger kids evenly spaced between the smaller kids. No way to get around without crawling through a fence and making a long detour through a neighbor's field. He is fast, and it's downhill clear to the man-gate at the corner of the road through the Kelley fence. He tries running at top speed swinging his lunch bucket. Sometimes they scatter, and he runs through and keeps going. More often, he picks himself up out of the barrow pit, clothes dirty, bits of weeds and grass in his hair, watching kids laughing and taunting as they run on down the road ahead of him.

Cliff gasped for air. He was cold even though he perspired in the hot afternoon sun as scene after scene of past harassment at the hands of Hector, Mr. Johnson and even his dad tumbled through his mind. Finally, the loop stuck and repeated with his dad's arm endlessly swinging first a belt then a razor strop...

Cliff stood up to stop the images. He stretched his legs and looked up the road. How much longer did he have to wait? He felt in his pocket and took out a shell. He rolled it back and forth between his thumb and forefinger. Still he did not load the rifle.

The sun hung high in the southwestern sky. Had he been there only a moment or for hours? *What if the teacher sent Hector home right after I left?*

He sat back down in his nest in the pile of broken tree branches. His rage still simmered. He felt slightly nauseated from the memories and images.

Cliff became alert at the sound of a rapidly moving car approaching from the direction of the school. It rounded the corner going too fast, sending a cloud of dust drifting up the slope toward the Kelley home. Through his one functioning eye, it looked like a pale blue 1950 Ford speeding down the road toward Cliff's hiding place.

Cliff froze. It was similar to the one Mr. Johnson had driven the last year he taught at East Lakeview Grade School. *Can it be?*

Cliff lifted the rifle and took aim at the driver as the car sped closer. The dark silhouette in the windshield looked like Mr. Johnson's narrow face. He kept the profile in his sight until the car was broadside, and he could see that it was a woman he had never seen before. The car sped on to the corner, took it too fast, sent a cloud of dust into the timber on the west side of the road, and sped south on its way to either Lakeview or Cortez.

Cliff shook as the adrenaline drained away. He had not pulled the trigger. He had not loaded a shell into the chamber of the rifle, but the impulse had been there, and it had been strong. He was certain that had it been Hector walking down the road at that moment, he would have loaded and shot.

Cliff shook his head to clear it. *What am I doing here anyway?*

"Everything you do has a natural consequence," his mother often told him. "Sometimes a decision is a good thing, and sometimes it's a disaster. Always consider the natural consequences of any decision you make." Her final advice to him during any decision was, "Ask yourself, what would Jesus do?"

What he contemplated would destroy not only Hector, Hector's family, Cliff's family, and all hopes and dreams for Cliff's future. Revenge would be sweet, for the moment, but according to his mother and father, the consequences would last for eternity.

Suddenly, Cliff got up from where he sat in ambush and ran back through the woods. He climbed through the fence and ran headlong across the alfalfa field back to the gunnysack and shovel.

He bent over beside the ditch trying to catch his breath and threw up. Heave after heave brought up nothing but bitter bile.

Did I seriously think about killing my classmate and the rest of them? Bully or not, surely there is a better way to deal with Hector than that, isn't there?

"Is there no hope for me?" he cried out bleakly.

He went to the irrigation ditch on the other side of the knoll and washed the bile from his mouth. He took a long drink of fresh water and looked back at the house. There was still no sign of his mother.

Cliff stuck the shovel upright in the sod bank of the ditch. He picked up the gunnysack and the rifle and continued down the lane heading south. He climbed through the fence that marked the south boundary of the farm, looked back across the farm toward the house once more, turned and entered the woods onto county land.

He did not look back again.

6
Monday, afternoon late
Between Kelley farm and Martinez Canyon

Every boy should have a place to go when he needs time to be alone, a favorite place to lie alone on a summer Sunday afternoon to listen to nature, watch ants work at their hill, read his book, or daydream. Cliff walked on autopilot toward his place.

He walked due south through piñon and cedar woods to a clearing where a mound of rubble rose above the surrounding trees. At the edge of the clearing was a very old cedar tree with a humming column of honeybees flying to and from a knothole on its trunk.

He dropped the gunnysack under the bee tree and leaned the rifle against the trunk. It was cool in the shade. A pile of stones, accumulated from numerous past visits, served as either a bench or a backrest. He sat down on the stones wearily for a moment listening to the calming drone of the bees.

Cliff's swollen eye hurt, and his forehead and cheeks burned under the bandages. Blood still oozed from his nose. He wondered if it was broken. Each time he took a breath, his ribs hurt.

He opened the sack and poked through what little he had brought from the house. The aspirin had helped, but the effects were wearing off. *Why didn't I grab a bottle of aspirin?* He hadn't thought through what he packed into the sack. *I should have taken time to make sandwiches and grab a water bag.*

The walk from Dog Town had settled his stomach, and he was a little hungry. Cliff selected a piece of jerky and bit down into the tough dried beef, but his jaw was so sore that he could not chew it. He exchanged it for an oatmeal cookie. He let the cookie melt in his mouth and swallowed it whole, including the raisins.

He was thirsty, but the nearest drinking water was back at the irrigation ditch. City folk would consider irrigation ditches unfit to drink out of, but he'd been drinking out of them all his life, and the water hadn't made him sick yet.

Cliff sat on the ground, leaned back against the stack of shaped stones and listened to the bees. He had a special attachment to this tree and the colony within. His first hive of bees had issued from it.

The discovery of the tree was, oddly enough, a result of his dad's odd mix of taskmaster and religious beliefs.

His eyes glazed over as he thought about his dad. He was a difficult man to understand. He was kind to his neighbors; polite, respected, soft-spoken and well liked. He was a guardian of the land, environment and neighborhood.

Cliff's dad was a teacher by nature. He had little formal education but was a self-taught mechanic, scientist, electrician, engineer, botanist and geologist. He had to labor over everything he read and that limited his reading to non-fiction.

He taught Cliff practical farming like surveying ditches to get maximum use of their water. Their surveyed ditches appeared to make water run uphill. Even their better-educated neighbors couldn't understand how Ed did it.

He taught Cliff how to catch native trout on artificial flies in Lost Canyon and Mancos Creek and how to hunt deer, dress and skin them and how to take care of the meat and hide, even how to harvest the tendons to make sinew and hooves to make glue. Together they searched for mineral rocks, agate, quartz, flint, turquoise, petrified wood and dinosaur bone that a friend cut and polished. They explored Indian ruins and discussed theories of how the Ancestral Puebloans had lived and why they had left the area 700 years before.

Most of all he had taught Cliff about the wonders of nature and to appreciate God's handiwork from the tiny insects, flowers, and trees to the majestic mountains and the nearby Grand Canyon of the Colorado.

The monarch butterflies' metamorphosis from caterpillars to cocoon to butterfly fascinated Ed Kelley. To him, it proved God's plan for righteous men. It was God's symbol for man's path from life on earth to an eternal existence as angels in paradise.

For all his wonderful qualities, his dad had a dark side. His quick temper, stubborn rigidness in his religious beliefs and stern discipline at home could turn him into a fearsome man in a heartbeat. He was a kind man most of the time, but he was not particularly affectionate. He relentlessly drove himself and his family. Only those closest to him saw his quick temper and mood swings.

Sometimes Cliff watched the other kids playing at school, and he realized that he didn't enjoy playing as they did. He did not really know how to play. They had fun for the sake of having fun. Cliff thought their games were silly and without purpose. Things he enjoyed were purposeful, not just to pass the time. The games he was required to participate in were not fun, but, thanks to Hector, were painful or carried the threat of pain.

Cliff felt as if he had no time to be a boy. He felt rushed to become a man too quickly.

Maybe Dad didn't learn how to play either.

~~~

His dad often told of the depression that hit rural America especially hard in the early 1920's when his family was struggling for survival. Ed had turned thirteen years old in 1920. Annual average farm income had dropped to $400 per family, and he had dropped out of school at the end of the seventh grade to help support his family of six siblings and two adults.
~~~

They had survived that depression and World War I.

Cliff's dad and mother had weathered the Great Depression, and the dust bowl years of the 30's and the rationing and sacrifices of the WWII years. Ed had escaped joining the army. As a farmer, he was valuable to the national effort. He would have claimed exemption on religious grounds as a Conscientious Objector if called.

He didn't believe in fighting, either in a brawl or in war.

Ed had begun farming on his own between the age of 12 and 14 in New Mexico. Out of those years, he developed a work ethic that dictated simply, "A man, who doesn't work, doesn't eat."

Etta Mae's picture box contained a faded brown photo of a skinny boy, who resembled Cliff, in bib overalls with a thin face and haunted eyes. On the back someone had scrawled in pencil, "1920, Ed Kelley, New Mexico farmer, age 13."

He expected his sons Charlie and then Cliff to begin carrying their own weight at the same age as expected of him.

If either of his boys complained or whined about the work being too hard for them to do at their age, he quoted "Paul in First Corinthian, Chapter 11, Verse 13. 'When I was a child, I felt as a child, I thought as a child; Now that I am become a man, I have put away childish things.'"

Cliff's dad was a religious man. "According to Genesis 2:2 'and on the seventh day God ended his work which he had made; and he rested on the seventh day from all his work which he had made.'" That had been the Sabbath on the Roman calendar. In his interpretation of the New Testament, the fulfillment of the old law had required that the new day of rest correspond to Sunday, the Christian day of worship.

Ed extended the "day of rest" tradition on Sunday to all his family. It was their "God-given" right. Some things required attention even on Sunday such as milking cows, and feeding the animals, but in general, the family farmed only in an emergency such as impending rain during haying season or threat of early frost killing a crop ready to harvest.

Everyone was to go to Church, or at least study the Bible, for an hour or so on Sunday morning. Ed did not believe in churches with rituals. He followed the ideas of a Nineteenth Century American religious leader, Thomas Campbell, who had preached returning to basic Christianity as practiced as nearly as possible to the churches in the times of the Apostles.

Ed found no references to instrumental music, and therefore believed only acappella singing was allowed in church. He found no reference to Sunday schools, ornament or graven images. Ministry was by the members themselves, not by a hierarchy. Because this eliminated most churches in Christianity, there was often no acceptable group available to meet with. Sometimes Etta Mae and Cliff went to Cortez to attend an established church of some size with a similar belief except for Sunday school and a hired minister. During those times, Ed stayed home and read his bible.

Other times if they heard of a like minded family or a family moved to within traveling distance, they traveled to Dove Creek, Yellow Jacket, Mancos, Durango, or even as far away as Farmington, New Mexico. Sometimes several families came together, each traveling from as far away as Farmington to meet somewhere in the middle. The meetings took place in a home and the families rotated. Those times were the best because usually there were other kids and potlucks.

If they traveled far and several families were involved, after services the men would move off to one side while the women set the food out. In summer, the kids played or talked. It usually depended on the age grouping. Inevitably, after the food settled for a half hour, the host distributed songbooks around the living room and an hour of singing began. Ed had called singing "a joyful noise." It depended on who sang. When the whole group sang some of the songs, it was the sweetest sound that Clifton ever heard. Noise was the most apt description of some of the songs. But, when the request came for Ed and Etta Mae to sing Amazing Grace, chills went up his spine. Their voices blended so perfectly. They had met in just such a meeting.

~~~

Regardless of whether they went to church or not, every Sunday yielded some free time for Cliff to spend on his own.

As Cliff grew older and gained more independence, he used his freedom to explore his universe, which extended as far as he could walk to and return in time do the chores.

Sometimes he had only a few hours of freedom and sometimes all afternoon. Cliff's exploration continued even during sunny winter Sunday afternoons. During cold and stormy Sundays, he whittled or read at the house. Sometimes he helped his mother at the suspended quilting frame, carefully hand stitching designs in a quilt or tying them.

In the summertime, his second most favorite past time was hunting bee trees. It was on one of those Sunday summer afternoon explorations that he discovered his first bee tree, the tree that he sat under at that moment. It was the first of several he had located.

All bee trees he had found were in cedar trees like the one in the clearing.

Unlike its shorter-lived piñon pine neighbors, the cedar tree had grown slowly for several centuries, until its girth was over four feet in diameter from the ground to the "Y" in the trunk that divided into an unruly mass of twisted branches. Patches of thick, gray-brown bark retreated from sections of the branches exposing white bleached wood. Dull, blue tinted, green needles and clusters of turquoise berries grew from the outer few feet of each twisted branch.

Repeated lightning strikes had charred and ripped away chunks of bark and wood.

Cliff had followed a "beeline", a fly-way, from the alfalfa field to the tree. That was the year he turned twelve. He had nagged his dad all the following winter for information on bees. They had visited a beekeeper,
~~~

and he had come home with a worn out smoker, a discarded hive and one broken frame. From that, he had duplicated a set of frames using the new Shopsmith with which his dad had built the farmhouse. The all-in-one tool was table saw, drill, lathe and sander. He had made good use of the table saw and disk sander. By spring, he had a freshly painted white hive with 10 frames strung with thin sheets of pure beeswax foundation embossed with the imprint of the cells. How could a swarm of bees resist settling into a new home like that?

He had visited the tree often that spring. The colony swarmed in late May, and he was lucky to discover it only hours afterward. The swarm still hung from a branch of the home tree, when he had arrived. He had raced home to get the hive, and with help from his dad, had brushed the three-gallon mass of bees from the branch into the open hive. The large healthy swarm had spread out on the frames, and Ed had carefully put the lid over the bees covering them and the frames in the hive. It looked as if as many hung on the outside of the hive as on the inside, but Ed reassured Cliff that they would join the rest of the swarm inside, or they would all leave. It depended on if they had captured the queen or not. They would know if the capture was successful when they came back for the hive the next day.

The next morning nearly as many bees issued forth and headed out to forage as left the parent cedar tree.

That had been two summers before. Since then he had captured more swarms and his apiary now counted six hives.

They'll be swarming again soon. My hives back at the house will be swarming also. I have empty boxes ready for all of them. I could have six more hives of bees by the end of June. If you haven't screwed that up too, Hector!

The bee tree and Ancient Puebloan ruins sat on government land a third of the way between the south Kelley fence line and Martinez Canyon.

The cedar tree spread its gnarled branches at the edge of an acre-sized clearing filled by rock and rubble, which he and his dad assumed were the remains of an Ancient Puebloan settlement. Perhaps it had been the ceremonial, religious or even the market center for the area farmers.

Under the trees surrounding the remains of the pueblo, there were numerous slight indentations in the ground and partially exposed rings of rock where pit dwellings had once housed a native population.

When Cliff visited the clearing on those warm Sunday afternoons, he was as fascinated by the mound of rubble as with the bees. In places, partially exposed stonewalls showed through the dirt and sagebrush. Archeologists had excavated similar sized mounds on Mesa Verde. From those he could visualize what lay below the rubble.

Cliff closed his functioning right eye and fantasized the ruin, as it must have been 700 years before. The soil that had drifted in over the centuries disappeared. Walls were complete again. Flat roofs were covered, and ladders once again projected through square holes in the centers. Women climbed ladders with baskets balanced on their heads, while children chased turkeys and each other around and through the trees. Throbbing drums accompanied a dancing Shaman with a hideously painted face, as he circled a fire.

He opened his eye and the drumbeats faded. It was silent again in the clearing. The only remaining sound was of the breeze rustling through the cedar and the hum of the returning honeybees. His dream was to someday to be a member of the archeological team that unearthed the mound inch by inch and catalogued the relics and secrets that had lain hidden for seven centuries.

Cliff visited the tree on many Sunday afternoons. While sitting in that spot, or while lying there, he would visualize his future as a "bee man", an entomologist, or an archeologist.

Unfortunately, the professional schools where one learned those professions were expensive. Penniless farm boys who graduated from one-room country schools probably could not pass entrance qualifications or afford the tuition. At least dreams were free.

Of more immediate concern than college four years hence was what to do in the next four hours when the sun went down. He had no idea what to do or where to spend the night.

He had combined hunting for bee trees with another favorite past time exploring the canyons that crisscrossed the Ridge. Discovering a bee tree in one canyon had led to his greatest discovery of all. It had happened last summer in Martinez Canyon, a quarter of a mile south of the clearing where he sat. Martinez Canyon was the longest, deepest, wildest, and the least known canyon on the Ridge.

He thought about the prairie dog and its burrow.

I really need a place to crawl into for the night. I need a burrow.

Maybe the answer lies within my discovery in Martinez Canyon. I vowed I'd never go back there. I've kept my promise to never reveal its secret, but after 700 year's maybe it could be a place for me to burrow in for the night.

There next to another bee tree was another Ancient Puebloan ruin of a different kind nestled, hidden, beneath the rimrock.

I've got to decide. The direction I take depends on my decision. Do I seriously run, or do I hide? I could hide in the canyon. Or, I can cross it and keep on going.

He couldn't decide.

It was only a short walk from the clearing to the rim of the canyon. However, if he wished to cross the canyon, he had to go east nearly a mile to the intersection of a draw that cut to the bottom of the canyon from the north. The southern slope was gentler and deer had worn a trail up that side.

Cliff listened to the bees droning above him as he tried to make up his mind. The sound was soothing, hypnotic. His head hurt and his closed eye throbbed making it difficult to concentrate. He nodded. He was tired and drained. He opened the sack, took out the saddle blanket and lay down on it. He pulled the gunnysack back under his head for a pillow and closed his functioning eye.

When he awoke, the headache was not as severe. The blood had fully clotted in his nose. He lay thinking about what he should do.

I can walk to the head of the canyon and across to the highway. Dad was a walker. He walked fifteen hundred miles the year before I was born, walking from New Mexico to Utah to Colorado looking for work. He walked from farm to farm, town to town before finding work with the Civilian Conservation Corps in Cortez. He walked back to Albuquerque, New Mexico, gathered Mom and Charlie, borrowed a car and drove them back to Cortez. While I was being born, he returned the car to New Mexico and walked back here.

He was a walking man. I'm the son of a walking man. I could be a walking man too, just like Dad. I could walk to Albuquerque and live in an alley like David Copperfield.

At highway 160, if I'm lucky, I can hitch a ride on a truck. If the driver goes east, I'll be in Denver by morning. If he goes west, I'll be in Albuquerque, Salt Lake or Phoenix. I can hitch a ride with a Navaho and live on the reservation. I can pass for an Indian. I've got black hair and a good suntan. Mom always says this face can pass for a Navajo. I'll have trouble explaining these bib overalls though. I've never seen an Indian wearing bib overalls. I'll have to explain that white people kidnapped me when I was a baby.

Who am I kidding? Who's gonna pick up a kid who looks about ten years old with a black eye, battered face, bloody nose and carrying a rifle? If I hitch, I'll have to ditch the .22. I hate to leave it behind.

What if I do get a ride? I don't have money. Will anybody hire a fourteen-year-old run-a-way? If I was big and strong looking like Hector, I could probably get a job. He looks like a sixteen or seventeen year old who can work. Look at me. A hundred pounds. I look more like a ten year old than a man.

Outside of doing a few farm chores, what can I do? I've never worked for anybody before. I've sold honey to the neighbors and baby skunks to the veterinarian! Otherwise, I've never worked for money.

I can hide out somewhere and steal enough to live on for a while. I'm pretty sure I'll be caught and probably be sent to jail. That's a great thought. That one really appeals to me! At least, I'll get three square meals a day.

Cliff absently picked at the clot in his nose and the blood began to ooze again. He wiped his hand on the gunnysack. *Doggone you Hector!*

It was the worst beating that he'd ever taken from anybody. Even the whippings he got from his dad didn't result in black eyes or a bloody nose; just welts on his butt. He felt the rage begin to boil up again.

The images began cascading through his mind again. *He was back by the road aiming the .22.* "Stop it!" he shouted. "Leave me alone!" He demanded. The images faded.

I should just go on back to the house. I should be proud about today. Today I stood up to you Hector. Most of the time you let others do the fighting. You goad the other kids into it or into helping you. I thought maybe if I stood up to you, you just might back down. I'll bet you would have, if it had been just you and me!

But, why should you back down? I put you on the spot in front of all the kids.

You are bigger than me. You didn't have to back down, and you knew it. But, even though I got whipped, I feel like I won too. First time in seven years, I should feel proud for not running and hiding from you!

So why am I running?

Do you know what? I'm not running from you any more Hector. That's not what really bothers me. You and Emilio are cowards. I've never done anything to you except be there. But tonight when Dad gets home from work, I'll get another beating. That's what bothers me.

Tonight when you get home Dad, why can't you say, "Finally you stood up to him. I'm proud of you!" Instead, you have your stupid rule, and you'll enforce it.

Today I refuse to be bullied. Not from Hector, not from you, Dad. Today, I refused to run from Hector. I tried to fight him back, but I can't fight you, Dad.

The only other thing I can do is leave. In the long run, you are more dangerous to me than Hector. I'm done with him. I can't continue to live with you!

If I had thoughts about using the .22 on Hector, will I begin having the same thoughts about you? I can't take that risk. Even though I'm afraid of you, Dad, I love you. I'm leaving your house to protect you from me.

Just the day before, on Sunday afternoon, Cliff had visited a point where the rimrock jutted out into the canyon. East of the point, the rimrock swept southward away from the main canyon. Land eastward sloped more gently toward the bottom of the canyon. A deer trail wound up from the creek near the base of the cliff formed by the rimrock.

On the north side of Martinez Canyon a draw that was more of a swale when it ran next to the east Kelley fence line had deepened and equaled the depth of Martinez Canyon as it intersected it directly across from the point. On either side of the draw's intersection, the north wall of the main canyon was sheer and the rimrock was thick.

The point on the south rim resembled an arrowhead jutting into the canyon. Martinez Canyon curved slightly to the south both east and west of the point. The point, commanded a view that extended for nearly a half mile in both directions up and down the canyon. It was on this point that the Ancestral Puebloans had erected a round stone lookout tower.

Small square windows allowed sentries to look up the draw, and up or down the canyon.

Cliff had sat with his back against the ruin of the tower reading his graduation present from Mrs. Campbell, a book about the Alaskan gold rush named *Smoke Bellow* by Jack London. It was a quiet place on the point. No one ever bothered him there. It wasn't a secret place. The tower ruin was a familiar landmark to most of the old-time residents on the Ridge. It was out in the open, but there was little reason for anyone else to be there.

The day before when he sat at the base of the tower, he had felt a sensation that he wasn't alone. He had put the book down and scanned the canyon as an ancient warrior might have done 700 years before. He saw nothing moving either in the draw or in the canyon. Finally, he saw the slightest movement on the opposite wall of the canyon to the left of the draw. There on a ledge so narrow it looked like a scratch, stood a goat watching him.

How long had the goat been there? It was some breed of domestic goat, so it must have run away from a farm somewhere. Where had it come from? Cliff tried to think of a neighbor who raised goats. Maybe Enrique Martinez had goats. His farm extended right up to the point on the same side of the canyon as Cliff sat. The Martinez family had owned land there for generations and the canyon originated on their original holdings thus the name Martinez Canyon.

Equally mysterious as where the goat had come from was how it had managed to get up to the ledge where it stood. The goat appeared to stand on a crack where the rimrock rested on the next layer of sandstone beneath it. The smooth face of the rimrock towered twenty feet above the goat and the layers below dropped half again as far to the rubble before sloping to the bottom of the canyon.

If the goat wanted to escape from people, it had come to a good place. There was water, plenty to eat and shelter in the canyon. The goat had everything it needed there in the canyon except possibly the company of other goats, assuming it needed company.

Maybe it was a sign. Maybe the goat was giving me the answer to my problem. Maybe his herd pushed him away and that's why he sought refuge in the canyon. If he can survive there, surely I can too.

Seven hundred years or so ago the canyons and farmlands around here supported a large population of natives. If I can figure out how to use what's there, the canyon should now easily support one lost boy and an anti-social goat.

I might not have the skills to make a living by earning money, but I haven't been asleep the past few years either.

Well it's time to, as Dad says, "Fish or cut bait."

It's too late to walk to the highway today, so I guess I just have one other place to go. Now let's see if I can find it. It has been nearly a year and that time I approached it from the creek. I had two good eyes to look for it. It's also too late to go into the canyon and try to retrace my steps. I'm not up to the climb this time anyway. I'll look from the top and with one eye. What are the chances? Oh, well.

Cliff rolled the saddle blanket and replaced it in the gunnysack, picked up the rifle, walked past the rubble of the Ancient Pueblo ruin and headed south the short distance to the rim of the canyon.

7

A Sunday afternoon, the year before Martinez Canyon

The summer of his thirteenth year, Cliff had followed another "bee-line" in the canyon in search of bee trees. He had discovered a bee tree, and even more remarkably, a small cliff dwelling on the north wall of Martinez Canyon. If he could find it again before dark, it would provide a temporary hiding place and shelter for the night. No one would disturb him there.

He had found the ruin on a hot summer Sunday afternoon. Cliff had fulfilled his mandatory two hours of Bible study by 11:00 o'clock that morning. They were in a spell when no other families lived nearby to meet with who met Ed's narrow measure.

Cliff had made mincemeat sandwiches, packed a makeshift knapsack with the sandwiches and water and headed to the lookout tower ruin on the point of Martinez Canyon. It was unusual to have such an extended amount of free time. Usually by the time the family arrived home from church, and had dinner, it was almost 2:00 o'clock, and he had to be back by chore time.

He had decided to use the extra three hours to explore Martinez Canyon. The canyon was largely unexplored because it had fewer access points than the other canyons. One intersecting canyon breeched the rim-rock that he knew of, in the final six-mile stretch before it emptied out onto the valley near Cortez. The closest breech he was aware of was the north branching draw opposite the point on which the lookout ruins stood.

Cliff had entered the canyon at the lookout ruin and walked down the trail about a quarter of a mile before coming to a pool in the creek bordered by a lush stand of yellow sweet clover. He climbed onto a small boulder by the water's edge and ate his sandwich.

An unusually heavy honeybee presence on the clover drew his attention. It was possible that bees from the old cedar bee tree might be coming to these clover plants, but the clover and alfalfa on the farm were in full bloom at the same time and were a lot closer. Why come to the canyon instead?

The thought of finding another bee tree sidetracked his original intent of exploring the canyon.

Cliff began by watching which direction a bee flew after filling her abdomen with nectar. After she left the blossoms, she flew into the air, circled and flew in a straight line out of sight at a westerly slant up the canyon side. He saw a pattern after observing several bees fly in the same direction up the slope. Was it a beeline? If so, was it to a tree on the slope? What if it was to a colony up in the rimrock? It could even be to a bee tree out on top.

Because of the high volume of bees, he guessed that the colony was fairly close by.

He set the boulder as the lower anchor point, climbed the slope fifty feet and moved horizontally east up-canyon keeping an eye on the patch of clover and the boulder. He heard no volume increase in the ambient sounds in the canyon. He changed directions moving down the canyon until he finally became aware of a steady increase in the volume of the distinctive droning sound of honeybees. He kept moving forward until the volume began to decrease again, and then he backtracked until once again he stood beneath the maximum hum. The "beeline"?

Standing in that spot, he spread his arms with his left hand pointing to the boulder and his right hand pointing to the rimrock, and he sighted up the slope to the top of the rimrock.

He tried to memorize the significant trees along that path, and he studied the very rim itself looking for a crack or hole where a colony of bees could make their home or that could serve as the upper anchor point of the beeline. There, appearing to stand on the very edge of the rim stood a snag. It was little more than a black line in the distance, but visible enough to work as an upper anchor point. Only when he neared the rimrock would he identify the mark as a dead or dying cedar tree trunk.

He had established a visible flight line up the canyon side, a reference line. Along that line, if the colony was in the canyon, it was in all probabilities located somewhere within a few yards of that line. The challenge was to find it.

He made his way further up the slope and again aligned himself with the boulder and snag and the droning sound was clearly audible above other sounds in the canyon.

Sheer sandstone, broken scree, and obstacles made it impossible to climb in a straight line up the steep slope. Cliff climbed steadily between boulders, snaking back and forth under the beeline, sometimes detouring hundreds of yards horizontally up canyon or down canyon to gain eight or ten feet in elevation around a boulder or over a shelf.

He methodically checked all likely trees along the invisible path and slowly worked up the slope.

Anytime he checked a likely candidate to be housing a wild colony of bees, but found none, he immediately checked the alignment, particularly if he could not see both the anchor points, and listened for the beeline to see if he were still on course.

After nearly two hours of hard climbing, listening and examining trees, and cracks in the sandstone layers, he had worked his way almost to the base of the rimrock.

He sat on an outcropping and looked back at the tiny boulder and yellow spot of clover in the bottom of the canyon. He was now close enough to see clearly the cedar snag on the rimrock. A rugged, twisted, gnarled old cedar tree battled for life against age and the elements on the edge of the rimrock.

He sat slightly to its right about 50 feet below almost to the base of the rimrock. He had not heard the beeline for the last half hour since detouring to the right of a wide crumbling slope under the ledge at the foot of the rimrock.

None of the trees, so far, was right for a bee tree. Only one candidate remained to examine, and he wasn't sure he could reach it. It was a huge old giant of a cedar at the base of the rimrock about a hundred feet to his left. He had been headed directly toward it before having to detour.

From where he rested, it looked as if he could only reach the tree by working up to the ledge formed by a sandstone layer ten or twelve feet thick, directly beneath the forty-foot rimrock layer and then crawling along the ledge to where it widened, and he could walk to the tree.

He couldn't get closer to the tree on the slope itself. On the downhill side of the tree, loose scree, and clay covered the steep slope. If he stepped out onto it, he would slide for a hundred feet or so down the canyon.

How the ancient tree had ever taken root in such a precarious position, and grown so huge, straight and tall, was mystifying. The tree hugged the ledge. He guessed it to be between three and four feet in diameter at the point where it began to divide about six feet above the surface of the ledge.

The layer of sediment the tree stood on flared forward from beneath the ledge. The tree's roots covered the entire space and its roots kept it from eroding with the rest of the slope around it. Cliff could not see what the slope looked like directly on the far side of the tree. On the near side of the tree, the flare extended along the foot of the ledge for what Cliff estimated to be about fifteen feet before it dropped off evenly with the front of the ledge.

It looked like the roots and duff had built up on the east side wide enough for a person to stand on, but access would have to be by ladder or rope.

Next to where he sat, a six-foot wide boulder had broken loose from the underside of the rimrock and crushed through the softer layer of the ledge sandstone. The block had settled down the canyon slope about fifty feet further leaving behind a chute, which had filled with rock and rubble in its wake. Had it tumbled, a significant rockslide might have created a dam across the creek some distance below.

The chute was too narrow and steep to eventually fill and become a trail access to the canyon. Mountain climbers might find it interesting, although it did not breech the rim cap itself.

Prudence dictated that Cliff leave now. He had gone as far as he could safely go.

Cliff could gain nothing by getting closer, other than verifying that it was actually a bee tree. He couldn't rob it. The best that could come of it was to know when to watch for a swarm. If he kept an eye on it from the top all through swarming season. If the swarm landed on a tree out on top. If he were right there within the six or eight hour timeframe before they flew again.

There were too many ifs to risk climbing any further. But, something nagged him to go the extra ten feet up the chute of loose rubble. He had come this far. *This is where I usually turn and run. I always take it to almost there... Facing Hector... Getting every last thing done without being told... Well why not finish this one, for once....*

Stubbornness was a Kelley trait. Ed liked to call it persistence.

No one knew where he was. He had just said he was going to go for a walk over to the lookout tower ruin at Martinez Canyon. His mom had just said, "Be careful."

If she could see me now, what would she say? "What would Jesus do?" Face it, If Jesus could walk on water, he could walk right up this chute, and he wouldn't have to worry about rocks shifting under him.

Kelley persistence kicked in. *Personally, I think Jesus would approve.*

He began climbing. In the last few feet of the chute, he felt the rubble settling and shifting under his weight. He wondered if a key rock would suddenly break loose and carry it, the loose rock and him in a thundering rockslide down the canyon side, gathering additional rock and boulders all the way, and finally burying him under tons of rock and rubble.

Once he got up to the ledge, if he got up, he had to think about getting back down. That would be ironic... I find the bee tree and then am buried in an avalanche and can't tell anybody about it.

Cliff was almost to the shelf when he felt the rocks begin to shift under him again. He reached for the edge of the shelf and pulled as he pushed and scrambled over the top. The loose rock under his foot slipped, settled another foot and stopped. He scrambled further onto the ledge, turned around, looked the way he had come and lay panting.

That probably wasn't the smartest thing I've ever done. He stared back down the chute he had just climbed. It looked twice as far down as it had appeared to be up. *How will I ever climb back down that thing,* he wondered. *In King Solomon's Mines, after all the jungle and hostile tribes Allan Quatermain and Elizabeth Curtis escaped from, they found the mines. However, the movie never showed how they got out. Unfortunately, this isn't a movie. I can't get away with that.*

Cliff crawled along the narrow ledge until finally it was wide enough that he could stand. He walked past a seep with grass and clover. He directed his full attention to the tree. He approached with caution. None of the bees at the clover patch had shown hostility, but he could never be too cautious at a bee tree.

Bees in the wild often mixed with wild strains and bad tempered colonies were often the result. If this was a hostile colony, guard bees would soon sound the alarm, and a few angry bees would dart at him. If that happened, he would back off. He wasn't prepared with veil, or long sleeves.

He had been stung plenty of times, usually because a bee had become trapped between his clothes and his skin, snarled in his hair, or he had accidentally mashed one. He did not react to their stings. But, too many stings and the collective venom could cause his body's neurological system to react as if he were bitten by a rattle snake.

As he slowly approached the tree, he saw a thick column of bees flowing to and from a black knot hole on the main trunk of the tree.

The entrance to the tree was about three feet below the surface of the ledge through a one inch knot hole that had rotted out where a small branch had withered and died then broken from the main trunk. The decaying knot had provided the breech to the cavity inside. It was now the bee entrance. The bee entrance faced south away from the ruin. The tree actually rubbed the front edge of the ledge. He moved closer to the tree and watched the bees hovering over the entrance before landing and crawling inside. An equal number crawled out of the dark cavity, onto the trunk and took wing. About half of those joined the column flying into the canyon and the rest flew up and over the rim. None of the bees challenged him. The bees in the tree at the pueblo on top were also very calm and easy to work with. *I'll bet they are part of the same original stock.*

At that point, the ledge was about eight feet wider from the face of the cliff than where it had appeared to be from below and further back than on down the ledge.

Cliff turned and examined the cliff behind the tree more closely. The overhang directly above him prevented him seeing the snag above. There in front of the tree he was standing in front of a shallow cave. He was not concentrating on the cliff, as he looked it over. He was thinking about whether swarms would fly out of the canyon or elsewhere within the canyon when the colony decided to multiply. He was also preoccupied with how to get back down the chute to the slope below.

The tree cast mottled shadows directly on the face of the cliff. That and chips, creases, cracks, and wrinkles where stone had flaked away all combined to create a richly textured surface. Nature did not often create straight lines. As his eye scanned the cliff face, a shadow fifteen or twenty feet above him caused him to pause. The dark shadow arched across the top as a cave in these rimrocks tended to be. The bottom edge was straight. A foot or so below was a row of circles about six inches in diameter spaced regularly across the width of the arch about a foot and a half below the edge of shadow. Four square shadows, about a foot square, were evenly spaced just below the row of circles. Their shape looked manmade.

He scanned the cliff face down to the shelf, and slowly it began to register that the face of the cliff in front of him was slightly different from the face of the cliff fifty feet to the left. Ahead and to the left of where he stood was another black rectangular shape. He brought his eyes into sharp focus. It was a doorway.

In an instant, he forgot about bees, bee trees, and getting down off the slope.

Set back under the rimrock overhang in the dappled shade of the cedar tree, was a stone wall plastered over with the same rusty brown clay that covered the canyon slope. The adobe blended perfectly with the sandstone rimrock. Broken shadows of the tree completed the perfect camouflage. Before him was one of the most perfectly preserved cliff dwellings Cliff had ever seen.

The builder had set the wall back from the front of the cave far enough to protect it from the elements and from the eyes of anyone standing on the rim above or on the canyon floor. The overhang protected the wall from weather's erosion, and the tree filtered and broke the power of the winds helping to preserve the clay plaster. The tree shadows and plaster would help hide it from view from the rim across the canyon.

An Ancestral Puebloan family or families over a hundred years before Columbus discovered America had gathered flat stones from the scree along the canyon side, broken them into building blocks, trimmed them, and carried them to the shelf, or lowered them over the rim to the shelf. Stone by stone the mason or masons had built the dwelling in the cave.

Each course of stone was laid with adobe mortar mixed from clay found on the side of the canyon. The finished wall likewise had been plastered with adobe mud from the canyon slope. Handprints were still visible in the plaster. Since the plaster was from the canyon and was the same color as the rimrock and the surroundings, it made the wall virtually invisible. The only unnatural feature of the wall was the doorway, which now appeared as a black rectangle.

Ed Kelley measured things two ways. When he needed exact measurement, he used a tape. When he needed approximate measure, he paced it. His pace was about three feet. He could reach six and a half feet. At the age of 13, when Cliff discovered the ruin, he had reached the same height and stride as his dad. Using the same methods of estimating measurement, he paced the ruin.

The front wall of the dwelling was about ten feet high and thirty feet wide and joined directly into the near vertical side of the cave on the right. On the left, the mason had built an end wall level with the top of the front wall and extending at a right angle to the back of the cave. He had then roofed the rectangular room with cedar poles. The roofing materials fill and final plaster coating had left a level roof on which the family could work and play.

Three cedar ceiling posts spaced evenly across the center of the room held up the ends of four even length cedar center roof beams that spanned the room from the end wall to a hole that had been chipped and drilled into the stone on the opposite wall of the cave.

The builder had placed smaller cedar poles about a foot apart at ninety degrees across the beams to create a ceiling. One end of each rested on the center beams and the other end protruded a few inches through the front wall. On dwellings with more than one story on Mesa Verde the front protruding poles extended out a couple of feet and were roofed to provide a kind of balcony.

From the center beams, similar cedar roof poles spanned the back half of the room to the sloping back of the cave. A hole was chipped into the stone to hold the back end of each pole, and another set of posts and beams had been set under them matching the center beams to hold up the ends of the roof poles to ensure the stability and strength of the roof.

A thatch work layer of willows and sagebrush across the poles and a coat of adobe mud was applied over that to create the roof, which, under the shelter of the cave and in the arid climate, had lasted from six to eight hundred years. On one corner of the roof, a small area was covered in a pile of flint chips suggesting that was where the hunter or hunters had knapped arrow or spear heads.

Cliff could just stand under the ceiling of the cave at the forward edge of the roof. The cave ceiling itself extended forward another eight feet or so. The cave lip was slightly arched over the ruin and dipped sharply to the ledge on the right side. *I'd like to be up here looking out across the canyon in a rainstorm. It would be like the time in Balcony House on Mesa Verde when the cloud burst hit, and we had to stay in there until it stopped. We watched waterfalls form on the side canyons, and a flash flood rush down the creek in the bottom of the canyon. The cave there was just like this. Oh, man!* Cliff had remembered.

Back from the opening, the cave ceiling opened to an additional five foot height, giving the dwelling a ten-foot ceiling at the highest point above the roof.

Access to the roof was by ladder. Rodents had long since eaten the leather holding the ladder together. Lying next to the wall were the remnants of the ladder that once provided access to the roof. Cliff had leaned one of the poles against the building and shinnied up it to the roof.

Access to the main dwelling was by a single rectangular shaped doorway nearly three feet high off the ledge. It was slightly narrower at the top. About a foot below the doorway was a small vent about six inches high and a foot wide. A thin flagstone over the top of the doorway supported the stones above the opening. Small square openings or vents were spaced around the top of the dwelling.

Benches were built into the inside walls all around the room, with spaces beneath them.

Inside the room, the distance up to the doorway was only about half as much as that outside, leading to the discovery that the floor of the room was filled in to level out the natural slope of the cave floor. Whatever the builder used; waste building materials perhaps, pebbles and dirt from the canyon side, gravel and dirt, it had been plastered over with wet clay, hardened, and worn smooth.

In the center of the room was a fire pit lined with flagstone. Fire blackened stones remained next to it. A fresh air intake, connected to the square hole under the entrance door, drew fresh air from outside. A flat stone in front of the opening inside the fire pit deflected the air from blowing directly on the fire. Around the outside wall near the roofline were four one-foot square openings that helped light the room and helped exhaust smoke from the room. This ingenious system allowed the doorway to be covered and a fire to burn without causing the room to fill with smoke or carbon monoxide.

A smooth, flat, piece of flagstone, clear on one side and blackened on the opposite side leaned against one side of the fire pit. It looked to Cliff like a stone griddle. Several worn grinding stones lay outside the doorway on the ledge. At the Mesa Verde Museum, they were labeled as *metate and mano*. One *metate* showed heavy use, the other was barely worn. Each had a hand-sized *mano* with flat grinding surface resting on it.

In the center of the floor was a small hole about three inches in diameter and two inches deep. In the *kivas* at Mesa Verde, the park rangers called such a hole "*Sipapu*", a spirit hole. They explained that it symbolized the passageway from which ancient ancestors of the Ancestral Pueblo had first entered the present world. Some older Native Americans still believed it was a pathway to commune with the spirits of the ancestors.

Several clay pots of various sizes shapes and ornamentation sat in one corner of the room. Around them were piles of squash necks and shriveled corncobs.

Rotted cords still hung from the ceiling poles. *Did they hang blankets to partition the dwelling into smaller rooms?*

On the far right side of the cave, ancient hands had chipped the stone floor to form a two-foot wide bowl nearly a foot deep, and it brimmed full of crystal clear sweet water. A trickle of water overflowed, ran out the side of the bowl and followed a path etched in the stone floor of the cave to exit through a square hole in the base of the wall in the front corner of the dwelling. The water flowed over the smooth stone, and the soil on the ledge absorbed it. A thick stand of clover and grass grew in the seep.

Green smudges along the canyon slope marked where water seeped from cracks beneath the rimrock. Most of the seeps produced only enough moisture to keep a few clover and grass roots nourished with none left over to spill down to the creek in the bottom of the canyon.

Cliff spent all of his available time there that afternoon examining the cave, and the ancient cliff dwelling.

He wondered how big the cedar was when the builder had constructed the dwelling, or if it had taken root there centuries later. The size indicated it was very old. Polished cedar slabs at Mesa Verde showed centuries of close spaced growth rings on trees such as this. This could have been a mature tree at the time the ruin was built and could have figured into the ruin's camouflage even then. Certainly, in recent times it had played a significant role in hiding the ruin from discovery.

After the discovery, he did not go back or share the discovery, even with his friend George. No one had looted it. That probably meant no one had discovered it before. The best way to keep it that way was to keep the secret.

~~~

For a year, he had resisted the temptation to revisit the ruin or to find the snag on the rim, and now he wished that he had at least located the
~~~

snag. However, he knew he was too weak to resist the temptation. Once he re-visited, he would eventually take something home and the secret would be out.

Only the unstable chute had permitted him access the previous summer. This time he wanted to gain access over the rim by rope, if he could locate the snag that marked where the ruin was located.

He had a firm image of the landmark burned into his memory, but he had viewed it only from the canyon. Would he recognize it at eye level when he saw it again?

He reached the rim as the sun began to settle low behind Ute Mountain. He had to choose right or left to begin the search: right down the canyon, left up canyon.

Deep shadows obscured objects on the canyon floor that might have helped him orient himself. If he could see the creek, he might recognize the boulder and pool that served as the lower anchor point where he had originally started to climb. The temporary loss of his left eye and the darkness in the canyon prevented that.

He was hungry, very thirsty and longed to drink from the cold spring of fresh water in the cave.

He went to the right examining all snags growing near the edge. Few trees, alive or dead, grew in the cracks and meager pockets of soil right up to the edge of the cliff, and he moved along quickly.

The sun sank lower. After a quarter of a mile, he turned around and went back. He had gone the wrong direction, or the old snag had finally fallen into the canyon. *If it is gone, I'll never find the dwelling again. The snag is the only reference I have to go by.*

Cliff began to panic as the darkness in the canyon deepened. He trotted back along the rim past the spot where he had begun the search and looked as far along the rim as he could see for anything familiar.

I should have given myself enough time to go into the canyon and tried to climb to it. However, things change along the creek too. I could have searched for the snag from the same perspective as I saw it the first time. But I was so sure that I would recognize it again up close!

Searching with only one eye was a terrible handicap. His left eye had been swollen completely shut all afternoon. His right eye was teary and stinging. It watered from the strain, and he constantly wiped away the tears. With no depth perception, decreasing light, and increasing desperation, he felt like sitting down and crying.

The damaged eye also determined how he searched. Without both eyes, he had to see everything up close.

He stopped and set the gunnysack down in frustration. *Maybe it was all just a fantasy. Maybe I just imagined it. I certainly dreamed of finding undiscovered ruins enough times, digging up buried Inca gold, and uncovering Coronado's Seven Cities of Cibola.* He sat down on the smooth surface of rimrock and stared into the dark canyon.

It was warm and still at dusk. Cliff closed his eye for a moment and breathed deeply, trying to get his panic under control.

He slowly became aware of a low droning sound, and with his eye still closed, turned his head to focus on the sound. It was low overhead and slightly to his left.

He looked to his left up canyon. Not more than twenty feet away on the edge of the cliff stood a twisted, stunted, windswept cedar. He studied it. The snag he sought had looked to be taller from below. However, the stance and branching did look vaguely familiar. It really wasn't a snag at all in the true sense of the word. This cedar had sprigs of green on the ends of its branches, but its location on the lip of the rim exposed it to winds and sand, and it had little soil to hold water. It was squat and twisted rather than growing straight and tall. Cliff suspected that it was very old.

He listened closely and looked out over the canyon. Darting black streaks, all going one direction came into focus.

The sound is honeybees returning from a nectar source to their colony after their final roundtrip of the day. The bees are narrowing their flight pattern as they descend down over the edge of the rim, homing in on the bee tree in front of the dwelling. This is the snag!

He lay down on his stomach, inched to the edge of the rim, and peered over the edge. Down below, was a large cedar tree. The tip of the tree came nearly halfway to the top of the rim.

Cliff removed the coil of rope from the sack, tied the end securely to the base of the snag and tested it. The snag, as he still thought of it, had put roots far back along cracks and dug into deeper soil seeking nourishment. It felt secure. He hung a chunk of dead wood on the end of the rope, tossed it over the edge and observed it swing back and forth, the end of the wood barely brushing the ledge as it swung.

Satisfied the rope was long enough, he put the rifle into the gunnysack and tied the end of the rope around the sack opening, and then he fed it over the lip of the rim and lowered it. The sack touched the ledge and the rope became slack when he let out the entire length.

Cliff put on his work gloves and straddled the rope on his belly. He had to force himself to slide over the edge of the rim and began lowering himself toward the ledge 40 feet below.

8

Monday afternoon, 4 p.m.
Kelley Farm

Mrs. Campbell drove across the cattle guard at the end of Ed Kelley's long drive way and parked in the circle drive in front of the farmhouse.

Etta Mae Kelley came around the house from the direction of the garden to greet the teacher, untying her sunbonnet as she walked. She wiped her hands on her apron and extended her hand to greet her son's teacher.

"Mrs. Campbell. So good of you to come. I'm just quitting in the garden for the day. Can you join me for a glass of iced-tea?" she asked. "Or I can brew a pot of coffee if you'd rather."

"Iced-tea would be very nice, Etta Mae. Your garden last fall was so lovely. I'm afraid I haven't begun to work on mine yet. It'll be a first priority next week when summer vacation begins."

"Well, the ground is only now getting warm enough to plant and put out starts. Down in West Texas my Daddy's cotton is already up and growing by now I'm sure," she laughed wistfully.

"Probably," Mrs. Campbell agreed. "This high elevation must present a challenge. We have an even longer season down in Lakeview just five miles away."

"And a thousand feet lower," laughed Etta Mae.

"What's your secret Etta Mae?" Mrs. Campbell asked.

"A hot bed with about a ton of green manure under it," Etta Mae laughed. "Every spring, about Easter, Ed builds a big hot bed for me, and I plant seed for everything that'll transplant in it. By now my tomatoes, cabbage, lettuce, cucumbers, squash, onions and the like are growing well and raring to go. I'll move the first of them before the end of the week. I'll have plenty of everything left over, and you are welcome to them when you get your garden worked up," Etta Mae offered.

"That's kind of you," Mrs. Campbell said. "I usually buy a few sets in town, but they're expensive. Your garden is huge. It would cost a fortune for you to buy all of your sets."

"I grow about all the vegetables we eat for the year," Etta Mae said as she led Cliff's teacher into the house.

Etta Mae poured two glasses of cold ice-tea from a pitcher she took from the refrigerator and handed one to Mrs. Campbell. The two sat at the kitchen table.

Mrs. Campbell looked around the modern kitchen. On a prior visit, Etta Mae had explained that Ed had designed and built both the house and the kitchen including the cabinets. The kitchen featured many of Ed's own innovations.

Her oldest son, Charlie, had done most of the farming allowing Ed to devote full time to building and finishing the house the year Ed and Etta Mae had built. The accrued debt on the three-year-old house and modern conveniences such as electricity and phone were the reasons Ed now worked in town to supplement the farm income.

Etta Mae was one of the few farm wives in the area who had the luxury of electricity in the house and thus the benefit of refrigeration, electric lights, instant hot water and other power appliances. Many farmers in the area had hooked up to the REA lines just to light their barns and heat their chicken brooders. Their homes were still without electricity.

Convenience came with a price.

Etta Mae took a long drink of her own iced-tea and waited for Mrs. Campbell to tell her the purpose of the visit, although she knew the reason.

"I came to see how Clifton is doing?" Mrs. Campbell said.

"Oh, I think he's OK. But, he looked pretty banged up when he came home," Etta Mae said. "I wanted to take him to the doctor, but he refused. I tried to get him to go lie down, but he wanted to go off and be alone for awhile. He reminded me of a hurt puppy that goes off into a corner and licks his wounds after a scrap. He's out in the field right now. His feelings were hurt as bad as his body."

Mrs. Campbell said, "I'm afraid I underestimated how serious things were between him and Hector Rodriguez. I thought Hector was mostly bluffing and was surprised that he would actually give Clifton a beating like that."

"That Hector has been nothing but trouble for Cliff for a long time," Etta Mae said.

"When I broke it up, Clifton ran out of there saying he was quitting school. He sounded like he meant it. We only have four days left until his graduation," Mrs. Campbell said. "Do you think he'll come back tomorrow?"

Etta Mae looked up. Her face was drawn. "I don't know. He keeps things bottled up. However, today he was different. He had a look in his eyes I've never seen before. It scared me a little," Etta Mae said. "He took his rifle with him when he left the house," she added.

"Are you worried about that?" Mrs. Campbell asked. *God don't let him do something stupid!*

"It's not unusual for him to take the .22 when he goes to the fields. He shoots prairie dogs and gophers with it. Sometimes he brings home a rabbit for supper. But, I didn't like it when he took it out today," Etta Mae said. "He's a good boy, but he's never been beaten up like that before. Even when he gets a whipping, it's not like that! Mrs. Campbell, did you send that boy home?"

"Yes. I kept him until I was sure Clifton was home, and then I asked your neighbor, Bob Harris, who was watching from across the fence, to escort Hector home with a message to Raul that Hector was not to come to school tomorrow. Why do you ask?"

"I was just wondering."

"The whole thing between him and Hector started last Friday on our field trip. I knew something was going on then. Clifton told me about it, but I hoped Hector would forget about it over the weekend, but apparently, he didn't. Ed's on the school board. Can he help out with this?" Mrs. Campbell asked.

"Unfortunately, Ed's not much help," Etta Mae said sadly. He's got this fool rule that if Cliff gets in trouble at school, he'll have to pay for it when he gets home, and no matter who's at fault. Therefore, Cliff is afraid that tonight when his father gets home, he'll get a whipping for getting into a fight. Ed says the boys ought to work it out between themselves, but I think things went too far this time. I want Ed to talk to Raul or even to call the sheriff."

"Well it really wasn't Clifton's fault. He should be able to go outside whenever he wants without having to worry about getting beat up. Usually he stays close and just avoids contact. Today he just seemed to make up his mind that he wasn't going to do that anymore, and he paid a consequence for it. I broke it up, as soon as I was aware it was getting out of hand, but it was too late. I had my hands full just holding Hector back long enough for Clifton to get away.

"If the other kids, especially Emilio, hadn't all gathered around and egged Hector on, I don't think it would have gone as far as it did, but you know how kids are. I kept Hector until he cooled off."

She thought a moment, undecided whether to tell Etta Mae. "Just before I sent him home, Hector said a peculiar thing to me. He said, 'That is the first time he ever stood up to me. Now maybe we can be friends.' What do you think he meant by that?"

"There may be a twisted logic to it. Something similar happened to their brothers when they were in the eighth grade," Etta Mae said. "Only in that case Charlie flattened Jorge with a chunk of firewood or something. Knocked him out with it. It drew blood. From that time on the two boys were all right with each other. Not pals, but at least they were on friendly terms."

"Do you suppose that is what this has been about all these years?" Mrs. Campbell mused.

"Surely not, but you never can tell," Etta Mae said.

"Anyway, by not running away, by actually calling Hector's bluff, Clifton put Hector on notice that he wouldn't be pushed around anymore. It's true that Hector won the physical part of the fight, but I don't think he'd want to have to fight Clifton all the time, because if Clifton is willing to fight back, and get hurt, he's smart enough to figure out how to whip Hector eventually.

"I think I understand what your husband has been trying to get across to Clifton by not taking care of the problem for him," Mrs. Campbell continued. "As painful as it is for us to stand by and see him get hurt, if Clifton gets strong enough to handle a problem like this with a guy like Hector, he'll be able to handle anybody who comes along. Ed's a little guy and little guys have to compensate in a world of big guys. I think he has been trying to get Clifton to understand that. Today I think Clifton grew. I hope that tonight when Ed gets home, he'll see that and act accordingly. Will he Etta Mae?" Mrs. Campbell asked.

"I hope you are right, Mrs. Campbell. I pray you're right," Etta Mae said.

"It's my observation, that although Ed is a quick tempered, stern man, he's a fair man," Mrs. Campbell said.

"That he is," Etta Mae agreed. "Most of the time."

"I really think that Hector will back off and may even make some move to make friends with Cliff. If he doesn't, then I agree that you should bring the sheriff in on it. I'll do whatever you ask me to do about this, Etta Mae."

"There was another thing I wanted to talk to you about, Etta Mae. When I first started here, Clifton was behind in his math skills. They were very basic. Not to criticize my predecessor, but times have changed and kids going on to high school have higher requirements than they did at one time.

"He can function, but even now he has just mastered compound fractions. In the fall, his classmates in the freshman class at the high school will be taking Algebra 1. I got him too late to get him caught up. He was just too far behind.

"We've talked about this before, and between us, I think we've done a good job, but we have a long way to go. I have lined up a tutor who can meet with Clifton once a week through the summer. Next Monday, I can check out the books the tutor will be using. On Tuesday, I can meet with Clifton and the tutor, and we can get him started. He can do the work at night so it shouldn't interfere with his work here on the farm. The tutor will come here to work with Clifton. I'm convinced that he has the learning skills to do it, if he sets his mind to do it."

"I'm sure he can Mrs. Campbell. What will a tutor for the summer cost?"

"I talked to the County Superintendent about this case, and he said the County will cover the costs of a tutor."

"I think he will jump at the chance Mrs. Campbell. You've been such a help to him. By the way, what did you think of his graduation project?"

"It was wonderful. It surpassed all my expectations. I gave it back to him today. I made lots of notes in it. I'm sure he'll share it with you. You must have given him plenty of help on it. He gave you high praise in the acknowledgments."

"I can assure you he did it all himself, but thanks."

Mrs. Campbell stood to go. "Please call me when he comes home tonight, and let me know that he's all right? Talk to him about the math tutor. Why not pass along the comment Hector made. I really do hope he'll come back tomorrow and finish the week. Are we still on for the graduation surprise up on Mesa Verde?"

"I think Cliff will enjoy it. I haven't let on we're planning it, so it will be a real surprise to him," Etta Mae said.

"I'm going to stop and talk to Raul after I leave here and tell him he needs to keep Hector home tomorrow," Etta Mae said. "You can tell Clifton he won't have to worry about being harassed for at least one day."

Etta Mae walked the teacher to her car and waved as Mrs. Campbell drove off.

Mrs. Campbell liked Etta Mae very much. Clifton was like his mother in many ways. Etta Mae had visited her shortly after the school announced that she was to be Mr. Johnson's replacement.

Mr. Johnson had taught at East Lakeview for many years. Until his arrival during the depression years, few teachers had survived a full year. Most had survived barely a month. Mr. Johnson had been hired at East Lakeview with two charges, bring it under control and teach the basics. That had suited him just fine. He had earned a reputation of being long on discipline and short on patience and subject matter. He taught the four R's: Reading, Riting, Rithmetic, and Rules.

Bullies like Hector had learned to work his rules to their advantage, and timid boys like Clifton had become victims of both the bullies and Mr. Johnson.

Mrs. Campbell remembered Etta Mae coming to her house. She had asked her to help her boy. He didn't need special attention, just occasional instruction and a supply of materials.

Working together, they had thrown books at him as fast as he could devour them, and devour them, he did. Mrs. Campbell discovered that he was a self-starter: He didn't play or become bored. He went on to the next lesson, as soon as he finished the first. If he had to wait, he read in a novel until she had time for him.

She had written on his first report card, "...he follows directions, even poor ones, better than anyone I've ever seen. He is self-directed. I only have to make the assignment, and he reads and understands the directions. He uses his time well."

Teaching to eight classes in a one-room school was like directing an orchestra. It required multi-tasking, coordinating groups of children moving from one subject to another, and doing the same for all eight grades.

She was a master teacher and member of a disappearing breed. Each year a handful of the one-room country schools closed, and the county bussed students to town. She had already been warned that East Lakeview was on the short list. Word was the school could be closed as early as the middle of the coming year if a transportation system could be worked out for distant students such as those on the Ridge.

Clifton's main deficiency was math. He had memorized the tables. He could do the basics. She had moved him forward until he was up to about the seventh grade level by town school standards.

When she showed him how to break complicated math problems into components, explained systems to him and why systems worked, he understood. She also taught him how to devise strategies for solving problems, but they had run out of time. Another year and she could have had him doing high school algebra.

She thought part of the problem was Clifton's fault. To protect himself from Mr. Johnson, he had tried to make himself invisible. He did this by staying busy. The busier and quieter he stayed, the less Mr. Johnson noticed him. As a result, he excelled in research and fell behind in math where he really needed the help. He had tried to pull that on her when she started at East Lakeview, but she made the time for him.

He loved to read and so did she. She had fed his thirst with literature from her home library, pulling books she had enjoyed in high school and even several thin books she had studied in college.

He even brought books to school checked out of the County Library. His mother took him there on Saturdays when she and Ed did their weekly marketing. He had brought several to school that surprised Mrs. Campbell such as *Ivanhoe* by Sir Walter Scott, and *Don Quixote* by Cervantes.

Mrs. Campbell knew that Etta Mae liked Zane Grey, and she and her son had read most of her collection together. He had also read books by Gene Stratton-Porter: *Freckles, Laddie, The Harvester, A Girl of the Limberlost,* and *Keeper of the Bees.*

Mrs. Campbell introduced him to epic poetry: *Evangeline* by Longfellow, and short stories like *Man Without a Country* by Edward Everett Hale. He also liked the novels by Nathanial Hawthorn, especially *The Last of the Mohicans* and *The Deer Hunter*.

When she found out he was interested in the Indians that had inhabited the Four Corners area, she searched for information on them and used some of that for his history and geography lessons.

He was quiet when he was around the other kids, but he seemed bright and perceptive when they worked one on one.

He loved to talk about bees. He told her about finding bee trees, and he had brought her honey from his bee hive. He was also proud of his artifact collection. He had found many of the artifacts (arrowheads, beads, bone awls and needles, grinding stones and stone axes) in the irrigation ditches on the Kelley farm.

He had an impressive knowledge of how the Indians lived on the farms and in the canyons of the Ridge and the area until the middle of the 15th Century. Much of that knowledge had come from listening to the rangers at Mesa Verde. He had excitedly told her of the artifacts, he and his family had found on the farm while digging the basement to their house.

As Mrs.Campbell drove down the county road toward Raul's home, she mused about the graduation project she had handed back to Clifton that morning. She had borrowed the idea from a professional publication. When she outlined the assignment to Clifton early in the fall, she had simply called it an eighth grade graduation project. He was to prepare a scrapbook to consist of a collection of pamphlets, booklets on Southwestern crafts, culture, i.e.; how they hunted, what they ate, plant and animal life of the Four Corners, geography, history and anything else that he wanted to include.

The finished product had all of that and more. Clifton had subdivided the scrapbook into three sections. Part I was titled INDIAN CRAFTS: Articles, booklets and summaries were on hide tanning, moccasins, pottery, basket weaving, clothing, weaving, flint knapping, and weapon making. Part II was titled PLANTS: edible, non-edible, medicinal, and fiber. Part III was titled RECIPES: for corn, seeds, beans, sunflower seeds, cattails, and making yucca soap.

I have to laugh at that title page, she thought.

He obviously practiced several times to center the words on the lines and then centering the lines on the sheet of paper. He got it perfectly on all but the last line. For some unknown reason, he miss-calculated the spacing, perhaps at the last minute, he had added a word. Instead of practicing the line on a separate sheet of paper, he must have guessed and when he saw his miscalculation, he started making the letters smaller and closer together to make them fit.

If he had made one more attempt at the page, no doubt it would be symmetrical also.

She thought about it and pursed her lips, *it somehow seems in character with other things he's done. He often takes things up to a point and then quits before getting it just right. I wonder why he does that.*

There was a rudimentary table of contents, index and acknowledgments.

In the front, he had acknowledged her for bringing her husband's sportsman magazines to school. From those he had winnowed articles on hunting with particular emphasis on bow and atlatl, arrow and spear construction; game dressing, tanning and meat smoking.

He had given his mother and father credit for taking him to the county library on Saturday afternoons so that he could research books and periodicals and to the County Extension office where he found racks of pamphlets and booklets on the native flora and fauna and Southwestern Colorado agriculture. If he asked a question they couldn't answer, they gave him the name and address of someone who could.

To the pages of the scrapbook, he had attached entire magazine articles, booklets and pamphlets. He had quoted in detail sections of books and longer magazine articles and cited them for future reference.

He had also illustrated some processes.

Mrs. Campbell spent considerable time annotating the pages and entries, writing suggestions on ways to improve the research or cite references to meet standards expected on research papers in high school. *He's going to astound the first high school teacher who gives him a research paper to do.* She had found it easy to heap praise on him for the massive effort he had expended. *The kid might be deficient in math, but he makes up for in research skills.*

She had reluctantly given the scrapbook back to him that morning before the lunch break. She had intended to go over it with him in the afternoon. On Tuesday, Wednesday, and Thursday, she would spend her time with him going over the work and answering questions about her written comments.

She was sure he hadn't had a chance to look at it before lunch. She noticed that he had taken it with him when he cleaned out his desk. She was very proud of his achievement. It had proven her theories on his ability to process information, do research, focus his attention, and make a plan and successfully complete it, if he kept with it.

Based on the success of the scrapbook she was convinced that if he worked with a math tutor over the summer, he would be right on target with his freshmen classmates come September. *That is assuming I see him again to get the summer program started.*

It was ironic that he might not come back and finish the week. She and Etta Mae had planned a special surprise for Clifton on Friday with a graduation picnic at Mesa Verde National Park. She had notified the parents of the younger grades that their summer vacation would begin on Thursday.

She and Etta Mae would just take the three fifth graders, two sixth graders, four seventh graders, and Clifton, the only eighth grader, up to the Park for the day. They were going to have a picnic lunch and present him with his certificate. What a disappointment it would be if he didn't come back to school for the rest of the week. It would have been the perfect ending of his school year for him.

9

Monday Afternoon, dusk
Martinez Canyon

When his feet touched the gunnysack, he looked down. As he had thought, the bottom of the sack rested on the ledge.

He wrapped his legs around the rope and slid down it, thankful for gloves to protect his hands from rope burn. Climbing back out would be another matter until his side healed.

He looked around. The ruin was exactly as he remembered it.

He stepped through the rectangular door opening, dropped the gunnysack next to the fire pit and went to the spring. He pulled his glove off, cupped his hand into the water and drew a brimming handful of cold, sweet water to his lips. It was still as pure and sweet as he remembered from last summer. He drank his fill. *Good thing this spring still flows. Without it, I couldn't stay.*

He glanced about the ruin. No one had disturbed it. The artifacts left behind by the Ancient Puebloan family were in exactly the same position, as least he thought so. Cooking tools around the fire pit, pottery bowls in the corner, shriveled corn cobs and squash necks still spilled around them. Fragments of rotted cordage hung from roof beams.

A few relatively fresh small animal bones littered the floor. Also, various sized animal tracks and dried scat disturbed the sand and dust. *How do they get in here?*

The biggest tracks in the dust were cat. That worried him. *Maybe Charlie was right, and cougars, bears, wolves and bobcats do live in these canyons. Charlie says they only come out at night. I guess they can go anywhere, even if people can't.* He was too tired to care at that moment.

Cliff stepped back outside into the twilight to rummage around under the cedar for dried needles, twigs and fallen branches to use for a fire.

It took several of the wooden matches to get a small fire going in the fire pit.

By the flickering firelight, he gathered the dry clean bones that littered the floor and stacked them. He threw the recently chewed ones, with enough gristle and fat to stink, out of the doorway onto the ledge. He would finish disposing of them in the morning.

Cliff unloaded the gunnysack so he could use it as a blanket. He placed the scrapbook, matches and .22 shells into a nook built high on the wall. He still had several loose shells and his pocketknife in his overall pocket.

He set the Mason jars with the cookies and jerky beside the fire where he could reach them. *Cookies and jerky for supper. Wow! Which do I have first? Dessert or main dish?*

He unrolled the saddle blanket next to the tiny fire and spread the gunnysack over himself. The sack was so thin and short it would be worthless as protection. The saddle blanket was too thin to be much padding against the hard floor. He finally re-rolled it and just sat on it.

It was warm, and the cave would cool slowly. The temperature dropped to near freezing at night, but the sun had heated the stone wall all day, and warmth would radiate back into the cave through the night.

So much has happened since breakfast this morning. I started the day at 5 a.m. sitting in a clean comfortable kitchen wolfing down scrambled eggs, bacon and pancakes and washing them down with tall glasses of cold whole milk. Now I sit 15 hours later in a cave a mile away on a hard, cold, stone floor getting ready to eat a piece of jerky for supper. How stupid is this?

He fished a piece of jerky from the jar and tried to eat it, but his jaw was still too sore to chew. He put the jerky back into the jar, took out a cookie and let it dissolve in his mouth as he stared into the popping cedar fire.

He bit into a raisin and pain shot up through his jaw. *I wonder if Hector knocked some of my teeth loose. Wouldn't it be just great if I lose a jaw tooth?* He chewed the cookie on the opposite side of his mouth, and it wasn't as bad. *When these are gone, I won't have anything to eat but jerky. What a mess.*

What are you gonna do now, Clifton? You gonna sit here and feel sorry for yourself all night? You could still go home, let Dad give you your whipping, go on to school tomorrow and everything will be back to normal. You could graduate from eighth grade, work hard all summer and go on to high school, just as you planned.

Mom must be worried sick right now. She's milked the cows. Dad's really mad now. He's set the water. I wonder if he found my shovel. He expected the water to be set when he got home after working all day. I guess it really wasn't fair to make him work two more hours, I hope he didn't take it out on Mom, but I'll bet he did.

I could still go home and say I got lost or something.

"Got lost where?"

"Out in the canyon."

"What were you doing out in the canyon? Don't lie to me!"

"Why won't you believe me?"

They wouldn't believe me. They never do. Why should they? They know when I'm lying. Sometimes I think I'm lying even when I'm not!

Cliff looked at the uncovered entryway. It was fully dark outside. He wouldn't be going anywhere now. Not tonight. He could hardly keep his good eye open, and he and the darkness were not friends.

The eye that still functioned filled with tears, and he put his head down on his arms. He had fantasized about running away and living in the ruin. It was a big adventure in the fantasy. Now he was here for real, and it didn't seem like such a great adventure. He couldn't stop the sobs that suddenly welled up in his throat. He couldn't remember crying like that for a while. Not since the bedwetting had finally stopped. Do I have to contend with that again too?

He lay down again on the saddle blanket, covered himself the best he could with the gunnysack and went to sleep.

~~~

"Isn't that boy home yet?" Ed asked when he came in the door from work.

"I haven't seen anything of him," Etta Mae answered.

"I came home as soon as I could get away after you called." He hung his hat and washed his face and hands. He dropped tiredly into a chair at the kitchen table. He spread his gnarled grease stained hands out in front of him. "Where could he be? He's never done anything like this before. Tell me again what he said when he got home!"

"He said he had quit school. He and Hector mixed it up at lunchtime. He had a bloody nose, his eye was swelling up and his rib cage was turning black and blue. I'm afraid he might have some broken. You know that Rodriguez boy won't leave him alone!"

"But he finally stood up to him! Good for him. It's about time. Maybe from now on Hector will leave him alone!" Ed said.

"But you've threatened to tan his hide if he fought back, Ed!" Etta Mae said in surprise looking at her husband.

"I don't believe I ever said that exactly. I've told him that I would give
~~~

him a lickin' if I caught him fighting on the school grounds if it could be avoided. There's a big difference there. I believe he needs to learn to take care of himself. I won't be there to fight his battles for him always. I'm not going to come running ever time someone says 'boo' to him. He's a little guy, just like me, and he can't win in a fight with his fists against a big guy like Hector. He has to be smart and use his body in other ways. Charlie tried to show him wrestling moves and holds, but he wouldn't take them seriously," Ed said. "But, I don't want him to go around picking fights either."

"So what's he supposed to do? Take a gun after him?"

"No! That's not being smart! He's got a mind. He needs to learn to use it! He can't use force as a first reaction. The Bible says..."

"...To turn the other cheek, right? You go tell that to Hector!"

"I was going to say that although he shouldn't resort to force, the Children of Israel were forceful when threatened. It sounds like to me that he told Hector today that when he gets backed into a corner he's going to come out fighting. He has to learn when to take a stand and how to make the other guy know he means it. I'll bet today he let the other guy know he means it, even though he got a bloody nose in the process."

"You should've seen him Ed. He was hurt pretty bad. But, the thing that was hurting him the most? That you wouldn't take up for him. That you were going to beat him some more when you got home. That's pretty much what he said. I could feel that was what was driving him away!"

"You think I'd beat my son after standing up to Hector?"

"That's the threat that he's lived under most of his life Ed!"

"But Etta Mae, I didn't want him picking fights and getting into trouble, but on the other hand, he has to learn not to run from it. Can't you see that?"

"All I can see, and apparently all he could see, is that you aren't there to back him up when he needs it most against a bully a lot bigger and meaner than he is!" She said coldly.

Ed looked at her tiredly. It was unusual for her to talk back to him. He started to protest and looked back at his hands. "I guess I had better give Sheriff Bill a call."

"What you going to tell him, Papa?"

"To keep a lookout is about all we can tell him so far."

"Now don't you make it any worse than it is!"

"How can I do that? I don't know what's going on yet!"

"Why don't you just drive around to the neighbors, and see if anyone's seen him. Maybe he's just visiting somewhere. You can call Bill in the morning, if he hasn't come back."

"He'd never go visiting without permission," Ed said. "Least wise, not normally."

"Ain't been nothing normal about today so far," Etta Mae said sadly.

Ed drove to his closest neighbor's first. They had not seen his son, but they would keep an eye out.

He drove down the road to the Rodriguez' home and entered the long dirt drive to the tiny adobe home. As Ed got out of the car and stood uncomfortably in the driveway waiting to greet his neighbor, he realized that although they had been neighbors for almost fourteen years, he had never been inside Raul's home. Even when he had rushed Raul's wife Inez to the hospital when their twins were born, she had met him outside the door.

Ed Kelley and Raul Rodriguez had become friends shortly after Ed and his young family moved onto their farm on Summit Ridge. Ed had stopped to offer assistance when he came upon Raul's old pickup truck stalled along the road to Cortez. Ed had a permanent toolbox in his pickup and an uncanny ability to diagnose and fix anything mechanical. He would soon gain a reputation of being able to lay his hand on a piece of machinery, close his eyes, bond with it, and know what ailed it.

In only a short time Ed had Raul's pickup up and running fine. He waved off Raul's offer to pay for his effort with the comment that neighbors were meant to help neighbors.

The next day at suppertime Raul had timidly knocked on the old Kelley farmhouse. When Etta Mae answered, with baby Clifton on her arm, Raul handed her a cloth containing steaming hot tamales his wife had made for the Kelley family's supper.

The friendship had grown from there. Ed and Raul had remained the closest of friends, and they helped each other out with no strings attached.

The two men were an interesting contrast.

Ed was slight of build, barely five feet two inches tall and weighing a hundred thirty pounds. His wavy shock of black hair was full of cowlicks. He had long bushy eyebrows and coarse black whiskers, which he shaved with a straight razor a couple of times a week and on Sunday. The hair, eyebrows and whiskers gave him a bit of a wild look.

Raul was a big man standing a little over six feet tall. He was muscular and lean weighing about two hundred forty pounds. Raul was a powerful man, and he worked hard. He could lift two, one hundred pound, bales of hay at a time, toss them on a hay wagon and do that all day long. His raven black hair was wavy and combed back. A thick trimmed moustache decorated his upper lip.

What Ed lacked in physical strength, he made up for with an understanding of the laws of physics. If he couldn't lift it, he knew how to lever it with his body or with the help of a makeshift tool.

Ed had two children, but came from a large family.

Raul was a proud man with a large family of twelve children.

Raul had once complimented Ed as, "The biggest little man he had ever known." The comment wasn't about Ed's physical size. It was about Ed's heart. He was a big-hearted man concerning his fellow man.

"Buenas noches, Señor Kelley, How are?" Raul greeted and shook Ed's hand.

"I'm good Raul. How are you and your family this evening?"

"I am sad that today there was trouble between our sons. I hope it is a matter of boys will be boys," Raul said, shaking his head.

"I'm afraid it might go further than that, but I've been reluctant to interfere," Ed said.

Raul listened as Ed explained what Mrs. Campbell had told Etta Mae about the fight at school between their sons and how long the hazing had been going on. "I came to ask if you have seen Clifton, or if you know if there has been any further contact between our boys after school?" Ed asked.

Raul's face turned a little red as he strode to the house, called Hector to the door and then took him by the arm and pulled him outside. He spoke rapidly and sharply to the boy in Spanish. Hector stood nearly as tall as his father.

Ed was surprised at how much the boy had grown. He hadn't seen Hector since the summer before. No wonder Clifton was so intimidated.

Raul looked back at Ed and made a motion to Hector.

He's telling him to come over and apologize, thought Ed.

Hector shook his head from side to side and spoke vehemently. The only word, which Ed understood, was, "*galena*", chicken!

Raul slapped his son across the face, turned him, opened the door and gave him a boot back through the door. He returned to Ed. "I am very sorry *Señor*. I am very surprised my other children did not tell me about it. I didn't know that my son was tormenting your son until Mrs. Campbell came here this afternoon and told us. She only told us about the fight. She did not give us details about their past together. The teacher said he can't go back to school tomorrow because of it. I have put him on notice that he is to stay away from your son and to leave him alone in the future. If he does not, he will answer to me!"

"I appreciate that, Raul. Your son is quite a bit bigger than my son in size. Hector has really grown up. It's a little uneven. Nevertheless, you and I should be examples to our boys that size should have nothing to do with how men get along together. I don't cotton to Clifton's fighting. If he refuses to defend himself, it's my fault, not Clifton's. I've always taught him to turn the other cheek."

"No. I don't want my son to be fighting either, my friend. If he shames you or your son, he shames me. You have my deepest apology. We will help you find your son! My whole family will help you to look. I mean all of us. I will come to your house in the morning and check to see if he has come back?"

"You are always welcome in my home my friend," Ed said.

"And you in mine," Raul said.

The two men shook hands and parted.

10
Monday, night descends
Martinez Canyon

Cliff and the darkness were not friends. His older brother Charlie and the neighbor kid, Larry, had made sure of that. When Cliff was still a toddler, the two boys filled their stories with fearsome bears, cougars, weasels, vultures, malingerers and other monsters, which came out mostly at night to prey on little boys. They had instilled the fear of the dark in him, and they saw that they could exploit that fear. Their fun loving pranks focused on that, as long as it worked. As it turned out, that was pretty much until Charlie left home when Cliff was eleven.

By the time he was old enough to realize what they were doing, it was too late. His fear of the dark was set, it had become a part of him, and continued so strongly that he couldn't sleep at night without a light shining in his bedroom.

Cliff's fear of the dark had begun in earnest at about the age of four, when his brother Charlie had asked to go up the road to get the mail one dark summer night, and Cliff had been naive enough to think Charlie might like his little brother to go along for company. How was Cliff to know that going to get the mail was just an excuse for his eleven-year-old brother to get out of the house to meet Larry up the road.

Cliff's parents had granted permission as long as older brother took younger brother along. So they had headed out, and Cliff could tell it was a mistake as soon as they were out the door.

It was a cool evening. The moon was up and shining just brightly enough to cast indistinct shadows from every tree, bush, fence post and a thousand other things, giving the landscape a ghostly appearance. Cliff wanted to stay close and sought out his brother's protection, but Charlie didn't want Cliff along, and he kept reminding him of it, walking so fast Cliff couldn't keep up and asking him, "Why can't you leave me alone and let me do my thing?"

When they got to the neighbor Larry's place, things worsened. The two older boys fed off each other. Larry loved to tease Cliff, especially when he was with Charlie. If Cliff had known Larry was going to be there, he would never have asked to go. Larry was the same age as Charlie.

The trip to the mailbox was uneventful. It was darker on the return trip, and the moon was brighter. The millions of stars that lit the clear sky at night in Colorado could not have been brighter and the gravel road between the mailbox and their house glistened like a ribbon of water.

It was strangely quiet that night. The frogs and insects, which usually sang every summer evening, were silent for some reason. "I can hear evil in the air," Charlie suggested. "Can you hear IT?"

Cliff listened and thought he could hear IT, whatever IT was.

Cliff's four-year-old mind began to set up scenes so vivid they seemed real, of swishing wings from a giant bird. They must have had wings that spanned at least fifteen feet.

The fear was confirmed with a commanding yell from big brother to "RUN CLIFTON!!! RUN CLIFTON!!! THEY ARE COMING TO GET US!!! THE VULTURES ARE COMING AND THEY LOVE TO EAT LITTLE BOYS. RUN!!"

Larry fell to the ground and began thrashing around screaming at the top of his lungs. "THEY'VE GOT ME! OH NO! THEY'RE GETTING READY TO EAT ME!"

Charlie flailed about the air as if fighting the beasts and continued to scream, "RUN CLIFTON!!"

Cliff ran for what seemed like miles with the monster vultures in hot pursuit.

When he had finally reached the house, he burst through the front door shouting, "Dad, Dad. Come quick. Get the gun!" He cried and tried to get his breath. His side ached and he clutched at it as he gasped for air.

His dad came running from the kitchen followed closely by his mom. "What is it? Is Charlie hurt?"

His mom tried to calm the sobbing four year old.

"Charlie may be dead! And it's right behind me. Get the gun Dad. The 30-30 Dad! Before it's too late!"

"What's out there?" His mom asked with concern as his dad hurried to the office for the rifle and shells.

"It's a vulture Mom! It's huge. It's right behind me. I think it killed Charlie! It'll kill you guys too if Dad doesn't shoot it!"

"What'd you say? A vulture?" He looked down at the sobbing boy. He relaxed, but a look of anger came into his eyes. He kneeled down to his son. "You don't know what a vulture is, do you son?"

"It's a huge bird Dad! And I think it killed Charlie. I heard him screaming!" Cliff said. He had stopped crying. Uncontrollable hiccupping began, as he tried to control his breathing.

"Son, a vulture is a buzzard," Ed said. "It's nothing to be afraid of. They're the size of a chicken, and they're asleep now, just like the chickens."

The back door opened and Charlie sauntered in through the kitchen and put the mail on the table. There was no sign of scratches and no sign of a struggle.

It suddenly dawned on Cliff that something was wrong.

Charlie had shrugged his shoulders, "We were just walking down the road, Larry, Clifton and me and Clifton just suddenly freaked out and took off. For the life of me, I don't know what scared him like that!" He said. "I guess his imagination is just too active."

"Cliff said you were screaming. What was that all about?" Their dad asked with a frown on his face. He turned back to Cliff to confirm his question.

Charlie caught Cliff's accusing eye and raised his eyebrow to let him know to drop it. If Charlie got a whipping for the prank, then he would get even the next time he babysat Cliff.

Even at the age of four, Cliff understood there were consequences for demanding justice. It had been a prank. There was no monster. Or, was there? Monsters came in all forms.

"I guess I must have 'magined it," he mumbled between hiccoughs.

His dad had looked at Charlie with a frown that was on the verge of a snarl, started to say something, shook his head and returned the .30-.30 to the office.

The beginnings of Cliff's fear of the dark were set. A vulture might be a buzzard and no larger than a chicken. They might sleep at night. However, mountain lions, wolves, bobcats, bears and coyotes didn't.

Charlie was seven years older than his little brother and had that much more advanced vocabulary. He constantly discovered new ominous sounding words that were perfect for teasing Cliff. One day he discovered the word malingerer.

Charlie even quoted the radio to add credibility when he told Cliff about "The Famous Rocky Mountain Spotted Malingerer. It killed three boys your age outside Colorado Springs last week. According to the radio, they go after fresh young meat and tear boys limb from limb just for fun," Charlie said. "You need to look out. The radio said a Malingerer was seen on the road between home and Cortez a day or so ago. You don't have to believe me. I'm just telling you what I heard."

After the Rocky Mountain Malingerer story, Cliff decided to find out finally whether Charlie was telling the truth or lying through his teeth by asking his mother, "Mom, have you seen any malingerers between here and town lately?"

His mother thought about the question. She was surprised, but pleased by how well Cliff's vocabulary was advancing. "Well, actually there were a couple of them walking down the road below the Stone's place on Saturday," she said, remembering a couple of hitch hikers that she thought were probably not where they ought to be. "Why do you ask?"

"Oh, nothing! I was just curious," he said. He went outside and sat on the steps for a long time. *Oh, my gosh! Charlie hasn't been lying to me. They really do exist,* he thought.

In time, Cliff's own vocabulary expanded. He knew that malingerers and procrastinators weren't animals at all, and were just part of Charlie's teasing. His brother no longer had power over him, but by that time, Charlie no longer lived at home. When Charlie lived at home, Cliff hated him for his teasing. Now that Charlie was in the Army and in far off Japan, Cliff missed him dearly.

~~~

Cliff came awake. For a moment, he felt disoriented. Except for a few
~~~

red coals that glowed beside him, it was pitch black.

He didn't know where he was. He reached for the soft cotton sheet and quilt, but his hand closed on rough burlap. The mattress was hard, not soft.

No nightlight glowed on the wall outlet.

Panic built in his chest and nausea began to boil up from his stomach.

He couldn't breathe. Frantically he felt around, his hand clutched the rough wool saddle blanket he lay on, and he began to remember climbing over the lip of the canyon rimrock and down the rope to the ledge and seeking shelter in the ancient cliff dwelling.

That memory was followed by a sudden succession of images cascading through his mind...*Hector sitting on his stomach...a fist smashing into his eye and face and ribs...protecting his face with his arms....* Cliff tried to open his left eye. It was sealed. His right eye was open but saw only blackness, profound blackness. *I'm blind! I'm blind!* His one eye frantically flicked here and there around the darkness until, it stopped at a block of black of a different intensity speckled with the Milky Way cloud of twinkling pinpoints of light.

The rectangle of Milky Way was strangely calming, because at that moment it was the only familiar thing in the blackness. He almost smiled, and then the images began again...*fleeing down the road from school...stumbling when he looked over his shoulder to see if Hector was following... grabbing the .22... hiding in the debris by the road... taking aim... the sound of the rifle shot... Hector falling into the prairie dog hole... fleeing from the scene of the crime...at Dog Town.*

He shook his head to clear it and stared at the rectangle of blackness that winkled and seemed to pulse in time with his rapid heartbeat. His hands clenched the edge of the blanket so tightly that his fingers cramped. Cliff focused on the rectangle of starlight and tried to relax his hands and slow his breathing.

His pulse calmed a little. "Darn it! Why didn't I grab a flashlight?" he cried out.

There's nothing to be afraid of. So why do I jump at every little sound? And why does the hair on my neck tingle and rise up. Why can't I control that? Why?

Cliff rearranged himself on the saddle blanket. It was just long enough to protect him head to toe from the cold floor. The gunnysack, however, was only three feet long and so his feet were uncovered, and it came up just past the pockets on his bib overalls. He slept fully clothed except for his shoes and socks, which he was trying to use as a pillow.

He closed his one still functioning eye and became still.

He drifted in and out of consciousness, until he became aware of a rustling sound and opened his eye. The hair prickled on his neck. Something was out there. *According to Dad, most wildlife is afraid of human beings,. I shouldn't have to be afraid of anything.*

"Get out of here," he yelled, hoping to scare off whatever thought it wanted to share the cave as a den for the night. The rustling sound stopped. From another direction came a faint sound of something moving within the cave.

I've got to figure a way to close that door, if I'm going to be here another night.

He couldn't go back to sleep.

Suddenly, a blood-curdling scream pierced the night and brought him to a sitting position. His heart raced in fear. He reached for the .22 rifle, and loaded a shell into the chamber with a trembling hand. He pulled the firing pin back into the cocked position ready to fire.

It had sounded like a child or a girl screaming. *I've heard that sound before when a bull snake squeezed into the rabbit cage? Mom thought it was me and Charlie fighting. Is that what I heard, a snake after a cottontail? Or is it a cougar? That's the sound cougars make in the movies. Isn't it?*

Cliff gripped the rifle, and pointed it toward the rectangle in the wall filled with twinkling stars. The muscles in his arms were tight, and he began to cramp. He lowered the rifle and flexed his hand. His breathing was shallow and rapid.

Breathe, he thought. He sat holding the .22 ready to fire into the darkness. Once more, he heard a rustling and a panting sound outside the door. He strained to hear. He had thrown out fresh bones earlier, some with gristle still on them. *That same animal must still use the cave as its den. Or some other animal may have been attracted to the smell of the rancid bones. I should have buried them.*

The snuffing sound came from the doorway. He raised the rifle with his finger on the trigger. A low growl sounded in the dark followed by a rumbling sound.

I know that sound. Purring? A cat? No cat I've ever seen purrs that loud. What kind of cat can purr that loud? Oh my gosh! It must be huge!

Slowly, a round silhouette with sharp pointed ears filled the lower part of the rectangle and rose to mask out half the twinkling starlight. The black silhouette paused and he was sure the outline was that of a large cat blocking stars in the Milky Way.

Cliff aimed between the faintly defined ears of the silhouette and pulled the trigger.

The silhouette disappeared and the milky cloud once again filled the rectangle.

The rumbling growl/purr turned to an instant snarl and a heavy body thumped to the ground outside the ruin. Rustling, scratching sounds continued for a moment, and it was quiet once more.

Reloading in the dark seemed to take forever. Reloading the single-shot was slow at best. Cliff fumbled in his pocket for another shell. He tried to distinguish between the front and back of the shell, and then attempted, with shaking hand, to load the shell into the .22. He finally found the mouth of the chamber, seated the shell, closed the bolt, pulled the firing pin out to the cocked position and aimed at the doorway.

He waited and trembled with the rifle ready for the intruder to block the twinkling star lights again. Adrenaline raced through his veins and his heart pounded.

He was nauseous and afraid he would be sick to his stomach. If he had only wounded it, the animal could leap through the doorway at any moment and attack with slashing claws and crushing teeth.

If only I had a light. Aren't they afraid of fire? I have to have a light. I've got to build a bon fire.

Cliff searched his pocket for a match. He struck it and used the light to gather leftover twigs into a small pile in the fire pit before the match went out. He struck another match, lit the pile of twigs and blew to get them started.

He felt better as he nervously grew the tiny fire with the remaining wood from the pitifully small pile he had gathered in the last remaining twilight the night before. Soon light and shadows from the little fire danced on the walls of the cave dwelling. He hadn't gathered enough wood to keep a fire going all night. If only the intruder would leave before it burned out.

Cliff sat on the saddle blanket staring into the fire. His blood pressure slowly fell when he heard no more threatening sounds. His pulse stabilized and his breathing slowed. He nodded and his chin dropped to his chest, as he slipped back into sleep.

In Cliff's dream, Emilio walked down the road, stopped, looked in all directions and barked, "All clear." Cliff took aim and fired then walked over and looked down the hole in the center of the road. He expected to see Hector lying at the bottom....

Cliff awoke from the dream and stared into the remaining embers, the dream still vivid in his mind.

How close had he come to doing as the dream portrayed. Suddenly, he worried. Had it been real? Had he actually done it? Was that why he ran? He felt his eye and his face. That part was real enough. The eye was still swollen shut, his nose clogged and sore, his ribs bruised and hurting. The beating had been real. He prayed the dream had not.

The fire burned down again as the night wore on. He had no idea what time it was. He was afraid to go to sleep again. He jumped at every sound and raised the rifle to fire.

Jumbled thoughts randomly filtered through his mind. *I should have gathered more wood before dark. Why didn't I bring a flashlight, a blanket, more food, supplies, money? What will I do when the .22 shells are gone? If I'm trying to keep out of sight, can I even use the .22 to hunt? Won't shooting draw attention here?*

Finally, he went to the doorway and looked outside. Although it was still very dark inside, the eastern sky was beginning to lighten.

He heard nothing moving, but he could smell something pungent nearby. He couldn't identify it.

A cold breeze blew down the canyon. He shivered as cold tendrils of current entered the doorway, lowering the temperature inside the cave.

He needed a coat. Even though it was spring, at a little over seven thousand feet in elevation, it got cold at night. The thin dry air did not retain heat. Even in the heat of summer, it was cool in the shade.

Cliff woke again just before dawn with the .22 still gripped tightly in his arms. He was stiff and sore. He didn't remember lying back down or changing the saddle blanket from mattress pad to blanket.

He had survived his first night in the canyon.

11
Tuesday daybreak
Martinez Canyon

Cliff stretched and looked out on the canyon. Trees and boulders on the opposite side of the canyon began to take on more definition in the early light of dawn.

He was stiff. Every muscle in his body ached from lying on the thin saddle blanket or burlap sack between him and the cold hard floor.

The bruises on his chest, sides and face were various shades of black, purple and blue and were painful to the touch. Thankfully, he couldn't see how bad his face looked. It looked even worse than he imagined.

He was hungry and groggy. His mouth was dry and tasted putrid from the blood that had drained back into his mouth from his injured nose.

His back ached from hunching by the little campfire through much of the night clutching the .22, aimed at the unprotected doorway. His muscles had been tense, ears straining for the returning sounds of scratching, huffing, growling and ominous purring.

Surprisingly, he had not messed himself when the animal appeared in the doorway or during his sleep. It was a good thing for he had only one clean change of clothing.

If he'd had anything in his stomach, it probably would have come up. Repeatedly, he'd told himself he had to be a man and face the darkness and what it held. However, that had only lasted until he had heard the scream and growl at the doorway and the snarl and scuffle when he shot at whatever it was. That had not been his imagination.

Cliff looked to both the right and left of the door opening. There on the ledge under the tree was the still form of a large spotted cat. He grabbed the .22 and aimed at the cat. It was very still in the dim dawn light. *I can't tell if it's dead or wounded.* He aimed at the tree above the big cat and fired. The cat didn't move.

He climbed through the doorway and slowly approached the inert body of a bobcat. It was at least as big as his shepherd dog Towser back at the house. Next to its head lay a dead cottontail rabbit.

Perhaps the dead rabbit solved the mystery of the scream. It had likely been the death throes of the rabbit, when the bobcat caught it and crushed its neck just down slope from the cave. Then the cat had brought it back to the cave to eat. Cliff's shot had been from no more than eight or ten feet. The .22 long rifle hollow point bullet was lethal at that distance, and he had hit the cat right between the eyes.

He turned the cat over and petted the luxuriantly soft fur. The animal had already shed its winter coat, and a glossy new spring coat had replaced it in preparation for the hot summer ahead.

Cliff would skin the bobcat that morning and save the pelt. *Too bad I can't eat bobcat. Dad always says don't eat meat eaters. But it looks like you brought cottontail for breakfast, thank you very much.*

Cliff picked up the rabbit. The cat had crushed its neck. Cottontails were safe to eat, and their meat was tender and delicious. Whenever Cliff caught or shot a cottontail, it landed on the dinner table.

A pocketknife was an essential tool for a farm boy wherever he went, and Cliff always carried one. His current pocketknife had three blades. The main blade was nearly four inches long, a graceful slim pointed blade, excellent for butchering and skinning rabbits. He seldom used the other two blades except for carving. All three blades held a keen edge, and he kept them sharp.

He could skin and dress a rabbit in no time at all. He had plenty of practice at it. The hide shucked backward off the body leaving the hair inward the skin exposed.

When he finished dressing the rabbit, Cliff tossed the head and viscera, minus the intestines, over the ledge as far out into the canyon as he could so the magpies or crows would clean them up. He squeezed the intestines clear and washed them outside the dwelling in the wastewater from the spring. He put the cleaned intestines with the skin to tend later.

Cliff took the rabbit inside.

He had taken various stones from the fire pit before building a fire the night before. There were several fist sized, round, granite river rock and a flat flagstone with a smooth clear side and roughened blackened side.

At home, his mother would cook the rabbit in several different ways. If it were a young fryer, she would fry it. If it were older, she would boil it and make soup with lots of tender rabbit meat. She did the same thing with chicken. Fry the young ones boil the old ones.

He wondered how the original inhabitants had used the stones. The flagstone resembled his mother's griddle in form. Would it function the same way if he balanced it on three of the river rock and kept coals under it? Could he get it hot enough to cook a rabbit on it? *I'll hold that thought for now.*

In the western books he read, the cowboys cooked wild birds over campfires on a stick.

He wiped the clear side of the flagstone and laid the rabbit on it.

Cooking the rabbit posed a problem. It was a little heavy to hold over the fire by hand with a stick, especially for as long as it would take to cook the rabbit.

One of his dad's favorite simple structures was the "A" frame. He used some variation of it to lift bales onto the haystack, lift butchered hogs over scalding vats and numerous other applications. *Why not use it here?*

Cliff cut two small branches from the cedar tree.

While the small fire burned down to a hot bed of coals, Cliff cut one of the cedar branches in half. Using the rabbit intestines as makeshift cording, he tied the two sticks together at the top leaving an inch or so extended above the binding to form a shallow "V".

He cut the second stick about three feet long and smoothed it. After binding the rabbit's legs together, he threaded the end of the stick between them and positioned the rabbit over the fire. He lifted the small "A" frame and rested the spit into the "V".

The flagstone now became a weight that he placed on the end of the stick on which the rabbit roasted.

The whole apparatus was somewhat precarious, but seemed stable enough to do the job at hand.

Cliff turned the rabbit occasionally. His mother had a rule that rabbit and pork were to be cooked well done.

Before sunlight flooded the canyon floor, Cliff was ready for his first meal in his temporary home in the ancient cliff dwelling. Breakfast would consist only of roasted rabbit meat.

No cold fresh milk. No biscuit and butter and honey for me this morning. Oh well, better get used to it.

He could have eaten all of it, but Cliff kept half the rabbit for supper. However, the meat alone did not satisfy his appetite. He was still hungry.

Water flowed from the spring in a trickle. The ancient architect had diverted its flow from spreading out across the cave floor by chipping and grinding a trough in the sandstone from the spring to a square hole in the base of the wall in the front corner of the dwelling near the corner of the cave and the ledge.

To keep the wall dry, the mason had extended the trough several feet past the wall to a natural indentation in the ledge where the water pooled before spreading out into the drifted soil that covered the ledge. Grass and clover grew in the damp soil on the ledge.

Cliff cut enough fresh grass to wrap the remainder of the rabbit and placed it in the gunnysack, which he stowed in the back of the cave near the spring, the coolest spot in the cave. The moist fresh grass in the breathing burlap sack would keep the meat fresh and the flies out. On fishing trips, this was how he and his dad kept fish fresh.

Cliff was inquisitive by nature. All his life he had learned from a father who was an intuitive and inventive farmer and a mother who was a nurturer, cook, gardener, gleaner and preserver. Both had survived starvation, depression, a dust bowl and two world wars. They perpetually prepared for the next big catastrophe just as for generations ancestors on both sides of the family had prepared.

Both his mother and father had tried to pass along their work ethic and values to him every day as they worked side by side in the garden or kitchen or surveyed an irrigation system in the fields, set water together, overhauled machinery, or hauled hay. They also taught him by example by assisting neighbors in need and treating others fairly, even though they were harsh disciplinarians at home.

Cliff had the day before him and nothing to do, but it was nearly impossible to sit still and do nothing.

Even though he had no cows to milk or hogs to feed or school to attend, he couldn't escape chores of another sort. He had to find more food. He had to take care of a bobcat.

He skinned the bobcat before disposing of the carcass. The pelt was too beautiful to waste. He folded it and set it aside with the rabbit pelt.

Cliff examined the naked carcass. It was smaller and less threatening without the thick spotted fur. Thick bundles of tendon along the back and legs enabled the big cat to leap great distances and gave it agility. Those same tendons when dried would unravel as thin threads so strong he couldn't break them by hand. *I can use these threads for all kinds of projects this summer.*

He trimmed the exposed tendons from the backs of the legs and neck of the big cat, and stretched the moist bundles of sinew next to the hide.

It was another useful trick learned from his dad. Ed Kelley always harvested the tendons from any animal he skinned. He dried the tendons, and sometime later, he pounded them to break down the sinew and wound the coarse threads into balls. On the farm, he repaired canvass, belts, and leather. On hunting trips, he made emergency repairs on packing gear and tents.

The downside of Ed Kelley's sinew stash was its smell.

Cliff carried the naked carcass to the wide end of the ledge and launched it as far out into the canyon as he could. It bounced off the scree, tumbled and disappeared near a scrub oak grove far below where scavengers could find it.

A flock of wild turkeys flew out of the grove where the cat landed and sailed above the canyon slope, circled and dipped gracefully to land on the trail by the creek. They strolled along the bank picking at grasshoppers and other insects as they moved along.

This is a surprise. I knew there are wild turkeys up in Mancos Canyon in the higher foothills, but I had no idea they lived this close to home. I wonder if Dad or George even knows they are here. What other surprises await me here in the canyon?

As Cliff watched the turkeys, he realized he was seeing out of both eyes again. Sometime during the night, the swelling had gone down. He had no idea how his face looked. The cuts on his forehead had scabbed over. His ribs were still sore and his breathing was easier.

At that end of the ledge, the exposed layer of sandstone that formed the ledge had broken off at some time eons before leaving an abrupt edge. The canyon wall also dropped off steeply below the rimrock, forming an "L" that plunged a hundred feet or more into the tumbled mass of rock in the canyon.

The ledge he stood on was one of many layers of sandstone that lay beneath the thick caprock. The canyon slope, in places, exposed layers of sandstone of varying thickness and hardness stacked like pancakes. Wind, frost, snowmelt, rain, slides and earth tremors had eroded each layer at a different rate.

The cave was part of that erosion. The spring had softened the sandstone, and over time, particles dissolved or washed over the layer that formed the ledge. Finally, the flow had slowed to the dependable small trickle of year around pure water supply that had made the pocket attractive to the ancestral Puebloans who had built there.

Thin layers fractured and sloughed into the canyon. Fine particles broke down even further through repeated freezing and thawing and built up a coating of clay on the slopes. Sand and dust blew in from the New Mexico and Arizona deserts depositing fine sand and soil on the slopes, on the clay, among the rock and in the pockets.

Shrubs and trees grew and roots grew tougher and spread, exerting force, buckling, crumbling the rock into smaller rock. Ironically, while the roots stabilized the slopes of the canyon, they destabilized the stone face of it.

Cliff carefully studied the face of the rimrock behind him. The Indian family or families who inhabited the ruin must have accessed it from the top. He assumed they would have needed ready access to their fields. However, they would have also needed access to the resources of the canyon.

The Indians on Mesa Verde had accessed some their ruins by cutting hand and toehold stairways right up the face of the cliffs.

He walked slowly along the ledge searching the face of the cliff for any sign of artificial or natural hand and toeholds. He looked from west to east into the sun. At that time of morning, the angle of the sun cast shadows on the surface emphasizing any irregularities.

When he approached the rope, still dangling from the snag above, he saw oval shadows about eighteen inches apart alternating on each side of the rope ascending the sheer face of the rimrock.

He examined closely the handiwork of an ancient one who had chipped and ground each toehold just deep enough to insert toes or fingers to support one's weight. There was no lip so that water could not collect in them.

Cliff placed the fingers of his right hand in the highest indentation he could reach and pulled himself up until he could put the toe of his left shoe into the lowest cup. Balancing there, he reached up to the next indent and pulled himself upright. He raised his right foot and fit it into the cup across from his left knee. *Whoever spaced these indents must have been about the same height as me.*

As he climbed, he hugged the face of the cliff. He was tense and his side hurt. It was a precarious feeling at barely ten feet off the ground. *How will it feel to cling like a lizard forty feet up this rock? How did some woman ever climb over the edge of the cliff carrying a deer or a child on his or her back? I'm not ready to find out. Not just yet. I'll have to use the rope.*

The rope hung down between his arms and legs. Cliff let go of the indent he held with his right hand and grasped the rope. He let go with his left hand and grabbed the rope above his right hand and began pulling his body upward while moving his feet from indent to indent to push himself upward.

He was too busy thinking about coordinating between pulling himself with his arms and hands on the rope and lifting his weight upward with his feet searching for the next indent on the rock face to deal with the pain in his rib cage, which built moment by moment.

Cliff pulled himself over the edge of the rim and stood up. *That was certainly a lot harder than coming down yesterday.* He looked down into the canyon. It was a beautiful morning in early May. The air was still misty in the canyon bottom making it appear further away. *If I'd fallen, nobody would have found me…* He looked away quickly.

It feels funny not to be finishing chores and getting ready to go to school. Sorry to leave it all to you Mom.

He pulled the rope up after him. *There's no use advertising while I'm away from it, in case someone wanders by.*

He untied the rope from the snag and hid it under a rock, then began walking along the rim up the canyon looking for a way to get down into the canyon.

The unbroken layer of rimrock on both sides of the canyon was the main reason Martinez Canyon was relatively unexplored. The surface of the rimrock was wavy with erosion, cracks, pockets, and irregularities, nevertheless, no adjoining canyons or significant breaks provided access to the slope below.

He didn't remember much about the route he had taken the summer before from the creek up to the bee tree ruin and back to the creek. It had required climbing a steep treacherous, slippery, crumbling clay slope. He had twisted back and forth between layers of horizontal sandstone, crossed rockslides and between boulders. Coming down he had not needed to follow the beeline, which made it faster.

That morning he had checked the narrow chute that had provided final access to the ledge where the ruin was located. He had expected to see it choked with rock from the ledge down to the slope below, just as it had been before. However, between last summer and now, the rock in the chute had settled or slid away, leaving a sheer wall of stone to climb, impossible without a rope or ladder.

It wasn't a major problem. He had decided that going down to the creek directly from the ruin was too difficult to be undertaken on a daily basis anyway.

He continued walking east along the rimrock toward the intersecting draw on the north side of Martinez Canyon across from the lookout tower ruin on the arrowhead shaped point. He knew that he could go down a trail into the canyon there.

The rim curved forming a viewpoint, and he walked out onto it to study the jumbled slope below and up the canyon from him. The canyon was wider and shallower than at the ruin, but it was still an imposing gash in the earth.

Willows and tamarack lined the creek below. A movement on the north slope caught his eye, and he watched intently and finally spotted three deer moving down the canyon side about a hundred yards away and two thirds of the way up the slope.

He watched them snake their way down the slope of the canyon and began to see a thin line. He followed the line back to the rim, but saw no break in the rimrock. He followed it back down the canyon. It was broken or obscured in many places by rock, brush or trees. He finally caught up with the deer's progress and watched them until they reached the creek, crossed it and walked down the trail next to the creek.

He lost sight of their trail in the grass and brush growing in the flat silt plain when they neared the creek.

Can that be my access to the canyon?

He left the viewpoint on the canyon rim, walked back into the trees and continued walking toward the east. Away from the irregular twists and turns of the rim face, he could walk in a straight line and make much better time.

He knew there was a very well defined deer trail in the draw that crossed Martinez Canyon just east of the tower ruin. It was the preferred route taken by the major deer migration. He had killed a deer there during the hunting season last fall.

The trail he sought was unmistakable when he came to it. Unlike the major trail in the draw, which was a couple of feet wide and worn deep, this trail was narrow and less defined. Sharp oval shaped cloven hooves had merely disturbed the soil. They ranged in size from a quarter to a silver dollar and pointed to and from the direction of the canyon. Cliff picked up a round pellet from a cluster among the hoof prints and crushed it between his fingers. It was still soft and bright green. The herd, probably just a resident family, had gone into the canyon only a short time before. From the sizes of hoof prints, he guessed the herd to be a mix of does and yearlings. A few mule deer hung around the area year around, rather than following the general migration from the foothills to Mesa Verde in the fall and back to the foothills and La Plata Mountains in the spring.

Cliff followed the trail to the rimrock. He was still much closer to the ruin than to the draw across from the lookout tower.

A car-width slice the full depth of the rimrock had settled beginning nearly 50 feet back from the face of the rim. It had tipped slightly backward as it slid, pushing layers of sandstone in front and out from it, leaving a chute backfilled with trees, brush, silt, debris, and trash. Over the centuries, drifting sand, soil and erosion had eventually sculpted the cut to the canyon slope. Animals seeking a path into the canyon had gouged a path as they angled back and forth across the slope of the canyon until they had a trail to the creek.

When the trail neared the creek, it became faint in the grassy silt. *That's why I never saw it before.* He marked the spot by focusing on the nearest willow grove, so he could find the trail again on the way back.

By the time he reached the creek, Cliff regretted not bringing the gunnysack. *I could have filled it with edibles for tonight and tomorrow's breakfast. However, the trip isn't a wasted effort. These bib overalls have deep front and back pockets I can fill and two bib pockets. Maybe they do have some advantages over jeans after all.*

Willows grew in groves interspersed with salt cedar or tamarack, as locals called it, all along the creek. He thought about the makeshift spit he had made that morning on which he had roasted the rabbit. It had been a challenge to balance the roasting stick on the rickety "A" frame. The cedar branch was not that straight and that became a problem when he turned the rabbit.

Willows grew tall and straight in tight groves all along the creek. There were few side branches until they were ten or twelve feet tall, and then they branched out to form a tangled mass. The canopy attracted magpies that flocked to the willow groves to build colonies of nests.

Cliff sat on the trail beneath a grove of willows and looked around. Willow, oak, and cottonwood grew along the creek and on the lower slopes. Clover, grass and asparagus grew on the banks along open stretches of the creek. Dandelions grew in abundance wherever the soil was a little moist. Cattails grew to the edge of the stream. As Mrs. Campbell had said on Friday, there was an abundance of food if a person looked hard enough for it.

As he sat there, he imagined what it would be like to shape a bow from a slender scrub oak trunk and making willow arrows. He would stalk the mule deer that came down the trail. In his imagination, he didn't have to acknowledge how difficult it would be to find a scrub oak growing straight enough to make a bow.

It was his first day away from home and at the ruin. Anything could happen. He could go home today or maybe wait until the end of the week. *They will be so happy to see me; they will forgive me for running away. Won't they?*

On the other hand, the sheriff could arrive by the end of the day. That will change the whole thing. I'll be in real trouble then. But, there isn't anything illegal in running off is there? If anybody did anything wrong, it was Hector. Wasn't it?

Cliff stood and began walking down the game trail next to the creek.

He finally recognized the pool and the boulder where he had found the beeline the summer before, and he searched for the snag on the rim. He did locate it and was surprised that it was just a thin line on the rock in the distance. *Good, the ruin is still invisible even when you know it's there. It's a lot faster and safer getting down here by the deer trail than directly down from there to here.*

Cliff walked on down the trail by the creek into new territory. The canyon grew deeper and the walls steeper, dashing any hopes that there might be an even closer way into the canyon.

He watched the creek for arrowheads and sign of fish. He saw no trout, but he did discover darting minnows among some of the shallow pools. *Water gets too warm for trout. I'll bet they're suckers. That's what they catch down in McElmo.*

He also found round nodules of flint, which had washed out of the layers of sediment in the canyon walls. He picked up a couple of fist-sized stones and several even smaller flakes and put them into his pockets. They were the same kind of stone the ancestral Puebloans had chipped into arrowheads and knives. Mrs. Campbell had used the same stone to start a fire.

He found no trail closer to the ruin than the one he had discovered to the east.

Along the way back to the deer trail, Cliff grazed and collected food. Tender asparagus sprigs as thick as his thumb grew in abundance. Dandelions were in full bloom, and yellow clover was just beginning to bloom on a few stalks. Lambs quarter, a very close cousin to spinach, was six inches tall. A new crop of cattails grew in the creek.

He cut the main shoot of a cattail and peeled away the leaves to the core to find the jelly like sap Mrs. Campbell had spread on Alicia's burn. He slathered it around his still tender eye and then over the bruises on his face and forehead. Finally, he ate the cucumber-tasting shoot.

He nibbled on crisp asparagus and cattail shoots, dandelion greens and dandelion blossoms. The bittersweet tasting dandelion blossoms pleasantly surprised him.

He packed a small bundle of asparagus into the front pocket of his overalls. He put fewer delicate cattail shoots into a back pocket. He filled one bib pocket with lambs quarter greens, dandelion leaves and blossoms.

Cliff put the two flint nodules back into the water. They were very uncomfortable to carry in his pockets. Besides, he needed the pocket room for food. He knew where to find them if he needed them.

Many of the seed heads on the dead stalks of last summer's cattails were still whole. He carefully cut one without bursting it and put it into his bib pocket. It would come in handy when he built the fire that night and in the morning.

His pockets were full, and he had eaten enough greenery to satisfy his hunger for the moment. He cut a willow shoot strong enough to use as a roasting stick to heat up the remaining half of rabbit. He started to trim it of side branches and leaves, and then he thought better of it. For now, maybe I'd better just not leave any sign behind. He took the entire willow and headed back up the trail.

About halfway up the slope he paused to rest on an outcropping of shale.

That morning he had noticed several pieces of shale lying outside the dwelling. The edges were chipped and when he fitted them together, they appeared to be shaped the approximately size of the doorway. He wondered if, when it was one piece, it had sealed the doorway when the inhabitants left the dwelling and if sometime in the following six or seven centuries it had fallen out and broken.

He had examined the masonry surrounding the inside of the door-frame and discovered a thin ring where adobe had mostly eroded away. He had looked carefully at one of the fragments. One side had a ring of adobe clinging to it, the other side had a thin layer of adobe plaster that matched the plaster remaining on the masonry wall.

Had that doorway still been plastered over when he discovered the bee tree, he might not have discovered the ruin while standing 10 or 15 feet from it 700 years later!

Cliff looked around the shelf where he sat. Thin layers of slate had broken and slid down the canyon side. He recognized the half-inch thick layers as the same material as the shale fragments on the ruin terrace. He picked through sheets of the shale and pulled fresh sheets out of the shelf where he had been sitting until he had found a piece that he estimated to be about the size of the doorway and carefully carried it out of the canyon and on back to the ruin.

It was not a perfect fit. It had broken into a roughly rectangular shape a couple of inches too narrow and several inches too short to fit perfectly.

He felt pretty smug about how closely he had guessed the size.

Cliff climbed through the door, walked to the spring, laid down on his belly and drank cold, pure water until he could drink no more. He just lay there for a while. It was cool in the back of the cave. The morning had become warm and then hot as the sun climbed higher in the sky. He had gone out without water. The water in the creek looked pure, but it drained off cow pastures, and he didn't know if it was safe to drink. Of course, he drank out of the irrigation ditch that ran through fields where the cows pastured all winter. The water that filled the pond that supplied the family drinking water had traversed farms and who knew how many cows had drunk out of it or crapped in it. He decided in a pinch, the creek was just fine. But, he knew it wasn't as sweet as the spring.

He drifted off for a short while, and when he woke, he felt refreshed.

It was warm on the ledge outside the ruin, but the cedar and lip of the cave provided shade. The sun was high enough in the sky that for the rest of the summer it would not strike the front of the dwelling at all. In winter, the face of the dwelling would receive full sunshine all day except for what shade the cedar provided.

Cliff sat in the doorway and looked out across the canyon.

He inspected his left eye. The salve from the cattail had soothed the skin and flesh on his cheekbone around the eye as well as the cuts and bruises on his forehead, nose and ribs.

The bruises around his ribcage were still angry purple and blue and were very sore, but he could breathe easily.

Too bad there isn't a salve for nightmares. If I could stop dreaming about shooting Hector it would help. Do I really have it in me to hunt another human down? Has Charlie's teasing, Hector's bullying, Mr. Johnson's rope and Dad's razor strop made me crazy enough to want to kill somebody? I don't feel like killing anybody right now. Would that change if I met Hector face to face? If so, I should get rid of the .22 now while I can control it.

Cliff chewed a couple of pieces of jerky at mid-day. His teeth were not as sore as the night before, and he was able to eat it. *I need to go easy on the jerky and oatmeal cookies until I see how I get along finding food out here. Mrs. Campbell made it look easy. I found enough for today, but if what I saw was it, my diet is going to get boring pretty fast. She may have made it look easier than it really is. And, I'm not sure I'm ready to east some of the things she showed us. These might come handy in a day or two if I'm still here.* He took the two jars with the remaining cookies and jerky to a nook high on the wall and placed them there out of sight.

He carried the slab to the door and stood it in place, holding it at the top to check the fit. He would need stops on both sides.

He used a thin sliver of the broken slate on the ledge to drill eight round holes as wide as his thumb in the narrow strip of adobe mortar between the stones around the doorway opening. Four were to keep the slate from falling outward and four were to keep it from falling inward. He cut eight pegs from the willow. To keep the slab in place, when he was inside, he inserted a set of the outside pegs. Then he placed the slate against them and inserted the inside pegs. The slate held in place with him inside for the night. If he wanted to keep out intruding animals, while he was gone from the cave, he would reverse the process. *Not bad,* he thought when he tried it out.

Cliff took the scrapbook from the nook and began to read the notes Mrs. Campbell had written in the margins. It was the first time he had taken time to look through the book since getting it back.

He smiled proudly at her notations praising his work, and he carefully read the detailed technical instructions on footnoting which he had largely ignored. He longed to sit with her and to go over the notes to understand fully her comments.

By the time he finished reading through the book and then reading some of the articles he had included, it was late afternoon. He put the book away and climbed the rope back over the rimrock.

Cliff gathered several armloads of firewood. He stacked the mix of clean burning cedar and pitchy piñon next to the snag. When he had enough for the night, he tied bundles of wood to the end of the rope and lowered them to the ledge. He had to descend to untie the rope and then climb back up to lower the next load. It took three roundtrips up and down the rope to get the wood down to the ruin.

Thankfully, the toeholds were there. He practically walked himself up the face of the cliff.

When he reached the ledge again, his rib cage hurt so badly he knew he could not make another trip.

Cliff sat on the saddle blanket in front of the fire. The second half of the rabbit tasted even better than the first half had at breakfast. He speared chunks of cattail shoots, dandelion root and asparagus sprigs on the willow shoot, and roasted them over the fire. While he waited for the wild vegetables to cook, he munched on dandelion leaf salad.

The fire popped and crackled cheerily. Shadows weaved and danced on the stone back wall of the cave.

"I wonder what Mom and Dad are doing right now?" He was almost startled to hear his own voice. He had not heard another person's voice for a day and a half.

Cliff was very tired. He had hardly slept the night before. He went to the door and looked out across the canyon. Now that he had something to put over the door, he could sleep more securely.

Before he went to bed, he placed the slate into the doorway. It fit well enough to give some sense of security. It would also help keep some heat inside the dwelling at night. Although it was warm during the day, it still dropped to near freezing every night. The air in the high altitude and low humidity held no heat.

He wished for a blanket and a mattress as he added a couple of pieces of wood to the fire. The saddle blanket helped insulate his body from the cold hard floor, but was no cushion. The sack gave the illusion of cover but was no blanket.

His clothes provided some warmth, and fire would cut the chill in the cave during the night. The fresh air intake vent for the fire pit and exhaust vents at the roofline assured the safety of the boy as he cradled his head on his arm and finally slept.

12

Tuesday Night, suppertime
The Kelley Home

"I'm worried Papa. I'm afraid something awful has happened to my baby," Etta Mae said as she set the supper table. "What else can we do?"

"I don't know, Mama. I talked to everybody in the neighborhood and the sheriff. The sheriff won't do nothing yet. It's only been a day and night. He thinks Cliff probably just run off, 'Kids do that,' Bill said. Bill's a good man, but he ain't much of a sheriff."

"Now that's not true. You know he does the best he can. But, I don't think Clifton would do that. Getting in a fight ain't no reason to up and run off. Things have been pretty good lately, ain't they?"

"I thought so," Ed said. "He ain't been complaining any. By the way, I found his shovel down by prairie dog town."

"Where'd he go from there, do you think?"

"I think we'd need to know why he'd up and run away to know where he'd go. If he went to any of the kinfolk, they'd of at least let us know he's safe and sound."

"I guess if he's on foot, he wouldn't have gotten there yet." Etta Mae poured the milk and put it on the table. "Come on and eat, Papa."

"I'm not that hungry Mama."

"You've gotta eat."

They bowed their heads and joined hands. Ed prayed. "We ask thou All Mighty Lord, to bless this food for its intended use of our bodies. And Lord, look over our two boys this night. Protect Charlie from harm and from evil and deliver him back safely to us from that far away heathen land of Japan. And, look after Clifton where-ever he may be. Forgive us if we did something to drive him away. And, forgive him if he done something that made him afraid. Help him realize the errors of his ways and help him do what is right in Thy eyes and do Thy will. In Jesus' name. Amen."

"Amen. I don't know what I'm going to do, Papa. The wheat planting has to be done. Water has to be tended to. Corn and beans have to be planted. I can't handle it all by myself. You're gonna have to hire somebody to help me, or take time off."

Etta Mae handed her husband the plate of fried chicken then the mashed potatoes.

"They don't take kindly to anybody asking for time off right now. If I even ask for time off, they'll fire me. Everybody wants their equipment running so they can get their stuff in the ground. If Cliff ain't back tomorrow, I'll talk to Raul and see if one of his boys is available," Ed promised. "Would you pass the biscuits?"

"I can't believe that your boss wouldn't cooperate with you on this,"

Etta Mae said. You haven't taken a day since you started there. It seems kind a sad that we have to go to Mr. Rodriguez for help when it was one of his boys who started this whole thing!"

"Raul is a hard worker, and he's taught his boys to be the same," Ed said. "What happens between our boys don't have to affect the way we adults act toward each other."

He ate in silence for a few minutes. "I've been thinking about something strange George was telling me today, when I stopped by his place. He said he was rounding up some stray heifers down in his pasture yesterday afternoon in that pasture, that joins our east slope fence line down in the draw. He found all but one of his heifers, and when he went looking for her, she had gotten down in the bottom of the draw that empties into Martinez Canyon. He said she was trying to reach some grass through the fence and was just too stubborn to turn around. While he was down there persuading her, he thought he saw someone up on the point where that old Indian ruin sits across the canyon.

"He couldn't tell who it was from where he stood. Of course, at that time of the day he wouldn't of expected it to be Clifton, because he should have been in school. He thought it was probably somebody come over from Mancos target shooting. When I told him Clifton was missing, he said it might could a been him."

Ed paused and took a swallow of milk. He wiped his mouth on his sleeve and continued, "George said, he figgered somebody was sitting up on the point target practicing. He'd be a tom fool to hang around there, if that was so. So he took off as soon as he got his heifer outta there before whoever it was took a shot at her.' He said he heard a couple of shots after he left.

"He said that particular place has become a problem lately, and he's gonna buy some no-trespassing signs and put 'em up around there," Ed said. "Even though it isn't on his property."

"He showed me where someone had been there, but it's just bare rock on both sides. We found an empty .22 shell there at the tower ruin. We couldn't find no tracks, but I kind of agree with George. Cliff talks about that point and the old ruin and asks a lot a questions about it. He kind a likes to go there and think, and I think he likes to go there during hunting season, because there's a deer migration trail that goes down the draw and crosses the canyon there.

"George and I think that's what Clifton might a done. From that point, it's a straight shot over to the highway. We think he could a gone over there and hitched a ride."

"You know that none of this would have happened if you'd stood up for him more often," Etta Mae said.

"What do you mean?" Ed asked.

"Like that thing at school yesterday. That Rodriguez boy had no right to go after him like that. He's been bullying our boy for a long time. Cliff's complained about it ever now and again and we didn't do nothing. You still treat Raul like he was your best friend! Why didn't you go to Raul a long time ago? Or why didn't you go to school and tell them to straighten that boy out, or you would go to the school board and have him expelled!"

"Don't start Etta Mae," he said quietly. "Boys are going to be boys regardless of what Raul or me say to them. We can't watch them ever minute! They just have to know the consequence of their actions and be ready to take them. Obviously, Clifton was not ready to take the consequences of his actions, and he just up and run away!"

"So you think it was his fault, and he ran away then? First of all, Evelyn Campbell said it was not Clifton's fault, and where do you think he'd go? How could he survive Papa? He didn't take no clothes, no food. You know how he eats. He'll starve in no time at all! He don't have any money. You think he'll hitchhike? What kind of man will pick him up? Will he become a thief? We have to go back to the sheriff, Papa."

"I don't know where he'd go. He might head out for New Mexico and my brother's, or to your sister's in Texas."

"He might go over to Durango or Mancos. But, he doesn't know anyone in those places."

"You gonna call Bill? He could put out a bulletin or something."

"I'm afraid to do that right now, Mama. If he knew Clifton has the single shot, he might put that in all those bulletins. If it says he's armed and dangerous, that would be a sure way to get him killed. I think we'd better handle it ourselves right now. I think it's different than if he's lost. If he don't want to be found, it'll be hard to find him. We really don't know where to look. We have to get hold of everybody we know and let them know that he's not in any trouble, and that he has to contact us."

"You know what we haven't talked about Ed? He looked like he could be hurt pretty bad, even if he wouldn't admit it. He might a gone somewhere and laid down and be hurtin' and can't get back. He was complaining about his ribs. What if he punctured a lung or something? What if one of those ribs was broken and worked up there and punctured his heart? I should have taken him to the hospital! Why didn't I make him go with me to the hospital?"

"OK, I'll call Bill about a search party."

"Good. And we've gotta do it right now, Ed!"

13
Tuesday Night, Martinez Canyon

Cliff opened his eyes. He heard a soft rustling sound from the direction of the spring. He didn't move. He couldn't have slept for long. The fire still burned brightly. Two beady eyes reflected in the firelight from across the room. Above the eyes was a pure white "V" stripe of hair. Skunk. *That's what I heard over there last night,* he thought.

The skunk had apparently come into the room through the spring's overflow opening. She had brought her family.

Cliff watched the dim outline of the animal followed by five little replicas with their tails arched over their backs. Mama was about the size of a house cat. She was coal black with a white stripe beginning as a V on her forehead and sweeping back in two stripes along her back merging into a single stripe that continued up the center of her arched tail. Her babies were marked the same with slight variations.

She lay down by the spring, keeping an eye on Cliff, while her brood took their places at the supper table.

Cliff had noticed fresh tracks in the mud on the ledge that morning. He had wondered how the animal had got there. He knew those tracks well. A skunk's main diet was small rodents and insects. A resident skunk would mean a mouse free environment. She wouldn't be especially interested in most foods he brought into the cave, especially if he didn't leave it on the floor. Skunks liked people. They seemed to enjoy being around humans. It took little effort to tame them. A skunk seldom used her scent on humans unless the human caught her in a trap or cornered her.

Almost every spring, a skunk family lived somewhere in the barn, under the granary, or in a corner of one of the tool sheds on the Kelley farm. Ed Kelley liked to have them around, because they kept the mice down. For Cliff they were a cash crop. He caught the young newly weaned ones and sold them to a vet in town. The vet removed scent glands, spayed or neutered them, gave shots, and sold the young skunks as house pets.

Rabies posed a problem in skunks in some parts of the country, especially in the southern part of the United States. But in the high country of Colorado in the 1950's Rabies was not considered a problem among any of the wildlife, according to the veterinarian.

Welcome mama, glad to have the company, Thought Cliff.

Cliff had never actually observed baby skunks nursing before. They competed for their share just like a litter of baby pigs. The skunks he caught were a few weeks older, weaned, and foraging on their own. *That's what I am, weaned and on my own. There is some parallel between their circumstances and my own. After this, I won't be so quick to catch another one of you.*

He thought back on the aimless day he had just put in. He wasn't committed to staying in the ruin. So much could happen. Like the baby skunks, he faced a perilous future in the canyon. He had no idea how mama skunk had made her way to the cave. She had obviously found some crack in the rock that she could crawl through. The baby skunks were probably safe as long as she kept them here on the ledge and in the cave. But out on the slopes of the canyon at night they would be fair game to the only predator without a sense of smell, the great horned owl that flew on silent wing through the canyons and on the table land alike. Skunk, young or old, also a nocturnal hunter, was a prime target. The powerful scent gland that would keep a cougar at bay was no defense against the silent killer from the sky.

What if I fall? What if I can't find enough to eat? What if I get sick? Here in the canyon I'll have no one looking after me. I don't know enough. I'm not strong enough to do this day after day.

I spent all day just finding a few weeds to eat. If I stay here, will it take all my time searching for food? This is how mom spends her life, isn't it? She runs a restaurant for us!

Breakfast, dinner, supper, and lunches for me and Dad.

Breakfast: bacon; biscuits, or pancakes; gravy, syrup, butter, and milk.

School lunch: two or three pieces of fried chicken; a couple of biscuits; and a boiled egg; or a couple of bologna or peanut butter and honey sandwiches and a pint thermos of cold milk.

Supper: fried chicken, pork, venison, or beef; potatoes; whatever vegetable is in season fresh from the garden (Brussels sprouts, cabbage, broccoli, spinach, or lambs quarter, asparagus, squash, zucchini, cucumber, tomato, green beans, peas (canned in the off season); biscuits or cornbread; pinto beans; a couple of glasses of milk; and for dessert, pie, cobbler, cookies or cake.

Mom seems to like watching Dad and I eat. What was it she said Sunday at dinner? He replayed the conversation in his head. *"I'll swan, Clifton, I don't know where you put it all. You must have a tapeworm a mile long. There you are just skin and bone after eating all that food."*

He smiled at the remembered conversation. He had teased back, *"I don't know Mom, but there is still a little space left in my left big toe,"* he had laughed. He remembered reaching for another chicken leg as he said it.

He closed his eyes and heard her voice again, *"Course that ninety pound frame needs lots of nourishment to lift a hundred pound bale of hay,"* she had laughed.

"Well, I don't exactly just lift them straight up off the ground, you know," he had replied. *"I have to kind of swing them up."* He smiled as he remembered saying that between bites of chicken.

"You haven't walked anywhere since you were knee high. If you ever slow down, you'll fill up like me. Anyway, you sure do burn away plenty. One of these days, if you keep eating like this, you'll blow up like a balloon. You'll get fat just like me and all your kin folk." He suddenly felt a lump in his throat. It was only his second night away from home and already he felt homesick.

He also realized that the hollow feeling in his stomach was hunger from thinking about all that food. But, there was no food in the cave other than the few remaining oatmeal cookies and jerky in the jars, and that he was keeping those as rations until a regular food supply started not as midnight snacks.

To get his mind off food, he looked back at the mama skunk and her brood by the spring.

I wonder if I should put another cedar branch on the little fire. I have enough wood to keep her burning tonight. However, if I move it'll scare her off, he thought. He really didn't want her to go. He really wanted some company, even if only a little member of the weasel family.

He looked over at Mama skunk and her brood. The firelight glowed in her eyes still. She was still as if asleep. Maybe she sleeps with her eyes open. She is a nocturnal animal. How does she do that with the babies? Will she leave them to hunt?

With the slate doorway in place and the skunk for company, Cliff relaxed and fell into a restful sleep.

14

Wednesday, morning
Martinez Canyon

Cliff awoke at dawn. Most of the light in the room came from the four windows near the ceiling, now that the door was partially covered. When he opened his eyes, he stared into the face of the mother skunk that stood within inches of his nose. He didn't move.

She cautiously sniffed his face and looked him over. Apparently satisfied he wasn't dangerous to her or her babies, she returned to her little ones who tumbled and wrestled a few feet away. She lay down and they immediately pounced on her and began nursing. Cliff watched contentedly until they finished breakfast and resumed their play.

Mamma stared at him intently and then began grooming the gleaming black fur on her chest. She stood, stretched, gave him a final glance, nonchalantly arched her bushy tail over her back and headed toward the water outlet with her brood lined up behind her. One by one they disappeared outside.

"See you tonight?" Cliff wistfully asked after her.

He had spoken to no one in nearly two days. Already he felt a little lonely.

There had been no repeat of the first night's terror. The slate in the doorway provided a feeling of security, which had helped immensely. Mama skunk and the fire had also helped.

The fire was nearly as effective as a nightlight in helping to calm Cliff's fear of the dark. For a second night in a row, he did not wet his bedding such as it was. Given the circumstances, he counted that as a victory. Maybe Monday night's crying jag was not an omen of bad things returning after all.

Cliff lifted the slate out of the doorway and stepped outside the dwelling onto the ledge. From where he stood, he could see light pink highlighting high wispy clouds over Mesa Verde. It would be another good hour before the sun lighted the canyon floor on that crisp spring morning. He climbed the rope to the top of the rim and admired the glorious sunrise lighting the sky behind Hesperus peak and the La Plata Mountains. From the ledge, he could see only the southern end of the La Plata's through the V of Martinez canyon. The sun would reach the northern end of the range at the beginning of summer. His favorite time was now when the sun rose from behind the highest peak still fully clothed in winter's white. He would have to climb out of the canyon for that view.

He had no coat, and it was cold. He was also hungry. The rabbit was gone. He would have to settle for roasted cattails, asparagus and dandelion root. It was not the most appetizing breakfast prospect, but it would have to do. He finally topped it off with one oatmeal cookie to sweeten his mouth.

After eating, he sat on the sill of the doorway. He had survived two nights. The first night had been worse than he thought it would be. The second night had been better.

He hadn't starved. Anybody could go two days without eating. He'd heard of people going without food for days and surviving. Some people fasted for weeks on purpose!

However, can I make it over time? I don't have any way to wash clothes, or cook food. I only have two boxes of shells and a box of matches. I don't have anything to sleep on. I don't have any money. Who am I kidding? I can't stay here.

~~~

Ed finished the last water set in the alfalfa and headed back to the house as the first golden sunrays broke over the Ridge. The air was sweet and fresh. It was chilly and crisp, and his hands were cold.

A cacophony of sounds greeted the sunrise. Swallow's sharp chirps announced their joy as they swooped through the morning hatch of mosquitoes. A meadowlark's melodious "whe he whe he spario" sounded across the hayfield. Magpie's "ack ack ack acked" from the willows and crow's "caw caw cawed" from the trees. Red wing blackbird's "cork a ree, a ka lee" sounded from the cattails along the ditch bank. The elm trees were full of hundreds of sparrows merrily chirping all at once as they flitted from branch to branch. The lone Rhode Island Red rooster finished his morning wake up crow from the top of the haystack in the barnyard.

Ordinarily, he would have felt exhilarated with such a sunrise and the joyous sounds of birds singing. All should have been good with the world. However, as he trudged back to the house, he didn't see the fertile gently sloping fields of his 160-acre farm springing to life after a long cold
~~~

winter. Instead, he saw plowed fields ready for planting, and there was no one to plant them. The help he had counted on was gone. The help was important, but more importantly his son was gone, and no one knew where to look for him.

Day after tomorrow school will be out for the summer, and Clifton would have been here all day, every day to do the spring planting. Finally, he's old enough to do a full man's work, he thought.

Just when things should get better, this happens. It's not the first time!

Charlie was a natural, even gifted, farmer and had he stayed, things would be far different now, he thought sorrowfully. His first son had received his letter from the US Army just before his eighteenth birthday, soon after he graduated from high school.

Ed had urged him to claim Conscientious Objector status. *If he couldn't stay and help me, at least he could have gone to a government work camp and served his time in safety, but he refused.* It had been hard to forgive that. Ed did not believe in the military, war, or fighting.

"Now history's repeating itself, but a lot sooner, and when I need him the most. Why? Is God testing me as he tested Job?" Ed asked aloud.

Etta Mae was hanging the milk pail as Ed opened the door of the porch. She nodded to her husband and went into the kitchen to begin fixing his breakfast as he cleaned up and changed into his mechanics clothes.

As Ed finished breakfast and prepared to say good-bye, an old pickup drove into the front yard. Two men got out and stood by the front fender waiting for someone to come outside.

Through the kitchen window, Etta Mae recognized Raul Rodriguez and his son Hector. "What you suppose they want," she said frowning. "You should run him off Ed. Tell him not to come back here after what that boy did to Cliff!"

"Now Etta Mae, you stay in here and let me handle this," he said.

Ed picked up his hat and slowly walked out to where his neighbors stood waiting.

"Morning Raul," he said and extended his hand.

"Good morning Señor," Raul Rodriguez replied.

The boy silently and sullenly looked at his feet.

"Hector!" Raul barked.

"*Señor,*" Hector mumbled without looking up.

"Hector!" Raul said again.

"Good morning, *Señor,*" Hector said again, this time looking Ed in the eye.

"Ed, Inez and I are very sorrowful that your boy has not come back home. My boy caused this to happen. He is very sorry and wishes to make up for it. Isn't that so, Hector?"

Hector continued to stare silently at his feet.

"Isn't that so, Hector!"

"*Si, Señor!*" Hector said.

Ed knew very well that Hector could speak English better than Raul and was surprised that he was using Spanish in his replies. Obviously, he resented being there.

"Until your son comes back safely, Hector will come here every day after school and do the work that your boy would have done. In addition, when school is out, if your son still has not come back, Hector will come here every day that Clifton is gone and do what your boy would have done. He will work hard, and he will be respectful to you and Señora Kelley.

"He will receive no money for this duty. I only ask that you could please feed him a noon meal. Hector is as big as a man, and he is a hard worker. He is part of a big family with many brothers and sisters, and he has a grandfather, a grandmother, aunts, and uncles. He has brought shame to us all by making life hard for another person who is smaller than he is, and who, he admits, has never done harm to him in return. He can bring back his honor, or he can bring more shame."

Ed started to protest, but Raul held up his hand to silence him. "I insist that you must let him do this. If he is not respectful to you, or if he steals from you, you must fire him. However, he cannot quit. You must work him hard and treat him as if he is the son that he took away.

"Do you understand, Ed? However, Ed, you may not lay a hand on him. If you become angry with him, you may fire him only. If it is unjust, he is finished with his obligation. If it is just, he will answer to me and his brothers and sisters, his grandfather and grandmother and his aunts and uncles. Do you understand *Señor?"*

"I don't think I completely understand why you are doing this. Boys are boys and sometimes they disagree. I told my boy he had to learn to get along and to learn to take care of himself. I told him he couldn't fight, but that he had to find other ways to solve problems."

"Oh, but *Señor,* my son is very big for his age. He must learn that gives no right to use his size to cause pain to another. His teacher said he beat your son badly. I told him he should go to jail, and I should call the sheriff myself. If he doesn't do these things, I will call the sheriff myself!

"He has always been jealous of your son, because your son is very smart, and he reads many books. My boy is also smart, but he doesn't read so well. Your son also has many nice things, because he is your son. You have a nice house, you have electricity, and you have a telephone.

"He is not old enough to understand these things. I didn't know, until now, how my son felt about these things, and that my son was causing your son so much trouble. Now my son will make up for his damage. He too must learn to settle his differences without fighting, ehh?" Raul said.

The elderly Mexican man held out his hand to the diminutive Anglo, and they shook.

Hector timidly held out his hand and shook hands with Ed. "I'll come by after school today," he said with downcast eyes.

"Etta Mae will show you what to do," Ed said.

"Si, Señor, Hector said.

15

Wednesday, midmorning
Martinez Canyon

As Cliff gathered cattail shoots by the creek, a movement in his periphery interrupted him. He slowly turned and looked up the south slope of the canyon. Fifty feet or so away under sagebrush, a cottontail rabbit sat staring at him. Cliff didn't move a muscle. Had he brought the .22 there would be a rabbit for dinner. It was an easy shot.

Cliff froze and waited.

Suddenly, the rabbit froze less than six feet away. The cottontail was small, about six inches long, half the size of a fully-grown adult. It had a small white spot of fur on its forehead. *It's probably out of its nest on its own for the first time.* Cliff barely moved. The young rabbit's only defense at that stage in life was to become invisible by remaining absolutely still.

Unfortunately, the human predator had already seen it. Cliff shuffled forward until he was within a yard away. He moved slowly down into a crouching position and dove. At the last second, the young cottontail tried to run, but it was too late. Cliff's hands closed around it. A frantic squealing sound erupted and Cliff cut it short with a sharp snap of the little rabbit's neck.

He laid the little fryer rabbit next to the cattails he had harvested and looked back at the sagebrush where the cottontail had first appeared. *I'll bet that's where the nest is. I wonder if there are four or five brothers and sisters hiding there. Mamma is probably already off somewhere else building another nest to have her next litter. Let's see what's over there,* he thought.

Cliff approached the sagebrush slowly, as quietly as he could, and smiled when he saw dry grass and fur. He knelt down and watched the grass. He barely touched the grass and could feel it pulse very slowly beneath his fingers. Under it were more remaining members of the litter. He cupped his hands and reached forward slowly then dipped his hands into the dry grass and hair and closed on another young cottontail as the nest exploded. Three younger cottontails flushed from the nest and ran madly in a zig-zag dash for cover among the nearby sagebrush and rocks.

Cliff snapped the neck of the second fryer and placed it with the first.

I can't believe the luck. Here is enough meat for two more days at least. This kind of luck at a moment like this just can't be an accident. A rabbit wouldn't just show up at that moment and give its life to me when I need it.

He knelt by the cottontail nest. He didn't know how to begin. He hadn't prayed with any conviction for two years. He felt that he had to acknowledge someone, or something, even if it was only the mother cottontail and her sacrifice of the two young rabbits to help him survive at a critical time. His neighbor and friend George Williamson had told him that an Indian hunter would customarily thank the game for giving itself.

George was partly responsible for Cliff's falling away from his blind beliefs that coincided with his father.

Do you believe in God, George?" Cliff had asked once.

"Well Cliff, you might say I am an Agnostic," George had replied.

"What is an Egnostic?" Cliff had asked.

"It's Agnostic, Cliff. An Agnostic is a person who doesn't believe in either the existence or the nonexistence of God or a god."

"So what do you believe then?"

"I believe that there is something taking care of all the creatures out there, Cliff, not just man. I believe that the worms in the ground, the butterflies, the skunks and the deer have something directing and watching over them. Maybe it is just Mother Nature. If we have a Heavenly Father, then they must have an Earthly Mother. How can one of them get along without the other? If we are going to take one of Mother Nature's creatures for our benefit then perhaps we should thank her for that," he had said.

Cliff had listened to his comments and digested them, and they had made sense. Cliff had many questions, and the two of them had discussed many things about religion when they visited. He realized that maybe the thing that had been bothering him since Monday was that he had killed one of Mother Nature's creatures at Dog Town without cause just because he was mad at Hector. He had felt guilty about almost taking one of God's creatures, Hector. However, he had forgotten about Mother Nature's creature, the prairie dog. He had killed many prairie dogs before that and never felt guilty about it. He couldn't let that happen again. Had Mother Nature through Mama Cottontail given him a second chance.

"Mamma Cottontail, I won't try to catch any more of them. I'm sure there are others to carry on. I'm leaving the rest of them for you. Thank you for sharing these two with me now. I've had a hard time this week so far. I won't waste anything. I hope your spirit lives long and safely, Mamma Cottontail. Heavenly Father, help me clear my mind and please take care of my folks. Earthly Mother, thank you for sharing your creatures with me," he said.

He didn't know what else to say, so he stopped.

It was with a light heart that he made his way back to the dwelling that afternoon. He felt stronger. His bruises were fading a little. His ribs were not as painful. The cattail salve was working on the cuts on his face and around his eye.

With fresh meat in the pack, he would eat better that night.

True to his promise to the mother cottontail, God or god and Mother Nature, Cliff wasted nothing of the two young rabbits he had caught with his two bare hands. He stretched the pelts and hung them alongside the one the bobcat had caught. He stripped the undigested food from the stomachs and intestines, cleaned them and set them aside to dry. He packed the remaining rabbit in fresh grass in the burlap sack and hung it in the cool back of the cave. It would be safe from insects and cool enough not to spoil overnight. He would cook it tomorrow and maybe save some for the next day.

16
Wednesday afternoon, late
Kelley farm

Hector stopped at the Kelley farmhouse after school as instructed by his father. He really didn't want to. He would rather be anywhere than here. His dislike for one *gringo,* Clifton, had spread steadily to include all *gringos* as the day progressed.

Actually, he had nothing in general against the Kelley family. His irritation was directed almost exclusively to the little *gringo* Clifton. He was such a little coward, but he talked so big, the *cabron!*

His father told him he had to do all the jobs that the *gringo* would do after school and if the *gringo* had not returned by the time school was out he would have to come every day and do his job all day long, perhaps all summer. It should be easy work. How much could the weak little *cabron* do? *I'm sorry he ran away, but it's not fair to make me miss helping uncle, he* thought.

Etta Mae had been dreading the hour when the Mexican boy would arrive. She had nothing against him or his family, but he was the reason for her son's absence. As far as she was concerned, she didn't want him on the place. It wasn't her deal. The men had worked it out. She would rather take care of the fieldwork and do the chores herself than have him around.

"*Si, Señora*. I can do it. If I can't understand it, I'll ask my father to help me," he said. He refused to admit to her that he had no idea what he would be doing. *If the gringo can do it, then how hard can it be?* He thought.

"When you're done with that, then come back to the house, and I'll show you about the milking and other chores."

He took the old pair of Ed's boots that she offered and went to the equipment shed to change from his school clothes to the work clothes he carried in a bag, and then he sauntered to the field.

He managed to close off the small head ditches that had been running overnight and all day. He created fresh ones that branched out into the small furrows that trickled down the slope.

Hector saw that Ed had repaired rows flattened by tractor tires or filled in by the dirt dug out by gophers. He checked the furrows in the new set he had started and as he did that, Hector began to understand the system and grudgingly to enjoy what he was doing.

"I have the cows in the pen already," Etta Mae said to him as he came through the gate. Usually Clifton brings then in from the pasture on his way in from the field. Tonight they came in on their own, because they were getting hungry, and they need milking. Clifton usually doesn't take quite so long to set the water," she said and immediately regretted her comment when she saw how tired and discouraged looking Hector looked.

She opened the barn door and poured grain in the trough in front of two stalls, as two Guernsey heifers trotted inside. She showed Hector how to fasten the stalls so the cows couldn't back out, as soon as they finished eating their grain, while he still milked them. "You ever milk a cow before Hector?" she asked.

"No *Señora*," he said.

"It isn't hard once you get the hang of it," she said.

Hector looked on in embarrassment as Etta Mae took a pail and a three legged stool and sat down facing the cow's udder and began cleaning and examining her.

He had older sisters, female cousins and aunts, but he had never heard a woman talk about such things as "teats" before. At age fourteen, he was entering an age where such talk was becoming interesting to his older cousins and uncles, but not in mixed company. Although he was looking at a cow, and the talk was about a cow's anatomy, he felt his face flush uncomfortably.

"Looks like this one teat is chapped," she said. She picked up the can of Bag Balm ointment that she had placed on the floor beside her, scooped a little out, spread it on the palm of her hand and worked it onto the heifer's chapped teat. "The secret here is to pull on first one and then the other on the opposite corner. As you pull down, squeeze a little. These Guernsey's are pretty easy, so the milk will come pretty fast. You have to be sure to milk them completely dry though. If you leave any, it will dry them up early."

She moved away and motioned for him to sit on the three legged stool, and after a few dozen tries, with not a drop of milk, there came a feeble stream, and then another, and after a few more pulls/squeezes he was drawing a full stream with each stroke.

A big grin broke over the boy's face. "I think you've got it now, Hector," Etta Mae said. You need to put more Bag Balm on that teat like I showed you now. It wouldn't hurt to work it into those blisters either," she suggested. She took the second pail and began milking the second cow.

Hector took some of the balm on the palms of his blistered hands, applied it to the raw chapped areas of the heifer's chapped teats and let the ointment work the pain out of his hands as well, as he continued milking.

The knuckles of his hands were still swollen and painful from working over Clifton on Monday. He had already spent three hours gripping a shovel handle, and now they wanted to cramp as he gripped and pulled the soft streams of creamy milk from the gold and white heifer.

Together, Hector and Etta Mae finished milking the four cows and fed the hogs, chickens and horses, and were carrying the milk to the house when Ed drove up.

It was dark. Ed got out of the pickup and took the two buckets Etta Mae carried from her. He and Hector, carrying two more buckets of milk, followed her to the house. Etta Mae opened the door to the utility room, and they set the four buckets down near the cream separator.

"How did you do today Hector?" Ed asked.

"I finished moving the water and learned how to milk a cow *Señor,*" he said.

"Have any problem with the water set?"

"I study what you been doing," Hector said. "I try to take care of it the way you doing it. I do the best I can. I am sorry if it was not very good."

"I'm sure you did your best," Ed said. I planned to be home early to help, but I went by to talk to the sheriff. That's why I'm late."

Ed put a fine mesh filter in the bottom of a stainless steel cylinder and then a cotton pad over the top of that and placed it into the top of a round stainless steel bowl sitting head high on top of a cast iron stand. Into the cylinder, he poured the first bucket of warm milk. "This filters out any dirt or dust particles that fell into the milk while you were milking the cow," Ed explained.

"This machine separates the cream from the milk," he told Hector. He explained how the separator worked as he assembled the cone shaped leaves onto the centrifugal head through which the milk poured. "At the proper RPM the milk will flow into the disks where it will be sliced and shredded into particles. The lighter fat particles will rise through the array of disks until they can escape through the highest opening and collect in the top enclosed pan where they will drain out the top spout into the cream-can. The heavier finer watery milk particles will find the lowest opening of the array and collect in the enclosed lower pan that drains out the lower spout into the five-gallon bucket here.

"We'll feed that to the hogs and calves. Etta Mae will also save some to make into cottage cheese. We'll sell the cream to the creamery in town. You like cottage cheese Hector?"

"I don't know Señor," Hector said with a shrug.

"First we'll draw off a gallon for the table." Ed selected a clean gallon jar from a shelf next to the separator and held it under the spigot on the separator bowl until it was full of the rich whole milk. He placed the full jar on the shelf. Then as an afterthought, he selected a second jar, filled it and placed it next to the first. Both jars would go into the refrigerator to cool and to keep fresh. "We'll skim about three inches of pure cream off this jar in the morning. That's what Etta Mae uses to make butter with."

He poured most of a second bucket of milk into the cylinder bringing the bowl back up to full.

"OK, Hector, now for the hard part. It takes quite a bit of power to get the centrifugal head up to speed." He pointed to a long crank attached to an axel protruding from the side of the cast iron frame just below the well where Ed had placed the assembled centrifugal assembly. A gear case drove a vertical shaft with a slot in the top over which they had placed the centrifugal assembly.

"You don't want to pull too hard to start, or you might spill the milk. The separator is bolted to the floor, but you could probably pull it loose if you pull too hard," he laughed. "Just pull on the handle nice and steady until it's going the right speed. Once the core is spinning at the right RPM you'll hear a pleasant hum, nice and steady. I'll tell you when and you'll come to recognize it. Here take hold. You can only turn it one direction. If you stop turning the handle, the assembly keeps spinning, as the handle disengages."

Hector bent, over took hold of the long handled crank and pulled it up as Ed moved aside. The crank didn't want to move, but Hector pulled steadily on the handle and the heavy assembly of thin stainless cones began to turn inside their cover of spouts. It took a minute or so for Hector to overcome inertia and get the separator core up to speed. Finally, Ed said, "There Hector, do you hear it? The sound has changed. That steady hum." He broke into the song scale he used when he tuned the church group before they sang a hymn acappella. "Do-re-mi-fa-so-la-ti-do-do-do-do-do… do you hear it Hector?" He asked as he held the note at doooooooo, the high "C".

Hector listened. The separator whined in perfect pitch to Ed's pitch. It was fascinating. The pitch was as steady and beautiful as the note of a bell or piano.

Ed reached over, turned the spigot and a stream of rich yellow milk gushed into the throat of the spinning separator core. Almost instantly a stream of pure white milk began to flow from the lower spout and cascade into the empty five gallon bucket. A moment later a thin yellow-orange stream began to emerge from the upper cream spout and flow into a shiny galvanized cream can.

"Ayee, look at that, *Señor* Kelley," Hector said happily.

The "C" note began to waver slightly as the milk-loaded core demanded more power. Hector instinctively pulled a little harder on the handle, the waver steadied and the hum was pure once more. He soon turned the handle with confidence. It took very little effort for the man-sized boy to maintain the speed.

Ed watched the expression on Hector's face. The boy was tall and he had to stoop on each downward stroke. It wouldn't be long until his back would be uncomfortable. At least in the beginning it was obvious that he had accomplished something, and he was feeling proud.

"As you turn it, keep an eye on the bowl. When it gets down close to empty, you can turn loose of the crank and pour in another bucket of milk. It won't lose speed in the time it takes to pour in another bucket of milk. You can easily catch up when you get back to the crank," Ed instructed.

As Hector cranked the separator, he looked thoughtful and then asked, "*Señor* , does Clifton usually do this watering every day and milk these four cows every night by himself?"

"Actually this spring when we started watering, he did the water set and did the milking and all the other outside chores both before and after school," Ed said.

"After school is out he will have the milking and chores done and then be on the tractor from about seven o'clock in the morning until five o'clock at night," Ed said. "Then he'll do the evening water set and evening chores. He will also take care of the pigs and horses each day. During the summer there will be weeding, hoeing, irrigating in the fields, and helping Etta Mae in the garden when she needs it. During the haying season, he'll mow hay, rake and this year bale it, and then work beside your dad loading and stacking it. That is if he comes back."

"But, he is such a little guy," Hector said. "I have been thinking for a long time he was just talking big."

"He is 14 years old going on 15, the same as you, but most people would think he is about eleven or twelve because of his size. So when he says he can do this or that, they think he is just bragging. Since you are a big guy for your age, it must seem even more so to you," Ed said.

"The work you did today? He does that every day," Ed continued. "He has to use tricks to do a lot of it, but he does it. I'm not that big myself, and I've had to learn a few tricks. I can't do things with strength alone, the things that come easy for most men, the things that are easy for you and are easy for your dad. I guess Cliff has learned a few tricks from me and is still learning," Ed said with a touch of pride in his voice.

Hector looked at Ed, as if for the first time realizing just what a small man Ed really was. "I am very surprised," he said quietly. He slowly began to understand why his own father respected this man the way he did.

He continued to turn the handle of the separator listening for the sound that Ed had made.

"Time to pour in the last bucket of milk," Ed said.

The process went smoothly, and Hector quickly returned to the crank and had it back to speed in a couple of turns. He seemed fascinated by the entire process.

The last of the milk trickled through the spigot, and moments later the last of the cream and milk dribbled through to the disks and out the ends of the spouts.

"You can stop turning now, Hector. You are all finished for tonight. The separator still has to be cleaned and sterilized, but it will take it a few minutes to run down. Usually Cliff cleans it after he gets cleaned up for supper. I'll take care of it tonight."

"I'm sure you are tired and anxious to get home. I'm sure you did a good job. I never met a member of your family who didn't do a good job and work hard."

Hector blushed, humbled by the compliment coming from Ed Kelley.

"Do you think your mother would like some of that fresh milk you milked tonight?"

"Señor?"

"Etta Mae why don't you fetch a jar of cold milk for Hector to take home," Ed said. "Remind Inez that in the morning she can dip off that cream and make some fresh butter out of it. If there isn't enough she might set it aside and she can add to what you bring home tomorrow night."

Etta Mae was ahead of him and came out of the kitchen with a gallon jar of milk cold from the refrigerator as well as a quart jar of fresh cottage cheese. "Why don't you give the young man a ride home, Papa," she said.

"No! No! I can walk," Hector protested.

"In the car," Ed said as he showed Hector outside, and they walked toward the pickup. Hector climbed in clutching his bag of school clothes, the gallon of cold whole milk and the jar of cottage cheese.

It would be a nice addition to their supper that night, and he was very hungry.

17

Wednesday, suppertime
Kelley farm

Etta Mae waited patiently until Ed returned from taking Hector home and finished his supper. She was anxious to know what he and the Sheriff had talked about after work that night. Ed looked tired and defeated. She hadn't seen him so down since Charlie had received his draft papers.

Now his second son had run away. His dream was for the two of them to get the farm going again and make it profitable. Now what could he do?

I've worked this farm like a man all the time we've owned it. How much longer can he ask me do to this? Etta Mae thought tiredly. *Should we revive the thought of selling it? We really can't think about it right now though, not with this hanging over us, I guess.*

"Papa, that was one of the hardest things I've ever had to do, being nice to that boy today."

"I know Mama. You look at a big kid like Hector, and you forget he's still just a boy like Clifton. It would be easy to come down on him hard and push him away, and we might lose both. I've told Clifton all his life that if someone slaps him, stand and turn the other cheek. I'd be a hypocrite if I can't do the same now. But, I agree, it isn't easy."

His wife continued to look tiredly down into her tired hands. Without looking up, she asked quietly, "So, what happened today?"

"I talked to Bill today," Ed began at last.

She waited.

"He's been asking around to see if anybody's seen him. He drove up around the Ridge and over around Dolores and Mancos. Nobody's seen anything suspicious or anybody fitting his description hanging around. He also stopped at the truck stops and talked to the highway patrol.

"He talked to George Williamson this morning early, and George took him down to the canyon where he saw the person up on the point.

"The Sheriff kind of agrees with me that it might have been Clifton that George saw. We both think that when he came home from school really mad, he might have gone over there and shot off a few rounds just to let off steam."

Ed poured another glass of milk.

"According to the Sheriff, George thinks Cliff is still in one of the canyons around here. George is going to go down and search the canyon by his place every spare minute he has this week.

"The Sheriff thinks Clifton probably walked from there over to Highway 160 and hitched a ride. It's about two and a half miles across the woods from there. He probably hid the single shot along the way and thumbed a ride. A trucker probably picked him up.

"A long hauler could have put him five or six hundred miles away by the end of a run. He could be in New Mexico, Arizona, Utah or even Nevada if the truck was going west. Or he could be in Denver, Wyoming, Nebraska, Oklahoma or Texas if it was going east."

Ed looked up at Etta Mae, "That's a lot of country to search, Mama."

He thought a moment, "Of course he could have just stayed on foot and be hiding out around here somewhere like George believes, but the Sheriff says that's highly unlikely. He said it has been his experience that a kid like that wants to get as far away as possible, as quick as possible."

"What would he do when he got there? He has no money, no clothes, nothing. How will he eat? How can he survive?" Etta Mae asked.

"That's how we started out, Mama," Ed said referring to their elopement and living in the hills of Texas hiding from her father. "Somehow we made it." Ed drained his milk. "I wasn't any older than he was when I went out on my own and made my first crop to help support my Dad's family."

"It was a different time and situation," Etta Mae said.

"I asked the Sheriff about his survival chances, and he said we'd be surprised how much survival instinct a kid his age has when it comes right down to it."

"It's a dangerous world out there, Ed." Etta Mae said. "I'm worried. I don't know that your family had to be as concerned about you back then, out on your own."

"I don't know about that. Maybe so, maybe not."

She stood and walked around the table to stand behind her husband, her hands on his shoulders. He reached up and took her hands in his. They both cried silently for their loss and for worry of their boy.

"I think you should pray for him now," she said.

18
Thursday, mid-day
Martinez Canyon

Cliff returned from the canyon with a fresh batch of greens. He cut asparagus, cattail shoot, dandelion root and clover root into chunks and roasted them over the fire. He would save the young cottontail, left over from yesterday, hanging in the burlap bag, for supper.

As he watched the green vegetables turning to a golden brown, it seemed strange that some of the chunks were missing. In addition, parts of the hand that held the willow roasting stick were missing. He blinked his eyes to try to clear them. When he looked around the dwelling, bits and pieces of the wall were clear and large sections were missing but not transparent.

He tried to speak. His voice sounded far away, and he could not understand the words he had spoken. He had to lie down. He moved away from the fire, lay down on the hard cold floor, curled up on his side with his head in his hands and closed his eyes.

The searing pain spread through his head a half hour later, and he awoke screaming. His head felt as if it would burst. He sat up and slumped over his knees clutching his forehead in the palms of his hands as tightly as he could.

The Doctor had called the first sign an aura.

First his vision was affected then his speech.

Later indescribable pain radiated out from his temples.

It affected his thinking and disabled him during each episode.

Sometimes, if he caught it soon enough, if he took aspirin, the pain did not develop as completely.

"I don't think the Doctor has any idea what causes it," Ed had said.

The Doctor had told his mother there was no known cause or cure for it. The doctor told Cliff it was his eyes, although he tested 20-20 vision according to the charts. "Perhaps it is related to stress," the doctor had said. "Perhaps you will outgrow it."

Outside the throws of the headache, Cliff could see perfectly. *If stress causes it, then I've certainly had enough of that lately,* he thought vaguely through the pain.

Cliff tried rubbing his temples with his thumbs to ease the pain. Disjointed thoughts and visions tumbled through his mind amplified by the pain. *Hectors' distorted raised fist, gigantic on the end of his arm; his dad coming toward him with the razor strop; the circle of kids jeering and cheering Hector on, their faces fading in and out; thinking of suicide, trying to decide on which bullet, bullets the size of his fist; killing the prairie dog without just cause; angering Earthly Mother Nature and Heavenly Father both at once; angering the mate of the bobcat, the bobcat that now stood in the doorway, gigantic head with foot long fangs hissing and snarling; forgetting to thank Mother Nature for sharing her little critters the cottontails; a baby cottontail looking at him with accusing eyes as he slowly pulls its skin over its back...*

A distorted rustling sound. Through the haze, he realized he had not placed the slate in the doorway. *The bobcat's returning*! He stared at the vision of a naked, snarling and hissing bobcat leaping through the doorway, and as suddenly as it materialized, it dissolved.

He had not banked the fire. He smelled charred vegetables.

Cliff shivered uncontrollably.

Canyon night sounds, amplified by the pain, surreal and frightening–a snapping twig booming like a falling tree. A branch crashed somewhere in the canyon. He listened for voices but heard none. Something prowled outside. The pain dulled all his senses but the hearing. Each sound thudded against his eardrums and intensified the throbbing in his temples.

The doorway was open. The slate was not in place. The hair bristled on the back of his neck. He crawled to the doorway and tried to move the slate, but it was too heavy. He was sure he had carried it from the canyon, hadn't he? He couldn't coordinate his hands and arms, and he couldn't remember how to insert the pegs that would hold it in place. He held the slate in his arms, and he cried in frustration.

He crawled along the wall, and pulled himself upright. He crabbed sidewise until he felt the .22 rifle and shells in the nook above it. He concentrated with all his might to drop the shells into his pocket. Then he stumbled to the floor and crawled back to the blanket clutching the rifle. He tried to remember what he had done with the shells then blindly searched for which pocket he had put them.

His hands shook, and he cried in frustration as he felt for the smooth surface of a shell and finally isolated one. The frustration mounted as he tried to load the shell into the breach of the gun. He dropped the shell, couldn't find it on the hard clay floor and had to remember which pocket all over again. This simple action repeated itself over and over again until he found no more shells, and he frantically searched the floor. An elusive shell finally revealed itself under his hand, and he managed to fit it into the breach. He studied the foreign object in his hands, bits and pieces fading in and out, and he held on to it until he slowly moved the round knob on the bolt forward and down, locking the shell into place.

The pain was so debilitating that a simple task, which he had performed hundreds of times before, had become a foreign task. In that state, he had no concept of the final task: cocking the rifle.

Finally, he was satisfied he was safe from the demons that prowled about the canyon. He searched for the saddle blanket, put the rifle down, sat down on the bare floor, rocked back and forth, clutching the blanket to his chest.

Mamma skunk grew more and more uneasy as the restless boy moaned and cried out in pain. She moved her brood further into the corner near the water overflow hole for quick exit, paused and then left the cave.

~~~

Hector Rodriguez knocked on the back door of the Kelley house promptly at 4:15 p.m.

He had already changed into his work clothes and wore a straw hat. He nodded to Etta Mae and stood uncomfortably until she spoke.

"Good afternoon, Hector."

"*Hasta lluego, Senora.* I will go to the field now. I will bring the cows when I come back," he said.

"Thank you Hector," she said.

"My *Madre,* she say, *muchos gracious* for the milk and cheese," he said.

"She is very welcome," Etta Mae said.

"I bring back the jars," he said pointing to the jars, which he had set on the step. He started to go then paused, turning, "Did you get word from *Señor* Clifton?"

Etta Mae stiffened, and her eyes flashed. She almost answered angrily, but she answered quietly, "No we have heard nothing." She turned and went back into the house, before he could see her tears forming.

Where could that cabron go? he wondered. *Man last night when my father told me Emilio will take my place with my tio, working the sheep this summer... I have to stay behind to work for Mr. Kelley to take the place of the gringo boy. It isn't fair. Why couldn't the little cobarde, take his beating like a man? Why couldn't he stand and fight. It is the way of men. It is the way friends are made! Why does he always run away? If he had a pair of huevos he could take it like a man. But, he always runs away. And I am paying for his cowardliness!* "If he had learned to be a man maybe we could be friends," he muttered to himself as he walked down the lane to the field.

"Now I don't think so. Man, I've got to stay here when it was my turn to go to the mountains! It's just not fair!" He said angrily. This time if I do find you, *cabron*...!

He slung the shovel off his shoulder and attacked the dry dirt angrily as he dug a new head ditch in the alfalfa.

While he worked, his mind wandered back to the incident that had put him on the course that had led him on a six-year journey with the missing *gringo*.

Six years before, at the end of Hector's first grade year, and as Clifton finished the second grade, their older brothers, Jorge and Charlie had faced off at exactly the same time of year.

Jorge, an eighth grader, was strong, stocky and good looking and everyone in school looked up to him. Charlie also an eighth grader was a slender kid of 14 about the same size as Clifton. He, like Clifton also thought he was big stuff and had been sweet on Alesha Lopez.

Jorge couldn't stand having the skinny *gringo* moony eyed over Alesha Lopez, and she made him even more jealous by talking to the *gringo*
~~~

during recess and lunchtime.

Finally, on a particular day in the spring, a few days before school was out, when the kids were playing catch-up, Jorge and Charlie both went after the same ball. Jorge tripped Charlie, in fun of course, especially to show Alesha how clumsy the *gringo* was.

But, Charlie hadn't thought it was funny, and he had a temper. When he got up, he had a piece of firewood with a rough knot on the end. Charlie had an accurate throwing arm, and he heaved it at Jorge, catching him behind the ear. The knot on one end of the stick either slightly punctured Jorge's scalp or scratched it enough to draw a large amount of blood.

Jorge went down hard.

Hector had cried when he saw his brother go down. He had lain so still on the ground, and Hector was afraid the *gringo* had killed him.

By the time Mr. Johnson arrived on the scene all the kids had gathered around, screaming and crying.

Jorge revived, bloodied, but not seriously hurt, and oddly enough, Charlie did not get a serious whipping from Mr. Johnson. That had been the worst insult of all.

Clifton had sidled up to Hector and given him "the look," and Hector had never forgotten it.

It had become a pride point to make Clifton pay for that "look" ever since.

Surprisingly after that, Jorge and Charlie had become good friends.

At first that had puzzled Hector, and then in his mind it had become an example of the order of things. Jorge had taken defeat like a man, and he had become friends with the man who had brought him down. He respected an opponent who stood up for himself. He had not lost face by doing it. He had remained strong. A better man had not brought him down; someone with guts enough to stand up to him had been brought him down. He could respect that.

Jorge had found other times and other places to prove himself. Now seven years later he was a successful businessman.

Clifton was supposed to take defeat like a man, and then we could become friends.

That was the way with men with cajones! But this Clifton, as we both got older, he just ran away. He did not stand and fight. The teacher made him play ball and compete, but he refused to defend himself. If Clifton had not run away, if he had admitted that I won the fight, maybe today at school we would have been laughing about it, si? The little gringo finally said "no" to me instead of running away. He fought back. But, he was unwilling to accept defeat like a man. We could finally have become friends. Then he ran away, not only from the fight, but away from home too! It was the ultimate cowardice!

There were so many rumors at school today. Emilio had even heard on the radio that a gringo boy was found by the road in New Mexico.

Oh, man! If that boy by the road is Clifton, is it my fault? Hector picked up the pace as he vented his anger and frustration on the dry sod and tough alfalfa roots as he prepared to turn water into the new trench he had just finished digging at the top of the slope next to the prairie dog colony in the center of Edward Kelley's farm.

19

Friday, 8 a.m.
Kelley farm

Evelyn Campbell crossed the cattle guard, drove up the lane to the Kelley front yard and stopped in the circular driveway in front of the house.

Etta Mae's face looked tired and drawn from worry. Mrs. Campbell wondered how long since she had slept. "Etta Mae, I can't stay. I have to get up the schoolhouse and open up. I assume you still have no word on Clifton."

"No, nothing yet. I'm just beside myself. I know something has happened to him. I can feel him, yet I don't know where he is. I know he needs me, and I don't know where to look," she said. She looked up at the teacher. "Evelyn, I can't help with the school plans for today."

"Of course. I told the rest of the kids yesterday the trip is off. They were disappointed, but they understood. They are worried about Clifton and sorry too. They all felt bad that things had turned out the way they have. I don't think they understood how serious what they were doing really was. They got caught up in something, and now they don't know what to do about it. They were really going after Hector and Emilio about the whole affair yesterday. Even the little ones were letting them have it. They were not saying anything in their own defense. Of course now that their parents know what was going on, they are catching it at home too."

"Well good. Of course it is too late to do any good now!"

"Yea, that's true. Isn't that the way it always is?"

"You sure you don't have time for a cup of coffee?"

"I wish I did. Oh, what if I'm a few minutes late. Of course I do!

Etta Mae poured coffee and uncovered a plate of cinnamon rolls that smelled fresh baked and placed it on the table. "Help yourself Evelyn," she said self-consciously. "When I am powerless to do anything else, I bake. This is Clifton's favorite."

"Etta Mae, the kids told me yesterday how they would like to spend this last day of school. I'd like to run it by you," Mrs. Campbell said.

~~~

When Cliff finally came awake after a fitful sleep, his head still ached but the vice pressing on his temples had finally loosened their grip and
~~~

images were fully formed when he looked around the ruin.

He spoke to mama skunk and his words were coherent. His hearing had returned to normal. He understood the words he spoke. He walked unsteadily to the doorway and looked out into brilliant sunlight. He was sure he had slept at least a day, through the night and into the morning of a new day. This must be Friday. It would have been his graduation day.

If he took aspirin before a headache, it lasted a shorter time. If there was no aspirin, the episode was usually more severe and longer. After each episode, his mom gave him tea to drink, and now he craved it. Unfortunately, he had none.

Cliff had stuffed his pockets with dandelion blossoms as he gathered in the canyon on Thursday. They had wilted, but he sucked on several and that seemed to sooth his headache a little. *If only I had a way to make tea.*

He walked to the end of the ledge relieved himself on the sand and scraped it over the side of the cliff. He was loose from the mostly vegetarian diet since Tuesday. He was hungry and felt dehydrated. *Thankfully, if it hasn't spoiled, there is still the cottontail in the sack by the spring.*

Two hours later Cliff's stomach felt full and content. The rabbit had kept well in the protection of the burlap, wrapped in the green grass, and hanging in the coolness next to the spring.

He had devoured dandelion root, asparagus, cattail, lambs quarter and half the cottontail. He had soaked the wilted asparagus and lambs quarter in the spring before stuffing them inside the rabbit and roasting the rabbit over the fire to very well done.

He craved something sweet and thought about his hives of bees. It was early in the season, but already the bees were collecting nectar from the first clover blossoms, dandelions and fruit trees. In the canyon, tamarack was in full bloom. If he hadn't left home, he could lift the cover on one of the hives and taste new honey.

It was Friday. If he went to school today as usual, he could graduate from the eighth grade. He was the only eighth grader at East Lakeview Grade School. He would have completed two more years of school than his dad. His dad was a full time farmer before he would graduate from the eighth grade. His mom finished two years of high school before dropping out to help her father on his farm in Texas.

Etta Mae had said Cliff should be proud of the achievement, whether he needed a certificate to get into Montezuma County High School or not. For sure, he would need a high school diploma and an exceptional grade average in high school to go to Colorado State University where he wanted to study archaeology and entomology, his two goals in life. However, that was all a moot idea anyway, because how was he, a farm boy, going to get enough money together to attend a school like CSU anyway?

For the first time since leaving home and school on Monday, he felt truly lonely and depressed. After each past migraine episode, he had gone through a similar period of depression. This headache particularly shook him, coming at the worst possible time.

I really want to see you Mom, Dad and Towser, He thought.

I want to see my friend George driving his John Deere tractor from his house to the mail box or around and around his field pulling a plow. I want to visit with George and talk with him about beekeeping and Indians and about Mother Nature while he drapes his arms over the fence and chews on a stalk of clover, or wheat or whatever else is handy. I hate to admit it, but right now, at this very moment, I wouldn't mind playing softball even with Hector Rodriguez!

Cliff leaned back against the smooth sandstone in the cliff dwelling doorway and pulled his knees up to his chest. He was on the verge of tears. He reminded himself each headache spell left him weak. He would get over it. He had always recovered before.

It was graduation day, the end of eight years in that little room a half mile up the road from his house. He'd spent a major part of his life there. In most respects, it had not been a pleasant experience, at least not for the first six years, but at least he'd honed his reading and 'riting there, if not much 'rithmatic.

He wouldn't give his two teachers all the credit. His mother had him reading and 'ritin' before he entered first grade. She had read to him from her mail-order subscription Saturday Evening Post or passages from Zane Grey while his dad read his Holy Bible at the kitchen table.

Cliff had enjoyed Zane Grey the most. Hearing his description of the American desert and badlands was like living in the canyon. The first words he began to recognize on the printed page and repeat to his mother were words from *Riders of the Purple Sage*.

Cliff was somewhat shocked to learn that in the first grade, he would have to read a book entitled *Dick and Jane* with such simple sentences as "See Dick. See Dick run." The stories he wrote for his mom were far more interesting and complex, and at least they had a plot.

Cliff smiled. "It's graduation day. Well, in some respects, I've graduated all right. I've graduated from East Lakeview Grade School right into a Zane Grey novel," he said.

He climbed out over the rim, this time without using the rope except keeping it between his arms and legs for security. He pulled himself up as he pushed against the toeholds. He climbed slowly and carefully and out over the top, reaching for the cedar tree as he crawled over the top of the rim. He stood and looked directly at the tree. "Look at me. I did it," he said. "No rope. Now one of these days I'll have to try going down without it. That's going to be a little harder."

Cliff walked restlessly along the rim up the canyon toward the trail. Instead of going down the first trail into the canyon, he kept going all the way to the Williamson Draw trail and walked down the deer trail on the western slope of the draw to the bottom.

The big mule deer could easily jump any fence the farmers put up, they preferred not to cross them if they could avoid it. Cliff had followed trails beside fences for what seemed like miles, until for no reason that seemed obvious; the deer merely jumped and followed the other side.

He had seen them stand flatfooted in front of the typical woven fence his dad and neighbors put up to keep cows and horses in their pastures, and seemingly without effort jump over.

Coming from this direction they didn't have to worry as George's fence was on the other side of the ravine. The trail went around it and on across the creek flowing down the bottom of Martinez Canyon. He followed it up the south slope to the flat land on top and circled back to the north facing rimrock on Martinez Canyon.

One of his favorite spots of Sunday's past was the old round tower ruin at the point overlooking the canyon from the viewpoint on the south side of the canyon. He had observed the goat from this spot. He had sat with his back against the tower and used many leisure Sunday afternoons reading and daydreaming there. There was no doubt, why the ancients had chosen the spot for their observation post. From there he could observe animal and bird life at the creek directly below and in both directions in the canyon.

He had no particular reason for going to the ruin that day other than it was familiar, and he had time on his hands. Down in the dwelling he felt a little claustrophobic. He felt restless, alone, lost. One moment he wanted to go home, the next, he was afraid to. He was not use to having idle time for several days at a time. Time did not pass quickly. He needed something to do.

He sat down inside the ruined tower. There was no roof. The wall facing the woods to the south had deteriorated the most. He looked up at the small windows in the crumbling walls, and imagined what it must have been like for a warrior protecting his village. *I wonder how he spent long lonely days waiting for a glimpse of an enemy. He must have gone stir-crazy. How did he occupy his mind? Were there two of them who spelled each other so one could sleep? How did they get food? Do you suppose maybe some beautiful Indian maiden brought them meals at noontime? Maybe their wives waved a piece of buckskin over their heads over at the pueblo or from a cliff dwelling, and the guy trotted home and ate corn cakes and tamales.*

It would help if Cliff had a book. It was hard to dwell on anything else when he immersed himself in an adventure taking place in some exotic land.

Cliff thought briefly of Hector and then slapped himself hard across the face. It stung. His face was still a little sore and bruised. It was too beautiful a day to spend hating Hector.

He got up and stepped outside the ruin. He sat down on the east side facing Martinez Canyon, which separated the Martinez farm on the south side of the canyon and his friend George Williamson's farm on the north side.

Cliff moved around the ruin to look up Williamson's Draw. It began as a gentle valley east of the Kelley farm and ended as a deep gully well inside George's pasture. In the last few hundred yards, it deepened and widened further until it opened into Martinez Canyon at the same level.

Cliff could see George's cows grazing up the draw on the east slope of the draw. Further east on the other side of a green mile wide timber swatch, he could see dust rising above the trees where a car moved along the Dolores-Mancos road.

He scanned the sheer wall down the canyon to the left of the draw where the goat had stood on Sunday. It was gone from its precarious perch. It could be anywhere in the canyon, or it could have gone home. *Couldn't make it here fella? Well don't feel bad. I don't think I can either. It was stupid of me to think I could survive down here. Did you go home? I think that's what I have to do too. I hope I haven't screwed up everything. What did they do to you when you got home? Beat you? Pen you up so you didn't wander again?*

A movement caught Cliff's eye. He looked hard at the lower part of George's pasture. A figure crawled through the fence at the corner of George's pasture and walked on down into the canyon. Straw hat, tall figure, slouching walk, he was sure it was George.

Cliff crouched low, moved around the ruin, crawled back over the crumbled wall inside, crept to the small window and watched.

George walked to the creek below the tower and looked up. He studied the tower ruin and the point. Cliff held his breath and didn't move a twitch. *Can he see me?*

George finally continued down the trail.

Cliff watched until George was out of sight then he left the ruin. He went up the creek a hundred yards and hurriedly gathered asparagus, cattail shoots, clover blossoms and dandelion root for supper. Then he crossed the creek staying off the trail, followed next to deer trail up the draw staying on hard ground or stepping on rocks. On top, he turned left into the timber and headed west.

He trotted all the way back to the snag, and lowered the sack of wild vegetables to the ledge.

He lay by the snag and watched the canyon floor for a sign of George. George Williamson was his friend. It was easy to talk to George. George had taught him about bees and Indians and many other things like the Indians' belief in the Great Spirit and Mother Nature. George and Cliff's dad were also good friends, but they disagreed on many things too.

What if he has his binoculars? He carries those binoculars everywhere he walks. I remember the eagle's nest he showed me on the crag in Big Canyon. I could count the pinfeathers on the chick's head. If he looks up here, he'll see the rope.

All week I've climbed this cliff using both the rope and the toe holds. This morning I climbed it without touching the rope. It was hanging there for a safety net. Can I climb down now without it? Is it time to fish or cut bait? If George finds me, I have no options. At least if he doesn't find me, I do have the option of staying away for a while longer, if I choose.

Cliff turned and untied the rope from the trunk of the cedar. He turned loose of the end of the rope and watched it disappear over the edge. He lay looking at the bare edge of the rimrock.

Forty feet below awaited the ruin and the unforgiving solid rock of the ledge.

He grasped the snag and held on with both hands as he turned around and scooted closer to the edge and let his legs hang over. The gnarled 12-inch tree grew close enough to the edge so that when he held on and extended his arms, he could barely bend over the edge at the waist. The right toe of his shoe found the top toehold carved into the face of the cliff. His knee bent slightly. Handholds continued forward onto the surface of the rim stopping just short of the snag. He released his hold on the tree with his left hand and grabbed the forward handhold on the surface. When he had a good grip, he lowered his dangling left foot into the toehold below and opposite his right foot and settled his weight into it. He slowly released his right handhold on the cedar and took a firm hold on the surface handhold below and opposite his left hand. Slowly, he lowered his right foot down to the next toehold.

He was now half holding onto the surface pockets and half with his toes firmly seated into toeholds on the front wall of the cliff. He rested and tested his balance. He breathed and slowed his pulse. He could still back out. He could still climb back up to safety and go home. The next two or three steps could be disastrous. Up to now, he had played it safe. As long as he had the rope, he had been safe. However, this was way more dangerous than saying "no" to Hector. If he lost his balance or lost his hold, it was 40 feet to solid rock and nobody knew where he was. Nobody would be there to pick up the pieces. He held his breath, turned loose of the handhold with his right hand, and reached down to grasp the next one.

~~~

"Good morning children, as we planned yesterday, only the upper grades are here today. Originally, we were going to have a graduation celebration up on Mesa Verde and a picnic. It seemed inappropriate to have a graduation celebration for a person who is not here and because of the circumstances of his absence." Mrs. Campbell paused and looked around the room at the quiet faces. *I met with all your parents this week, as you know. They well understand what Cliff was going through,* she thought. *They have suffered similar treatment themselves. You don't need a lecture from me this morning.*

"This morning, however, we can do something constructive. A member of our student body came to me with a suggestion. I took it to Mrs. Kelley this morning, and she thought it was a wonderful idea. She was moved by your thoughtfulness.

"I am going to ask Hector to come up and talk to you about HIS plan. Hector?"

Hector Rodriguez slowly rose to his feet and self-consciously went to the front of the schoolroom. He was accustomed to manipulating others to do his bidding, but from the sidelines. For a moment, he avoided eye contact and looked above all the students sitting in the room. More than
~~~

half were direct relatives; brothers, sisters, cousins, aunts or uncles. He finally took a breath and looked at their faces.

"I think we kids have explored or played in just about every hiding place around here. We know every abandoned shack, car, cave, chicken house, potato cellar, and even the Indian ruins in the canyons. We have climbed up every tree that makes a natural tree house, and checked out every hiding place we can walk to or ride to on our horses. In our games, we are accustomed to hiding and finding each other. It's our favorite summer time sport. We are also reasonably good trackers. If we go out there today and search for that *cabron...*," he paused and blushed and the kids all laughed. He was so used to calling Clifton cabron in a negative sense as "bastard or worse" that it slipped out when in this case he had meant it in the kinder meaning of "friend or comrade" as he used the same word toward Emilio and the other boys. "I meant our *compañero.* If and he is close by, I think we can find him. What do you say?"

"My sister and I will search the Little Canyon. It is close to our house and we know it," volunteered Felix Munoz.

"I'll help them," said Ignacio Chavez

Mrs. Campbell wrote their names on a list to keep track.

So it went until the entire lower half of the Ridge was covered from the front slope of the Ridge half way to Cortez to the west, Lost Canyon to the east, the bottom and sides of Big Canyon to the northwest and to the rim of Martinez Canyon to the south.

"Emilio and me live down towards the old coal mine and where the junk cars are dumped. We'll get our horses and cover that area," suggested Hector.

"Mr. Williamson is searching down in Martinez Canyon today," Mrs. Campbell said. "He knows the canyon, according to Sheriff Kirkendall. I have permission of farmers for you to check old buildings and cellars that are out of sight of their homes and that no one is using. When you go to the farm where you are going to search, it is a good idea to go up to the house and knock on the door. They will be expecting you. That way if they have a dog, they can keep it in the house while you are there.

"Each of you is to come back here to the schoolhouse by 4:00 p.m. Do a good job. When you have searched your area and checked in, you will be finished for the school year. On the porch next to your lunch pails is a box of oranges. Also there is a box with a special treat that Mrs. Kelley sent along for you. Be sure to read her message when you stop for your lunch or snack. Good hunting. It will be a special day, if we find our graduate today."

Students went out the door with their lunch from home and an extra orange provided as a treat by Mrs. Campbell. They also each received a tinfoil wrapped oatmeal cookie with a note that said, "Thank you" from Mrs. Kelley.

At 9:15 AM, 13 students ranging in age from nine to 14 years in age spread out from East Lakeview Grade School to thoroughly examine every nook and cranny on the immediate five square mile area of Summit Ridge.

Among them Porferio Ortega, Ignacio Chavez, Ana Hernandez, Felix Munoz, Emilio and Hector Rodriguez would search on horseback.

Porferio, age 13 took 11 year old Hermano Rodriguez. Felix, 12 teamed up with nine year old Carmen Munoz. Ana, 13 teamed with 10-year-old Katia Guzman.

Maria Rodriguez, and Cecilia Ramirez, both 9 and Carlos Hernandez, 10 went with 11 year old Adolph Ramirez on foot to the nearby farms to check the outbuildings, including one old fallen down chicken house in the lower wooded area on the Kelley farm.

Mrs. Campbell crowded Porferio, Ignacio, Ana, Felix, Hermano, Carmen, and Katia in her car and delivered them to their homes where they could saddle up and begin their search.

She then dropped Emilio and Hector at home where they saddled their horses and struck out down the county road.

She returned to the schoolhouse to close up the building for the summer and to wait as one by one the students checked in and made their report.

It was possibly a futile effort, but it gave the kids a sense of atonement for their insensitivity toward Clifton over the past years.

20

Friday, morning
Martinez Canyon

George Williamson chewed a dry clover stem. The bitter juice was to his liking, although actually, he would have preferred a sweeter, milder dry alfalfa stem, but it was a little early in the season to find one that hadn't gone through the winter. Many of his fellow farmers chewed tobacco products. Why buy tobacco when clover and alfalfa grew all over, and he'd never heard of anybody getting a mouth full of cancer from chewing clover?

George considered clover a kind of miracle plant if one were careful with it. In some ways, he preferred it to alfalfa for his livestock. However, clover was more dangerous. Either one would kill a cow if they ate too much of it green. When clover fermented, it formed crystals with the same chemical make up as Warfrin, rat poison, a blood thinner. This happened when clover fermented in a silo, inadvertently chopped with green corn, stored as silage or if baled before properly dried in the field. Live stock that ate clover fermented under any of those conditions could bleed to death internally and die.

When the round brown seeds matured and dried, they were flavorful and his wife spread them on bread crust, like sesame or poppy seeds. She ground them and added them to flour when she baked. On the other hand, he simply chewed them raw or toasted.

He used fresh or dried cloverleaves for tea and especially liked clover tea at bedtime when he had trouble sleeping or when he had tension headaches. They had mild analgesic properties that were nearly as effective as aspirin.

~~~

George was the unofficial veterinarian of the neighborhood. If a neighbor's cow wandered into a green alfalfa or clover patch and bloated, he sent for George. George would rush to the cow's side. First, he would put a stick in the cow's mouth like a horse's bit, tie a rope around each end and loop it up around the heifer's ears. George hoped that keeping the cow's mouth stretched open would cause her to belch out the gas captured and expanding in her stomach. As a last resort, he would puncture the heifer's stomach with his pocketknife to release the pressure. He had to puncture the stomach in exactly the right spot, and there could be complications. It was an act of faith to allow George, not a licensed vet, to perform the procedure, but by the time the farmer could contact a vet and get him out from town, a bloated cow would be dead. George did not save every one of them, but his record was good, and he had the vet's blessing and approval.

Farmers called on George to perform or supervise other procedures such as assisting mares and heifers with difficult births and with neutering calves, colts, pigs, and sheep.

George had seen the same wide-eyed enthusiasm in Clifton Kelley as he had in his own boys, and he looked forward to visits with the boy when Clifton came to ask about bees and Indians or just stopped by to pass the time of day. George enjoyed the position more as an uncle to the boy than just being a neighbor.

George was the source of much of Clifton's information on bees and beekeeping. He also helped shape much of Clifton's view of the world.

Ed Kelley's view of the world was somewhat narrower and much of that view was religiously oriented.

George was skeptical of organized religion. Although he didn't advertise it, he was agnostic. If he worshiped anything, it was Mother Nature. He envied the relationship the Native Americans had with nature. He worshiped Mother Nature, in his way. He was accepting of all religious viewpoints and accepted what religion did for the human spirit. He did not accept the idea that world religions should be competitive.

Ed Kelley accepted no religious viewpoint as valid except fundamental Christianity. Within the fundamentalist movement, only a very narrow literal interpretation of the King James Version of the Holy Bible was ac-
~~~

cepted.

Ironically, Ed Kelley's fundamental beliefs were rooted in the philosophy espoused by the 19th Century religious leader and reformer Thomas Campbell. Campbell had rejected all denominations and religious ritual and followed Christianity strictly, as he interpreted it by the New Testament. This wasn't so different from George's non-secular belief except that it rejected all other culture's beliefs.

"Do you believe in God?" Cliff had asked George one day.

George had looked around at the mountains and the thunderheads in the brilliant blue Colorado sky that day. He and Clifton were walking in the dry land pasture on the Kelley southeast corner. Clifton had just shown him the stone circle that marked an Ancestral Puebloan ruins, he had uncovered. Next to it a barrel cactus with brilliant waxy orange blossom grew. A few moments before, they had stopped to admire Indian paintbrush and sago lilies. "Clifton, when you see all these wonders of nature, how can you not believe in something wonderful. The question is not whether I believe in God. It is whether my God is better than someone else's God. Is my God better than the God of the Ancestral Puebloans who were walking these canyons when the Christ was preaching a new religion? Is He better than the Navajo's? Or the Ute's? Or the God of the Jew's, the Muslim's, or the Hindi's? Who is to determine whose God is the one we should pray to? Should we thank some King or Prince 400, 600, a thousand years ago for choosing which one 'True Word' to save for us, or should we condemn him for burning all the other alternatives? Was he in any better position than me to speak to my God?

"Did not God create all the creatures including us. Therefore, doesn't that make us all brothers and sisters? If we take a creature's life, should we thank God for providing it for us? If the cougar takes our life, who is to say that afterward, it doesn't thank its God for providing our life so that it can survive?"

Clifton had not argued with him, but had listened thoughtfully, and George had noticed that the talk of hunting had diminished when they were together.

Cliff had asked intelligent questions and required him to justify his answers and back his answers with reason and logic. With George, he could do this. With his dad, he could not.

Ed Kelley and George Williamson did hold one common philosophy however; every man should be his neighbor's keeper, and be a steward of his neighborhood. When a neighbor called, they stepped forward. Neither man waited for the call, if he was aware of a need. When a neighbor was in need of help, Ed Kelley as well as George Williamson were blind to their neighbor's religion.

George had watched his neighbor Ed Kelley from the time he had moved his young family next door. He was the only farmer without roots on the Ridge. But, in the few short years that he had lived there, Ed had built a reputation of being honest, open, and an asset to the community.

Anyone with a broken piece of machinery or stalled automobile could call on Ed to fix it. When it ran again, they would offer to pay for his time, but he never accepted. If a part was required, they went after it. "It will all work out in the end," Ed would say as he wiped his hands on the rag he always carried with him.

George admired Ed, a man with little formal education, who had figured out how to work within systems using his native practical understanding of how things worked. The guy was tenacious. Etta Mae said he was stubborn, but George thought persistent was more apt. Ed had petitioned the county for gravel on the road leading up from Cortez. When that failed, he got elected to a non-paying position on the County Board of Commissioners, and in that role helped convince the county to gravel the dirt road from Cortez up to the Ridge. Furthermore, in that position he used his influence to get the Rural Electric Association and the telephone company to bring their service to the area. He accepted a position on the Lakeview School board, and he took on the job of maintaining the East Lakeview schoolhouse and peripheral buildings: outhouses, fuel shed, cistern, teacherage, and playground equipment.

Unfortunately, George had watched that Good Samaritan philosophy and stewardship taking so much of Ed's time helping everyone else out that his own farm was neglected, and it put more pressure on Etta Mae, young Charlie, and then finally after Charlie was drafted, a growing pressure on Clifton.

Improvements such as electricity gave Ed more efficiency such as electric motors to run power equipment in the shop and to run an elevator to lift bales up to the haystack and such.

Although the convenience of power equipment gave Ed extra time, he had to use the extra time on a job in town to help pay the extra expenses of the modernization. The other farmers in the neighborhood refused to hook up to the power lines and phone lines that ran by their farms. In so doing they also escaped the extra expenses of the conveniences and the cost of the appliances and machinery. More and more neighbors, including himself, were having phones installed, but that was about it.

George and his father before him had learned that life could be good, if they could make a good crop every year, and if prices held every year. However, usually if they made a good crop, prices dropped. If prices were up, crops were marginal or failed altogether. It seemed that about once in every seven years both prices and a good crop coincided.

He and his wife still lived in the ramshackle house where he was born. He farmed with an old John Deere tractor that ran well. They lived simply without electricity, cooked on a wood stove, read by lantern light and retired early each night. Within the marginal fluctuating income the farm produced, the farm was debt free.

Although they had their differences in philosophies, they also shared many and had become close friends. They respected each other, and if he had any influence on his friend's son it was because he answered Clifton's many questions as honestly as he could and qualified them with disclaimers that they were his, George Williamson's, ideas and opinions. They were not to be taken as superior to Ed's ideas or opinions in any way, and his father's guidance took priority in every way. George was just a sounding board.

~~~

George knelt down and dug up a section of clover root with his pocketknife. He scraped it clean, cut off the hair-like tip and chewed on it like a stringy carrot as he walked along the creek on the southwest corner of his place. He would begin looking where, at the spot on Monday, he had seen a lone figure sitting on the point of rimrock overlooking Martinez Canyon. Had he realized at the time that it might have been his young friend Clifton, he could have gone to him and perhaps talked to him.

Now he knew the boy was injured. Undoubtedly, his feelings were hurt, and he was angry. George thought he probably could have talked Clifton into going home with him. He was good at working with injured creatures including boys with hurt feelings.

~~~

As he walked, George thought about how he could best help his friends and neighbors Ed and Etta Mae. It was planting time. The soil had just been reaching the right temperature to sprout corn, spring wheat, barley, potatoes and beans.

He and most of the neighborhood farmers had started planting during the week while Ed and Etta Mae tried to find their boy.

Ed worked full time in town now to meet his bills. He couldn't afford to quit and work on the farm. Ed had talked all winter about how this was the summer when his second son would be able to do the bulk of the farming, and maybe they could finally catch up. George had worried about the amount of expectations Ed was placing on 14-year-old Clifton's narrow shoulders.

George had seen how proud and confident the boy had acted when his dad talked about him doing the farming. Then he had seen the uncertain look in the boy's eyes when he thought no one was looking. He knew Clifton didn't have a lot of self-confidence. He tried too hard to please, and he wagged his tail like a pup when he received a compliment. He was a little too quick with an "I'm sorry," when he couldn't quite get something done well enough for his dad's approval.

The older boy, Charlie, had been a good farmer and was a hard act for Clifton to follow. Clifton was more of a dreamer and George didn't think the boy's heart was in farming. The boy was curious about archeology. That would be good field for him if he could afford the tuition in four years.

Now the boy had gone missing, and George considered it to be partly his fault. He should have been more curious about the lone figure, if indeed it was Clifton.

When the Sherriff came by that morning George had asked, "Which canyons have you searched here on the Ridge?"

"None of them yet," Sherriff Kirkendall had answered.

"Why not?"

"Why should we?"

"For one thing, he might be living down in one of them."

"Where would he get a cockamamie idea like that?"

"He talks about it all the time," George had said.

"So let's say this idea is valid. Where is this most likely to happen? The only ruins I know about are over in Lost Canyon."

George thought about that for a moment. "No I don't think he would go there. Yes, there are a number of ruins there, and they are probably the best ones, but they were also the most well known. It would be easy to check them out. I think they should be checked out. But, I don't think he would go there. I've never heard him say anything about them. I don't think he hangs out there at all."

"Any ideas then?"

"I think if I were going to put money on it, I say he is right over behind my place in one of the cliff dwellings in Martinez Canyon."

"From what you say about his interest in Indians and all, I don't think it is too farfetched to consider that he might hide out in a ruin like you are suggesting, but this close to home? This is not very characteristic. If he were a little kid maybe, but his age? I doubt it. How about McElmo canyon?" Bill had asked.

"There is no doubt that there are plenty of ruins down in McElmo," George had agreed. "But that's a long way off."

"Tell you what Bill, I know Martinez Canyon as well as anybody. Why don't I give it a good once over and see if I find any clue that he might be down there, and if there seems to be any reason to search it further, I'll let you know."

"Sounds good. I'll get someone to ride up Lost Canyon from Dolores to the train crossing at Millwood. I'll have someone meet him there with a trailer to bring him home. He can ride the canyon and give the ruins a look over. See if there are smoke stains and so forth.

"I think that I'll get a group together and check out the McElmo area. The Ute Agency search and rescue team can make a go up the canyons they have mapped out. They know pretty much where to look. Of course, there are hundreds of square miles down there, and they say there may be thousands of undiscovered ruins in that area. He could be anywhere if he puts his mind to it. We have people who have gone on the lam down there that have never been found."

~~~

George climbed through his fence and walked to the creek that flowed through the intersecting Martinez Canyon.

His thoughts were on the conversation that morning with Sherriff Bill
~~~

Kirkendall. George's convictions were founded on the many conversations he had shared with the boy about living off the land.

The idea of living in one of the caves wasn't so bad, actually. Man had lived in caves from before the dawn of civilization. At one time, the canyon and the surrounding top lands had supported a large agricultural population. The boy was very inquisitive about how the Indians had lived, what they had lived on, about Indian lore and where the ruins were.

Ed looked east up the canyon and west down the canyon. Directly across from where he stood was the point where he had seen someone on Monday and heard someone shoot. The ruin of the round tower stood on that point. He stared at the tower for a few moments trying to think where Clifton might have gone. The trail he stood on led directly to highway 160 probably not much more than a couple of miles away.

The crossing there was deadly for motorists and deer alike through the months of September and October as deer worked toward the safety from guns and toward the mild winter climate and of winter grazing grounds on the slopes of Mesa Verde. The reverse migration began in May and early June as they came back through on their way to the foothills and the La Plata's.

I guess he could have gone over there and caught a ride. Some trucker would probably stop and pick him up. For sure, an Indian or a farmer would pick him up. They'd take him for a kid out rabbit hunting or someone whose horse ran away, He thought.

But, why did Cliff run in the first place? George kept coming back to it. *One fight with another kid shouldn't have been enough to make a boy like Clifton run away from home.* His thought turned to the boy's dad. *For all his qualities as a good neighbor, Ed has a temper. I'll bet he sometimes takes it out on his boy.*

Ed has been planning on Clifton to do the day to day farming this summer. The Kelley farm is one of the largest tracts under irrigation on the Ridge. It has the most shares of water of any of the local farms. That is a big responsibility for a grown man. I'm confident the boy knows enough about farming and Ed would be directing it. But, what if any of a thousand things were to go wrong, including most that would be out of his control, such as surprises Mother Nature might have in store?

How understanding might Ed be? I wonder if Clifton has been bothered with the same question. If that was Clifton sitting there on that rock, was he thinking about who'll be held accountable if he can't pull it off this summer? Is that what he's afraid of? Was he afraid of the consequences of letting his dad down?

Ed is also a pacifist. He was furious when Charlie accepted the draft instead of claiming CO status. He practically kicked Charlie out over it. Could it be that Clifton is afraid of his dad over the fight with the Mexican boy?

George thought of his own youngest boy Scott. How he might have reacted under similar circumstances and pressure. *Would Scott have gone far away? Would he have stayed close? I'd bet the farm, the boy would stay close.*

As he walked, he examined the trail, bushes, grasses, cattails, and willows for any sign that anyone had been there recently.

At one spot, George stopped to investigate grass on the north side of the creek. It was disturbed, he assumed by deer coming down that side of the canyon. He scanned the slope for a trail and could see intermittent sections of a small deer trail. He couldn't distinguish any marks on the rock or grass other than deer tracks, so he returned to the main trail and continued.

Something was different about the deer tracks on the main trail. The local deer herd used the trail as their main thoroughfare up and down the canyon. George studied the tracks on his hands and knees. Something had spooked them recently, to be cautious in this area. They had veered off, hesitated, milled about and then continue down the main trail. Underlying the tracks was a disturbance that may have been boot tracks, but he couldn't be certain because of new overlaying deer tracks in the dust.

He studied the willows and cattails. Were broken twigs the result of magpies building nests? Deer browsing? Were the gaps between stalks natural? He didn't think so. Were deer alone responsible? He couldn't tell.

Mule deer grazed at the tender alfalfa fields on the top land during the twilight hours and dawn and returned to their bedding grounds in the canyon by day. Their sharp hooves kept the trail well stirred up as they moved back and forth. Only fresh tracks were sharply defined. They nibbled on fresh shoots as they went along. He saw nothing that looked like the sharp edges of knife cuts.

George walked down the stream until after noon, further than he had gone in years. He finally turned around and began retracing his steps where the creek emerged from the lower slope of the Summit Ridge plateau about a mile east of highway 160 and five miles east of Cortez.

He spotted the remnants of several small cliff dwellings under the cap rocks on both slopes of the canyon, but none appeared to be especially well preserved. He climbed up to the most promising of them and saw no sign of visitation. Every dwelling he knew of in this canyon and elsewhere in the vicinity were all thoroughly looted.

He thought he detected a hint of cedar smoke. It was faint. He became aware of it far down the canyon, and once he caught the first whiff, he smelled it from time to time until he reached the draw where he had entered the canyon. He couldn't actually be sure it came from the canyon. It could have come from someone burning brush from newly cleared land on top.

It was also possible that someone in McElmo had burned a pile of cedar branches on a recent afternoon. Smoke from that burn would have flowed with the warm air up through the canyon toward the foothills and the La Plata Mountains where it cooled and returned as cold air that evening or the next down the same canyon or Lost Canyon. There were no barriers, and thus few inversions to stop the airflow from between the mountains and the desert.

Streaks ran down the face of the rimrock caused by natural pollution and stains from water running over the side after rainstorms and snow melt. A black streak above a cave was not necessarily proof of a fire beneath. He saw nothing around old ruins or caves that looked like fresh smoke stains when he studied a few especially black streaks with his binoculars.

In the late afternoon, he finally quickly walked back up the trail toward his own place. He still had an eerie feeling that somewhere in the canyon was his young friend Clifton. There was no sense of foreboding that Clifton was in any danger or hurt. He would come back repeatedly until he was sure, one way or the other. He was re-assessing his idea that Clifton was hiding out in an Indian ruin. He could have been wrong about that. His memory could have deceived him. None were as well preserved as he had remembered. He had obviously transposed some of the ruins from somewhere else into Martinez Canyon.

However, that didn't mean that he hadn't set up camp in an overhang or something.

Chores waited. He had also decided to make a visit to several of his neighbors to see if he could organize a planting party for Sunday at the Kelley place.

It was payback time!

21

Friday, mid-morning
West of the Rodriguez home

Hector and Emilio rode together down the county road west of their respective homes. Their ponies were of no discernable breed, but they in good condition and well groomed. The two boys went everywhere they could on their horses. The opportunities were many in the summer, as fences existed mainly around the perimeter of the farms. They had free access to the thousands of acres of the county, state and federal lands and the canyons.

The time was growing near, when they would have to join their older brothers and sisters working. For the past several summers, they had been carefree and were encouraged to explore and develop their horsemanship skills. If they eventually spent time in the mountains as herders, they would need all the skill they could learn.

"Emilio, here is where I will turn off. I am going to check out the old cabin at the coal mine. In addition, there is an old shack at the homestead further to the west. After that I will ride back along the canyon and see if I see anything or smell smoke or anything. I'll meet you back at the schoolhouse, and we can ride over to Lost Canyon.

"OK. I will check out that bunch of abandoned cars off the road down by the big ditch. He could be living in any of them. That's where I would go if I ran away. Then I'll ride over to the end of Little Canyon and up Big Canyon to the road and back to the schoolhouse from there." Emilio said, pointing to the northwest toward the confluence of Little Canyon and Big Canyon. Felix and Ignacio were riding Little Canyon with Carmen, Ana and Katia. They had decided that Big Canyon was too deep to search, and they didn't know the ruins in it. There were many little ruins further down in Little Canyon they could check.

"*Adios*," Emilio said, and he continued down the county road for another half mile before turning off to the right and following ruts to a clearing choked with abandoned junk cars.

Hector left the county road to the left onto a lane that disappeared into the trees. He rode a quarter of a mile down a winding dirt lane over washed out rock, exposed by erosion, to a cleared area where the brown sandy soil was sprinkled with chunks of rock laced with coal.

He and his father, like many Ridge residents, visited the site each fall to dig free coal. All it cost was aching backs and blisters from a day of breaking away layers of shale to get at the thin layers of coal. An unknown miner sometime in the past had abandoned it leaving behind only a weathered, leaning shack.

Hector dismounted and looked at the padlock on the weathered shack. It was rusty and showed no sign of tampering. There were no tracks in the dirt and piñon needles around the shack.

He peeked through cracks between the boards over the window but could see nothing in the darkness inside.

Satisfied that the runaway Clifton had not visited the shack, he remounted and moved on.

A half hour later, he made the same determination at the abandoned homestead farmhouse a mile west, and he pointed Diablo south toward Martinez Canyon.

The sun was well past high noon when Hector arrived at the rim of Martinez Canyon. He had crossed a smaller less well formed draw that a few miles later to the west opened into a marsh known as Totten Lake.

When Hector arrived at the canyon, not far from where it emerged from the southwestern edge of the Summit Ridge Plateau, he stopped briefly to eat his lunch, drank water, and eat the foil wrapped cookie. *Mrs. Etta Mae and Mr. Ed have been kind to me the past two days. They have sent milk home each night for my family and a jar of cottage cheese. My family really likes that cottage cheese. I wonder why Mother doesn't buy more of it? Maybe it is expensive in the grocery store. Why did they give us the milk and the cheese? Why do they want to be my friend? Do they admire me, because I am big and strong, and their son is so little and weak? However, I see that he could do all that I have been doing. So how could he be so weak? Maybe he is strong too. Maybe I misjudged him.*

He stood, wiped his forehead and remounted Diablo.

A half hour later, he moved slowly but steadily up the rimrock on the north side of Martinez Canyon. The afternoon was warm and the air was clear. He looked at the La Plata's ahead. He dismounted and walked. Diablo did not like to walk close to the rim of the canyon. It had narrowed and deepened along this stretch of the canyon. So far, he had seen nothing; no tracks, no unusual marks on the rock to indicate anyone had come along here recently.

He glanced at an ancient looking cedar very close to the edge and wondered how it could survive and how many more years before it gave up and fell over the edge. *Maybe I should give it a little nudge.* He dropped the reigns and walked over to the snag, put his shoulder to it, set his feet and pushed.

The snag held firm. It had withstood the elements for more years than his family had been on the Ridge going back for several generations. Its roots had spread wide seeking nourishment and stability to sustain its sparse growth.

"Tough old *cabron*. You remind me of my grandfather," Hector laughed, admitting defeat gracefully. He walked back to Diablo, led the pony further back from the edge, remounted and picked up the pace. *This is a waste of time. Señora Campbell said this Canyon is being searched from below.*

He turned the horse back toward the timber; rode past the big pueblo ruin just south of the Kelley fence line, turned left and continued toward the county road.

He had visited Uncle Ignacio for a week last summer, and they had sat around the campfire after the evening chores. In the moonlight, they watched the sheep spread out below them on the meadow below timberline. The nights were cold in the high altitude and the air was thin. His favorite time of all was when Ignacio took the guitar and began playing sad ballads. He said the sound of the guitar and his voice kept the sheep calm and the coyotes away.

When he saw the gate at the county road, the peaceful vision dissolved. The reality sank in. We are not going to find him.

~~~

When Cliff awoke, the sun was at the midpoint between the lookout tower on Mesa Verde and highest peak on Ute Mountain. He had lain on the narrowest end of the ledge next to the chute where he could see the creek at the bottom of the canyon. He had apparently dropped off to sleep in the warm sunshine and slept on a good part of the afternoon with the warm sun beating down on his back. The straw-hat shaded his head and face.

This end of the ledge gave him an unobstructed view of the trail in the bottom of the canyon for a glimpse of George, if he passed by. He could see the trail from the other end also, but there he exposed himself to anyone looking down from the rim. On the narrow end, he could not be seen from the top of the cliff.

Cliff continued his vigil until the sun nearly reached the head of Ute
~~~

Mountain before he gave it up. He waited until after dark before starting a fire. George might be waiting anywhere for the tell tale signs of smoke. If that was Hector up on top this afternoon, he might be waiting at the edge of the timber for my head to pop up over the rim out of curiosity, just like a prairie dog.

So they are searching for me here now. Is it just George? Was that Hector on his horse on the rim this afternoon? If I'm going to stay here, I'll have to be really careful now. A scratch mark on the rock, footprint in the mud, and they will be all over it.

22
Friday Night
Kelley Farm

Sheriff Bill Kirkendall turned across the cattle guard at the entrance to the Kelley driveway and followed the lane to the front of Ed and Etta Mae's house. Ed met him at the front door, relieved him of the roll of maps and his hat and ushered him inside to the dining room table.

Bill saw Hector Rodriguez turning the long handle of the cream separator in the utility room off the kitchen and waved to him.

"Bill," she said as she handed him a cup of coffee.

"Etta Mae," he nodded.

"Anything?"

"Afraid not. I was just about to show you where all we've gone, and who all we've talked to. We've an 'all points' out in Colorado, New Mexico, Utah and Arizona. Posters have gone up in all the truck stops and bus stations in Colorado, New Mexico, Arizona, Utah, Nevada, Oklahoma and Texas. There hasn't been a word reported to the State Patrols in any of those states that checked out. There was a boy found in a ditch down in New Mexico, but they identified the body as a local Navajo boy.

We've contacted every household here on the Ridge and not a single one has reported seeing Cliff or reported anything missing or out of place.

"The kids up at the school conducted a search today. Evelyn checked in. She said the kids went around to every hiding place, abandoned car they knew of, cave, Indian ruin in the canyons they played in, and even in farm buildings that are not used and are out of sight. They all reported to Mrs. Campbell and she called me at five o'clock this afternoon. Nothing. The only thing they found was some old Ute guy who was sleeping one off in a car clear at the end of the canyon down almost to Lakeview. He told Emilio, 'He didn't see no white boy lately.'"

The three friends digested all that information and looked over maps of Montezuma County, primarily Summit Ridge.

Bill unrolled a Forest Service map and sipped his coffee. "Do you think he would head up to the hills? You mentioned he liked this Lost Canyon country?"

"I had a rider ride from Dolores to Millwood here," Bill said. "That's where I had him picked up. He didn't see any evidence in the ruin area in the lower part of Lost Canyon. It was a superficial look at best, but you'd think that after a week, there would be fresh smoke stains if he's been burning a fire."

"He likes fishing up about here." Ed pointed to a dot on the map. We go there every summer. We drive this Forest Service road to here," Ed said. He traced a thin line on the map to Summit Lake. "This elevation is where piñon and cedar gives way to ponderosa pine. The road crosses a stretch of ponderosa to Lost Canyon, across to the north side then on up the north side through blue spruce and quaking aspen to a trail head up the canyon. From here it's about a mile and a half down to the bottom of the canyon where we fish."

"But Bill, he couldn't live down there. As far as we can tell he's just got the clothes on his back," Etta Mae said. "As Ed says that is blue spruce and aspen country. Right now there is still snow on the ground up there."

"Mama thinks he may have taken a box of matches, but she can't remember if there was a box in the cupboard or not. It's still freezing up there every night and nothing to eat," Ed said. "He didn't take a fishing pole or tackle that we can tell. I just don't think he'd do that. He may be desperate, but I don't think he's irrational."

"You've checked all his relatives?"

"We've called all that have phones. We contacted his aunts and uncles in New Mexico, Oklahoma, Arkansas and Texas. Even so, how could he get there this soon? Our nearest relative is in Farmington, New Mexico. I guess he could have walked to there by now, but it would have been a long dry walk. Problem with that is Mesa Verde between us.

"You know Bill, we think that Cliff may have been seen by George on Monday," Ed said.

"I think so too. It was too much coincidence in time, for it not to have been Cliff. No one saw any cars out there, and we didn't find any tracks. So that would have put him in the Martinez Canyon area," Bill said.

"Etta Mae and I have also been talking a lot about how he thinks. He loves Mesa Verde and the ruins up there. He has said he could live like that. I think he fantasizes about it. About all he talks about is Indians and Indian ruins. There are two places where there are plentiful Indian ruins, Mesa Verde and McElmo. I've taken him to ruins in some of the back canyons down there where no one ever goes, they are so hard to find, and they're harder to get to. There are still squash shells and cornhusks in some of them."

"It was in a ruin in that area where one of the farmers discovered the bowl filled with the beans they have in the museum up at Mesa Verde. Etta Mae and I think he wouldn't go to Mesa Verde because there are too many people. The tourist season won't open until Memorial Day, and he couldn't mingle with the tourists until then. The Rangers would spot him, and it's too heavily patrolled up there," Ed said.

"I'll put posters around up there just in case," Bill said.

"That's a good idea, Bill," Ed agreed. "But we think he more likely would go to McElmo. He likes it down there. It's warmer down there already. Think about it. The elevation is 7000 feet up here, between 6500 and 6000 feet in Cortez. McElmo is about 5,000 feet and the sun on all that bare sandstone heats up the bottom of the canyon, so they have an extra month, or month and a half, of growing season. They already have cherries and apricots coming on down there. There would already be definitely more for him to eat. Furthermore, the quickest most unobtrusive way to get from here to McElmo would be to pick up the creek in Martinez Canyon, follow it to McElmo creek and just stay on it straight on through Cortez and down into McElmo."

"So you're saying we should concentrate our search on McElmo?"

"It's my thought," Ed said.

"George and I had this same conversation this morning.

"Also he thinks we should be looking around here as well as McElmo. In fact, he spent today checking out Martinez Canyon. He called me when he got home and said he couldn't find anything that he could hang his hat on, just as I expected. But, I'm still skeptical about all this Indian ruin business. It still makes more sense to me for him to have high tailed it on over to 160 and thumbed a ride. Some trucker looking for company..." Bill paused and looked from Ed to Etta Mae. "I'm sorry to say this, but we have to face reality, some trucker or someone without the best of intentions might have been glad to pick him up going either direction."

Ed shook his head. "I think he's too smart to take a chance like that. He's never thumbed a ride in his life."

"Well Ed, back to your theory about McElmo. We're talking about hundreds of thousands of acres of badlands and canyon country down there. We have hardened criminals who have disappeared down there and have never been found by even the best hunters and trackers the Utes and Navajos have, and believe me, they don't come any better."

"Unfortunately, I realize that, Bill. We aren't talking about a criminal who has a habit of running from the law. This is the first time my boy has ever..., and I emphasize..., ever run away!"

"I understand that. So, he talks about Indians. That's a childhood thing. Lots of kids do that, but few run away to become one. Not even Indian kids do that anymore."

"He doesn't just talk about them, he studies them," Etta Mae said. "I'll show you what I'm talking about," she said. She excused herself and went to the back of the house to Clifton's bedroom. She returned after a few minutes, her face blanched. She slumped into her chair. "It's gone! Cliff took his scrapbook with him! I can't find it."

"Scrapbook?"

"Bill, there was enough information in there to help him actually live off the land in this region."

"Do you think he's been planning this for a while?"

"I don't think he's been thinking about it consciously. However, it might have been in the back of his mind once Mrs. Campbell made the assignment. Maybe that's why he chose that topic," Etta Mae said.

For the next hour, the Sheriff listened and jotted down information that Ed and Etta Mae could remember about what kind of information Cliff had collected. He became more convinced as he listened that the Kelley's were correct that the boy might have run away with a fantasy of surviving off the land somewhere.

He was also convinced the boy wouldn't last two weeks.

The Sheriff would focus on the likely places the boy would go, according to his parents. That would be two or three branch canyons in McElmo. Bill spread a different section of the detailed county map on the table and penciled in the areas where Ed and Clifton had climbed to various cliff dwellings.

"I've already contacted the Ute Agency about having their search and rescue team search in McElmo. The area you marked is not on their reservation. It is a long shot. There are literally thousands of small cliff dwellings in those side canyons in McElmo and other canyons that feed the San Juan. I hear there are more up on Ute Mountain on the Ute Reservation. Many are inaccessible and unexplored. It could take years to thoroughly search them all, and he could never be found, if he doesn't want to be found."

"How about Etta Mae and me show you where we think he might a gone, if he went to the Canyon?" Ed asked.

"That would be great. Want to meet me at the office in the morning? How soon can you be there?"

"Soon's we get the chores done and get around."

"See you then."

As Sheriff Kirkendall folded the map, Hector called through the utility room door, "I'm all finished."

Bill looked up. "Hello Hector."

"Buenos Noches," Señor Sherriff, Hector said.

"I heard you were helping here. How is it going?" Bill asked.

"Oh, I'm learning a few things. I'm learning how to milk a cow," Hector said with a smile.

Etta Mae took a gallon of milk from the refrigerator and handed it to Hector.

"I'm ready to leave now. Can I give you a lift home?" Bill asked.

"Si Señor," Hector said. "That would be very nice. I will get my school clothes."

"Meet you at the pickup," Bill said. When Hector disappeared out the door, Bill asked, "How is he really doing?"

"He's doing fine," Ed said.

"Does he bear watching?" asked Bill.

"Mrs. Campbell said it was his idea for the kids to search for Clifton today," Etta Mae said.

"That's right," answered Ed. "I think he's really sorry Cliff is gone, although it is self-serving. His dad brought him here and commanded that he work. I don't think he should be here without pay and come Monday, I'll talk to Raul about where we go from there. Hector's a good worker, but it isn't fair to make him work against his will and for nothing. But, for now I am respecting Raul's desire to make a point with his son."

"Well, you two work it out between you. You've always seemed like good friends. I want to see you keep it like that."

"Depend on it Sheriff," Ed said.

~~~

They were the eyes of Satan come for him. He had killed Hector. He was damned to hell! The nightmare was vivid. He had pulled the trigger and seen Hector fall and had turned to run but had been surrounded by human sized prairie dogs dressed in black coats. Each stared at him with blood red eyes, their pointed noses aiming at his heart. Overhead a cloud formed and from it two vaguely formed faces emerged that he felt were, female and male; Earth Mother and Heavenly Father. Angels darted at him from every direction. He couldn't escape. Black clouds descended over the landscape and the sound of coyotes and frogs came at him from all directions and blood red eyes swooped in on him suspended on twenty foot wings with talons and razor sharp teeth and claws clutching at him, coming to take him to hell. He tried to run but his feet were glued to the road. He got down on his hands and knees and tried to pull himself along, but no amount of strain would pull him from that spot. He struggled to sit up but now a rope was twisted around his neck, and he tore at it. The gunnysack finally came away in his hands, and he felt along it for a hangman's noose, but found none. Cliff awoke in the middle of the night drenched in sweat. It was very dark. Two dark red eyes stared at him from two feet away. The hair rose on the back of his neck. He couldn't breathe. He gasped and gasped again for breath and stared at Satan's eyes again, and they didn't blink or move but stared steadily back until finally a spark popped free and sputtered across the fire pit.

His eyes focused on the fire pit, and he slowly remembered where he was. He tried to relax and to breathe normally again. The vivid images of the nightmare remained. He could feel his heart pounding in his chest.

He stood, felt his way to the doorway and lifted the slate to the side. He stepped through the door, walked down the ledge toward the broad end and relieved himself over the edge.

A thin moon hung over the canyon casting just enough light that he could faintly make out rock and trees on the opposite canyon wall and the shiny ribbon of water far below.

Is it only Friday night? Is it truly only my fifth night in this cave? Why do I feel as if it has been weeks already? Is it my last night?
~~~

Noises drifted up from the canyon. Owls whistled and hooted. Branches moved and sighed in the breeze. Twigs snapped as creatures stepped or slithered over them. A breeze blew gently through the canyon and around the rimrock making slight moaning noises.

In the distance, a trucker shifted gears as he guided his big rig up the long grade out of Mancos Canyon several miles away, the still night air amplified the sound and the face of the Mesa Verde escarpment bounced it all across the plateau and valley at its feet.

Cliff returned to the ruin, slid the slate back in place and returned to the saddle blanket. He put another piece of cedar on the fire and tried to go back to sleep.

23

Saturday Morning after breakfast
Martinez Canyon

Cliff got up on Saturday morning, washed his face and sat in the doorway looking out into the canyon. He could get use to it here: the view out over the canyon and the blue green Mesa to the south, and up on top he could add to that view, the Sleeping Ute and the La Plata Range. But it was not to be. Sometime in the wee hours of the night, after awakening from the nightmare, he had decided to go home. It was time. He had played scene after scene in his mind, rejecting most alternatives in their entirety after he viewed them. Some ideas he liked and parked them in a compartment in his mind to revisit. Finally, he had hit on the one he liked best. He had played the plan several times and saw no major flaws. It would work. After that, he had slept for a time.

His plan was simple. Today was Saturday. They always went to town on Saturday. He would put the planter on the tractor and plant beans until time to set the water. Then he would set the water and have it done before his mom and dad got home from Cortez. He would ask for their forgiveness. If they forgave him, then life would go on as planned. If they did not forgive him, then what? He would search his mind, check the lesser plans and see if one fit, decide on the spot and act on it.

After grocery shopping, they would sell sacks of pinto beans, wheat and or corn to the mill. If Etta Mae needed flour or cornmeal, they would trade some of the wheat or corn for it. They usually tried to time their morning to arrive at the sales barn at lunchtime. There they could eat and check out the flea market before the livestock auction turned to the calves and pig sales. If Ed took an animal in that day, he would check it in when they arrived that morning, and hang around that afternoon to pick up a check. It was a social event every Saturday where farmers and their wives gathered to share information and friendship.

Usually on those Saturday afternoons, Cliff's parents parked him at the library in town, or if he had a spare quarter, at the movie theater next door for the Saturday afternoon matinee. It depended on the matinee. Once the matinee had been a Janette MacDonald and Nelson Eddy musical. The billboard had shown a Canadian Mountie and a beautiful woman. How could he have known that there would be little action and much operatic singing?

Cliff didn't know if he had messed up their weekend routine or not. His plan depended on their following it. If they didn't go to town as usual, he would have to decide whether to just walk up to the front door and knock or walk in. He didn't know what their reaction would be if he did that.

To know for sure if they followed the custom, he would watch the road to see if they went to town.

Before leaving, Cliff tidied the cliff dwelling and put everything back exactly as he had found it. He ate the few left over cattail and asparagus shoots and set the slate inside the door. He could find something more to eat at the house.

He tried to remember how his dad had cut gunnysacks to make their fishing creels. He slashed the gunnysack and did a credible job without destroying it. He packed all he had brought with him back into the bag and checked that nothing remained. He put the .22 into the bag butt first, tied the straps around the barrel, then tied the sack onto the end of the rope and carried it all out to the ledge. Cliff tied the end of the rope to the back suspender of his overalls and carefully climbed the vertical face of the cliff using the hand and toeholds. The rope trailed out behind him.

When he reached the top, he hesitated. Was Hector or someone waiting? Were they hiding in the trees, waiting for him to expose himself? He had no sentry to bark "all safe!" He inched over the edge and stood. He examined the trees, waiting for someone to rush forward. Moments passed. He tried to blend with the snag. He waited tensely.

Finally, he tied the end of the rope to the trunk of the snag and pulled the bag up after him. He untied the rope, put it into the bag, put the strap over his shoulder, picked up the rifle and stopped 20 feet forward. There on the bare rock were fresh U shaped scrapes from steel horseshoes. There had been someone there yesterday.

"I wonder what Hector would have done if he had spotted me. If I make him miss out on going to the mountains, and he catches me out here one of these days, what will he do? He'll really be mad then. If he catches me, I'm going to have to be ready to defend myself, that's for sure. Luckily, he should be gone by tomorrow or the next day."

He headed home, the long way around.

Cliff walked along the rim down the canyon and cut across the timber to intersect the county road just below the Stone residence.

The Stone's were the last neighbors on the road before it dipped from the Ridge down into the Lakeview valley. It was a walk of about a mile and a half or two miles from the ruin to the road and another two and a half miles through the woods from there to his folks' house.

Cliff waited out of sight in the woods until he heard a vehicle rattling down the beginning of the long grade toward Cortez. From his vantage point, he watched as a pickup bounced into view on the dusty washboard gravel road.

Cliff recognized his dad's dusty, green, Ford pickup and then saw both his dad and mom as they came closer and closer. He choked back a knot that welled up in his throat. *Despite everything, I miss you. I love you guys. Could you forgive me if I stopped you right now? If I ran out into the road and waved you down and climbed into the pickup with you?*

He stood rooted to the spot, undecided as the pickup slowly, noisily rolled by. He had hesitated too long. He burst out of the woods and ran into the open shouting, "Wait for me! Wait for me! Wait…!" then fell to his knees, and sobbed.

Inside the old pickup, neither occupant saw the figure through the dust coated rear window nor heard the shouts through the loud road noises caused by the rough road.

Clifton stood. The dust drifted into the timber across from him.

He crossed into the woods on the other side of the road, walked mindlessly on toward Little Canyon, and followed it up behind Raul's house to another smaller canyon-draw that ran through the northwest corner of the Kelley farm.

At the bend in the county road that cut off the northwest corner of the farm, he crossed it and entered the narrow strip of timber between the alfalfa patch and the road. Between him and the road was the cleared area where he had lain in wait for Hector in the brush pile. *I can't believe I did that,* he thought as he looked at the site of his near crime. He looked down at the single shot in his hand. *I surely could not have pulled the trigger. No matter how much I hated that guy, surely I couldn't have done it, could I?*

He turned from there and went on to the house. He passed through the man-gate in the fence behind the outhouse, walked past the root cellar and on by the house. His old dog Towser looked up at him, wagged his tail weakly and went back to sleep.

Cliff kneeled, petted the old dog and lifted his head. They had gone everywhere together. They had explored, played, herded cows in the right-of-way. Towser had been his best friend, especially out in the fields all summer. The only time Towser couldn't go was when Cliff hunted skunks.

Cliff walked down the familiar driveway to the lane that separated the barnyard from parked machinery, equipment sheds, shops and field access. He checked the tractor. Oil, gas, and water levels were good. He tipped the hoppers on the two-row planter, and swapped the corn disks for bean disks. The disks dropped the proper number of seed per foot in each row.

Before attaching the bean planter, he went to the granary to make sure his dad had brought home the seed. He set the gunnysack of clothes, saddle blanket, scrapbook and the .22 down inside the door of the granary and checked on the seed. He wanted to go into the house, for a piece of jerky and maybe a cookie, but he couldn't let himself get sidetracked. He had to do this right.

Cliff left the sack in the granary and went back to the tractor to attach the planter and take it around to the fill the hoppers. Before he could start the tractor, he heard a vehicle clatter across the cattle guard at the county road entrance to the driveway leading up to the Kelley home.

You've come home early! I'm not ready yet!

His sack and .22 were out of sight in the granary. His folks had not had time to get to town and come back. It had to be someone else. He stepped into the oil shed next to where the bean planter was parked, across the lane from the equipment shed and the tractor. *It'll be easier to hide in here, if it Mom and Dad, until they go into the house, and I can slip away or figure out what to do. It's probably someone just dropping by. They'll surely leave when they see no one is home.*

He had just closed the door of the shed when he heard approaching tires crunching on the gravel. Instead of the pickup turning into the circular drive and parking at the house, it continued straight and stopped between the oil shed where Cliff hid and the equipment shed. He peeked through a knothole expecting to see the green family Ford pickup, but instead a different pickup truck rolled to a stop no more than six feet in front of him.

Raul Rodriguez opened the driver side door of his old beaten up 1948 Chevy pickup and got out. Hector got out the other side.

What the…? What are they doing here? They don't have any business here! Cliff wondered angrily.

He started to open the door and challenge them. Raul reached back into the bed of the pickup and removed his shovel and a pair of boots.

Hector walked across to the equipment shed on the other side of the lane and came out with an old pair of Ed's boots and Cliff's shovel. The two chatted in Spanish as they put on their boots and then walked down the lane, through the gates and followed the fence toward the north alfalfa field next to the timber.

Seething in anger, Cliff waited until they were out of sight, before he left the oil shed. Raul had worked for Ed Kelley before when he needed a hired hand, usually during haying season. Hector had never worked for them. Bile rose in his throat. *They don't belong here! Why didn't Dad hire someone else instead of him? Anyone else! Dad just doesn't get it, does he! He's actually already replaced me with Hector?*

"You want Hector Dad? OK You got him! Damn you!" he swore, perhaps for the first time aloud in his life.

He had brought home everything that he had carried away on Monday. He stomped away from the oil shed and stood in the lane staring at Raul's truck. His shoulders slumped. The adrenaline drained from his system.

They don't care if I'm gone. They've already given my job to my worst enemy. I hate them! I was right to leave the first time!

On impulse, Cliff dashed across the lane into his dad's workshop. Tools littered a workbench made of 2x4's set on their sides and running the full length of the south wall of the shed. Along the opposite wall were freestanding tools such as grinders, a welder, vise, and forge.

His inventive dad never threw anything away. He dropped old worn out files into a bucket. The high-grade steel made good blades for weed cutters and knives. Several half-finished knives lay near one of the grinders. Cliff had watched his dad carefully grinding and tempering a large old rasp wood finishing file into a heavy-duty knife. Much grinding would be required before it matched the Bowie knife sketch that Ed had tacked over the grinder. Already it had a sharp edge. All it needed was a handle before it was safe to use. Ed had said he was waiting for just the right elk horns to finish it off. He had already drilled the holes to attach them. It had waited for a handle for as long as Cliff could remember.

He grabbed the knife, a pointed keyhole saw hanging from a nail and a small metal sharpening file, like the one he used to sharpen his shovel, and dropped them into his gunnysack.

He went directly to the house from the shed, feeling like an intruder, even a burglar when he stepped onto the front porch. It wasn't home anymore. *They've already replaced me with Hector!* He went to the shelves of canning jars, selected six of the quart mayonnaise jars with lids, and carefully put them into a fresh burlap sack along with the file-knife, file and saw. He resisted the temptation to go into the kitchen one last time and replenish his cookie and jerky supply. *If I took canning jars, Mom would miss them. She'll never miss the mayonnaise jars because Dad helps himself to them all the time.*

He left the house and went back to the equipment shed. He looked around and went to the cabinet in the corner of the shop where he kept his beekeeping supplies. Quart jars of comb honey remained of what he had robbed from his hives the summer before. He took a jar, and carefully placed it in the sack. It would be the heaviest thing in there on the return trip to the cliff dwelling.

Cliff looked at the new smoker he would leave undisturbed on a front shelf in the cabinet. *I guess I won't get to use you this year. What will happen to my bees? They will be swarming soon, and I won't be around to take care of them. Will Dad think to put supers on the hives? I still don't have foundation strung in all the frames. I still had so much work to do. He won't have time to do all that and to check them from time to time.*

Cliff looked around the narrow closet as he turned to go, and he saw the old smoker in a back corner behind a hive waiting for repair. It was rusty and the bellows need replacing. The smoker was a homemade one that Ed had made for him out of a two-pound coffee can. The hinged lid was in the shape of a funnel. Fixed to one side was a three inch by six-inch pine slat a quarter of an inch thick. Both the slat and the coffee can had half-inch holes drilled in the side facing each other a half-inch from the bottom. Ed had fixed the slat to the coffee can with four metal feet. A second three by six inch slat was hinged to the fixed slat at the bottom. Ed attached thin flexible leather to the sides and top of the slats to form bellows. Squeeze to blow, release the slat to suck in more air. Squeeze for a puff of air through the hole in the bottom of the can to keep cotton rags or cedar bark smoldering and producing smoke, which issued from the spout of the funnel shaped lid. Smoke directed over a colony of bees, calmed them so that they would share their honey with the beekeeper. *It's not as sleek as the new manufactured smoker Mom gave me for Christmas, but it got the job done. If those bees decide to get up tight or swarm, that old smoker might come in handy.*

He picked the old homemade smoker out of the corner and along with it took the long bladed knife that he used for cutting through the comb. It was thin and heated quickly so that it sliced through beeswax like butter. *I don't know how I might use this, but then I don't know how I'll use half this stuff. What am I doing?*

He walked out of the shed and saw Raul's pick up parked in the middle of the lane.

It broke his heart.

He ran back to the granary. With a pang of guilt, he opened the door and stared at stacks of seed grain, beans and corn Ed had brought home from the Farmers Coop during the week. He stood immobilized by them. *This morning I planned to come home and start the planting two days early. The original plan was to begin on Monday morning. I was supposed to back the tractor up to the door and fill the planter or grain drill and put the first seed of spring into the ground. It's the most exciting part of the farming process.*

For weeks dad and I walked the fields deciding what crops would be planted in which fields, how the rows would be angled, how furrows would be oriented, and which ditches needed to be re-aligned. We planned everything for the first Monday after school was out. With luck, the soil would be just the right temperature to plant the first seed.

As planned, the sacks of seed were neatly stacked in preparation. All was in readiness except Cliff. Cliff had gone AWOL. *But I came back in time. It was you who jumped the gun, Dad. You who couldn't wait to replace me with Hector!*

There is still time to stay. I can fight for my right to be the man of the farm. What can Hector and his dad say or do? Adrenaline pumped through his veins once more, and he felt the urge to run into the field and demand that the two leave his farm immediately! *Dad can't afford to pay you to work at this place for the summer!*

Then he felt the rush fade, and he felt almost faint. He drooped in the granary doorway. *You know what? It's your choice Dad. You always say 'make your bed, lie in it! If you want Hector and Raul to do the work instead of me, then that's your choice!"*

Disheartened, he took four more used but good burlap sacks from the tall stack, rolled them and put them in his sack. The sack bulged. He couldn't put anything else in there.

He had all he could take back to the ruin with him. He now had a second sack full.

He really wanted white muslin flour sacks that he could use as a mattress liner to fill with cattail seed fluff, but Etta Mae had taken all of those to the house to use for dishrags and towels or even to sew into aprons or skirts.

He stubbornly resisted going back to the house. The next best thing was a short stack of old sheets that Etta Mae had retired. They would be used as rags at calving time or for multiple purposes with the livestock. He took one of the sheets, put it with the sacks and left the rest undisturbed on the shelf.

He filled four of the six quart jars with pinto beans from the nearly empty bin. The other two jars he filled with shelled corn from last year's harvest.

He looked around. On a shelf by the door was a packet of needles used to sew up full or torn burlap bags. Five remained in the set of six. One needle was stuck into the cardboard core of a spindle of jute twine, which Ed used to tie sacks. Cliff took one of the slender six-inch needles. It had a slightly curved, triangular head to penetrate the weave in the heavy burlap sacks and provided a gripping surface to pull the twine through the heavy fabric. The long oblong slotted eye was large enough to take the jute twine. One leg of the eye was thick and sturdy while the opposing leg was thin and cut at an angle to facilitate threading by pulling the twine across the thin spring edge and snapping it into the eye. The rounded pulling end of the eye allowed the twine to be pulled tightly without cutting it.

The sharp leading end of the eye allowed the farmer to cut the twine. Cliff had watched his dad sacking grain. He could sew a sack of grain and stack it all in one continuous motion. Snap a needle onto the trailing edge of a spool of jute; grab an "ear" of the full sack of wheat; throw a loop of jute around it; quickly sew a dozen tightly looping stitches across the top of the sack, cinching each tight; bunch an ear on the opposite side; loop a circle of twine around it and punch a line through; cinch it tight; punch an anchor stitch; then jerk the jute back against the leading end of the needle to cut it; all one continuous movement; without breaking the rhythm, toss the sack onto a wagon or a neat stack to be hauled away later.

Cliff wound off yards of the jute twine into a ball and cut it free of the cone. He stuck the needle through the ball, put the ball, and needle into the original sack with his clothing.

He was anxious to leave but took one last look around, when he spotted Ed's worn packsaddle, used when he took the horses elk hunting in the mountains. Hanging on the back of the saddle were the camp saddlebags.

Cliff checked the pockets in the right side bag and found boxes of weatherproofed matches. Ed had poured paraffin into new, full boxes of wooden matches completely imbedding the matches inside blocks of waterproof wax. In rain or snow, all he had to do was break a match free and it would light, even if everything else in the pack were soaked. In only a week, Cliff had nearly used up his initial box of matches, and he was relieved to see a new source, which he added to his sack.

The left saddlebag held a spare hunting knife. Cliff tested the eight inch curved blade. It was sharp. The leather scabbard was dry and stiff but sound. He felt around in the bottom of the saddlebag and found a whetstone in a box. Cliff dropped the knife in its scabbard, and the whetstone into his front overall pocket.

He picked up the .22. He now had two heavy gunnysacks to haul back to the ruin.

Somewhere in the back of the granary was a bundle hanging on a wire that contained the fishing bags he and his dad had carried the summer before. He took it down and removed the sacks.

Any trace of fish smell had long since aired out. He dumped all the stuff out of his original sack onto the floor. He had pretty well mangled it that morning. He divided the contents of it and the new sack between the two former gunnysack-fishing creels. He added the original, now useless sack to the bundle and tied it back up where he had found it.

He looped the straps of the two used fishing bags over his shoulders, settled the heavy load under his arms, picked up the .22, shifted his load for balance and straightened up.

He stepped outside the granary. *I wish I'd known I wasn't staying before I came here this morning. I wouldn't have brought anything with me. Now I've got to take it all back and more.*

It would be a long walk with a heavy load. Straight down through the lane in the middle of the place to the ruin was only a mile. He couldn't take that route without Hector and Raul seeing him. Backtracking through the woods, the way he had come that morning, was a good five miles.

The two sacks now bulged with new inventory; some of it, like the honey, beans and corn were heavy.

There was another way to get home, and it was not much further than down the lane. He could walk up by the pond and cross the ditch that ran the ridgeline to the south fence line. A row of willows grew along the ditch. No one had cleared the willows since Charlie left for the Army, and they were growing thick. If he went that way, Raul and Hector would not see him, although he would be visible to anyone on the east. If he spotted anyone, like George over to the east he could step into the willows and into the ditch if necessary.

As he headed toward the east and the row of willows, it struck him that all he was setting out to start housekeeping with, in earnest, he now carried on his back and he still had to solve the problem of how to cook most of it.

~~~

How quickly things can change. It had all been so clear that morning. The way to return with honor had been within his grasp. Seeing his mother and father drive by on their way to town without him had given him even more determination to set things right.

Then Raul and Hector had driven up as if they had belonged there. *You betrayed me, sold me out, and replaced me with the very one who whipped me in front of the whole school and Mrs. Campbell. Maybe for a day or two, I just wanted you to carry my shovel Dad, so you understood I was doing something important for you. I could have made life easier for you. You could have made life more bearable for me too, Dad. Instead, you just replaced me with him, just like that!*

He hadn't dwelt on Hector for the last day or so. Hearing Hector's laugh Friday, and seeing Hector up close again, brought back memories of torment by him. Punishment because of Hector, images of the fight and of times he had suffered at the hands of Hector or a pack of kids encouraged or manipulated by Hector went through his mind.

He felt confused and angry again as he carried the heavy load back to the ruin.

Cliff lowered the sack and rifle to the ledge and dropped the rope after it. He climbed down the toeholds to the ledge, transferred everything inside the door and placed the slate over the opening.

He lay down on his stomach at the spring and drank. Then he just lay there in the coolness on the hard clay floor.

After a while, he moved to the saddle blanket and sat. He thought over the emotional high and low moments of the day and then of the week.

He sat staring into nothingness all afternoon never leaving the ruin.

Afternoon turned to night.

He did not build a fire.

He sat in the dark room. With the doorway covered and no fire, the darkness became profound. The faint Milky way starlight hardly filtered through the four small windows near the ceiling.

His fear of the dark intensified, but he fought it as images and rolling thoughts also grew.

Hector is carrying my shovel now. I suppose he will begin driving the tractor Monday and planting the crops. That is costing money that Dad doesn't have. What does Hector know about farming? Mom is doing my chores now, or will she be driving the tractor planting the crops in my place? Or she will be teaching Hector.

It is all my fault.

The thoughts rolled through his mind on an endless loop until finally he nodded, and lay down. Sleep came fitfully.

~~~

The dream began shortly afterward. In the dream, Cliff sat cross-legged on the point overlooking the canyon where he had spotted the deer slowly making their way down the canyon slope. A surreal sunrise was developing over his left shoulder between the peaks of the La Plata Mountains. A wispy thin layer of clouds in layers of vermilion, red and pinks spewed across the sky from behind the huge blood red disk of ole Sol and spread out across the south covering the canyon and the land between it and Mesa Verde. The brilliant psychedelic colors reflected off the sandstone, making the canyon rimrock glisten like a thick layer of freshly hardened and broken milk chocolate sitting atop crumbling thin layers of sugared molasses wafers, freshly stacked, pressed and warm. A dusting of snow on the north facing slopes lay in patches on scraped edges of crumbs, sugar and cinnamon flaked off to gather along slopes and around the smooth butter finger colored sandstone boulders on the canyon floor.

Even in his dream, he was hungry and wanted to go into the canyon to feast on the gigantic delicious confections spread out before him.

Cliff sat in his bib overalls, denim shirt and straw hat. His glossy black hair had grown longer.

He looked down into the canyon where wild turkeys sailed back and forth, and deer grazed contentedly along the willow-lined creek. Unafraid, grouse and quail scratched, fluffed and pecked in the sand and dust around him. Long tailed black and white magpies hopped about carrying on a conversation with chipmunks, and a family of skunks.

A hunter, lithe, athletic body built for endurance, no taller than Cliff, dressed only in breechcloth, with bow in hand and arrows in a quiver slung across his shoulder, stepped out onto the point in front of Cliff.

A slight breeze rippled through the man's long, straight, raven black shoulder length hair.

He reached into a leather pouch tied to a thong at his waist and, extending his right arm, he pointed to the north up the canyon. He began chanting and released a few grains of yellow pollen, swept his arm to the east, released a few more grains of pollen, paused and then swept to the south, repeated the ritual and turned to the west to complete the circle, he lifted his hands to the sky, and pointed down to the earth. He continued to chant as he went through the ritual.

Cliff had never thought of up and down as directions, but the hunter appeared to.

Cliff was an observer not a participant in the ritual.

The man turned to Cliff and nodded to acknowledge his presence for the first time. He clapped his hands together, and then he spread both arms wide and turned his back on Cliff to face the canyon. He began a new chant and with his arms wide he turned in a complete circle to encompass all that surrounded them; the mountains, the mesa, the canyon, the sleeping giant Ute Mountain and the psychedelic sky. Then the hunter turned and pointed to Cliff. He paused and slowly resumed the chant.

The hunter stepped, dipped his shoulder, turned, stepped, dipped his other shoulder, and turned the other way as he chanted there on the point. Cliff became aware of a low throbbing, drumming sound and a chorus of voices coming from the canyon and echoing off the distant escarpment of Mesa Verde. The throbbing drumbeat, chorus and chant mesmerized him as the hunter stepped, dipped, turned, stepped, dipped and turned the other way. Cliff seemed to float to his feet and in perfect synchronous movement with the hunter stepped, dipped and turned. Cliff couldn't understand the words of the chant, but the meaning came to him as clearly, as if the hunter, the drums, and the chorus from the canyon spoke to him in English. Cliff opened his mouth and began to chant in a language he could not understand but in harmony with the hunter and chorus and in time with the drumbeat. It seemed natural and Cliff was unafraid as both he and the hunter stepped out over the rim of the canyon and continued stepping, dipping, and turning on the wispy psychedelic clouds over the canyon.

The clouds shimmered and undulated, and joined a whirlpool of color that slowly receded back into the blood red orb of the sun as Cliff struggled to open his eyes. The straw hat fell down around his face. He gasped for breath, finally tearing the band away and forcing his eyes to open. He lifted his hands to his face and in the faint glow of the red embers of the fire pit recognized the gunnysack in his hands. He sat up.

The strange dream and brilliant colors lingered in vivid detail. It was infinitely different from the nightmares of the past few nights or any dream he had ever experienced before. He felt no fear, no anger, only a feeling of hope, well being and optimism.

Who was the hunter? He was so real. Although he seemed like a powerful figure, he was non-threatening.

I don't remember ever dreaming in color before.

Parts of that landscape and clouds looked like candy. Man, I'd die for a big dime size Butter finger candy bar. He suddenly craved something sweet.

How had he understood the meaning of the chant? But, he hadn't understood the actual words, he had somehow understood the meaning. It was like a poem running through his mind. When he first woke there were verses and many lines, and he tried to remember them all, but they began to fade away.

Cliff felt an overwhelming panic to write down the meaning while he could still remember as much as he could. He chanted the verses over and over to not forget them while they lingered in his memory, but each time he repeated, he forgot several.

He felt next to the fire pit for a cattail seed head, pulled a tuft of cotton and placed it in the cold ashes. He felt for twigs and covered the cotton. The stack lit with one match. He added sticks to that and finally a rich piñon knot and a larger cedar stick.

He reached in the nook for the scrapbook, and it wasn't there. For a moment, he stood in horror. Had he lost it? Then he remembered that it was still in the gunnysack by the door.

The first page of the scrapbook was a blank sheet of paper. *I have to write it down, but there is nothing to write with. Why didn't I bring a pencil? A simple lead pencil. I don't have a pencil, but I do have a piece of lead. He felt in his pocket for a .22 bullet with a soft round nose of pure lead.*

He grasped the bullet between his thumb and first finger and printed the only verse that remained in his memory:

"Adversity presents
Unique opportunity
A moment of time,
In God's wilderness,
Use the time wisely."

He closed the scrapbook and replaced it in the nook where he had kept it all week. A feeling of peace settled over him. He lay back down on the saddle blanket, cradled his head on his arm and went back to sleep. Finally, for the first time that week and many weeks before, he slept soundly and restfully through the rest of the night.

24
Sunday, early morning
Kelley farm

Etta Mae carried the last bucket of milk to the house and prepared to run it through the cream separator. Ed was in the field finishing the morning water set. It was Sunday morning and in better times, he had considered it a sacred day for church and rest. With Clifton gone, and pressure to get crops into the ground, there would be no Bible study or rest on this day.

Hector and his father had taken care of both morning and evening chores and the watering on Saturday, so that she and Ed could take the day to look for their son.

They had lost most of the day Saturday with Sheriff Kirkendall in McElmo Canyon. Ed had directed the sheriff to the end of a barely passable road in a box canyon. They had walked for an additional couple of miles before climbing to cliff dwellings high up on the canyon walls. They had seen other complete dwellings that they couldn't reach without ropes and climbing gear. They assumed Clifton wouldn't have been able to get to them either. There had been no evidence he might have been to any of them.

They had searched until dark and returned home discouraged past their usual bedtime.

Etta Mae assembled the centrifuge and set it on the separator shaft. Over that, she assembled the trays, which directed cream to the cream can and milk to the five-gallon slop bucket.

She poured the first three-gallon bucket of warm milk into the strainer in the bowl on top of the separator and began turning the crank handle to bring the centrifuge up to speed.

She had gone through the motions hundreds of times before. It took little mental process to maintain the speed by monotonously turning the handle, and Etta Mae's thoughts turned to her son. *What was he doing? Where had he spent the night? Was he cold? Hungry? Safe? In danger? It had been some week. She had lost one baby in his infancy and another to the U.S. Army. Had she just lost a third?*

The "chuga, chuga, putt, putt, putt" sound of a John Deere tractor approaching the house broke through her reverie. She turned the flow of milk off and stopped turning the handle.

She peered through the back door as a green and yellow, tri-cycle shaped, John Deere tractor driven by their neighbor, George Williamson, drove down the driveway and disappeared on the lane past the front of the equipment shed. Drawn behind the tractor was a wheat planter. The distinctive popping of the John Deere slowed, and backfired as the heavy flywheel, mounted on the side of the motor, lost momentum and finally coasted to a stop.

A few minutes later, another neighbor, Bob Harris who lived on the neighboring farm between the Kelley's and the schoolhouse, on his dark red Farmall with a bean planter topped the driveway and pulled in behind George's John Deere. Close behind the Farmall was their neighbor, Sam Royce, from across Little Canyon on his Persian Orange Allis Chalmers B pulling a grain drill. Ralph Frederick, from up the road toward Summit Lake, on his Ford appeared in the drive with a bean planter. Rounding out the parade of neighbors was Enrique Martinez on his red case V with a corn planter mounted on the back.

The farmers climbed down from their tractors and stood visiting with each other.

They were obviously ready for work. Sam and Enrique wore Levi jeans. The rest wore overalls. All wore straw hats. Bulging, weeping, canvas water sacks hung from the fenders of their tractors. They were dressed for a long day of work in the field.

Etta Mae was surprised that Ed hadn't told her they were having help. She hadn't prepared to feed extra people for dinner.

A few minutes behind the tractors, cars and pickups began arriving driven by the wives of the farmers. The vehicles swept around the circular driveway and stopped in front of the house. Women headed for the house carrying heavily packed baskets.

A pickup driven by Raul Rodriguez with his wife and son pulled in behind the last tractor. While Raul and Hector joined the men, Raul's wife, Inez, headed to the house with her basket.

All the farmers greeted Raul with handshakes and slaps on the back. A couple of the neighbor farmers good-naturedly conversed with him in Spanish. They teased Hector, who shyly teased back. Although still a boy, Hector was as big as the biggest of the farmers.

Inez called to Hector, who went to the house at her wave. She only had to point at the porch where Etta Mae was turning the separator. Hector motioned for her to let him take over. Etta Mae moved aside and he expertly caught the handle. He checked the bowl. It was still nearly full. There were still two buckets full of milk on the floor. Etta Mae left him with it and joined the women in the kitchen. Hector had turned the separator handle for the past four evenings and continued with confidence.

Ed came hurrying through the gate from the field with his shovel over his shoulder and approached the group of men. The caravan of tractors and equipment assembled in his equipment yard puzzled him.

"George, Sam, Enrique, Ralph, Bob, Raul. Morning to you," he said.

"Ed," George and the rest returned the greeting.

"So what's going on?" Ed asked.

"Well, Ed," George began. "We thought you might can use some help."

"That's kindly of you, but I can take care of things, thank you," Ed said. "We don't need your feeling sorry for us over here."

"Feeling sorry for anyone doesn't even enter into it, Ed. Well, Ed, we figure it's payback time," George said.

"Over the years, you've taken time to keep every one of these old tractors running and every piece of equipment here fixed and working right," Ralph said. I don't recollect that you accepted a penny for it."

"Now you've got a problem. You need some time to be concerned about it. You just have to show us where you want the seed planted, and today if you have everything in stock, we think we can get it all in the ground," Sam said.

Ed looked dumbfounded. He started to protest, but saw the looks on their faces.

Bob held up both hands to shush him. "Now Ed we want to do this. You've never taken a dime for your time helping us and now, as George said, it's payback time. It's what neighbors ought to do."

Ed gave up. "Etta Mae and I are mighty appreciative. The seed is in the granary."

With the sole of his shoe, he smoothed out an area in the dust of the lane. He broke a twig from the elm tree at the corner of the machine shed, and in the dust, he outlined his fields, the slopes, and the direction of the runs.

"Beans will be planted in the east field, on the west draining slope. I'd like corn here on this south slope draining northwest. Wheat and barley on the west slope draining to the east."

When George had contacted the other farmers, they had agreed the kind of planter to bring so that each crop was covered. He knew pretty well, what their preferences were so each would be planting the kind of seed for which they were best equipped. As Ed sketched where he wanted each crop planted, his neighbors studied to see where they would be working that day. Afterward they all walked to the gate at the lane leading to the fields and climbed up. The little bit of elevation helped so they could see each area as Ed pointed out the various slopes that he had just drawn.

After Ed answered all their questions, he humbly said, "Gentlemen, I'm much obliged."

"Well, what are we standing around for?" Bob Harris asked.

The farmers pulled their tractors into a line in front of the granary where Raul and Hector helped them load their grain drills and planters from the seed stock, and one by one, the tractors exited the barnyard for the fields to begin planting. By 8:00 a.m., five dust clouds rose into the air.

Last to the field was Ed on his own Ford with the corn planter on the back.

Raul and Hector loaded the remainder of the sacks of beans, corn, wheat and barley seed onto the pickup. They followed the tractors down the central lane, and parked next to Dog Town in sight of all the men.

When a planter or drill ran low on seed the farmer stopped and waved his hat in their direction. Raul immediately drove over the unplanted ground to him, and he and Hector refilled the planter. The driver took time to relieve himself in the shade of the tractor, get a drink of water from the water sack, and as soon as Raul drove the pickup away, got back on the tractor and continued either circling the field, if planting grain, or working back and forth if planting corn or bean rows.

Back at the house, the wives busily rolled out dough for light bread rolls, picked young frying roosters, peeled potatoes, gathered lambs quarter in the orchard and in general prepared the noon meal while they caught up on neighborhood gossip.

They tried to keep the conversation light and away from the question uppermost in their minds. What they really wanted to know was what was happening in the search for Etta Mae's son? When they broke for coffee at midmorning and sat around the dining room table. Etta may set out a tray of cinnamon rolls.

She finally told them what she knew. She told them about their search among the ruins in McElmo the day before and the theory that Cliff might be trying to live somewhere in one of the ruins.

Each of the women had her own theory to share.

"George goes along with that idea, but with a little difference, Etta Mac," Lorreta Williamson said finally.

Etta Mae set her cup down, "Oh?"

Loretta looked at the other wives shyly. She weighed whether to say more. She had listened to Etta Mae's report of the search the day before and the official search going on in McElmo using the Indian search and rescue unit from the Ute Reservation. It wrenched her heart. George had told her his theory and told her to keep it on the cuff, but Etta Mae had a right to all the hope she could get. "George thinks your son never really left."

"What?" Etta Mae asked. "Never left? Does he think we made this up?" She asked incredulously.

All eyes were suddenly on Loretta.

"Of course not! He thinks nothing of the sort. Of course, he is gone, but George thinks he's nearby, that he never really ran far away! He thinks that Clifton is hiding out around here somewhere. Maybe in one of the canyons here on the Ridge like Martinez Canyon, not down in McElmo. He's searching the canyons around here when he can. He checked out Martinez Canyon behind our place yesterday."

"Did he see anything?"

"Well no. He walked the full length of that Canyon. He said something wasn't quite right down there, but he couldn't put a finger on it. He thought he smelled something like cedar smoke from a campfire, and something was wrong with the deer tracks in one area, but he couldn't quite figure it out. He'll be going back again to take a look," she said. "George has good intuition. I've seen it before. And when he gets into something, he doesn't turn loose easily. He'll keep going down into that canyon until he is absolutely certain."

"Did he tell the sheriff?"

"They did talk about it and will continue to keep in close touch about anything he finds. However, I think he wants to look some more first before he gets anyone's hopes up. He knows that canyon like the back of his hand, you know."

"If only it were so," Etta Mae sighed. "If I just knew where he is and that he is OK, I could live with that.

~~~

He was hungry and there was nothing left in the cave to eat except the quart of honey. He cut an inch square of comb with his pocketknife and put it into his mouth dripping some onto his chin in the process. He bit into the comb, mashed the sweetness out, and savored the wonderfulness of it all as the smooth honey ran down his throat.

Nothing on this earth is this good. He chewed the wax and let the honey roll around in his mouth and then trickle down his throat savoring the taste as long as he could draw it out. When only the wax remained, he chewed it until no taste remained. He worked the wax into a ball, took it out of his mouth, and put it into a corner of the nook with the jar of honey.

He licked the knife clean and licked his chin as far down as he could reach with his tongue. Then he wiped the rest off with his finger and licked his finger. He washed his face in the spring and rinsed his mouth. Last, he ran his dripping fingers through his hair and shook out the water.

The honey began to put energy into his system and sweetened his outlook.

He sat down and put his socks and shoes on. His socks smelled ripe. He needed to wash them with soap. Just rinsing them each night wasn't enough.

Cliff climbed the vertical face of the cliff out over the rimrock using
~~~

the toe and handholds. Tied to his back was the .22. The jute had already come in handy. He was on his way to the canyon to hunt a rabbit for breakfast. *To heck with the noise. If they hear it, let them. School's out. Half the kids on the Ridge will be out shooting rabbits now.*

No cloud marred the perfect deep blue Colorado sky. The air was crystal clear and the La Plata Mountains looked close enough to walk over to this morning.

For the first time in a week, he felt at peace with the world. He had awakened fresh.

He had hummed a strange chant as he washed his face and climbed the rope and then suddenly a thought came to his mind.

"Adversity presents unique opportunity, a moment of time in God's wilderness, use the time wisely."

Images of the dream began to unfold. The message. He vaguely remembered writing it down, or had he dreamed that too? *It seemed to say you have an opportunity to do something instead of sitting around feeling sorry for yourself. You can take the opportunity to become self-reliant. Time is short. Move on. Earth Mother and Heavenly Father have provided you a wilderness now use it.*

He recalled parts of the dream. The vivid psychedelic colors, the Indian hunter and the dance; ancient voices echoing from the canyon and a message that seemed to be communicated to him either from spirits in the canyon or from his own subconscious.

His bruises had mostly healed. Only faint tenderness remained in his ribs. The scabs were ready to drop off his forehead and cheeks. He was healthy by nature and usually healed quickly. His only recurring physical complaint was the occasional migraine.

He had walked only a hundred yards or so before the sound began to break into his thoughts. At first, he thought the sound was bees swarming at either the cliff dwelling bee tree or the pueblo ruin bee tree, but when he got to the tree in the clearing, everything looked normal. The steady column of workers coming and going to the fields was uninterrupted. No brown cluster hung from a nearby branch, and no bees swirled around the tree. Everything was business as usual.

The droning sound came from the direction of the farm. He walked on toward the north. The sound grew, and he recognized it as several tractors working together. The closer he got to the south fence line the more able he was to distinguish individual tractors like John Deere's one cylinder popping, and high pitched four cylinder engines of Fords, Allis Chalmers and Farmalls.

There was nothing unusual about hearing any of the familiar tractors as they were the neighborhood workhorses, but it was odd to hear them all working together, especially on a Sunday morning.

Dust rose above the various fields on the Kelley farm. On Saturday, the fields lay bare ready for planting. Cliff had plowed the fields after school and on weekends after the fall harvest finished. As soon as fields were free of snow and frost in late April, he had gone over them with the disk and harrow to smooth the soil for planting. For the past two weeks, he and his dad had checked the soil temperature and moisture content almost every day to decide when it was time to plant. They had finally decided he could begin on Monday after school was out.

Cliff recognized George Williamson planting wheat on his John Deere. Ralph Frederick and Bob Harris were planting beans. His dad and Enrique were planting corn. Sam Royce was drilling barley.

Cliff moved along the edge of the woods for a better view of the activity.

In one day, the neighbors were doing the job that would have taken him possibly two weeks to finish. They were all experienced farmers and had worked out their own efficient systems. He watched in fascination as Ralph, planting beans, waved to Raul. The pickup started up and headed across the unplanted part of the field toward him.

Cliff watched Hector lift a hundred pound sack up to the planter hopper, fill it, and carry the remainder of the sack to the second hopper and fill it. Ralph tipped his head back and drank from the water bag without getting off the Ford. As Hector carried the empty gunnysack back to the pickup, Ralph started the Ford and was already continuing up the slope finishing off the row of pinto beans he had started. The whole stop had taken only minutes.

If I'd been planting by myself, I'd of had to drive from the field back to the granary to refill. I'd of dipped beans out of a hundred pound sack into a bucket, carried the bucket to the planter, poured the bucket into the hopper, gone back to the granary for another bucketful to finish one hopper and then two more buckets for the other hopper. It would have taken me over a half hour to refill the planter and get back to the field. Ralph and Bob will finish planting the beans today easy. It'd probably take me more than two days.

They'll work hard but have fun today. Mom and the other women are probably cooking a big dinner right now. At noon, they'll all gather around for lots of food, good conversation and farmer jokes. They'll have pies and fresh homemade ice-cream, and then they'll go back to the fields for the afternoon or until they are done. No one'll get into trouble if a few beans or corn get spilled, or if a row is a little crooked.

Cliff stood under the piñon tree watching the activity. He ached to be part of it. This time he would have liked to be part of the team.

But, if I hadn't taken off, that party wouldn't be happening.

I probably should have stayed yesterday, but I didn't. I should walk out of these woods and join the planting crew now! That's what I should do. I see Dad driving the Ford tractor. I could walk up, flag him down and offer to take his place on the driver's seat. "Hi, Dad," I could say, "How's it going?"

I'm sure he'd be just fine. It's probably the perfect opportunity. How could he take off his belt and give me the whipping I probably deserve right there in the field in front of all those men? All would be nice, "Glad you came back son, so good you are safe, ta da, ta da, ta da." Then all the men would go home at the end of the day.

No Mom and Dad are going to be OK Their friends are helping them out. They haven't forgotten all those favors dad did them over the years. Good for them. Getting it all in the ground is the hard part. Harvesting it will be the next big one. We'll see if they come around again.

I'll just keep an eye on it from a distance.

Cliff turned from where he stood watching the activity from under a piñon tree. He gripped the .22 and walked back toward the canyon. They were making plenty of noise. No one will hear me if I shoot. He parked himself near the creek in a grassy area and waited. A visit to the creek by a flock of grouse was his reward for waiting. His excitement rose as he watched the chicken size game birds pick at insects and greenery, then settle in the dust in the trail and fluff the fine dust up through their feathers.

The flock flew, but left one member behind when he fired. He would have more trouble picking the bird than skinning a rabbit, but then again, if he skinned it, he wouldn't have to pick it. It was easier to skin the bird while it was warm. He did so, packed it in fresh green grass and packed it in the bottom of the burlap bag hanging around his shoulder. He kept the skin with the feathers attached. He would finish dressing the grouse back at the cave.

He picked an ample supply of shoots from the asparagus growing along the bank and in the cattail marsh. He also stripped clover blossoms to dry when he got back to the cave.

~~~

As the sun climbed overhead, Ed glanced more frequently toward the house. It was nearing dinnertime. The wives would have spent the morning preparing a hearty noon meal to feed the farmers who had generously given up their day of rest to put his crops into the ground on time. His heart swelled with gratitude toward his neighbors' generosity. They had worked hard all week in their own fields, and now they were here on their own day of rest helping him.

He smiled as he saw the familiar white cloth begin waving from the back porch a few minutes later, and he relayed the message by stopping his tractor, standing on the seat and waving his straw hat, until he got answering waves from all the others.

He finished the row, killed the motor and waited beside the tractor until Raul made the rounds gathering the men in the back of the pickup, finally stopping for him last. He crawled over the tailgate and sat down on a sack of beans among his neighbors for the bumpy ride up the lane to the farmhouse.

The only things they brought to the house with them were their water sacks and their appetites. When they returned to the field, Ed would load a barrel of gas into the back of the pickup so the tractors could be re-fueled without having to drive them back to the house.

The men took turns washing the dust off their faces, hands and necks
~~~

under the faucet at the corner of the equipment shed. Several complimented Ed for his ingenuity in piping running water down to his house and outbuildings from the pond.

"Didn't the original house sit right where the reservoir is now?" Sam asked.

"As a matter of fact, it did," George answered. "It sat up there on the highest spot on Ed's place, right out in the open. Nearest tree was that cottonwood that's still there on the ditch just down from the pond. The best idea Ed ever had was moving his house down here by the timber. He's sheltered here from the southwest and north winds. And by moving down here, he can bring his water down from the reservoir by gravity."

The women had the big kitchen-dining room table set, when the men marched through the back door. A fresh white tablecloth covered the extended dining table. Etta Mae pointed to it. "Seat yourselves," she said. The men randomly seated themselves, each leaving a spot next to himself for his wife.

"We miss Dulcina today," Sam Royce said.

"She sends her regrets, Enrique said. "She had already promised Angelina that she would take her to Durango to a concert for her graduation present. She has had the tickets for several months. It is a traveling show. They went early for church and are spending the day. They excused me to help our friends Ed and Etta for the day."

"And we thank you for that," Etta Mae said, pulling out a chair for him.

The table was soon loaded with a pot of pinto beans, bowls of mashed potatoes, cottage cheese and fresh boiled greens (lambs quarter weeds picked from the edge of the garden, as the spinach was still too small to pick). A plate piled high with light bread buns, a heaping platter of golden fried chicken, a big platter of *tamales* and a casserole dish of *enchiladas* rounded out the main course. Condiments included a large saucer of fresh churned butter, a pitcher of cold milk, a smaller pitcher of sweet cream, a bowl of red chili powder, salt, pepper, homemade catsup, sorghum syrup, white and brown sugar, home canned jalapeño peppers and a small dish of ground red chili pepper.

The women finally sat down by their husbands and Ed gave grace. Around the table were Mormons, Catholics, reformation fundamentalists and George the Agnostic. It was a long prayer, even for Ed, as he included especially heartfelt thanks for his neighbor's generosity and capped it with, "And Heavenly Father look out for our son Clifton, wherever he may be. Keep him safe from harm and return him soon to us. Please let him know somehow that he is loved and that his loved ones and neighbors wish his speedy return. In Our Savior's name, Amen."

Even George joined the chorus of Resounding "Amen's" repeated around the table.

Etta Mae and Raul's wife Inez started to rise from the table.

"Where are you two going?" Ed asked.

"Well I need to wait the table," Etta Mae said nervously.

"Me too," Inez said haltingly. Her English was poor, and he doubted that she had ever sat at a table with so many Anglo neighbors before.

"Now you both just sit and enjoy your meal. I think we have everything here we need until we're ready for those pies," he said pointing to the counter where several fresh baked pies cooled.

The chatter was friendly and mostly about the coming growing season. There was general speculation about the chances of favorable weather and prices. Sam Royce turned to Inez and spoke to her in Spanish. She beamed and spoke back at some length.

Enrique translated to the rest of the table. "He asked Inez how it is to raise twins. She told him it is double the trouble but twice the love. Fortunately she has many helpers as the twins are the youngest." He paused and Inez said one short sentence. "So far," he laughed.

"How are your girls doing, Enrique?" Ralph Fredrick asked.

"Well, I have two families as you know. My older daughters are grown and married, and from them, I have six beautiful grand children. I have grandsons now although they will not carry my name. And I have my young family. She was, what would you say? An afterthought? Dulcina and I thought we were through raising children, and we could sit back and spoil our grandchildren and send them home with their parents and then, surprise! Angelina came along. What a precious gift from God. This fall, she goes to high school. Then I will have to get my double barrel 12 gauge shotgun loaded with birdshot. By the way, Ed, your boy and my Angelina were eating fish together at the fish fry last summer. When he comes home, you'd better watch him. He might come home with a seat full of buckshot one night."

Everyone around the table laughed heartily.

Enrique turned to Hector. "And the same goes especially for you, young man!"

Hector blushed, but just ducked his head as his dad reached over and mussed his hair.

Hector ate and watched his mother and father with the Anglo neighbors. He had not wanted to come today. He had expected these people to blame him for the trouble. However, no one had said anything or acted ill toward him. He felt at ease, more so than he had expected. They treated him well. He had worked that morning as an equal among the men. This morning he was prepared to see the other men treat his father as a servant, but it was not happening that way. Respect had been shown to both his mother, father and to him.

Raul had bossed the other men around when he needed to get the tractors in the right position for them to refill the planters. He had been there with the seed as they needed it almost exactly as they ran out. It had been beautiful to watch the cooperation and trust the men had for each other.

The other reason he didn't want to come this morning, was that he didn't want to see his mother be a servant to the other farmwomen. But he did not see that at this table. His mother's *tamales, enchiladas* and *tortillas* were among the first platters emptied. They were actually almost all gone before the platters got to him. She sat at the table with the other wives and was a participant in the conversation, thanks to the Spanish-speaking farmer, her proud husband and their neighbor Enrique.

"You ever think about cooking *tamales* like these and selling them?" Ralph Frederick asked Inez.

Sam translated to her.

"No, no," she said covering her mouth with her hand, embarrassed by the compliment.

"She is a very good cook," Raul said seriously. "However, she has many mouths to feed at home. Someday when the children have all gone, maybe she will open a small *cantina*. It is her dream."

"You'll have at least one steady customer," Sam said in Spanish and again in English.

The conversation continued good-naturedly until finally George asked the question they all wanted to ask, "What's the status of the search, Ed?"

All conversations stopped. Ed put down a half-eaten chicken back and said slowly, "Nothing yet. Sheriff Kirkendall turned the Ute Search and Rescue unit loose down in McElmo yesterday. They are checking out ruins in the area where Clifton and I have explored before. We thought he might have headed there. They should know soon if anybody has been back in there. We went down yesterday, but we didn't see anything. It's a big country and we don't know what kind of instincts he has for this kind of thing. We just know that he took a book that he put together, as a school assignment. It has a lot of information on how the Indians lived, and what they lived on. That's all we have to go on."

Raul translated simultaneously in a quiet voice to Inez.

"I took a good look at Martinez Canyon yesterday, Ed." George said slowly. "I kind of thought he might just stay a little closer to home. It'd be a little tricky getting past Cortez to get down into the canyon, wouldn't it?"

"We think he'd travel some at night. If he hit McElmo creek and followed it, that would take him right on through Cortez. I don't think anyone would even notice a kid walking along the creek in town because kids walk along there all the time."

"Funny you should think he would travel at night. If I recollect correctly, seems like he was pretty much afraid of the dark," George said.

"I'll say," Etta Mae said. "I've never seen somebody as afraid of the dark as he is, thanks to his brother Charlie. If he's down in one of those canyons at night, he's got to be terrified. I just can't believe that's where he is. I don't know, but that's where Ed and Bill think, and that's where they're looking. We don't know where else to look."

I had a really funny feeling yesterday," George said. "I had this feeling that he was nearby. I couldn't pinpoint where, but I think he's closer than you think," George said. "I thought for sure he was watching me."

Hector was very uncomfortable with the talk. Everyone knew what spark had ignited the situation. He suddenly wanted to be excused, but he couldn't ask that, nor could he just get up and leave.

"Where do you think he would go?" George asked suddenly, turning to the boy. "If it were you, where would you go?"

Hector felt all eyes turn to him. "Well, *Señor,* he must eat, and he must sleep. He cannot work. Maybe he hides. When nobody is looking, maybe he comes out and takes something to eat. Maybe he sleeps in a barn or a hole in the ground at night. There are old buildings all around," Hector said. "Maybe one of those."

"Tell them what you and the kids did the last day of school, Hector," Etta Mae said.

"The kids in the neighborhood know where every hiding place is," he said. "When we play games, or when we explore, we find every place there is. So on Friday we went out searching. We went every were. Emilio, and Ignacio, Porferio, Felix, Ana, and me took the horses and the younger kids either went with us or searched on foot."

"That was a good idea," Ed said. Mrs. Campbell helped to organize them, and as you know she got permission from you guys and the other local farmers for the kids to check old buildings that aren't used much more anymore and are out of sight."

"So did you find anything?" George asked.

"No, *Señor,*" Hector said. He was very uncomfortable and his face was beginning to sweat. "But I think we must keep on looking. We looked in all the places we knew."

"Thank you Hector," Ed said. "We appreciate all the effort you and the other kids put in."

"Thank you, *Señor,*" Hector said.

"And now Etta Mae I think it time for some of that mince meat pie. You like pie Hector?"

"I don't know that pie," Hector said.

"You're in for a treat," Bob Harris said. "Nobody makes mince meat like Etta Mae. It's her secret recipe.

Ed looked at his neighbors sitting around his table enjoying each other's company as they ate their dinner after a productive morning in the fields. A tear rolled down his cheek as he spoke, "The only thing that could have made this a more perfect day would have been if Cliff had come walking out of the woods this morning and joined us."

"Amen!" the men and women echoed.

"I wish for that too." Hector said. "I am so sorry, Mr. Kelley and Mrs. Kelley," he whispered.

"So Enrique, you think if Ed brings out his old guitar you might play a little something on it while this dinner settles?" Sam asked.

Enrique smiled. "Well since Dulcina wasn't here to help the cooking, but I ate my share, I suppose I could play for my dinner."

While Etta Mae poured coffee and the other wives cleared dishes and served pie around the table, Enrique tuned the old guitar that Ed handed him.

He began strumming it, and for 20 minutes, he played and sang ballads. The lyrics were all in Spanish. Most of the men and women around the table, except for Raul, Inez and Hector, were not familiar with the music. Nevertheless, they enjoyed the mood, the music and the camaraderie. Enrique's voice was full and rich, and he sang with feeling.

Finally, he began to lightly slap the body of the guitar with his hand alternately as he flicked the strings with the back of his fingers and settled into a flamenco rhythm and nodded to Raul and Inez.

Raul stood and held his hand out to Inez, who also stood. Raul bowed to her, and they posed, and she began to slowly dance around him. Sam Harris began to clap in time to the rhythm of the guitar.

The Mexican man and his wife seemed to feed off the obvious enthusiasm of the other couples as they danced their version of the classical Spanish dance until Enrique, accompanied by Sam, finished with a flourish.

Everyone applauded and Enrique handed the old guitar back to Ed with a compliment on the guitar's sound.

They had a job to finish.

~~~

Cliff stood on the ledge and stared at the busy column of bees coming and going into the bee tree. How he envied the worker's lives. They all knew their tasks and did them without question.

He walked to the dwelling, stepped through the doorway and leaned the .22 against the wall next to the dwelling entrance. He unslung the bag with the grouse and greens, carried it to the back of the cave and hung it there to stay cool.

When the coals were ready, he washed the bird and used the same spit he had used to roast the rabbits. He suspended the plump bird over the hot cedar coals and stared listlessly into the coals as he turned the bird occasionally. After it was done, he sat on the doorsill eating. It was good, but his appetite was gone.

He wrapped most of the meat along with the greenery in the grass, put them back in the bag and hung them in the back of the cave to keep. He went back to sit on the doorsill then moved inside and sat on the floor. He turned, put his arms on the sill, lay his chin on his crossed arms and stared past the bee tree cedar and across the canyon.

How often have I been ashamed of you, Dad, for giving so much time, effort and resources to our neighbors without hesitation or charging them for it? They took advantage of you. Every time I tried to point that out to you, you cut me off with, "Do unto others, as you would have them do unto you..."

I didn't understand that, but I guess the neighbors did. Obviously, they respected you for it, and that's why they're out there today. They sure ain't out there
~~~

for me! Why couldn't they have just stayed away for a few days and let me come back on my own and do my job?! But, how could they know? They didn't trust me to do the right thing, obviously. "Use the time wisely.."

Is that it, there wasn't time? What if it rains next week? What if it rains tomorrow and the crop wasn't planted? Then what? So if I had been at home what difference would it have made? I guess all would have been well. It would have been God's will. Well maybe this was all God's will too. What do you think of that? What about it God? Is this your plan? Is this some kind of practical joke? Dad says the earth is only 5,000 years old and the Bible proves it. However, we find petrified dinosaur bones down in McElmo Canyon. It takes a lot longer than 5,000 years to create petrified bone. When I ask Dad about that, he explains it as God's way of testing our faith. So what is this? Another practical joke? My faith hasn't been all that strong lately anyway, so sure I failed, but Dad's faith has always been strong. Are you testing his? Am I just some piece being moved around in a puzzle to test Dad's faith?

Cliff turned. He sat down on the floor, faced inside the ruin and stared, unseeing, into the back of the cave. The dark shadows there more closely matched his thoughts than the sunny warm colors in the canyon.

Visions of the past summer began to march through his mind. *Under the cotton wood tree reading Zane Gray… oblivious to water pouring down gopher holes… "I don't know why there are burned spots in the alfalfa Dad!" ...an arm raised with the belt descending… "it must be blight in the corn Dad…" "It'll never happen again, I promise"…slipping a book out of the house a few days later… dreaming about riding across the purple sage with Zane Gray… cool shade and soft grass under the cottonwood… precious water running freely through the culvert, escaping unused into the canyon…*

Hector, Emilio, Maria, Ignacio, Felix, Porferio, Carmen, and the others milling around the school grounds playing in small groups, unable to play softball because he decides to take a whipping again and refuses to play… Mr. Johnson sitting inside the schoolhouse supervising… without total participation, there aren't enough kids to field a team… ha, ha, ha, play rough, you don't play... Take that.

A team! I didn't want to be on the team. I was last to be chosen. I got hurt. You didn't want to be my friend. Then I didn't want to be yours. I just wanted to be left alone! If we couldn't be friends, why couldn't you just go away?

The family is supposed to be a team, but when we do something that requires teamwork, I'm the one they sent to run get whatever they left at home. It seems like I always miss out on half of whatever the rest of the team is doing, half the time, I can't find what they forgot. They forgot it, they should go get it!

This summer I would have been a part of the real team. They were depending on me. I'm not sure that I could have done it. Now, I have already let them down before I got started. Now I'll never be able to prove that I could have done it. I've done it again… water escaping into the canyon…

Why was Hector walking down the lane with my shovel? So what's up with him? Hector has been bragging about going to the mountains to help his uncle with the sheep. He's been bragging about that all year. He's been really proud that he was finally old enough to go. Maybe being out there with my shovel wasn't his idea after all. Wouldn't that be interesting? From the way he talked, I didn't think any amount of money would have kept him away from the mountains. Is his dad making him carry my shovel? Have I messed up his life too? Why do I care? A few days ago I set out to kill him. He went after me first!

A week ago I waited by the road ready to shoot Hector, a member of a family. What would that have done to Raul and Inez, Maria, Pitina, Cesar, Margaret, Hermano, and the rest of his family? Would that group of neighbors be out there today having a planting celebration helping my dad if I'd shamed our name by carrying through with my impulse?

I'm glad there are no mirrors here. I don't want to see this face!

Why is the conflict between Hector and me only at school?

I've been to his house, and Hector or his brothers or sisters have come to my house with messages from Inez or Raul. It was Hector who came galloping up to the house on his horse with a message for Dad to come quick, when his mother was in labor and had to go to the hospital. Dad took her to the hospital, and she had the twins.

I delivered messages to Hector's house several times. I didn't want to, but not because of Hector. It was their dogs. Everybody is afraid of their dogs. His mother Inez doesn't speak very good English and so Hector, Maria, or Pitina had to translate for her. No one ever invited me inside the house except Mary. Once, Mary insisted I come in out of the hot sun while she translated the message to her mother.

As Mary translated the note, I looked around the little house. I realized fourteen people lived there. It wasn't much bigger than this cave. It looked like the inside of this dwelling too. Raul must have made it out of mud bricks from the field next to the house. The floor was dirt just like the floor here in the ruin.

Hector's mom was cooking on a wood cook stove. She had a washtub and a washboard hanging on the wall outside the door. Maybe she was heating water on the stove to hand wash clothes for her twelve kids every day. Every time we drive by, we see clothes drying on the long lines next to the garden. Dad said Inez waters the garden with grey water from the kitchen, baths and laundry. I wonder if the same tub of water is used for the whole family to bathe in. No wonder Hector has been looking forward to going to the mountains this summer to help his uncle with the sheep. I'll bet I've messed that up too.

Mrs. Rodriguez and Mary were nice to me that day. Inez offered me a drink of cold water. I was surprised that a dirt house with a dirt floor could be so clean and orderly. How can Hector's mother raise twelve children, feed them and send them to school clean and in clean clothes each day?

That day I went home feeling embarrassed by the conveniences that my family enjoyed: electricity, phone, concrete floors, indoor running water, electric water heater, shower, gas cook stove and electric lights.

Is that why Hector and the other kids hate me? Do I give them the impression by word or attitude that I think I'm better than they are? Probably.

Don't they understand how lucky they are to have that big family to depend on, and how lucky they are to have each other to talk to and to help each other?

Cliff looked at the .22 rifle leaning against the wall. *It would be so easy.*

I won't be the one who will have to clean up the mess if they ever do find me! It might be another seven hundred years before an archeologist has an interesting time trying to figure it all out.

Tears ran freely down his face. He had fought against being a part of the group effort. Well, now it looked like there was no choice. The group didn't need him or want him.

That winter Mrs. Campbell had given him a thin book to read entitled, *The Man Without a Country*, By Edward Everett Hale. The patriotic story was about a fictional character, Philip Nolan, tried in 1807 as an accomplice to traitor Aaron Burr. Nolan renounced his nation during his trial saying, "Damn the United States! I wish I may never hear of the United States again!" The judge granted him his wish and convicted him to spend the rest of his life on war ships of the US Navy in exile with no right to ever again set foot on U.S. soil and with no mention ever again made to him of the country of his birth.

When Cliff had read it, he had thought it an interesting story and was touched by the ending when the old dying Philip Noland showed an officer his room, which Nolan had made into a shrine of patriotism.

Cliff stared at the cool water in the spring in the edge of the cave and looked around the dwelling. *Is this to become my prison within sight of home? Had Mrs. Campbell sensed that I was somehow heading toward a life of exile and isolation by avoiding being part of the group?*

I am not a traitor, or am I? I suppose to my father, I am. He put pressure on me to accomplish something that would have been worthwhile to me and to my family, my team, and I ran away, just as I always ran away from Hector's challenges. Now it's too late.

My sentence has been handed down. Am I too 'a man without a country?'

Book II

Monday June 1, 2000
After the lockdown, Before third period
South High School,

The lock down ended. The alleged shooter at Northside High School was in custody. Three students were confirmed dead. Twenty-three were injured and had been transported to the two local hospitals. Six were in critical condition and undergoing surgery. Ten were in intensive care.

Police had confirmed that Mrs. Emma Whitley, French Teacher at South High School, mother of the alleged shooter, Zack Whitley, was dead from gunshot wounds at her home.

Psychologists and school district counselors had descended en mass on North High School. A few were diverted to South.

Stunned South students filed out of classrooms into hallways. Students who ordinarily would have hardly acknowledged each other an hour and a half before, embraced wordlessly, comforting each other in their shared loss of innocence. They joined the stream of students who flowed down the stairways and out the doors into the sun-drenched courtyard.

The lock down had lasted through the first period class and most of the second period. Strict adherence to schedule was suspended for the day. Bells were quieted. The dismissal announcement had offered an hour for students and staff to assemble in the gym for a general update and assurances that they were safe. Students could use rest rooms, call home and visit with counselors who had set up tables in the cafeteria.

Many of the students had drawn art and written messages to place on the school sign in front of the street entrance and in the hallway outside Madame Emma Whitley's room as a show of affection and respect.

The announcement said the class schedule would resume at 11:00. The rest of the day would run on a shortened class schedule. Teachers were to postpone scheduled final exams for the day. Privately, teachers were counseled to grade students on credits accumulated so far in lieu of a final if a student missed an exam, especially if it pertained to a senior in good standing.

Mr. Clifton Kelley locked his classroom door and walked downstairs to the faculty room near the main office where teachers were gathering from all parts of the building.

Subdued greetings replaced the usual upbeat chatter and by-play that commonly welcomed anyone entering the faculty room.

He filled his coffee mug with the strong institutional brew and filled a paper plate with cheese and crackers.

Traditionally, teachers dropped by the faculty room between classes, during their preparation periods and at lunch time during the final week of school, as the secretarial staff maintained a continuing smorgasbord of snacks all day long.

Clifton hadn't thought he would have an appetite after the emotional experience with the prolonged first period class. Surprisingly, he felt exhausted and almost weak with hunger. He sat down with the plate and coffee in the corner of the room and watched his colleagues.

He looked from face to face as they poured coffee, made tea or took juice from the little refrigerator. Some filled a plate with snacks, or grazed, seemingly oblivious to what they were doing.

John, a math teacher, took a handful of grapes and visited quietly with Larry, a history teacher. John was a retired Army officer, and now chairperson of his department. Larry's social studies classes were legendary. Other teachers occasionally used their prep time sitting in on his classes to study his techniques. Younger staff members sought out both teachers for mentoring and classroom advice.

Ingrid, a special needs teacher and local coordinator of the Special Olympics Program was on the phone as usual.

"Four more days to go for you, huh, Cliff?"

Clifton turned. Steve Boyd, the Crafts' teacher, balanced a paper plate of fruit on top of the coffee mug in his left hand. In his right hand was a sheaf of papers. He was in the act of sitting down without upsetting the delicate balance of coffee and plate.

"Yea, looks like it," Clifton replied. "If I hold together that long."

"Emma and you are going to leave a big void around here," Steve said. "You picked the right time to retire. Wish I was going with you."

"You got that right about Emma. I don't know that my absence will be noticed that much," Clifton said. "My kids were devastated about Emma this morning."

"Yea, and it still hasn't really sunk in."

"You know I was just looking around at the people in this room. This isn't a magnet school, or a performing arts school, or a rich school in an affluent neighborhood. It's a solid, ordinary, neighborhood high school in a blue class community. I can't think of a finer bunch of people," Clifton said. "Nowhere would we find a higher level of talent, and professionalism, and dedication than has gathered to teach at this school. If what happened to Emma had happened to you, or John, or Larry, or Craig out in P.E. or any one of the sixty-five other men and women here...." Clifton said before his throat closed up and he choked.

Steve set his cup down, reached his hand across and cupped Clifton's hand. "I know..."

Clifton looked down at that hand clasped with his in friendship. He closed his eyes. *Thank you Heavenly Father and my Guiding Spirits here on earth for your help. I've been fortunate to have lived and worked alongside people like these. I admire them and they are my friends. As I sit here among my friends sharing our grief in this loss of a beautiful friend, mind, and colleague, I thank you Heavenly Father and Earthly Spirits for looking after me and giving me a second chance back when I considered taking a life and giving up on my own. Without your help and intervention, I would never have known her or these people or have worked among them. Like Zack, I was harassed, I felt alone, and depressed. I was on the outside, believing I would never belong. Please look after Zack. Please help him now.*

The Cliff Dwelling, Martinez Canyon
The Kelley Farm
Summit Ridge, Colorado
Summer 1954

30
Clover Tea
Martinez Canyon

Saturday had begun for Cliff with a decision to return home to his family with a prayer for forgiveness for worrying them.

However, he had seen those high hopes for forgiveness dissolve as he watched Raul and Hector arrive to take his place in the fields, and the following morning neighbors had shown up on their tractors to do his job planting spring crops. Instead of risking public humiliation rather than a reunion, he had fled back to the cave unseen.

He cried and raged out of control until finally, in the middle of the night, the migraine returned for its second visit of the week. Excruciating, throbbing pain began in his right temple and spread to the left. Nausea turned to heaves, until he laid panting and writhing on the cold hard floor. He stood and made his way to the doorway, stepped over the sill and stumbled to the edge of the cliff in the faint moonlight.

He beat his fists against his temples and screamed, "Why God? Are you sending me some kind of message? Just give me the strength to throw myself over the side into this canyon! I will gladly do so! Just tell me why you've selected me to bear this! Please help me!" His screams, amplified by the room behind him, echoed from canyon wall to canyon wall.

Other restless spirits, ancient and not so ancient, paused in their restless wandering and streamed toward the long forgotten dwelling of the Ancestral Puebloans and whispered among themselves between the agonizing cries.

Cliff slumped to the pebbled surface of the ledge and stared into the dark shadows in the canyon. The moonlight and Milky Way cast only barely enough light to mark the edge of the cliff in front of him and dimly outlined the rocks and trees below. He needed only to lean forward, close his eyes and let go. He willed himself to do it, but could not.

"I don't even have the courage to do this right!" he sobbed helplessly. He crawled back to the doorway and pulled himself up, over the sill and back into the dwelling.

Mamma skunk and her brood slinked from the cave and took shelter in the rocks along the ledge outside, leaving the boy to his private agony.

Cliff called for his mother, wanting her there to hold him with ice wrapped in wet towels pressed to his throbbing forehead. Finally, blessedly, he fell into fitful sleep.

He lost track of time. It may have been sometime Monday night or Tuesday morning before dawn or even Wednesday before the vise finally loosed its grip, and he could finally process how to build a fire.

He lay on his stomach and drank from the pool of cold water. He had an overwhelming thirst for tea and aspirin. Acting on instinct, he went to the corner of the ruin where the Ancient Puebloan family had abandoned bowls in a variety of sizes. Some smaller bowls had apparently covered larger bowls as lids. He selected a small one, decorated with the same grey-white background with black markings like hundreds of fragments he had found on the ground and in the irrigation ditches on the farm and around the big pueblo ruin.

Into the bowl, he emptied one of the quart jars of pinto beans. He rinsed the jar and filled it half full of clean water. He went out to the ledge where the clover bloomed in the overflow from the spring. He picked spires of yellow blossoms and dropped them into the water until an inch of the water was yellow.

Back inside by the fire pit, Cliff used a stick of firewood to rake a small round stone, a river rock, one of a half dozen left there, to the side of the pit and up over the side to the top. He held the hot stone balanced on the top while he held the jar next to it and tipped it into the mouth and let it drop down through the clover blossoms to the bottom of the jar.

For a few seconds, the water boiled up around the hot stone, settled to a few bubbles and then slowly the bubbles subsided as the water heated.

He felt the jar after a few minutes and the water was hot. He washed the stick and used it to stir the blossoms into the water then let it steep as he nodded by the fire.

Cliff roused himself, raked the soggy clover blossoms out of the jar with the stick, lifted the stone to the mouth of the jar far enough that he could grasp it with his fingers and removed it. He tasted the tea. It was strong, tasted good, was still hot, and he drank it all.

He rolled out the saddle blanket. For two days and two nights, he had slept on the cold clay floor. He laid down on the blanket and drifted back into fitful sleep.

He had developed a taste for clover blossom tea from his mother who brewed it in season, flavored with wild mint. She brewed it by the gallon in a glass jar by pouring the freshly gathered blossoms into water and setting the jar in the south kitchen window and letting the sun warm the water and brewing it naturally.

It was a fortunate choice for Cliff as, next to aspirin, it was the closest herb available in the canyon to sooth the effects of his migraine.

When Cliff awoke, he remembered his mother's sun tea and started the quart jar to brewing out on the ledge. An hour after that he sat wearily, but calmly, in the doorway of the ruin absorbing the heat of the noonday sun sipping clover tea.

31

On his own
Martinez Canyon

Cliff was weak and dehydrated. He sipped tea and drank from the spring until he began to feel normal again and hungry. He was sure he had lost a day, but thought it might have been more.

He vaguely remembered waking and looked at the doorway seeing daylight, and the next time he had looked, it had been dark. The next time he had awakened it had been light and then dark again. So had he lost a day, two days? Did it matter? Why did he need a calendar? Why did he need time?

He took down the jar of honey, cut an inch square block of comb and chewed on it. The sugar in the honey would provide energy almost instantly. He had used it for just that purpose many times in the past.

Cliff remembered the uneaten grouse hanging in the back of the cave. It was cooked and that was the coolest part of the cave, but he didn't trust that it was still good. He didn't taste it, but threw it over the edge of the cliff.

Cliff looked at the jars of corn and pinto beans. He had carried them all the way from the house, but he wasn't sure how to cook either of them yet. A big bowl of beans and cornbread sure sounded good right then. The very thought made him salivate.

He wondered if he could soak beans and cook them the way he had made tea with a heated rock in the jar. That would require changing the rock too often. The jar was too small. It would break if he tried to cook directly on the fire with it. He needed a metal container of some kind.

Today he would forage in the canyon for greens and maybe a rabbit, but he had to figure out how to cook beans and corn.

Cliff took the .22 down from its pegs, selected shorts, and a couple of long rifles and put them into his pocket. He had tied a jute twine around the stock and barrel, so he could carry it on his back. He washed the gunnysack-fishing creel and slung it over his neck with the bag hanging under his right arm. He hung the coil of rope over his neck also. He would hide it on top to use when he returned.

He went out the door, placed the slate into position in the doorway and climbed out of the canyon to forage for the day. As he walked toward the canyon entrance, it was with a different sense of purpose. He looked about him. The effects of the migraine had worn off. The air was clear. The sound of the tractors was gone, except one in the distance. He heard frogs in the canyon and birds calling in the piñon trees.

I'm on my own now. I'm not just marking time until I go back to the house. I can't go back there whenever I need something. Either I find it here, or I do without it. Things will never be the same again. I have matches and the rifle today. Today I'll use the rifle if I have to. I only have a few shells left, and I've gone through the matches quickly. That's it. Mrs. Campbell taught us how to build a fire without matches. I have to find a quartz stone. I saw them in the creek the first time I went down there. I'll rest up today. That's it. Time to fish or cut bait. Or as the dream said, "Adversity presents, unique opportunity, a moment of time, in God's wilderness, use the time wisely."

32
Dutch oven
Miner's Shack

Cliff walked along the rim going over the mental list of things he needed besides food. The gunnysack bag hung from his neck down under his arm to carry home whatever, he found.

He had debated bringing the .22. He needed meat. The hunt the day before had yielded only a couple of frogs, although there were plenty of greens. Cottontails were plentiful, but they came out early in the morning and toward sundown. He hadn't seen any more grouse.

The strongest motivating factor now was keeping from being discovered because of the noise.

I'm way too close to home. I need to get further away. If Dad finds me here, he'll kick me home so fast my head'll swim. My rear end will be clear up around my neck before we hit the south fence line. But, where can I go? I'd starve up in the mountains, and I don't know my way around down in McElmo. Somebody would see me sure if I tried to get through Lakeview or Cortez. I don't think I could climb Mesa Verde, and I know I couldn't walk up the road up there without being picked up. For now, I'm better off just staying here where I know my way around. That's what I need to do. And, stay out of sight and be quiet.

Other than today's groceries, I need to find a way to cook besides on the spit. If I can find a can, maybe a coffee can, or an old coffee pot, or a quart fruit or juice can in good condition, I can hang it over the fire and boil water, stew, or beans in it. If I find a pot of some kind, maybe I can put it directly on the fire or coals.

Cliff also needed storage. It was too early in the summer for much to be coming on, but he was already thinking of the time when he could gather seeds, grain and beans. He would have to store whatever he gathered. The growing season was short. The winter was long. If he couldn't create storage in the short summer months, then no matter how much he gathered, it would go to waste. Life on his own would be over. He had to begin finding ways to store things. But, he had to take it one day at a time. *Today I have to find simple cooking utensils.*

Cliff followed the canyon as it ran southwest for a half mile, then he cut due west across the timber and across a wide shallow swale that ran roughly parallel to Martinez Canyon. He walked for nearly a mile until he intercepted a narrow even more shallow draw that drained from the north. He knew that this draw began just south of the county road.

A game trail followed this draw to the swale, crossed Martinez canyon and continued on to Highway 160, crossed McElmo Creek and up to Mesa Verde.

He turned up the small northern draw and followed the bottom of it until he arrived at his destination, an abandoned coalmine.

In the past, Cliff and his dad had visited the old surface mine to dig coal for their stove. It was not a very high-grade coal and had many impurities. It was also back breaking work separating it from the vein and loading it into the back of the pickup.

It was hard to justify calling the operation a mine. The vein broke through to the surface of the draw when erosion wore through the thin layer of rock concealing it. To get to the coal, people shoveled and pick-axed the dirt and rock off the top of the vein and kept working back into the bank of the draw. There was no mineshaft as such. The exposed gash grew wider with time. By then it was more of a series of gashes in the bank rather than a continuous dig. When the covering layer of rock and dirt became too deep to move easily, the local residents moved to the side and started uncovering a new layer of coal. The top layer of rock and dirt was shoveled and pushed over into the adjoining abandoned trench where no more coal was to be found.

When locals had enough cash, or the snow or mud was too deep to get to the old vein, they went on to the working mine near Cortez where they could back up to the chute and have it loaded for them.

It looked as if no one had visited the vein since winter. Cliff ignored the dig and headed to the abandoned shack. The original miner had eventually boarded up the ramshackle shack and left when it became obvious that the vein of coal was not a commercial grade. The shack was fifty yards up the draw by the narrow road.

Cliff noted that a horse had walked around the coal site and up to the shack, or possibly down the road and around the shack and then by the dig.

While his dad had shoveled coal into the pickup, on their last visit more than a year before, Cliff had peeked through the boards covering the window of the shack. He was pretty sure he had seen a pot inside the shack. He thought it had been a coffee pot hanging on the wall. He had squinted and peeked through every narrow crack he could find trying to get a clear view, but all he had been able to see were vague shadows.

The miner had nailed boards over the small window and put a padlock on the only door when he left. Cliff reasoned that the miner must have planned to come back and claim his household goods later. However, he had never returned.

Narrow batten boards were nailed over the cracks between clapboards on the walls and roof. The whole shack was weathered and warped, and the whole structure leaned. Every deep snowfall caused the shack to lean even more.

Some neighborhood couple had carved hearts on the door with their initials and arrows through them inside, but otherwise there was no other vandalism. There didn't appear to have been any attempts to breach the shell of the cabin.

The neighborhood was a generally safe place and most residents didn't bother to lock their doors when they went to town or left the house. Folk trusted each other, and Cliff had never heard of anyone being robbed. His folks never locked the house when they went out. He didn't have a key to the house, and never needed one, when he got home from school and no one was there.

It was ingrained in him that everyone's home was off limits. It bothered him to be going into the abandoned miner's house like a thief, but in his mind, it would not be stealing, if he took something that abandoned long ago. He would not vandalize. He would leave the cabin the way he had found it. He would only take any items that he could use for survival.

The single set of horse tracks stopped at the house. He examined them closely. They were a day or two old. He tested a pile of horse dung, and it was dry. He guessed it was several days old, maybe a week. Someone had stopped, and it appeared as though the rider had dismounted and led the horse to the window, re-mounted and ridden away. They looked the same size and shape as the marks on the rock near the snag. The timing would have been about right.

I wonder if it was the same person looking for me? I'm sure it was Hector's laugh I heard. He was being pretty thorough.

Cliff examined the hasp of the lock. The rusty old screws give a little in the dried out weathered wood. He worked on the screws with the blunt end of the pocketknife blade and soon had them loose enough to remove all four by hand. He put them in his pocket and opened the door.

What he saw was a great disappointment. In his mind, he had begun to picture a fully stocked room with everything that an old miner would need for housekeeping. He had begun to imagine the miner would have just walked away leaving it intact, much the way the Ancestral Puebloans had left the ruin with the pots in the corner, the grinding stones by the door and the heating stones in the fire pit. Maybe there would even be a guitar hanging on the wall. He couldn't play one, but he wanted to learn how to play. Ed had promised to teach him to play his old guitar, but they had not got around to it.

What Cliff found was the shell of a cabin stripped bare of everything including the coffee pot he thought he had seen.

The shack was just one room with a homemade table in the center, a bunk bed along one wall and a small cast iron cook stove backed to the wall next to the door. Next to the stove was a tin bucket half full of fist size chunks of black coal. The bucket was too rusted to be of any use.

The Kelley's burned coal at home, and coal was used at the schoolhouse. It burned hot and for a long time. Cliff placed several chunks of coal in the gunnysack. It might be an interesting source of fuel to try.

Only one item remained in the cabin that interested him. On the floor next to the stove sat a twelve-inch cast iron Dutch oven. The wide, five inch deep Dutch oven would be a valuable solution for his cooking needs if he could get it back to the dwelling. However, at twenty-five pounds, one quarter his own body weight, it was dismayingly heavy, and he was several miles from home. He debated whether it was too heavy to carry back to the dwelling, but he had to have it. It would solve many of his cooking needs. He had watched both his parents cook in such an oven. The best biscuits he had ever tasted were the ones his dad made in the Dutch oven at camp. It served as oven and pot. The lid appeared to be in good shape. The lid had a flange around the top side to hold hot coals when it was used as an oven. Or, inverted the lid could be used as a griddle on a bed of coals.

Cliff looked the pot over carefully for a sign of rust. He rubbed his finger over the inside surface. It came away clean. He turned the lid on it, and it turned true and tight. It was a fine pot and worth the effort to get it back to the ruin.

The only other possible useful item was a set of wooden bed slats that remained in the frame of the crude bunk. Each pine board was about four inches wide, a half-inch thick, and four feet long. They were worn smooth on one side, and he thought they had potential for any number of things. He might use one as a blank from which he could fashion an atlatl spear thrower. If they split straight, he might use them for spear blanks. He placed the slats, Dutch oven, and coal outside the hut. He would pick them up after he looked for a tin can he could use to boil water in.

He fished the screws from his pocket, replaced them in the hasp and tightened them better than he found them. A glance would not reveal that someone had tampered with it, and that it was no longer secure.

He had another stop before returning to the ruin. He had plenty to carry already with the unexpected Dutch oven find, but while he was in the neighborhood, he thought he might know where he could find a coffee can. It wasn't an ideal place to rummage through a trash pile, but it was a trash pile that belonged to the one man on the Ridge with a coffee reputation.

He walked up the quarter mile long, narrow, washed out lane that had once been the access road to the coal claim from the county road.

When Cliff reached the main road, he stayed in the woods out of sight as he walked along it east another three quarters of a mile to the first home one came to on the Ridge.

It wasn't really a farm as the owner had no water rights and grew no crops or produce. The small two-acre parcel had only house, several out buildings, pig sheds, rabbit hutches, a hen house, and ramshackle barn that also served as a garage. The rest of the property had never been cleared.

It belonged to the Stone family, a large family of eight, ranging in age from six months to fourteen years.

Freida Stone stayed at home while Elmer worked in town.

In some ways, the cluttered place was no trashier than any other place on the Ridge, including Cliff's own. It was fairly typical, in fact.

One difference in Elmer's and some of the other places might have been that Elmer was not as handy with tools as some of the farmers, so much of his building program was more haphazard. He had turned most of it over to his boys who worked with enthusiasm but had little direction and no plans to go by.

What appeared to be junk was scattered around the out buildings, which themselves were careless works of odd sized boards nailed in place with little regard to neatness or uniformity. Crudely sawn ends were either too short to reach all the way to the corners or were too long. They spliced short boards. Spacing between boards was inconsistent. Random piles of old buckets, tires, and junk leaned against the walls and spilled out of the sheds.

Elmer had parked every car he had ever owned somewhere behind, in front of, or beside a building or shed. When a car quit running, he pushed it as far out of the way as possible and left it there to rot. He then bought another vehicle, usually just as old, at a used car lot in Cortez, and brought it from town to run until it too quit.

Cliff approached the outbuildings from the backside of the place nearest the woods. He expected to see a kid pop up from any direction at any time. It was too bad school wasn't still in session.

The older kids went to school at West Lakeview. They refused to attend East Lakeview Grade School where Cliff had attended. Their presence would have helped even out the number of Anglo vs. Mexican kids. Their house was only a few hundred yards down the road from the Rodriguez home. Instead of having his kids attend East Lakeview, the neighborhood school, Elmer chose to transport them the extra five miles to West Lakeview, which had two rooms, and which divided the grades by one through four and five through eight.

Ed Kelley explained it as a matter of convenience. Elmer dropped the kids off at school on the way to work and picked them up on the way home. Cliff was close enough to East Lakeview Grade School to walk. Both schools were in the same district. Parents could send their kids to whichever school they preferred. The district provided no transportation to either school.

Cliff had begged Ed to drop him off on the way to work and pick him up on the way home too, but Ed went to work earlier than West Lakeview school opened, and he came home much later than school let out.

Cliff assumed that Freida was home with all eight kids: six months, eighteen months, three and a half, five, seven, nine, eleven, and thirteen. He checked the sun. It was nearly noon, and he guessed she was inside the house with them fixing lunch. That would be a good thing, because the dogs would be hanging close to the house hoping for a hand out, if they were anything like Towser.

The fact that he heard none of the kids playing or running around, could mean they had all gone to town. However, if they were gone, the dogs would be wandering around outside somewhere and could be on him in an instant.

The dogs were his biggest worry. If they were outside, they would smell him or hear him, investigate and probably attack. They had a bad reputation and his parents had cautioned him to avoid walking by the Stone Place because of the dogs. He did know that the dogs chased the pickup truck almost every time his parents drove by the house.

He stayed well back from the main house and surveyed the activity around the place. Chickens of every breed and color combination scratched around the outbuildings. Several ducks and geese waddled around the pigpen and yard. A big black and white spotted rooster noisily chased a red hen over and around several cars before he caught and briefly mounted her. He released her and crowed loudly before proudly strutting off to scratch among other busily feeding hens where he could select another victim. The chickens, ducks and geese made so much noise that Cliff didn't think any slight noise he made would be noticeable to anyone in the house, if anyone was home.

Not far from where he stood, was a shallow depression, perhaps a feeble attempt one of the boys had made to dig a hole for the trash. Cans, paper, old catalogues, magazines, bottles and cardboard were piled haphazardly into the depression. It was in plain sight of the road, but away from and out of sight of the house.

He had still neither seen nor heard the dogs. Usually when a car drove by, if the dogs were outside, they sprang from the porch outside the front door and gave chase. Cliff slipped closer to the junk pile. He had several trees spotted that he could climb quickly if he heard the dogs coming. If they treed him, he might be safe from them, but he would surely be discovered then.

He bent low, keeping as much of the shed and old cars between him and the road and house as possible. He constantly swept the yards for sign of the dogs.

He was looking for any clean coffee can, or other large can, and possibly jars.

The Stones were Mormons as was most of the Anglo population on the Ridge. As far as Cliff knew, George and his wife and the Kelleys were the only Anglos living on this side of the Ridge who were not Mormon.

According to Cliff's Mom, Freida Stone was a good Mormon who abided by most of the tenants of the religion. She had visited the temple in Salt Lake City. She also had complained even to Cliff's mom, who was not Mormon, that Elmer couldn't enter the temple because he, of all things, drank coffee, forbidden to their religion. He not only drank coffee, he drank lots of coffee. She was sure he drank coffee to spite her.

George had told Cliff that Elmer drank coffee directly from the pot and by-passed the mug. He usually laughed when he said that, and so Cliff knew it was probably an exaggeration. However, it was precisely why he was poking through the trash pile at the Stone residence that day. He knew that it was the one trash pile on the ridge, outside the Kelley and Williamson trash piles, that was likely to have a coffee can.

Most metal containers would rust inside almost immediately, because of what they had contained. But, the coffee's natural oils protected the inside metal, and if he found one recently discarded it should be like new.

So far, there were still no sounds from the house. No dogs. No kids. He relaxed slightly. He had been at the trash pile for only a few seconds and knew that he had to be quick. The kids could erupt from the house at any second, and he had to be out of sight. Each second he remained at the trash pile, he was vulnerable.

He moved a cardboard box. Beneath was the familiar red Folgers emblem on an empty two pound can. It was still shiny inside. *Pay dirt!!*

Like his mother, Mrs. Stone would throw jars away only if they had nicks in the rim and wouldn't hold a seal. A nick would have sharp edges and be dangerous. Pickle or mayonnaise jars were not usable for canning and some people threw those away. The jars were not manufactured to stand the extreme pressures and heat required for home canning vegetables and fruit. They were sold with a solid lid that couldn't be resealed. However, they were reusable for dry storage. Most homemakers just threw them away after they accumulated as many as they needed.

Off to one side, half buried under papers and magazines, he saw the corner of a square one gallon can. He pulled it out from under the mess. The label had peeled away. He twisted off the cap and smelled. It had held molasses. The metal still seemed good. He would find out for sure when he cleaned it out. He set it aside with the coffee can.

Cliff resisted the urge to dig deep into the pile, because it would make noise and only newly discarded trash would still be good. Also, if he disturbed the pile it would be impossible to put it back into its original state. As he turned to leave, he spotted a flash of white porcelain under a piece of rotting trash. When he pulled the trash aside, there lay a large porcelain coffee mug with most of the handle broken off. The cup itself was intact. Next to it were a couple of quart mayonnaise jars with solid lids screwed on. Both jars and lids seemed in good shape and were clean.

He quickly placed jars, coffee can and molasses can into the gunny-bag, backed away from the junk pile trying not to leave any more tracks than possible, turned and went back toward the woods. He had been in and out of the trash pile in less than two minutes by his estimate and that two minutes was far more than he wanted to risk.

The body of a 1938 Chevy, resting on blocks with no wheels, sat rusting under a piñon tree at the edge of the woods, and he saw a goose waddling from beneath the derelict car. She ambled nonchalantly back toward the rest of the geese, ducks and chickens. Cliff searched for her nest under the fender from where she had emerged, and there he saw a round impression in the dust with four large clean white eggs inside. One was still warm. He took the warm egg and two more of the cleanest and placed them in the mayonnaise jar, then ducked back into the woods and headed across the timber directly toward the miner's shack to retrieve the Dutch oven and wooden slats.

As the cacophony of poultry sounds began to fade in the background, he heard a sudden frenzy of barking followed by several excited voices yelling. He paused to listen. He realized his heart was beating hard and fast.

"Come back here Roscoe, Butch!" a high-pitched boy's voice screamed after one of the dogs. The dogs quieted a little, and Cliff picked up his pace as he picked his way more carefully through the trees.

He didn't relax or begin to breathe normally until he had the Dutch oven and bed slats in hand and the chunks of coal in the gunnybag and had been trotting away from the miner's cabin for a half hour and had heard no more sound of either dogs or kids in pursuit.

33
Fresh meat
Martinez Canyon

Cliff cut nearly in a straight line back to the ruin from the miner's shack to reduce the distance of the return trip. He calculated the distance he would walk by the time he reached the ruin. It would be somewhere between six to seven miles. Half that distance would be carrying a 25-pound Dutch oven.

He was nearing the snag when he passed under a large, spreading piñon tree and saw the telltale sign of a porcupine. Rough grey brown bark chips with an alternate side of smooth fresh yellow sapwood lay on the ground. He looked up into the tree were a porcupine busily chewed away the outer bark to get to the cambium layer, the soft layer next to the harder wood of the tree trunk. Through the cambium flowed nutrients from the roots to the needles of the tree. It was the tree lifeblood and prime food source for the porcupine. When the porcupine chewed a circle around the tree, crowning it, nutrients could travel no further. The tree above the circle would begin to die immediately. This young porcupine had nearly crowned the stately old piñon tree. It was too late to save it. The herbivorous animal ate whatever it could find, plant, fruit, berries, and roots, and in winter survived primarily on the cambium of trees. It was in that period of transition between spring and summer before many seeds and berries were available and the inner bark was still attractive to the animal.

Cliff set the heavy Dutch oven aside and shucked the gunnybag, selected a bed slat, and began climbing the tree. When he was close enough to use the board as a pry bar, he poked at the animal to prize it loose from its hold on the trunk of the tree.

The porcupine slapped at the slat and moved around the trunk to get away from the annoyance, but persistence eventually won out, and the porcupine lost its grip and fell, bounced off several branches and broke smaller ones before hitting the ground with a thud. It rolled to its feet and began ambling off.

Cliff scrambled down the tree and headed the lumbering porcupine off. The animal ran on four stocky legs nearly obscured with long coarse grey-brown hair. The same coarse hair covered its head beginning behind its eyes and combed back over its back mixing with long deadly quills. The quills began along the neck. The head itself had no quills.

The rodent stood a foot tall and resembled a large watermelon with a small head and a tail covered with long coarse hair.

When it tired of Cliff's harassment, it stopped, turned its tail to Clifton and raised it defiantly. It tucked its unprotected head beneath quilled front paws. Cliff avoided the tail, which whipped around whenever he approached. He would have to turn it over to get a whack at the head.

The porcupines' vulnerable points were the head and belly, neither protected by quills.

Cliff ran around the animal, darted in and shoved the slat under the front quarters of the porcupine, lifted and nearly flipped the animal over. The porcupine scrambled to keep upright to protect its belly and for just a moment, left its head unprotected.

Cliff swung the bed slat catching the porcupine on the back of the head with the edge of the pine slat. The fight was over.

Cliff slit the bare belly of the porcupine, and the animal was not difficult to skin. Cliff did have to be very careful, however, as the quills were as sharp as needles and could be dangerous and very painful if they punctured his skin.

He left the quill covered hide and entrails under the tree for the magpies. He removed the bed slats, cup, jar, coffee can, and molasses can from the gunnybag and lined the bottom with fresh chips from the piñon tree. He placed the carcass of the porcupine on the bed of chips in the bag and replaced the items from the Stone family junk pile on top.

Cliff had carried the bag over his neck and let it hang down his back on the way home from the miner's shack instead of tucking it under his arm. The bulky gallon can was not heavy, but it was awkward. Carrying it that way would choke him with the porcupine's dead weight.

He decided to try carrying the bag like a hobo pack. He tied the shoulder straps to the end of a bed slat and lifted the bag to the crotch of the piñon tree. He balanced it while he put the slat through the straps of the bag and put it on top of his shoulder and draped his arm over it. The bag hung down his back while his shoulder carried the weight. The body of the porcupine conformed to his back while the cans and jar rode on top. He picked up the remaining bed slats with his right hand, tucked them over his shoulder with the hobo bag and grasped them with his left hand along with the slat that balanced the bag.

He picked up the Dutch oven with his right hand and continued toward the ruin.

He was tired from the long march. The wearier he became the darker his mood. By the time he reached the last quarter mile of the snag, the excitement over finding the cans and Dutch oven, had slowly turned to guilt. *What am doing out here? I stole from a neighbor today while a woman like my mother tended her brood inside her house, not knowing I was lurking around outside. What am I becoming? My parents taught me better. Would they be proud of me tonight? I don't want to feel like a criminal.* He almost felt nauseous from the thought of it.

Cliff was hungry. He had never worried about food before. Just a short distance away was all the milk, meat, bread, honey, beans, vegetables, and fruit he could eat and a loving mother to prepare them for him.

He suddenly felt a terrible weariness come over him. It took a great effort to place one foot in front of the other. Earlier in the day, he had taken care to leave as little sign as possible that he had walked there. Now he was so tired he didn't care if he left tracks through the woods or if he dragged a mark on stone.

One foot in front of the other.

One foot in front of the other.

Finally, he stood at the snag. Forty feet below, snuggled into the cave beneath the rimrock on which he stood, was the dwelling and now home.

With leaden limbs, he removed the rope from under the rock where he had hidden it, tied it to the snag and then tied the end of the rope to the Dutch oven handle. Into the Dutch oven, he placed the gunnybag. He tied the strap around the rope to secure it and carefully lowered both over the edge down to the ledge.

Then Cliff grasped the rope, crawled over the side of the cliff and climbed-walked down the face of the cliff to the ledge. *Thank you Heavenly Father and the Spirits of the Ancients for the toeholds today. I couldn't have made it down this cliff without both you and the rope.*

He untied the Dutch oven and sack, and carried them to the dwelling. When he removed the slate door cover and climbed inside with his treasures, mamma skunk and her little ones turned from the spring and faced him with their tails on alert.

His face lit up. "Hi Mamma," he said. "Welcome back. I didn't see you last night." He made no move toward her, but she remained on alert, as he began slowly removing the items from the sack. Cliff found the cup with the broken handle and turned to the spring.

"Mamma, I sure need a drink of water," he said. Cliff had earned a few dollars over the past several summers by catching young skunks and selling them to the veterinarian in Cortez, and he knew their habits and characteristics. They also found human company acceptable, which was one reason they made good pets.

They were myopic, docile animals, very self-assured in their abilities to protect themselves with their exceptional scent glands. Their first line of defense was to bluff. If that didn't work, then they used their scent defense as a last resort. The veterinarian removed their scent glands more to protect household pets from them than because their human owners needed it.

Cliff walked halfway across the room then dropped to all fours and crawled on hands and knees toward the spring. Mamma skunk faced him and hopped stiff legged toward him a couple of hops, her tail arched over her back. It was a defensive motion that Clifton knew well.

He stopped and waited for her. She held her ground for a moment and then turned, and followed by her little ones, pranced toward the exit hole. About halfway to the exit, she stopped and again faced him.

Cliff slowly crawled to the spring, dipped a little water, took sandy silt from the bottom of the spring and scoured the inside and outside of the porcelain cup and rinsed it in the overflow trickle of water. He filled the cup, sat back and tasted the ice-cold water.

It was so much easier drinking from the cup while upright than lying on his belly and lapping it or sucking up a mouthful at a time. He drank and looked at the mamma skunk, which by now had lain down and was nursing her brood.

"Thank you for sharing Mamma. I really needed that."

A little refreshed, Cliff built up the fire. He was pleased that he could now build a fire with one match at a time. He placed the chunk of coal next to the fire pit. Several times, he had thought about lightening his load by throwing it away. One day soon, he would try burning it in an open fire and see if he could carry a fire over until morning with it. There were many places in the canyon where coal veins broke through the surface of the slopes.

He hoped the vegetarian porcupine would be sweet and tender. His dad had told him that, like a bear's, as they got older the meat became strong tasting. He judged by its size, this was just a young one, so it should be tender and sweet.

He washed the porcupine in the spring overflow, removing any of the piñon chips that clung to it and washed out the cavity.

Cliff cleaned the coffee can the same way that he had cleaned the mug, filled it full of water and set it next to the fire to let it begin to heat. It had held two pounds dry weight and was twice as tall as the one pound cans that his mother bought. *Maybe the stories are true about Elmer and the amount of coffee he drinks.*

Should I use the Dutch oven to make my first batch of stew? Or, should I try for a smaller batch and use the coffee can? I need to clean the Dutch oven too before I use it. I can make a small batch in the coffee can. Quick and dirty. I think I'd better do that today and work on the Dutch oven later.

At the creek that morning, he had dug both clover and dandelion roots. The dandelion roots were nearly the size of carrots, although more gnarled and stubby. Clover roots were more slender, but ran deep into the mud of the creek bank. He had washed them off in the creek. He had eaten some of them, carried some in the gunnybag on the trip to the cabin and had them for lunch and as afternoon snacks.

Using a pine bed-plank from the miner's cabin as a cutting board, he chopped the remaining dandelion and clover roots into chunks and dropped them into the coffee can.

The freshly cleaned porcupine lay on a damp gunnysack. He began peeling away the flesh from the ribs and dropping the strips onto the bed slat next to the vegetables.

When he had all the meat he needed for supper, he hung the carcass from a ceiling pole in the back of the cave where it was cool. It he would take care of the rest of it after supper.

After the water boiled in the can for a few minutes to sterilize it, he moved it with a different bed slat over to the overflow and emptied it. Then he used the porcelain cup to put two clean cups of water in the can and returned it to the fire. As soon as the water began to simmer, he added the roots and meat, and he leaned back to wait until it all became tender.

Mamma and her brood slept contentedly where they had stopped just inside their exit. He expected they would go out at sundown to forage for grasshoppers and insects in the grass outside the ruin.

He really didn't have any way to eat his stew once it was ready. That morning he had brought back a few small willow branches to the ruin. He selected a small stem from the stack of branches, skinned the bark off it and sharpened the end.

He speared a chunk of dandelion root and tasted it. It was a little bitter, but it was tender. He carefully scooted the end of the pine plank under the coffee can and removed the simmering container from the fire pit.

With his gloved hand, he tipped the can and poured a half cup full of the broth and raked chunks of meat and vegetables out of the coffee can into the cup. He set the can back near to the fire to keep warm while he ate.

Using his sharpened willow, he speared chunks of root and meat and ate them. *These aren't bad. The stew would be better with a little salt, but anything tastes pretty good when I'm hungry. Maybe a little chili powder would be good. I'm surprised how good the dandelion root stewed up. I like it better this way than roasted. This meat is as tender and sweet as anything I've ever eaten.* He poured the remainder of the stew into the porcelain cup and settled back on the folded saddle blanket contentedly.

Until this stew, everything he had eaten in the past week had been raw or roasted over the spit. *Now all I need are a couple of biscuits,* he thought.

He still had the rest of the porcupine to process, but his stomach was full. He felt drowsy. He was tired from the long walk and carrying the heavy Dutch oven. He would lay back for just a moment. A few hours of daylight remained.

34
Making jerky
Martinez Canyon

When Cliff woke, it was late afternoon and there was still work to do after cleaning the coffee can he had cooked the stew in and the cup he had eaten it from. *This must be how Mom feels every night.*

He felt rested and invigorated after the nap and the stew.

He thought the best way to preserve that much meat was by making jerky out of it. That would require a frame or frames.

He had enough smaller willow branches to make two frames. He used the four longest and sturdiest willow pieces for the corners to build frames about six feet tall that would straddle the fire pit.

He used jute twine to tie the three-foot horizontal rungs to the vertical end pieces, which he tied together at the top on both sides to create a self-supporting "A" frame.

With the "A" frame in place, he retrieved the cleaned porcupine from where it hung. Cliff began cutting the meat off in thin strips and hanging them on the frames. He wanted the strips to dry and cure over the smoldering campfire of cedar.

Although the work went quickly, Cliff needed to finish, because he would run out of light soon. He didn't care how pretty the work was, he only had to impress himself.

The growing dullness of the pocketknife blade began to slow him down. It was a fine wood cutting blade not intended for digging dandelion roots and clover in the mud and soil.

In the future, he would carry the heavy homemade file-blade for digging and save the pocketknife for better use.

Cliff started to sharpen the pocketknife on the whetstone from the saddlebag. He didn't really have time to do a good job of that right now with the fading light. He closed the dull blade and returned it to his pocket.

He retrieved the hunting knife from the nook where he had placed it when he had unpacked the gunnysack on Saturday. He felt the blade edge. It was sharp but needed work before it did any better than the pocketknife.

He started to return to the whetstone, but remembered the piece he had pasted into the scrapbook about the Indians' use of flint. The article said a flint knife was sharper than steel and that some modern doctors in the middle of the 20th Century were experimenting with obsidian blades in place of steel for surgical procedures.

He went outside and climbed to the roof. He had come up here the night before and watched the sun go down over Ute Mountain.

On the left corner of the roof, was the remnant pile of a flint knapper's workshop. Most of the flint flakes were tiny and glinted where they poked through the layer of dust. He had raked through the pile with a stick, and while most of it consisted of small flakes, a few were clamshell sized shards. He took one shard that fit the palm of his hand and returned to the down stairs to test it. The edge was razor sharp.

To his amazement, just as the article said, the glassy stone cut the porcupine flesh much better than the pocketknife, and he quickly finished cutting the remaining meat off the porcupine's bones and loaded the strips of meat onto the drying racks.

The jute twine holding the drying racks was strong. The horizontal rungs sagged under the weight, and the entire frames leaned slightly, but they held together.

His eyes were heavy and his arm would hardly function when he cut the last remaining meat off the porcupine's bones and hung the strip on the frame.

He gathered several scraps that he had set aside, cut them into smaller pieces, placed them on the end of a bed slat and carried them over toward Mama skunk. She rose from where she had been watching him and faced him as he drew near. He placed the slat on the floor and slid it toward her then backed away. She waited until he had returned to his blanket before she walked to the slat and sniffed the fresh meat, then daintily picked a morsel up with her teeth and returned to her brood. They sniffed her muzzle and began trying to take it away from her. She chewed it and kept her face away from even the most persistent of them until she had swallowed. This time they followed her to the slat and began attacking the remaining pieces of meat.

35

Hygene concerns
Martinez Canyon

At last, Cliff lay down on the saddle blanket. As he had on previous nights, he would sleep in his clothes. His feet itched. He had to get out of his shoes and socks.

When he took his socks off, he was greeted with an aroma that mamma skunk might have found offensive. His underwear was also ripe. He took it off too and hung both the socks and underwear outside the door to air out over night. At home, he changed into fresh underclothing every night. Dirty socks and underwear went into the laundry. However, he hadn't been home for almost two weeks.

The cave would be warmer that night because he would keep a small fire burning all night to cure and dry the porcupine meat. He took off his shirt. It was dirty and smelled sweaty. He had slept in a shirt every night because of the wool saddle blanket. It scratched his bare skin when he laid down on it. The burlap sack was equally rough on his skin. The overall front bib protected his chest, the back flap and suspenders protected much of his back. Under the present circumstances, he appreciated their utility.

He had resented wearing bib overalls to school the past couple of years when all the other boys had worn jeans. His mother had promised that somehow she would buy him jeans with a belt when he began attending high school.

Right at that moment, jeans and high school seemed unimportant. What he wished for were sheets, a soft mattress and a blanket.

Cliff's last thoughts before drifting into sleep were as important as the food collection, *hygiene could become the biggest challenge I have to face, if it isn't already. I haven't washed my teeth since the last day I went to school and my mouth tastes like crap. My feet itch, and I'm raw between my legs. I really need a bath. It's warm weather now and hot weather is ahead, and I'll be sweating more. Maybe tomorrow I can take a swim. That's about the time George will show up. They're probably watching all the swim holes now.*

The overalls weren't a problem. He was use to wearing overalls for several days at a time between each laundry.

In the days before they had running water in the house, he had been too young to be working out in the fields in the summer time. Once a week, usually Sunday morning, everyone took a bath in the tub in the kitchen using the same water. They soaped and wiped off before getting into the tub, soaked stepped out, soaped and scrubbed some more. The water stayed surprisingly clean through the whole process.

By the time Cliff worked every day out in the fields, Ed had installed running water with a shower on the porch. When Cliff returned from the fields each evening in the summer, the last thing he did before supper was shower. The dust and sweat from a long day riding on the open tractor melted away down the drain. One of the hardest things so far about living in the canyon was putting on the same sweaty, soiled clothes. He could adapt to the diet he faced, but he was afraid of the idea that raw sores might develop on his feet and the inside of his legs if he couldn't keep clean.

He had overheard conversations between his parents that even some modern day Navajo Indians in the mid-1900s were still using yucca root for shampoo. The men and women he saw at the sales barn on Saturday afternoons had beautiful, black, shiny clean hair.

One resource the canyon and surrounding area had in abundance was yucca.

He was sure he had a pamphlet in the scrapbook that extolled the virtues of yucca for soap, fiber, medicine, maybe even food. It was too dark to read the pamphlets that night, and his brain was too tired to comprehend anything he read anyway. He would check it out in the morning.

He awoke periodically and added cedar to the fire. About half the time when he awoke, coals still glowed brightly and radiated heat into the dwelling. Each time he woke, he looked at the doorway. The slate slab was in place protecting him and his drying meat.

If he could keep the nightmares at bay, sleep should be sound and easy.

During one of his waking moments, in the glow of the fire, he saw Mamma skunk return from foraging. He saw her dim shape and white stripe move to the spring and heard her lapping water. Five little white sets of stripes moved to her side, nuzzled her, and urged her to settle for them to nurse, but first she ambled toward Cliff. He lay watching her as she approached his feet and sniffed them. She wriggled her nose, rubbed her snout with her paw, and returned to her young where she settled into her usual spot and allowed them to feed.

"OK, Mamma, I get it! Tomorrow everything'll get washed!" He agreed.

~~~

Cliff awoke in the middle of the night drenched in sweat. It was very dark. One dark red eye stared at him from two feet away. The hair rose on the back of his neck. He couldn't breathe. It was the fiery furnace of Hell. Satan had delivered him. He had killed a man. He was damned to hell! The nightmare had come true!

He gasped for breath and choked. He coughed and sat up without taking his eyes from the red eye which never blinked, but stared steadily back at him. He regained his breath, swallowed and cleared his throat. A tiny spark spun off into the fire pit, and a faint curl of smoke wafted up from the red coal.

His eyes shifted upward to the strips of meat hanging between the glowing coal and himself, he slowly realized where he was, and he
~~~

breathed deeply and began to relax. The only recollection he had of the nightmare was the feeling of dread and the knowledge that he had killed someone. *Did I actually kill someone, or did I just desire to kill someone? Is there a difference? I didn't really do it, did I?*

He stood and felt his way to the doorway, removed the pegs and set the slate aside. A thin moon hung over the canyon casting just enough light that he could faintly make out rock and trees on the opposite canyon slope and the shiny ribbon of water far below.

Is it only my second week in the cave? Why does it feel as if it has been weeks already?

Noises drifted up from the canyon. Owls whistled and hooted. Branches moved and sighed in the breeze. Twigs snapped as some creature stepped or slithered over them. A breeze blew gently through the canyon and around the rimrock making slight moaning noises.

In the distance, a trucker applied Jake brakes as he down shifted to keep a heavy rig under control down the long grade into Mancos Canyon. They were all sounds that were becoming familiar.

Cliff set the slate back in place, pushed the pegs into their holes and returned to the saddle blanket. He put another piece of cedar on the fire and tried to go back to sleep.

~~~

Mamma skunk lifted her head to observe the restless form, checked her brood, and drifted back off to sleep. Being nocturnal by nature and having eyesight at night equally as good as in the daytime, she had closely inspected the sleeping form and his smelly feet again, eaten another piece of meat that had not made it to the drying frame inspected the willow frame and drank more water. She returned to the drying meat, pulled a strip off the lowest rung of the frame, and returned to her brood to eat it.

Fortunately for Cliff, she could not climb up to the nook where he had placed the three goose eggs in the mayonnaise jar. She had a particular fondness for eggs.
~~~

36
Boiled egg
Martinez Canyon

Glowing cinders remained to rekindle a morning fire. He was pleased that he would not have to use a valuable match. Of course, he had tended the fire all night. The chunks of coal he carried from the miner's shack lay by the fire pit. He would try burning a chunk that night. In the stove at home, coal carried the fire through the night. *I hope this will work in an open campfire. If I can use some of the coal that's available in the canyon, and if it will carry through the night, that would really be good, especially this winter.*

He had brought a sample of coal from the cabin. He had not tried it the night before because he was afraid the oily coal smoke would contaminate the drying meat.

Cliff looked forward to breakfast.

When he built the fire up, he placed three stones in the edge of the fire so that he could balance the cooking stone on them. The round river rock had rested to one side of the fire pit. The cooking stone was a flat flagstone left leaning against the fire pit by the original cliff dwellers. He had decided they probably used it as a kind of stone griddle. The equal sized river rock were large enough to elevate the cooking stone above the hot coals and provide a cook surface.

As the fire burned down to coals, he raked them under the stone to heat it up.

He filled the coffee can half full of water, placed it on the cooking stone and added one of the goose eggs he had taken from the Stone residence the day before. He knew one was fresh and hoped the others were too.

It didn't take long for the water to boil. Water boiled quickly at 7,000 feet elevation. For every 500 feet in elevation, it took one degree less to boil water. Therefore, instead of water boiling at 212 degrees, as it would at sea level, it boiled at 198 degrees on the Ridge. A five-minute hardboiled egg at sea level was only hot inside at seven thousand feet. He had observed his mother boiling chicken eggs many times and under her direction had boiled eggs on his own. She usually boiled her eggs eight to ten minutes from the time she dropped them into the boiling water until she took them out. The goose egg was nearly twice the mass of a chicken egg.

His mom also had a clock to guide her intuition. He had none.

The water merrily boiled away, literally. He had no more dandelion root, clover root, asparagus or cattail shoot. It was time to replenish his supply.

Before building the fire up, he removed the frames from over the fire, still loaded with the dried meat. He stood them against the wall to unload later. He selected a piece of dried meat from one of the frames and chewed on it while the egg boiled.

The smoke had given it flavor. It wasn't bad. It was chewy. The only way he had to judge it was by the jerky his mother made. He guessed this jerky was a little drier. It should keep.

He waited for what he guessed to be ten minutes. The egg might or might not be hard-boiled, but at least surely, it must be cooked enough. He didn't like soft-boiled eggs. He liked them well done.

Cliff laughed aloud. It startled him to hear himself laugh. He realized he hadn't really laughed for a long time. He wasn't sure when the last time he had laughed. "When someone else was doing the cooking, I could afford to be choosy. Now that I'm doing the cooking, I can't be choosy any more. Mom would love that!" he said.

His mother often complained about high altitude cooking. She was born and raised in the lower altitudes of Texas and learned to cook there. The high altitudes of Colorado had forced her to relearn how to cook.

Etta Mae did not like her son to leave anything on his plate. If he did so, she reprimanded him and threatened that he would have to take over the task of cooking for the family.

"It's not because I didn't like your cooking that I'm doing it myself now, Mom," he said as he removed the can of boiling water from the cooking stone with the bed slat and carried it to the overflow and poured it out, water, egg and all.

He retrieved the cooling egg and refilled the can half full of fresh water. He set the refilled can back on the cooking stone, added a few chopped pieces of dried porcupine strips and waited for the water to boil into broth.

While he waited for the egg to cool, and the broth to boil, he stripped the dried meat off the racks. The strips that had hung limply on the willow frames the night before were now firm and stiff. It was a good trial run. Usually his mom did the meat drying. He knew that the meat should reach a certain dryness to keep from mildewing. Yet, it shouldn't be too dry either. This batch would be a good test because there wasn't so much meat that it would last very long.

He removed the remaining eggs from the mayonnaise jar, placed them in the highest nook, and packed as many pieces of the dried meat as would fit into the jar and screwed on a lid. He packed the remaining mayonnaise jar and the Mason jars in which he had brought jerky and oatmeal cookies from the house.

He had not planned to touch the Ancestral Puebloan pottery that had been left in the corner of the ruin, but the jars brought from the house on the last visit to the farm still held corn and beans. No doubt, some of the pots had also contained corn, beans and seeds at one time for the original family before they had deserted it.

Cliff carefully lifted a small pot inverted over the mouth of another small pot. The second pot had contained sunflower seeds. He reached into the pot and took out a handful of the ancient shriveled seeds. They looked the same as the seeds he would see later in the summer on the sunflowers growing profusely in abandoned fields and where the hoe and cultivator had missed them in the wheat and corn. On close examination, he could see where insects had bored into each shell and eaten the kernels.

He poured the empty husks out, set the pot and its covering pot aside and examined another set of pots. The pottery was plain on these pots, unlike broken pottery around the ruin, which was decorated with black markings on a white background. It was as though they had taken the best work with them and left the more ordinary work behind. A second pot had contained another kind of seed that the insects had also reduced to empty hulls. He couldn't identify the original seed. When he lifted the pot out of the silt that surrounded the base, he realized it sat on a bed of small, shriveled corn cobs.

Cliff had already emptied one jar of pinto beans into a bowl to free a jar to make clover tea. He divided the remaining three jars of beans into the first pot and one of the newly cleaned pots, and the two jars of corn into the other third pot.

Irregular rectangular shaped indentations, usually about half the thickness of the wall and from six inches to nearly a foot high and eight to ten inches wide were built into the front masonry wall of the cliff dwelling. These nooks were perfect for storing a small pot, a jar or similar sized object. The jars of jerky went into the nooks high up so that mama skunk couldn't get into them. He also set the pots with the beans and corn high up on the wall and inverted the small bowls over the mouths just as the original inhabitants had nearly seven hundred years before to keep the rodents out. It hadn't kept the insects away, but Cliff would use the beans and corn before insects could do their damage.

He stuffed a few pieces into his bib pockets for lunch. All the meat on the porcupine had shrunk to fit into nine one-quart jars, not as much as he'd thought it would.

Cliff poured the broth into the broken handled cup, peeled the egg which was a little on the soft boiled side, and sat on the sill looking out across the canyon. It was a peaceful and quiet morning. Magpies called from down in the willow grove by the creek. The overnight crispness had not burned off and a faint mist rose off the creek and dissipated before it hit the rim of the canyon.

37
Yucca Root
Between Martinez Canyon and Highway 160

He bit into the goose egg. It was delicious. He sipped the hot porcupine broth and chewed the morsels of wild meat, as he read in the scrapbook all about yucca, and how the Native Americans had used the root of the yucca plant for soap.

The scrapbook was open on the doorsill and turned to a pamphlet he had collected at the Extension Service. The pamphlet consisted of six over sized sheets of paper folded in half and stapled in the middle. Unlike many of the Extension Service Bulletins, printed by CSU, this pamphlet had apparently been prepared by a missionary serving in one of the mission schools on the Navaho reservation.

The pamphlet was a mixture of scholarly descriptions and poorly reproduced photos of a missionary demonstrating digging, preparing and using the yucca root as soap, and of her gathering, preparing and using yucca leaves and their fiber for clothing, mats and baskets as taught to her by Navajo friends.

Cliff had a long history with the small local yucca plant. He had broken loose the tallest centermost leaves, which wrapped tightly around a needle pointed stalk that was the perfect substitute for a sword or lance in fantasy duels. Only in his own versions of challenges, unlike Don Quixote's mad raving against windmills and dragons, Cliff's fantasy duels were against opponents resembling Hector Rodrigues, his teacher Mr. Johnson, and occasionally even his dad.

The outer leaves of the plant were trough shaped which caught and directed rain and melting snow water down into the plant's roots. The roots gathered and stored water in three ways; a large fleshy storage root, a network of small roots directly below the soil surface that gathered water quickly before it ran off or evaporated, and a long taproot that extended as deep as the plant was tall or more to collect and store water further down.

The part of the plant that Cliff needed to collect for soap was the storage portion in the lower trunk and the upper part length of the taproot. Removing all that would still leave plenty of side roots to replenish the plant, as more plants would grow from lateral roots left in the ground and any remaining taproot. The plant was built for survival, as any farmer in the area knew when he tried to clear a new pasture where they grew.

According to the pamphlet, sun-drying the roots was easy as one merely had to slice the root into chips and spread the material thinly on a clean surface and leave them in direct sunshine until all of its moisture evaporated. The root could, either fresh or dried, be used for soap, bathing, brushing teeth, or laundry. To produce suds, one only had to swish a piece of clean root around in water. Or, the root could be grated, put into a cloth bag, and the bag could be dipped into the wash water.

The soapy water was good for shampoo or laundry detergent. Unlike a grease based soap, no rinsing was required, a vital aspect to desert hygiene.

The missionary reported that it was very gentle on the skin and made the hair shine.

The pamphlet stressed that it was good for washing delicate items or work clothes alike. It said the root had medicinal properties as well, and could be used as a poultice for broken bones and sprains, treatment for skin lesions, inflammation and bleeding. It could be steeped as a tea for internal health.

~~~

After cleaning his breakfast cup, Cliff brought the *mano* to the doorsill. The *mano* was the hard, flat, hand sized stone the original homemaker had used to grind corn and seeds on the *metate.* The *mano* seemed to be a harder granite rock more like the river rock found in the Dolores River. The rock in Martinez Canyon was softer sandstone. The *metate* was a square of softer flagstone with a trough worn down by the harder *mano* and corn kernels from grinding.

Cliff used the *mano* as a grindstone to sharpen the heavier file-knife blade. Digging dandelion and clover roots had dulled the pocketknife blade, so he would not use it for that any more. He had used the whetstone to bring it back to razor sharpness. He did not want to wear out the precious whetstone on the coarse large blade file-knife.

Ed had sharpened the file-knife on the grindstone. The edge was sharp, but because it was rough like thousands of tiny saw teeth, it would dull quickly. It needed to be finished with a smooth edge. As he honed the blade on the smooth granite, he dampened the stone continually and added a little sand to form a paste. He checked the edge as he worked and was pleased to find that, although it was not as efficient as a regular whetstone, the *mano* stone slowly brought the file steel to a razor sharp edge. *The file steel should hold up to digging out a yucca root just fine.*

Cliff looked out over the canyon side as he worked. Numerous small yucca plants dotted the open spaces on the slope between the dwelling and the creek. The dense plants spread their stiff spiny leaves, beginning at the ground, and spreading out in one to two-foot radiuses. Needle sharp tips on each leaf protected the plant and gave sanctuary to tiny birds. Each successive row of leaves pointed at a higher angle until those at the center were nearly vertical, protecting the center where every two years a flowering stalk appeared.

Fortunately, he had a good pair of work gloves. Each fall Ed traded their deer and elk hides for tough elk hide gloves. In a normal summer, Cliff and Ed each went go through two or three pair. The pair Cliff had brought with him to the ruin was new so the palms still had all the original
~~~

thickness and strength.

The leaves were also serrated along the edges. Even with the gloves protecting his hands, he shuddered to think how his arms would be scratched, if he didn't go about it right.

He studied the nearest plant, which grew below and to the left of him. It was out in the open, and it required deep soil in which to grow. Taking one out would be obvious because he would have to disturb a fair amount of ground around it and on the slope below it. He looked at the few other yucca plants, and all were out in the open where they got plenty of sun. He couldn't remove any of them without calling attention to someone working there.

"If I had my shovel, this job would be a snap," he said. During the summer, his shovel went everywhere with him. With it, he brought down tall, tough sunflowers, dug channels for water, dug fencepost holes, excavated Indian ruins, cut through sod and cleared brush. The list of chores he put the shovel through every day went on and on.

He already felt lost without the shovel and was tempted to make a trip back to the farm to try to sneak it away. "As far as I know Hector is using it. I can't take that chance," he said to himself. "And I refuse to steal one away from a neighbor."

I wonder what the Indians used. Did they have shovels? He looked back at the poorly copied photo of the missionary. In her hand, she held an Army shovel. When Cliff saw that he laughed out loud. *I guess Coronado probably had shovels with him when his band of conquistadors came through the Southwest looking for the Seven Cities of Gold. The Indians around here left two-hundred years before he arrived. On Mesa Verde, they were irrigating their cornfields. That means they must have been irrigating their cornfields right here too. It would be hard to irrigate a field with a stick. They must have been using something like a shovel.*

Cliff put several pieces of jerky into the bib pocket of his overalls. He debated emptying the jar of sun brewed clover blossom tea and carrying water in it, but the thought of coming home to a fresh jar of tea won out. Surely, I won't be gone that long. If I am, I'll have to take a chance on the creek water.

He looped the gunnybag over his neck. Inside he put an extra gunnysack to carry back the leaves. He put on his straw hat, checked that he had his gloves in his back pocket and set out for the day's excursion.

There were two goals that day; yucca root, yucca leaves and more miscellaneous roots and vegetables for supper that night and breakfast the next day.

Rather than walk along the rim, it was closer to enter the timber and walk straight through to the draw that intersected Martinez Canyon from the north across from the tower ruin. There he picked up the deer trail that crossed the canyon, followed it up the south slope and out across the area between the canyon and Highway 160.

The area between the canyon and the highway was a roughly pie shaped wasteland of sagebrush, piñon and cedar. It was bounded by the Mancos--Dolores county road that crossed Martinez Canyon a half mile east of the tower ruin, ran south a half mile, turned east a mile then ran due south for three miles to merge with Highway 160 at Hallersville. As far as Cliff knew, Hallersville's only claim to fame, other than it being the entrance to Mesa Verde, was the caged bear named Nehi at the filling station. People bought the bear soft drinks. His favorite was one called Nehi so that's what he became known as.

Washes, gullies and ravines crisscrossed the strip of wasteland, but there were no creeks or springs as far as Cliff knew. His knowledge of the strip was from looking directly down on it from the "Knife Edge" road on Mesa Verde, which provided a thousand foot high bird's eye view of the farm, roughly 8-10 miles as the crow flew from the view point on the Knife Edge. Martinez Canyon, Big Canyon, Little Canyon, McElmo Creek, feeder draws and swales, and in the distance, Lost Canyon--the whole of Summit Ridge spread out at in a 180 degree panorama.

No one farmed the wedge of wasteland. From the viewpoint on Mesa Verde, it appeared as one unbroken olive green mass, unmarked except by a several game trails that crossed it and a web of dry washes. A few junky homes dotted small one or two-acre home sites along the highway, but they did not intrude far into the area.

No roads crossed to the canyon or intruded into the pie shaped area.

The point of the wedge ended in a narrow western end bordered by the edge of the Summit Ridge plateau, the creek from Martinez Canyon as it merged with McElmo Creek and flowed under highway 160.

Cliff followed the deer trail out of the canyon. As soon as he reached level ground, he left the trail and angled to the southwest into the wasteland for a quarter of a mile before stopping.

Although Cliff was now in unexplored territory, he was not afraid of getting lost. When he could see above the piñon and cedar, Mesa Verde stood tall to the South, Ute Mountain to the west and the La Plata to the east. His internal compass was so accurate that he could find his way to within a few yards of where he wanted to come out the other side of a relatively dense timber as long as least one of those landmarks was visible long enough in the beginning to orient himself.

He stopped on the slope of a wash where a large yucca and two smaller plants basked in the sunshine. He chose the larger plant because it made sense it would have the larger taproot. This plant also grew with some separation from the others. Most of the yuccas in the area were squat reaching barely knee high. A few grew waist high like the one he would dig. The smaller two plants sent lance-shaped leaves out from the base of the plants and crowned almost immediately with almost no trunk. His target yucca had a trunk that grew to a little more than 12 inches before crowning and center leaves that reached above his waist.

Cliff pulled on the elk hide gloves and faced the plant. Stiff needle pointed leaves hugged the ground in a three hundred sixty degree circle around the plant. It was an old plant and the lower several layers were dry and dead looking. The root was well protected. He gingerly reached into the stiff fronds and grabbed a leaf as close to the base as he could reach.

Cliff pulled sidewise, and the first leaf pulled away more easily than he expected, as did most of the first row of leaves.

The second row required more twisting and pulling before the individual leaves finally peeled away from the trunk. As he peeled each leaf away from the trunk of the plant, he stacked it to one side before peeling off the next. Each succeeding row slightly overlaid the row above it. It was the opposite effect of the way a house was sided with each board overlapping the board below so the water drained off without penetrating the interior. If one tore the siding off a house, he began at the top and worked down. It was ingenious how the plant protected itself and how nature had equipped it to collect water. It would have been impossible to remove the leaves starting at the top. The plant's defenses were formidable.

It reminded him of the porcupine. Attacked from above, the animal was virtually indestructible. However, its belly was vulnerable. The yucca was the same. Its belly was vulnerable. By fighting through the very bottom row first and getting them out of the way, he could pull down each row exposing the row above. Before long, he had the leaves of the denuded trunk/stalk stacked neatly a few feet away from the plant. His arms itched as the needle points repeatedly pricked through the denim shirt. Serrated edges of the leaves sawed at small bits of skin when he reached in to grasp another leaf near the trunk and his shirt pulled back.

The trunk tapered from the crown at a diameter equal to his wrist to more than the diameter of his bicep muscle at the point where the trunk grew from ground and continued as the taproot.

The only leaf or leaves remaining on the crown was the tightly rolled center spike that Cliff liked to use as a "sword" or "lance" when he played fantasy medieval war games. Usually he had to remove it by reaching as far down into the center of the yucca as possible and grasping the spike and wrenching it free. This time he would cut it off without breaking it.

The file-knife was keen, but the outer skin of the yucca trunk at the crown was tough. Cliff worked to cut through it just below the crown of the plant where the final rows of leaves had circled the crown and had pointed nearly straight up. He grasped the trunk with his left hand and sliced with his right hand. The knife had no handle, and so he did not have a good grip on the knife, but he sawed through and left a clean cut.

The exposed tip of the trunk was fibrous and pulpy. Moisture began to bead on the moist surface.

Cliff's hand ached from peeling away the leaves and cutting through the trunk. He removed the gloves and stuffed them into the back pockets of his overalls. It was thirsty work and the morning sun was warm, likely to become very hot by late afternoon. The nearest trustworthy water was back at the dwelling.

Cliff looked at the stump and the moisture beading on the freshly cut surface. He tentatively licked the top of the trunk and tasted it. It was bland and pleasant enough. The whole trunk and root were supposed to be a water reservoir. Cliff took out his pocketknife and sliced a chip of the pulpy heart from the trunk. He pared away the rough rind and took a small bite. It was moist and sticky. He chewed it. It was bland tasting and juicy. Despite the heat, the liquid was cool. He sucked out the liquid, swallowed and spit out the pulp.

He sliced off several more chips from the top of the trunk. He pared one and put the chip in his mouth and the rest of them in his bib pocket. The chips didn't seem to dry out very quickly. It was like carrying slices of apple. He had heard of slicing into a barrel cactus and using the juicy pulp as a thirst quenching source but had never thought of yucca in that way before.

The ground around the yucca was hard. When summer rains came, often a hard pounding cloudburst, sometimes accompanied by hail, washes like the one in front of him filled with runoff and became roaring torrents that ran for a few hours then dried up again until the next downpour. A wash like this was the best place to look for arrowheads. It was time to take a break before attacking the hard probably rock filled soil around the taproot.

He picked up the nearly two foot long round center spike and walked down the slope into the wash as he pared and chewed the yucca chips one by one until his thirst was satisfied. He also noticed how fresh and clean his teeth and gums felt when he was through.

Eroded areas, such as the sides and bottom of the wash, were usually good arrowhead hunting grounds. The bottoms of dry irrigation ditches were also good places to look. Cliff skimmed the ground for flashes of white or glass and triangular shapes or straight edges. He walked for a hundred yards or so, turned and walked back on the other side of the wash. His eyes constantly scanned the lower edge of the wash for any shape that didn't seem to fit the surroundings. A shape that didn't conform, a thumb-sized, serrated edge, finally rewarded him. It was a wedge of flint. It was heavy, thick and longer than his thumb. It was large enough to have been used as a spear point for big game.

Cliff made it a game to guess if a point might have served as an arrowhead or spear point. Was it used to hunt birds or game? Arrowheads were tiny, the size of a dime or nickel and more delicate. Back at the farmhouse, he had a beautiful mounted collection of delicate points that matched photos of those used for small game such as rabbits or turkey, grouse, quail or doves.

He saw no sign of broken pottery in the wash. Back at the farm, small pieces of broken pottery lay on the ground and in the irrigation ditches everywhere. This desolate piece of ground must not have been worth much even six hundred years before, he thought.

As he continued back to the yucca, he almost stepped on a half set of forked horn deer antlers. Bucks dropped their rack each year and grew a new pair with an additional point. He carried the antler back to where he was harvesting the yucca. It could come in handy.

He began digging the taproot. He wanted to keep it in one or two pieces if possible. He stabbed into the soil around the root with the file-knife. When he hit rock, he dug it out with the file-knife and cleared the dirt out with his gloved hands. The hardpan and rocks made digging slow. Cliff decided knife and hands were not efficient digging tools.

He had to stop frequently. He cut chips off the top of the trunk to chew for water and chewed jerky for nourishment. Unfortunately, the dried meat increased his thirst, but it maintained his strength. As the sun neared its zenith, he noted that although the hole around the taproot was nearly as deep as his arm length, the root continued on hardly diminished in diameter.

He was glad to see increasing moisture in the soil, however. The soil had also changed. It was actually more like the loam on the farm at that depth.

The top layer of soil was rocky, and it would have been hard to dig through even with a shovel.

Once when Cliff stopped to rest, he broke a clod of dirt apart. It was hard and had especially resisted his hammering through it. Just a month before, the whole area would have been practically impassable during the end of the spring thaw. The mud would have clung to his shoes in a gooey viscous mess. Layer upon layer of clay would build up on the tires of a vehicle trying to drive across it. Most vehicles would become mired within a hundred yards.

When the snow melted and the mud dried up, what had been an elastic layer would again become a solid hardpan. Rain would run off into washes and gullies and become flash floods rather than soak into the clay.

The relatively thin layer of soil became soaked during the slow snowmelt, froze, thawed and froze repeatedly each spring. Over the centuries, it had broken down to a fine layer of clay. Sand and dust blew in from New Mexico and Arizona and settled to add new layers that broke down during the next spring thaw.

A network of roots in the soil close to the plant allowed organic material from the plant to infiltrate it. Water draining from the leaf network could drain down into the tap root system. A few inches outward from the plant, the clay capped the soil.

"Is this the clay the Ancestral Puebloans used for their pots?" Cliff wondered aloud. He knew that the clay they used was not very strong, and that they recycled broken pottery by grinding it and adding it back to the clay they used to give it body and strength. If they didn't have broken pottery, they added degraded sandstone. He set aside a couple of the hard clods to take back to the dwelling to test them as potential pottery clay.

He chewed another piece of moist root as he dug out another six inches of root and called it quits. Finally, he broke off the taproot. The taproot continued down into the ground. Side roots hung from all sides of the hole in which he crouched. He guessed that each of those roots could potentially grow a new plant.

When he and his dad had cleared a corner of a field where numerous yucca plants grew, within weeks little yucca had sprung up around where the mother plants had grown. He imagined the same would occur here. By summer's end in place of this plant would be a half dozen newer plants competing for the same space.

Cliff broke the root into three equal pieces, each almost the length of his arm, scraped off as much of the soil as possible without scarring the skin and placed the heavy pieces in the bottom of the gunnysack on top of the antler, and clods.

Cliff cut the needle points off the leaves, made stacks, and tied the stacks tightly at each end with a split leaf. He fit individual stacks into the spare gunnysack. Several smaller tattered lower leaves had spider webs and egg sacks on them, and he left those behind. The sack of bundles of green leaves was bulky and heavy.

He back-filled the hole, smoothed the soil over it and cleaned the area, scattered the remaining leaves over it, and oriented himself to intercept the deer trail somewhere close to Martinez Canyon. It had taken all morning, and he was hot and sweaty.

The file-knife had worked well, but he had to put a handle on it soon. He would see if he could make handles out of the antler.

Cliff could hardly wait to get back to the ruin to try out the root for soap. *I have to keep track of how long the root lasts. If it actually works as soap, I need to dig enough to dry it and store it to use when I need it even through the winter.*

~~~

When Cliff reached the bottom of the canyon, he went down the trail next to the creek. He stopped to gather wild vegetables before climbing back out the north side of the canyon. He dug dandelion roots, tops, and flowers. As he dug, he nibbled a tender dandelion leaf, flicked away bees and other bugs, and ate several flowering heads for their sweet taste. He also dug sweet clover roots.

He rinsed the roots in the creek before placing them in the gunnysack, keeping a dandelion root out to chew on the way home. The dandelion root was slightly bitter and oozed a bit of white sap, but it was juicy, and he was hungry. His rabbits loved them as much as they loved carrots. He ignored the slightly bitter taste.

He cut a bundle of cattail shoots. They would keep for several days. He would try putting the bundle in the cold water of the spring and see if they would stay fresh longer there.

Asparagus was at its peak, and he gathered a bundle of fat spears bigger around than his thumb.

He stripped handfuls of blossoms from yellow sweet clover and filled
~~~

his overall pockets. He wanted to conserve the blossoms on the clover growing outside the cave as much as possible for times when he couldn't make it down to the canyon. A jar of sun tea would be ready when he got back to the dwelling.

Cliff's mom occasionally made sweet clover tea. She also made coffee from parched and ground dandelion root when she ran short of coffee grounds.

He didn't drink coffee with his parents, and they didn't offer it. They inferred that it was strictly an adult drink, and that the caffeine might be harmful to him as a growing child. Funny. His dad had reminded him just a few weeks ago that it was time to put childish things behind him now that he was a man.

However, when his mom drank tea, she poured a cup of tea for him also, and iced tea was a summer staple. He thought it also contained caffeine, but he didn't question the contradiction. She experimented with iced mint, clover and dandelion blossom tea if she didn't have English tea available.

Without cow's milk to drink, clover or dandelion tea seemed a good alternative.

Cliff looked longingly at the creek rippling its merry way along between grassy banks. There were few places where it pooled. It slowed and widened in areas and willows and cattails took advantage of it, but he didn't know of pools deep enough for swimming. It didn't matter. He didn't know how to swim. He reached down and ran his hand through the water. It was ice cold.

Right now, more than swimming, he needed a drink of water, and it was still a ways from the cave. The water was surely as good as the water in the irrigation ditch. He kneeled down and dipped water up to his lips with his cupped hand. He sipped the cold water. It tasted ok. He drank just a little to get him to the cave. *I could have sucked on a few more yucca chips, but I think they are much too valuable to use for water.*

The problem with water on the Ridge was the cold. Creeks, rivers, lakes were cold. The pond was their drinking water.

Kids in McElmo have it good. McElmo creek's warm and there are plenty of pools where kids swim down there. Sometimes I wish I'd grown up down there. I think kids down there have more fun. However, then they do have rattle snakes…

He looked around before heading home, and realized that he stood next to a patch of "lamb's quarter." Although it was a weed, it was actually a cousin of the domestic garden spinach. At his mom's direction, he gathered it for her in the spring to use as fresh salad, or she cooked it as a substitute for spinach. It tasted about the same. He gathered a handful, put it in the sack and headed for home with a full gunnysack of yucca leaves on his back and the gunnybag under his arm full of vegetables and the yucca root.

38
Laundry
Martinez Canyon

Cliff cut an inch section of the ugly yucca root and put the remainder aside. He had two pairs of socks, two pairs of underwear, two tee shirts, a couple of denim outer shirts, and two dirty pair of overalls to launder.

He had not worn underwear that day, but he couldn't go without socks in the work shoes without wearing blisters on his feet. If he wore blisters, he would be in serious trouble. He usually didn't wear a shirt at all, but today he had worn a denim shirt because of the yucca leaves.

The Dutch oven was the only available vessel he had in which to soak his clothes. He folded his overalls and tried to fit them in the Dutch oven. One pair fit at a time.

He filled the coffee can with water and placed it on the cooking stone in the fire pit to heat. The two-pound coffee can held about two quarts of water.

While he waited for that, he placed the one-inch yucca root disc on the *metate,* and with the blade of the knife, he cross cut the face a quarter inch deep in quarter inch squares. Then with the *mano* he mashed the surface to a pulp.

When the water began to simmer, he removed the coffee can from the fire and poured an inch of water into the Dutch oven. Cliff swished the pulpy surface of the yucca chip through the water and light suds began to form. He dipped the overalls into the Dutch oven and then turned them over and poured the rest of the hot water over them. He put the warm lid on the Dutch oven and left the work pants to soak. While they soaked, he went back to the spring for more water and put it on to heat for the next pair.

The molasses tin was a rectangular shape about three and a half inches by eight inches by nine and a half. The label had come off. The pour spout was in the corner of the three and half inch end.

Cliff used a .22 bullet to draw a cutting line on the surface of the tin. He would cut out the side next to the pour spout. He placed the can on the flat stone surface of the doorsill for stability. He managed to cut the side out of the tin can in several passes. The heavy blade of the file-knife cut through the light weight tin and sliced a relatively straight line.

He used a little of the hot water heating in the coffee can and yucca suds from the same chip to clean the molasses out of the tin can. It didn't have as large a capacity as the Dutch oven, but it held water, and it was clean. The coating of molasses and the cap over the spout had kept the inside shiny bright.

He added socks and underwear to the new molasses tin washbasin and let them soak, occasionally swishing them around with a willow stick. After what he guessed to be a half hour, he fished the overalls out of the Dutch oven and squeezed the water back into it.

The water was brown and foul. He poured it over the ledge onto the dirt under the bee tree and refilled the Dutch oven with fresh water. He didn't bother to heat it, but swished the root around the cold water raising more suds. He dipped the overalls into the water and kneaded them thoroughly then wrung as much water out as he could and hung them on the drying racks to dry. He refilled the Dutch oven with fresh hot water and into it went tee shirts and the outer denim shirts to soak.

He wrung out the socks and underwear and rinsed them. He was not surprised that the water was foul after the wash, but after the second rinse, it was almost clear.

The socks felt clean and fresh for the first time since he had taken them out of his dresser drawer. The pamphlet had been correct about the cleansing effectiveness of the yucca root. *Too bad it is so darned much trouble to dig out,* he thought.

He rinsed the denim shirts, squeezed the water out and then rinsed the tee shirts.

Last, Cliff pulled off the overalls he wore and put them to soak in the Dutch oven.

Then he heated a new coffee can full of fresh water and poured it into the molasses tin-basin, soaped it, and using the clean tee shirt as a wash rag, he washed himself all over the best he could. Last, he dipped the yucca root into the water and using the pulp end as he might use a bar of soap, he lathered his hair and then with the broken handled cup, he poured the rest of the water from the Dutch oven over his head and wiped the excess water off his shoulders with the t-shirt.

There was no place to rinse his hair or body. The little crudely printed bulletin had said yucca root soap required no rinsing. He felt refreshed for the first time since his Sunday night shower at the house, the night before he ran. He vowed that this would become a daily ritual. Later in the summer, perhaps the creek water would be warm enough to bathe in, but this early in the summer, the creek water was ice cold.

Cliff looked at the denim shirts, pair of overalls, tee shirts, socks and underwear hanging on the meat-drying frames where he hoped they would be dry by morning.

If a pair was dry enough, he would put on the driest pair of overalls to sleep in that night and wear them the next day. The next night he would put on a clean pair and launder the dirty pair. He would do the same with underwear and socks. Each night he would go to bed clean and fresh.

It was suppertime before he had finished the simple task of laundering five items of clothing and taking the equivalent of a sponge bath.

~~~

Before supper, Cliff, still naked, climbed the toeholds to the rim top. He walked back into the timber to relieve himself. He brushed back duff under a piñon, much as a cat would, and relieved himself into the hole. When he was finished, he covered the waste. He went to a different tree each time each day. This was what he did while working in the fields or when he accompanied his dad fishing.

The rangers at Mesa Verde explained that archeologists found human waste along with corncobs, broken pottery, and other trash in the trash heaps on the slopes downhill from cliff dwellings. They usually concluded their description with a comment on how it must have smelled in a large community, especially in summer.

He was uncertain what to do during the winter.

Every home on the Ridge had an outhouse. Most homes had only a cistern for a water supply except for Cliff's family who got their water from the reservoir. However, water was not plentiful enough for a flush toilet.

He could hardly build an outhouse on the ledge.

When his dad had been ill for several weeks, his mother had tended him. She had collected his waste in a special pot and carried it to the outhouse. Cliff decided that was the answer. He would make a waterproof pot or basket. When winter arrived and snow began to fall, like the Ancestral Puebloans, he would pour it over the ledge. There were several places where anything he dropped would land in a scrub oak stand or far down the canyon slope.

39

Cornbread and pinto beans
Martinez Canyon

Cliff sat on the doorsill sipping hot clover blossom tea heated in the coffee can, warmed up from the sun tea brewed the day before. It was a beautiful morning. He thought about climbing to the rim and watching the sunrise over Hesperus.

He felt clean and fresh. He had slept in clean underwear, overalls and tee-shirt. When he got up, he had fresh clean socks to put on. He had even rinsed his shoes with soapy water and they had dried odor free over night.

He didn't itch this morning. His hair felt clean and fresh. He had combed it out with his pocket comb the night before. *The missionary was right. That yucca root really works.*

I've already put on a can of beans to soak. I've got stew beginning to simmer
~~~

in the Dutch oven. Tonight I'm going to have beans and cornbread. If I can learn how to make cornbread in here, then things will be ok once again.

Cliff had done nothing with the corn since bringing it back to the ruin.

Now seems the right time. Supper will be a feast of cornbread and pinto beans. Umm good. He had no idea how long it actually would take to cook the corn. It would be strictly an experiment.

The beans were another matter. They would have to soak and then cook. At best, they wouldn't be edible until that night. When his mother needed an emergency batch of beans, she boiled the beans for a few minutes, and then let them soak in the same water for as long as she had time, and then she changed the water and cooked them for half a day. Or, if she had even less time, she cooked them in the pressure cooker. In the future, he could soak them all night, cook them in the morning and have them ready for lunch. They would simmer by the fire in the coffee can.

The corn bread would provide Cliff starch and carbohydrate. The corn would also complete the missing amino acids lacking in the pinto beans to make them a complete protein source. Etta Mae knew this. Cliff loved both corn bread and pinto beans and so got the full protein. But he didn't know that was the reason she served them together. He had heard his father preach the virtue of pinto bean's protein value, however.

These beans would provide me all the protein I need. I'll bet if I had enough pinto beans I wouldn't have to worry about finding meat at all. Unfortunately, if I only eat beans, I'll run out in a few weeks. There won't be more until almost winter.

He filled the porcelain cup full of beans, poured them into the empty coffee can, filled the can half full of water, and set the can on the coolest end of the cooking stone in the fire pit. The beans would almost triple in size as they soaked.

About mid-day, he would pour the water out, rinse the beans, put in enough water to cover the beans and put the can back on the cooking stone to simmer all afternoon. He would also break several sticks of porcupine jerky into pieces and add them to the beans for flavor. Each time he returned to check the fire he would also check the water level and add water if it got low. By suppertime, the beans should be tender enough to eat.

Cliff finished his tea and checked the stew cooking in the Dutch oven. He had mixed chopped asparagus, cattail shoot, dandelion greens, lambs quarter, porcupine jerky, and water and it simmered the way he wanted it. He lifted a piece of jerky with his pocketknife and blew on it until he could taste it. The piece was still chewy but would add flavor to the vegetables. He lifted the Dutch oven away from the coals, fished out the vegetables into the cup, and ate them using the willow stick to spear the pieces or to loop them into his mouth. He scooped the liquid up, drank it and felt satisfied with a hot breakfast.

Mama skunk came over to see if he had something for her, and he gave her a piece of jerky. She had become bolder after the present of meat scraps. As she became friendlier, one of the young ones followed along.

Cliff gave it a little piece of jerky too. The other four youngsters stayed on their side of the dwelling, preferring to play or doze, still too shy to be friends with the human.

Although it was a whole day before suppertime, Cliff decided not to wait until then to learn how to make corn bread.

He carried a few kernels of corn outside the dwelling to where the grindstones leaned against the front wall. He wiped the least worn *metate,* grindstone base, clean with his sleeve and put a small handful of kernels in the trough. The hard dry kernels slid forward under the *mano* when he applied pressure to them and pushed forward. He lifted the *mano* and looked at the kernels. They were as whole as when he put them on the *metate.*

Cliff tried cracking the kernels into smaller pieces one by one with the *mano.* The pointed edges of the cracked kernels kept them in place as he again put pressure on the *mano* and rubbed it back and forth over them. After a few passes they began to grind steadily down to finer and finer meal.

Is this how the mother of the house did it long ago? She must have had so much practice that she didn't even have to think about what she was doing. I wonder if she used that stone and her little daughter used this one. What was their life like? This is really hard work!

He didn't know how much corn to start with. The initial grind produced a small handful of meal, which he raked off the end of the *metate* into the porcelain cup. He scraped the stone clean with the hunting knife and carried the cup inside.

Ed Kelley had a knack for mechanics and Etta Mae was a natural born cook. Cliff had not yet developed instincts for either skill. Undoubtedly, his mother could have looked at the meager amount of cornmeal and have thought of myriad ways of turning it into a gourmet dish.

Cliff thought back to his mother in the kitchen making tortillas. He remembered her pouring water into corn flour and then forming balls of dough, which she rolled out with her rolling pin, and then putting the flat thin dough on the griddle. He thought she used waxed paper to transfer the rolled dough to the griddle. He couldn't remember if she added any other ingredients like an egg, salt or soda to the cornmeal. It didn't matter. He had nothing else to add anyway.

He added a little water and then more until the cornmeal formed dough around his fingers. He shaped it into a ball and tried to press it flat between the palms of his hands, but it kept sticking to his palms. He finally gave up and scraped the dough back in the cup.

He rubbed the dough that clung to his hands into little balls and pressed them back into the dough in the cup. He closed his eyes and brought back the image of his mother in the kitchen. Flour. She had put flour on the board that she had used to roll out the tortillas.

He took several more kernels of corn, returned to the grinding stone and ground them down to as fine a meal as he could get, scraped it into his palm with his knife and returned to the fire pit.

This time he spread the fresh corn meal on a bed slat board. He pinched the dough into a ball again and took it from the cup. There was still corn meal on the palm he had used to transport the meal to the slat. He noted with satisfaction that the dough did not stick to his hand this time.

He placed the ball of dough on the spread out corn meal in the middle of the bed slat board and began pressing the dough out into a thin corn cake with his thumbs. When it began to crack around the edges and threaten to fall apart, Cliff picked it up on the hunting knife and his fingers and transferred it to the hot cooking stone next to the can of simmering beans.

I'll bet the Indian mother was able to pat these cakes out in her hand just like that and toss them on the stone and they never stuck to her hand. Pat, pat, pat, back and forth, and onto the stone they go, yo, ho, yo, ho!

He had no idea how long to cook the three-inch diameter piece of dough. The stone was hot enough to raise a drop of water into a dancing ball before it boiled off into steam.

When the thin corn pancake began to look dry around the edge and crack, he used the hunting knife to turn it. It broke in half during that process.

The corn cake didn't rise up and turn golden like corn bread, which was a disappointment. It just started looking more and more like dried out dough and continued cracking around the edges as it cooked.

Cliff broke off a piece to cool it enough to taste. Without salt, it was bland. It was dense, not fluffy and crumbly like Etta Mae's cornbread. It was more like eating a thick tasteless tortilla or pancake.

He ate the morsel and waited only a short time for the second side to cook before removing it from the stone to the wood slat to cool. *Maybe it will taste better if I use it to soak up some of the stew gravy or crumble it in the stew. On the other hand, maybe not.*

~~~

That evening he tried a new batch of cornbread, which turned out about the same as the morning's experiment. This time he made three of the little cakes.

He slid the can of beans to the edge of the cooking stone and then off onto the bed slat and moved it away from the fire pit. He held the top of the can with his gloved hand, tipped the coffee can to pour the cup nearly full of pinto beans, moved the can back to the cooking stone and added more water to let them keep simmering. The cup of beans had indeed grown to nearly three times their original bulk. He would have enough beans for the next day. Unfortunately, they would also occupy the coffee can so he didn't have it to heat water to do the evening's laundry. But then again this evening he had only a pair of socks, and a pair of underwear to launder. He could do all that in the Dutch oven after dinner.
~~~

He sat on the saddle blanket and dipped pinto beans with the stiff corn cake.

In a former life, he would have pushed aside the tasteless corn cake. Now he forced himself to eat it. It was different from eating beans and cornbread at his mom's table, but he thought the food value was probably the same when he got down to it.

At his mother's table, he would have had catsup and a bowl of chili powder to spice up the pinto beans. The cornbread would be fluffy and doctored up with fresh butter. He would wash it all down with a tall glass of cold whole milk.

This would be a little better with ketchup on it, but I'll take it. He drank from a mason jar and picked up the second half of a corn cake. He carried it, the cup of beans and tea to the doorsill and sat in the late afternoon sunshine. There he finished eating while he soaked up sunshine and rested. It had been a good day.

40
Sipapu
Martinez Canyon

Cliff heard a rustling and looked down. His little friend nuzzled his hand looking for a handout. He had put a small piece of the corn cake in his bib pocket just in such case, and he held it out to his little black and white friend. The creature daintily accepted it with his front paw and teeth and moved away a foot to eat it. Then it moved forward again and accepted Cliff's petting and scratching behind the ears before prancing back to its siblings and mamma.

Cliff continued to watch the mama skunk and her family.

The babies have grown in just the time I've been here. I think she's weaning them now. It won't be much longer before she sends them out on their own. I don't know how to feel about that.

Mamma skunk and her brood had continued to make the dwelling their home base. He had cultivated her friendship with morsels of dandelion and bits of dried meat. He liked having her company, and her presence reassured him. She had become his friend of sorts. He talked to her when she was around. She had apparently grown used to him and ignored him when he walked around the ruin. She hardly lifted her tail, when he walked right by her anymore.

The green vegetables Cliff brought to the cave had begun to attract an occasional deer mouse. Mamma was an excellent mouser and caught every one. The human and the little mammal had an amiable and functional relationship.

Cliff had named the friendliest baby Moonbeam. Following the night-time theme, he called the others Star Light, Star Bright, First Star and Milky Way. They were most active at night and slept most of the day. Each was distinguishable by subtitle differences in the white stripes on their foreheads, backs and tails.

Moonbeam in particular was very adventuresome and friendly and ate from Cliff's hand. So far, she was the only one brave enough to let him scratch her behind the ears. *I'm sure you are a she, Moonbeam, because you preen so much of the time and flirt with me. I'm going to miss you most of all when you leave me.*

Cliff smiled as he watched the skunks. Mamma skunk had shown up the first night, almost as if she was there to keep an eye on him and to protect him against the things he feared most in the night with her presence and powerful scent gland. His fear of the dark had been realized the first night by the visitation of the bobcat. But even the bobcat had given up its supper to provide breakfast for him that first morning. He still had its hide as a reminder that he could overcome his fear of the dark.

He thought about the young cottontails sacrificing themselves to keep him alive by revealing their den to him the week before. It had come at a very opportune time. He had been afraid of everything. He thought he was losing his mind. Then it was as though Mother Nature stepped in to take care of him. Maybe it was both his Heavenly Father and Earthly Mother.

The cottontails had shown up on an afternoon when he really needed meat. He had made a promise: *Mamma Cottontail, I won't try to catch any more of them. I'm sure there are others to carry on. I'm leaving the rest of them for you. Thank you for sharing them with me now. I had a hard time this week. I won't waste anything. I hope your spirit lives long and safely. Heavenly Father, help me clear my mind and take care of my folks. Mother Nature thank you for sharing your creatures with me.*

He had made a promise that day, and he thought about it at some time every day.

Cliff still struggled with fear of the dark. Each night was a challenge. Some nights were not so bad. Sounds in the canyon still woke him, but with less and less frequency.

Dangers of the night were no longer an abstract concept. They were real. A false step in the dark and he could fall hundreds of feet. In just two weeks time, he had seen the tracks of bobcats, lynx and even sign of a mountain lion in the canyon. He heard coyotes nightly. He hadn't seen one of the big cats or a coyote yet, but their fresh tracks were in the dust and in the mud along the creek. He'd seen deer kills that only a mountain lion or pack of coyotes could have brought down. From the dwelling, it was only 15 miles to the high slopes of the LaPlata Mountains. Who knew what large predators grew in the forests there or how far their territories extended?

It seems like my life in this canyon is becoming more dependent on these little critters all the time.

His thoughts flashed back to the dream of the man and his message. *Was it just a dream?*

What are those sounds out there really? Are they spirits talking to each other? Are those really owls and coyotes? Aren't the coyotes supposed to be tricksters? Or, are those the spirits of the ancient hunters and shaman discussing this new intruder in their canyon? The hair prickled on the back of his neck as he thought about it.

That night when he awoke, he listened to the breeze blowing through the rocks and trees and the great cedar tree outside. *I can hear the drumbeats and the chanting again.* He listened more closely. *No, I guess it is only the frogs down at the creek. Or is it?*

He was very aware that only a few feet away from where he spread the saddle blanket each night, a round hole had been drilled into the clay surface of the floor. In *kivas* on Mesa Verde, the rangers called similar holes *the Sipapu.* It was the spirit hole, the portal through which the First People of the Ancestral Puebloans had emerged from the underworld and the portal through which the Ancestral Puebloans communicated with their ancestors.

Cliff and his neighbor George had talked about Mother Nature. George and Ed's concepts of Mother Nature were different. Ed spoke of Mother Nature in vague terms as God's handiwork. George spoke of Her as on a near level with God, as a caretaker of the spirits of the non-human living flora and fauna on earth and even beyond that to the very earth itself. She was God's counterpart on Earth.

Cliff had asked George if that was so, then how could George eat Mother Nature's creatures and bounty. George had said that he should always ask permission first of the game he hunted and if granted and he took it, use all of it, never waste it. He must make the animal or plant proud of the way its meat, its hide, or its fiber was used, and any parts that he couldn't use properly should be made available to Mother Nature's other creatures. When George died, he wanted his body made available for Mother Nature's other creatures even if they were the worms in the earth. George used the term Mother Nature and Earthly Mother interchangeably.

George also said that if he was going to survive on Mother Nature's creatures, then he had to be willing to sacrifice his life to protect Mother Nature's creatures. He had spent much of his adult life doing just that.

Ed Kelley believed that only man, among all other living things, had a soul. All other life had been created to be overseen and if necessary consumed by man. No other living thing had a soul. He owed nothing to the other creatures, but he believed he was a caretaker and as such it was his duty to treat them humanely. So who was right? Mother Nature with a spirit in man and all living things? Or did man alone have a direct link to God?

Dad believes that God created nature to be dominated by man. He believes in God, and Jesus, and something he calls the Holy Ghost. Dad prays nightly and at every meal. He goes to Church every Sunday if he can find anyone else who agrees with him. To Dad we walk with those spirits looking over our shoulders at all times. And he believes their angels are everywhere looking over us too. The animals, plants and earth are on their own.

Two years ago, when I was 12, I walked down the aisle and was baptized. For a while, I thought I felt a spirit following me around. I talked with it and asked it to help me through difficult times in life like with Hector and Mr. Johnson. And I think it helped a little to have enough courage to "turn the other cheek," as Dad said. Then when things began to get bad with Dad, and I asked for help, the spirit disappeared. I prayed to him to soften Dad's heart. But, how could I ask God or Jesus or the Holy Ghost to help me against my dad? Dad was praying to them too. I know that Dad must have been asking the same spirits to straighten me out.

Cliff had become confused and had given up inside. He had begun to go through the motions. When the family went to church, he had no choice but to go along. But, the joy was gone. The bright light had gone out, but Cliff hadn't quit believing in God. After all there was a lot out there in nature that was wonderful and beautiful, but he wasn't seeing much wonderfulness in human nature. Why would God forsake all that was beautiful and put it at the mercy of merciless humankind?

The nature that compelled him to believe in a Heavenly Father and Mother Nature were in the order and wonder of the bee colony and the beauty of his columbine flower bed, the blossom of a prickly pear cactus, the delicate petals of a sego lily, the faint fragrance of the alfalfa patch, the sunrise over the La Plata Mountains, and thunderous lightning storms over Ute Mountain.

He had listened closely to George talk about Mother Nature and tuned out long dreary droning sermons on Sunday denouncing fellow Christians and their heathen activities like youth activities, dancing, and Sunday school. He had turned to the chapters in the Old Testament and read the stories about David vs. Goliath. In that story, he visualized himself in the role of David and Hector as Goliath. When he read the stories of Solomon, he thought of Ed and George. In the Book of Job he wondered if the message was to himself, and if he was patient long enough, would he survive and prevail.

He became more interested in George's philosophy of world religions when he read about the crusades in the stories by Sir Walter Scott in *Ivanhoe* and *The Talisman*.

If George is right, the spirits of hundreds of generations of Native Americans could be roaming the canyon. The canyon and the four corners region were occupied with civilized people for several thousand years before Jesus walked the earth. Even if George is wrong and Dad is right, there could still be the souls of all the Indian people who lived in this canyon over thousands of years out there, couldn't there? If George is right then they might be happy souls. If Dad is right, I guess their ghosts walking the canyon might be in some form of Hell.

Dad used to read to us that the prophets in the old testaments got their messages from spirits through dreams. Could that still happen? I'm not a prophet, but could I still get a dream from a spirit?

The hunter or shaman, or whoever he was, in the dream seemed to be giving me permission to be here, but he also seemed to be giving me a duty. He just pointed to everything and told me to take care of all of it,

'Adversity presents
Unique opportunity,
A moment of time,
God's wilderness,
Use the time wisely.'

But, he didn't say anything is for the taking.

Cliff moved over next to the Sipapu and sat down on the floor facing it. He leaned forward toward the hole in the floor and started at it. As if he could communicate with the man through the Ancient portal, he said, "So, I'm trying to do as you said. If you let me live here, I will try to make you proud. I'm trying to stay clean and healthy, I'm trying to learn something new every day and I'm trying to accomplish something every day. If you are a guardian of this place, I will make you a promise. I will only take what I need. I will waste nothing, if I can understand how to use it. If I promise to do this, will you help me? Will you show me how?"

He moved back to the saddle blanket, laid down and drifted back to sleep.

The breeze blew a little more softly through the branches of the bee tree, the frogs sang with gusto down at the creek, an occasional cricket joined in. A great horned owl called "whaWho-whowho" in the cedar bee tree outside. On the south rim of the canyon, a pack of coyotes began to yip and howl.

41
Routines
Martinez Canyon

Each morning I face a new dawn, the world around me looks fresh and new, and I feel refreshed and ready to face new challenges.

Mamma skunk and all but one of her brood left last night and didn't come back this morning, but Moonbeam was curled up near me when I awoke. Mama skunk has never left her alone with me before. Is Moonbeam a free agent now, has she chosen me?

I've read about some tribes sending boys on a quest to find their totem. Have I found my totem? How should I feel about this? They searched for bears, mountain lions or eagles. What does it mean to have a skunk as a totem? I'll always be a little stinker? Cliff smiled at the thought.

My headache hasn't come back, thank goodness. I'm so tired each night, I'm asleep when my head hits the floor.

Life is good for the moment. I don't feel as afraid right now. I look forward to dawn each morning. I can greet each dawn with new appreciation and anticipation. Time seems to fly by each day.

Days are getting hotter. But that doesn't seem to have much effect on the cave. It is very comfortable inside. Nothing much seems to change the temperature of this mass of rock.

~~~

Cliff had established several routines and made rules for himself during the first weeks in the ruin. The first week had been chaos. By the end of the week, he realized staying in the ruin amounted to no more than an unrealistic fantasy and he was ready to go home if he could do it gracefully. That first week he had not kept a schedule or routine. When he woke up in the middle of the following week and faced the reality that he couldn't gracefully go back, he made his mind up to build a new life.

Before he could go out into the world and compete, he had to build himself up to compete with it. If it took all summer or if it took a year, then so be it. To survive he had to have a plan. His mother and father didn't just live day by day. The orchard he and his dad planted were seedlings that came up to his three-year-old waist. Seven years later Ed had let the first fruit go to maturity on the young trees.

Cliff had captured his first swarm, not by accident, but by careful planning and observation.

If his future had suddenly landed into his own hands instead of continuing in the hands of his parents and teachers, then he had to take care not to screw it up.

The days took on a pattern that gave form to his new life. He made an informal list in his head. He had no tablet to write the list on and no pencil to check each task when he completed it.

Get up and build up the fire.

Greet the day with a cold cup of tea using the last cup from the sun tea made the day before.

Put a new jar of water and clover blossoms, dandelion blossoms, mint leaves, or charred and ground dandelion root out on the ledge to make sun tea.

Pour out the water the pinto beans had soaked in overnight and cover the now plump beans with fresh water. Move the can to the cooking stone to simmer through the morning.

Cook a morning stew in the Dutch oven.

Go to the canyon to gather vegetables for the evening meal and next day breakfast. Bring back either willows or other material for later use.

During the heat of the day, use the coolness in the dwelling to learn to do one new thing such as build a trap, make a tool, make fiber from yucca leaves, turn fiber into rope, make a basket, work clay, make a clay pot, learn to tan the rabbit hides.
~~~

Late afternoon, gather firewood. Stockpile enough firewood to last all through the winter.

Prepare evening stew. Make corn cake to go with beans.

Bathe and then launder yesterday's clothes. Hang them to dry.

Study the scrapbook to learn more about survival tools, traps, hunting weapons, etc.

Turn in when it gets dark.

42
Trapping
Martinez Canyon

Cliff lifted the corn *tortilla* from the cooking stone with the hunting knife. It was more of a thin corn cake than a tortilla. *I'll bet I've made a hundred of these so far, and they don't look or taste any better than the first one. I can't keep thinking how much the taste would improve with a little fresh Guernsey butter on it.*

He made the corn cakes more palatable by spreading a little honey on them, but he would have to cut back soon, or he would run out of the delicacy.

He spooned the porcelain cup full of pinto beans that had been simmering all morning. Into that, he crumbled the corn cake and used the cedar spoon to scoop the beans and corn cake into his mouth. He ate raw cattail shoots that tasted like cucumber, and asparagus spears in between mouthfuls of beans.

Cliff set aside time to work on making at least one thing each day. He was trying to learn to use the Dutch oven lid as a cook surface. However, things seemed to want to stick to it more than they stuck to the stone. He needed fat. For now, the lid served a better purpose as a lid for the Dutch oven. He could heap it with coals to help cook whatever he put inside.

One day he carved a wooden spoon to make it easier to dip from the Dutch oven or coffee can into the porcelain cup, and to eat soup or stew from the broken handled cup. He chose a piece of dried cedar wood from the stack of firewood. The wood was hard enough that it did not absorb the moisture in the soup. It was easy to whittle and smooth. He liked the texture of the wood and appreciated the finished look. He had whittled horse's heads and objects out of pine boards before but had not tried whittling out of dead wood like cedar.

Cattails would be available all summer, and continued to be abundant, but they would go to seed soon, and the shoots would not be nearly as succulent. Dandelions had bloomed out and the leaves were no longer tender and sweet, but he still dug the roots.

One of the afternoon chores had been to make a wooden handle for the file-knife. He used a piece of red cedar. Fastening it was the challenge. Ed had drilled holes in the shank that he planned to use to fasten the elk horn handles. Cliff drilled matching holes and used damp sinew. He wound the sinew in bands around the wooden handles and through the holes and threaded the ends back beneath the bands. As the sinew dried, it shrunk and bound the wood tightly against the shank. The thin bands fit comfortably in his bare hands. Having a handle made the file-knife much easier to use as a digging tool.

He ate the roots raw like carrots and chopped them into the stew. Lambs quarter greens were now leggy and in bloom. They would be loaded with seed in the fall. Sparrows loved them. His mother gathered the seed and used them instead of poppy seed.

He missed the lettuce that was probably coming on in his mom's garden.

Cliff charred some of the dandelion roots, ground them and used them as an alternative to the clover tea.

Cliff set aside a small piece of corn cake for Moonbeam and used the last piece to sop the inside of the cup clean. There was no meat in the beans that night. The porcupine jerky was gone. He had searched for other cottontail nests in vain. For the past week, his protein had come solely from pinto beans, and they wouldn't last much longer, unless he could get a supply of meat coming in.

He had built a working trap, tested it several times, and it worked each time. From that he had all the components assembled for three traps.

If the traps didn't work, he would have to use the .22, at least occasionally, even if he risked discovery, until he made them work or found a place where they worked.

Charlie had shown him how to make his first "four point" trap. With it he had caught the mean old red rooster and several chickens before his dad caught him at it. He had caught a whipping for using the trap on the farmyard poultry. His dad had explained that it was inhumane because it used a noose. Cliff had argued that it was not as inhumane as leg hold metal traps, and that if he caught a fryer chicken in it the fryer would get its head wrung off anyway so what was the difference. He had nearly caught another whipping for "talking back."

Strong fine rope was required for the noose on a "four-point" snare. He would use some of the jute twine from the granary. In time, he would try to make his own twine. He had the raw material in the stack of yucca leaves that continued to grow in the back of the cave. He was learning how to extract the fiber from the pulp of the leaves already, but he had not tried to twist it into cording.

The simple trap had four parts: the noose; an upright leg about fifteen inches long; a horizontal trigger/bait stick; and a trip stick.

When assembled, these three sticks formed the figure **4** and were the trap's tripping mechanism. Bait was stuck onto the end of the horizontal trigger/bait stick. The prey dislodged the trigger stick from the notch in the upright, releasing the catch (trip) stick. The catch stick held tension on a twine bending the branch of a nearby shrub or tree. When the tension released, the branch snapped upright. Tied to the branch was a twine, which looped to the ground and encircled additional bait in a noose. When the branch snapped it would usually tighten around the prey's leg.

Depending on the size of the prey and the strength of the branch, the prey could be lifted into the air where, if caught by the leg, it could dangle until its cries brought the trapper or other predators for it. If the trapper had to use a smaller sapling or brush, the snare might only be strong enough to keep the bird or animal from flying off or running away. It was important to check the trap often because nearby predators would respond to the cries of a tethered prey. In that case, the hunter might only find feathers or blood and hair for his trouble.

For each upright, he cut a two-inch diameter willow piece a little over fifteen inches long and squared it. He sharpened the end of each peg and hardened the point by bringing it to the near charred stage in the fire. He next squared the top so he would have a surface to pound it into the ground. He laid it on the floor and marked it about an inch down from the top. With his pocketknife, he made a vertical cut a quarter of an inch deep the full width of the peg and opened the cut a little steeper than 45 degrees.

He laid the upright peg on the floor with the notch facing forward. Cliff would drive the peg into the ground about halfway. He cut the notch for the horizontal bait stick about an inch above the halfway point. He cut that notch at a forty-five degree angle on the lower side and straight across the top and two-thirds the depth of the peg.

For the horizontal trigger/bait stick, he had squared a one-inch willow and trimmed it a couple of inches longer than the upright. It would lie horizontally in the notch in the upright. He tapered the trigger stick so that the bait end came to a point. He notched the opposite end about an inch from the end of the stick. That notch would cradle the trip stick. The trip stick was short and held the end of the twine from the tree or bush that would tighten the noose and the end of the noose itself.

Last, he cut the trip (catch) stick, the forty-five degree angle of the **4**. It was just short of half the length of the upright. He cut the end at an angle to fit the notch on the end of the horizontal bait stick. The other end fit into the notch near the top of the upright.

~~~

The morning routines were completed, it was time to set the traps.

After Cliff's first week in the ruin, the rope had not dangled from the face of the cliff. He now carried it out with him when he hauled wood back to the cave or lowered other heavy items to the ledge.

He also used it to access parts of the canyon from the ledge rather than
~~~

walking a mile up canyon and following the deer trail down. It was still an easier climb down into the canyon from further up, but there were things closer by that he could use, like firewood.

On one of those forays, he had discovered that right below the ledge was a shelf where a variety of large birds liked to sun and fluff their feathers in the dust.

He wedged a chunk of firewood with the end of the rope tied to it in a crack at the edge of the rock chute at the end of the ledge. The components of the traps were in the burlap gunnybag hanging over his neck and down under his arm. He climbed down the rope in the chute to the rocks and stepped over to soil. From there he was able to traverse downward across the canyon slope to a spot where a couple of days before, from a little higher above and to the side, he had observed quail and grouse sunning and dusting their feathers.

In the dust were numerous bird tracks of all sizes. Among those of the smaller game birds, were a few larger tracks that he hoped might be those of the turkeys he saw gliding along at dawn and dusk around the oak groves in the canyon.

He selected a branch on an oak sapling as a spring pole, set up a **4**-point trigger, spread the noose/loop, scattered a few precious kernels of cracked corn around within the loop and jammed a piece of fresh dandelion root onto the point of the trigger/bait stick. A prey could trip the trigger either by picking at the bait on the end of the bait stick or brushing against the end of the bait stick as it pecked at the bait on the ground within the noose.

Cliff was afraid that as soon as he left, magpies would come eat the corn. He didn't think they would eat the root. He didn't know if turkeys would eat the root or not. The domestic turkeys on the farm would eat anything like that thrown to them. He would check the trap just before sundown to see if he'd caught anything or not.

The narrow level of dusting soil that the game birds frequented stretched around a fifty-foot ribbon shaped curve bordered by scrub oak. Cliff set all three traps along the shelf so that none was in the sight of the others.

Before returning to the dwelling after setting the traps, Cliff examined the slope between there and the canyon bottom.

He had not been to the creek directly from the ruin since the discovery the summer before. The canyon was deeper here than at the deer trail up canyon and had been more difficult to climb.

He surveyed the slope looking for a way down to the creek and decided that it was futile to attempt it. The previous climb had been from his left up-canyon. If he went to the canyon directly from the ruin, he would have to go down at a slant to his left when he faced the canyon. He was certain he could do it, but it would hardly be worth the effort. Carrying much weight out of the canyon here would be nearly impossible because of the steep climbs. It would be very dangerous for him to attempt it alone and repeatedly. Getting to this ledge from above was easy enough, but no further. He headed back up the slope for home.

When he reached the ledge and approached the dwelling, a large grasshopper flew from almost under his foot startling him. It landed on a clover stalk in the foliage growing outside the wall of the dwelling. Tall orchard grass, fescue and clover grew in the silt that had blown in from the desert and settled in the seep. Birds drinking in the puddle from the spring had deposited the seeds in their droppings. The grasses and clover seeds had taken root. After many eons of summers, a miniature oasis grew on the ledge.

Additional water seeped from under the caprock to augment the meager runoff from the spring. Without the shade from an overhanging cave, the exposed clover and grasses benefited from the hot sun and the reflected night heat from the rock face. Yellow clover with roots in the cool damp soil grew to its full seven-foot potential and covered itself with bright blossom.

The foliage attracted grasshoppers, butterflies and other insects, which had in turn attracted Mamma skunk. Now that Mamma was gone, Moonbeam hunted grasshoppers and garter snakes in the oasis and deer mice when they came into the dwelling. Cliff had never discovered the skunk's secret passageway to the ledge.

Cliff left the greenery alone in his foraging, except for green grass when he had fresh meat. Then he cut enough green grass to help keep the meat cool and protect it from flies. Unfortunately, since the porcupine he hadn't needed to cut any grass. The area was also a constant supply of clover blossoms for tea, although he collected a majority of his clover blossoms whenever he went to the creek. When they matured, he would harvest as many of the clover seeds as he could wrestle from the birds. As the clover came to full bloom, he was beginning to harvest all of his fresh blooms from the oasis and dry what he brought back from the creek. The dried blooms would serve as tea during the winter.

Most of all, he enjoyed the fragrance the clover blossoms brought to the cave every evening and the sound of the honeybees working the blossoms during the day.

Cliff was aware of the big grasshoppers and the role they played in the mamma skunk's pantry, but he hadn't given them much attention as he walked by, and he was startled by the big insect which immediately began to devour a leaf on a stem of the clover plant a few feet away.

Cliff removed his straw hat and crept forward, barely moving until he was close enough to strike. He drew back just far enough to gather momentum and swung the hat forward. The force of the air swept the clover stalk carrying the big grasshopper off the stalk and onto the ground at Cliff's feet where the hat completed its sweep and covered it. He reached under the hat until he felt the hopper's wing, and closed his fist around the insect. He pinched off the head and put the hopper into the bib pocket of his overalls.

It took only a few minutes for Cliff to catch a dozen large, plump grasshoppers. He removed their heads as he caught them.

He returned to the dwelling with his catch.

The baking stone was still hot over the coals of the breakfast fire. Cliff rinsed the hoppers, pinched off the bone-like legs at the joint below the fat thighs, dumped them on the cooking stone and stirred them around with the hunting knife as they sizzled and popped. He ground enough meal to make a corn cake, mixed it with water, pressed it out and put it on one end of the baking stone to bake.

When the corn cake was done, he scraped the browned grasshoppers onto it, folded it over, closed his eyes and bit into it. The compliment of soft cake and crunchy grasshoppers was satisfying, if he didn't think too much about what he was eating.

He spooned beans into the cup and alternated between the corn cake/grasshoppers and pinto beans. *What a nice lunch. Mrs. Campbell said grasshoppers are a good source of protein. If the traps don't work then this might work. There are plenty of them down in the canyon and out on top. I don't need the .22 to go after grasshoppers.*

Hunger overcame any other thoughts about taste. The only real problem with grasshoppers was there weren't quite enough to satisfy his appetite. His family had meat for almost every meal. Since moving to a solitary existence in the canyon, he had become primarily a vegetarian. He missed having meat with almost every meal. *I took these grasshoppers from Moonbeam's pantry. If the traps don't work, and I have to begin eating more grasshoppers, six at a time won't do it. I could wipe out her supply in no time. I would have to range out for them. I think it would take a lot of time and energy to catch enough grasshoppers to live on. Or I can begin using the .22. Even if I use the .22 the shells won't last long. I suppose I could go after ants. There are quite a few ants here in the canyon. Yummy! I read that ants are even higher in protein than grasshoppers.*

Late in the afternoon, he went down to where he could see if there was action at the traps. He didn't see the usual number of birds sunning and dusting. Either they were shying away from the traps, or something was spooking them.

As he approached the first trap, he could hear rustling and struggling sounds. He picked up his pace. A bird of some kind was in the trap. As he feared, it was a black and white magpie, which had come to feed on free corn. The bird was snared by its leg and was not injured. It flew to the end of the tether and landed in the top of the shrub that imprisoned him. Cliff released him, and it flew squawking toward the willow breaks at the creek. *You go bird. Tell the rest of them to leave the corn alone in the traps, or you'll get your scrawny neck caught!*

When Cliff arrived within sight of the second trap, he stopped and stared in amazement. A bronze turkey hen dangled by one leg from the noose. Cliff fished the pocketknife from his pocket as he approached. She had been hanging quietly until she saw his movement, and then she began flapping her long wings once more, trying to take off. He moved forward quickly, grabbed her wings, and got his arms around them, folding them back against her body so that she couldn't flog him with them. She was strong, but she had been struggling and was tired.

Cliff wrapped the twine around the second leg and tied a simple half-hitch knot in it to immobilize both legs so that she couldn't rake him with her sharp toenails. He turned her wings loose, and she hung from the scrub oak spring pole. She flapped her powerful wings, but with both feet bound, she was helpless. Cliff opened the long straight blade of his pocketknife, pinched her jaws open, quickly inserted the blade into the roof of her mouth, stabbed into her brain, pulled it back, turned it to her throat, severed her artery and turned her loose.

She was dead instantly. Her wings flapped a few times from muscle spasms as she bled out cleanly. While the hen turkey finished draining her life spirit onto the canyon slope, Cliff went to the next unsprung trap, disassembled it and put the components back into the gunnybag. He collected the trigger mechanism at the turkey site and collected the trap the magpie had tripped and returned to the turkey.

A turkey! I think turkeys were really important to the ancient ones here, maybe more important than cottontails. Was this another message from Mother Nature? From the spirits of the ancients?

She was a handsome bronze and grey bird. She was smaller than the domestic turkeys Etta Mae raised each summer, even though those were the same color. He untied her from the oak spring pole and lifted her full weight. He guessed she weighed at least ten or fifteen pounds. Cliff had seen the flock feeding on green food and insects along the creek and where they had scratched for acorns that had fallen from the scrub oak the fall before.

Cliff laid her down and arranged her. He stood humbly before her and faced to the north as the hunter had in the dream. He pointed to the east up the canyon. He swept his arm to the south, paused and then swept to the west. He paused and pointed to the ground and to the sky to complete the ritual. He had no way of knowing what the ritual's exact meaning was to the man in the dream. His dream state might have conjured it up from a cowboy and Indian movie matinee scene, but in the context of the dream the rite seemed to imply to Cliff that the universe was watching, and that he should acknowledge that.

I thank you Heavenly Father and Mother Nature for sharing your creature, this turkey hen with me today. I will not waste any part of her. I will not hunt or trap any other of your children except to survive. Let her spirit stay with me and help me understand as she helps me survive, he thought.

As he picked up the turkey and began climbing the slope, it nagged at him that he was breaking laws against poaching. *I know there are laws against hunting out of season, and that this isn't turkey season. I don't even know if there is a turkey season. Do laws and seasons outweigh a person's right to survive? I need to ask George about this. I know there is no season on porcupines. Why is it different to kill and eat this turkey than to kill and eat the porcupine, if*

I'm going to eat it or starve? If I was going to kill it for fun or to sell, well now, that might be different.

Cliff tied the rope around the hen's legs, climbed up to the ledge, lifted her up and carried her back to the dwelling thinking about how he would prepare her for cooking.

~~~

Picking and dressing turkeys was not new to Cliff.

Ed and Etta Mae grew a small flock of domestic turkeys each summer and marketed them in town at Thanksgiving each fall. It was a part of their fall cash crop, and they had repeat customers they could depend on. During the summer, the turkeys were also useful in the beans as they kept down grasshoppers, bugs and caterpillars that caused crop damage.

He and Etta Mae had worked out a system for harvesting their little flock of Thanksgiving turkeys. In the week before Thanksgiving, they would have to catch, slaughter, pick, clean and deliver 35 to 40 turkeys to their customers. Some years those days late in November came after snow was on the ground and the work had to be finished outside in cold weather. Cliff remembered standing in the cold with his feet turning to ice and snow falling around him while his parents labored over the steaming birds.

At picking time, Ed used a small 40-gallon barrel. This barrel sat beneath a block and tackle hanging from an apple tree in a straw covered area in the corner of the orchard. An hour or so before work began, Ed gathered apple wood and built a fire under the barrel and heated water almost to boiling. The barrel was just the right size to dip a big turkey into several times to scald it for picking.

Ed would lift a heavy 20 to 30 pound live turkey to a rope where Etta Mae would fasten a strap around its feet. While Ed continued to hold the bird still, she would insert the knife in the same way that Cliff had butchered the wild turkey. While that bird was left to bleed cleanly, Ed transferred a turkey that had already drained to the block and tackle by snapping a hook into the strap around the turkey's feet, tightening the rope, and releasing the strap from the first rope. The bird then swung over the barrel where Ed dipped it several times into the hot water, lifted it and transferred the bird to another rope. There Ed and Etta Mae picked the turkey and removed the pinfeathers.

The feathers went into a full size barrel. While the turkey hung from this rope, Etta Mae opened the turkey, removed the entrails while Ed brought fresh water and washed it down. That bird was then left to dry while they moved back to the turkey pen to round up the next victim.

~~~

Cliff considered how he would clean the turkey hen. The largest container he had was the Dutch oven. He could heat water in it, but he could hardly immerse the turkey in it. He had picked chickens and seen his parents pick turkeys and even the past two years had helped pick the turkeys. Hot water loosened the feathers.

It took a pretty good size pot to scald even a fryer chicken. It would take a canning size pressure cooker or the barrel to scald a turkey.

His mother skinned mallards when Ed brought them in from time to time. *I think that's the way to do it.*

Now that he had the turkey, he saw the unexpected prize of her feathers. In his review of the journal, as he now began to think of the scrapbook, he returned often to the articles on spears, bow and arrows, and the spear thrower, the atlatl. All of those hunting weapons used feathers for the arrows and spears. He still had the grouse wing and tail feathers. He had also collected magpie feathers from a carcass he had found, but none compared to the wing and tail feathers of the turkey hen.

Cliff wiped the slate he used as a door covering and laid the turkey on it on her back. He used the pocketknife to cut through the skin above the breastbone. Unlike the domestic turkeys Etta Mae raised, which had a plump breast, this wild turkey had very little breast development. Cliff wondered about that, then wondered if it had to do with this turkey's ability to fly long distances skimming over and along the slope of the canyon above the trees, scrub oak, and sage, whereas the Kelley flock of domestic turkeys were earth bound with their off balanced, front heavier weight development. Early in the summer, they liked to roost in trees around the barnyard, but they couldn't fly as such. The domestic turkey chicks that his mother ordered each spring were bred for meat production and were not meant to be released to survive in the wild.

He lifted the skin with his fingers as he cut along the front of the neck to just under the head. He cut the skin around the neck under the skull up to the comb on both sides. He peeled the skin off the neck gently using the piece of flint to help where the skin wanted to stay attached to the hen. His fingers did most of the work.

He cut all the way around the base of the neck so that he could peel the skin off the neck.

To remove the rest of the skin and feathers, he cut the skin down the center of the back from in front of the wings to in front of the "preacher's nose" as his dad called it. He cut through the fatty tail, leaving the skin and feathers attached to the skin of the back, legs, and back half of the stomach. This whole section was the hardest to skin and required the most use of the flint to cut loose the skin from the flesh.

When he was done, he opened the cavity and removed the crop, cleaned the gizzard, took out the intestines and found the egg sack, the oviduct.

It had not occurred to him that she might still be laying. He thought that laying season for most of the game birds was long over, that the young would have incubated, and they would already be out on their own.

He stared at her ripe egg chamber, the long elastic tube from her ovaries to her vent. A fully formed, ivory colored, egg was up against her vent opening. She must have been within hours of adding it to her nest. Another egg lay in the next chamber up the tube, the shell already formed, but chalky white, ready to descend. Up the tube from it were other eggs in progressively earlier stages of formation.

He removed two fully formed eggs with hard shells. Both were nearly the size of the goose eggs he had stolen from the nest at the Stone residence. A semi-transparent film covered the third egg in succession, and it held together when he removed it. He realized it was the film beneath the shell when he removed the shell on a hard boiled egg. He was able to remove two other smaller eggs in their transparent film sacs. *Why would you be getting ready to sit a nest this late in the summer? Your chicks should be half grown by now.*

He placed the two eggs with shells in a basket. The eggs with tough membrane he carefully placed in a separate container. The smaller eggs he put into the porcelain cup.

He had seen this before when Etta Mae had told him to catch an old laying hen that she thought had stopped laying eggs, a "stewing hen," she had called her. The hen had had a couple of eggs in her tube. Etta Mae had said she should have had a full tube of eggs if she was still a good layer. Now Cliff knew what she meant.

Cliff looked at the meat. It would sustain him for several days. He would eat some of it fresh today and smoke the rest as he had the porcupine. He would eat the eggs. The eggs without shells he would eat tonight. The others he would in the next several days.

I am so sorry Mother Nature for killing one of your Mothers and keeping her from laying her eggs and raising her babies! I am so sorry that I didn't let her go. I didn't think. I won't set the trap there again. I guess I won't set the traps anywhere again. I will find a way to hunt where I can see what I'm hunting. If I can't survive that way, then I'll give up eating meat. Please help me Heavenly Father and Earthly Mother.

43

Robbing the Bee Tree
Martinez Canyon

The quart of comb honey brought from the beekeeping supply closet that Saturday in May was gone. It had not lasted long. It had served as a constant source of energy in those first weeks before he began to settle into a rhythm in the cliff dwelling in Martinez Canyon.

He missed the sweet goodness of the honey, and the chewiness of the freshly secreted wax. Pollen was an acquired taste, but he had eaten it. After beginning to work with bees, his pollen intake had grown. He had no allergies to any of the plants on the farm.

He had no intention or desire to destroy the tree. It was much too valuable. The tree shielded the ruin from view, and protected it from the elements. He only wanted to take a little honey and leave the colony alone to keep manufacturing more.

George Williamson's present to Cliff on his twelfth birthday, had been a reprint of Langstroth's thin book with drawings and dimensions for hives and removable frames, the basis for the boxes and frames Cliff had made in his dad's shop.

Cliff had built several modern hives with supers based on Langstroth's hundred year old model of tiers of boxes each containing ten removable frames. The lower box was the colony's brood chamber. Upper boxes or supers, were for storing honey. He would collect honey by driving the bees down to the brood chambers with smoke, removing the full supers, and replacing them with empty supers. The frames were strung with thin sheets of beeswax foundation, held in place with wire, on which workers would build new honeycomb to fill with honey.

A strong colony might fill the equivalent of four or five deep supers in a summer season or twice that many shallow supers where Cliff lived on the Ridge. The shallow supers were for comb honey. When he harvested for comb honey, he cut the capped comb from the frames, and he placed it into wide mouth pint or quart jars and filled around the comb with strained pure honey. He harvested comb honey only on new comb. Deep supers were used for extracted honey. When the frames were full and capped, he cut the caps off, set the frames into a centrifugal extractor and whirled the honey out. The empty combs were replaced into the super and put back onto the hive to be refilled. The extracted combs were used again and again. As long as the combs were in good shape there didn't seem to be a limit to the number of times they could be used, although they did get dark and brittle over time. The deep supers were the most efficient way to produce honey.

Cliff had purchased a special screen with a grid just wide enough that a worker's body could pass through, but a queen's swollen abdomen could not. This was placed between the brood chamber and the supers. The screen provided free access to workers from the brood chamber to the supers above and kept the queen from laying eggs in the comb among the honey in the supers. In a fixed space, such as a tree, the walls of a building, or crevasse in the rimrock, the queen had free access to comb throughout the chamber, mixing the brood and honey.

The only way to get to the honey in the bee tree was to cut the tree down, or cut a slab out of the tree to gain access to the chamber. A breeched chamber was vulnerable to bees from other bee colonies, birds, other insects such as wasps and yellow jackets, and animals.

The government regularly inspected hived bees for disease. If a disease was discovered, the colony was removed and destroyed. If a bee tree became diseased, and died out or was robbed and left open for other bees to rob, the disease could spread to a healthy colony.

After a bee tree had been breached, the bees gorged themselves on honey and collected on a branch. Scouts went out to search for a new home and returned to report their recommendations. Through some form of consensus reaching process, the decision was made and the scout's directions were followed to the new tree, barn, hollow log, crack in a cliff, or beehive to start a new colony.

Cliff had acquired a hive of bees that way when George, Ed, Charlie and Cliff had robbed a cottonwood bee tree.

The entrance to that tree was rotten at the junction of the trunk of the cottonwood and a ten inch lateral branch. It was Charlie's idea to hook a chain out about 15 feet onto the branch and pull the branch off sideways. "It will pull off a slab of the tree trunk from the branch down and open up the hollow so you can rob it," he had reasoned. "All you guys will have to do is go in and scrape out the honey."

Ed and George had helped Charlie hook the chain to the branch, to the cable and to the tractor.

Cliff's recollected his dad's last instruction to Charlie as, "Take the slack out of the chain slowly, then ease off on the clutch and pull the branch off the tree without shaking the tree up any more than necessary. Hopefully, it will peel a slab right off like you said."

Cliff had remained in the pickup, on his dad's orders, while all this was going on. He had the window rolled down to hear what was going on. As soon as Ed and George joined him, Ed had rolled the windows up tight. It was a sultry summer afternoon and although the pickup truck was parked in the shade of another cottonwood, it was hot in the closed cab.

Charlie might have intended to follow his father's directions. He cinched the drawstring of the veil that he wore over his straw hat. He pulled on his gloves and started the tractor nearly 50 feet distant from the tree. Even at that distance from the tree, he looked nervous. The three in the pickup saw Charlie pull the hydraulic lever that operated the drawbar on the Ford tractor, causing it to lift.

"Why's he doing that?" George asked. "At that height, when he tightens the cable it will pull the front end off the ground. He won't have any control!"

"No! Charlie!" Ed said and sucked in his breath. He grabbed for the window handle to wind it and shout, just as Charlie pulled the throttle to full open and popped the clutch.

The tractor leapt forward, the cable/chain, which had until that moment lain slack on the ground, snapped tight into the air and the front end of the tractor reared high into the air like a bucking bronco. With a loud crashing popping sound, the branch ripped off the cottonwood along with a two-foot wide strip of trunk and ragged chunks of bee comb. The front end of the tractor bounced to the ground, throwing Charlie across the steering wheel, which he hung onto for dear life, and spurted forward. Charlie dropped back into the seat and managed to steer the tractor back onto the track across the grass made earlier in the afternoon with the pickup. Bouncing and whipping along behind were the branch and slab of tree trunk throwing off chunks of bee comb and bees. He never slowed down, he said, until he got back to the house.

It was the last time he had driven the tractor before reporting for Boot Camp.

A sudden boiling cloud of bees came out of the cavity of the cottonwood looking for something to fight. The pickup sat about 20 feet away from the tree and the swirling mass of hate homed in on it. For minutes, the living cyclone circled the vehicle with an angry roar.

Cliff was stunned and frightened. There was no mistaking what that roar meant. Those millions of bees wanted to murder all three of them. Plain and simple. And if they could get into the pickup, they would. They covered the windows and the windshield but the cab was tight.

Fortunately, the onslaught lasted only a few minutes, which seemed like hours to Cliff, and then the cloud began to dissipate and the bees began to return to the tree. The sound began to change from one of extreme anger to what Cliff thought might have been mourning. The bees were returning to the tree to gorge themselves with honey in preparation to evacuate.

Cliff was devastated. He felt like crying. He had looked forward to capturing the bees and starting another colony in the hive he had built. He was sure the queen was lost somewhere along the road. It was like Charlie to screw up their plans with some foolish hotshot stunt like that.

It didn't help that George couldn't stop laughing at the Vaudeville-like comedy that had played out in front of him. Ed still fumed from his place in the driver's seat. He was angry that Charlie in all likelihood had panicked at the last moment, ruined the tree and wasted most of the honey.

The bees returning to the tree from along the road where they had separated from the slab being dragged behind the departing tractor joined those returning from foraging in the fields, and the mass of brood bees preparing to evacuate. Collectively they began forming a swarm cluster on a branch of the mother cottonwood tree.

Ed, George and Cliff had waited safely in the pickup until the scene at the tree looked quiet and a minimum of bees still flew around the pickup. Ed fired up the smoker, and they donned veils and gloves and stepped out into the hot sunshine. They were soon scraping the honey and brood from the cavities of the tree that had peeled back. Smoke from the smoker hastened the evacuation process.

Afterward George placed Cliff's newly built empty beehive with frames of beeswax foundation under what had become a huge swarm cluster of bees. Cliff had stood back as George gently brushed the mass off the branch. They fell down in clumps onto the frames. When they were all off the branch and crawling all over the frames of new foundation in the new empty box, George had placed the cover on it, and they had left the new hive under the tree for the night. George told Cliff that there was still a chance that the scouts might have located a spot and might still convince the queen and her committee to leave the readymade hive. They couldn't force them to stay.

Ed, George and Cliff had collected the buckets of honey and brood and gone home.

The next morning when Cliff checked the new beehive, a steady stream of bees emerged from the entrance and flew off toward the hayfield, as a steady stream of bees arrived with their legs yellow with pollen. It meant the colony had adopted the hive as their new home. That night Cliff and his dad had returned to collect the new hive and relocated it to the orchard near the house. It was hive number two. Hive number one was a swarm from the bee tree near the pueblo ruin between the cliff dwelling and the south fence line of the farm. Both hives were put into service during the twelfth year of his life. He now thought of himself as an experienced beekeeper.

In the days Cliff had come to live in the dwelling, he had studied the tree trying to decide how to approach it. One day he would dismiss the thought of trying to penetrate the tree, as the task seemed formidable. Another day he lay on the ledge three feet away from the entrance of the bee tree looking at the steady stream of light brown and black bees crawling from the knothole out onto the trunk, lifting off, flying in a corkscrew pattern into the air and entering the beeline. Incoming bees narrowed their approach and landed inches away from the hole and crawled inside, carrying their heavy loads of nectar and pollen. He visualized the immature workers inside greeting the incoming workers and assisting them unload the nectar into half filled cells of thin uncured juice while other newly hatched workers fanned their wings to evaporate the moisture from filled cells before other workers secreted new wax to cap them.

Ed had helped him build a small, two-frame, glass-sided, observation hive. They had established it in a window of the little office where his dad kept his guns and the bookkeeping records for the farm. The workers crawled through a tube to a cutaway in the corner to exit to forage for nectar and pollen.

Cliff had watched the queen laying eggs, workers tending brood, fanning nectar into cured honey, the entire process. He had watched hour upon hour, fascinated by the harmony of the society of the little colony on the other side of the glass.

Finally, after vacillating day after day, he had mapped the tree closer, tapping the trunk on the three accessible sides trying to determine where the hollow was located within the tree and where it was closest to the outside of the trunk.

The position of the tree made physically working on it a huge challenge.

How the tree had ever taken root in such a precarious position, and grown so huge, straight and tall, was mystifying. The tree hugged the ledge. The layer of sediment the tree stood on flared forward of the bottom of the ledge. He guessed the cedar to be between three and four feet in diameter at the point where it began to divide about six feet above the surface of the ledge.

Cliff tied the rope about a foot out from the main trunk of the tree onto a branch that pointed out slightly at an angle from the ledge and hung out over the canyon. He climbed down the rope and maneuvered around the tree to the east side where he could stand at the foot of the cedar. On the downhill side of the tree, loose scree, fine sand and clay covered the steep slope. The tree was large enough that he couldn't reach around it to hold on. If he dug his fingers into the rough cedar bark, it might peel off if he lost his balance.

When Cliff looked directly down from that spot as he hung by the rope, it appeared that the face of layer the tree stood on had fallen away in chunks at some time in geologic history. He guessed the tree had grown to some size before the last slide had occurred. *I wonder how long it will be before this knob and the tree will all fall off into the canyon.* The tree and its roots covered the entire bulge and wedged into cracks along the face of the shelf below it and even under the bulge itself. Roots spread laterally between the layer it stood on and the ledge above it. The flare extended along the foot of the ledge toward the west for a few feet. He could stand on that with one hand on the face of the ledge and one hand on the tree, but there was not enough room to balance and work. On the east side of the tree, Cliff estimated the shelf to extend about fifteen feet. It flared the width of the root base, five or six feet wide, and narrowed to even with the ledge above around fifteen feet away.

A person could stand and work on the roots and duff on the tree's east side, but access to that small space would have to be by ladder or rope.

Cliff moved the ladder used to access the roof of the dwelling down to the shelf around the tree, but it was unsteady, and he was afraid to climb down it. He withdrew it. He didn't want to risk losing the ladder. *That's silly. I'm worried about losing the ladder. I guess I'd be on that ladder if it went over. I guess if that happened, I wouldn't have to worry about anything else. The only problem would be if I just hurt myself real bad and had to lay there for days or weeks in pain until I died. I'd rather be stung to death! Wouldn't it just be better not even to risk it?*

He climbed down the rope and smoothed the dirt, shale, and tamped rock into low places and tested it. *It should hold the ladder now.* He climbed out, lowered the ladder and for insurance tied the rope to the top of the ladder. He warily climbed down.

He looked at the tree differently now as he stood looking at the tree's east side at the level that he would work at it. Oddly, that side of the trunk was bare of bark. The wood was weathered gray. Something had scarred the tree there, possibly a lightning strike, or fire had burned the bark off.

The entrance to the tree was about three feet below the surface of the ledge and on the southeast side of the tree a quarter of a turn away. Cliff had estimated the layer that made up the ledge to be about ten feet thick. Cliff's height at last measurement was five feet tall. He could reach to just over six feet. When he reached to his fullest extension, he was short almost a foot of reaching the bee entrance.

It made sense that the knothole would lead directly to the cavity in the tree, perhaps the cavity was a direct result of the puncture, the knothole. So anywhere near and below the knothole was a good guess.

The smoothest, flattest area of the trunk was also on the east side of the tree facing up the canyon.

The tree was thick enough that for the core to be hollow, the outer hull could still be a foot thick and still have plenty of room for a strong colony. There was no way of telling where the exact location of the hollow space. When he knocked on the trunk, the east side sounded like it was the thinnest and caused the most reaction from the bees.

Cliff wanted to remove a twelve-inch square plug from the trunk of the tree, cut out a small section of comb, and replace the plug. If it worked, the bees might even replace the comb, and he could pull the plug occasionally and get new honey. It was not an accepted practice in primitive bee culture. It could only work if many unknowns were met.

He gathered the tools by the tree: hunting knife, honey knife, keyhole saw, file-knife, Dutch oven with lid, smoker, cedar bark, fire making materials, jar of water, gloves and all the gunnysacks in case he had to retreat inside one in an emergency.

It was not a good situation. He had little room to work. If things turned mean, he couldn't escape easily. He would have to climb the ladder to get away from them.

This is not a good idea. All kinds of things can go wrong with the plan. The bees can turn mean and come after me.

He pulled the straw hat a little tighter on his head to keep them out of his hair. He tied twine around his pant legs over his shoes against any crawling bees then pulled on his gloves and tied twine around his shirtsleeves at the wrists over the gloves. The only thing without some protection was his face. Usually he wore a screen around his face. George never bothered with a screen. As far as that went, George never even bothered with gloves. However, George did use smoke.

The biggest defense was the use of smoke. That was where the old homemade smoker came in. Cliff twisted and worked at a long strand of cedar bark until it was shredded, then wound it back and forth into a bundle that loosely filled the smoker can. He broke open a cattail seed head releasing a handful of filmy seed in their cotton parachute packing and packed this around the end of the cedar bark bundle.

Cliff had stopped using matches to make fire. The few he had left were safely stored in a nook awaiting an emergency.

Taking a quartz nodule and a square horseshoe nail from his pocket, he struck the face of the nodule over the white wad of cattail seed. It only took a couple of strikes before a trail of smoke rose. He blew on it until it flamed, then pushed it down into the can and squeezed the bellows until a good cloud of smoke emerged through the funnel shaped top. All it took to keep the bark smoldering was an occasional puff of air.

The bee entrance was on the south side of the tree from where he would cut the plug and nearly a foot above his reach.

He moved the ladder around the tree as far as he dared and as far as he could level it. The rope remained tied to the top. If the ladder tipped, he could grab the rope, pull himself to safety in the tree and retrieve the ladder. By climbing a rung, he could reach far enough to puff smoke into the entrance of the bee tree periodically. That kept the smoker going and began to calm the few bees that came around to his side to see what he was doing.

It was the very best time of the season to rob the bees as the flow of nectar was at a peak. During the peak flow, bees were the least aggressive. When the flow was the slowest in early spring and fall, their aggressiveness was much more noticeable. It was just like the human economy.

The first step was outlining, about eye level, a twelve-inch square on the bare tree trunk and then with the file-knife gouging a small hole in the upper left corner of the square. When the hole was an inch deep, he began sawing back and forth at the hole with the pointed tip of the keyhole saw making the hole deeper. Slowly, the cut lengthened along the line with the grain.

The blade worked deeper and deeper into the soft wood until finally it broke through. He was in luck. The trunk was no more than three inches thick at that that point.

He began working across the grain from the same hole to complete the corner. When that corner cut through to the cavity, he moved to the opposite corner and started the process all over again.

He continued working around the square, a corner at a time, trying to keep the saw blade from penetrating into the cavity further than just the thickness of the trunk. After starting all four corners, he returned to the upper left hand corner and cut across the grain to meet the right corner.

It was very slow, tiring, cutting with the fine toothed saw. The blade of the keyhole saw was flimsy, and the stroke was short. He had to take frequent rest breaks and pauses to blow smoke through the entrance and check the sound of the bees to be sure they continued calm. Eventually, the thin blade arrived back at the upper left corner.

The block, although sawn all the way around, still felt firmly attached. Comb was either anchored to it, or the cap was still attached to the interior of the tree. If the plug was still attached to the interior, he was finished.

He blew smoke all the way around the narrow cut, but couldn't tell if any smoke actually penetrated through to the cavity. When he put his ear to the incision, he could hear the hum of bees inside the trunk.

Now came the critical part. He had no veil. He had gloves to protect his hands, and the shirt would protect his body, although an angry bee could sting through the light denim cloth if it really wanted to. The bib of the overalls would protect his chest, and the back flap with the suspenders came pretty far up his back. But, still there was no protection for his face.

He had worked with his bees a great deal over the past two summers, and he respected them, but he wasn't afraid of them. George said that they could smell fear. He had been stung before, but he had never had a reaction to the stings. Usually when he was stung, it was his own fault because he had accidentally mashed one or allowed one to become tangled in his hair.

Cliff had to keep them smoked well and read how they were reacting. Angry bees made a very recognizable sound. If he heard that sound, he would abandon the project immediately, get back inside the ruin out of sight and use the gunnysacks to cover his head if necessary. He was at a disadvantage if escape was necessary. He would have to climb the ladder to get away. There was nowhere to run. He had about eight feet one way to move in semi-safety, and he couldn't afford to panic. If he dived over the edge he wouldn't stop for several hundred feet. It might be a smooth slide, but there was nothing to stop him but brush, trees, and rocks. It was not an attractive escape alternative.

He focused his attention back on the plug. *Stay calm Clifton. They can smell fear. I wonder if Hector could smell my fear. Why can I stand here where there are hundreds or thousands of bees that can sting me and potentially kill me in an instant, and I don't really feel fear of them, and the thought of facing Hector made me sweat and fear him? He wasn't threatening to kill me. I could have talked to him. I can't talk to these bees.*

There was potentially a great deal of danger there, however, and he had to proceed with caution. Wild bees were unpredictable. If they were only a generation removed from a domestic hive, they should be relatively calm. They had shown no aggressive tendencies yet. But, they might be all over him when he broke into their brood chamber.

He heated the blade of the honey knife on the hot barrel of the smoker and then ran the thin twelve-inch blade through the saw cut into the comb inside, cut all the way around the square, and withdrew it. He had run into no hard wood obstacle. Hopefully, the plug was being held in place only by the combs inside.

Sweet, cured honey covered the knife when he withdrew it. He licked the blade with pleasure. He had never tasted that particular flavor before. It was very mild and the color was almost clear. The main source of nectar, besides the clover, in the canyon now must have been the tamarack bushes. Bees had covered the pink blossoms.

Cliff used the tough file-knife to prize one side of the wood square and then the other until he felt something give. He slowly began working the plug outward until the wood was free and the dripping edge of the comb appeared.

A few bees tried to squeeze around the plug. The hum inside grew much louder. He puffed smoke all the way around the perimeter of the plug. He puffed more smoke into the entrance and the hum subsided slightly.

"There you go guys. Go on back to work now. I'm just going to borrow a little and leave the rest for you. You're going to run out of space in there soon anyway. This will give you a little room."

He puffed more smoke all the way around the cutout and waited for a few moments. The hum there quieted slightly more. He worked the wooden plug out another inch. Bees crawled out of the hole, over the wood, the comb that clung to it, and his glove. It was still a non-threatening group of workers. No bees were on the offensive yet.

"Great! We're almost there!"

Cliff gently puffed smoke onto the workers and most of them retreated inside the cavity. He continued to drive stragglers back inside until he had a little over eight inches of exposed comb. The layers of comb clinging to the square had broken loose unevenly from the comb inside the cavity and dripped honey from broken cells.

What Cliff finally held in his hands was a twelve-inch square of honeycombs. Six rows of combs twelve inches high had broken free nine inches back into the cavity and clung to the plug. The mostly seasoned dark brown combs had caps of fresh pale golden butter colored wax so the new honey in them was cured. The new caps meant the honey had been gathered that spring, even if it was stored in older combs. Some brood was also scattered in patches throughout the exposed comb. One mostly new comb looked freshly capped on both sides and contained little brood.

Unlike in a hive with removable frames and manufactured wax foundation that guided the formation of the combs into straight rows, the wild combs were more haphazard and joined in curving sections to fit the curving interior shape of the tree.

He puffed more smoke into the hole to keep the bees as calm as possible while the plug was out just before he removed the plug of honeycomb completely from the tree. The plug was heavy and he had to handle it with both hands. As soon as he had it free, he turned the plug up so the wood carried the weight of the combs. The Dutch oven was at the base of the tree. He set it down on the Dutch oven quickly. He hit the hole with smoke to keep bees from boiling out of it, although it was not as bad as he feared.

He smoked bees off the combs on the plug and most flew back to the tree.

Cliff used the honey knife to cut the block of combs loose from the cedar plug into the Dutch oven, and he immediately refitted the plug back into its original position in the tree trunk.

Cliff put the lid in place over the Dutch oven and draped his tee shirt over it to prevent bees from gathering on the exposed honey. A few crawled out from under the shirt and flew back to the tree entrance.

He pressed willow wedges into the saw cut around each side of the plug to hold it firmly in place. The next time he needed honey all he would have to do was remove the plug and carve out new comb. At least that was the theory.

Later in the day, he would prepare piñon pitch by heating it into a gooey gum and pack it into the cut around the plug, sealing it against ants and insects that might invade the colony.

Everything had worked better than he could have dreamed.

The Dutch oven was heavy, and it wasn't the easiest thing to carry it up the rickety ladder up the ten feet to the ledge. *I should have retied these rungs before I started up. If this thing slides out from under me, and I lose the Dutch oven and all the honey after all this work then man…!* He made it to the top of the ledge and set the Dutch over the top. He climbed over and carried the heavy pot of precious honey through the door and set it down inside.

"Now you stay out of this until I get back, Moonbeam. There will be plenty of treats for you in this when I get back," he said. He took a stick of turkey jerky out of the pot, tossed it to his pet and returned to the ladder.

He set the smoker, still emitted a narrow tendril of blue smoke, down and placed the tools next to it. He stood in front of the tree with his hands at his side and his head bowed humbly before it. Then he turned to face the north, pointed up the canyon to the east, swept his arm to the south, paused and turned to the west, pointed to the earth and then to the sky. *I think you Heavenly Father and Mother Nature for letting me share this sweet honey with your Queen, workers and drones. I took only a little. I didn't damage their home, so they can continue to live and work safely. I will not revisit them until this honey and wax are used. I will not waste any part of it. I will protect this tree and all your children within it to the best of my ability. Let their spirits stay with me and help me understand as the product of their labor helps me to survive.*

~~~

He was very satisfied with his work and set about cutting the comb into strips separating out brood and pollen as he went. The one section of comb that was new with new caps he cut and laid in the former molasses tin separate from the rest of the honey. He further separated pollen into the porcelain cup. Brood larva he fed to Moonbeam. He mashed the remaining comb and honey in the Dutch oven and let it sit to drain overnight.
~~~

Cliff had visited the Ancestral Puebloan pottery in the corner of the ruin once before. Now it became imperative to do so again. The jars were again full of jerky from the turkey hen. He wanted to transfer it to the pottery and the honey to the jars. He could store jerky in a pot, and it would have no real impact on the pot. All he wanted to do was keep the jerky dry and clean. He had no idea what impact the honey might have on a pottery bowl.

Cliff carefully lifted a small pot inverted over the mouth of a pot that would hold probably a gallon of liquid. He carefully emptied and wiped the pot clean and emptied the jerky from the four quart jars into it and placed the pot up on a nook and covered it with the original pot-lid.

After a rinse, the four Mason jars were ready for the almost clear, mild tasting honey. After the honey had drained out of the crushed comb, he would melt it into wax cakes. The older combs were dark and brittle, while new combs were softer and golden brown. It didn't matter how old the wax was, once melted it was all the same. As it melted, the impurities tracked in by the workers, such as pollen, floated away leaving golden brown wax. He could make candles out of it. He could waterproof leather with it. There were endless uses for it.

He transferred the section of comb honey to a quart jar by itself and screwed a lid down tight. It had the mild almost clear honey that he could not identify. *If I do make it out of here on good terms, this would make a good peace offering with my Dad.*

That night when Cliff made the corn cake, he mixed a little honey into the dough. The stew had smoked turkey and wild vegetables. Instead of crumbling the corn cake into the stew, he spread honey on it.

44
Yucca fiber
Martinez Canyon

Cliff's first serious experiment to make rope was to have cordage to make a carrier for the spear thrower and spears.

He had made many combined root digging and leaf gathering expeditions. Yucca root and leaves were a supply he could harvest in the early summer when not much not else much was happening.

With yucca fiber he could also make baskets to store beans, corn, and seeds, which would begin to mature in August and continue through October. Once they began to mature, there would be no time to make containers. He experimented with various leaves and barks and decided that yucca leaves were the most versatile. From yucca he could make rope, baskets, and crude cloth. When he gathered the roots, he had brought home all the leaves that were in reasonable condition.

It didn't take long to accumulate the large stack of leaves, which dried in the back of the cave.

The instructions for processing yucca advised soaking the leaves until the pulp rotted away leaving the fibers free. He couldn't afford to tie up the Dutch oven or the molasses tin for days at a time so he looked about for a natural solution.

He discovered a natural tub-like pothole down the ledge past the toe-holds near the end drop-off. It was filled nearly full of blown in sand and trash. Cliff cleaned it out and discovered nicks and scrapings and gouges along the sides. Although the indentation appeared to be natural, man had deepened and enlarged it for some purpose. The sides of the bowl showed signs that fire had burned there too.

Cliff filled the tub with yucca leaves, weighted them down with stone and then filled it with water. After a few days, most of the fleshy material had rotted away, and it smelled terrible. *If they used this for the same reason, this must be why they had it clear down here. I'll bet they used this tub for soaking deer hides also. They might have just filled it with water, let the sun heat it and bathed in it.*

He removed a leaf and the plant material squeezed out easily. He carried the remaining fibers in the Dutch oven back to the runoff and rinsed them until they were almost clean of plant material. He wrung the bundle of fibers out and rinsed them again and even more plant material and short fibers rinsed free. When they were clean and all odors were gone, he hung the thin hank of fibers on a peg and began processing the rest of the putrid tub of leaves the same way.

Cliff was tired and stunk by the time he finished the last leaf and scooped the water out of the tub with the Dutch oven and rinsed it out with fresh water. Even Moonbeam would have nothing to do with him. He wondered if it had been a good idea to use the only cooking utensil he had to move the putrid water. But, fortunately, the pot cleaned up and with a thorough scrubbing was odor free with help of yucca soap.

He heated water and took a sponge bath using plenty of yucca suds, cooked a good supper and stopped for the night.

He examined his day's work by firelight. Hanks of yucca fiber hung drying from pegs. The soaking method had left the fibers softer than the test he had done by pounding a dry leaf to remove the plant material. Those fibers were coarse and stiff.

The next day Cliff carried a hank of fibers to the water and rinsed them, letting them soak for a few minutes to soften the strands. He carried them back to the fire pit and separated out small bundles of fibers the size of matchsticks.

To make simple cording he held each end of a bundle a foot apart and twisted clockwise with each hand. The fibers twisted into a cord until suddenly a kink formed in the middle.

When he brought his hands closer together and kept twisting, the kink rotated on its own in a counterclockwise direction for several rotations.

Cliff threaded a willow stick through the loop in the end at the kink and wedged it in between two rocks in the fire pit to hold it firm. He now had two bundles of fibers to work with.

He twisted each bundle of fibers clockwise keeping them twisted into a tight cord and at the same time twisted the two cords counterclockwise into a two-ply cord. As the original bundle began to run out of fibers he layered another bundle parallel to the bundle being replaced and continued twisting. First one bundle had to be replaced and then the other.

He twisted the individual bundles and twisted them together into the combined cord trying to keep the diameter of the cord uniform as it grew longer until he had a thin strand of two ply rope about ten feet long. Cliff coiled it and started a new strand.

When he had two ten foot lengths, he tied both to a stick and began twisting them into one four ply rope. He doubled the rope in half and began twisting it around the stick wedged in the fire pit rocks. The finished four-foot long eight ply rope was a little under a half inch in diameter.

When he tested the eight ply rope, it was very strong for its size. He couldn't break it.

45
Atlatl
Martinez Canyon

Cliff stood on the lip of the rimrock facing the La Plata Mountains to the east as the first rays of the sun broke over the one lone sharp rocky peak to the left of the range of majestic peaks. The lonely sentinel, not as tall as its sister peaks, but shaped much like a giant shark's tooth, which gave it its name, was the last obstruction to the sun announcing summer's arrival. *It's the beginning of summer around the 20th of June already. How can that be? It has been about six weeks, since I left home. Oh, well, I'm not dead yet. I wonder if they are still searching for me.*

~~~

He finally resorted to using the .22 a few times. He began taking the rifle with him when he visited the wasteland southeast of the tower ruin to dig the yucca roots. Cottontails didn't venture far from the creek into the dry land area, but he was usually able to spot one or two on the return if he timed the return toward dusk, or if he left early in the morning, their favorite feeding times. The only things he saw out in the wasteland any time of the day were quail, doves and occasionally a jackrabbit. He couldn't eat
~~~

jackrabbit, and he couldn't afford to risk a bullet on a quail or dove. They were hard to hit, and if he got one, it would provide only one meal.

In the stretch of the canyon between the tower ruin and the trail out of the canyon, he was a mile from the Kelley house, a little over a half-mile from the Martinez home and a half mile from George Williamson's home. All three could hear a .22 shot if they were listening for it.

The .22 was the most likely thing that would draw attention to where he was if he used it very much. He had spread his ammunition out on the floor of the nook so that he had an instant inventory, whenever he walked by it each day. That morning there were 20 shells left, fewer than half the number when he left the house. Fortunately, he seldom missed. He had to learn to hunt in another way, and soon, or there would be no more meat in his stew.

~~~

Cliff sat in the shade of the cedar reading a handout from Mesa Verde on the basic mechanics of the atlatl spear thrower.

The Museum handout showed several examples of the spear throwing sticks in their exhibit. The Mesa Verde pamphlet attributed the name Atlatl to the Aztec, although it said there was evidence that Homo Sapiens had used the device for as long as 400,000 years.

The previous summer Cliff had watched a docent's atlatl throwing exhibition and had even attended a little craft workshop conducted by a Museum staff member on how to make an atlatl from a tree branch.

The handout was from that workshop. According to the handout, "The twenty-five inch long stick extends the throwing arm, enabling a skilled thrower to cast a spear with enough force to bring down big game at fifty to a hundred feet."

The docent had admonished the onlookers to be extremely careful if they tried to make and use an atlatl, "because they are an ancient *deadly* weapon." He had looked each of the young people in the eye as he repeated the word "deadly".

The handout suggested using cedar, but Cliff used willow.

~~~

Since early in his sojourn he had accumulated willows at the ruin by bringing home two or three whole willows each trip if he could. In dense groves, they grew tall and straight with few limbs until they were eight or ten feet tall. At the root level, the trunks grew to an inch and a half to two inches in diameter. At 10 feet, they were about an inch in diameter. The canopy of branches was an array of small branches covered by long narrow light green, which darkened as the summer progressed. Lower leaves turned brown and fell in late summer and through the fall covering the ground and water with leaves. *There are enough willows in the canyon that I'll never run out of raw materials,* Cliff thought every time he visited the willow groves in the canyon. He randomly chose willows from up and down the creek, always cutting them below the water line, or down beneath the soil line to hide their disappearance from George when he strolled down the trail.

~~~

To make his first atlatl, he selected a willow with a half-inch long stub of root at the butt end. He cut off a length of the willow two and a half feet long. He tapered the stick away from the root end to leave most of the weight at that end. The tapered end would be the handle end.

Cliff drilled a hole all the way through a couple of inches from the handle end with the point of his pocketknife and reamed it out to about a quarter of an inch in diameter. He cut a willow stick four inches long, peeled the bark off, trimmed it to fit the hole and tapped it half way through.

In the aiming position, a spear would be nestled in the groove against the spur, pointing forward through the V of the first and second fingers holding the tapered end of the stick. The little finger would press against the cross peg stop. The thumb and third finger would hold the spear in place as his right arm prepared to throw the spear.

Cliff scraped and smoothed the throwing stick with the heavier file-knife.

When he was satisfied that his atlatl looked as good as the one in the pamphlet, he hung it and set about to make spears for it. This would be much more difficult.

As he had trimmed willows to make drying frames, traps, hide stretchers, and other uses, he had set aside the straightest most uniform sections of willows at the point where they became about three quarters of an inch in diameter and were straight up to six feet long and were still at least a half inch in diameter. He had tied these blanks into bundles and set them aside.

From a bundle, he selected a half dozen of the straightest blanks. He carefully trimmed any knots flush with the trunk and stripped off the bark. He heated and straightened sections that were bowed. He tested their straightness against the level floor, straightened more, until all were as straight as he knew how to make them.

Cliff notched the smallest end of each spear blank and fitted the V notch on each spear to the V shaped hook on the throwing stick.

To check each spear's balance, he wrapped his second, third and little fingers around the tapered end of the atlatl with the peg against his little finger. His forefinger and thumb extended above the shafts to hold the spears in place against the spur at the butt end of the thrower.

The throwing stick extended another two feet back from his right hand, in effect, extending the length of his arm by that much. As each
~~~

spear blank pointed forward across his cheek, he raised his left hand straight in front of him. The spear blank, rested on his left thumb just forward of the center.

After Cliff was satisfied with the balance of each blank, it was time to add feathers to each of them.

Cliff had carefully preserved the feathers from the hen turkey as well as the grouse.

He brought the pot containing the wing feathers down from its resting place. For practice, he selected several short and damaged feathers, saving the longer prize feathers for later when he learned what worked. Cliff worked to fletch only one spear at a time.

He noted that the feathers of each wing curved the same direction and selected three feathers accordingly. For his first spear, he used grouse feathers.

He ruined the first feather by trying to peel the feathers away from the spine. They peeled away but curled up and were unmanageable.

He sharpened the pocketknife to its very best edge.

He was successful this time as he split the spine of the feather dividing each feather into two rows of veins, which swept back away from the point, which had attached the feather to the wing. The upper row of veins was nearly twice the height as the lower row. He discarded the lower row of veins and used the taller dominant row.

He cut three equal lengths and trimmed the veins back a half inch on each end. He loosely tied the three feather lengths in place onto the small-notched end of the spear shaft using wet rabbit sinew. Cliff looked at the shaft from the end and carefully positioned the feathers until they were an equal distance apart. It wasn't until they were in place that he fully realized why the feathers on an arrow or spear should all be from the same wing. The veins of the feather curved like a gentle wave. In this case, all three curved to the right, so they worked together to spin the arrow, just as the rifling in a gun barrel rotated the bullet to make it travel true to its mark.

With the three feather lengths in place, he cinched the sinew tightly around the half inch of the spine that projected past the veins of the feather on each end. As it dried, it would snug down firmly in place holding the spine against the wood of the spear shaft.

The larger blunt end of the spear was the front, dart end. He had already created several darts or points.

Cliff selected bone rather than flint for points on the darts using a long hind leg bone of a rabbit for raw material. Flint would have been the preferred raw material but Cliff had not mastered knapping and did not want to use the few precious arrow heads he had found.

The bone was about the size of a school pencil and was tough and hard. He used the file he had brought from the tool shed to bring the end to a point. Four inches from the point, he began filing around the bone tapering it to about half the original diameter and extending the taper to within an inch of the sharp point. When he was satisfied with the taper, with the keyhole saw he cut the bone at the small end of the taper opposite the point.

This he fitted into a six-inch long willow dowel. He drilled a hole in the center of the end of the dowel as deeply as he could with the pocketknife just large enough to fit the taper of the bone point and chipped away at it until the bone seated snugly with the front pointed inch protruding.

To affix the point, he poured a small amount of melted pitch into the hole and pressed the tapered end of the bone point into the hole. The pitch anchored the point tightly in place as it cooled.

He then wrapped the dowel tightly with soaked sinew. As the sinew dried, it shrank around the wood and that protected the dowel from splitting upon impact.

Because he tailored each point to a dowel, Cliff didn't have to worry about uniformity. However, the dowels were to be interchangeable with the spears so the spear sockets and the dowel tapers had to meet some standards or the system wouldn't work.

The tapered dowel pressed, with no pitch, into a sinew re-enforced hole in the blunt end of the spear. In theory, it was much more time consuming to make a spear and more difficult to carry a large number of spears. However, a hunter could carry a variety of darts, and select the dart to fit the size and type of animal he encountered. The hunter could throw the spear at a game animal. The spear would imbed the dart deeply enough to wound the animal mortally. The spear would separate from the dart and fall away undamaged to be used again immediately. The dart and point would remain in the animal to weaken it and cause it to bleed to death.

It would be much easier to carry a dozen or so darts in a pack and only two or three of the more cumbersome spears.

Cliff fashioned a belt out of the four-foot, eight-ply, yucca fiber rope to go around his shoulders to hold the spears. He put half the darts in a bib pocket of the overalls and left the rest in the ruin.

He placed the spears butt first in a knapsack similar to the creel gunnybag, but made to hang down his back like a knapsack. This sack hung from straps that went over his shoulders rather than around his neck. He tied a loop in the belt that would fall in the middle of his back for the fletched end of the spears. The spear thrower hung down through the loop with the heavier spur end down inside the knapsack and the finger stop cross piece across the loop. He tied the belt around his back, under his armpits, up over his shoulder and around his neck. The spears extended up above his head out of the way, leaving his hands free when he climbed out over the rimrock.

Cliff felt different when he stood on the rim of the canyon the first day he went out to practice with the spears and thrower.

He took the atlatl and a spear out of the knapsack. He looked down into the canyon and surveyed his domain with a different eye. He was a hunter now, even if he had yet to throw the spear for the first time.

He walked along, vigilant now, about where he walked, choosing hard ground, avoiding dry branches that might break and slow his passage.

He watched for areas where birds or rabbits used dusting stops to fluff dust up into their feathers or fur to drive out mites or fleas. Turkeys, grouse, rabbits and quail used them.

Cliff balanced the practice spear in the groove on the top of the crude spear thrower. He checked the notch on the spear to see that it was nestled into the spur hook on the atlatl. He did not mount a dart with a bone point to the spear. He would be throwing for practice. He did mount a blank dart to protect the dart socket and to maintain the balance the spear would have with a pointed dart.

At a small open area of sagebrush, he practiced throwing the spear for the first time.

After a few throws, he tried practicing with the atlatl without a spear.

Then he positioned the practice spear on the thrower.

He wrapped his fingers around the tapered end of the atlatl with his pinky finger tight against the cross peg. His forefinger and thumb extended above the shaft holding the practice spear in place against the spur at the butt end of the thrower.

On the first attempt, the spear flew off to the side. It wasn't much better on the second or even the third or the tenth throw.

He continued practicing that day until he ran out of time and until he began to understand the logic of the various movements involved, the spear flew more accurately, and his confidence began to rise. He began to understand how he had to place his feet, when to release the spear, and how to aim. At that point, he had to stop for the day. *I thought it would be easier. The docent had made it look easy. Maybe it was the way I made my atlatl. Maybe the docent spent years mastering the art of using the atlatl. I'll probably never be able to kill anything with this thing. It's probably just a waste of time.*

The next day he was at the same spot, as soon as he had taken care of the daily chores and had a good portion of the rest of the day free. To his delight, his arm and brain had seemingly continued to work on the practice in the intervening time, and his first throw was better than anything he had thrown the day before. When he went home that night, he was very tired and his arm was sore, but he felt exhilarated. He had made progress, although he was far from hitting anything with it.

In the middle of the next day, he brought the spear up to his extended left hand, which pointed to the target. His eye fixed on his left finger and the spear point. He placed his left foot forward and his right foot at a right angle. He drew his right arm back behind his shoulder. He stepped forward and brought his arm forward rapidly in an overhand sweep, releasing the spear with a snap as it became horizontal.

The spear leapt forward and slapped into the ground a hundred feet in front of him with great force right on the target. He broke into a grin that spread into a silent laugh. He retrieved the spear and looked about for another target.

A sagebrush bloomed fifty feet away. He could usually stalk to within twenty-five feet of a cottontail. His goal was to become accurate enough to hit a cottontail at that distance.

He took aim and threw the spear, and it sailed over the bush. The next time it fell short. The next time it fell harmlessly to the right. Each time he threw, he got closer. The sage was many times the size of a cottontail, and it stayed still.

He would have one throw at a rabbit. They normally spooked, ran a few yards and froze, depending on their ability to blend into their environment for protection.

With each throw, he experimented when to release, how hard to throw, how to swing his arm, and continued until his arm began to get sore. He stopped for the day. It was the best day yet. *I can do this. I can learn to hunt with this thing. I can't believe how much force it has. If I can build enough accuracy and start putting cutting blades on the darts, I'm not going to have to worry about having enough meat. And I won't have to worry about ammunition.*

Dare he think about deer? Mule deer were plentiful. He saw fresh tracks wherever he went, but he seldom saw the deer themselves. They ate from all the farms in the area. The farmers didn't necessarily see this as a good thing, but there wasn't much they could do about it. The deer were protected with seasons, and a license was required to kill one. Most farmers killed their limits each fall without leaving their farms. Some likely had fresh venison throughout the year.

When he foraged, Clifton's vigilance became even greater when he came to eroded areas, washes, and around where there was sign of cliff top dwellings. That vigilance was rewarded with finds of arrow heads of various sizes and shapes as well as beads, a bone awl, another *metate* grinding stone, a couple of *mano* grinders, and a stone axe. Each of these he carried back to the dwelling. Some of the arrowheads were the size of a quarter, and heavy. Others were fine, the size of a dime and intricately flaked. Some may have been for spearheads and others for arrows. Some were obviously for big game and others for birds or rabbits. Most were broken and had imperfections. He assumed they had been discarded. He found several that he could use, and he bound a couple to darts. He tipped most of the darts with bone. Practice darts had points hardened in the fire.

Each day he practiced until he could drive a spear through a six-inch space in a sage blossom at twenty-five feet. He now carried the atlatl, three spears, and darts with bone points, wherever he went. He no longer took the .22 from the dwelling. It was only a matter of time now before he had an opportunity to throw at a live prey.

46
Maggie
Martinez Canyon

Cliff climbed the spreading old piñon tree to the highest branch that would support his weight and crawled out on it to just beneath the mass of twigs that made up the magpie nest. He slowly pulled his legs up under himself and rose to grasp the branch where the magpies had built their nest. He stretched around to where he could see through the entrance. The massive nest was a coarse, bulky, domed over structure of piñon sticks at least three feet high. Inside was the actual nest made of mud, grass and hair.

There were two entrances, one facing him and one on the opposite side. He hoped to find six to nine, fresh, greenish grey, brown marked eggs. He wanted to take half of them back to the dwelling to mix with his corn cakes. He had found other magpie eggs in the willow grove nests. He never took them all. When he added a couple of eggs to the corn cakes, they were more flavorful and fluffy.

Instead of eggs, he stared into the eyes of four pin-feathered baby magpies, which seeing movement, raised their open beaks and began begging noisily. He was several weeks too late for fresh eggs at this nest. He also needed to get away from the tree quickly or face the wrath of an angry mother magpie that would ferociously defend her nest and babies with sharp talons and beak.

He started to lower himself back to the branch that he stood on. Then on impulse, he reached in and took the largest, strongest looking bird from the nest. The bird continued to squawk loudly, begging for food with its head tipped back and its beak wide open. He put the struggling infant into the middle bib pocket and climbed down the tree.

Before he dropped to the ground, the mother landed at her nest and began squawking and in a few minutes, other magpies began to arrive to set up a cacophony of "yak yak yak yak" and "mag, mag, mag, mag" calls back and forth. He dropped to the ground, and as he began walking away from the tree the baby bird quit squawking and rode quietly. A few magpies followed from treetops for a way and slowly returned toward the nest tree, and Cliff walked on with his captive.

On the way back to the ruin, Cliff caught several grasshoppers and pinched off their heads. He mashed one of them between his fingers, spit on it to moisten it and touched the baby bird's beak. It immediately opened its mouth and raised its open beak hungrily. He dropped bits of the crushed grasshopper down the bird's gullet. It gulped them down and became quiet again.

The magpie's natural diet was beetles, wasps, ants, caterpillars, cutworms, grasshoppers, eggs, other bird's nestlings, carrion, mice and human food scraps. Cliff assumed that the baby's diet could be any of those things partly digested, mashed or shredded to simulate the way mother magpie would present food to it.

Cliff had tried several times to raise baby magpies. Each had lived a little longer as he had learned how to feed them, until the one he had raised last summer had survived until fully grown with mature plumage. The last bird was older when he took it from the nest and although it survived, it did not imprint with Cliff as completely. He had named it Maggie, and it had learned to speak its name. Then it had escaped when he had accidentally left the latch to its cage undone. Possibly, the intelligent bird had undone the latch itself. For a few weeks, it had hung around the yard and then disappeared.

Cliff built a crude cage of willows, more to protect the baby magpie from Moonbeam than keeping the bird from escaping. Moonbeam was very interested in the newcomer and watched intently as Cliff chewed grasshoppers, mixed in a few grains of sand with his fingers then dropped them down the bird's gullet.

When Cliff settled down for the night, he placed the cage next to himself. Moonbeam, as usual, curled in the crook of his arm and snuggled her nose up to her human friend's nose. *Heavenly Father and Mother Nature I thank you for sharing your children with me. They will be fine companions. They will help me in my loneliness. They help me want to survive. Please give little Maggie the spirit to survive also. I will take care of him and feed him, even before I feed myself. I can see intelligence behind his eyes. Let me be his friend and he be mine.*

The bird required frequent feedings during the day. Cliff carried him along wherever he went. He rode comfortably in the middle pocket in the bib of the overalls. Cliff was careful not to mash him. He kept the loose pocket propped open with a short thin willow stick arched around the pocket opening. Cliff lined the pocket with ground up cedar bark that he changed each morning and night to keep the pocket clean. At night, Maggie stayed in the cage.

After a few weeks, Maggie had lost most of his pinfeathers. Permanent feathers had begun to replace the pinfeathers and the long black tail feathers had begun to grow in. His white breast feathers were coming in and black neck and back feathers were becoming sleek and iridescent. It wouldn't be long before he would want to try flying. Until then he had the run of the cave when Cliff was there, and he hopped everywhere and examined everything. The intelligence behind the eyes became more apparent each day.

Clifton talked constantly to both Maggie and to Moonbeam. Maggie perked up when spoken to and listened intently, cocking his head from side to side.

He had no way of telling whether the bird was male or female. It was hard to tell even in the adult birds, which was which. Unlike some of the songbirds and jays where the females were drab and the males had more elaborate plumage, the main difference Cliff saw in the magpies, a member of the crow family, was the size. The males were larger. But, it just seemed natural to think of Maggie as male because of his playfulness.

The mischievous bird began to play with the skunk before it could fly. He would hop up to her and groom the skunk's fur then peck her and hop away as the skunk ran after him. It was obvious that it was play and there was no threat of retaliation.

Cliff's loneliness lessened as he laughed at the antics of his two black and white companions and talked to them constantly as friends. The cage now hung from one of the roof beams as Maggie learned to fly short distances, and he had free access to it. After a great deal of soul searching, Cliff took the door off it.

Friends didn't jail friends, but he prayed that the bird would stay.

47

A Different Perspective on the Night
Martinez Canyon

On the darkest nights, Clifton fought his fears. The sounds seemed magnified and echoed off the canyon walls. As the summer solstice passed, there were many more sounds in the canyon than upon his arrival in May. The slate door covering kept out few of the sounds. Each night as he lay on his mats, he listened to the sounds and began to isolate the originators of each; owls, frogs, crickets, cicadas, snapping twigs, turkeys on their roost, cats, foxes, badgers, coyotes, pack rats, and mice rustling through the brush, and occasionally the sounds of a kill.

As he identified the familiar creatures, he became less afraid. Images of strange beasts, horrible bears and giant flying monsters faded and images of Mother Nature's children replaced them. He had seen their tracks and many of their faces. They were real now, not fantasy. He and they were all part of Mother Nature's family. He was coming to believe that he shared their spirits, and that they wouldn't harm him. He had begun to identify with them. He, like they, was on his own scavenging for his daily meal. For the first time he understood the passage in the Bible, "give us this day our daily bread." He wanted to ask someone if that prayer included the animals, bees and ants and all the rest. If he went back to the farm, would he be able to spray the corn for his dad? He had begun to think about the difference in the turkeys eating the bugs, caterpillars and other and poisoning them.

He began to get up in the night. On nights when there was enough moonlight to see, he would remove the slate door cover and sit on the doorsill with Moonbeam on his lap looking out across the canyon and at the rim of Mesa Verde in the distance. Instead of being afraid of the sounds, he came to welcome them and find them comforting. He was no longer alone on these sleepless nights. It also helped that in addition to Moonbeam, a few feet away in his door less cage perched his newest friend Maggie.

~~~

When Cliff first lay down to sleep each night, Moonbeam curled near him. However, soon after her human friend drifted off to sleep, the young skunk became active. She silently checked out nook and corner of the cave. She sniffed the air, then she inspected all the passageways to the cave for intruders such as little deer mice attracted to the smells of cooking, and greenery or meat brought to the cave. Moonbeam was a very efficient hunter and few if any slipped by her. If an elusive mouse slipped by one night, it rarely survived another night if it remained in the cave. If she found nothing, she went outside and hunted the oasis or followed the ledge to the narrow crack in the rock through which her mother had led her and her siblings to the slope in search of voles and crickets until her hunger was satisfied. After filling her tummy, she made her way back to the cave, careful to avoid the watchful eye of the great horned owl, and snuggled close to her friend Cliff where she slept soundly until Cliff awoke at dawn.

She slept most of the day while Cliff and Maggie foraged outside the dwelling.

~~~

Even on the few nights when the moon was completely absent, away from artificial lights, there was an amazing amount of light at night. The thin clear Colorado sky was ablaze with the cloud of stars, the Milky Way. On those moonless nights, a few creatures came out an hour or two earlier and dined and came out again at dawn. However, they preferred to hunt and to dine by moonlight.

As the moon progressed through its phases to the full moon, it became almost as light as the day. At sundown most creatures woke up, came out of their dens, oak groves, cattail breaks and burrows to feed.

Finally, one night, Cliff became bold enough to climb out of the canyon over the rim. He walked through the timber to the fence line at the south edge of the Kelley farm.

He could see that the corn, beans and grain were growing rapidly. It was the best time of the year when everything was growing, and although the weeds were not taking over yet, they were growing too. It was time for plowing. He enjoyed the plowing process. It cut down on the drudgery of hoeing later in the summer during the really hot days.

Plowing was a cultivating process. The tractor, carrying a frame supporting an array of heart shaped plows, straddled two rows of corn or beans at a time. The plows drew soil up around the roots and stalks of the corn and bean plants destroying weeds between the rows and covering the small weeds that grew up in the corn or bean row. The added soil would help retain moisture and protect the roots from the very hot July and August weather to come. The resulting ditch between rows also became the furrow for irrigation. It was time to plow. Who would do it, he wondered, his mother? Or would they have to hire it done? If so would they call on Hector?

Even with this method of cultivation, later in the summer the corn would require hand hoeing to get rid of sunflowers and careless weeds that escaped the cultivators by growing in beside the corn or beans.

In the grain, smaller heart-shaped plows made furrows two feet apart. The object was not to mound dirt, but to create water passage through the grain. They would spray the weeds with 2-4-D a broadleaf herbicide. Because the grain was a grass, the 2-4-D would not harm it or inhibit its growth while it killed the sunflowers, morning-glory, and carless weeds that grew up as soon as it was watered. If Ed couldn't afford to spray, he would have to hoe the grain by hand.

As Cliff looked out over the farm, he realized that two months before he would not have had the courage to sit out in the dark alone like this enjoying the view. He would have been terrified of the dark.

He was getting better.

48

Etta Mae Dreaming of the Dreamer
Kelley Farm

Etta Mae did the cultivating. She had been her father's right hand and the most valuable field hand until Ed Kelley had stolen her away. Driving the tractor up and down rows plowing corn was very much easier than picking cotton or driving a team of horses planting peanuts.

She adjusted her bonnet to shield her face from the Colorado sun. Even with the bonnet's shield, her skin had long ago become dry and parched. One might have guessed her age to be older than her age of forty years. Low humidity, high altitude and ultra violet rays all conspired to suck the vitality out of the skin of her face. Clifton's disappearance had taken much of her remaining spirit.

Her thought shifted to a question he had asked after their last visit to Mesa Verde. "Mom, did you realize the First People entered the world through the *Sipapu?* That's what the Ranger said the Indians believed. Was that like God creating Adam and Eve in the Garden of Eden?"

That had been a hard one. It had been easier when he had burst through the door to announce finding his first bee tree, or the first bone awl he had found in the pit house.

At the end of the row, Etta Mae expertly pulled up on the hydraulic lever to lift the array of cultivator plows out of the ground as she simultaneously stood on the left brake, freezing the left rear tire in place, swinging the tractor around into position to go up the adjoining two rows of corn.

Setting her course up the rows, satisfied the plows were at the right depth to throw soil to the exact height to cover weeds without covering the first leaf of the corn stalks, her thoughts returned to her missing son.

Clifton was like her in so many ways. Charlie had been like Ed. Charlie had been a good farmer and mechanic, able to work with livestock, raising champion Four-H beef, competing in farm activities, able to plow all day and proud of his accomplishment, able to repair equipment, overhaul engines, welding and inventing time saving tools that made life easier on the farm. Yes, he was just like his father.

Clifton was a dreamer. He preferred to read Zane Gray and dream of riding the purple sage. He would read Sir Walter Scott and dream of jousting alongside King Richard or camping with Robin Hood and his merry men in Sherwood Forrest. He read Miguel de Cervantes and dreamed of jousting windmills with Don Quixote.

Mrs. Campbell had been a Godsend.

Unfortunately, he tended to neglect his chores, the quality of his work in the fields was erratic, and he devoted far too much time to daydreaming and reading the novels that he concealed in various retreats around the farm. She had hoped that he would grow out of it, but no amount of disciplining from his father had had much effect. The discipline that Ed meted out was severe, and she could see that instead of changing Clifton's habits it was breaking his will. She had worried about him, even before he ran away, but had felt helpless to do other than try to support his dreams. It had been partly her fault for feeding his thirst and encouraging that side of him. Now he was gone. It was her fault.

She sighed and her tears mixed with the dust that rose around her as she neared the end of the row.

49
Fishing
Lost Canyon

Cliff awoke to gunshots; rapid-fire, staccato, machine gun fire. It sounded like a war zone. It was not late enough in the year to be the hunting season. The sound was not close, but sound carried far in the still, thin, clear morning air. From the cave, he couldn't tell the direction of the shots. He lay on his mat for a moment after quiet returned. Moonbeam stood on her hind legs at the doorway, her ears twisting back and forth listening, and her tail arched defensively.

Maggie cowered in his cage.

He had totally lost track of time. Surely, it couldn't have been seven weeks since the fight and the afternoon when he had come close to taking another human's life. He had no doubt that if Hector had come down the road that afternoon, he would have pulled the trigger, he had been that full of rage. He realized he had not thought about it for a while, and he no longer re-played the fight in his mind.

July fourth would be about two weeks after the solstice.

The Fourth of July had been one of his favorite times of the year. Ed would put a board in the head gate diverting most of the water into the reservoir to fill it. He would leave a small head to run down the central ditch clear to Raul's so that he could fill his cistern, and water his garden and little patch of beans. In exchange, Raul would milk the cows and do the chores so the family could go fishing. Sometimes George and his wife Marilyn would go along too.

The family fishing hole was in Lost Canyon high in the mountains where quaking aspen and blue spruce grew. The campsite was at the end of an unimproved dirt Forest Service road. A trail led to an ice cold, crystal clear creek a mile or so below. They usually got up around 3:00 A.M., milked the cows, did the chores and drove up before dawn.

They arrived at the campsite at sunrise in time to assemble fishing gear and walk to the creek getting there as the sun hit the water. The creek was narrow enough in most places to jump across. Pools and beaver dams made the fishing ideal for Cliff's willow fishing pole and Ed's old split bamboo fly rod.

Etta Mae and Marilyn stayed behind to set up camp, talk, walk and relax.

When the men reached the stream, they decided who would go upstream or downstream. Usually Cliff and Ed stayed together and Charlie and George fished together. At noon, they changed directions, arrived back at the trail by mid-afternoon and headed back up the long trail to camp.

The trout were native brookies and none got above seven or eight inches. They were scrappy and plentiful. Ed rigged two flies on Cliff's six-foot leader and often two trout would strike at once. They would stop at noon to share a lunch of candy-like seeded raisins, canned sardines and crackers. Fish went into burlap gunnysack creels, "gunnybags".

George had shown Ed how to make the burlap creel by cutting a burlap sack down each side an inch or two back from the side seams of the sack. George tied the resulting two straps at the top to form a neck strap. He had cut fresh green grass and put it into the bottom of the bag; sprinkled water was over the grass and tucked the side flaps back over the grass. It provided a cool moist environment for the fish they caught and kept the blowflies away.

Every hour Ed and Cliff cleaned the fish they caught.

Cliff smiled when he remembered the first time Ed had made him a "gunnybag". It had nearly reached to the ground. Ed had shortened the straps to fit his short frame. The gunnybag he had brought with him from the granary was the one he had used last July Fourth.

At the end of the day, Etta Mae and Marilyn would have camp made when they finally took those last weary steps at the top of the trail and saw that wonderful spiral of blue smoke.

According to the forest service trailhead sign, it was one and a half miles from that point to the creek. Cliff was sure that it was twice as far coming back out as it had been going in that morning. Fortunately, it seemed as though just as he reached the point of exhaustion either Ed or George would call for a short rest stop saving him from begging for the same. He was proud of the fact that he had never had to ask for a rest.

The fire would be burning, cut balsam boughs spread to act as a kind of mattress for the blankets. There were no tents. They slept under the trees and stars where they could smell the campfire smoke and hear the breeze rustling through the restless quaking aspen. A fishing trip had never been rained out.

Those were Clifton's fondest memories.

It was there at Lost Canyon that Cliff had discovered his favorite flower, the Colorado blue columbine, the state flower. He had transplanted several to his "mountain flower garden" at the house to enjoy all summer, not just for one or two days each summer. Everyone told him it couldn't be done, but he tried anyway. He had dug a clump of blooming wild strawberries and columbines and transplanted them into a little pocket space where the porch extended out from the northeast end of the old house. The area was shaded from the hot southern summer sun. In summer, it received an hour or so of morning sunlight and was shaded for the rest of the day. There and on the north side of the house, snow slid off the tin roof, accumulated and packed into ice. It was slow to melt, as it was shaded from the sun by the new house in the morning and by the old house during the day.

Cliff had asked for the space to start a mountain flower garden, and Etta Mae gave him the roughly eight by ten area to tend. It was a weedy eyesore. Domestic flowers wouldn't grow there. It was the middle of June before the ground thawed. It nearly duplicated the conditions the wild strawberries and columbines had in the mountains.

The strawberry vines immediately thrived and put out new runners. Just as his dad had said they would, the columbines had wilted and died.

The next spring, when the snow and ice finally melted off the mountain garden, among the strawberries Cliff had begun to see a new growth around the dead columbine stems. By the middle of June, every blue columbine plant flowered as brilliantly as it had on the trail leading to Lost Canyon Creek. He did not cut the stems back as the flowers finished their bloom, but left the seed stems to mature. It wasn't until the first snowflakes fell that the seed heads bent under the weight and spilled their black seeds onto the earth at their feet. The next spring those seeds sprouted and spread. After several years the whole garden was a mix of columbine, strawberries, and flags added later from the Lost Canyon trail.

~~~

As the sound of the fireworks faded, Cliff wondered what had become of his little garden. It would be in full bloom now if anyone was giving it a little water and keeping the weeds away from it. He guessed it was one more chore left to his mom. His dad had never shown any interest in any of the flower gardens. Flowers were his mom's province with Cliff helping out. The wild flower garden was strictly Cliff's.

Other than the columbines, Lost Canyon held particularly poignant memories of his dad patiently untangling the fine six-foot leader when it frequently become entangled over willows or brush growing by Lost Canyon Creek.

Furthermore, burned into his memory was the delighted expression on his dad's face when a trout flashed at a fly and the line tightened.

His dad had been patient with him, as Cliff learned to catch trout on artificial flies. When fishing was slow in the middle of the day, they panned for gold in the gravel bars along the creek. The gold they found was low grade, but it was fun to discover.

On those days by the creek, there was no discipline, no scolding, no correction, just a dad and son enjoying nature together.

During those two days each year, he and his dad talked. He could ask questions, and he felt close to his dad. He saw the man that most people saw all the time.

~~~

Cliff stared at the poles in the ceiling of the dwelling and stared at the scrub oak lattice work holding up the solid clay roof above it. A few empty baskets hung from the poles already. He wiped the tears that had begun streaming down his cheeks. It was the first Fourth of July he would miss spending with his family. He wondered if they were in Lost Canyon fishing without him that day. *Or are they out in the field working because, I'm not there to help them?*

~~~

The two men carried their old split bamboo fly rods unassembled in canvass bags in their hands. They carried burlap sacks freshly into converted into fish bags under their arms.

George was responsible for carrying on the yearly tradition of going fishing on the Fourth of July. Ed had planned to just stay home and get some work done on the farm. With Clifton gone, the work had piled up and despite Etta Mae's best efforts; he had much to do each weekend including Sundays. He really couldn't afford a day away to go fishing. Hector had continued working for Ed, but he or Etta Mae had to teach Hector everything to do. He worked hard, but he wasn't as efficient as Cliff as far as Ed was concerned. That even included the time it took to shake Cliff out of his daydreaming.

"I guess it's a moot question now. I hadn't thought about it. I thought I had four years to prepare for it."

"Ed, you've got to take a breath. You need to take a couple of days and relax. You've been going at it five days a week in town and coming home to work another half a day and then a full two days each weekend. A man can't keep this up. You and me are going to go fishing," George had said and that had been it.

The two men walked down the trail into Lost Canyon in the crisp, thin, mountain air. The dew on the grass sparkled in the first glimmers of sunlight. A cluster of Colorado blue columbines, their outer five pointed sky blue petals surrounding five pure white rounded inner petals stood welcoming the day at the foot of a forked, white and black clad quaking aspen.

"This is what brought me to this country and then kept me here, George," Ed said. "You see those columbines and smell this aspen and blue spruce, and you'd never know that we're only 20 miles from the edge of the high desert, canyon lands or badlands."

"Yeh. No place like it that I've ever seen," George agreed.

"There is only one thing missing, George," Ed said as he stared down the trail ahead. "Clifton loved this place. Those columbines back there? He thought they were the most beautiful flower on earth. He wanted to transplant some of them back to the house. I'd heard that they wouldn't transplant, and that they wouldn't grow at lower elevations, and I told him that. He tried it anyway, and darned if he didn't get them to live and even flourish. That boy had more determination than anybody, when he set his mind to it. The contradiction in him is so many other times when he started and didn't follow through...."

"Why are you speaking of him in the past tense?" George asked.
~~~

"What do you mean George?"

"Ed, Cliff isn't gone. It's true he isn't here with us today, but he's not dead. At least we don't know that he is. We can't be thinking that he is gone forever. It sounds like you are beginning to think of him as gone for good!"

"We haven't heard a word. There hasn't been a clue. No sign of foul play. No sighting. No nothing. What am I supposed to think?"

"You of all people can't give up faith, Ed. You have been an inspiration to all of us in the depth of your faith in God. Don't lose that faith now! You have to know that you aren't alone in this. Your God is looking after that boy in your absence!"

"You know George, I've tried to do right by my family and friends, but I went wrong with my son. I didn't pay close enough attention to him. I was looking right through him. He was trying to tell me, and I wasn't listening. I grew up in a different time. My dad was a severe man, and I was the oldest son in a big family. I had to become a man when I was still a boy. I didn't have time to be a boy, to dream and to do what my dad considered foolish things. I'm afraid I turned out to be my dad. I wasn't there for my boy, and now I'm being punished for it."

"Is that what you think Ed? Do you think God is punishing you?" George asked. "How does that square with your faith? If you feel you've done wrong, can't you ask forgiveness? Does your faith require your punishment be the death of your son? I can't follow that Ed. And I don't believe you should either."

"I had a talk with Raul the other day, and what I found out was that his boy had been bullying Cliff for a long time. Raul didn't know that either until one of his children told him about it. When he confronted Hector about it, Hector admitted it. Hector told him why he had done it and there was a peculiar logic to it, I guess, if you are a kid. In some ways, it wasn't so different from mine in the way I disciplined him, I'm afraid. The boy told his dad. He wanted to be Clifton's friend, and he thought by constantly going after him, in the end it would make him strong.

"I also found out this summer that the teacher, whose discipline I supported, was being too heavy handed and quick to discipline for frivolous things and was being manipulated by Hector and the other kids. It was all a cruel game. He was a victim of bullying at school by the kids, and unnecessary discipline by the teacher for several years, and I was a participant rather than his advocate. Clifton tried to tell me that, and I refused to listen. Instead of making him strong, we were all beating him down.

"I feel horrible about this George. I can't blame him for running off, and if he never comes back to me, I can't blame him for that either. I want to ask his forgiveness, but I may never have a chance now!"

"That's a pretty big admission, Ed. I'd say that what you have to do is wait. Give him time now. I wouldn't give up on him, Ed. The thing is, I like to think that I'm a pretty good friend of your son, and you know what? He has never complained to me about your being too hard on him.

He blames himself, mostly for his own behavior. He's a good boy, and he's resourceful. I have a feeling, he's doing all right, wherever he is, and whatever, he's doing. I have a gut feeling, when he gets things sorted out, he'll come back on his own terms and the two of you can make your peace. Just be prepared at that time to do the right thing."

"I pray every night that you're right, George."

"Just don't let that faith, that you've had for so long, and that has carried you through so much, waver now."

They walked down the trail in silence for a while quietly enjoying each other's friendship and the beauty of the blue spruce, aspen canyon side.

"So Ed?" George asked, "What's happening to Clifton's flower garden this summer without him there to take care of it?"

"I've been sprinkling it every morning just like he did. I figure it's the least I can do. I want it to be nice for him when he does decide to come home. Those little mountain strawberries are the sweetest things you ever tasted. I guess that's one way of telling myself that he's OK, and that I have faith that he's coming home."

"Good for you," George said. "When you get ready to go through the bees, give me a holler, and I'll come lend a hand. What's he have, about six hives now?"

"That's right."

"It's about time to add supers. Did he make any this winter?"

"He made three for each hive, and he has the foundation strung in all the frames ready to go, I'm pretty sure."

~~~

Cliff wandered about that day thinking about his family and the camping trips and fishing with his dad. He thought about the columbines, quaking aspen and coolness of the mountains. He loved the ferns, grass and flowers that grew on the damp hillsides where abundant snow in the winter and more frequent summer rains produced a different climate than here on the edge of the high desert.

He stopped and sat on a weathered cedar log at the edge of a rocky outcrop. In front of him, a prickly pear cactus spread flat hand sized pads. A waxy, brilliant yellow blossom competed with the sun in intensity. Growing under nearby sagebrush profiting by both the shade and taking nourishment from the shrub's roots grew an orange Indian paintbrush.

Cliff smiled. Mother Nature just couldn't resist dropping a tiny spot of color in the most random places just to cheer him up.

Cliff looked longingly at the LaPlata Mountains and the green foothills on the north eastern slopes a little to the left of Sharks Tooth where
~~~

the head waters of Lost Canyon Creek began. It was a 20-mile drive by road to the trailhead down to the canyon. He could walk that in a good day if he could stay on the road. For him to stay out of sight, he would have to follow the canyons, and stay in timber, avoiding the numerous farms between the ruin and where the heavy timber began. It could take a couple of days and there were many unknown risks that he might be observed. If he took the safest route via Big Canyon, over to Lost Canyon way down toward Dolores, then walked up Lost Canyon until he reached the mountain portion, the distance could easily be two or three times as far as Lost Canyon twisted and turned this way and that on it's way to the Dolores River.

Alas, he couldn't go up there and spend the summer fishing and enjoying the cool mountains all summer, as tempting as that seemed. Winter was coming and those few baskets hanging from the roof pole should be joined by many others and all had to be filled before snow fell. Seven weeks had gone by all ready. He mentally figured out how much time he had left: July, August, September, 12 weeks. When October arrived, it could begin snowing anytime after that.

50

Basket Making
Martinez Canyon

Cliff's main task each day after breakfast was to forage for food. Maggie was now his constant companion. At first, he had ridden in the bib pocket. Then as he grew and pin feathers had turned to permanent feathers he rode on Cliff's shoulder. When he gained enough confidence to learn to fly, he flew in short bursts from the shoulder to bushes back to shoulder, shoulder to branches back to shoulder, shoulder to ground and back to the shoulder.

It was great fun to explore and forage with the magpie. At first Cliff had been afraid that Maggie would fly away to join others of his own kind, but he seemed to have little interest in the others. Cliff had taken Maggie from the nest soon enough to imprint fully with Cliff. The wild magpies called to Maggie, and they chattered back and forth in active conversation, but as Cliff moved on Maggie moved along with him.

"It is no wonder people find you members of the crow family spooky. The raven was a good subject for Edgar Allen Poe," Cliff said to Maggie and laughed.

The crow family, to which Maggie belonged, was considered to be the most intelligent of all the birds and Cliff was aware that many Native

American Nations considered the Raven, also a member of the crow family, to be a sacred bird. He wasn't aware that the raven was considered a sacred bird by many ancient cultures worldwide, even the first bird off Noah's arch was sometimes reported to be a raven. Crows, and magpies invented tools to help them in the search for food. Cliff was intrigued by their conversations as he passed under trees where they congregated while Maggie rode on his shoulder. They seemed to be calling down to his friend who answered then. He listened to their talk and realized that there were subtle inflections and combinations in their "yck, yack, yac, mag, mag, mag."

Maggie would listen and answer. A different magpie would answer, or several magpies would answer in turn. Then Maggie would reply.

When a magpie flew in from somewhere else a quick conversation would ensue among the assemblage of birds and the flock would take wing.

Cliff knew that bees had a high-level of communication. A worker who discovered a new nectar source communicated the location to a distant field through an elaborate dance. The huddle of fellow workers looked on and on the conclusion of the dance took wing, following the set of directions to the source.

As he watched the magpies converse, he realized they were probably doing the same thing as the bees only they were communicating in the same manner as human beings, through verbal language.

As Cliff foraged for food, Maggie also hunted and brought big fat grasshoppers to Cliff, who added them to the pouches of seeds he collected. By this time, Maggie gathered all his own food. What he brought to Cliff was surplus. Maggie was an expert grasshopper hunter and Cliff added some of them to the stew or roasted them and ate them whole. He offered a portion of the stew to Maggie and to Moonbeam each night.

Moonbeam was also self-sufficient but enjoyed sampling Cliff's food when it was offered. Cliff had begun to add crickets, red ants, worms, maggots and frog legs to the stew. As he foraged, he carried a mayonnaise jar in the gunnybag into which he put the insects Maggie brought to him whether they were alive or dead.

The canyon was their supermarket.

Into the gunnybag went larger items such as greens, prickly pear leaves and pears, cattail shoots, dandelion roots, wild onions and asparagus, before it went to seed and put up lacy fern-like stems. Into his pockets and pouches went clover blossoms for tea and sage, grass, clover and dandelion seeds as they matured.

The seeds on the earliest blooming clover began to mature, and he gathered them when he got to them before the birds did. Fortunately, there was plenty for everyone. Dandelion seeds, likewise, were abundant until their season ended. As one plant's season ended, another began to mature.

As summer progressed, a variety of grass seeds matured. Timothy, orchard grass, rye grass, and fescue all grew tall and lush along the ditches on the farms and along the creek bank. As the tall stems and leaves matured, the deep green slowly faded to a light tan. The seed began to fill and swell and were doughy when he tested them. Following the change of color by a few weeks, the grass seed heads turned down and the seed fell free when he rolled the heads between his hands.

He learned that by grinding the seeds and blowing away the chaff he had rich nutritious coarse flour that he could either add to the stew or cook with cornmeal and an egg into a tortilla. There was a ready supply of magpie eggs most of the summer. He never took more than one or two from a nest. The prolific birds produced several broods per summer and were in no danger of extinction.

Dandelion seeds were easy to gather before the wind disbursed them. He grasped them by their umbrella heads in one hand and broke the dangling seeds free with the other hand. The tiny seeds, when ground and added into the corn meal, tasted like poppy seeds.

Soon, the dandelion blossoms and seed were gone, but the foliage remained, marking the location of their roots, which he continued to dig. Cliff ate some of the roots raw. He also charred some of them and ground them to make a coffee-like drink. He had dandelion root, cloverleaf or clover blossom tea every night.

When he returned from foraging, Cliff emptied the mature seeds from his pockets into separate baskets. He watched the contents of each little basket grow as a miser watches his coins.

In addition to yucca root and leaves, if there was room left in the pack, he filled it with cedar and sage bark taken from trees and bushes along the way home. He never removed a noticeable amount from any one tree or bush to prevent revealing his presence.

~~~

Cliff had begun trying to attempting to weave baskets almost immediately after moving into the ruin. The first results were crude affairs of willow and grass leaves.

For his very first attempt, he had used four thin green willow twigs each about a foot long. He had cut a V notch in the middle of each one-half way through, tied them together at the notch, bent them upwards forcing them into a basket shape. He tied the stakes to a willow hoop to keep them in place and wove blades of grass in and out of the stakes to fill in the sides of the baskets. The opening of the basket had been the size of his fist, and it was six inches deep. Unfortunately, the bottom was pointed, so it wouldn't stand up.

He bent the stakes of the next basket. The willow twigs were very flexible while they were green and formed a graceful U. He stayed with that form for the next several attempts.

Besides grass, he tried weaving willow bark through the vertical
~~~

stakes. The result was heavy and slightly ugly. He used it to store his balls of yucca twine.

He had no teacher except the scrapbook and experience. Cliff began to appreciate the fact that being the only student in his class in grade school had been a bonus after all. He had become a self-learner. He had learned to read critically and how to follow directions accurately. Directions in the one article on basket making were sketchy, but there were a few drawings and grainy photos.

Baskets would answer a need for storage for most things. Tiny seeds such as dandelion or lambs quarter were problematic, as they would work into the weave of bark baskets or just leak out.

He studied one crude looking, fragile pot that had been left in the ruin. It looked burned and he realized the marks on the outer surface looked similar to a basket weaving.

This gave him the idea to mix and kneed a ball of clay and press coils of it into the inside of a basket, building up a thin wall from the bottom up to the brim. He smoothed it, covered it and set it aside to dry slowly. Unfired, it would not hold water, but if it didn't crack apart, it would be suitable to store fine seeds, nuts or other dry goods. The clay would also resist rodents from chewing through the grass or bark to get to the seeds.

He even burned away one of the baskets. The finished pot wasn't pretty, but it was durable. It didn't fire hot enough make it waterproof, but it was useful for dry storage anyway. He left the rest of the lined baskets unfired with the woven material in place to strengthen them.

As he created each basket, he strung three cords of rope through the upper rim and hung each one from the ceiling poles.

These early clay lined baskets became the storage containers for the seeds he brought home from foraging each day as summer progressed.

One morning he stood on the top of the rimrock waiting for the sun to rise at the far north end of the La Plata Mountains. He had begun to ask Mother Nature's help before beginning each basket. He held one up above his head. *Heavenly Father and Mother Nature please breathe the spirit of the willow, sage, cedar, yucca and plants into these baskets. Please keep their spirit strong so the baskets will protect the seeds and food I store in them. And keep their spirit strong, so they will be pleasing to look at as well. Thank you for helping me survive.*

~~~

As the days passed, he tried to calculate the quantities of things he would need to survive the winter if necessary, and how to store food. Winter was still two and a half to four months away, but he couldn't wait until the last minute to prepare. Fall could linger or it could change overnight. Most of what he was currently eating would not store through the winter except for the seeds, and the charred dandelion root. He could use the dried yucca chips for soap but he couldn't eat them.
~~~

When the time came, he would try to glean from his dad's corn and bean fields and if necessary from the neighbors. Some corn and beans always went to waste, and after harvest, his dad turned the cows in on it. A couple of nights foraging would give him all the corn and beans he needed for the winter. He was confident of it. He could glean potatoes and fruit. Several old orchards were within his range. No one cared for them or pruned them, but they still produced some fruit he thought, although he didn't know if the fruit was any good. The apples were probably wormy, and they would rot quickly. All the gathering would go to waste if he didn't have enough storage containers to store the food safely to last through the winter.

~~~

A large worry loomed ahead. Cliff's overalls were both wearing out, and he was out growing them. His underwear was getting tighter and one sock had a hole in the heel. He had alternated wearing and laundered each pair of clothes, but constant scrambling over rock, digging yucca root, and climbing in and out of the canyon every day was far more abusive wear than he would have given them under ordinary circumstances.

He was growing. His muscles were filling out. His toes were cramped in his shoes.

51
Atlatl First Kill
Martinez Canyon

In the still early morning hour, Cliff crept silently forward with the atlatl at ready. Twenty feet ahead sat a cottontail rabbit, frozen in place, blending in with its surroundings. Cliff had affixed a dart with a bone point to the blunt end of the spear. He held the shaft between the forefinger and thumb of his right hand, the tapered end of the spear thrower between his palm and three fingers.

He had practiced for weeks until he was accurate about eighty percent of the time. Lately, he had hit objects the size of a tin can at ten paces, roughly thirty feet. However, until this moment he had not had the opportunity to cast a spear against a live animal.

He had not used the traps again after catching the hen turkey. He had made a promise to hunt only what he could see, so that he could choose what to take. He had also put the .22 away as an emergency backup. His shell supply was nearly exhausted.

He had gone out with the atlatl every day, but the cottontails weren't
~~~

coming out in the daytime. He had seen a few late in the afternoon or early in the morning, but always at a distance.

That morning Cliff had sat by the *Sipapu* and asked Mother Nature to share another of her creatures with him. He didn't dance or chant, but spoke with his heart. He had told her his plight that morning. He felt fine and had not lost weight. He hadn't had meat for a while. But, the beans were gone as well as the cornbread. His diet lately was mostly a kind of bread by grinding grass seeds and mixing in roasted grasshoppers, crickets, red ants and carpenter ants. He also mixed the grasshoppers, crickets, red ants, carpenter ants and frog legs into his stew. He thanked Mother Nature for loaning him Maggie who brought him most of the grasshoppers and crickets.

Now here he stood with a cottontail in his sight within casting distance.

He took the stance he had practiced repeatedly, drew back, stepped back on his right foot and then forward on his left foot as he moved his arm forward in an overhand sweep, releasing the spear with a snap of the wrist as it became horizontal and aligned with his sight. The dart tipped shaft shot forward decisively and pinned the rabbit to the earth.

Cliff ran forward to grab the rabbit before it got away. The dart had gone clear through the neck of the cottontail, breaking the spinal cord. It was still attached to the shaft. He pulled the dart and spear free of the dead rabbit and examined the bone point. It was undamaged and ready for use again. The kill had been swift and clean. Mother Nature's gift had not suffered.

Cliff lifted the rabbit to the north, east, south and west, lifted it toward the sky and dipped it to the earth. *Heavenly Father and Mother Nature I thank you for sharing this rabbit with me today. I will waste no part. I will hunt only to survive.*

He put the spear aside, skinned and cleaned the rabbit leaving the head attached. He turned the pelt inside out and placed both it and the meat in the gunnybag with the liver, lungs, kidneys and heart still inside the body. He squeezed the intestines clean and coiled them inside the sack to keep them from drying out. The inedible viscera and feet he placed in the crotch of a tree for the magpies and crows to clear up.

Cliff was elated with his first kill. The cottontail was a little smaller than the domestic white Dutch rabbits he raised in a hutch in the farmyard, but the meat was the same.

The spear had struck the rabbit with an amazing amount of force and Cliff was convinced that if he used a dart with a good flint cutting point he could bring down a small deer. He already had several such darts made up using found flint points. Nevertheless, he knew it was a big leap from killing his first rabbit to hunting his first deer with a spear.

52
Tanning Fur
Martinez Canyon

Cliff had read and reread everything he had on tanning. The articles tried to make it sound easy. He knew that it was not. He knew that he had a long learning curve ahead.

He had tried several times to tan rabbit hides, and the results each time had been disastrous. Each hide had become a putrid mess that he had finally taken to the pasture and buried. As he read the articles in the journal, he realized he had tried to tan the rabbit pelts as if they had needed the hair removed first. In fact, the rabbit pelt should not have been tanned with the hair left on. They were more suitable as a fur pelt. If he were tanning a deer hide, he would need to remove the hair. Each kind of hide or pelt required a different procedure.

Most of the pamphlets and magazine articles were complicated, and he read them carefully to see if he could understand what he had done wrong in summers past. It became almost immediately apparent where he had made many mistakes.

From the beginning of his stay in the dwelling, he had stretched every pelt including that of the bobcat intruder that first night. So he had an ample supply of pelts, but he did not have a supply of the chemicals the articles called for. His best hope was in a few paragraphs in a sports story that had appeared in the sports section of the Cortez Sentinel during the hunting season of the fall before.

Stephan Zacharias, an old timer in the area, had described how he and his dad had tanned hides, back in the day, before anyone could purchase all the chemicals through a taxidermy supply catalogue. He had claimed the best chemical came from the animal itself, the brain. Zacharias had simply said, if you are tanning a deer hide, soak it in wood ash over night and scrape off the hair then soften the hide with the brains of the deer that had produced the hide if it were available. Let it almost dry then rub it down with brain soup, wrap it in a damp towel or sheet to rest overnight, then rub it dry over a board until it was soft. If it was a pelt, just wash the fur and skip the hair removal step. The rest of the procedure was the same.

The recipe was as vague as most of Etta Mae's recipes. She jotted down the general outlines, but all the specifics were in her head.

The rabbit pelt was still soft. He knew from all the other readings that he first had to make sure the pelt or hide had to be free of any flesh, fat or membrane. They all suggested scraping with warnings not to cut the hide.

The pelt was still a tube just as when he had shucked it off the rabbit. Keeping it tube shaped made it easy to stretch, as all he had to do was bend a green willow in half and insert in through the hide turned fur side in. When he let the willow try to return to its normal straight position, the wood stretched the hide tight. A stretcher stick between the ends of the willow kept the tension on the willow as it dried.

He left the pelt in the tube shape and with fur side in slid it over a bed-slat. For a scraper, he used a piece of thin shale. A number of such pieces were scattered around the front of the cave on the ledge. They weren't like other rocks on the ledge or on the rimrock He assumed the original occupants, perhaps for use as tools, had brought them there.

Clifton removed all the fat and membrane. Then he washed the skin with soapy water. After cleaning the skin side of the pelt, he turned it fur side out and shampooed the fur. He wrung the excess water out and hung it so the fur would dry while he prepared the brains.

Cliff hacked the rabbit skull open with the file-knife. He scooped the brain out with the wooden spoon and dropped it into the coffee can, added water to cover the brain and set it on the cooking stone to heat. He heated the brain and water until they were warm, and then he mashed the grey mass and mixed the brain and water together with his hand until it resembled a grey soup. He added a half cup of water and mixed it in thoroughly.

The fur was dry by that time, and he turned it back inside out exposing the skin, which he let almost dry.

At that point, he cut the pelt open so that it lay flat before he began to knead the brain mixture into the skin with his fingers. He continued until he had covered the entire skin, and the skin was soft. He quickly re-rubbed the surface of the entire skin with another thin layer of brain soup.

While he was applying the brain soup to the skin, he was heating water in the Dutch oven. He dropped a t-shirt into the water, fished it out with a willow stick and let it drain, and then wrung it out. He lay the freshly brain rubbed skin on the hot t-shirt, rolled the skin up in it, and set it aside to rest for several hours.

While the rabbit skin rested, he covered the remaining brain mixture and set it in the coolest part of the cave high enough that Moonbeam couldn't reach it.

That night right after supper, he unrolled the t-shirt and checked the pelt. It was soft and pliable. For good measure, he rubbed the remainder of the brain soup into the skin again and worked it in with his hand, and then he rolled it into the rinsed and re-soaked t-shirt again and set it aside to rest for a final time.

The next morning Cliff unwrapped the pelt and wiped the brain solution off with the freshly soaked t-shirt the best he could and hung it up to dry while he laundered the t-shirt in fresh yucca shampoo.

The skin was drying quickly and he had to soften it before it was dry. He did this by drawing it back and forth over the smooth rounded corner of the doorsill. The friction on the stone helped to finish drying the skin and soften the fibers at the same time.

The finished pelt was a lovely soft grey-brown rabbit fur. It wouldn't go far, but enough of them would make a beautiful coat.

When the skin was dry, he hung it high so Moonbeam couldn't get to it.

53
Tanning Continues
Martinez Canyon

The first rabbit taken with the atlatl proved to be no fluke. Cliff's hunting and stalking skill continued to improve. He practiced constantly, and his aim and accuracy continued to improve.

He didn't hit every rabbit he threw at, and he had to spend time each day repairing and replacing the bone points. He had yet to throw a dart with a precious flint point, saving them for the time when he might hunt something larger.

Cliff gained skill and speed in tanning and the string of grey brown pelts grew.

~~~

About a half mile below the Stone residence began a section of the road a quarter mile wide where mule deer crossed from the Big and Little Canyons on their way to Martinez Canyon and on to Mesa Verde. Although the main crossing times were in the fall and early spring, it was a dangerous place to drive through at night any time of the year if one drove too fast. Any resident hitting a deer was encouraged to call the county to report a collision as soon as possible so that the county could pick up road kill deer to use in the school cafeteria or at the jail.

Cliff visited the deer crossing below the Stone residence, whenever he could looking for a road kill deer that was not mangled in its encounter with a vehicle.

He had found several, but the vultures and other scavengers had already discovered their mangled carcasses. The county quickly removed any that still had usable meat.

One morning Cliff arrived at the road at dawn and walked the edge of the woods where he had a clear view of the road, and he could quickly duck out of sight if he heard a vehicle coming. As it had become his habit, when he reached the road he walked east on the south side of the road until he came close to the Stone residence then he crossed to the north side and walked west. The deer at that time of the year were trickling in from the north. It seemed early. Usually they approached the road, froze when a car approached, and sometimes leaped into the road just as the car was broadside. Those that were thrown aside and that had died instantly fell either into the north barrow pit or alongside that side of the road. Occasionally, one leaped clear over the front of a car or truck and only hit a thin leg or legs on the hood in passing, breaking a leg or landing in the middle of the road then limping on across and sometimes collapsing in pain on the south side, either in the cleared area or in the timber.

As on other mornings, Cliff found nothing that morning on the North
~~~

side of the road but a dead porcupine. He crossed back to the south side of the road below the deer crossing and walked eastward to complete the circuit. That is where he came upon the fawn.

The fawn had not fallen by the side of the road, so the county did not pick it up for its meat. It had made it just inside the woods before it died. Unfortunately, it had been dead long enough that Cliff was afraid to use the meat. He dragged the carcass further into the woods and skinned it. He took the head, opened it up and cut away all the tallow from around the intestines, heart and liver, took the hide and returned to the ruin.

Tanning the fawn hide, he realized, was a much bigger job than tanning a rabbit pelt because he had to remove the hair. The old man had said soak it in ashes.

A more official sounding guide suggested soaking the hide in a lye solution. A sidebar said "purists" should use wood ashes. He had an ample supply of wood ashes cleaned from the fire pit.

The article instructed him to soak the hide in a tank or wash tub. He could use the natural tub in the rock of the ledge where he regularly soaked yucca leaves to rot off the leaf material to get to the fiber.

At that moment, the natural tub was full of rainwater. All he had to do was add ashes, stir them in thoroughly, add the hide, and stir it until it was coated with the ash grit, weight it down and let it soak overnight.

The next day he spread the soaked hide on the flat surface of the doorsill and began scraping the hair off using a shale scraping stone. The loosened hair still required work to remove, but he persevered. Next he turned the hide over and scraped and cut away all the fat and membrane tissue from the inside of the hide before he could begin applying the brain mixture and working it into the hide.

~~~

After working on the hide for three days, he was satisfied that he could do no more. It was a soft rawhide colored leather. In the newspaper article, the old man had said simply smoke pelts and hides to waterproof them.

The literature said that to make pelts water resistant one had to smoke them. Smoking would not actually make them waterproof, but if they got wet, they might become stiff when they dried. If he smoked them, then they would dry soft. If he used the pelts to make clothing, he would get them wet plenty of times.

He constructed a tripod over the fire pit, and fastened the fawn hide and rabbit pelts over it until it resembled a tipi. The skin side of the pelts faced inward. He built a small smoky fire in the fire pit and kept it going all night. The tipi captured the smoke within, and it permeated the pelts, turned the fawn leather to a golden brown. Fresh air carried the smoke from the top of the tipi out exhaust vents at the eves of the dwelling at the roofline keeping the cave itself relatively free of smoke.
~~~

54

Preparing for winter
Martinez Canyon

As he and Maggie foraged for food and supplies each day, Cliff considered what he would need if they lived in the dwelling over the winter. Hypothetically, they needed to store enough to last one person, a skunk and a magpie from as soon as early October until late May. On the other hand, it might be as little as late November until the end of April if it was a mild winter. He needed to store enough food to last for six to eight months. He wanted enough for nine.

About now, a mile away at the farmhouse, Etta Mae would be canning vegetables from the garden. Seven quarts or 20 pint jars would go from her big Presto pressure canner at a time to be stored in the floor to the ceiling shelves in the basement. Behind the house was the man tall high earthen mound with steps facing the house leading down to the underground root cellar. Into that cellar each fall Etta Mae and Ed put sacks of root vegetables: carrots, beets, turnips and potatoes; squash: banana, hubbard, and acorn; and apples. From the center pole hung bacon, hams, and muslin cloth tubes packed with sausage. Deer quarters hung there until consumed. Freshly slaughtered hogs and beef hung there until they were processed.

Ed's cellar was his pride and joy. Most of his neighbors had root cellars, some similar and some more primitive, and they used them mostly to store potatoes if they were built away from the house.

Ed and Etta Mae were both from families who had survived not only two wars and depressions but also the dust bowl of 1930 to 1936. The first years of their marriage were on the run from the effects of the dust bowl that had destroyed the farms of their youth in Texas and Oklahoma. The memories of those horrible years of starvation and hardship were burned into their core. Each year Etta Mae grew many times more produce than her family could consume and canned enough for several families.

His parents did not talk about that part of their early life. They were generous to a fault with their surplus garden produce. He had argued that they could sell it, but they shut him down when he mentioned it. He had said something to Mrs. Campbell when they talked about U.S. history, and she had given him a thin book to read. It was the *Grapes of Wrath* by John Steinbeck. It had helped him to visualize what they had lived through a little better, but still he had not lived in it.

~~~

Cliff turned his attention back to his own situation.

During the wintertime, he could possibly depend on finding a few
~~~

rabbits in the snow. But, that was about all. If things got rough, he might raid a neighbor's granary but with snow and mud on the ground all winter long it would be impossible to hide his trail. Stealing from a neighbor was an admission of failure. This time he would not fail. He might be a coward, but he was not a thief.

He would also have to store a winter's supply of fuel. How would he do that without an axe? He had found several stone axes. He would have to put a handle on one to use it. Probably, that was what he would do. Either way the chopping was going to draw attention. He was already cleaning up most of the dead fall in the area. The firewood stockpile in the space outside of the dwelling was growing every day.

He had until the first snowfall to prepare for winter.

The number of rabbit pelts grew daily. Once he learned how to use the atlatl, and his stalking skills improved, he could have accumulated more, but he had promised he would take only what he needed for survival. Recently, he had taken two per day, one in the morning and one in the evening. He ate half of one as fresh meat each day and dried one. He didn't know what the shelf life of the dried meat would be. There did not seem to be a shortage of cottontails. It almost seemed like the more he hunted of them, the more there were.

By managing the brain tanning soup, he also managed to tan the bobcat pelt and the other pelts he had taken before he had learned how to tan them.

During the hottest month of August, Cliff covered the doorway with a mat woven of cedar bark stretched over a frame that fitted the doorway more like an actual door. It was much more convenient than lifting the slate into place all the time and the mat allowed more air circulation.

~~~

Cliff began designing a coat to make from rabbit pelts. He used one of the denim shirts he had brought from the house. It was now almost too tattered to wear. However, by disassembling it, he could understand the shapes he needed for the sleeves and how they were attached.

He selected pelts for color and quality, squared and fitted them together and punched fine holes along the edges using the a long thin thorn end of a yucca leaf.

He selected a rabbit rib bone and used a sliver of flint from the pile of flint fragments on the roof to pierce the large end creating an eye to hold the tough sinew threads saved from rabbit tendons.

He had already practiced sewing together inferior pieces of pelt, making pouches that he now used when gathering seeds.

The coat turned out better than he had hoped. He had no mirror, only his reflection in the spring, to see how it looked on himself.

He added a collar, cuffs and then pockets using a strip of bobcat fur. It looked good and was very warm. He could only wear it when he first got
~~~

up in the mornings. It would be very comfortable in winter.

He had pelts left over and made moccasins to wear around the dwelling. They were soft and luxurious with the hair against his skin. They were a welcome change after the tight fitting work shoes, but they were much too soft to wear outside on the rough rocks. For that, he needed durable leather such as buckskin to protect his feet.

His work shoes were already wearing sores on his feet because they were too tight. In frustration one day, he cut the toes out of his right shoe so that his big toe would be free when he walked. That made it awkward to climb up the cliff face, so he took his shoes off and climbed barefoot. When he reached the top, he wondered why he had not done that from the beginning. He had a much better grip on the rock with his toes than with the toe of the shoe.

Cliff tried cutting a piece of fawn skin slightly larger around than his foot and attaching laces that crossed over his foot and up around his ankle and tied around above his ankle. The flesh side of the skin was against the skin of his feet. All the skin did was protect the sole of his feet from grit, pebbles, piñon and cedar needles.

His feet breathed, and after an attempt or two, the makeshift footwear stayed in place regardless of his pace. His feet toughened and when he walked around the ruin at night barefooted, after a while he didn't notice small pebbles and such bothering him when he stepped on them.

When cold weather came, perhaps he could protect his legs with leggings made from rabbit pelts, but if he had buckskin, that would be even better. He thought the perfect combination in the dead of winter would be a buckskin coat over the rabbit coat and buckskin leggings over rabbit fur leggings. His coveralls were becoming tattered and would be useless by winter.

55
The Deer Hunt
Martinez Canyon

As Cliff's skill with the atlatl grew so did his confidence. His weight and stature were still disadvantages in one sense, but what he lacked in sheer strength, he made up for in accuracy.

He became more convinced each day that he could bring down a deer if conditions were right.

He was afraid of wounding a deer that would run off, die and not be found, or worse be found by someone who would question why an animal had been wounded with a primitive spear. He also was worried about killing a deer out of season.

He knew how to harvest a deer. However, all of his kills before were with a rifle that met the minimum standards set by the State of Colorado and during the hunting season set by the State of Colorado. He had promptly tied a tag to the designated leg.

The preceding fall he had shot a large doe in the alfalfa field, which dressed out at 250 pounds. He had collected her with the tractor and trailer, brought her to the house, and hung her up with the help of a block and tackle. His mother was home and had helped him dress the deer.

At the same time, his dad was hunting with George up the Rio Lado, a tributary of the Dolores River.

If he killed a deer now, he would have to dress it out and skin it on the ground. He couldn't hang it up by himself without block and tackle. He would have to be very careful to keep from ruining the meat by getting it dirty.

He began planning seriously for a deer hunt using the atlatl.

He convinced himself that his winter survival was more or less dependent on killing at least one deer, perhaps two, not only for the food but also for the hide or hides. If he could not, then he would have to consider returning home and facing the consequences, whatever they may be.

If he did decide to return home, the longer he procrastinated the more severe the consequences were likely to be. *Also if I decide to return home, I may as well swallow my medicine in time to go to school.*

~~~

Clifton studied the deer trail he frequently used to gain access to the canyon. It regularly brought a small herd out of the canyon to feed on his dad's corn and alfalfa fields.

He followed the tracks down the trail into the canyon and located the patch of scrub oak where they sometimes bedded down during the day. From the tracks, it appeared that there were several does, yearlings and
~~~

fawns born in the spring. Earlier in the spring, the does would have left the fawns hidden in the canyon while they foraged. However, by now, the fawns accompanied their mothers when they went to the fields.

Before dusk, he hid in a piñon tree near where the trail emerged through the gap in the rimrock and watched for the herd to appear. Soon an old doe appeared leading a string of young does, yearlings and fawns up the trail out of the canyon. A couple of the yearlings had barely begun to grow spikes.

The trail led through the woods to the fence along the south side of the Kelley farm where the deer cleared the fence and proceeded into the corn where they tasted an ear here and there before continuing on to the alfalfa. During the early evening, they gorged themselves on alfalfa then bedded down under the piñons between the alfalfa and county road to chew their cud and sleep. Just before dawn, they again gorged before returning down the trail to the canyon to the protection of the oak grove to chew their cud during the heat of the day.

He stood perfectly still.

Cliff checked the deer trail every day for several days to see exactly when they returned to the canyon. The first day the doe seemed nervous and stopped to sniff the breeze before she proceeded past the gap. The second day they didn't come out of the canyon. On the third day, they were back on the old trail. They returned from the fields each day about a half hour after dawn.

It was light enough to see how to aim and cast.

He was in the tree waiting before dawn the next two days and the deer walked on by without hesitation. The next day they approached from the canyon, halted and sniffed the air. Finally, they turned and bounded back the way they had come in their stiff fourlegged lope and disappeared through the gap back into the canyon. Cliff returned to the ruin discouraged. They had discovered him. He would go back one more day to see if they would come back. The next day as he hid in the tree late in the afternoon, they emerged from the gap and walked on by without a second glance.

The following day Cliff practiced throwing from the tree at a point on the trail about fifteen paces from where he stood. The branch he stood on was about ten feet above the ground, and at a ninety-degree angle from the trail. Smaller lateral branches grew from both sides of the main branch. When he faced away from the gap in the rimrock, he could put his left foot on the lateral branch behind him for bracing. The lateral branches on each side grew about eighteen inches apart along the main branch.

Cliff cut willows long enough to span the lateral branches and created a foot wide platform on each side of the main branch. His plan was to stand against the trunk of the tree with the atlatl and spear at the ready in his right hand. He would be leaning against the tree bracing himself with his left arm when the deer came down the trail toward the gap heading toward the canyon at dawn. He would wait until they passed under him.

Usually the lead deer was the old doe followed by another doe or two and the fawns. Last were the yearlings.

He would wait until the does and fawns had passed then he would assume the throwing stance, take aim and wait for one of the yearlings to come into view 20 to 30 feet ahead. He imagined placing the dart through the lungs of one of the yearling bucks. He would aim at sending it through the side of the animal just behind the front shoulder as the animal passed by.

If he injured the animal, it would more likely continue into the canyon to die rather than run out into the farmland to die and be discovered there by a farmer.

If he had enough force to penetrate the rib cage, the dart would not have to go deep there to collapse the lung. If the dart collapsed the animal's lung, it would literally suffocate. Death would be practically instantaneous, much swifter and humane than making it bleed to death after running into the canyon. This was Ed's favorite shot when he hunted elk.

The next morning finally came. Cliff said a silent prayer to the Heavenly Father and Mother Nature asking their permission to take one of their sons. He drank a cup of cold clover tea and was in the piñon tree before daybreak awaiting the deer's arrival at the break in the rim.

He didn't have to wait long before he heard the soft sound of hooves on the trail and their snorts from exertion. He faced the gap, his back to the trail coming from the fields. He tensed, imagining the deer moving in a line led by the old doe heading for their day of rest in an oak grove in the canyon.

Cliff watched the old doe come into view below him. She seemed unaware of him. He had a six foot spear knocked in the atlatl. All he had to do was step back from the trunk onto the narrow platform, lift the spear, aim and throw all in one motion. He had to be absolutely silent as their huge mule ears could pick up any sound.

The procession moved forward under him, does, fawns and now the yearlings.

He picked the first yearling buck that came into view under him. He was nearly the same size as the does. Spikes three or four inches long were already showing on his head between his constantly moving long ears.

Cliff silently moved away from the trunk of the piñon into position. He had aimed and thrown the atlatl so many times that moves were automatic. He had good hand eye coordination. His eye aligned the spear on the target, angled the atlatl and spear up slightly for the distance it would have to travel, and adjusted for the elevation. Cliff lifted his elbow level above his shoulder and drew his wrist back behind his ear.

His eye fixed on a spot behind the right shoulder of the yearling as he stepped forward on his left foot and brought his wrist forward with his body. As his arm reached its forward extension, he snapped his wrist and released the spear.

Almost in the same instant, the herd leaped forward in a series of stiff legged jumps with all four feet hitting the ground together covering the remaining distance to the gap in the rim and disappearing instantly.

The yearling leaped with the others, but on his first descent, he crumbled to the ground. The spear had struck right behind the shoulder and plunged the dart deep, the razor sharp flint point slicing through both great lungs, causing them to collapse. The young buck tried to regain his footing, but he couldn't breathe. He staggered to his feet and fell once more, bleated once and fell to his side onto the protruding spear shaft, snapping it off.

Cliff scrambled from the tree and ran to the side of the buck, popping the snap of the hunting knife scabbard as he ran. As soon as the buck lay still he grabbed it by the neck, dragged it away from the trail onto the duff under the piñon. He cut the jugular vein and let him bleed out. As the yearling's spirit flowed onto the ground, tears flowed down Cliff cheeks, and he first raised his eyes to the red dawn of morning. "Thank you Heavenly Father," he dropped his eyes to the piñon and cedar duff where the yearling lay, "and Mother Nature, for giving me this creature for my survival. I will make full use of his flesh for the survival of my flesh and will make his covering into my covering. Without it, I couldn't survive the winter to come. Thank you for continuing to guide me and providing for me."

When the blood flow ceased, Cliff immediately prepared to dress the buck by undressing himself and hanging his clothes on a branch to keep them clean. He could wash his skin later. It would be hard to wash blood off his tattered clothing.

He propped the buck on its back and opened the abdominal cavity, careful not to puncture the intestines. He turned the deer on its side, cleared the heart, lungs and liver free of the intestines and put them back inside the abdominal cavity to take home.

He carefully trimmed all tallow away from the stomach and organs. The tallow was an important part of the harvest that day.

He carried the mass of intestines, lungs and organs to the rim of the canyon. There he systematically emptied the intestines of their digested food and set the empty membranes aside. He slit the stomachs, dumped the chewed and un-chewed cud and kept the stomach lining. Miscellaneous organs and glands and the musk gland he dropped over the canyon edge for the magpies, crows and others to scavenge. He hoped it would help keep them away from the site for a while, as he processed the carcass.

He returned to the yearling carcass with the intestine and stomach lining and folded them into the cavity with the heart, liver and scraps of tallow.

Although it had cooled down overnight, it would get hot that day up on top. He had to get the meat to the cave so it could cool as soon as possible, or it would spoil.

He had to skin and quarter the buck immediately to transport the meat to the cave.

He moved the now much lighter yearling to beneath a tree with a sturdy horizontal branch high enough above the ground that quarters of meat hung from it would be temporarily safe from scavengers. He would have to make several trips to the cave to carry it all there. While he transported each quarter, the remaining would be vulnerable from ground and air until the last piece was in the cave.

Cliff had been so positive that he would be successful in the hunt when he set out that morning that he had brought his knives, rope and gunnysacks to process the kill.

Removing the hide from the yearling while it was on the ground was more difficult than if it were hanging. The hide was very important. He needed it as much as the meat. He skinned the head to beneath the chin and up around the base of the ears.

It took longer to skin the deer on the ground, but he took his time.

The only puncture in the hide was the small half-inch hole behind the right shoulder left by the dart.

The hide shielded the meat from the timber floor and kept it clean as he worked. As soon as he cut the hide loose of the carcass, he began quartering it.

Quartering the carcass was the hardest task. The only way he could carry it back to the dwelling was to quarter it. The meat would not cool down in the heat of the day out on top. Although it was still early in the day and a slight breeze was still cool, the days were hot at midday. Temperatures could soar to over a hundred degrees by mid afternoon. However, it was cool in the cave even in the hot afternoon, and the meat would cool down while he processed it.

Cliff tied a length of yucca cord around the hoof of a hindquarter, tossed the other end over the branch and pulled it tight against the trunk of the tree. He turned the deer up onto its back with the foot into the air, pulled the slack out of the cord and re-tied it at the tree trunk. When he had the quarter cut clear of hide and the rest of the carcass, it would swing clear of the ground.

He worked the hindquarters free with the knife by cutting to the ball and socket that joined the hindquarter to the hip. When the quarter swung free from the limb, he wrapped it in a burlap sack. Then he lifted the haunch and tightened the cord until it was up high up against the branch, took out the slack and re-tied the cord at the tree trunk. The quarter was as secure as he could make it from ants, magpies, crows or even possibly coyotes or whatever else might come by, until he could carry it down to the cave.

He repeated the process for the other haunch and the two front shoulders.

Last, he removed the back strap and tenderloins and separated the rib cage halves from the neck. The neck and head he left in one piece, and hung them from the branch along with the ribs. These he hung without wrapping them because he had only enough sacks for the front and hindquarters.

It took the rest of the morning to carry the meat to the cave and hang it. The best meat went first.

He took the quarter sections out of the burlap sacks and hung them to cool from the roof poles in the coolest part of the cave. The yucca fiber rope proved to be strong enough to hold the weight. He left three of the quarters inside burlap sacks. The meat could breath and cool and yet be protected from flies. He used one sack to transport the neck and head and the two rib sections. Those he had to hang without the protection of the burlap. When he had the head and rib sections transported, he put the shoulder quarter back into the sack.

As he made the last trip with the hide and prepared to lower it over the side of the rim, the sun suddenly dimmed and a chill wind began to blow. He looked up from tying the rope around the bundle.

Huge angry looking thunderheads boiled and spilled over Mesa Verde and moved northward over Summit Ridge. Lightning flashes streaked down from the black underbelly of the clouds. The sky to the west as far as he could see was very dark also. While transporting the meat to the cave, he had been oblivious to the changes occurring in the sky.

He hurriedly finished tying the rope around the hide and lowered it over the side. He untied the rope and tossed it down after the hide, and scrambled down over the rimrock and moved the hide inside. He started to fasten the mat door in place and on second thought lifted the slate into place against the dowels. The mat served well on summer nights, but it was not strong enough to withstand strong gusts of wind.

He had barely finished inserting the last dowel before the wind hit, followed by lashing rain blowing in at an angle that drenched the face of the dwelling and the slate door covering in spite of the cliff overhang.

"And it's not even Fourth of July, Moonbeam," he said to his black and white four legged companion. "That's when it usually wants to rain. That's when we could turn the water in the pond and go fishing." The young skunk had retreated to the back of the cave at the first sound of thunder, and curled up with her tail over her face and ears to resume her nap.

Maggie sat wide-eyed and indignant in his cage. For the first time since he had reached flying age the cage door was closed. "Hey Maggie," Cliff said. "Are you hungry? Clifton's got treats." He opened the door and put small slivers of liver into the cage for the magpie.

The bird waited to be sure it wasn't an idle promise, and the door would remain open, before he responded. "Clifton got treats?"

The temperature dropped rapidly as the cloud burst dumped torrents of ice cold rain onto the high plateau and into the canyon. The wind howled around the rimrock and through the canyon. It shook the trees, and rain splashed through the gap over the slate door covering.

Inside the dwelling, Cliff stirred the coals on the fire. He filled the coffee can with water to heat to brew hot tea. That evening he would fry up a thick slice of liver on the lid of the Dutch oven. He had the combination of fat and meat together at last.

He put fresh water in the Dutch oven to heat so that he could take a bath and wash off the blood. The yearling's blood stained his hands and arms and smeared his belly and legs. His clothes still hung clean in the tree where he had processed the deer. There would soon be no sign that anything had happened under the tree or on the trail. The rain would soak the blood into the duff. Birds, animals, maggots and insects would scavenge the viscera scattered on the canyon slope in a day or two. Mother Nature's creatures all participated in the cycle.

When the wind died down and the rain settled to a steady downpour, Cliff opened the doorway letting in the fresh sweet smell of the rain. The temperature dropped inside the cave with the door open. Cliff felt fresh with clean hair and body after a bath.

Still naked he climbed out over the face of the cliff with the rain beating down on his back. He felt primitive and free as he gripped the cuts in the stone face with fingers and toes. He felt exhilarated by the knowledge that he had brought down a deer with one of the most primitive of hunting weapons. He stood on the rim of the canyon and looked out across the flat timberland to the Mesa Verde escarpment. Through the sheets of rain, it was only a ghostly outline in the distance. Occasionally rolling thunder broke the sound of the rain. He looked up the canyon and saw the water rising in the creek. It was already over the banks and was the color of the rimrock.

He turned and dashed up the canyon to retrieve his clothes from the tree where they hung.

Cliff felt chilled when he reached the dwelling with his clothes. The rain had slackened but continued. The rainwater was cold and the temperature dropped, he put on the rabbit fur coat and enjoyed its warmth.

He washed the heart and liver. During a lull in the rain, he raced outside and cut fresh grass. He packed the heart and liver in the damp grass, packed them in the gunnybag, and hung them from the ceiling in the back of the cave.

I can already smell that liver frying. Too bad I don't have any onions. I wonder about those little wild onions? It would have been awful good with beans, seasoned with cedar berries and sage leaves. Oh, well, it won't be long now until new beans are ready.

He inspected the hanging meat. The air temperature in the cave dropped with the icy rain that lashed the canyon. The meat would cool well in the draft of cold air coming through the fresh air ventilation shaft and door and exiting through the roof vents. In the corner rested the folded hide that he wanted to turn into buckskin moccasins and leggings.

~~~

It was dark in the cave because of the heavy clouds when Cliff sat down with a thin cake of seed mixture and a thick slice of fried venison
~~~

liver and cup of refreshing clover blossom tea. It had been a long and tiring, but successful and satisfying day.

A little later Cliff kneeled near the *Sipapu*. Maggie, now full of scraps and liberated from the cage, hopped to Cliff's knee and then up to his shoulder. He leaned forward and twisted his neck to look up into the boy's face inquisitively.

"Hi friend," Cliff said.

"Hi friend," Maggie said.

Cliff reached into his tattered shirt pocket and took out a corner of the bread scrap he had saved for his feathered friend. "Your friend got a treat," he said as he gave the morsel to Maggie.

Maggie took it and swallowed it in one bite.

"Friend got treats," he said.

Moonbeam waddled over and joined her two friends. She fawned against Cliff's leg then walked around to the other side and climbed into his lap and curled up to be petted.

Heavenly Father and Mother Nature thank you, especially for these two little friends, Cliff thought.

Cliff finally spread his sleeping mat and curled up on it. He was joined by Moonbeam, who offered her neck to be scratched then curled up on her back against her human friend's face with her bushy tail curled forward between her legs and belly. Maggie flew back to his cage. Cliff put his arm around his little skunk friend and looked up at Maggie in his cage. About all he could see in the flickering firelight was the white belly of the bird. But he saw enough to tell the well fed magpie was already sound asleep with one leg lifted up under his wing, his beady black eyes closed. Within minutes, Cliff's eyes closed.

The rain stopped, the clouds drifted on north, and the stars came out. A frog began croaking somewhere down near the creek, soon joined by others. If one listened closely, the chorus sounded like voices chanting an ancient prayer of thanks for the summer rain. Cliff dropped into a deep contented sleep.

~~~

The dream began. *Cliff sat cross-legged on the ledge outside the dwelling. The air was fresh from the afternoon thunderstorm. The last rays of the setting sun lingered over Ute Mountain.*

Cliff wore the rabbit fur coat trimmed with bobcat collar, cuffs and pockets, fawn skin breechcloth, buckskin leggings and moccasins to ward off the cold. The straw-hat he had worn in his first dream now sported a turkey feather in the leather band. He looked down into the canyon. Where he had seen wild turkeys sailing back and forth, and deer grazing contentedly along the willow-lined creek in the first dream, he now saw deep snowdrifts.

Maggie sat on one knee and Moonbeam sat on the other. All three listened intently to their friend the hunter.

The hunter's lithe, diminutive body was now dressed in cotton clothing. The
~~~

finely woven fabrics had intricate designs woven in. On his feet were light moccasins built for travel. He was no taller than Cliff and other than pouches that hung from a strap at his waist; he carried only bow and arrows in a quiver that hung low on his back.

A slight breeze rippled through the man's long, raven black shoulder length hair.

He spoke in an ancient language to Cliff through Maggie and Moonbeam. That his two animal friends could speak and translate for him seemed perfectly normal.

"We have been watching you. You have done well. You have used the time wisely in the Great Spirit's Wilderness," Maggie translated.

"Can you tell me what the Great Spirit is?" Cliff asked.

"What do you think it is?" the hunter asked.

"My dad thinks it is God, Jesus and the Holy Ghost. Is that correct?"

"Yes," Maggie translated.

"George said it is Mother Nature, is that correct?"

"Yes," Maggie translated.

"How can it be both?" Cliff asked.

"For your dad, it is what he needs," the hunter said. "For your friend, it is what he needs. What do you need?"

"I need to know, which is true."

"You are searching, my friend. When you came here, you were a broken spirit. You were wondering and in danger of being lost. You have learned. You still have much to learn and decide for yourself what works for you. Your dad bases his belief on a new system. Your friend bases his ideas and thoughts on an ancient system. They both learned in their own ways. You are forming your thoughts in your way. In your body courses the blood of ancestors who held both the new and the ancient beliefs. While you are here, listen and learn.

"You are not ready to go home yet. You still have more 'time to spend in God's and the Great Spirit's wilderness, continue to use the time wisely. Listen to your two little friends, they are wise," the hunter concluded with a smile and fed morsels of food to each from his pouch.

As in the first dream, the mysterious hunter stood, reached into a leather pouch, and extending his right arm, he pointed to the north. He began chanting and released a few grains of yellow, swept his arm to the east, released a few more grains of pollen, paused and then swept to the south, repeated the ritual and turned to the west to complete the circle. He lifted his arms to the sky, and then lowered them to the earth. He continued to chant as he went through the ritual.

He clapped his hands together, and then he spread both arms wide and turned his back to face the canyon. He began a new chant and turned to the east and panned to the west to encompass all that surrounded them, the silhouette of the La Plata Mountains, the mesa, and the sleeping giant Ute mountain. The sun had set and they were in the time between dusk and night.

The hunter too stood in silhouette with the last rays of light in the background as he slowly stepped, dipped, turned, stepped, dipped and turned the other way as he chanted there on the ledge in front of the dwelling. Cliff was aware of a low, throbbing, drumming sound and a chorus of voices coming up from the darkness of the canyon. He was once again mesmerized as the hunter stepped, dipped his shoulder, turned, stepped, dipped his other shoulder and turned the other way as he chanted. Cliff floated to his feet and began moving with the hunter, stepping, dipping, and turning.

This time Cliff didn't need to understand the words of the chant. Cliff opened his mouth and began to chant in perfect imitation of the chorus of frogs down by the creek who sang in time with the ancient drumbeat.

56
Making Jerky
Martinez Canyon

The air was fresh and cold the next morning. The sound of rushing water rose from the canyon floor as excess water drained away from the cloudburst of the day before.

High cotton clouds floated lazily across the deep blue sky. They could be harmless or they could quickly build into towering thunderstorm clouds in the afternoon. It was a typical pattern about that time every summer in August. It could get hot outside very quickly that morning.

Cliff had been up at dawn cutting long thin quarter inch thick strips of venison, first from the neck and ribs. He cut off all the meat from the neck and head and left the skull hanging. He would remove the brain when it was time to tan the hide.

He filled the Dutch oven first, and then he filled baskets with strips of meat. When the sun reached the ledge, he began hanging the strips of venison on drying racks. When he ran out of racks, he built more.

The hot beating sun reflected heat off the face of the cliff. A slight breeze sucked the moisture from the meat and by late afternoon, the first batches of jerky cracked when he bent them. He gathered the strips into clay lined baskets, tied gut membrane over the mouths, covered them with woven lids and hung them inside the cave. As thunderclouds began to gather late in the afternoon, he stacked the racks inside the cave to wait for the morning when he again reloaded them with fresh strips of venison to dry.

Drying the meat was only the first process. He knew that he couldn't live only on dried meat. However, he could preserve it that way temporarily until he could further process it.

His mother always used either lard or tallow when she cooked. He had questioned that once, and she explained that fat was a necessary part of diet. When she cooked beans, she put a spoonful of lard into the pot. Or, she put a square of bacon fat into it to cook down as the beans simmered.

He had not processed any of his stores of dried rabbit into pemmican yet because he had no source of fat. The meager amount of tallow from the road kill fawn had been barely enough to cook with. He hoped that just as the yearling had the right amount of brain to tan its hide, it would have enough tallow to process a major amount of the meat. The yearling had dined all summer on deep grass and other excellent forage, was well filled out, and fat. There should be plenty, if he worked out the proper proportions.

Cliff had saved the beeswax from the bee tree. He planned to try making pemmican as a final step in preserving the meat, and using the wax to seal it. According to the recipe, it would last for years if sealed properly. He had a half page cutting in the journal. The very nonspecific recipe simply said powder meat, (venison, beef, buffalo, bear) mix with suet, (tallow) nuts, berries, wrap in cheesecloth, dip in suet or wax. Eat raw or cook in a stew with corn meal or vegetables. Carry as travel food or use as preservative for winter stores. Note: Very nutritious, if used with cornmeal, and vegetables, provides complete diet.

If the beeswax worked, he would convert as much of the dried meat to pemmican as he had the tallow to go with it.

It had remained cool in the cave that day and the hindquarters and shoulders continued to cure.

That night Cliff dined on stew with chunks of heart.

~~~

He finished supper and sat back with a cup of tea. It had been a very long day, and he was satisfyingly tired. He would sleep well that night. Moonbeam curled at his elbow, and he affectionately cupped the animal's head and caressed the glossy hair. He ran his fingers through the long bushy tail hair and collected loose hair that shed. He had begun collecting all the hair the skunk shed and wound it into a ball. Perhaps he could weave it into something later. "I always wanted a cat, Moonbeam. . I thought if I live trapped a cat at Harris's barnyard and brought it home, Mom and Dad would fall in love with it and I could keep it. I got it home OK. When I turned it loose it ran under the barn, and I only saw it occasionally. The closest I ever got to it was when it started coming out when I milked the cows. At first, I put a cup down for it. After a long time, it got so that I could squirt a stream of milk out at it, and it would lap the milk right straight from the cow. In some ways, you are kind of like the cat I never got to have in the house, Moonbeam."

A few feet away, in the firelight, Maggie pecked and pulled on a piece of venison scrap. Each time Clifton spoke, he looked up and cocked his head. His vocabulary increased daily. He now included "Hello Maggie," "Hello Clifton," "Hello Moonbeam," "Pretty Boy," "Pretty Girl," to the original "Clifton got treats?" It wasn't enough to carry on an intelligent conversation, but it was a human sounding voice.

Cliff's looked at the Sipapu, as he seemed to do more and more lately. It was the gateway to the underworld in Indian lore, the portal, the pas-
~~~

sage used by the first people to come to the surface of the earth, the spirit gate, the place one returned to when they died. It represented the connection from the surface to the inner world. Is it the equivalent of the Pearly Gates? Or, can their spirits go back and forth through this symbolic portal? Wouldn't that be neat? Go to the other side and visit with Grandma or Grandpa and find out what should be done. Or, maybe talk to St. Peter himself and then come back here and do something about it. A two way Pearly Gates. I like this idea. Probably, that's the reason I've never heard of it before.

His family was only a little over a mile away, probably sitting down to supper. His dad was probably asking God in Jesus' name for forgiveness for whatever shortcomings he had, whether he was aware of them or not. He might even be asking for forgiveness for Cliff's shortcomings.

Cliff looked hard at the *Sipapu*. It was about three inches in diameter and almost perfectly round. Someone had drilled it into the hard clay floor covering down to the stone cave floor. On Mesa Verde the *Sipapu* was located in the ceremonial *kivas.* This dwelling must have supported only one family, and there was no room for multiple rooms and a *kiva.*

Cliff thought about last night's dream. He had almost forgotten the first dream. It had haunted him for weeks and then slowly faded. So much of this dream had been similar, and yet it was much more. *The hunter seemed to be telling me there is something watching me that all of this isn't just an accident, and he spoke through Maggie. According to George and the Rangers, the Indians held crows to be spiritual beings. Maggie is a member of the crow family.*

Am I thinking about all this because from the time I could listen to a story my mom read me Bible stories, and I saw my dad reading his Bible? All my life I've been surrounded by religion. George talks to me about Mother Nature almost as though She is a religious figure. I wonder what I would be thinking right now and wondering about, if I had never heard those stories Bible stories or heard George talking. Would I have had the same dream?

Those he now communed with were two children of nature. Both were intelligent, bright-eyed creatures. Each had powers he did not have. One could fly; one could defend herself with a powerful acid/scent. Without their companionship, he thought he would lose his mind with loneliness.

He pondered his place in his universe during the many nights as he sat considering his circumstances.

He felt thankful, but who to thank? He couldn't thank himself. He had merely reached out and taken what had been provided.

Were Mother Nature and God the same thing? Why would a prayer offered while staring at the floor of a church save him, but not one offered to a hole in the floor of a cave? Surely, one place was as good as another. His dad had often said, "Speak to your God in private, not on the street corner."

When his dad prayed at each meal, he began his prayer with, "Heavenly Father."

He had begun thanking both God and Mother Nature early in his experience living surrounded by nature.

In the dream, the hunter had said his dad was right and George was right. He had said Cliff wasn't ready to go home, 'You are forming your thoughts on little information. You are not ready to go home yet. You still have more time to spend in God's and the Great Spirit's wilderness. Continue to use the time wisely.'

The hunter referred to aboriginal blood coursing through my body. Was he referring to my mother's Comanche and my father's Choctaw great-grandmothers? Could that possibly be affecting my dreams and thoughts?

57

Buckskin and Moccasins
Martinez Canyon

Killing the deer provided many additional items to Clifton's inventory of resources. He had a full larder of jerky. He saved some of the bones to turn into tools. The tallow was vital for cooking and his plan to convert the jerky to pemmican.

As he had cut the deer into quarters to transport it to the cave, he had removed the bundles of tendons in the back of the legs, along the spine and neck. He kept the bundles of fibers as long as possible. When they were dry, he pounded and separated the bundles of tissue into individual strands of sinew that he wound into a ball. He used the coarse natural threads to sew together anything he made with leather. He fletched spears with it and bound together anything that didn't require rope.

Among the pages in the scrapbook was a page from a coloring book, a color—fold up plan for "Apache" moccasins. He had made a pair from rabbit pelts. The soft fur next to his feet was luxurious, and he wore them while in the dwelling. Using the same pattern, he cut a pair from the neck of the deer hide. They weren't really all that much more comfortable than his simple sole protectors, but they would be warmer come winter.

At first, they were uncomfortable because the sole was flat and offered no arch support, but they protected his feet from stones, piñon needles and cactus spines. He made a second pair large enough to wear over his rabbit pelt moccasins for cold weather.

Cliff continued to reduce yucca leaves to fiber, tediously twisted the fiber strands into cordage of a few strands and wound it into balls. He built a simple weaving frame from willows and on it wove a course, primitive cloth from the yucca cordage and from that made a shirt. It was a far cry from the denim work shirt he had worn from the house.

He wove two pieces of cloth just wider than his shoulders and as long as his shoulders to mid way between his waist and his knees. He sewed the two pieces together at the top across the shoulders, leaving space for his head to pass through.

Rather than sew the sides together, he sewed on bands at the bottom on each side and about three inches apart up each side. When he put the shirt on, he could tie it loosely around his torso for ventilation. If it was cold out he could tie the bands tightly, overlapping the cloth on both sides, and it was quite warm.

He had walked away from the house with two denim shirts, one on his back and a spare in the gunnysack. He had taken one apart to use as a pattern for the rabbit pelt coat. The remaining denim shirt was tattered from climbing through the rocks and brush and now hung useless from a peg on the wall.

He wore the new yucca shirt around the ruin when it was cool in the evening. During the day, he usually went without a shirt.

In his spare moments, he began twisting fiber into cordage and winding it into yarn for further weaving. It had taken many evenings by the firelight for Cliff to wind enough cordage to weave enough cloth for one shirt.

Weaving he could do during the long days when he would be shut into the cave during the winter. Gathering leaves and reducing them into raw fiber would become almost impossible come cold weather.

With that done, he turned his thoughts to leg protection.

In spring and fall, Ed rented the pasture, the timber triangle corner of the farm cut off by the county road on the northwest corner, to a rancher from McElmo for an overnight stop. Every summer the rancher took his herd of a couple of hundred Hereford cattle to summer range in the LaPlata Mountains. The cows tanked up on water and alfalfa hay from Ed's haystack. The cowboys set up their bedrolls in the edge of the timber with the cattle, built a campfire and cooked their supper and breakfast there.

Cliff had looked forward to the cattle drive each year. He visited with the cowboys, and they told him stories around the campfire. Usually one of the cowboys was a Navajo and the other was a brother of the rancher.

Cliff was interested in the 30-30 Winchester saddle rifles they had holstered on their saddles, their jangling spurs and chaps.

Most of the drive from McElmo up to the Ridge was on and next to the road in the right of way. The only time they encountered fences was when farms abutted the road. The chaps protected the men's legs from the sagebrush they rode through to keep their charges moving.

They covered the men's jeans from the crotch to the ankles on the inside of the leg and on the outside, they reached to the belt which held them up. The men wore them over their form fitting Levi's jeans.

Cliff measured his legs and transferred the measurements to the hide using charcoal. To his disappointment, the hide would only make a chap for one leg. A chap did not completely enclose the leg, but was held over the leg by several short leather straps that ran under the leg and buckled to the opposite side, enclosing about three fourths of the leg. Cliff's chaps would completely enclose his legs.

He wanted them to taper from his crotch to his ankles on the inside and from his ankles to his waist on the outside of his legs. A narrow buckskin belt tied around his waist and through a loop on the outside of each legging would hold them in place.

He had never worn a belt before.

The buckskin did not lie flat, but humped the middle where it had draped over the deer's spine. Cliff left the charcoal drawing for a chap for his left leg on the hide adjusting it so that the front of his leg conformed to the deer's spine area on the hide.

He used leather outside that drawn area for the moccasins and a belt.

Cliff had an immediate concern than leg covering. The two pair of underwear he had taken from the house, the pair he wore and a spare pair, were now in sad shape. He had grown. They were too tight and the daily washing was far more frequent than the manufacturer had intended. Recently, he had worn no underwear at all when he went out. He had not become accustomed to that. It worked as long as he could wear the overalls, but now it was time to retire the overalls.

From the fawn hide, he cut a breechcloth about a foot wide and as long as the hide to loop over the belt in back go down between his legs and loop back over the belt in front and hang down in front to protect his modesty. As he made the simple garment, he wondered why bother. He hadn't seen anyone. He assumed no one had seen him. That was the idea of the garment, wasn't it? Of course, winter was coming, and he would need it for protection then.

He laid aside the outgrown underwear and worn out overalls for good.

It felt strange to Cliff the first morning that he stood in breechcloth held up by a buckskin belt. On his feet were the moccasins. On his back, he carried the burlap knapsack. Spears and spear thrower protruded from it up past the back of his head.

On his head, he still wore the sweat stained straw hat, which was becoming too small. His hair now brushed his shoulders. When he didn't need the hat, he tied his hair down with a headband to keep it out of his face.

When it got cold, he would need a cap and ear protection.

It was warm enough that he didn't need his legs covered. At first, he missed having protection against the brush and rocks, but after a while, the sun toughened his skin, and he didn't scratch as easily.

At first, he missed the spacious overall pockets. To replace them, he hung a variety of rabbit skin pouches from the belt in which to put various seeds that he collected. He also hung the hunting knife scabbard and fire making tool pouch on the belt. He made several pouches from the scraps left over from the fawn hide. These he carried from long thin straps around his neck. From the thicker yearling leather, he made a scabbard for the homemade digging knife.

Cliff had no mirror. He caught only glimpses of himself in the creek and in the spring.

In his current outfit, with a magpie perched on his shoulder and a full-grown skunk at his heel, he would present an odd sight to anyone he might meet on the trail.

Another imperceptible change had come over him. When he had entered the cave he had walked and sat slump shouldered with eyes downcast. Although he spoke with excitement at new discoveries, his usual manner was very quiet. He was timid around nearly everyone except his neighbor George and his teacher Mrs. Campbell.

As he walked the trail on that summer day, anyone meeting him would have seen a young man with his head held high, walking confidently and swiftly along with a smile on his face. His bright eyes were full of humor, as if he had gained a secret knowledge.

58
Angelina Martinez
Late summer 1953

Cliff stayed close to home most days, but through the summer, he roamed the area from the snag east to the old watchtower ruin at the point across from the draw at the corner of George's farm. From there he walked to highway 160 and sat out of sight watching trucks power by heading to Durango and points south to Farmington, Albuquerque, Amarillo, Oklahoma City, or from Durango on east to Pagosa Springs, Wolf Creek Pass and to Denver. Other trucks coming from the east roared on toward Cortez where they either headed south to points in Arizona or New Mexico or north into Utah.

He wondered what his life would be like if he could catch a ride on one of the big 18 wheelers and ride off into a new world. Then he took stock of his clothing and knew that if he walked out of the woods, up to the highway and held up his thumb, it wouldn't get him a ride. He might get a few stares or laughs.

One afternoon he nervously followed the woods almost to the Martinez farmhouse in hopes of catching a glimpse of Angelina.

He did not see her, but he did find the family trash dump where he found two cardboard boxes full of discarded quart mayonnaise jars and pint jars with the label printed in Spanish. They were not reusable as canning jars. *So I wonder if Dulcina Martinez cans vegetables from her garden like Mom does.* The jars were clean and the original one-piece lids were in place.

The Martinez farm was one of the larger farms on in the area and under irrigation. It had been in the Martinez family for several generations, and was one of the original homesteads on the Ridge. Most of the Mexican families of the kids that Cliff attended school with lived on small places with gardens. They made their livings working for others. The Martinez family was the exception. Cliff's mother referred to them as Spanish rather than Mexican. Cliff didn't know the difference. In his mind the two words, Mexican and Spanish were interchangeable. *I wonder what kind of house Angelina lives in?* He was afraid to get close enough to see the house. *I wonder if they have dogs. I'll bet they have dogs. I didn't ask her about that.*

On the discovery trip, he carried as many jars home as he could in his burlap knapsack and underarm gunnybag. All the way home he told himself that he would be satisfied with the one trip, and that he couldn't be greedy. However, by the time he got home, he knew that he had to go back for more.

He was a little disappointed that he hadn't caught a glimpse of her. She was his age. She would have graduated from Mesa Verde Grade School near Hallersville, at the entrance to Mesa Verde probably the same day he would have graduated if had stuck around East Lakeview another week.

He thought she was pretty. The last time he had seen her was nearly a year ago. *She must be even prettier now.*

What would I have done if I'd seen her? I couldn't have called out to her. Surely, she knows that I've gone AWOL. Would she turn me in? Would she keep my secret? It is too much to even imagine. If the tables were turned, and I discovered she was hiding out, I know I'd let it slip. This last trip has to be my last trip, period. If I hang around here trying to catch a glimpse of Angelina, I'll be caught. She probably would not like that, and Enrique would probably shoot me.

~~~

He had become aware of Angelina at the annual County Extension Service fish fry at Summit Lake the previous summer. He had actually known who she was, but thought she was just one of the other Mexican kids on the Ridge and hadn't given her much attention. After all, Mexican kids in general didn't seem to want to have anything to do with him.

That had changed, when at his parent's urging, he had entered the organized games. As it turned out, he and Angelina were the only kids in the thirteen-year-old bracket.

"Do you want to be my partner," She looked at his tag, "Clifton K.? My name is Angie Martinez." Angelina had asked as teams organized for the sack race. All participants wore a tag with a large number, letter and first name. The number designated age, the letter was the first letter of the last name and helped match the participant's and full name on a ledger.

The tags helped to organize the activities quickly and fairly, at least by age.

Cliff had looked at her tag, "Sure Angie Martinez. Cliff Kelley. It looks like we are the only 13's here." They had just finished a short dash, which she had won. He had out run her in the longer race just before that, but just by seconds. "You're really fast."

"I had older sisters. I had to learn to run at an early age to keep up,"
~~~

she laughed. "Or keep away from them!"

"So how does this race work?" He asked.

Just about that time the college intern in command of the youth activities called their attention and began handing out oversized gunnysacks.

"So, we both get in there and run?" Cliff asked.

"I don't think that's how it works," she said. If it is we are going to be a little crowded in there. You ever been in a sack race before?"

"No. And if I had, I probably wouldn't have been in there with a girl," he said blushing.

"What's the matter? You think I'm going to bite?" She teased.

"No. I just, well, you know…" he stammered.

"Hey, it's OK. Truth is I've never been in a sack race with a boy either. All the sack races I've ever seen were with one person, one sack. I've never seen a team sack race before. So, we just have a few minutes to learn how to run in this. Got any ideas?"

"OK, listen up everybody, the organizer called. This is how this is done. In the team sack race, you each put a leg in the sack. I assume you all know enough to be facing the same direction," he laughed and looked at them, as though they were city kids or something.

The assortment of farm kids laughed and waited. The organizer called his assistant forward. They each stepped into the sack, one with the left foot and one right, cinched the sack up and both stepped forward. "See how easy that is?"

"Well, I think we can walk that way, without getting tangled up," Cliff said.

"Let's try it," she said.

She put her left leg into the sack, he put in his right leg, and they pulled the sack up in front of them.

The first attempt landed them in a pile on the ground. She had fallen on top of him. His first impulse had been to push her off, but he had not. She had untangled herself from him and the sack and helped him up.

"I think I've got an idea," she said. "Let's try it again."

"Everyone on the line!" The intern called. "We've got to walk together, lifting our feet with the sack and letting our feet push it forward," she said and they practiced that as they moved into position in line.

"I think it will work," Cliff said. "Let's start off slowly, and when we hit our stride speed up. I think if we don't fall, we'll be OK We might even win this thing."

"On your mark! Get set! Go!"

Angelina and Cliff nearly toppled on the first sack step forward, but they corrected.

"Grab the loose sack corner in your left hand and bring it over to your right hand," she said. She grabbed the surplus sack on her side in her right hand, pulled it forward and over to her left hand. With the sack tightened around their two legs rather than flapping between their legs, they began synchronizing their steps more accurately and progressed slowly toward the finish line. "You had a good idea, Angie," he said.

She looked at him and nodded. They were synchronized. They picked up the pace, began running, gaining speed and crossed the line with space to spare ahead of the next competitors a mixed 15 and a 16-year-old couple. Several of the teams still struggled to hit a stride back near the starting line.

"We won!" Cliff had exclaimed as they jumped around and shucked out of the sack to accept their blue ribbons.

"The three legged race is next. Think we can do it again?" Angelina asked excitedly. "It's pretty much the same idea."

"Why not!"

This race was similar, only in place of a sack, which allowed each individual to move his or her legs within the sack; their legs bound loosely at the ankle.

Angelina watched a couple of girls struggling to walk. Although bound at the ankle, they tried to walk independently of each other. "You are going to have to put your arm around my waist," she said as she grabbed his hand and placed his arm around her lower back. She put her arm tightly around his waist. "OK Now hold tight enough that we are like one person walking," she said.

"Ready?" Cliff asked. "You're right. This is the way a three-legged person would walk, although, personally, I've never seen a three legged person before," he laughed. "Can we run this way?"

"You bet we can. We won the races when we were running independently. Now if we can keep in sync, nobody's going to touch us!"

They had lifted their bound legs together and stepped forward then stepped forward with their free legs.

"You know, Angie if we get out of sync while we are running, we are going to go down hard," Cliff said. *I wouldn't have minded losing the race that way at all,* he remembered thinking.

"I'm left handed. That's why I got on this side when they bound us. I noticed you step out with your right foot all the time. I think you're right handed. Right?"

He nodded in the affirmative.

"I think that this is going to work just fine for us."

But they had not fallen in a tangle of arms and legs.

They had walked away with another blue ribbon each.

Until that time, he had given little thought to girls. He had actually given up on making friends with almost anyone his own age. The Mexican girls at East Lakeview Grade School drew Hector's scorn if they dared to be more than cordial to Cliff. In earlier grades before Hector had become the head honcho around school, there had been older kids who had done the same. There had been a subtle shunning. In the first few grades, he had been eager to learn Spanish and had asked the other kids for the Spanish words for objects. When he did that, before the kid could answer he would hear the phrase, *"No le diga!"* whispered or *"Callate la boca."* If the other little kids had been ready to or perhaps even eager to share with the Anglo kid, he or she would suddenly find something to do or someone else to do something with.

There were few youths in the church in town or the families they met with. Even if there were, transportation was not available to put them together. The church did not provide or encourage youth parties, dances, or socials.

Angelina, Angie, was different. She was not shy about talking to him. She made him want to talk to her. He had found himself laughing and talking easily.

They went to the picnic table where her parents had set up and Angelina gave her ribbons to her mother Dulcina. She had introduced Cliff to her mother.

"May we go get in line to eat now Mama," she asked. Her mother had given her permission with a wave of the hand and a smile.

"Come on Cliff Kelley," she said. "Let's go get some fish."

Over deep fried trout, they had talked freely about East Lakeview and Mesa Verde Grade Schools and books they had read. He was amazed and delighted that she had read at least as many books as he had. Her favorite poem was "The Raven," by Edgar Allen Poe. Her favorite author was Mark Twain.

She wanted to become a veterinarian.

She had a pony. She could imitate most of the birds on Summit Ridge. She played the guitar. "I am learning to play the flamenco style from my Papa. He and Mama like to dance that. Sometime you have to come to my house and see them dance. I will play the guitar for you."

"I'd like that. My dad has an old guitar, but he doesn't play it much. He promised to teach me, but he puts it off."

She didn't think it was ridiculous that he caught skunks, had hives of bees and hunted for bee trees. She was interested in looking for bee trees with him next summer.

He had asked her if she would go to MCHS when she graduated from Mesa Verde Grade School. She had hesitated and said she might go to Mancos High School, but she had not really wanted to talk about it that much.

Although she had dressed like the other Mexican kids on the Ridge that he had known all his life, and she spoke with the same accent, the resemblance seemed to stop there. Her eyes were blue green; her hair was a medium blonde. Her skin was fair.

Most of all they were in sync.

This is the way it should be, he had thought at the time.

On the way home from the lake, Cliff had asked his mother why she thought Angelina might choose to go to Mancos High School instead of MCHS. Her parents would have to take her to the bus at Hallersville. If she went to MCHS, they could turn around and go home each day. If she went to Mancos High, they would have to drive an extra five miles each way. It would be another two years before she could drive herself.

His mother had told him a strange thing.

She had said, "I think most of the kids at Mesa Verde Grade School are Anglo. Do you think that she might be having some of the same problems there that you are having up at East Lakeview?"

"But she's pretty, Mom. She's doesn't even really look Mexican."

"Dulcina and I had a good visit up at the lake too. She's almost as worried about her daughter, as I worry about you. Angelina carries traits of Dulcina's ancestors' back in Spain. Enrique too carries enough traits of their mother country that they have produced daughters who like Angelina are beautiful girls who have blue eyes and blond hair. Unfortunately, here in the backwoods we don't have as many families who don't have the mixed Indian blood. Neither one of these groups seem to know enough about the world to know that many women in Spain and Mexico look like Angelina and her sisters.

Anglo kids are not treating her as one of them, and the Mexican kids don't treat her as one of them. It is a loss to both bunches of kids because she is a graceful, talented young lady," Etta Mae had said. I'm guessing she might want to go to Mancos to get away from some of the kids she has been going to school with.

She had looked at Clifton with a smile on her face. "Why all this interest in Dulcina's daughter, Cliff?"

He had blushed and changed the subject. But, Etta Mae had given him much food for thought.

Unfortunately, the Fish Fry was late in the summer, and it was too late to create a way to see her again before school started. That late in the season he did not have free time on the weekends and when winter set in, Sunday afternoons were short.

The experience had left him with a desire to see her again. They had much more in common than he had imagined. Now he had missed the opportunity to take her looking for bee trees this summer, and had heard her play the guitar. He never would, unless he could get out of this mess.

If I can survive this on my own, maybe someday I'll be able to just walk up to your house and ask to be invited in to sit down and talk to you like the man I'm supposed to be Angelina Martinez, he sighed.

59

Baskets and pots
Martinez Canyon

Cliff continued to use willows for the framework of baskets and yucca, grass leaves, cedar, sage and willow bark woven around the frames as filler. His technique and skill continued to improve. He experimented with designs using different kinds of grass to provide shades of gold and brown for ornamentation so the baskets weren't so ugly looking.

After he made his first deer kill, he filled several of the baskets with jerky. He checked the jerky often to see that it was all right. He found no sign of spoilage so far. Humidity was low even in the cave. The problem would come in the wintertime. When he had found jars at the Martinez dump, he transferred as much of the jerky to them as possible. He sealed each jar with slightly moistened rabbit gut, tied it off with sinew, let the gut dry and put the lid back on, if he had a good lid. If he had no lid, he used two thicknesses of the rabbit gut.

Smaller tightly woven grass baskets were filled with grass and weed seeds. He worked on baskets at night by firelight. If there was enough moonlight, on warm summer nights he sat outside on the ledge or on top of the roof and worked. He needed little light to weave the grass in and out of the frames. Each basket had a woven cap.

He also made clay pots and experimented firing them in the fire pit with varying success. He couldn't built a fire hot enough and maintain it in the fire pit without overheating the dwelling. He was afraid to build a big fire outside and maintain it for a long time because it would attract too much attention.

The most successful firing he made was using the natural tub in the ledge where he tanned hides and separated fibers from yucca leaves.

He made a coiled pot about ten inches in diameter at the widest and six inches at the mouth standing eight inches tall. He dried the pot in the cave first and then moved it outside into the shade on the roof for a week. The next week he moved it into the sunshine and let it continue to dry. It had dried up to that point without cracking. He had followed directions in grinding soft sandstone and adding it to the clay to give it some body and therefore strength before rolling it into the long thin rolls that he had wound around the base to form the walls of the pot. The morning that he decided to begin the firing he placed three stones in the bottom of the pit and balanced the pot on them. Between and around the stones he arranged twigs and bark as fire starter. He also arranged smaller wood around the perimeter of the pit, just enough to get a small fire going. He did not want to build a hot fire to begin with but to heat the pot slowly.

Cliff transported several coals from his breakfast fire to the pit and placed them under the pot to start the kindling. The fire caught and slowly spread throughout the pit and quickly burned down to embers. He fed sticks to the coals randomly around the perimeter and between the stones under the pot. Throughout the day, he continued adding wood until the pit was full and the fire burned hot. He looked into the center of the blaze at the pot in the cage of burning cedar. *I wonder how the Ancestral Puebloans brought their fire to a temperature high enough to turn the clay to stone. I don't know how much hotter I could can it without a furnace. I wonder if they had ovens. I don't remember seeing anything at all on that. How long did they have to hold it at that temperature?*

The cedar burned hot and clean and produced little smoke, although anyone walking within a half mile could have smelled it. In the hot summer afternoon, heat waves distorted the atmosphere and the slight smoke would not be very apparent to anyone looking across the landscape toward Mesa Verde. One would have to be looking directly up or down the canyon to spot it. Cliff depended on this set of circumstances to work with him. He kept the fire stoked through the afternoon and evening and far into the night and finally let it begin to burn down to coals in the wee of the morning. As it cooled, he criss-crossed the pit with longer pieces of firewood that reached across the pit and covered that with burlap sacks to trap as much heat inside the stone pit as possible to slow the cooling.

He was dismayed at the amount of fuel it had taken to fire the one pot. He couldn't afford to do another firing at that rate of fuel consumption.

He didn't disturb the pot until it was completely cool two days later. The surface of the pot was hard and brittle sounding when he tapped it. The outer surface was rough from the ashes and fire. It was not glazed so it had a raw look. There were no cracks through the sides or bottom of the pot. He filled it with water and set it on the floor by the fire pit and when he checked it later, there was no dampness around it.

Cliff didn't know if the pot was in a state potters would refer to as bisque or biscuit. Cliff didn't know that much about it. He did know that this pot looked very similar to the more crude pots the inhabitants had left behind. His craftsmanship was not as refined. The walls of the pot were thicker. But it was substantial. To make sure it was waterproof he coated the inside with hot pitch.

The pot became a main water heating pot as he filled it each morning, set it on the end of the cooking stone and left it there. It slowly heated as the fire cooked his breakfast. Cliff dipped out warm water to bathe, wash his clothes and clean his spoon and knife. He replenished what he used, as he used it, and it slowly warmed to be ready again when he needed it. He did not use it as a hot drinking water source.

60
Collecting and Roaming
Martinez Canyon and Lost Canyon

He robbed the bee tree once more later in the summer. He found fresh new comb and cured honey in the block. The bees had firmly attached the new comb to the face of the block and had been built down from the comb above. When Cliff cut around the block, it came out cleanly. It was hardly attached at the opposite end this time. Several rows were not built completely out to attach to comb but were rounded and finished. Because the nectar flow was on the wane at that time of the summer, this time the bees were a little more uneasy, and several bees wanted to challenge him. Also his clothes were no longer in very good condition, and most of his body wasn't protected. It would be his last time to rob the bees, this season at least.

The second honey harvest did produce more honey than brood. The flavor and color were definitely clover. During the late summer, there was less pressure to build up the colony size to multiply and divide and more pressure to build up the store of honey for the winter.

Cliff was thankful for the additional wax and it was all new wax so he could enjoy honey in the comb. He could enjoy chewing the honey out of it and then use of the wax again as a seal around balls of pemmican.

~~~

A few jars were free that had been used to store jerky, enough to now become honey storage.

He had already pounded and ground most of the best venison jerky into powered meat and mixed it with tallow. The mixture of dried meat and soft tallow with ground sunflower, clover seed, and wild currents, turned out pretty well. He made them into compressed balls about the size of his fist as his instructions suggested. He didn't have cheesecloth as the recipe suggested, so he tried instead cradling a ball with thin strands of yucca cord, dipping each ball quickly into melted beeswax and removing it. He didn't leave it in the beeswax long enough to melt the tallow. He set the balls aside to cool. He had peeled back the wax covering on the first ball to check it. The wax had hardened into a tough, thin full protective coating. He had dropped the peeling back into the wax to re-melt and use again.

He had used a large percentage of the tallow from the yearling deer to convert the jerky to pemmican and still had wax to spare. Those balls of pemmican were now back in the baskets that had held the jerky before he had transferred it to the jars. His instructions had said pemmican stored in this manner would last for an indefinite time.

~~~

Once, over a two-day period, he and Maggie roamed to the north. Cliff left the atlatl and spears at home.

He followed his usual route to the deer trail across the county road and followed timber to Little Canyon, down to Big Canyon and followed it to Lost Canyon. From school it was only two and a half miles to the rim of Lost Canyon. It was nearly six miles via Big Canyon. He came out on the rim of Lost Canyon a little further down the canyon than if he had gone to the canyon directly north of the schoolhouse.

It was a deeper more significant canyon than Martinez Canyon and from the rim where he first gazed into the canyon it was only between four and five miles down to the confluence of Lost Canyon Creek and the Dolores River. The conquistadores had named it the "River of Sorrows" reportedly because they had seen a weeping Indian woman on the banks of the river. Gold and silver mining in the upper tributaries had opened the Dolores River and added the Southern part of the state to the Gold Rush.

The Rio Grande Southern Narrow Gauge railway connected the town of Dolores, Stoner, Rico, Ophir, Telluride, Placerville, Ridgway.

From Dolores to Millwood, Mancos, and Durango where it joined the Denver and Rio Grande narrow Gauge.

The Ancestral Puebloans had built their cliff dwellings in the lower reaches of Lost Canyon and in the cliffs of Dolores canyon below the confluence of the two canyons. Evidence of their farms and surface dwellings dotted the sloping lands to the west of the Dolores and Lost Canyons and between the minor canyons on the Ridge.

Cliff and Maggie explored the canyon and ruins for two days. There were numerous ruins, all explored, dug, plundered, very close to farms and families. While he was there, he finally got to see the little steam engines pulling long lines of stock cars or mix rows of stock cars, freight cars and coal hoppers. He even saw the funny looking half bus, half car Galloping Goose motor railroad car go swaying up the track on its way from Dolores to Mancos. Charlie had ridden the Goose to Stoner once to go fishing.

He had heard the whistle on the steam engines while working out in the fields on days when there was no breeze and sounds carried. The whistles had been mysterious, and he had fantasized they were calling to him to come and go with them to far away exotic places.

The upper reaches of Lost Canyon in the blue spruce and quaking aspen forest was Cliff's favorite place to fish. He loved it there among the ferns, blue columbines, blue flags, and crystal clear, ice cold stream where the brook trout waited.

There near Dolores, the canyon walls were dry and the vegetation was scrub oak, piñon, cedar and sagebrush. That part was familiar. It was like Martinez Canyon but on a wide scale. However, there were too many people around who could remember the search earlier in the summer, assuming the sheriff had actually searched this part of the country. *My clothes are a dead giveaway now. I can't fit in as a kid from town or a tourist. Anglo kids don't go around dressed in a breechcloth. If somebody sees me, I'll probably be arrested for indecent exposure.*

He had to duck and hide from other kids and hikers several times.

When he was safely back in Martinez Canyon, he was glad to be home. Moonbeam welcomed him as though she thought he wasn't coming back. Maggie had accompanied him all the way.

~~~

He went out each day dressed in moccasins, breechcloth, knapsack and straw-hat carrying the atlatl. He came back most nights with a fresh cottontail, fresh vegetables and raw materials. When his hunt was unsuccessful, he broke strips of jerky into the Dutch oven with his greens, cut off a shaving of tallow and dropped it in and a while later settled back to reflect on that day and consider what he needed to do the next day.

~~~

Cliff observed and stalked the wild turkey flock relentlessly. He needed more feathers to maintain the spears and to make replacements for those that were broken or damaged when he hunted. He had considered the turkeys as pretty stupid when he observed the domestic variety on the farm, but the wild ones were difficult to stalk. He could find them, but he couldn't creep up on one close enough to get a clean throw at one.

He finally discovered the flock's roosting trees and speared a gobbler one night at sundown as they came home to roost. The meat was a welcome change from venison and rabbit, but most important of all, it provided prime wing and tail feathers for fletching his spears.

~~~

Each morning when he went out, he checked up and down the county road below the Stone residence looking for road kill. As summer closed in on fall, the time drew nearer for the fall migration from the foothills to Mesa Verde. At the sound of the first shot of hunting season, the migration would accelerate and inevitable collisions between deer and vehicles would increase. While collisions between deer and cars were regrettable, Cliff saw this as an opportunity to obtain another hide if he found another road victim that hadn't been mangled too badly.

He foraged for food in the canyon during the day and along the ditch bank on the south fence line of the Kelley farm at dusk and dawn. Grasses and grain were maturing. Summer was on the wane.

~~~

Once he had watched from concealment in a scrub oak grove in the canyon as George Williamson inspected the canyon trail, willow groves and cattails. Cliff continued to be careful in his harvests in the canyon and not to revisit any one willow grove, or dig cattails in the same place too often. George's manner or body language didn't seem to indicate he had found any signs of Cliff's presence in the canyon. This was not the first time he had seen George inspecting the trail and creek. He had to be ever vigilant or someday George was going to catch him out in the open.

What would George do if he found me? Would he go straight to Dad? Would he understand why I'm here? Maybe I should go down there the next time I see him and talk to him. I could have him go to Dad and arrange for me to come home.

61
Sunflower Seeds Near Martinez Canyon

Cliff's summer work and preparation began to show dividends. The baskets began to fill.

He had filled several small baskets with mature, black, dried clover seeds.

He began gathering the tiny lambs quarter seeds, and then careless weed seeds.

Clifton gained a new respect for the sunflowers, which before had been his bane when he had to hoe them in the corn, beans and grain. The scraggly branching, tough fibered, weed produced numerous seedpods from two to three inches in diameter ringed with bright yellow petals. The plant produced flowers over a broad timeframe and as older blossoms lost petals and seeds matured, new blossoms opened and turned their faces to the sun. The brown centers each produced a handful of small seeds that birds flocked to. The triangular seeds were smaller than the seeds sold in the grocery store, and they were tedious to shell. However, when he crushed them on the *metate* with the *mano* and blew away the husks, the broken kernels remained.

Cliff had run out of corn and the corn growing in the field was only turning from milk firm. Kernels would not begin to dry into hard kernels until fall about the time of the first frost.

He tried roasting a cupful of sunflower seeds and ground them, husk and all, into meal. He prepared dough from the sunflower seed flour and cooked it the same way he had cooked the corn cake. It was delicious.

The common wild sunflower grew everywhere. He gathered seeds along fencerows, in fallow fields, and at the edge of the dry land timber on his dad's place. Sunflowers that had missed the hoe in the irrigated areas on the farm were much larger and wouldn't mature until later. The smaller stunted plants in the dry areas had matured much earlier, but the seeds were just as full and just as plentiful.

He filled all of his pouches full of the seeds every time he went out. In one field, he shook the seed from head after head into the knapsack, took them to the dwelling and returned to the patch of golden yellow for more.

As the heads on each sunflower matured, there was a narrow window of opportunity to harvest seeds, as flocks of birds descended on each patch of mature seed and fields of sunflowers were stripped of the tasty treats in a few hours.

He didn't feel badly about taking his share. The crows and jays were mobile and could range far afield in their search. His lack of transportation and circumstance limited him to a very small area..

Book III

School Shooting
Monday June 1, 2000 the week of graduation, South High School after school

Mr. Clifton Kelley walked out the door of South High School and headed toward the parking lot across the street from the front of the school. Parallel to the street and set back toward the school about ten feet from the sidewalk, was the school sign built by students in the industrial arts program.

It was an elaborate metal structure with the letters cut out of steel, and the school mascot engraved on each end. The unfinished metal had rusted to a fine cinnamon brown. It was a landmark in the community and a statement to the strength and stability of the school with a history going back to the settlement of the town before the turn of the century.

Clifton walked by the sign and turned to it as he went by. He broke into tears. The school sign had become an instant memorial to the school's beloved teacher as well as to the victims of sister school, North High School.

Hundreds of pieces of paper; full sheets and tiny scraps, with comments and drawings had been attached to the face of the sign. On the grass in front of the sign were thousands of flowers. They ranged from elaborate floral sprays, delivered by townspeople and the flower shops, to a single dandelion in a science class beaker.

A steady stream of cars drove by slowly as townspeople and students leaving for home after school, waved or saluted solemnly to the display.

Clifton paused briefly to read some of the comments and smile at some of the drawings.

This display must be nothing compared to what is going on over at North.

Some people have written off this generation, but if they come by here, read these, and see the deepness of their feelings and ability to express them, they might change their minds.

The Cliff Dwelling, Martinez Canyon
The Kelley Farm
Summit Ridge, Colorado
Fall 1954

62

Hector Rodriguez
Summit Ridge

School would begin on Tuesday. Hector would have come down from the mountains the last week in August, to prepare for school if his summer plans hadn't been changed for him when Clifton Kelley disappeared after that stupid fight at school. Instead of going to the mountains, he had spent the summer farming for Mr. Kelley. He would be paid for his hours when the beans and grain were combined.

Hector had argued that his uncle needed him, but Raul had said, "Your uncle and Emilio can handle them. You will work this summer to undo a terrible wrong, and then you will finish school," Raul insisted. "And then next year you will go to high school. If you study, I will send you to Ft. Lewis when you graduate. None of our family has ever finished high school before. I am saving so you can go to Ft. Lewis. When you are paid for your summer work, it will go into a savings account to help."

Hector was finished farming for the summer. Ed had given him the weekend off to prepare for school. "I am going for a ride," he told his mother.

He went to the corral, saddled Diablo and rode down their lane to the county road. He had to admit that working outside all summer in Ed Kelley's fields had been interesting, although he had often dreamed of the freedom of riding all day in the mountains without encountering a fence all day, day after day. He was not looking forward to being confined within the walls of East Lakeview Grade School when the weather was still fine.

He rode the mile and a half up the road to the schoolhouse to the cluster of mailboxes. As he rode along, he wondered what kind of year it would be. He would be an eighth grader, one of four. He would be the leader again, of course, but it wouldn't be the same. What is a leader with no one to lead against? The *gringo* was gone. He was going to have trouble with Emilio. Emilio would come down from the mountain a big man, while Hector had spent the summer a lowly farmer. Emilio might have some thoughts about taking over the leadership.

According to his father, no one had seen the kid since that day when they had fought. He had felt remorse all summer over that fight. It had been stupid. His father and *Señor* Kelley were good friends. His father had been very angry with him for fighting the *gringo* boy and had forced him to do the boy's work for the summer. He and his family had helped to plant the Kelley's crops the day before Hector was to go to the mountains. Hector had been embarrassed to be sitting at the Kelley table eating their food and being treated with respect after what he had done to them.

At the end of that day when they planted the crops, he had offered to stay and help on the farm until they found their boy. Señor Kelley had thanked him and told him he would be glad to have his help, but he would insist on keeping hours on him and paying him in the fall when the crops were harvested.

The thought of the fight had been with him often throughout the summer. Hector secretly fantasized that one day he would find the boy and bring him home and everything would be fine between the two families. He of course would be a hero after all.

Hector gathered the mail and turned the horse toward home. He thought about his father's plans for him; the idea of going to high school and then to Ft. Lewis Junior College. He and his *tio* had talked about raising sheep. His uncle knew everything about sheep; lambing, sheering, protecting them from predators, doctoring them, moving them about their summer pasture in the mountains, and when to start them back down to the winter pasture in the Valley. Why had his father chosen him to go on to school instead of following his uncle into the sheep business?

Hector rode south from the mailboxes to the corner at the Kelley farm and turned west for the short distance past the piles of brush and broken trees the county road crew had left inside the Kelley fence. He had no way of knowing that Cliff had lain in wait for him that Monday afternoon in the spring after their fight. Cliff had arrived at least an hour after Hector had been escorted by there by Bob Harris that afternoon, after Cliff had angrily left the school. If Cliff had stayed a half hour longer, Hector's brothers and sisters would have come along and perhaps paid the price for Hector's behavior.

A half mile further at the southwestern corner of the Kelley farm, Hector stopped the horse for a moment. He looked out across the Kelley's fields ripening in the sun. He had had a hand in irrigating cultivating and tending those fields. He felt proud of the way the pinto beans, corn, and alfalfa looked, in spite of himself. He looked on southeast beyond the farm at the tract of timber. Over there lay Martinez Canyon and on the other side of that Enrique Martinez' farm.

The day before, Dulcina Martinez and her daughter Angelina had visited his mother Inez. Angelina had grown up some over the summer. She was a year ahead of him in school, but they were close to the same age. She told him she would be a freshman at Montezuma County High School this year. But that didn't matter to him as much as it seemed to matter to her.

He had wanted to talk to her, maybe kid around with her, but she was more interested in hanging around with her mother and Inez.

He had hung around the house, finding things to do; polishing his school shoes, and pretending to read a magazine. Finally, he had gone outside and waited around to see her again, when she and her mother left. He wanted to see her again. Too bad she had attended Mesa Verde Grade School. He didn't know if her hair was natural, or if she was coloring it. Was she trying to prove something to the Anglo kids? Those Anglo boys in town were going to be all over her. Too bad they'd get a head start on him.

He searched for an excuse to visit her home that afternoon. He thought about cutting through the woods on county land on the south side of the Kelley fence line. He thought he could ride clear through to the Mancos-Dolores road, which went right by the Martinez place. He thought he had heard she had a pony. Maybe he could talk her into going horseback riding with him.

63
Harvest begins
Kelley Farm

That same early September morning when Cliff woke up, there was a still chilliness in the air. He looked out the doorway and down into the canyon. Twilight reflected off a mist that hung over the creek. He shivered in the cold air that seeped into the dwelling, and he replaced the mat cover and donned the rabbit skin coat and the fawn breechcloth.

The fire had gone out over night. He gathered fire-making materials together. He still had the box of wax-coated matches from the saddlebag, but he was determined to keep those in reserve in case of emergency during the winter. For now, when the banked fire didn't make it through the night, he made another from scratch with flint and horseshoe nail. He only used the fire to cook during the summer.

He took a pinch of cottonwood cotton from a basket and a pouch that hung next to it and returned to the fire pit. He took a small piece of twisted cedar bark, ground it between his palms until it was fluffy, broke twigs and stacked them on top of the bark. From the pouch, he removed a flint nodule and horseshoe nail. He held the flint above the cotton fluff and struck the stone sharply with the nail. A healthy spark flew off and landed in the fluff. Cliff blew gently on the glow and smoke rose, then a tiny flame. Cliff placed the cotton fluff under the cedar bark and continued to blow gently, and in a few moments, bark and twigs began to burn.

He had tried various ways to make fire and had given up on most of them. He had tried spinning a stick between his palms. The end of the pointed stick creating friction in a pocket on another stick only produced blisters on the palm of his hand.

He had built a bow that twisted the friction stick back and forth much faster without using the palm of his hand. This had actually produced smoke, but he had not been able to coax fire from it.

Mrs. Campbell had demonstrated striking a nail across flint to produce a spark. He also knew that muskets used flint across iron. Also, he had produced showers of sparks sharpening shovels on the abrasive grind stone.

There was a pile of flint fragments on the roof of the ruin. Most were remains left by the original inhabitants of the ruin. A few were from his own experiments at knapping nodules gathered from pools in the canyon.

He had tried striking flint against a rusty horseshoe he had found on a fence post. Surprisingly the soft metal of the horseshoe produced the best spark. On one of his yucca harvesting trips he had found a square horseshoe hail. It was made of the same soft iron as the horseshoe and produced an excellent spark. It was also lightweight. He carried the pouch wherever he went.

Fire started best when a spark landed in cottonwood or cattail fluff.

The huge broadleaf cottonwood trees had put on green clusters of grapelike seedpods in June. Each marble size pod contained seed tightly packed in cotton. As the pods dried on the tree and their three petals opened, they released a puff of cotton, which carried seed to far places on the wind. The cotton made good stuffing in chairs or pillows if gathered in enough quantity.

Cliff gathered gunnysacks full of the pods just before they opened and carried them back to the cave.

He filled the largest empty ancient pots with the nearly bursting green pods and let them dry.

He planned to remove the husks as they burst and move the cotton to one or two of the burlap bags to use as a soft cotton mattress. He had to continue harvesting cottonwood balls because the soft fluff compressed so much. He had hauled bag after bag of the cotton to the cave until he had enough for a thin mattress.

He made a sack of the bed sheet from the granary and stuffed it with the fluff. He now used it as a thin mattress to replace the saddle blanket. It wasn't much softer, but a little.

Early in the experiments with cottonwood fluff, he discovered that cotton was good for more than padding.

When he began experimenting with the flint and horseshoe, he struck sparks into a number of different media; ground up cedar bark, pitch and cattail seed. He got smoke and was able to coax a flame in the powdered cedar bark when he struck a healthy spark into it. He got an instant flame in the cattail seed, but it burned fast.

The cattail seed fluff resembled the cotton in cottonwood seedpods, and he retrieved a fist-sized ball of it. When he compressed a twist of the cottonwood seed, it looked like cotton. He struck a spark into it and the spark smoldered, smoked and as he gently blew on it, flamed. He added crushed leaves and twigs and soon had a fire going. It was more reliable than the cattail seed and much more abundant for a short time. When he had collected enough for the mattress, he continued collecting the cotton as a fire starting media.

The cottonwood seed went into baskets, which he covered and hung far from the fire as his primary fire starter media.

The cottonwood seed went into baskets and they were hung safely as his primary fire starter.

~~~

Cliff rinsed the clay pot, filled it to two thirds full from the spring and set it close to the middle of the cooking stone to heat. The first cup of the fresh warm water would be for his morning tea. The rest would be a start for his morning hygiene, and to wash his dishes. At first he had been cautious about drinking water from the pot, but as time went by he began using just enough for his morning tea. He continued brewing sun tea in a quart mason jar for the rest of the day.

The remains of the cottontail that Cliff had cooked the night before hung from a cord suspended from the ceiling. Cliff reached up, removed it, squatted by the tiny fire while he tore off half the back, and rib section and handed it to Moonbeam. The other half he handed to Maggie who took his half and flew to the top of his cage. He kept the remaining front legs and neck quarters for himself.

"I think it may have frosted last night, Moonbeam," he said thoughtfully as the three companions ate their breakfast. "That means the piñon nuts will begin to fall, the beans are ready to combine, the wheat is ready to thresh, and the corn is about mature. We are going to be busy, busy, busy. Maggie and I'll go check it out today. It must be September sometime. I should have been getting ready to walk down to Lakeview to catch the bus this morning right about now. I wonder what today would have been like?" he said wistfully.

Three months before, he thought he had his life laid out for him. He had looked forward to entering high school in Cortez; MCHS, Montezuma County High School. There were nearly 400 students there compared to the 23 at East Lakeview Grade School. He assumed a little more than a hundred classmates were in the freshman class.

He had looked forward to friends, long talks, football games, marching bands, walking uptown at lunchtime. It would have been a drag walking the six miles to the bus every morning and home the same six miles every night, but he could have handled it. Actually, Charlie had cut the distance to about four miles by walking down the small canyon that began as the draw that cut off the corner of their place, ran into Little Canyon which emptied into Big Canyon, which emptied into Lakeview valley near the bus stop.

It was all a moot point now. He had worked many scenarios' in his head where he enrolled in high school in Mancos where nobody knew his family, but he would look a little out of place with long hair, moccasins, a yucca fabric shirt, rabbit skin leggings and a breechcloth. He certainly didn't have money to buy school clothes. He had nothing to sell except maybe some pelts or his pet skunk. That wasn't going to happen.

He debated going to school for even one day in his outgrown overalls and tattered work shirt, but he knew he wouldn't be able to stand the teasing, and he would attract too much attention. Besides, they probably wouldn't give him the books without his parents there, so he couldn't try
~~~

it. He really wasn't acquainted with Mancos High School and he would have to ask too many questions. And, certainly THEY would ask too many questions. He would have to use a fictitious name. What if they demanded proof of identity?

His brother had attended MCHS, and he thought he might be able to make his way around there without having to ask questions.

However the was frost meant it was too late anyway. School was already in session.

~~~

Moonbeam curled up on her nest of cedar bark and went to sleep. Cliff shed the rabbit coat, donned the knapsack, hung his knife on his belt, gathering pouches around his neck, and tied a buckskin pouch containing his darts around his waist. He put the atlatl spears through the loop around his shoulders and into the knapsack. He went out the doorway and refastened the door behind him.

Cliff shivered in the still cold air. With Maggie alternately flying circles overhead and riding on his shoulder, he climbed the cliff face and headed through the woods toward the south fence of the Kelley farm.

He slipped over the fence into the wooded dry land corner of the place and from there into the tall corn field and walked down the row between stalks. They had begun to dry and turn brown. The full plump ears hung downward. He broke an ear free and peeled back the husk. The kernels were beginning to wrinkle, but they were not yet completely dry and hard.

If he picked ears now, they would probably dry and keep, but it would be better if they could mature on the stalk for another week at least.

It would not be long before his mom and dad would drive down the rows with the wagon behind the tractor. His mom would drive while his dad ripped the ears off the stalks and threw them into the wagon. His dad had built high sideboards on three sides of the wagon so that the ears hit them and bounced back into the bed. The sideboard on the one side was lower so that he didn't have to throw high over it.

A contract cutter had already chopped about two thirds of the field into ensilage. The entire corn stalk was chopped while the stalks were still green and the ears were plump. When one tall sided wagon was full, it pulled out of the way and the second was pulled in its place to catch the chopped corn as it streamed out a chute at the side of the chopper.

The loaded wagon then headed to a dug out pit silo Ed had prepared next to the barnyard. The wagon dumped its load and went back to the field ready to take its place for more. Each successive load ran over the preceding load, compressing the chopped ensilage in the pit. The whole chopping operation took about two days.

When the pit was full, Ed covered it with tarps and then spread a thin layer of soil over the tarp to hold it down. The green fodder was left to ferment slightly. During the winter months, Ed fed the slightly fermented
~~~

green ensilage to the milk cows giving them a sweet, fresh, green fodder to supplement the dry alfalfa hay.

The portion of the cornfield left to mature produced dry kernel corn that was ground and mixed with wheat and barley for hog, chicken, horse and cow feed. A very small amount would be ground into corn meal for Ed and Etta Mae's cornbread.

Unknown to Ed, it would also provide a staple of his son's diet, if Cliff could manage to pick some of it ahead of them without their awareness.

Checking the beans was more risky as the field was nearer the road and the stalks were only knee high. But the field was on the northern slope of the valley that ran down the southern third of the farm. He would not be visible from the house and would only be visible for a minute to a car driving by. If he heard a car he could lie down between rows, and he hoped he would be invisible there on the ground.

He moved out of the standing corn and across the bottom of the draw to the end of the bean field. A swath about twenty feet wide where the tractor turned at the end of the rows was not cultivated. Grass and weeds competed with the beans for moisture there. The only vines that grew in that swath were those where the planter had dropped seed as it was being raised from the ground while the tractor began its turn. The tractor tires ground the seeds into the dirt at the ends of the rows. Vines that came up grew haphazardly and would not be harvested.

The vines were less luxuriant than those in the cultivated rows where they had been irrigated and soil had been thrown up against the stems to conserve moisture and kill competing weeds. Those vines had some maturing yet before harvest. In the dry swath, the weeds and grass had sucked the moisture from the uncultivated soil and vines were stunted. Those vines had matured early and the pods were dry enough to harvest.

He stooped down to the first vine and carefully pulled a rawhide colored pod off and broke it open. Tan beans with brown, splotchy, splatters spilled out into his palm. They were as plump as their cultivated and pampered cousins would be in another week or so.

He placed one between his molars and crunched down. It shattered between his teeth. They were hard and ready. He began pulling pods from vines and dropping them into the knapsack.

It seems fitting that you come with me. You are the misfits in this field. The seed sewn here fell among the weeds and dry ground and and were not tended. The sunflowers and careless weeds competed with you for every drop of water and sucked the life out of you all summer. Nevertheless, you survived. You won out didn't you? And in a few days when they come along to harvest the crop, you know what? They were just going to run right over you and smash you into the ground. All they would have been interested in were those beans over there. Well, you come with me. You can help me survive the months to come. I will appreciate you more than you can ever know. Mother Nature and Heavenly Father put you here for a purpose. They spilled you here so I'd find you and harvest you and have your nourishment this winter. And I'm not going to forget it. If I can survive this, then maybe it is a sign that I should be keeping an eye out for others who have been out among the weeds and looking for someone to help them.

Cliff continued to gather pods until the knapsack and all the pouches were full. He could have carried away many more beans if he had shelled them there, but he didn't want to leave behind the husks of the pods.

Up in the rows the vines met in the middle of the row. It would be a very good harvest, partly the result of the deep soaking rains back in July. The rain had arrived at the perfect time when the vines were growing at full growth speed. If the price held, his dad had made a good decision to plant a large field in pinto beans. Some years he planted only enough for their own consumption.

Cliff would make repeated trips to that part of the field to try to salvage the rest of the beans that would be run into the ground when the row beans were combined. He probably had the rest of the week. He would check the moon that night. Maybe he could come back after dark.

64

Harvesting Piñon Nuts
On top outside Martinez Canyon

On his way back to the dwelling Cliff passed by the pueblo ruin and the bee tree where he had captured his first swarm.

Between the pueblo ruin and the canyon were many large old piñon trees. Flocks of magpies, jays and crows were beginning to gather on particular trees. Impatient birds were beginning to peck half open cones to get at exposed nuts. Others hopped around beneath trees scrambling for nuts as they hit the ground.

Cliff hurried to the dwelling with an excited Maggie following along calling to his cousins all the while. "Maggie, don't get any ideas about running off with one of those flocks," he warned. "You have a pretty good thing going here, you know."

Maggie bird cocked his head and eyed the man that he had bonded with. "Clifton got treats?" he asked.

Cliff laughed and dug a small piece of jerky out of a pouch that hung from his waist and tossed it to his friend. "For you always," he laughed.

Cliff hurriedly emptied the knapsack and all of his containers into a large basket prepared for bean storage, and coaxed Maggie into his cage.

He gathered the burlap sacks and went back out over the top to the piñon tree that attracted the most jays, crows and magpies. He assumed they had homed in on the tree with the most abundant and largest nuts.

He spread the burlap sacks under a branch and climbed into the tree. Protesting birds flew from the trees, circled and flocked to the nearest tree to continue their raucous protests.

From his perch on the main branch, he shook each smaller lateral branch he could reach that extended over the sacks. A hail of nuts and cones hit the burlap sacks underneath him. When he had shaken all the smaller branches he could reach, he climbed down and consolidated the nuts, cones and needles that had landed on each sack by pouring them into one sack.

He repeated the action until he had gone completely around the tree several times climbing higher each time. By the time I'm finished with the tree and the gunnysack is full of nuts, cones, twigs, and needles I'll be lucky if there is a gallon of nuts in the bunch.

Many of the cones on that tree and the trees around him had not opened so each tree he worked would continue to drop nuts. Most of the nuts he had harvested should be good. The birds, squirrels and chipmunks would have their turns.

Before dark, he had filled and carried to the dwelling three full gunnysacks. In the next few evenings, he would sort through the sacks, removing empty cones, trash and needles. Cones that had not opened he set aside. Some would open in a few days. If they did not he would char them in the fire pit. When they were charred, he would open them with a knife. The nuts would be roasted. The charring burned away the pitch. The debris from the trees would make good kindling. He would make other trips to the piñon trees as long as nuts continued to fall.

65

Road Kill

The County Road below the Stone Residence

The atmosphere changed. A slight haze hung over the landscape, nights were frosty, yellow and brown leaves rustled dry on the cottonwoods. Red oak leaves clung to scrub oak. Small acorns covered the ground attracting squirrels, chipmunks, blue jays and turkeys. Leaves on corn stalks had withered after hot, still, September days. White husks were wrapped less tightly around hard yellow rows of mature kernels. The silk, pollinating purpose long ago accomplished, hung dry and brown, from the ends of the dangling ears.

Indian summer hung in the air as an expectant prelude to the winter just ahead. Cliff had noted how thick Moonbeam's coat had become. The fur on cottontails likewise had grown much thicker and luxuriant. His dad had said one could tell what kind of winter was ahead by observing the animals. If the horses' hair was shaggy, for example, they were preparing for a hard winter. Cliff was nearly finished in the summer-long pursuit of gathering of food to weather out a long hard Colorado Rocky Mountain winter.

His remaining concern was warm clothing.

The annual migration of deer from the mountains onto the plateau and lower foothill valleys had progressed from a trickle to a flood with the first shots of hunting season on October first. A few days before at dawn, shots sounded from different directions. Cliff could tell which hay fields the deer herds had stopped to graze in overnight. A few shots echoed off Mesa Verde at dusk. It was a signal that hunting season had opened. It was October first, and hunters would roam the woods and canyons shooting anything that moved for the next month. He had to be careful and lay low or he could become a casualty himself.

Most out of state hunters went to the mountains. The gunshots he could hear were from local farmers and their kids who probably didn't even put tags on their kills if they didn't see anyone around.

Cliff had seen increased activity on the deer trails. The small herd that inhabited the canyon and local farms year-around had been lost in the transient herds that passed through. Those transients each spring and fall grazed on the now harvested alfalfa fields, helped themselves to any standing corn or waste left in the field, grazed the ditch banks, scooped up acorns in the oak groves and moved on, depleting the food supply for the local deer population.

They would spread throughout the canyons, mesa tops in the Mesa Verde National Park sanctuary, or drop into the warmer canyons such as McElmo, spend the winter and then migrate back into the high country in April and May.

Particular stretches of roads and highways along the migration path became treacherous for deer and drivers alike during the weeks of the migration. Signs at each end of the crossings and intermittently within each warned drivers to watch out for deer crossing those stretches of road. Nevertheless, each morning a mangled body lay on the roadway, beside the road, in the barrow pit, or occasionally a few hundred yards off the road if the deer almost cleared a vehicle before being clipped and only crippled.

The westerly most trail crossed about a mile below the Stone residence and continued past the abandoned miner's cabin where Clifton had found the Dutch oven.

The large mule deer were heavy enough to cause serious damage to a vehicle in a collision.

It was a very busy season for Cortez body shops, emergency rooms and occasionally mortuaries.

Motorists were encouraged to notify the sheriff's department to pick up fresh road kill if carcasses weren't badly damaged. Usable meat was delivered to the county schools or jail. Otherwise, carcasses were disposed of at the rendering plant. It was against the law for the driver to take the meat home.

Although Cliff had walked the road as often as he could on the off chance of finding an injured deer, the chances had improved many times over with the opening shots of hunting season.

Cliff arose early each morning before dawn to be at the county road as soon as he could see. He followed the road down the hill away from the Stone's home, checking each side of the road from the barrow pits to inside the timber a few yards for any deer that might have been hit or injured during the night. He watched, for not only actual carcasses, but also sign of blood or tracks, sign of an injured animal.

The first few mornings were for naught, but eventually he came upon a large doe in the edge of the woods on the south side of the road. He felt her neck. She was dead, but still warm. She had been struck only moments before he had arrived at the road.

Cliff pulled her further into the woods before another vehicle came along, and continued dragging her carcass deep enough into the trees that he could work without being seen from the road. The area was on the slope of the draw that led toward the miner's cabin. The ground was rocky. He was careful to leave no drag marks or blood trail behind.

If the sheriff's deputy knew what he was looking for and the exact spot to look for it, he might be able to find where she had fallen and where she had bled. If he checked further down the washed out rocky road they would see more blood where she had been dressed out. There was no trail in between to lead him from the first spot to the next.

She had lost no blood in the collision. That was good. The drag marks were not very obvious on the hard rocky ground and timber floor. It was a gamble whether the driver would call the sheriff's office and report it or not and how accurate the location given would be.

Daylight grew into sunrise as Cliff skinned the doe. The hide was in good shape. One front quarter and the ribs were badly bruised. He assumed she had been hit there and the impact had collapsed her lung or damaged her heart. The only part he took from there was the tallow. The neck and three other quarters were salvageable.

He set the damaged meat aside to take to the shallow part of the canyon and leave there for Mother Nature's creatures to dine on. He would keep the head for the brains to tan the hide. The hindquarters, one front quarter, one side and most of the neck he kept for the meat. They were a bonus. The tendons hide and tallow had been his main objective.

As with the deer he had killed in the summer, he let the hide protect the meat from getting dirty as he cut the carcass apart. Before he separated the quarters, he trimmed off the tendons along the backbone and the back of the legs to separate into sinew later. It would take several trips to transport everything back to the dwelling. He could only take a quarter at a time.

It was a lot further from there to the dwelling than from where he had killed the yearling. It would be a long hard day. Fortunately, the weather was not so hot, so he wasn't so rushed from that, but there was more chance of discovery. Hunting season had opened and there could be people roaming the woods now. That could also be a problem. He had to be alert. Some of the hunters from town were known to shoot at about anything that moved in the woods.

If the driver had reported the collision with the deer to the authorities, the sheriff would dispatch someone to pick up the meat immediately while it was still fresh. If the sheriff did come back and found a butchered deer, he could launch a poaching investigation.

Cliff worked quickly. He took each quarter further back into the woods and hid it up in the crotch of a piñon tree.

Cliff checked the site, making sure he had left no footprints. He took one last look around before collecting the hide, head and tallow scraps and heading back to the dwelling.

He would hang all the meat in the new room that he had finished building on the end of the dwelling. It wasn't fancy, but it matched the original building and it had a door. The weather was cold enough that he would not have to process the meat immediately. It could hang there until he finished with the corn and potatoes.

~~~

The sheriff's department pickup drove slowly along the county road. The deputy scanned the barrow pits and right of way on either side for the body of the reported doe. The deputy drove to the Stone residence and knew he had gone too far. The report said the deer collision had occurred about a mile below Stone's place. He had seen nothing yet. The key word was "about" a mile. That could cover a lot of territory.

The report was probably reliable coming from a Ridge resident. The caller said he had a bent fender and bumper to take care of because of the collision. The caller had thought the deer was probably in or near the barrow pit on the south side of the road. The deputy guessed that probably the impact had only injured the doe and she had dragged herself off to die. The coyotes, crows, magpies and buzzards would take care of this one. He sure wasn't going to go off looking for it.

He turned around in the Stone's driveway and picking up speed headed on down the county road toward Cortez.
~~~

66
Potatoes and Apples
Kelley Farm

"We can probably live without potatoes, but not apples Moonbeam," Cliff said. "You have never tasted an apple have you? You haven't lived until you've sunk your teeth into a sweet delicious apple and let the juice run down your chin. It will taste so much better than those grasshoppers and mice you eat," Cliff laughed.

Either potatoes or apples will keep all winter if we do it right. I'm going to need something to offset all the dried food I'm going to be eating. The problem is how to get to them. The potato patch and the apple orchard are very close to the house. If anyone is at home, it'll be impossible to visit either the potato patch or orchard during the day without the chance of discovery.

Cliff had lost track of what day of the week it was from nearly the beginning of his stay at the ruin. It could take days and there was the chance of discovery finding a time when both parents were gone.

He looked out the doorway. *It's going to get cold again tonight. It seems to get a little colder every night.*

That morning when he stood on the rim and looked up and down the canyon, he was aware that Mother Nature had visited the canyon with her paintbrush. The relatively drab green piñon and cedar, turquoise sage, tans, grays, browns, umbers and rust colored sandstone and scree were now spotted with bright splashes of red oak groves, brilliant yellow cottonwood tree and willows leaves.

It had been clear and bright out the night before; bright enough that he had filled a gunnysack with full pinto bean husks bursting as dropped them into the sack. They were from the swath at the foot of the bean field where he had gathered husks during the day. He had still been able to see the creek in the bottom of the canyon and details on the slopes when he got home sometime in the middle of the night.

It occurred to Cliff that he was becoming like the denizens of the canyon. It was more comfortable and safe to use the night when he could see and hole up during the day.

Maybe the moonlight is the solution. I have a better chance of digging potatoes and picking apples by the moonlight. I doubt that Dad has replaced Towser. He didn't care about the dog that much anyway. Towser didn't recognize me the last time I was back there, he was so old and feeble. I doubt made it through the summer. Even if he did, old Towser's so deaf and blind he won't bark and wake Mom and Dad. I can be in and out of there long enough to pick a few apples and dig a few potatoes without their knowing.

Several varieties of apples grew in Ed's tidy orchard; red delicious; winter banana, which didn't really get sweet until they had been in storage for awhile, usually about mid-winter; Jonathan; and McIntosh. Cliff liked the taste of the red delicious, but they didn't keep well without getting mushy. The Jonathan, McIntosh and winter banana kept very well.

Cliff waited until the moon bathed the canyon before setting out. It was a mile walk from the snag to the set of gates separating the fields and the farmhouse yard containing the equipment sheds, house, garden and orchard.

The potato patch was on the field side of a fenced lane that gave the livestock unsupervised access from the barnyard to the timbered pasture behind the house. The potato patch was directly across the lane from the garden.

The orchard was located between the garden and the back of the equipment sheds and machine parking.

Cliff kept the equipment shed between him and the house until he could check for lights. All the windows were dark. His parents were usually in bed asleep by 9 or 10 p.m.

He tasted a Jonathan apple. It was tart-sweet and came away from the tree easily when he tugged on it. On the ground were apples that had already fallen. They were still good, but they wouldn't keep as well, because when they fall from the tree, they bruised and would soon rot.

Etta Mae would pick up the best of those apples and make applesauce from them. Before she finished canning, applesauce would fill almost one full shelf in the cellar. She would give away most of the good apples to neighbors and gather up the apples she didn't use and give them to the hogs.

Cliff filled the gunnysack nearly half-full of ripe Jonathan apples and stopped. He left it under the tree while he went to the row of McIntosh and tasted one. It was sweet and crisp. He filled a sack to half full. He could carry a full sack of apples but it would be awkward to carry a full sack from there to the dwelling. It was easier to carry two half sacks to evenly distribute the weight. He tied the ears together on each side of the tops of the sacks and kneeled down between them. He thrust his head between the two sacks so that a sack hung in front of his chest and the other down his back. With the weight evenly supported on his shoulders, he stood and headed out of the yard, through the gates and down the lane past Dog Town.

Cliff carried the heavy apples to the south fence, into the woods and left the sacks, still tied together, hanging over a branch as high off the ground as he could reach.

There were other of Mother Nature's critters out there that liked apples and potatoes who would enjoy filling stomachs with an unexpected find in the middle of the night if they could reach them.

During the summer, Etta Mae had begun digging immature "new" potatoes, as she needed them, to mix with English peas, a favorite dish for the hired hands during haying season. Since September, she had dug mature potatoes, one hill at a time as a vine began to wilt. Her scattered digs throughout the patch would disappear when Ed would plow the field, turning the red tubers up so they could quickly picked them out off the top of the ground and sacked for transport to the market or to the cellar.

Cliff had often accompanied his mom when she went to the potato patch for her daily needs after the potatoes were essentially mature. Her method was to pull the vine and pull off the potatoes that clung to the roots. Half of the potatoes from each vine remained in the ground. She knew when Ed plowed the whole patch the rest would be harvested. She didn't need to take the time to dig them. But she put the tops down to mark the hill so that if Ed was concerned that gophers were working the patch or something, all he had to do was walk over to the blank and check. Often that hill was next to a hill where she had dug out a few "new" potatoes back in midsummer without disturbing the vine itself. She had left those vines to continue feeding the remaining potatoes still attached to the roots of the vine.

Cliff checked the moon. He had several hours of moonlight left. He went to the granary and "borrowed" six more used gunnysacks. If he didn't use them all, he would have them at the dwelling for other uses.

With the digging knife, he loosened the dirt around the dead vines, which Etta Mae had pulled. A dozen or more large red potatoes and several smaller ones remained in the ground at each mound.

At each hill he dug, after removing the spuds, he replaced the soil and left the dead vine that Etta Mae had pulled on top of the soil. He hoped it would not be apparent that anyone had visited the patch besides his mom. He dug until two sacks were each about a quarter full. A full sack of potatoes was supposed to weigh 100 pounds. He thought he could carry 50 pounds of potatoes, about a half sack, a half mile to the woods each trip, especially if he balanced the load. He was sure that the apples had weighed that much or a little more.

Cliff tied the sacks together as he had the apples, put them over his shoulders and headed back down the lane toward the woods. He hung the potatoes on the branch next to the apples.

He rested for a while, snacked on a ball of raw pemmican and drank from a jar of water that he had left under the tree earlier that night.

He made one trip back that night while there was still light, this time to the equipment shed. Once he entered the shed, it was pitch dark out of the moonlight. He couldn't turn on a light. The boards merely butted against each other, and at night when the light was on, it lit up. The shed was visible from his parent's bedroom window and if lights came on, they would wake up. He felt his way around the tractor, benches, and tools that Ed had left where he had used them last, until he reached the cabinet in the corner where he stored his beekeeping supplies.

Cliff located the latch and opened the double doors. If Ed had not gone into the cabinet and re-arranged it, he could locate what he wanted in the dark. He felt along the top shelf for the smoker to orient himself. It was not there. Slowly he moved his hand along the shelf and stopped at a jar. He lifted it. It was heavy. He usually didn't keep honey on that shelf. So Ed must have moved things around. *Why did he do that? Has he moved my things out and is using it for something else now? I wonder if he gave it all away, or sold it all.* He continued blindly inspecting the shelf but found nothing but jars. He moved down to a lower shelf and there felt the smoker and other beekeeping tools.

His hand finally touched a round, waxy surface. He reached for it with both hands and ran them over and around a large round cake of wax. He carefully closed his hands around the two years accumulation of melted beeswax from his hives of bees and clutched it to his breast as he latched the door and picked his way back out the shed into the moonlight.

Cliff walked directly back to the ruin with the cake of wax. He pulled the rope up and tied the end to the cake, lowered it and used the rope to walk down the face of the cliff. He seldom climbed down with the assist of the rope anymore. However, tonight he was so tired, he wasn't sure he could climb down without it.

Cliff was exhausted when he stepped through the doorway into the dwelling. He thought about resting for an hour and returning for the potatoes and apples. But, he lay down and was asleep instantly. He brought the apples and potatoes to the cave early the next morning and stashed them.

He returned that night and made enough trips from the patch to the woods to fill one full gunnysack full of potatoes and one full gunnysack of winter-banana apples, which wouldn't be good to eat until mid-winter. He had not made a noticeable difference in either the potato patch or the apple orchard. Each potato vine pulled by Etta Mae had still yielded such a quantity of potatoes that it had not taken that many hills to fill his sacks.

As Cliff approached the snag with the last two partial sacks of apples over his shoulders, he didn't feel guilty for having taken them. He didn't feel as if he had stolen them.

I helped set out the young trees in the orchard. Together, Dad and I staked the orchard so every tree would be exactly the same distance apart in every direction. That way we could maintain them with the tractor by disking in any direction. Any direction made a row. I always thought it a miracle that when I walked along the end of the orchard the rows changed as I walked along.

Together we pruned the trees during the winter, hauled the branches off and burned them in the spring. When I got old enough to drive the tractor, I got to keep the soil beneath the trees worked up and free of grass and weeds. I learned to irrigate by being in charge of watering the trees regularly.

During part of the summers, when I was younger, I sat in those trees, especially the cherry trees, shooting at the robins, first with the bb gun to keep them away until Charlie or Mom could pick the ripe fruit. Then I graduated to the .22 with birdshot. That's where I learned to shoot straight. There were whole flocks of robins and blue jays wanting those pie cherries and big sweet cherries.

That is my orchard too.

It was also my idea to locate the potato patch where it is. That was a big patch of bindweed and thistles and I went to work on it with a hoe and 2-4-D, cleaned it out, plowed it up enough times and built it up until it would make a good potato patch. That is my potato patch too. I worked for it.

Cliff thought of the times he had cut sprays of blossoms and made flower arrangements for the dinner table. After he had captured the bee swarm and put his hive under the apple trees, he had watched the vast increase in the bee activity in the blossoms and had noted the additional fruit the trees bore.

He had even learned to separate out early apple, pear and cherry blossom honey from the little orchard from the later, stronger, clover honey. The fruit nectar honey in the comb had been one of his dad's absolute favorite treats.

When Cliff had first tasted the honey from the bee tree at the dwelling, he realized that the honey was from the tamarack growing along the creek in the canyon. It was very localized and his bees at the house didn't gather enough nectar from that source to make an impression. He had put a square of comb aside to share with his dad.

I remember dad's expression the first time he bit into a new comb of honey from my first hive. A smile had creased Cliff's face. *I really miss my dad.* He had thought.

~~~

It was still light and Cliff could see plainly by the time he got the second night's sacks back to the snag. He stood on the lip of the rimrock preparing to climb over the side. He realized that he had felt no fear the past two nights. He again lowered himself over the rim into the dark shadows in the canyon.

The dark had truly ceased to be his enemy. He had had no nightmares in weeks. The sounds of insects, birds and animals had long before ceased to be terrifying to him while he was safely in the cave. Now he felt that he had overcome his fear of the dark outside the protective walls of the dwelling as well.
~~~

67
Presence
Kelley Farm

"I felt his presence last night Daddy," Etta Mae said. She and Ed sat at the breakfast table sharing their coffee before he left for work.

"I woke up and I couldn't go back to sleep. I couldn't hear or see nothing, but I felt him near. I got up and went to the window. The moon was out. It was almost as bright as day. The La Plata's were bright with fresh snow. I looked to see if he was out there. I couldn't see him, but I could feel him. I know he was out there. A mother can feel these things." She took a sip of coffee.

Ed thought she looked more calm and relaxed than she had any time since Cliff's disappearance. "What did you feel?"

"I felt that he wanted to reach out to us, but didn't know how. But, most of all, I felt he was OK. I felt he was stronger. I felt like he would come back sometime in his own good time. When I looked out across toward the mountains, do you know what image came to my mind? I pictured him arranging a spray of apple blossoms into a flower arrangement for the dinner table."

"Today I think I'll make apple sauce. I think those Jonathans are nice and ripe. You want apple pie with your supper Ed? Why don't you bring home some ice-cream?"

"We haven't had ice-cream all summer, have we Etta Mae."

"No, we haven't. It hasn't felt right."

"Is there any of that comb honey in the cupboard I could have with this last biscuit?"

68
Corn
Kelley Farm

Cliff had gathered all the pinto bean husks from the vines growing in the weeds and grass by the time the combine and tractor pulling it ground the vines into the dust. As Cliff had predicted the "volunteer vines" in the turn swath was a waste product. They could only be harvested by hand, which he had done.

Every year shortly after the pinto bean harvest, a neighbor or two knocked on the door and asked if they could glean the harvested bean field. They were given free access to the field and the neighbor, usually a mother and several children, would descend on the field with buckets. They were looking for spots where the combine had stopped.

If the combine stopped to clear a clog, empty the hopper, or for any other reason that caused the combine to stop for a few minutes while still running, a mound of dirt, chaff, ground leaves, and beans would build on the ground beneath the combine. The combine would move on and the mound stayed. It was not worth the combine's crew trying to rake through the mound to salvage the beans spilled there.

The gleaners raked through these piles, their nimble fingers plucked the good beans out, into their buckets and by the end of a patch, they could have several three-gallon buckets full of beans. The beans were large and hard and the birds left them alone. Any left would be plowed under when the fields were worked later, either that fall or the next spring.

Cliff knew that the combine usually stopped at the end of rows to empty the hopper when possible so he looked for the mounds of spilled beans there and salvaged what he found. He left the rest of the field for the usual gleaners.

~~~

Clifton made a trip to the cornfield the night after visiting the apple orchard. The night before, he had detoured past the field to check it out. At least half the remaining stalks were bent over nearly to the ground. His dad and mom had already begun harvesting the ears. They would harvest a few rows each evening after Ed got home from town. Ed only had a short time each day before dark now, so he would do most of his farming on the weekend. It would take one more weekend to finish the cornfield.

By the remaining moon light, it was hard to find the ears that his dad had missed. Ed had taken the full, well-formed ears. After all the crops were in, the cows would be turned in on the fields and they would graze on any partially filled out ears and nubbins they could find before eating the stalks. Whatever was left of the stalks would be plowed under the first
~~~

thing in the spring.

The nubbins were what Clifton sought. Each stunted ear produced fewer than half the number of kernels of a normal ear of corn. At least the kernels were the same size and had the same food value.

He walked down one row of bent over stalks.

His bare legs were cold and the dry stalks scratched his legs. He had to make leg coverings soon. He had the hide now to make the kind of leggings he wanted from the road kill deer, but he had to tan the hide first. That would have to wait until he had the corn in.

Ed had picked most corn stalks clean, but enough stalks had half-formed ears that Clifton's gunnysack slowly began to fill. He could take anything left on the bent over stalks now that Ed had picked them. He tested only the first few to see if they had enough fully formed kernels to be worthwhile before he pulled the ears and dropped them into the sack without inspection.

For the time he had remaining light, Cliff managed to half fill a gunnysack five times with the nubbins and haul them to the nearby dry land woods where he emptied it under a tree. When he finished that night, he carried a sack home with him. He would return for the rest of the ears early the next morning, hopefully before the birds discovered them. They were a sorry yield for the work and bulk. The same quantity of ears, had they been full ears of corn would have yielded a bushel or so of kernels. He doubted if all these nubbin ears would much more than fill the Dutch oven.

He wasn't going to have enough corn. One good ear of corn would equal three or four or more of the nubbins.

The good part of it was the fuel that the cobs would provide. None of it would go to waste.

He had gleaned over the portion of the field that his dad had picked. He would return to glean more after Ed picked the rest of the patch. The rest of the field would be easier if he picked it in daylight. But, it would be too risky. *I think Dad is picking the best of the nubbins too. He usually doesn't do that. He usually lets the cows clean that up.*

He could pick the standing stalks because he could conceal himself better within the rows as he worked. But it would also be obvious to his dad if suddenly there were no small ears when he picked the rest of the field. There was less moonlight each night. The cows could be into the field before the next three quarter moon arrived.

It was a dilemma. Finally, he decided that he would go back to the cornfield during the daytime, probably at dawn, and take the chance that his dad wouldn't notice the absence of half-filled ears. *I'm going to have to beat him to the best of the half filled ears or I'm going to have to take a few of the full ears. Otherwise, I'm going to be short of corn. I was depending on having enough corn this winter. If I'm alert, I shouldn't be spotted in this field. Dad will be leaving for work. Mom will be busy in the kitchen or finishing the chores. Hector is back in school. There is no reason for Raul to be coming around.*

69
George
Martinez Canyon

George did not give up the idea that Clifton might be nearby. He had visited the canyon on numerous occasions looking for clues. He had not seen anything definitive. He had looked closely at willow groves and cattail stands. Over time, he recorded changes, such as holes in the willow stands where on a previous trip only one willow or two were missing.

He studied the plant life as the season changed. Occasionally he found clover plants with stripped stems where there should be blossoms. Deer didn't eat only the bloom, did they? He searched his considerable knowledge for an animal or bird with an affinity to clover blossom that stripped the blossom only.

He did not discuss his findings with Ed, although they visited occasionally, even though they both were busy with their harvests. He didn't want to get his friend's hopes up over suspicions, only to have them dashed when he couldn't confirm his suspicions.

On this October morning, George took his binoculars to the point near the Indian tower ruin. He studied the canyon floor and slopes as far as he could see from there to the first bend in the canyon.

After awhile he moved along the south rim, stopped and studied the canyon with his binoculars. He saw nothing out of place. Wildlife went on grazing, hunting, burrowing, flitting about or diving on their prey. It was not what he would expect if man walked among them.

George moved past the next bend, the deepest part of the canyon, and again lifted the glass to his eyes. He sat down with his back against a piñon for support, pulled his legs up so that he could rest his elbows on them to steady the binoculars.

It was a beautiful spot in the canyon. Scrub oak painted the lower wall of the canyon side crimson red. Along the meandering creek, willows and cottonwood were dropping yellow leaves. The creek barely ran at this time of year with irrigation ditches dry. A trickle of water from natural seeps kept pools full in the dry time such as this. It was chilly even though the sun shone. *It feels like winter is coming. Glad I wore my jacket today. Sure is pretty down there. Glad I came this way to see that. Should have brought my camera.*

I may as well head home. Maybe after one more look down the canyon. It was a valid idea, but I just don't have enough evidence. Oh well, it hasn't been a waste of time. I always have time to see Mother Nature at her best. You've outdone yourself this time Old Gal.

Out of the corner of his eye he saw movement near the creek in the bottom of the canyon. He turned and stared at the spot and, after a few moments, thought it had been nothing but the flash of a bird wing.

George holstered the binoculars, prepared to stand and go a ways further down the rim. More movement riveted his attention to a spot on the canyon floor. He felt for the binoculars without taking his eye off the spot. He slowly brought the high power binoculars to his eyes and aimed at the spot. His heart beat rapidly. Standing in the shade of a tree about twenty feet from the creek was a man. His black hair, held back out of his eyes with a headband, fell almost to his shoulder. He was bare except for a plain leather or cloth breechcloth and moccasins. He wore a brown knapsack on his back.

In the man's hand was some kind of stick or spear and he was apparently stalking something. Suddenly the arm and hand moved in a blur almost too fast to see as they arched upward and forward and a flash arched forward. George moved the binoculars to see where the hunter had thrown.

Next to the stream was a rabbit with a spear pinning it to the ground.

George was puzzled that, after the man had thrown, he still held a short stick in his hand. Was it to aid in throwing the spear?

George moved the glass back to the man who moved forward quickly to take the rabbit by the neck while he removed the spear. Then he broke the struggling rabbit's neck. George watched as the man hung the rabbit from a shrub and cut the skin around the neck. Then he clipped the feet and pulled the skin backward, leaving a naked rabbit body. He hung the skin over a branch and quickly slit the belly and removed the entrails, stripped them and rinsed them in the creek. He pulled grass from the creek bank and stuffed it into the knapsack and placed the rabbit on the green grass.

The man lay down by a small clump of young willows and cut one stem off under water. Without stripping the bark or thin branches he bent it into a U and pulled the rabbit skin over it, skin side out. When he released both ends of the willow, they stretched the skin tightly. The man placed the stretched skin into the knapsack with the rabbit.

George studied the man intently. He was small and slim. Was he a man or a boy? It had been a little over five months since Clifton's disappearance. Would his hair have grown so much? He thought back to his own boys at that age. He had cut their hair regularly once a month and yes, if either of his boys' hair had been let go, it would be at least that long.

The man kneeled by the creek and washed his hands. Suddenly he looked up and slowly scanned the south slope of the canyon and then shaded his eyes and scanned the rim until he paused. He seemed to stare directly into George's binoculars.

George was sure he couldn't be seen by naked eye from that distance, because he was in the shadow of the tree. He sat still holding the binoculars on the man's face. It was Clifton. There was no doubt about it. George studied Clifton's face. His cheeks were full, his legs had filled out some. There was a healthy glow about him. He was obviously not starving or in poor condition, from what George could see.

How is he staying warm down there? He's been gone, what...May...October...nearly six months..., he counted on his fingers. *It looks like he's grown some. I'll bet his shoes and clothes don't fit him anymore. Where did that outfit come from? He killed that rabbit sure as shootin'. Could he kill a deer? I can't believe he could do that. But I don't know...*

George watched with curiosity as Clifton dropped his intense stare and lifted the rabbit from the knapsack and one by one faced the four cardinal directions and then motioned to the heavens above and the earth below. His lips were moving as he performed the ritual.

George heard, "Yak, yak, yak, yak, mag, mag," directly above him and a magpie launched out of the tree that George sat under. The long tailed black and white bird circled the tree, sailed into the canyon and landed on Clifton's shoulder. "Yak, yak, yak, yak, mag, mag," echoed up from the canyon. The two seemed to speak to each other.

George almost shouted down to his young friend, and then thought better of it. He might frighten him. He should race home and tell Ed about his discovery.

The boy put the knapsack back over his shoulders and with the magpie riding on his shoulder he turned and walked down the trail by the creek, turned a corner and was out of sight.

He has to be living nearby. George scanned the north slope looking for caves under the rimrock. He saw none. *Is it important? The boy has obviously devised and mastered a successful hunting device, and he is making clothing. He seems to be thriving. The look on his face was direct and alert. The timid, unsure look seems to be gone. He walked proudly with his shoulders back and his back erect. If I hadn't seen his face, I would not have known it was my young friend.*

I can't interfere here now. The boy is OK. That's what matters. If I tell Ed, he will be down here beating every bush until he either finds Clifton or chases him off. I think I should try to keep an eye on him from time to time and leave him alone.

Although George had decided to leave Clifton alone for now, it still nagged at him that Clifton might be going into winter without warm clothing to wear.

I think there are still winter clothes in my son's closet. If I left a bag of them here what would his reaction be? Would he accept them and take them back to where ever he is staying? Would it scare him and make him go somewhere else. He looks good, but I don't know his frame of mind. If I left him clothes, should I leave a note with them?

If I bring clothes back, I'll have to tell Loretta. It would kill her not to tell Etta Mae. I don't think Etta Mae could stand to know that her boy is living this close to home and not go to him. On the other hand, it would lift a huge load off her shoulders to know he is all right.

George hurried home. He had made up his mind and changed it numerous times. When he walked into the house, he picked up the phone and put it down before the operator answered. He went to the kitchen where Loretta removed gleaming jars from the pressure cooker.

"There's a bowl of peaches in the cooler," she said. "Seemed a shame to can the whole basket. They are especially sweet this year. The produce manager at City Market said this is the last of the McElmo peaches this year. Where you been all afternoon. I was about to call the Sheriff and have him send a posse out looking for you," she chuckled.

"Down in the canyon looking around," George said looking in the cooler. "You get ice?"

"Already put in. You see anything down there today?" She asked.

"There still a closet full of winter clothes up in Scott's closet?" He asked, avoiding her question.

"Yea, we keep a full set up there for when he comes home on the holidays. It'll be snowing then. And, there's still some up there that he's outgrown. I've been thinking of taking a bag full to town for one of the churches to give away. It's getting colder these nights. Why are you asking?"

"Just wondering. It's only a month before Scott comes home for Thanksgiving. Ned will probably bring along what he needs."

"About all Ned will need is to get to town to see Marilyn," laughed Loretta. "You still didn't say what you found in the canyon today," she pressed. She studied his face intently as she asked. He wasn't telling her something. He had found something. Well if he was going to keep it from her, he had another think coming.

70

Initial Contact
George Williamson's residence

Dear Clifton,

I believe I observed you hunting down by the creek yesterday. Obviously if you are this close to home and have been for nearly six months now, you are not ready to come home. That is your business and your folks'. I don't know how ready you are for winter. If I am meddling, then forgive me. I do it with only my very best of intentions.

This bag contains clothes that Scott has outgrown. If you can use them, you are welcome to them. If you don't need them, then you may do what you want with them.

If you are living in this canyon and we get a deep snow, it can get pretty dangerous down there. Remember our conversations on how the aboriginals communicated. I will watch this part of the canyon every day this winter. If I see smoke that seems to be any kind of a signal, I will investigate.

You are on your own as long as you want to be. If you need my help in any way or want to talk, you signal me somehow, or you know where I live. Unfortunately I don't know where you live.

Your Friend always.

George Williamson

P. S. I miss you my friend, and I know I speak for your Mother and Father who miss you and are ready to take you back, no questions asked, any time.

~~~

George carried the sack of clothes wrapped in a water proofed tarpaulin down the canyon to the spot where he had seen Clifton the day before and hung the bag from a rope about six feet off the ground from a cottonwood tree branch. He tied the rope back to the trunk. It would be easy for Clifton to untie it and get it down, but more difficult for an animal to get the bag down and destroy the contents.

Within the bag were warm jeans, flannel shirts, mittens, cap, lace up boots and overshoes. Scott was a bigger boy at 15 than Clifton, but not so much so that the clothing wouldn't be warm and serviceable if he chose to use them.

George looked around the area. He shook his head. There was no sign at all that Clifton had been there the day before. He even wondered if he was in the right spot. He checked the south rim with the binoculars and was certain that he saw the tree that he had sat under. He scanned the north rim looking for any shadow that might be a cave, or wisp of smoke from a fire. There was nothing to indicate the presence of a ruin or a place where anyone might have hidden out over the summer.

He turned and made his way back up the trail by the barely trickling brook.

~~~

From the cover of thick scrub oak, Cliff looked out at George retreating up the creek. He had been halfway down the canyon trail when George came into view a few minutes before. He had dropped to the ground and frozen in place. He watched George walk on down around the bend. When George was out of sight, Cliff hurriedly descended the trail to the scrub oak and noiselessly followed George down the canyon until George stopped and hung a bag in the tree and left back the way he had come.

Cliff had not been so close to another human in months. He waited for a few minutes until George was gone before he approached the bag.

Is this some kind of trap? If I touch this, will it yank me up in the air just like I caught the turkey? George wouldn't do that. What was he up to? That was him up there yesterday then. I knew it. He's trying to tell me something.

OK George let's see what you've got for me. I'll see whether it's worth taking home.

~~~

It took nearly an hour for George to circle back to the tower ruin and down the south rim to the spot where he had spotted Cliff the day before. He trained the binoculars on the tree. The bag was gone.

I will have to assume it was you who took it Clifton. Now the next move is yours.

71
Annex
Summit Ridge

It began like a ghost roaming the canyon in the night with a light snow dusting over the plateau. It soon turned steady. Large flakes silently draped the landscape in pure white.

Cliff awoke that morning to a steady snowfall. He had prepared all summer for the arrival of winter. But, he felt a moment of panic. It was way too early. Had he prepared well enough? Had he brought in enough wood? He had wanted to gather much more.

He surveyed his winter preparations. He had stockpiled wood and kindling. He also had a pile of corncobs and husks, piñon cones, and bean pods for fuel and kindling.

The baskets were full of corn, wheat and barley; beans; piñon nuts; sunflower, sagebrush, clover, and grass seeds. A basket of dried yucca root chips would provide for his shampoo and soap. Dandelion and clover root had been parched and stored for tea. Sacks of potatoes and baskets of fresh dandelion roots, if they kept, would serve as vegetables. Baskets of apples would provide him fresh fruit all winter if he could keep them from rotting. Other baskets were full of jerky and pemmican. He had three quart jars full of honey. Beeswax candles hung by their wicks from a peg on the wall.

In preparation for winter, Cliff had added another small room to the left end of the dwelling. Perhaps original inhabitants had used the open portion of the cave for wood storage. Perhaps the space had awaited another family or families to build there, or they had left it open for a future *kiva*. On the other hand, maybe a larger room would have been impossible to heat.

He had roofed the annex in the same manner as the original dwelling with poles, four pieces of deadfall branches, across the ceiling to hold up a layer of brush thatch then canyon clay. The poles also served as hangers. His roof poles weren't as neatly cut and trimmed as the ones in the dwelling. They were dead branches he had hauled in, originally for firewood. He had fitted a stone axe with a handle and used it sparingly to remove
~~~

side branches. He did not try to chop down trees or chop up firewood past rudimentary breaking up chunks of wood. It was a laborious process, so he tried to find wood already in sizes that required no further sizing.

The doorway was just wide enough to step through and tall enough to put a leg through and duck under.

Cliff had constructed a door from the butt ends of willows and lashed them together with rawhide to make a strong door against any marauding creature that might visit. He hinged it with bailing wire. The latch was also bailing wire taken off a fence post on his dad's fence line.

With no heat in the room, it would remain cold, tempered by the almost constant temperature of the cliff stone. He intended to shovel snow inside to compact into ice if necessary to counter any warmth from the sun shining on the face of the room during the low slanting days of winter. He had stacked the room with firewood, leaving room above to hang meat if it became available.

The addition would also serve as a protected cold storage room if he could bring down an additional deer if he decided to go after one. Temperatures were below freezing every night. He had hung the road kill doe in there and it was cold enough that he had not had to dry any of it. He was cutting off slices of meat, as he needed it. Depending on the year and temperatures, his dad did the same thing when he got a deer at the end of season after cold winter set in.

The new room blended with the ancient wall as he plastered over the front side with mud from the canyon slope, as had the original builder of the main dwelling.

72
Leggings
Martinez Canyon

Winter had begun early, and if this continued, it would be unusually harsh. Successively deeper snowfalls followed the early snowfall. Colder temperatures and wind that blew in from the desert and high plains, accompanied the storms. He would need all the protection he could get from wind and moisture when he went outside.

The yearling hide taken in the summer together with the road kill doe hide at the beginning of hunting season should produce enough buckskin finally to make a complete set of leggings.

Cliff finished tanning the hide, a task made much harder than in the summer when he worked in the warm sunshine out on the ledge. He had no other place to soak the hide to loosen the hair than the natural tub in the rock on the ledge. He carried warm water through the snow to the pit and partially filled it, added ashes and folded in the hide. Then he added more warm water to finish filling the pit. To keep the pit from freezing over, he rotated warm rocks to the pit every few hours throughout the day during the soaking period. When it came time to scrape the hide, he took it to the dwelling and worked on the floor near the fire pit.

To make the hides waterproof he smoked them together. The smoking also turned both of them from a raw cream color to a rich golden brown. They could get wet or even soaked, but they would dry soft.

Cliff had begun his self-imposed exile in the cliff dwelling over six months before with two changes of clothing. He had worn out both sets. The two pair of worn out bib overalls now hung worn on a peg on the wall.

Cliff had begged his mother to buy him regular jeans held up with a belt, such as the Mexican boys wore, instead of the loose fitting overalls held up with suspenders. When he went to town with his parents, only a few of the other farm boys his age wore them. He suspected that was because they were tough, cheap, and it took a long time to outgrow. It was the sure uniform of boys living out on the farms. Even Hector wore jeans held up with a belt.

The overalls with deep side and back pockets, and bib pockets had proven invaluable to him during the summer as he gathered food in the canyon. Now one of the worn out pair would serve a last function as a pattern for a pair of leggings.

Maggie and Moonbeam were curious and he almost expected Maggie to tell him how to proceed. They watched Cliff measure his leg against the leg of the outgrown garment and mark the difference in length on a willow stick. Cliff put on the overalls. His waist and leg size had not changed much and the cut of the garment was roomy. The main adjustment was the length.

Cliff spread the pair of overalls on the floor and Moonbeam promptly lay down on them and curled up. "That is not a new bed for you girl," Cliff laughed. "We have some work to do here. Why don't you come over here by the fire and make yourself comfortable." Cliff lifted his little friend and moved her over to the warming blanket. Moonbeam left the comfort of the warming blanket and returned to his place next to Maggie to supervise the operation.

Cliff removed the bib by ripping the seam that held the bib at the waist in front and cut the braces off the back.

He then unbuttoned the fly and ripped the seam down to the crotch and up the backside splitting the right leg from the left. Then he slit each pant leg down the seam on the inside of the legs. This gave him patterns for both a right and a left legging.

Cliff studied the hides. They did not lie flat like a piece of woven cloth. The worn overall cloth had stretched and had warped much like the hide. He arranged the right pattern on the road-kill doe hide first to follow the natural shape of the hide. The hide naturally wanted to fold over the back of the deer. He placed the fold at the inside of the leg over the natural fold on the hide. The lacing and fringe, if he chose, would be on the outside of the leg.

He allowed for the inches he had grown in height, added two inches to the width an inch overlap on the outside of the leg for lacing the leather together where it met after folding around his leg. He traced around the pattern with charcoal.

He also had to allow room for another garment to be worn beneath the legging such as the rabbit pelt leggings he had made in the fall or the jeans that George had left in the bundle of clothes.

A faint pattern drawn in charcoal was still visible for the left leg on the yearling hide. Cliff had taken measurements from the overalls when he had originally tanned the hide and realized he didn't have enough leather for a full set of leggings. At the time, he had drawn that pattern he still wore the overalls and could not afford to tear a pair apart He placed the left overall pattern cloth over the drawing and compared how close he had come in his original drawing. It would have worked. He made a few adjustments.

After checking the two the patterns on the leather, Cliff made a cup of tea and studied them. He folded each around his legs testing whether they were roomy enough and if there was room to lace them together. He couldn't afford to make a mistake. He made adjustments in each pattern to make them match.

When it seemed that all measurements were correct and adjusted, he put on the rabbit skin leggings and folded the buckskin over his leg again. If it really got cold, he could layer the rabbit skin under the buckskin. It would be like wearing heavy long underwear.

Among the pack of clothes that George had left were several pair of Levi jeans. He selected a pair and pulled them on. He rolled up the cuffs to the right length and wrapped the right legging hide around his leg again to test it for fit. It was the tight enough to keep out a draft, but not too tight to restrict movement.

He made slight adjustments, punched a thin hole at the top of the seam line he had drawn and at the bottom and tied the buckskin around his leg with sinew to test the fit one final time before cutting it.

The slightly adjusted pattern would work. He held his breath and began to cut the leather.

He cut one edge of the pattern straight to within an inch of the marks for the lacing. He left the opposite edge raw. That would be the outside of the legging and the edge could be finished in fringe if he chose, or it could be space to make allowance for growth or mistakes.

Cliff used a bone awl to punch holes a half inch apart along a seam line that followed the seam in the denim pattern.

He chose buckskin lacing to fasten the legging together rather than sinew. The thin sinew was strong enough, but he was afraid it would cut the leather. The leather smelled good, whereas the sinew smelled foul when it got wet.

He used a sharp edged piece of flint to slice lace from the straight edge of the buckskin scrap. After he laced the legging together, he trimmed the flap on the front edge, leaving it wide enough for a fringe or adjustment later.

He had added three inches to the top of the pattern to fold over and lace. This created a loop through which he could string his belt to hold the leggings and breechcloth up.

When he was satisfied that the fit was good, Cliff repeated the process for the left legging.

When both leggings were finished, he put them on over only his breechcloth and bare legs. He put on his fur coat and moccasins and stepped outside into a cold, blowing winter day. Snow whipped down the canyon on an icy wind. He put his hands in the coat pocket.

Cliff had used one of the denim shirts for spare cloth to patch the sleeves and tattered areas on the better one. He wore the shirt tucked down beneath his belt. The coat hung to mid thigh on his legs sealing his torso from cold air.

If that doesn't work, I guess I'll have to fall back the on the pair of jeans George left me. They'll protect my 'family jewels' as he calls them, and be warm under the leggings. I'd like to make do without using them, but it would be an easy way out, if I need to go out and it gets really cold or storming bad.

He had enough pelts and leather left to make a head covering and mittens. In another day, he would be ready for whatever the elements wanted to throw at him.

He felt good that he was ready to face whatever the Colorado winter wanted to throw at him. *Thank you George. I think I'll begin wearing my first pair of Levi's.*

73
Warming Table
Martinez Canyon

As winter descended on the plateau known as the Ridge, cold became the enemy. Every night the icy cold air flowed down the slopes of the snow-clad La Plata Mountains, seeking the lowest levels, the canyons, river basins and draws to flow westward toward Cortez and on around Towac at the south end of Ute Mountain and McElmo Canyon on the north end. On sunny winter days, the air warmed in the lower warmer climes of Arizona lifted and circled back to the La Plata Mountains in the east to be cooled and returned that night to the lower lands.

Cliff leaned back in his willow back support. He laughingly referred to it as his chair, although it had no legs. His feet were warm under the table with the blanket tucked around his waist. Maggie sat in front of him waiting for a scrap.

On clear sunny days, Maggie accompanied Cliff when he went outside. The bird made short flights out into the snowy landscape, but he seemed glad to return to the warmth of the cave.

As Cliff worked, or when he took breaks from his work, he coached Maggie. He taught him new vocabulary words, and practiced him through all the words that the bird knew fluently. The magpie picked up new words and phrases amazingly fast, and he imitated Cliff's voice perfectly. By winter, the young magpie knew enough phrases that they could hold a conversation of sorts, whether the bird understood the meaning of the words and phrases or not. It didn't really matter. He had an uncanny way of imitating yet substituting. Cliff thought sometimes the bird understood very well by his choice of phrases.

A conversation with the magpie would go something like:

"Hello Maggie."

"Hello Clifton."

"How's it going?"

"Fine, thank you."

"Maggie, where's Moonbeam?"

"Out to lunch."

"Is Moonbeam pretty?"

"No, pretty Maggie, pretty Maggie!"

"You're so silly!"

"Silly Maggie, silly Maggie!"

Cliff talked to the bird constantly, and the bird was a good listener. Cliff discussed his ideas and thoughts and in the process of brainstorming without argument from the black and white bird that only occasionally interrupted with a word that he carefully imitated, Cliff began to understand himself better. He began to add new concepts and to discard old ideas, many of which stopped re-occurring in his nightmares after awhile.

Life was good for the moment.

~~~

As the weather cooled, Cliff had soon learned that it would be impossible to keep the cave warm. He couldn't overcome the base temperature of the stone that made up the cave and walls as it began to cool. He could heat the air, but the drain on his wood supply would deplete it long before winter was over.

As he had dwelled on this problem, memory of a letter from his brother to his mother began to make sense. PFC Charlie Kelley had described a Japanese warming table.

Detailed letters from Charlie stationed in Japan were full of the exotic customs on the far off island nation. One of the curiosities he had described was a heating table the Japanese called the *kotatsu. "These people are the cleverest people on earth Mom,"* Charlie had written, *"They take a coffee table and sink a charcoal burner in the middle of it. Then they cut a hole in a blanket to fit around the burner, and put it over the table and let it drape over the floor all around. The heat from the charcoal burner is captured under the table. The family sits on cushions with their legs under the table and they pull the blanket up around their waist. They wear a happy coat to keep their upper body warm. On top of the blanket that covers the table, they put a hard removable top, with a hole cut out for the charcoal burner. They use that as their kitchen table to eat on in winter. When they aren't eating, it's their study table. In winter, it's the center of the family activity. They heat water for their tea on the charcoal burner and even make soup on it while they keep warm. I love it."*

The warming blanket was made of burlap sacks. Cliff had taken six of them apart, laid them flat and sewn three together to make the top, three for the bottom. He had sewn them together on three sides and filled them with a three-inch layer of twisted and crushed cedar bark for insulation. He sewed the fourth side together and quilted it with the six-inch burlap bag needle and jute twine. He imitated his mother who quilted by tying her quilt tops, batting and backing together with a grid of hand tied knots about a hand's width apart. The colorful yarn contrasted with the colors with the pattern on the quilt.

He built a square frame table of willows and elevated it on legs at each corner. It was just tall enough that Cliff could put his legs under it and use the top as a work surface. The table was about two feet by two feet square.

Inside one corner of the table, he built a pocket framework that hung suspended beneath the surface of the table. It would support two or three of the round river rocks that had been in the fire pit when he moved in.

Cliff used rocks for the heating element by heating the river rock and placing them in the pocket, then covering the whole table with his burlap-warming blanket. work surface was placed on top of that. The heated stones were hot to the touch, but not hot enough to cause a fire. The blanket hung to the floor and trapped a pocket of warm air beneath the table
~~~

just as Charlie had said. Cliff could slide his legs under the table, and as Charlie said, work or eat and keep warm. With his lower body warm, it wasn't difficult to heat his upper body with the rabbit skin coat.

When the stones cooled, he slid the top to the side, lifted the corner of the blanket back just far enough to reach in, take out the rocks and replace the blanket to keep the heat from escaping. He put the stones in the coals of the fire, removed hot stones from the coals and dropped them into the cage in the warming table, replaced the blanket and top.

He didn't have to keep the fire burning nearly as hot to keep warm. He wasn't heating the air in the entire cave. The warming table conserved fuel and the cooler temperature in the cave better preserved the foods stored in the baskets. Charlie's letters complained about the Japanese custom of not heat their houses and how cold they were.

There were enough round stones available in the fire pit to have half of them heating while the other half radiated heat under the burlap blanket. It took a very small fire to keep the stones heated. The same small fire kept the cooking stone hot so he had hot water for tea or washing and he could simmer beans all day or cook in the Dutch oven.

It was uncomfortable to spend long hours sitting on the hard floor with his legs stretched straight out in front of him with his back unsupported so Cliff built a chair with a willow framework. He soaked dry willow stalks for several days in the overflow until the wood was wet enough to bend as he heated them. When he had the willow bent into a shape he wanted, he tied the stalk with rawhide to hold that shape until it was completely dry. It took two willow stalks to form the complete frame back and seat of a chair. Shaping the willow, cut during the summer, was a skill he had learned while struggling to straighten willow blanks for spears. It was a matter of soaking the wood, heating it and cooling it.

The wood was tough and it took patience to make it conform to the shapes he wanted, but in the end, he prevailed. He had to soak heat and bend, let dry and cool, soak, heat and bend. When he was finished, he had the crude shape of the seat and back of a chair. He bound the ends of the willows together where they met, and he wove the webbing for the seat and back out of yucca cording.

He bound two lengths of willow to the bottom of the seat framework on each side to elevate it off the floor a couple of inches, so he would not be sitting directly on the hard floor. He smiled contentedly when he sat down with his back supported when he leaned back.

When the chair was finished, he placed it facing the warming table. He sat down, punched his feet and legs under the table, pulled the blanket around his waist and relaxed. He was warm. He had his two friends to keep him company. He was content.

He wove the tabletop of cattail stalks strung between willow frames. It was rigid enough to support the loom, or hold his knife and needles while he carved or wove baskets, and it served as a dining table.

Moonbeam loved the warming table. She either curled on top of the blanket or snuggled half under an edge and slept through most of the days. Maggie spent his days standing around the table or hopping around the floor near it. Just as in the Japanese homes that Charlie had described in his letters, the warming table very quickly became the center of activity for the three.

Maggie hopped down from the table and pecked at the sleeping Moonbeam until she was awake enough to play tag around the ruin.

Cliff watched them and laughed at their antics.

He looked over at the note on the corner of the table and picked it up. He had read it over and over. *George knows I'm here and has left an offering. He signed it "My good friend" and "Your friend always." He has offered a way out as a negotiator. But, he won't have to be the one to live with the consequences. And, what about the curious last part about Mom and Dad ready to take me back with no questions asked? Dad might not ask, but can he forget? Can he change?*

I've changed. I can't live with Dad the same way we did before. I don't think that Dad could live with that. If I live under his roof, then I am at his command. I don't think that I can be a partner with him. If I make a mistake, then I think he will resort to the same kind of punishment he always has. I'm not ready to accept that anymore. I know that George didn't raise Scott that way. I asked Scott.

But, it is nice to know that if I'm hurt, and I can make a fire, I can signal him. I should probably let him know I got his package.

74

Second Deer Hunt
On the trail outside Martinez Canyon

Cliff wavered about going after a second deer. He wasn't sure he needed to. The road kill deer had provided meat that he hadn't expected. A hide was his priority, and the fresh meat was a bonus. He wouldn't let it go to waste.

This animal too would be illegal only in the sense that he had no way to purchase a five-dollar license, which would entitle him to tag two deer; a doe and a buck or two bucks. At least he didn't think season was over. He thought season lasted clear into November down here in the foothills.

He had fixed flint points to four of the darts. They were ancient but were as lethal as the steel broad head points modern bow hunters used. The indigenous people of the area made the knapped points, as Cliff had been unable to master knapping points for himself. For that, he had come to realize, he needed a teacher.

~~~

Cliff had discovered fist sized nodules of flint during his first explora-
~~~

tion of the canyon. Over the summer, he had collected a number of them from pools in the creek. It was the same material the Ancestral Puebloans of the canyon had used to make their projectile points.

A pile of chips from the same kind of stone remained on the roof of the dwelling where, Cliff assumed, the warrior/hunter had once knapped points for his own hunting weapons. Edges on the fragments were as razor sharp 700 years later as the day when they were flaked off a nodule or finished point.

Throughout the summer, Cliff had attempted to learn how to reduce the nodules into blanks that he could knap into spearheads.

The scrapbook had only one very sketchy article on flint knapping. It was virtually useless and he gave up trying to understand it after reducing one of the nodules to a useless collection of shards, and acquiring an angry gash in the palm of his hand.

He had finally produced a rough thumb sized piece from one the shards that looked like a double edge serrated knife blade. The edges were razor sharp. It might have been about right if he were putting a point on the end of a shovel handle or something. It was too clumsy to mount on a dart.

Even though he had not produced a usable point, he soon had a collection of exceptionally sharp edges that he could use for carving, cutting leather and scraping.

~~~

This time he would go for a mature animal. He had gained enough confidence in his hunting skill and ability to process the meat of a larger animal from his first kill and in processing the two road kill deer. The game trail, which in the summer was a minor path for the small resident herd, had become a temporary major arterial for the migratory herds that visited the area hay fields and then continued their journey across the canyon and on out across the wooded area south of the canyon to Mesa Verde.

He could use the same perch in the piñon tree he had used before. He had tested the narrow platform, and it was still solid.

~~~

The morning of the hunt, he awoke to a steady snowfall. Big swirling flakes obscured the opposite side of the canyon. He almost abandoned the hunt that he had prepared for over several days. Then he convinced himself, it was now or never.

Cliff donned warm rabbit fur moccasins and over them a pair of buckskin moccasins. He put on the Levi jeans, and buckskin leggings, threaded his belt through the hoops to hold them all in place and tied the jeans over the top of the moccasins. Last, he put on the rabbit fur coat.

He rolled the burlap sacks and tucked them into the knapsack on his back. Finally, he hung a buckskin quiver that held the atlatl, spears and darts over his neck. He picked up several coils of homemade rope, the rope George had used to hang the offering of clothes from the cottonwood and stepped out of the dwelling into the cold silent snowstorm.

This hunt probably wasn't extremely important to his ability to stay in the canyon as far as meat was concerned, but the early winter could mean a really long hard winter and the extra meat could be important. If he were successful, he would have one more hide. He could use the hide for all kinds of things.

First, he checked the hand and toe holds that were his usual climb out of the canyon. They were damp but no snow had accumulated in them so far. At the first sign of snowfall, he had fastened the long rope to the snag and let it hang down the cliff in front of the toeholds. The rope was his safety line to the top of the cliff face when it got icy, and he still used the rope to lower loads down to the ledge, although in fair weather he never left the rope hanging from the snag. He put on his old worn work gloves, took hold of the rope and climbed out.

This snow may change everything. I don't know if it will be helpful or not. However, it will make it really hard to hide tracks in the snow bringing the meat home. The deer will be on the move all day. I guess I'll have more than one opportunity. He set out for the deer trail and the stand.

Fresh tracks led down the trail into the canyon. A steaming patch of snow on the trail let him know a small group of deer had passed that way only a few minutes before.

Cliff climbed into the tree. He had fitted four spears with flint point darts. He fitted a spear to the atlatl and waited. This would be only the second time he would use a precious stone head on a dart. His first deer kill had also been with a flint spearhead. *Maybe it will be good luck.*

Cliff did not have a long wait. He leaned against the tree looking back up the trail. The varicolored rabbit coat blended with the bark of the tree, and he hoped it masked his scent. A string of does and yearlings appeared as grey ghosts and then were more clearly defined plodding along through the now densely falling snow.

Cliff very slowly and deliberately turned against the trunk to face down the trail so the deer would pass below him. He raised the atlatl to the aiming position slowly as he moved into position. The deer would emerge below him and move forward toward the gap, which the snowfall now obscured.

He wanted one of the big older does or a full size buck. As with the yearling, he would aim at the area behind the right shoulder in hopes of sending the dart through both lungs. If he could collapse the lungs, the animal would go down. It would literally suffocate on the spot.

The head of one of the largest does emerged through the snow below him and passed on to the right of the tree. He waited until she was twenty feet forward. He tipped forward on his left foot and thrust his right arm forward rapidly with all the power he had, and with a snap of his wrist he let fly.

The doe saw the movement and leaped. The spear glanced harmlessly off the side of her front shoulder as the doe dodged and leaped into the air. The herd bounded toward the canyon disappearing into the veil of snow leaving the hapless hunter alone in the tree with the snow swirling around him. Cliff scrambled from the piñon and retrieved his spear. It looked no worse for the wear. He removed the dart and replaced it in his holder.

What am I doing out here? I should be back at the dwelling hunkered in. I don't need this. He retrieved his knapsack and turned toward home.

It was snowing so hard he could hardly follow his tracks on the way back to the dwelling. He could only see a few feet in front of him. It was dark and he felt closed in. He felt a touch of panic. It would be very easy to lose his sense of direction. *What if I can't find my way back?* He stopped. If he strayed to the north, he should run into the Kelley south fence. If he went too far west, he should come across the county road. If he strayed too far south, he should find the canyon. However, the road turned, he could go west for miles without hitting a road. Hitting the fence was only a half-mile opportunity. He looked back at the white covered ground for his tracks and could no longer see where he had come from the ruin.

Cliff began walking again. He avoided looking directly into the snow but looked at the ground ahead as far as he could see it. He had to know if he neared the rimrock. He moved slowly and looked behind him and the tracks trying to determine if he was walking straight or not. *I think I'm doing OK. I'm going back to the ruin. The canyon is to my left. I need to turn slightly to my left.* He consciously turned slightly to the left and looked behind to see that his trail did actually turn. *I've been walking long enough to be nearly there. Why haven't I come out at the rim already?* Cliff made a deliberate quarter of a turn and very slowly began walking. He constantly scanned 180 degrees, turning his head slowly trying to penetrate the snow as far out as he could. In places, the trees came quite close to the edge of the rim. In others such as at the snag, the distance to the nearest tree was fairly wide. He had walked only a short distance before he realized he was out of the trees. He froze. He looked behind him. He walked backward in his tracks until he saw a tree to his right and then to his left.

The canyon had to be in front of him. He turned to his right, walked to the next tree and walked to the left of the tree. There were no more trees south of it. He was very near the rimrock.

Was he down canyon from the snag or still up canyon from it? How could he tell? When it was clear he knew all of the trees in the immediate vicinity of the snag. Now they were all ghosts. He wasn't sure he could identify them in bright sunshine covered in snow.

Cliff looked at the piñon he had just passed. He moved over to it and tested the mound that had grown around the perimeter of the lower branches. He ducked under and slid down the well to the area next to the trunk. In the dim light, he could see a wall of snow around him and a canopy of green and snow above. Snow from earlier snows had sloughed off the branches and accumulated around the base of the tree creating a well that was a natural shelter from the storm. I'll wait here until it clears enough for me to see where I am. I could get lost out there or stumble over the edge into the canyon if I don't watch it.

~~~

Cliff awoke. It was silent. He looked around and for a moment, he did not know where he was. In front of him was the trunk of a piñon tree. All around him was white with bits of green needles and twigs.

He turned over, stretched to the branch above him and dug beneath it. The snow was hard and crusty. He pulled out the hunting knife, dug through and finally could see gray outside. The snow had slowed and it was lighter. He dug a hole large enough to crawl through.

Cliff slogged forward through snow nearly to his waist to the canyon rim and looked out across to the other side trying to get his bearings. He was slightly past the snag. He retraced his tracks to the timber, turned to the right and walked back to the east. There was no trace of the tracks he had made earlier that day. Not more than a hundred yards east, between the piñon's, he saw the snag.

Like it or not he saw little choice but to walk out of the timber and descend the rope. If someone cruised the rim, he or she might wonder about it. *No use making it too easy for them.* He walked to the snag as though he had walked out of the timber to look at the canyon. He walked down the rim twenty feet, stopped and looked out at the canyon and walked back into the timber. Then he stepped back into the same footprints he had left coming from the west. He followed in the same footprints to the point where he had walked out of the timber to the snag, walked back to the snag and climbed down the rope. If he had any hope of getting out of the canyon during the winter, the rope had to stay. He had to live with that, even if it meant discovery.

~~~

George and Scott kept a steady pace on the snow shoes across their pasture, removed the shoes to climb through the fence, stepped back on the shoes, fastened them and continued down the draw toward Martinez Canyon.

"So you saw Clifton down here only once all summer Dad?"

"I actually saw him once back in early October. I went through that canyon probably once a week all summer. I charted every willow grove and cattail stand for some clue that he was cutting down in there. I was sure that he was, but he was darned sneaky about it. Problem was the deer. They graze on the willows too and they walk through stuff, and so it's not as if every broken bush had to be by Clifton's hands. I also noticed an extra ordinary amount of yellow clover with the blossoms stripped. When I told Loretta about it, she immediately said, 'He's making tea out of the clover blossoms!' That's the one clue he didn't hide. He didn't cut the clover blossom stem off when he stripped off blossoms."

"So what are we looking for today?" Scott asked.

"I'm not sure. It's treacherous down in the cañon with the snow. I'm curious if the deer have beaten a trail out of there yet. I'm wondering if he's moving around down in there. I wonder if he's leaving a trail. I keep a lookout everyday for signals of distress. I have to have faith that he's OK and that if he needs help he'll put up some smoke. It's his choice that he's down there somewhere."

"I can kind of understand that," Scott said. "We got along pretty well. He told me some things about the way things were at school and the way Bob Harris's boy Larry teased him. It was bad enough when Charlie was around and even worse when Charlie wasn't around. I told Larry to knock it off, and that if I heard Clifton complain any more, I'd call Sherriff Kirkendall, but I don't know if it helped. I think Clifton was a good kid, but I worried about him. I liked that he could talk to you. I think he looked up to you."

They walked along in silence, their snowshoes making the only sound swishing along in the snow on the south bank of Martinez Canyon. They stopped near the spot where George had observed his young friend in the fall. George removed his backpack and from that a thermos. He poured hot coffee for his son and a cup for himself. He handed the glasses to Scott.

"He was down about one o'clock on the bottom of the canyon. I've figured out since then that he had made an atlatl and was using it to throw a spear. He killed a rabbit with it, so apparently he had learned to use it. He was wearing a breechcloth that looked like leather. I'm sure he wasn't wearing it when he walked away from home. See anything down there?"

"There are tracks along the creek, but they look like deer tracks from here."

"Look along the slope in both directions and see if you see any black streaks in the new snow that might be caused by smoke."

"Why do you think he would necessarily be on that side of the canyon?"

"If he's in a cliff dwelling, I think it would be built on the side of the canyon where the farms were. I don't think the Indians farmed this area from here to the highway. I know that whole area between this canyon and Lost Canyon is covered with evidence of farming during that era. The Cliff dwellers skillfully used the sun, and when they could, they located ruins to face the south to catch the winter sun. All the ruins I know of are on the south bank in this canyon."

The two men, father and son, ate a sandwich, put their cups and thermos away, shouldered the pack and began their journey home. They were comfortable with each other.

"We got time to walk the north rim?"

"We can go a ways, but Mom is waiting for us back before too late."

George missed his sons while they were away at the University and relished the visits home for the holidays. Quiet walks, talks, and the knowledge that they had the foundation to meet life head-on regardless what it might be.

They snow shoed the South rim to within 500 yards of the cedar snag with the frozen rope tied to its base before turning back heading for the camaraderie and warmth of home, family and Thanksgiving dinner.

75
Thanksgiving, Cortez
Martinez Canyon

Ed and Etta Mae Kelley left the house after the chores were finished and navigated the freshly plowed, washboard county road to Cortez where Bill Kirkendall and his wife Shirley warmly greeted them..

Shirley, a tall attractive woman, took the basket containing the mincemeat pie fresh from Etta Mae's oven that morning, and greeted their guests warmly. "Etta Mae Kelley, come in this house. I've been anxious to meet you for a long time. I've heard so much about you from Bill. Come on in the kitchen. I've got the coffee ready. We can have a cup, and we can get caught up while the men go to the living room and keep out from under foot," she laughed.

Etta Mae was a little shy at meeting strangers at first, but she warmed up to the Sherriff's wife immediately.

Bill took their coats and hung them in the entry closet as the women disappeared down the hall.

"Etta Mae, Bill had a piece of your mincemeat pie up at your place last summer. He came home just raving about it. He said it was nothing like mine. He would rather I not bother with mine, as a matter of fact. You want to share with me. Or is it a secret?"

"We'll it's nothing secret. I usually make up a pretty good batch at a time. Each year we butcher a couple of hogs. When we do, I take those two hogs heads and cook them in the pressure cooker, sometimes half a head at a time, depending on how big they are.

"Then I remove most of the fat; add about the same amount of cooked ground beef or venison if I've got it. I like to use venison best. I salt these when I cook them. To this, I add about half as much ground raw apples as I have meat, couple quarts of cherries, couple pounds boxes of raisins, and couple pounds of currents. I add cinnamon, nutmeg, cloves and allspice to taste and I have to admit I like the taste of cinnamon. Oh, and a small amount of vinegar and sugar, enough to suit my own taste. When all this is mixed together, I add enough water to keep it from sticking and cook it until the apples and raisins are tender.

"By now I've got about two big 16 quart canners full of mincemeat simmering on the stove. I can all that in quart jars. When I want a pie, I open a quart and place it in an unbaked pie shell, cover it with a crust and bake it at 425 degrees up on the Ridge. Down here you'd probably cook it the same temperature, until brown."

By the time Etta Mae had reached the halfway point in the recipe, Shirley was laughing. When Etta Mae finished, Shirley was nearly pounding on the table. "You don't even have that recipe written down, do you Etta Mae?"

"Well, I kinda do. Of course it changes a little each time depending on various things, like how big the hogs' heads are."

"My mom cooked like that," Shirley said. "She just had an instinct for what would work. And, sometimes it didn't work. But, most of the time that was the best grits we ever had. I'm dying to taste that pie."

"Nothin says you have to wait until after the turkey," Etta Mae said. The men will never know. And if they do know, if they know what's good for them, they'll keep it to themselves."

"Good idea, how about a little slice of that pie while we enjoy this coffee," Shirley said. She handed Etta Mae a kitchen knife and took down two saucers.

Bill and Ed sat in the front room. Ed looked around the room at various mounted heads of mule deer, elk and big horn sheep. "You have quite a collection there, Bill. There must be quite a story in that big horn. What did you use on it?"

"Come on I'll show you," Bill said. He ushered Ed toward his office where he kept his hunting rifles. "I want to thank you for bringing the fresh turkey for today's Thanksgiving dinner, Ed. It will be quite a treat. I understand you free range them on your farm..."

~~~

In Clifton's fourteen and a half year lifetime on Summit Ridge, never had so much snow accumulated so early in the winter.

His only calendar was the sun's position at sunrise and sunset: more precisely sunrise. That morning the sun rose through the gap between the southern end of the La Plata Range and the eastern end of Mesa Verde. In a few more days, it would reach its most southerly extension at Winter Solstice. It had to be around the end of November or early December.

Are my parents getting ready to gather with friends for Thanksgiving? Or is it already over?

"What do you think Maggie? Should we have a Thanksgiving dinner? I could make you a piñon nut pie. Moonbeam, how about bobbing for apple cores? Don't you think that would be fun? All three of us have many things to be thankful for."

Maggie flew across the room, landed on Clifton's shoulder and pecked at his ear playfully. Then the glossy black and white bird stretched around Cliff's face and looked into his man friend's eye, "Man friend got treats?"
~~~

he asked.

Clifton laughed and held out his hand for the long tailed bird to hop onto. He placed the bird down on the floor next to the fat black and white skunk who playfully swished her tail at the bird then hopped stiff legged across the room followed by the playful magpie.

Cliff never tired of watching the bird and animal at play. Cliff sat with his legs tucked under the warming table. He pulled the burlap blanket up around his waist. He picked up the piece of crooked red cedar from which he had been carving a spoon with a handle that arched gracefully up and away from the bowl of the spoon into the long necked head and beak of a bird like Maggie. He held it up and examined it and realized what made the magpie distinctive was the tail not the neck and beak. This spoon more resembled a duck or heron. So much for art, he thought. He finished smoothing the bowl of the spoon and set it aside.

Thanksgiving dinner isn't a bad idea. I have plenty to be thankful for. If the first thanksgivings were to celebrate a successful harvest then it would be appropriate. My harvest has been successful. So far, none of what I harvested has gone to waste. So far, I have survived against a few odds in seven months of solitude. I also am thankful that I did not wait for Hector down there by the road. Now my conscience is clear. This hard work here in the cañon is a lot better than breaking rock on a chain gang or sitting in a cold cement cell somewhere, and I'm thankful for that. I could go home today if I wanted to. If I had killed Hector, I couldn't. I'm thankful for that.

I don't think much about him anymore. At least he doesn't scare me anymore. He may be bigger than me, but that tree out there full of bees is bigger than me too. I didn't show them fear, and they cooperated with me. I think I can stand beside him now and not show fear, and I am thankful for that.

I haven't had a nightmare for a long time.

Look at all this. I did this. No, I didn't do all this. I wouldn't have stayed and done this without you, Maggie and Moonbeam. Oh, yea, you my Indian friend. I know you are out there watching and listening. You told me to keep working until I was ready. I know I'm not ready yet. I couldn't have done it without you, Dad. You taught me how to do a lot of this, and you, Mom. You taught me a lot of this too. George you made me question and think about the Great Spirit and Mother Nature and think about how they fit in with Dad's God. I'm thankful for that.

Mother Nature you sent me the bobcat and your little creatures for friends and to eat.

I have so much to be thankful for. I'm not afraid of the dark anymore. Charlie, you've lost your grip on me at last. Now I can concentrate on the things that I learned from you that were good. Maybe I can start forgetting about the bad

I am most thankful also that the headaches seem to have gone away!

"Come on Moonbeam and Maggie, I declare this Thanksgiving Day! We are going to have a feast!" Cliff said excitedly.

Moonbeam and Maggie ceased their play at Cliff's outburst, ambled, hopped respectively over to the warming table and looked up at Cliff expectantly. Usually such an outburst from their human friend meant treats.

He turned back the warming blanket, pulled his bare legs out from under the table and stood.

He stepped into the Levi jeans and tied the belt. He put on the buckskin leggings, fastened the belt through the loops and tied it, put on and laced his coat, pulled on buckskin moccasins, rabbit skin cap and mittens and stepped outside.

Snow swirled around the front of the dwelling and the wind moaned down the canyon. He checked the rope hanging down from the snag. He had anchored the trailing end with a heavy stone it to keep it from blowing out of reach. Ice coated the rope. He whipped it against the face of the cliff and ice broke loose, but he doubted that he could climb it right then because of the ice that still clung to it.

Cliff undid the door to the annex storage room and cut a lightly frozen venison steak from a hindquarter.

He re-entered the dwelling, kept the coat on but shucked out of the leggings, mittens, and cap. It wasn't freezing inside the cave, but it was far from warm out from under the comfort of the warming table.

He put the steak on a clean flat stone near the fire to thaw while he assembled ingredients into a basket: a sliced potato, a handful of shelled piñon nuts, a sliced apple, a handful of soaked corn kernels, and a half cup of soaked pinto beans.

The Dutch oven had been heating next to the fire with coals on the lid. He removed the lid, dropped a chunk of deer tallow into the bottom of the oven and smeared the bottom, and then he dropped the steak in, seared both sides and turned it with a wooden fork. He added water and the sliced potatoes. He ground aromatic dried sagebrush leaves between his fingers, scattered them over the meat and potatoes and added the piñon nuts. Every morning when he got up he put that day's beans to soak. That morning he had also put corn on to soak. He added both beans and corn to the pot.

He replaced the cover on the Dutch oven, refreshed the coals on the lid and left it to simmer.

While he waited for the meat and beans to cook, he resumed carving a small figure of a skunk out of red cedar.

Later in the afternoon, but earlier than they usually ate their supper meal, Cliff began preparing the Thanksgiving dinner.

On the metate, he cracked sunflower seeds and raked away the husks. He added wheat, corn, sage seeds and a mixture of grass seeds and ground the mixture. In a carved cedar bowl, he mixed the coarse meal with water, honey until it was dough, and then spread the dough on the flat stone next to the fire that he used for baking.

The only guide he had for how long to cook anything was texture, taste and logic. If the meat was tender and the vegetables were soft, it must be done.

Cliff tested the steak with the wooden fork and hunting knife. He let it simmer until the usually dry venison was moist and tender. The potatoes were soft and just the way his mother served them.

Cliff cut the venison into small pieces in the Dutch oven and filled the carved bowl, which now doubled as a serving dish, and set it on the warming table.

The warming table was multipurpose and served as work and dining table. The cattail mat protected the blanket on table. The table was elegantly set. A crude beeswax candle in a small clay pot burned brightly in the center of the table. Light was dim in the dwelling because the snowstorm made the day dark and gloomy outside and inside. He kept doorway closed to preserve the meager heat produced by the small fire. The only light coming into the dwelling was from the fresh air/smoke vents along the ceiling line. That outside light was so faint that the candle was the main source of light for the dinner.

The bed slats from the miner's cabin had served many purposes over the months. One now became a table for his friends. He served up bits of cooked potato, venison steak, kernels of cracked corn for Maggie and boiled corn for Moonbeam, pinto beans and raw potato peel for them both.

Moonbeam and Maggie dug in with gusto, sampling everything on the pine board as Clifton watched in amusement.

He smelled the sweet aroma of the red cedar bowl that he held cupped in his left hand. In his right hand, he held the magpie-faced spoon that he had finished carving that morning.

He looked across the fire to the *Sipapu*. It seemed to shimmer in the firelight and to call to him to offer thanks before he ate.

"Heavenly Father and Mother Nature," he began. "We have gathered here to celebrate this Thanksgiving Day. You seem to have combined your forces to help me to survive by bringing me together with your children, this beautiful mammal and this intelligent bird. They are my friends in this lonely place. You sent me nightmares and headaches to test me and for me to conquer. You are teaching me how to stand on my own. You are teaching me that I need to be strong to survive.

"Heavenly Father and Mother Nature, thank you for sending us the food that we are about to eat. I pray that you have provided as abundantly for my father and mother. Please sooth their hearts and help them to understand that in some way, someday, I will make up for the anguish that I have caused them, and I will make them proud, and one day soon, I will give them hope."

He didn't know how to end his recitation, and so he hesitated and then finished, "In the name of everyone Heavenly and earthly who is responsible for this wonderful world and this wonderful life, Amen." He stopped and saluted his two friends who had hesitated politely in their eating while he talked.

He tasted his food, and it was better than good. It was wonderful.

76
After the Storm
Martinez Canyon

The storm finally broke and the sun rose in the gap where Mancos Canyon cut through a gap between foothills and the east end of Mesa Verde. When the sun's orb touched the Mesa it would be the beginning of winter.

Snow lay deep everywhere he looked. Big fluffy blankets clung to trees. Layers outlined the ledges on the canyon walls. Piñon trees were layered; cedar trees were mounded; sagebrushes were bumps in the snow. Everything was dazzling white. Except for on the face and lip of the rimrock, snow wouldn't melt until spring.

As soon as the sun came out and hit the edge of the rim snow began to melt. Water dripped over the face of the cliff. Ice-cycles formed in cracks where water had trickled and dripped after the first snow.

At mid-day, the sun was only a few degrees high over Mesa Verde and the rays shone directly on the face of the ruin at full force, although dappled in some places by the evergreen cedar. That warmth radiated heat into the cave during the day and continued to some slight extent during the night. The face of the cliff, the rope and toeholds warmed even more because they were not in the shadow of the cedar. The ice melted out of the toeholds and the rope dried a little. He estimated that he might be able to climb out on top by mid-day.

As Cliff had hoped, by noon the rope, hand and toeholds were clear.

Without the rope, Cliff could not climb out even though the toeholds were clear. When he reached the lip, he still had to fight the accumulation of snow before he could stand on top. The rope gave him something to hold onto as he struggled to break through the front of the snow pack.

Eventually the heat from the direct sun on the edge of the snowpack would cause the front edge of the snow to break off and fall into the canyon. Along most of the canyon, it fell and slid or tumbled across ledges, stopped or created small slides that rolled or slid on toward the canyon floor. In the area of the dwelling, the ledge caught much of the snow that slid off, and it added a layer on top of the snowfall accumulation on the front of the ledge.

Fortunately, the dwelling was set back from the front of the cave far enough that little snow reached the doorway. The small avalanche of snow landed eight feet forward of the dwelling wall, so the effect was to create a barrier of snow between the dwelling and the canyon. Cliff had no snow removal tools, but except in the last few feet to the rope, he didn't need it.

The remaining front edge of the snow on the rimrock would melt back gradually until he had room to crawl over the front edge of the rimrock and stand. At that time, he could climb the face of the cliff without the rope as long as the toeholds were clear. In the meantime, with the rope attached to the snag, he could break through the snow barrier and escape without having to wait for several days or weeks of sunshine to melt it back from the edge.

He debated whether to go any further than the rim. *If I make a trail out from here, anyone who flies over or walks by will be able to see it. Surely, no one is still out looking for me. I doubt that anyone is wandering around in this much snow.*

His curiosity won out.

It was a changed landscape above. He had not been out since the latest storm had begun nearly a week before. The top layer of new snow was over a foot deep. Beneath that was the frozen surface of an older snow fall that had packed, melted a little and frozen. Each layer had packed, the surface crust had frozen, and the accumulation continued with each snowfall. He estimated a total snowpack in places of nearly four feet. Drifts in the open were even deeper.

The pits around large piñon and cedar trees had completely closed. The wells, like the one he had taken shelter in after the failed deer hunt, were deeper after the snow sloughed off the trees.

The snow from earlier snowstorms had melted back a few feet from the cliff edge in both directions, and he could walk in the shallower snow, but it was very dangerous that near the edge of the cliff. The chance of slipping over the edge was too great. He looked back at his trail. When he returned to the ruin, he would come from the opposite direction so that the trail would seem to follow the cliff. In a few days, if the weather stayed clear the new snow should melt away from the lip of the rimrock again and he could follow the rim without leaving sign.

He walked in a direct line to the nearest timber.

The top ice layer, a foot below the surface of the new snow, held his weight. As he entered the woods, he found a multitude of tracks made by birds, mice, rabbits, a large cat and coyotes.

It would be a hard winter on Mother Nature's creatures. If the cold and lack of food didn't get them, a predator surely would.

In winters past, he had actually caught rabbits barehanded in snow conditions such as this. The trick was to find a fresh track and follow it to the base of a sagebrush. If the trail went in and didn't come out, the bunny was resting or hiding in a hollow beneath the bush.

Cliff followed a fresh cottontail track to a low mound. The track disappeared into a natural tunnel beneath branches hidden under the snow. Cliff lay down in the snow and reached into the tunnel as far as he could with his bare hand until his fingers felt warm fur. His fingers closed on enough hide to get a firm grip, and he jerked the rabbit from the hole and grabbed it along the back with his other hand. The startled rabbit kicked and struggled but couldn't free itself from the boy's grasp.

Cliff pulled the rabbit under his arm and calmed it. Back at the dwelling, he had plenty of frozen meat hanging in the annex, and pemmican and jerky in the dwelling.

He wasn't hunting for food today. He had promised Mother Nature to take only what he needed to survive.

Cliff smoothed the rabbit's fur back and put it down on the snow next to the sagebrush expecting it to return to its shelter. He looked around. Other predators might be watching. If he turned it loose, and the rabbit dashed across open ground, it might be caught at an unfair advantage. At least he would have a chance to run for it. It was the rabbit's choice. He suddenly regretted disturbing the rabbit just to satisfy his curiosity.

"I'm sorry," he whispered. He turned the rabbit loose and started home.

77
Christmas
Martinez Canyon

The sun came up in the gap through which the Mancos River rounded the eastern end of Mesa Verde. It had risen there for several days and Clifton could detect no movement either further south or back toward the north as Earth paused for Winter Solstice. Christmas had arrived.

A package rested in a cornice of the nook in the wall. The wrapping was yucca fiber woven on the Navaho loom. Woven into the design were skunk and deer hairs, rabbit fur and magpie feathers. The fabric was folded over a framework of thin, bent, willow shoots and tied in place with soft buckskin lacing. Inside the package were Cliff's best two carvings. Both were from red cedar knots. One was of a skunk and one was of a magpie.

For several days, he had debated about how to deliver them. He wanted to just walk up to the door and hand the package to his parents, but he didn't yet have the courage.

He needed an intermediary, but who could that be? He could trust no one. *Well I guess I can trust George, but I don't want to trouble him and maybe put him in the middle of something.*

He woke in the middle of the night unable to go back to sleep, his mind thinking about the package he had lovingly put together. He got up and walked to the doorway, moved the thick mat door aside and looked out over the snow berm on the edge of the ledge and across the canyon at the Milky Way lighted snowscape on the other side. The sky was so clear the Milky Way looked like the drifting clouds of a summer afternoon. *I wonder how many millions of suns they represent and if any of them have earths like the one I'm standing on circling them. Was it a night this clear that stirred the minds of shepherds 2000 years ago to search for a baby in a manger in the Holy Land?*

Just 10 nights before the moon had reflected on the new fallen snow nearly as bright as daylight. Tonight, so far, the moon was absent.

It would appear as a sliver sometime later during the night. Combined with the faint light of the Milky Way he could see well enough to get to the house and back, but it would make navigating more difficult. It came up a little earlier and a little brighter each night. He would try tomorrow night.

Cliff slept restlessly, awoke early and fixed breakfast for himself, Moonbeam and Maggie. It was still warm under the warming table. Cliff had begun spreading his sleeping mat with the lower half under the table at night. The stones held heat for several hours at a time with the added insulation above them. He got up each night around midnight to add a little wood to the fire and change the stones to get through to dawn.

He had few mandatory chores on the long winter days. He heated water, took his morning bath and washed his hair. He bathed moonbeam and put the wash pan of freshwater down for Maggie to bathe. He had encouraged the bird to bathe in the wash pan, from the day the bird was let out of the cage, to keep him out of the spring, and he had continued to use the pan as an adult bird. Cliff cleaned Maggie's roost and Moonbeam's litter and washed the morning dishes.

He checked his gift again and put it back in the nook. Tonight he would attempt to deliver it.

Cliff polished a red cedar carving of the replica of moonbeam that he had been working on for several days. He thought it might be his best work yet, or at least as good as the figure in the gift box. Moonbeam was very interested in the miniature of herself and studied the wooden likeness. Maggie pecked at the arched wooden tail and hopped back as if expecting the tail to suddenly arch higher and threaten to spray him. "What's the matter Maggie?" Cliff laughed.

"What's the matter Maggie?" Maggie imitated. "Clifton got treats?" Maggie asked.

"For you always," Cliff said. He reached into his pocket and pulled out a small piece of jerky and tossed it toward the magpie who caught it in the air.

The time passed slowly that day, and he was restless.

Finally the new moon rose. The cloudless sky was awash with the Milky Way. The thin crescent moon and Milky Way reflected off the snow and would give just enough light for Cliff to find his way to the house and back.

He closed the door cover, stirred the fire, added wood and finally dressed to go out. He had on his warm woven undershirt, rabbit skin coat and hood, buckskin leggings over Levi jeans, moccasins, rabbit fur under moccasins, and mittens. The cloudless sky meant it would get very cold that night.

The sun had been down for some time. It had to be the middle of the night. At that time of the night, there was not likely to be traffic on the road.

He climbed, bare handed, out over the top, put on his mittens and walked in tracks already in place to the nearest piñon tree. There he lifted the branches on the side facing the canyon and slid down into the well next to the trunk. Earlier in the day he had dug an escape hole on the opposite side. He wiggled through the hole and stood in the snow berm surrounding the tree, carefully turned to his left facing down canyon and walked just inside the tree line but keeping the canyon rim in sight. He walked until he judged he was about due south of Raul Rodriguez's place. There he turned to the north and walked on through to the road.

He came to the road west of the Rodriguez driveway and had to walk by it. The Rodriguez's dogs barked when he passed by, but they didn't come to investigate. He didn't know if the dogs would bother anyone walking by their place or not, but that night they huddled in the cold near the house.

Cliff walked up the road. The county kept it graded almost to the gravel. A remaining thin layer of snow had turned to ice as vehicles traveled over it. Chains were required for any vehicle that dared try to pull the long grade up to the Ridge and then navigate the many short grades out of swales, draws and canyons. The chains were very noisy, and he would have plenty of warning if anyone approached. He left no tracks on the hard icy surface.

He stopped when he crested the top of the ridge, at the southwest corner of the Kelley farm. In the distance, dim moonlight outlined the Kelley farmhouse and outbuildings. He continued up the road at a trot, constantly alert for the sound of traffic coming behind him or car lights coming toward him.

Cliff crossed the cattle guard and walked up the ruts of the familiar driveway. He stopped at the top of the slope even with the house. The windows were dark. He watched for movement and the sound of a dog. He was sure his dog had not survived the summer. No dog came to greet him. *Apparently, it is as I thought, they haven't replaced Old Towser. Why am I not surprised.* He walked on down to the equipment shed, staying in the car ruts, leaving no tracks.

Ed usually kept a tablet and pencil in the shed to make lists of parts needed when he worked on engines, or to write down new labor saving ideas or improvements.

Cliff turned on the light over the workbench. The tablet was right where his dad usually kept it. He removed a sheet of paper and began to write:

Dear Mom and Dad,

Merry Christmas. I am fine. Please don't worry about me. I am getting well in spirit, and I am healthy. I will come home to stay one day when you can be proud of me. Please accept these Christmas gifts for now.

Know that I love you.

Clifton

He folded the paper and slipped it beneath the buckskin lacing that bound the gift-wrapping in place. He replaced the tablet and pencil and turned off the light.

Cliff walked in car ruts to the path that led to the house, and then he followed the snow packed path to the back door. He stood for a moment in front of the familiar door. *I should knock and wake them. I'm sure the door isn't locked. I could walk in, crawl into my bed and have a hot breakfast tomorrow morning. Bacon, eggs, milk, maybe pancakes and warm syrup, butter, conversation, hugs... .*

He placed the package between the storm door and the backdoor, turned and retraced his steps to the driveway. He hurried down the driveway before he lost his nerve. Tears began to freeze to his cheeks. He crossed the cattle guard to the county road and trotted all the way back to the corner of the county road next to the Rodriguez driveway where he had intended to come out earlier. He cut off the road there and walked toward the canyon until he thought he was half way, and then turned east until he was sure he was past the snag.

In the distance, he could see ghostly image of Mesa Verde in the combined pale moonlight and Milky Way to give him his directions.

He walked to the edge of the timber and keeping the rim in view in the moonlight he walked west with a row of trees between him and the clear rimrock until he intersected his trail at the beginning point at the piñon tree. He wanted anyone following his trail from the road to assume that it was continuous from the road to the canyon and back to the road. Unless they had some reason to, they should not suspect that the trail had originated in the canyon and returned to the canyon. At least he hoped they would think so.

He ducked back through the hole under the piñon and exited out the other side. Carefully he walked back to the snag in the same tracks.

78
The Gift
The Kelley Farm

Morning dawned at the Kelley farm pretty much the same as any morning except that Ed did not have to go to work. He had a leisurely breakfast with his wife.

Christmas Day fell on Saturday that year. The shop had closed on Thursday to allow the employees Christmas Eve off. It would reopen on Monday. Business was slow but would pickup right after the first of the year as farmers began to schedule work to be ready for the first time they could get onto their fields for soil preparation in the spring.

The day before a long letter had arrived from Charlie. Charlie wrote wonderful letters about his Army life in Japan. It was as good a point in time as it went in the Army. The Korean War was in an Armistice stage. The troops were still a major presence on the base in Kyushu, Japan, but he had seen no action other than training, drills, weathering a typhoon, and wandering the countryside when he had leave.

Ed and Etta Mae did not celebrate Christmas. Their celebration was in the resurrection not the birth. To Ed the actual birth date and place were in dispute and had been set by the Roman Catholic Church to pacify pagan warship. The Christmas tree was a prime example. He had tolerated it when Cliff wanted a Christmas tree, but he had not participated in the celebration. There had been no fake Santa Claus at the Kelley household and no prancing reindeer, although Ed had secretly enjoyed listening to Etta Mae read the classic Clement Moore poem "The Night Before Christmas" to Clifton when he was a child.

They had used the season in a purely secular sense to keep their sons from feeling left out of the spirit of the season by ordering clothes and shoes, caps and mittens.

Each year Etta Mae dug into her box of handwritten recipes for popcorn balls, date roll, fruitcake and peanut brittle candy.

When Clifton had reached six years of age and he could handle a hatchet, he had declared he wanted a Christmas tree and had brought in a little piñon tree. He had decorated it with popcorn strings and hung crayon colored walnut shells glued together with a string in the center as the hanger.

From that time on, he had cut a piñon tree every year for a Christmas tree.

That morning no tree stood in the corner by the fireplace. Etta Mae had made peanut brittle and date roll.

She would present Ed with a new plaid shirt on Christmas morning.

It was winter and there was not much to do outside. He had the day to read, study the Bible and rest up. There was a jigsaw puzzle started on the end of the dining room table. He might be able to talk Etta Mae into a game of dominos later.

Etta Mae would lower the quilt frame and work on that for a while.

But now it was time to do the chores. Ed donned his heavy coat, overshoes, hat and gloves and opened the back door. An unusual looking wrapped package fell to his feet. The screen door was open. Something blocked it so that it wouldn't close. He looked to see the address and almost fainted when he opened the note stuck in the binding and saw the signature on the note.

Dear Mom and Dad,

Merry Christmas. I am fine. Please don't worry about me. I am getting well in spirit, and I am healthy. I will come home to stay one day when you can be proud of me. Please accept these Christmas gifts for now.

Know that I love you.

Clifton

He stumbled back into the house and cried hoarsely, "Etta Mae, it's Clifton! He's been back! He's....!"

"What? Where?" She cried.

"A gift! He left a gift!" Ed said excidedly.

"Where?"

"Here!" He gasped. "He left a gift on the steps."

"Are you sure it was him?" Etta Mae cried.

"There's a note. Look!"

Etta Mae read the note hurriedly. "That can't be Clifton," she said. "Is it a practical joke? How.....?"

"I don't know mamma!"

"Why don't you open it?" she said.

Ed carefully opened the wrapping. "What is this material Etta Mae?"

"It is some kind of fabric," Etta Mae had said, examining the weaving. "It's more like a tapestry of some kind."

"Oh my gosh! look at these!" Ed said. He placed the two carved objects on the table. The two figures were lifelike in their realism. The skunk and the magpie seemed to be looking up at an admirer with impish, expectant looks on their faces.

"Do you think Clifton carved these?" Etta Mae asked.

"I think he did," Ed said. "You know skunks and magpies were his two favorite creatures."

He turned the magpie over. On the base, carved in tiny letters was a phrase:

Clifton got treats?

Inscribed on the underside of the skunk figure base was:

Moonbeam,
Christmas 1954,
Clifton Kelley

Ed reached for Etta Mae and they held each other for a long time. "He's alive and well. It says so here in the note. Why do you think he didn't come in and stay, Papa?"

"I don't know. He must have his reasons. But thank the Lord he finally let us know."

"We've got to call the sheriff. He must be near. Maybe we can find him and bring him home!" Etta Mae said.

Ed was silent for a moment as he read and re-read the note. "No, I don't think we should do that. He says *'I will come home to stay one day when you can be proud of me.'* I don't know why he is saying that. Doesn't he know we've always been proud of him? But, he is promising to come home on his own terms in his own time. I think we should respect that," Ed said.

Etta Mae was surprised at Ed's suggestion. "But Daddy, I can't stand the idea that he is nearby and I can't see him and have him here with us!" Etta Mae said.

"I know, mamma, but he left for a reason and is obviously trying to work it out. If we go after him with the sheriff, assuming we could find him, and bring him home before he is ready, we may lose him for good," Ed said.

Etta Mae cried silently, holding herself as if in pain. She rocked back and forth. Finally she stopped, dried her eyes and said, "I guess you are right. If he has been safe all this time and is reaching out to us, then we must respect it. But I don't like it."

79
The Revelation
George Williamson's Farm

"We got a gift and note from Cliff, George," Ed told his neighbor. "I guess you were right all along. He has to be nearby."

"What did the note say, Ed?" George asked.

Ed repeated the message Cliff had left with the gift. "What do you think George?"

"What are you going to do?" George asked slowly.

"Etta Mae thinks I should call the sheriff and search again. We might find his tracks in the snow," Ed said.

"And what do you want to do Ed?"

"Well, I don't know. I think it might be a good thing to leave him be," Ed said. "I don't think he's ready to come home."

"Ed, there is something you should know," George said.

George turned and looked Ed in the face. Their eyes met. "I know where Clifton is," George began.

"You what? You're hiding him from me?" Ed asked incredulously.

"No! No! Nothing like that!" George hurriedly assured his angry friend and neighbor. "I would never do something like that behind your back. You know that."

"Then what...?"

"I kept going down Martinez Canyon looking for clues, and your son was very careful and clever about not leaving any. However, they were there if you knew what to look for. One day I watched the canyon with my binoculars, and I saw him. I followed him, with the binoculars, until he disappeared from my sight. I didn't see where he is living."

"How did he look George?" Ed asked.

"Well. He looked well. He looked great. He's growing and he's fleshing out some. His face looked healthy and alert. And Ed, he walked proudly. I watched him kill a rabbit with a spear! It was a deliberate and skilled throw. I think he was using an atlatl like the one in the museum at Mesa Verde. He wore moccasins and a coat of what appeared to be rabbit skins. He's turned into a real hunter!" George said. "I'd say he is living his dream of living off the canyon as the Indians did."

"Why didn't you tell me about this before?" Ed asked.

"Ed something serious caused that boy to leave. But, he didn't go far. He has a reason to be there. I was afraid if I told you, you might rush in to find him. If you involved the sheriff, it would be more like a quest to capture him," George explained. "I was afraid if he thought people were searching for him, he would leave and we really wouldn't see him again. You have to believe I'm trying to do right by you, Etta Mae and your boy. I've gone back a few times, but I haven't seen him again or found where he lives, but I'm sure he is still there.

"Right after I saw him, I left some clothes hanging in a tree right where he was hunting. They were some of Scott's winter clothes that he outgrew when he was about Clifton's age. They disappeared the same day. He must have been watching me.

"Ed you have to believe that this was the most difficult thing I've ever done, withholding this from you."

Ed said, "I guess the important thing is that he's healthy. You know that I went out on my own at his age. It was the depression and Papa needed me to go out and get any kind of work to help the family. I guess there ain't much difference. I'll leave him be. I don't think I'd better tell Etta Mae though. She wants him back here now! I don't think she could live with the knowledge that you know where he is."

"I think she might be a lot better off knowing that he is alive and well, don't you think Ed? I think it would be better for her if we broke it to her now. I think we can explain why he should come home on his own. We'll keep monitoring him. You'll want to come with me next time," George offered.

"I'd like that," Ed said. "Well then, let's go talk to Etta Mae."

Book IV

Monday June 1, 2000
Hometown of South and North High School
The Home of Ed and Etta Mae Kelley

Clifton pulled into the driveway of the suburban ranch house and killed the motor. He smiled with satisfaction at his parent's well-groomed lawn. Four Colorado blue spruce competed for space beside the sidewalk fronting the street. They were a long way from their native forest home, but they thrived in the lushness of the regularly sprinkled lawn.

Etta Mae opened the door before he could knock, and her worried face softened when he stepped through. She clasped him tightly. "I saw the news on television son. I worried all day. What's the matter with kids these days? Were you in the cafeteria when that boy went berserk?"

"No Mom, it wasn't our school. It happened at North High School," Clifton said gently. "I'm at South." He led her over to her chair. "Everything is under control now."

"I thought you might call and let me know you were OK," she said.

"Well, I thought about it, but I thought you knew there were two schools," Clifton said.

"You know how us old people are, names don't mean much. A school is a school, you know. All I knew was there were pictures of police at a local school. Daddy kept saying don't worry none! But, I couldn't help it."

"Where is Dad?"

"He's out in the garden somewhere. He's always out there doing something. We ain't eat half of what he grew out there last summer. I told him why 'don't we just skip the garden this year. Things grow down here without half trying at it.' But, he said, 'No we got to get it planted.' He's already brought in the first batch of radishes. I got some washed for you to take home to Angelina."

"Thanks Mom. Last summer I don't think we had to buy any vegetables at all after Dad's garden came on," Clifton laughed.

"Darn fool thinks more of that garden than he does of me," Etta Mae said.

"I thought about the old place today," Clifton said. He looked at his mother. Her face had fewer wrinkles now than she did when she was forty. The milder more humid climate wasn't as harsh on her as the dry, high altitude had been. "Do you have any idea what ever happened to Hector Rodriguez?"

"Whatever brought him up?" she asked. Etta Mae thought for a moment. She looked around the room and picked up the magazine she had been reading and put it in a rack and straightened the afghan on the recliner. "I haven't thought of Raul and any of his family in years. Hector went on to Ft. Lewis for a couple of years, and I'm trying to think if he transferred to another school from there. I believe he went to work for the Extension Service in Cortez. Ed would know about that I expect. Why do you ask about him?"

"Today's shooting brought back a lot of memories, I guess. I was just wondering. I guess Hector was probably partly responsible for my going into teaching in the first place."

The screen door slammed, and Ed Kelley walked into the kitchen. He took off his shoes, washed his hands, hung his straw hat on a rack near the kitchen door and joined his wife and son in the front room. "How you be?" he asked, and hugged his son tightly.

"Oh, I'm holding on," Clifton said. "How you doing, Dad?"

"Sick abed, upstairs and in the head," Ed laughed. "Heard you had some excitement at school today."

"It was a pretty rough day," Clifton said, tears filling his eyes. "One of our best teachers who was also a good friend of mine was killed by her son last night…" The dam broke. He sat down on the couch, put his head down and sobbed.

Etta Mae moved to the couch, sat down beside him and put her arms around him. Ed stood watching for a moment before joining them. He sat on the other side and put his own arms around his son and wife.

"We heard on the television what happened," he said quietly. "He was just a boy, wasn't he?"

"Yes. He was just barely fifteen years old. He was just finishing his first year in high school. He was just barely older than I was when I almost did the same…."

"I'm not sure I understand…," Etta Mae said.

"I never really told you the whole story Mom, Dad…"

"We've always thought there was more than just a school fight that sent you running into that canyon," Ed said.

Winter of 1955
The Cliff Dwelling Martinez Canyon
Summit Ridge, Colorado

80

Deep Winter Fantasies
Martinez Canyon

The previous eight winters hadn't been as bad at school. He rather cherished the time each year when snow finally covered the ground to stay and the long stormy days kept the 20 to 30 students cooped up the tiny schoolhouse called East Lakeview.

The community had erected the school building many years before Clifton's family bought their 160-acre farm, a half-mile away. The concrete gray, stucco, wood frame building required no paint. In places, the plaster had broken so Cliff could see the chicken wire that held the stucco to the frame beneath.

Someone had painted the wooden window frames white, but the paint had cracked and peeled long before Cliff began a student there.

The only light came from the four tall windows on each side. On dark, snowy winter days, the students could hardly see their lessons in the dim interior.

The one room schoolhouse stood on an acre of land in the northeast corner of Don Harris' farm where the county road from Cortez intersected the Dolores to Mancos road. It was ten and a half miles northeast of Cortez, eight miles southeast of Dolores, fourteen miles northwest of Mancos, and five miles east of West Lakeview.

A couple of miles up the road to the northeast stood another one-room school in another district. Ten miles southeast, near the intersection of the Mancos to Dolores Highway and Highway 160, stood Mesa Verde Grade School.

Why two schools stood so close together and in two separate districts seemed a mystery to Cliff.

Fifteen feet to the left of the front door, next to the fence was the concrete lined cistern. On the southeast corner of the grounds stood the teacherage, a tiny building containing a bed and cook stove. The teacher could live there free of charge. The only time that a teacher actually lived there while Cliff attended the school was during heavy snow weather. Since all the students walked to school, the only one who had to worry about how to get to the school was the teacher.

After every snow, the big road grader came up the county roads clearing them so that anyone with chains could navigate. However the teacher occasionally stayed overnight in the teacherage if a big overnight snow was predicted.

The center of the schoolyard was the softball diamond used in the fall and for a short time in the spring. During the time when snow was on the ground, it became the setting for a large round circle game and other snow activities.

The girls' outhouse occupied the far southwest corner of the grounds and the boys' outhouse occupied the far northwest corner nearest the road. After a succession of Halloweens when someone hauled the outhouses from over their stands to lay them in front of the schoolhouse door, Ed Kelley and Don Harris had built concrete block outhouses that withstood Halloween pranksters.

The schoolhouse held five rows of desks with five desks per row. On the south side of the room, the row of little desks accommodated the first and second graders. The row on the side parallel to the north wall had the largest desks for the upper grades. On the west end of the room was a blackboard that spanned wall to wall.

In the center of the room just in front of the entry door stood a potbelly stove with a metal shield around it. The stove burned coal and wood and heated the entire building. During his eighth grade year Cliff had received ten dollars a month to go to school forty five minutes early to build a fire and have the building warm by the time the teacher and students arrived during the cold months.

The front door faced the county road that wound up the Ridge from Cortez. Between the front door and the main room was a small porch, also built by Ed Kelley, made of concrete blocks where students hung coats and overshoes and stored their lunches. A set of bookshelves was the library: a few extra textbooks, an old set of encyclopedia and a few discarded books from the county library.

The teacher had no duplication machine so the blackboard served that purpose. Beginning on the left end were lists of spelling words: Five words for the week for the first and second graders; ten words for the third and fourth graders; fifteen for the fifth and sixth grades and twenty words for the seventh and eighth grades. This took up the left half of the black board. Math problems filled the right side for the younger grades to copy.

Cliff and the other students were to copy the words and math problems for their grade level into their tablets the first thing Monday morning. When the last student finished copying, he or she could erase the board.

During that day and the rest of the week, they were to memorize the words. At times during each day, there would be drills and tests on them. Usually the students who were a grade or two ahead would drill and test the students below them.

Mr. Johnson had a kind of duplication process called a hectograph that he could use once every 24 hours. It was a laborious process. He made a master with a purple carbon-like paper. He placed the master on the hectograph tray, which contained a gel material transferring the purple "ink" to the gel. If Mr. Johnson was careful placing a clean sheet of paper on the gel and gently rubbing it, he could make a dozen copies of poor quality. Mr. Johnson had to clean the gel with mineral spirits after each set of copies and let it dry for 24 hours. He used it sparingly for art projects for the first and second graders.

By the time Cliff reached third grade he was spending a great deal of time drilling the first grade students in both spelling and math and in turn being drilled by someone in the fifth grade. He had daily spelling tests with words read to him by the teacher or an older student.

Math drills were like competitions. Several students went to the board and either Mr. Johnson or another student orally dictated a problem to solve. The competition was to see who could solve it first. If a student made a mistake, or was the last to solve the problem, he/she had to sit down and another student would take the place. The challenge was to see who could last the longest. Each spring, selected teams of students loaded into Mr. Johnson's car to travel to countywide competitions in spelling and basic math computations between the county's country schools.Each grade had a different number of students. Through most of his eight years, he was the only one in his grade level.

During the winter confinement, he was able to interact with the other students and the teacher. Interaction, of course was in English. Other than the math competition, he was on equal footing. Drilling the other students was a form of play, and it was a one on one interaction between him and the other boys and girls alike that was fun and non-threatening. Even drilling Hector with spelling words was entertaining, not a competitive task. During those brief moments, there was a truce between them.Cliff had enjoyed the times when there had been fresh snow. The competition ceased and together all the kids had created snowmen, angels, and had a wonderful time playing in it. One favorite game was a large circle game with a safety zone in the center. Adventurous students could venture out into the outer ring where a person who was "it" could chased them. If one was "tagged" then he/she became "it" and began chasing someone else in the outer ring. Four spokes connected the ring with the center safe zone to provide an escape. No one could be tagged in the safe zone. Tagging was by touch. Nothing was thrown. Because Cliff was fast, he could play that game safely as the person chased or as the "it".

Marbles was a fun game he had enjoyed that they had played inside during the winter. At lunchtime, they used the open space in front of the desks under the blackboard. The boys liked to play keeps. A student drew a circle on the floor and each player put a marble inside the ring. Players took turns shooting at the marbles, and if a marble the player hit rolled outside the ring he could keep it and got another shot. The marble he shot with also had to roll outside the ring or he lost it and did not get the following shot.

Ed Kelley believed keeps was a form of gambling, and he forbade Cliff to play it. On those grounds, he had to refrain from participating and Mr. Johnson did not interfere.

Occasionally a girl joined in the marble playing. Hector was the most competitive of all and delighted in knocking other marbles out of the way by shooting at them with his. Since he was very good at shooting keeps, he always had his pick of good marbles to use. He also had enough force in his thumb to break another kid's marble occasionally.

The best thing about this game though, was that everyone was on pretty even ground, as it was a game of skill not just brute strength. Hector had the power, but his aim wasn't that much better than anyone else. Cliff beat him as often as not, which was one more coal on the fire between them.

He had to admit that although those years with Mr. Johnson had been brutal, particularly at the beginning and end of every year, during the winter months he had experienced the most interaction with others that he had had in his lifetime.

He had been safer during his seventh and eighth grades, as far as outside participation in sports was concerned but Mrs. Campbell's methods of teaching were different and so he had not had the tutorial participation that he had experienced with Mr. Johnson. She had not called on him to test younger students with flash cards for example. She had let him use that time to read and do his own projects.

~~~

Cliff missed his books.

In wintertime, when snow blanketed the fields, a farmer could take time between morning and evening chores to sit by the fire and read a book without feeling guilty.

He could finally relax with a book in plain sight, during the daytime, read to his heart's content and not have to worry that he was neglecting some field or fence line. Now Cliff had nothing to read except the precious few pamphlets and magazine articles in his scrapbook.

Cliff had read and re-read each article and clipping so many times, he had them memorized, and they were becoming fragile. He had been so busy through the summer and fall that he had not had time to think about leisure reading. In the evenings there wasn't enough light to read by, and he was usually too tired to stay up anyway.

The days were short in the dead of winter. If the sun came out, it shone directly on the front of the dwelling and through the ventilation holes up near the roof giving dim light to the dwelling. On those days he dressed warmly and sat outside for awhile in the sunshine. The berm of snow and ice on the front of the ledge, cut the sunrays from hitting the lower part of the dwelling wall, but the roof was clear.

On those days when Cliff could see well, his hands busily removed tiny chips from intricate woodcarvings to create the look of hair or feathers. The close work tired his eyes in the dim light so he preferred to do that kind of work only in sunlight.

On dark days when snow swirled through the canyon, winds blew and the sun did not filter through the cloud cover, Cliff occupied his day inside weaving cloth from yucca fiber, talking to Maggie and Moonbeam, or basket weaving. They were activities that he could do in even dimmer light.

It was during those hours when his hands needed less supervision
~~~

that his mind wandered off to other things and other worlds. In his mind, he drifted the mighty Mississippi with Mark Twain and rode the desert with Zane Grey's Ranger Dick Gale on Blanco Sol from *Desert Gold.*

Cliff may have had no books to read at the dwelling, but the books he had read in the past three or four years or listened to his mother read to him before that, provided plenty of material for vivid fantasies. During the long gloomy days in the cave, while he wound grass and straw around willow staves into baskets, and wove yucca fiber into cloth, he created elaborate, vivid chapters of chivalrous medieval fantasy in his mind.

He peopled his fantasy freely with heroes and heroines from Sir Walter Scott and Miguel Cervantes. It was his fantasy, and so he included himself and the neighbor girl that he secretly admired although he had only briefly met her once.

She was Angelina Martinez the girl that he had met at the Summit Lake Fish Fry the summer before. They had competed in games together and against each other. They had talked during lunch and again several times during the afternoon. They had laughed together and she had said they were "in synch." She was the first girl he had ever met who seemed interesting to him.

Had I not gone into seclusion, we might be sharing freshman classes together during these long winter afternoons or even walking uptown at lunchtime to share a malted milk at the drug store soda fountain. That afternoon at the lake, we planned to look for bee trees "next summer." The summer that became my summer of disappearance! "Damn you Hector! You screwed that up too. Damn you!" He shouted. I wonder if she remembered our date? If I return next summer, will she be willing to give me another try?

Cliff worked Angelina into his cast of characters. She was Lady Angelina de la Martinez of Barcelona. He was Sir Clifton Kelley Esquire; Noble Knight Templar in the service of King Richard. In the fantasy, on Sir Clifton's return from the crusades fighting beside King Richard, he goes on a quest to rescue the Lady Angelina de la Martinez of Barcelona, held prisoner in the castle of the dastardly Count Hector Rodriguez.

Sir Clifton leads a group of valiant knights including, Sir Ivanhoe, Don Quixote and his sidekick Sancho Panza, Robin Hood and his Merry Men, Knight Templar Dick Gale on his war steed Blanco Sol and several other knights against the castle. The rescue is successful after many battles and duels. Lady Angelina is freed unharmed by none other than Sir Kelley himself.

In the end of the fantasy, Sir Ivanhoe and the Saxon princess Lady Rowena, rejoin their Saxon clans in England. Sir Clifton Kelley and the Lady Angelina Martinez are married and unite the Irish and Spanish Kingdoms and Don Quixote finally has a chance to defend his Dulcinea del Toboso's honor against an advancing army of windmills.

The very complicated fantasy occupied his mind for days as he created art with his hands. He carved intricate animal faces from the wood with his hands while his mind created jousts, sword fights, castle sieges, kidnappings, and romantic walks with Angelina Martinez in Sherwood Forest. There were roundtable discussions about honor, chivalry and religion with Clifton having to play each part. At the roundtable his advisor is the grand wizard to the court, George Williamson.

He tried to position Maggie and Moonbean on the warming table so they could play a part but they wouldn't cooperate, so he gave up.

His knights were chivalrous and honorable and came to the defense of the downtrodden and bullied. The opponents were evil and took advantage of the weak and helpless.Obstacles the knights overcame included dragons and hostile bands of knights and outlaws.

Ed and Etta Mae had sometimes dropped Cliff at the movie theater on Saturday afternoons while they did their shopping and trading or went to the livestock auction.

There he had seen Robin Hood played by Tyrone Power and Ivanhoe played by Robert Taylor.

Cliff's mental image of Robin Hood in his fantasy was Tyrone Power and Ivanhoe was Robert Taylor. The ethics in the fantasies were drawn from the authors Zane Grey, Sir Walter Scott, and Miguel Cervantes. In his mind, the good rode white horses and wore white over their chain mail armor. The evil knights wore black and rode black horses. The steeds resembled the retired workhorses such as the two who grazed contentedly in his dad's pasture. Romantic interludes in the fantasy featured long walks and talks in Sherwood Forest or the gardens of Barcelona.

81

Deep Winter, Developing Art
Martinez Canyon

In summer and fall, when he was not out foraging, he had used whatever time he had to make fiber out of yucca leaves, cedar, sage and willow bark. After he had separated the fibers from the leaves, he separated strands, twisted them into yarn or cordage, wound it into loose balls and stored them in baskets for later use. He had even made a fine cotton-like yarn by twisting and spinning cottonwood and cattail seedpod fluff. The quantity was small but the yarn was soft and delicate.

He used cordage to bind the rows of grass or bark together in baskets and twisted strands together for rope or twine to hang baskets from the roof poles.

Later, when he had produced enough baskets to store food, he had time to learn how to use the loom and balls of yarn.

Harvest time was long over. Snow now kept him inside the cave for long periods at a time.

He now had time to use the balls of coarse yarn. The small loom sat on the top of the warming table and he wove either cloth with finer cordage or heavier blanket thickness pieces with heavier cordage. Whatever he produced on the loom was a warm natural brown color. He had no idea how to dye it to create colorful designs. However, he could experiment with designs by alternating twine made from different sources.

He based the little Navaho loom he used on one from a pamphlet showing construction plans for a loom of any size. The example called for natural cedar. Back in the summer, he had hacked down several small scrub oak to build the basic frame. Without nails, bolts and screws, he had to lash parts together with wet rawhide.

The loom was small. The largest piece he could weave was about twenty-four inches wide and about thirty inches long. It was a simple structure. He used the scrub oak to build a sturdy rectangular framework about three feet wide and five feet tall.

He used willows for the crossbeams. He strapped the top beam to the front of the outer frame. A free hanging willow dowel about six inches wider than the frame hung from the top beam by cord tied to the right end of the top beam and laced down to the dowel, back over the top beam, and down to the dowel several times and ending at the left end of the top beam.

A second willow dowel the same length as the hanging dowel was tied with loops just below. From it the warp was strung to a willow dowel fastened by loops to a dowel attached to the foot of the outside frame.

The pamphlet showed how to string the warp and how to make a simple design using different cording or colored cording.

He used a long, thin, pointed, flattened willow stick to thread the woof thread back and forth and another willow to keep the warp threads separated and to press each woof thread down snug against the preceding thread. It was simple and primitive but the result was a tightly woven cloth or heavier blanket.

He found that weaving cloth on the loom or weaving grass through willow uprights to make a basket to be totally relaxing and satisfying. His thoughts were free to roam, fantasize or contemplate God, Nature and his place in it.

Most of all, he felt relaxed and peaceful. He also realized one day that he felt good about himself and all that he had done.

He had not had a serious headache since the debilitating one the night he had returned to the cliff dwelling for good.

He had enough raw materials for baskets, carving and weaving using firewood, baskets of cordage, willow and sheaves of long stem orchard and timothy grass gathered from along the creek.

Cliff sat for hours at the warming table alternating between whittling and weaving grass leaves and stems or straw around willow frameworks into small intricately designed baskets embellished with hair, feathers, beads and yarn.

He had saved hair and feathers shed by Moonbeam and Maggie and from birds and animals taken as food. He made beads from rabbit, bird leg and bird wing bones sawn into thin disks. The hard bone began to wear down the teeth in the keyhole saw and he finally had to lay the saw aside. He polished the end of each bone on damp sandstone before cutting off each thin disk. The soft center of the small round beads were easy to hollow out. He polished one edge and sewed the rough edge to whatever he was making. The polished white bone beads shone almost like ivory.

Cliff enjoyed playing with Moonbeam and Maggie. They became his favorite models to carve into figures from cedar knots and gnarled pieces of sage and piñon firewood.

At first, the carvings were strictly utilitarian spoons, forks and bowls. He carved the first pieces because he needed utensils to get the food out of the Dutch oven into his cup, and then from the cup into his mouth.

Then he began to embellish the handles of spoons by carving them in the shape of bird's necks and heads. At night as he gazed into the fire, he began to see shapes in gnarled pieces of sage and cedar. Then the shapes became faces of birds and animals to him, and they seemed to struggle to become free before they burned and split apart. He began to imagine freeing the faces of the creatures from the gnarled pieces of firewood.

The first carvings were crude. However, as he struggled to bring out the faces and free them from the wood his intent and intensity changed. Improvement slowly began to come with each carving as he began to understand the wood and how to handle the three blades of his pocketknife. He kept the blades razor sharp and the blades began to grow thin from the constant sharpening.

He used the hunting knife to rough-in detail in the wood, but the knife was worthless for carving any detail.

By accident, he had discovered that the sharp edge of a fragment of flint cut leather better than a knife. The same was true of cutting or shaving wood. The curved edges of the stone flakes allowed him to cut delicate grooves to simulate hair or feathers. The sharp stone edges were also useful for scraping edges down to a velvety smooth finish.

82
Snow Shoes
Martinez Canyon

Cliff climbed the snag and surveyed the piñon/cedar timber in front of him. Deep snow covered the landscape. Heavily loaded piñon trees sloughed cascades of snow at the slightest breeze to build the fortress-like ridge of snow even higher around their perimeter. Sagebrush that dotted the landscape had disappeared to become merely bumps in the snow.

Cliff had thought the snow was deep back in late fall before the solstice, but it had only been a preview of things to come. He had never seen this much snow on Summit Ridge. It was like the photos he had seen of New England in his mother's Saturday Evening Post.

He stepped out from the snag onto the surface of the snow and sunk down to his waist to the frozen surface of the previous snowstorm.

Once the first snow of the season fell, the ground stayed covered until spring. The usual pattern was snow, clearing for a few days, settling, surface melt and freezing, more snow, settling, surface melt and freezing, and so on.

Until this three-foot or so snowfall had a chance to settle and the surface melted and froze, there would be little movement on it.

Even then, it would be treacherous to walk on. The ice crust would not support the sharp hooves of deer. When a person or animal broke through the surface, the snow beneath would not support their weight and they floundered. Anything trying to get around off a packed trail would have to fight for every foot forward. Heavy animals such as deer and cattle would be in trouble this winter.

For the rest of the winter snowshoes would be required for anyone trying to get around in snow this deep.

Cliff struggled through the deep snow back the few feet to the rope tied to the snag, backed to the cliff edge and descended to the dwelling.

Clinging snow covered his leggings, moccasins and Levi jeans. *George I will have to hug your neck next time I see you for these jeans. I'd be freezing my butt off if it weren't for them.* He removed them, hung them to dry, and hurriedly slid his bare legs under the warming table. The rabbit skin coat would have to dry while he wore it.

Moonbeam climbed up onto the blanket on his lap and Maggie flew down to the table in front of him, cocked his head and inquired, "Clifton cold?"

"Brrrrrr," Cliff said and shook his head as he blew air through his lips and then laughed. It was a game they played.

"Brrrrrr," Maggie imitated shaking his head and bobbing up and down.

Cliff tried to remember how snowshoes were made. His dad had bought them both used snowshoes at the livestock auction two winters before.

The livestock auction sales barn opened for business every Saturday. Before the afternoon auction people brought their used household goods, farm machinery, small animals, and junk to be traded and sold. Junk went into a flea market. Nice things were auctioned in the morning. The snowshoes went into the flea market.

They were old and most of the webbing was missing on all but one of the shoes. One pair was smaller, the other was full size. Ed Kelley had been intrigued by them and had bought both pair for a dollar. No one else wanted them, because they required extensive re-webbing. Ed was confident he could repair them and visualized in his head how he would do it before he made the owner an offer for them.

One snowshoe still had most of the original webbing intact. From it, Ed duplicated the webbing scheme in the others.

Down in the foothills of Summit Ridge, the snow rarely accumulated to depths making snowshoes necessary. They weren't needed for any utility purpose on the farm. Ed carried them with him when he packed into the mountains each fall to hunt for elk and found them very useful.

Cliff had learned to use the smaller pair on Sunday afternoons after fresh snowfalls. With them, he had been able to go farther and explore an entirely different world in the wintertime without breaking through the layers of ice every few feet.

On the warming table in front of Cliff lay the framework of a primitive pair of snowshoes that he had shaped out of willow. They resembled crude elongated tennis paddles. They didn't exactly match, but they were close in size. They had started out as two straight one inch in diameter willows. Hours of soaking, heating and bending had resulted in the shapes he wanted. Shaping them had not been as complicated as shaping the chair.

Before fastening the trailing ends together with sinew, Cliff braced each frame from side to side in front and behind where his shoes would fasten. Then he squared the edges of the frames to make them lighter.

The complicated webbing process was similar to webbing the seat of the chair at the warming table. Cliff stretched the slightly damp yucca cording from the front of the frame to the forward brace and then wove cording from side to side. He likewise tied cord at 90 degrees from side to side and then wove cord at 45 degrees to the braces and from side to side. From the rear brace, he strung the webbing from side to side and at 45 degrees from the brace.

He tied thongs through the webbing next to the front brace looped them over his moccasins, crossed and tied them behind the ankle to hold the snowshoes to his feet.

Cliff strung the cord while it was slightly damp so it was more flexible. When it dried, it would conform to the shape of the framework. It would not shrink and warp the framework. When it got wet, it would not loosen.

~~~

Cliff ventured out with the new snowshoes the next day after morning chores. Maggie flew ahead up to the snag and waited for him. The snowshoes hung from his shoulder along with the atlatl/spear quiver. Both hung outside the worn burlap knapsack.

A slight breeze kicked up fine grain ice and swept it along the surface of the snow creating very slight riffles along the surface when he emerged from behind the cliff face and stood on the rim of the canyon. In front of him was the wall of snow. He kept a firm grip on the rope.

Cliff climbed the snag, took the snowshoes from his back and placed them on top of the snow. He gingerly stepped off a bleached branch onto the left snowshoe and put his weight on it. The collection of webbing and willow slightly sank into the snow as he put his full weight onto it. He balanced on his left leg and stepped over onto the right snowshoe. The two shoes fully supported his weight on the surface of the snow.

Cliff wrapped the thongs around his moccasins, tied them and tested the shoes by stepping forward. They held to his feet the way he wanted as he struck out along the canyon rim toward the east, keeping just inside the tree line.

When he arrived at the gap where the deer trail led out of the canyon he was not surprised to find that the snow where the trail emerged from the canyon had not been broken. After previous snowfalls, the trail had soon been well broken and used.

He followed the slight indentations where the previously broken trail wound back into the timber toward the farm. Nothing heavy such as deer or coyotes was coming out onto the deep snow yet. The only tracks he saw were bird tracks. There was little exposed food for them.

Maggie flew to a piñon and then hopped down to the mound of snow surrounding the overhanging evergreen branches and disappeared down the inside slope of fallen tree-shed snow into the well next to the trunk. Cliff ducked under branches and slid down into the hole with Maggie. Snow had drifted clear to the trunk of the tree and had frozen, but it was shallow next to the trunk. Fallen needles and cones covered the first snow that had fallen back in November and December. The newest snow had not drifted into the space.

Eventually rabbits would take shelter in clear areas such as this and come in to browse on twigs. Rodents might come in and dig for left over piñon nuts or hidden caches of nuts that piñon jays had hidden and forgotten about.

Cliff now knew from his experience after the failed deer hunt in the fall, that if a sudden storm came up while he was away from the cave, he could escape the wind and weather by taking shelter in such a place. Now each time he left the cave he had the waterproof matches encased in paraffin with him. He could probably start a fire with the mass of small dead branches that usually clung low to the ground to the trunk of such trees. *I*
~~~

was so lucky that doe ducked when she did. The way the snow turned out, I would probably have ended up wasting most or all of her.

Cliff climbed back out and circled back to the ruin.

Later that day, for the first time since the deer migration began, he heard coyotes yipping.

83
Coyote
Between Martinez Canyon and the Pueblo Ruin

Cliff heard a rabbit's scream and knew a predator of some kind had either made a kill or had it cornered. He fitted a bone tipped dart into the end of a spear, loaded it onto the atlatl and moved quietly in that direction. Perhaps a fox had a cottontail cornered. If he could drive it away, Cliff might be able to take the rabbit himself. The fox could run down another rabbit more easily than he could.

It was impossible to be silent in the snow, but he moved slowly and as quietly as possible on the snowshoes. The soft new snow was quieter than the crusty frozen surface which lay three feet below it. The snow had settled and could now support small animals, but it had not formed a hard enough crust to support a man or large animal.

He heard a threatening snarl ahead. Something had interrupted the predator. Cliff maintained cover between him and the sounds, until he was very near. The snarling match elevated in volume and viciousness as he stepped from behind a piñon tree and viewed the action. A silver fox had killed a jackrabbit. Fresh blood covered the white snow where the fox had begun to tear the belly open. Standing a few feet from the fox and his kill stood a large coyote, head lowered, and fangs bared, moving in on the fox. The coyote looked lean and hungry.

Cliff had heard an increasing number of coyotes in the canyon and on top since the last snowfall had ended. He had heard them occasionally in the summer. They had followed the deer migration down onto the plateau and on toward Mesa Verde in the fall. He thought the Coyotes had followed the deer on to their wintering grounds on Mesa Verde.

Either they had suddenly returned or possibly, they had been there all along, but they had kept out of sight. He knew from tracks, there were many inhabitants or visitors to the cañon that he never saw. The last few days and nights, their calls seemed to be all around, both out on the top and in the canyon.

The fox was silver with a black tipped tail. He would have been invisible, if he were just standing in the snow. When Cliff saw fox in the summer, they were reddish grey.

Cliff supposed the fox would be no match against the bullying coyote if it continued to stand its ground. That was Mother Nature's business, and it was not his place to interfere as long as they were no threat to him; however, the coyote was a large animal and was too close to Cliff for comfort. Cliff raised the atlatl into position to aim and throw in his own defense if necessary until the coyote left or until it allowed Cliff to move quietly away. The snowshoes made it difficult to turn in place and subtly slip away. Instead of leaving the scene, the snarling coyote suddenly turned, crouched and with bared teeth lunged directly at Cliff. In the same instant, Cliff aimed and threw.

The distance closed between coyote and boy until it was little more than the length of the spear as the spear cleared the end of the atlatl and impacted the coyote's chest. The needle sharp tip drove through skin, muscle, lungs and heart.

The coyote crumbled to the ground at Cliff's feet.

Cliff trembled, as he stood rooted to the spot. It was the first time he had used the weapon in self-defense. He gasped for breath. Everything had happened so fast he had not had time to think, only to react. His knees felt weak, and he leaned against the tree. *What if I'd missed? I could have been badly injured. No knows where I am. Could I have reached help if the coyote had reached me?* When his breathing returned to normal, he removed the spear. The dart portion remained imbedded in the coyote's heart. The animal was lean, but its winter pelt was heavy and glossy.

The coyote was slightly smaller than its cousin the wolf. The size differences the same as Bob Harris's border collie to a German Sheppard. The animal was in good condition, although lean. It did not appear to be diseased. He had never heard of a person being attacked by a coyote. Had the animal felt cornered? Cliff had not backed it into a corner. The timber was open on all sides for its escape. The fox blocked its way on one side, but not directly behind and was no match in size for a coyote anyway. *The animal must be pretty hungry and thought I was going to compete for the rabbit.*

The fox grabbed the rabbit and disappeared as soon as the attention turned to Cliff.

Cliff kept the Coyote's head attached to the hide when he skinned it. He left the carcass there to provide food for other hungry predators and birds that would find it. Already magpies and crows were calling back and forth, spreading the word that food was available.

On the way back to the dwelling with the coyote pelt, Cliff worried about the animal's attack. It was very uncharacteristic, he thought, that a coyote would attack him rather than run away.

Coyotes usually were either solitary or ran in very small packs. They were the ultimate survivors. They ate rodents, rabbits and carrion. They lived in the mountains and on the desert. Like the goat he had seen across the canyon from the tower ruin up the canyon from Cliff's dwelling, the coyote could climb the canyon slopes and ledges. No place was out of reach to the coyote, it seemed. The previous winter the newspaper had reported that with the extinction of the wolf in Colorado, the coyote was growing in size without the wolf to compete for food.

Cliff worried that if a pack of coyotes were in the area and they were that hungry, they very well might seek out his meat cache in the annex. There wasn't much left on the bones. They couldn't come over the rimrock, but they might try to come up the canyon side as he had when he first discovered the cave. They were wily and agile. Surely, their sense of smell was acute.

His location was a good deterrent, but coyotes had lived in the canyon for centuries and weren't to be underestimated. If the bobcat had made the cave its home, a coyote probably could get to it, if it set its mind to it.

I hope Dad's livestock is safe. I assume in this snow, Dad has them in the timber behind the house where he can feed them hay and keep an eye on them. What about the other farmer's livestock? Will they know the coyotes are coming in and getting desperate? Should I signal George now?

He spent the afternoon reinforcing both the door on the annex and the main dwelling.

84
Invasion
Martinez Canyon

Moonbeam alerted Cliff by running to the doorway and looking up, sniffing. Never before had he seen the skunk do that. He seemed very agitated. Then he heard a scratching sound outside.

He pulled on the coat and leggings and considered the .22. The spear had dropped the coyote that morning. He doubted the .22 would have. The .22 could kill a coyote, just as it had killed the bobcat the first night he was in the cave, but at close range, it didn't have enough stopping power to stop a charging dog. Also, he could throw two spears in succession faster than he could load a second bullet into the single shot .22.

He took up the quiver of darts and spears and fitted a dart to each spear. He took the atlatl in his right hand and loaded a spear into it. In his left hand, he took the quiver, went to the door and listened. Moonbeam wanted to go out. If the coyotes were out there, they would kill him, even with his powerful scent to protect him.

"No Moonbeam, you have to stay here," he said. With that, he quietly unlatched the door and peered out into the moonlight. Dark shapes milled around the ledge near the door to the annex. *If they destroy the remainder of the venison hanging in there, and if they get a whiff of the pemmican stored in here, my life in the cliff dwelling is over. I may as well pack and go home.*

He could not throw through the doorway in that direction. He lifted the quiver of spears through the doorway and stepped through pulling the doorway closed behind him to keep the skunk inside. He pulled four spears with darts attached out of the quiver with his left hand. The fifth was in the atlatl ready to throw.

The largest coyote scratched at the doorway to the annex fifteen feet away trying to tear it off its hinges. The animal was about the same size as the one that had charged him that morning, about the size of a border collie. It was also thin and hungry looking.

Without warning, Cliff aimed and threw. The coyote at the annex door yelped and limped the opposite way on the ledge into the darkness. The spear fell free, leaving the deeply imbedded dart. The others animals swirled around in confusion. The snow and ice berm constricted the space on the ledge giving the coyotes little room to maneuver. One turned toward Cliff, snarled and charged, as Cliff threw a second spear. The spear and dart lodged in its chest wounding it fatally.

The pack ran away from him into the snow and darkness and disappeared toward the end of the ledge where there was no escape. It was a long drop to the canyon slope on that end of the ledge. He loaded another spear and readied to throw. Without warning or sound, they appeared again in the dim moonlight and rushed toward him. He hurled a third spear, which brought down a third animal before the remainder of the pack rushed by him, and then he heard them below the ledge on the canyon slope below.

The two coyotes in front of him were dead when he examined them. Unaccounted for was the big animal he had hit on the first throw. It was potentially the most dangerous. It might still be on the ledge and badly wounded. He should not permit a wounded animal to suffer.

Cliff slowly moved down the ledge until he saw the dim shape of the coyote lying on its side. The animal snarled when he came near. Cliff went back to the dwelling for the .22 and one of the ten precious remaining rounds.

He dragged all three animals to the door of the annex and left them there. He would skin them the next morning.

~~~

The first thing Cliff did the next morning was follow the tracks of the retreating coyotes to see how they had accessed the ledge. The chute that had given him a way to the ledge the first time was now filled with snow. The pack had scrambled up it and onto the ledge and had retreated the same way.

I have to warn Dad and George and let them get the word out that their cattle is in danger, if they don't already know it. George knows I'm here. I can't believe that he hasn't already told Mom and Dad about it. He probably has. They know I'm around here somewhere. It would be too easy for them to follow my tracks in the snow if they were really trying to find me now. This is too important, a lot more important than me.
~~~

He warmed tea and sat at the warming table thinking about how he could warn the others about the Coyote's behavior without coming in. *Am I ready to come in? Why not come in now? Isn't one time about as good as another?*

He looked at the coyote hide folded in the corner. Outside were three more coyote that he would skin as soon as it was light. He would tan them and make a coat out of them to replace the rabbit coat. He was content in the ruin, at least for now. *I haven't spoken to another human in probably eight months, maybe nine. I'm not sure I remember how, not that I was all that good at it before I came here. I still have a voice. I speak to Maggie and Moonbeam every day. Is it all nonsense?*

In the very dim glow of the fire, he could only barely make out rows of baskets hanging from the roof beams. To him, they were works of art. What am I doing with my life? Am going to spend the rest of it like this?

Cliff didn't like the feeling of uncertainty. It was an old familiar feeling, but one that he had not felt recently as he busied himself through one long winter day after another.

However, right now I have to decide what to do about contacting people about the coyote attack. Cliff left the warming table and found the note from George.

Remember our conversations on how the aboriginals communicated. I will watch this part of the canyon every day this winter. If I see smoke that seems to be any kind of a signal, I will investigate.

The Indians long distance communications, according to George was by smoke or fire. Fire by night and smoke by day. George had told him that the Ancestral Puebloans had an elaborate network of signal locations on highpoints throughout the regions that they staffed, and by smoke or fire they could send signals rapidly by relay. *However, although I might send up a smoke signal, we never established where you might come to, or when you might look out your window each day or what day of the week that might be. I think I need to be more forward than that.*

He turned the note over and with the lead point of a .22 bullet printed:

Geo. Coyotes attacked. Killed 3. I OK.

Warn Dad & others about Coyotes. Livestock.

Thanks. Cliff

He sewed the note to the back of a rabbit skin and at first light; he climbed out of the canyon, stepped onto his snowshoes and set a steady pace east toward George Williamson farm. It was bitter cold in the stillness before sunrise. He had no way of knowing the actual temperature. His dad had an outdoor thermometer at the barn that Cliff checked every morning when he milked the cows. The previous winter about the same time, the temperature was several degrees below zero at dawn. It felt at least that cold this still frigid morning. The surface of the snow was frozen, and he made good time through the trees. Ordinarily he would have to remove the snowshoes to climb through the fence, but he walked along it only a little ways and merely stepped over it in a spot where the snow had drifted over the top of the barbed wire strand above the woven wire.

Cliff came out of the woods near George Williamson's barn. He had taken the shortcut from the Kelley farm to George's house many times before, but usually in the summer time. He saw no activity around the house. George's dog raised no alarm. He assumed George had taken him inside for the night. George did not work in town, so he did not have to milk the cows so early.

Cliff slowly glided beside the barn to the door. He had to be quick. He was in plain sight of the house if George looked out the utility room window. Cliff quickly tied the rabbit skin, holding the note, to the door handle and went back around the side of the barn the way he had come. George should find his note when he came out to milk his cows after breakfast.

Cliff reached the trees behind the barn and headed for home. He looked behind him. The wind was blowing fine ice and snow particles across his snowshoe tracks filling them in. They were already becoming dim, but they would be visible enough to track for a while if anyone wanted to follow him.

~~~

Despite their lean hungry condition, the coyote's heavy winter coats were long and glossy. There was no sign of disease when he skinned them. Before setting out to deliver the note, he had carried the three animals inside the dwelling so that they would not freeze before he returned.

The deep snow must be driving them to their boldness, not some disease. The four coyote pelts tanned beautifully. The four hides made a warm coat to replace the rabbit coat made from many pelts. He had taken the rabbit pelts in the summer when they were not in prime condition.

Although the heavy snows and unusually cold winter were a dangerous time for Cliff, the coyote invasion and the coyote attack out on top earlier had turned from potential disaster into a providential gift of material for a better coat.

He had no way of knowing what the reaction had been to his note. He had every confidence that George had passed on his warning to the neighbors and that they would take precautions to protect their livestock if they weren't already. He liked to think he was out on the front lines, a kind of sentinel and that he had sent up a warning to protect his people.

Cliff salvaged the collar and cuffs of bobcat fur off the rabbit coat, and reused them. He attached short bones with polished ends to the front for fasteners. To complete his ensemble he embellished his buckskin mocca-
~~~

sins by trimming the tops with bobcat fur.

He had no mirror in which to admire himself, but fancied he looked pretty handsome in his new coyote coat, rabbit fur mittens, buckskin leggings, Levi jeans or fawnskin breechcloth (depending on the occasion), and buckskin moccasins.

Both Maggie and Moonbeam seemed to approve.

85

Desert Wind
Martinez Canyon

The wind began blowing from the southwest through the gap between Mesa Verde and Ute Mountain. It started as a few lonely moans among the sandstone and then increased into a howl that woke Cliff in the middle of the night. The day before, Cliff had stood on the rimrock at dawn watching the sunrise over the long slope of the south peak of the La Plata range. It was nearing the vernal equinox. The actual calendar date for the spring equinox was March 20. It was a mile from where Cliff stood and the front window of the Kelley home where Ed had charted the sun and the La Plata range by the calendar. Cliff didn't think a mile to the south would make that much difference. However, he didn't have a printed calendar to test it.

The cold wind carried fine dust that drifted across the ice-encrusted snow.

White snowdrifts turned reddish brown.

It didn't let up for twenty-four hours.

Another twenty-four hours went by without change.

Cliff didn't go out. He huddled half under the warming table trying to concentrate on keeping his hands busy. The incessant moaning and howling wind in the canyon and through the cliffs made him want to scream. He wadded small balls of cotton fluff and put them into his ears to keep out the sound, and that helped, but he began thinking about the tiny seeds that the fluff contained and took it out. What if a seed sprouted in his ears? He put on his head covering and tied the thongs under his chin to pull the flaps tight against his ears. That helped shut out the constant, dreary sound.

He chanted and sang at the top of his lungs and soon grew tired. He tried sleeping, but sleep was fitful.

He kept a small fire going to heat the warming stones.

Dust hung in the air in the dwelling. He could see it in the rays of weak filtered sunlight streaming in through the eve vents.

He tasted the dust. Mucus filled his nostrils, and it was gritty when he blew it free.

His eyes felt puffy and scratchy.

After the first couple of days of wind and dust, Cliff lost his will to do his exercises or keep to his daily hygiene routine. The only time he went out was to empty the clay pot of his waste. On the third day without a break in the wind, he awoke early and listened to the mournful sighing wind, which periodically increased to moaning and howling before settling back to steady sighing and moaning through the trees and canyon.

Cliff tried to get his mind off the dreary, depressing wind outside by re-creating his fantasy of the dramatic rescue of the Angelina de la Martinez of Barcelona being held prisoner in the castle of the dastardly Count Hector Rodriguez. However, he couldn't. He tried fantasizing walking through his vision of Sherwood Forest Angelina Martinez, which helped for a while, and then his thoughts began to dwell instead on Hector. For an entire afternoon, he thought about Hector for the first time in weeks, actually for the first time since in the busy fall harvest season. The dreary wind and dust brought on a depression and with his sinking spirits, the door opened to Hector.

He began to think about what if he was to encounter Hector again. How would he handle it? He only knew he would not run away from him. He was not afraid of him now. However if he was forced to confront him, he needed a plan. The last year or two that Charlie was home they did more together. "Do you want a piece of me little brother?" Charlie would ask playfully. Charlie would be lying on the bed or the floor and Cliff would pounce on him. In nothing flat, Charlie would have Cliff's arms pinned and Cliff would be crying "uncle."

Charlie would teach him the "secret hold", that never worked. He had won every time because he was a lot bigger. But, for the first time in Cliff's life his brother was playing with him, after a fashion. He did not cry when Charlie made him say "uncle." He hadn't felt as if Charlie was trying to hurt him. They were beginning to develop a different relationship.

"So Maggie do you think that if I could figure out those holds that Charlie was using on me and practice them, I could put them to some use, someday?"

Maggie sat lethargically on his perch. He had hardly eaten when Cliff prepared food for him that morning. Moonbeam curled next to him at the warming table. Her appetite was off also.

He felt like a prisoner. He couldn't leave the cliff dwelling because it was worse outside where the wind whipped the particles of dust and sand against the skin like sandpaper.

He had weathered all that Mother Nature had thrown at him without giving up, but the wind and dust was the greatest test. He seriously considered abandoning the cave and trudging the mile home where the house was tighter.

He had heard both his parents talk about the dust storms back in Oklahoma and New Mexico before they moved from there to Colorado.

According to them, it was like this for months on end. No wonder they left. Has it come here? Will it last for months? Was this what drove the original inhabitants away from the dwelling?

Cliff remembered one other dust storm in the past. He had been in the field hoeing, concentrating on the small weeds between rows of corn, eyes fixed on the ground and daydreaming as he moved along. When he came to the end of the row and looked up, the world had changed. Hanging at eye level was an opaque, yellow/red cloud. He had to bend slightly to see under it. The air was clear below it. As he stood there, the cloud lowered inch by inch. When he stood, his head was in the cloud and he could see only a few feet in any direction. He had ducked down and it was clear. It was eerily silent. Birds that had earlier called to each other and sung merrily, were silent.

Suddenly, he had become disoriented. The row of corn was the only reference. He had got down on his knees and sighted up the row. The field was on a slope and the bottom of the cloud was level. The row disappeared twenty feet up the slope from him. Down slope, it was clear to the bottom of the draw. He was at the end of the row almost to the bottom of the draw at that time.

The cloud slowly settled to the ground. Cliff knew he couldn't wander off the place without running into a fence. He had no idea in what direction the house lay from where he was. He was totally lost on his own farm. Cliff had heard of people getting lost in blizzards, but he had never thought about dust causing the same condition. At least in the dust cloud he wouldn't freeze to death as he might in a blizzard.

The origin of the dust storm was miles away, perhaps hundreds of miles away in the New Mexico or Arizona desert. The wind had picked up hundreds of tons of dust and carried it thousands of feet into the air, and when the wind dwindled in strength, the dust dropped out of the air as a silent cloud to drift in a mass of particles almost too fine to see with the naked eye. Collectively the particles settled silently as dust fog onto the ground.

It had taken hours for the air to clear. It had been a hot summer day. Cliff had walked to the end of the row at the lowest point, lain down, and gone to sleep in the shady furrow between the rows of corn rather than wander around lost. It had been near dusk when the air cleared enough to see where he was, and he had picked up his hoe and walked to the house to his near frantic mother.

This time the wind was not only blowing down in the desert. It blew in through the gap between Mesa Verde and Ute Mountain and swept across the Ridge.

The wind blew through the spaces around the ill-fitting door and in through the open vents.

The wind carried the fine dust until it entered the dwelling and lost force, moved across the room with the current and then sifted out over everything in the ruin. Fortunately, Cliff had covered every basket and pot to protect contents from rodents. The covers now protected the contents from dust.

Cliff wondered how the original inhabitants of the ruin had coped with this late winter or early spring wind and dust.

During the months of inactivity, Cliff exercised several times a day by doing push-ups, sit-ups, stretching and running in place. He walked almost every day regardless of temperature, if he could climb up the toeholds to the top of the rimrock. When he couldn't climb out, he paced back and forth on the ledge.

After sitting under the warming table for an hour at a time, he felt his legs and back stiffening, and the series of exercises loosened him up and made him feel fresh. During the time of the dust storm, he changed the exercises somewhat to include lunges and dodges. He imagined that he was sparing with someone. Over the course of the months that he had been in the cave, he had lost most of his anger, but he had not lost a sense of reality. The reality was that when he rejoined the real world, he would probably have to face the same people he had run from. He would have to face them and stand tall when he did it. He focused on the space in front of him. "You want a piece of me little brother?" Cliff waited and then dropped to the floor and kicked out to the side and rolled away.

Moonbeam woke up and backed away in alarm.

The new sense of purpose to his exercises took his attention off the wind a little, and he shook off some of his depression.

He stretched and tossed a moccasin at Maggie's perch eliciting a startled, "Clifton got treats?" He shook the lethargic Moonbeam awake.

"Hey you critters! Up and at 'em! We can't sit around and mope all day waiting for this wind to die down. It's breakfast time. Come on get out of bed!"

Cliff built the fire up, made a cup of tea and began making breakfast for himself and his two friends.

Moonbeam was almost a year old. He expected that she would be finding a mate soon. He hoped she would stay around after her tryst and have her brood in the dwelling where he could see them.

Cliff had never had a conversation with anyone about sex, but as a boy growing up on a farm he had observed the mating of rabbits, pigs, cows and horses. Neighbors brought their heifers to be bred by Ed's bull. He had put the male rabbit into the doe's hutches, observed them mating then returned him to his own hutch. He had helped deliver the results of those matings; the calves, colts, piglets, bunnies and lambs. He assumed the process was the same for humans. It would be a natural course of things for Moonbeam to find a mate. . She was free to come and to go. Her mother had left her there with Cliff soon after she had weaned Moonbeam and her siblings. He assumed the mating process was an instinctive thing.

Moonbeam had put on nearly as much weight as her wild brothers and sisters who at that moment still slept in dens under the snow sleeping and waiting for the spring melt to clear the passageways so they could emerge and seek mates. They would have put on all the weight they could back in the fall to keep their bodies nourished while they lay in their dens through the winter. Moonbeam had been awake and active in the cave all winter long with her human caretaker. Her steady diet, thanks to Cliff, had continued all winter.

Cliff checked his wood supply. All the wood he had stored in the annex was gone. He had started using the wood stored in the main dwelling. At the current rate of consumption, he would have to begin foraging for wood before warm weather returned but hopefully not until after the snow had all melted.

The supplies of piñon nuts, sunflower, sage and grass seeds, corn and beans were fine. He would have corn and beans to get him through the summer. Fresh wild vegetables would begin to come on in another six weeks or so soon after spring thaw. He had enough pemmican sealed in beeswax to take him through until early summer. As he finished his inventory, he felt he was in good shape for food.

He continued to occupy himself during the days by carving, exercising, weaving and also repairing and improving damaged darts and spears in anticipation of spring when he could hunt again.

Cliff finally woke to silence one morning. Moonbeam stirred and ran to the door as Cliff sat up and looked around trying to identify what was different about that morning. There was no wind. It had stopped. He checked the marks on the floor. After the third day, he had begun marking the days since it had begun to blow. He grouped them into weeks. It had been nearly three weeks since the incessant wind had begun blowing off the New Mexico-Arizona desert.

He opened the doorway and looked out across the canyon. A brown fog hovered in the air. He could hardly see the cedar tree in front of the dwelling. Dust filled his lungs. He closed the door to keep it out but it continued to filter in through the fresh air vent he had not covered and around the door. He covered his nose with a piece of yucca cloth to filter out the dust.

The dust slowly settled as the day wore on and he could breathe easily again. When he coughed the phlegm was filled with red grit. The dust covered everything in cave. He shook dust off the baskets and pots. He shook out his bedding and blanket.

When he climbed out on top, dirty reddish brown dirt covered the beautiful white snow. In places, the beginnings of sand dunes had accumulated on top of the snow.

The sun rose from just to the right of the tallest peak of the snow covered La Plata Mountains. Spring equinox had occurred sometime around the beginning of the dust storm. It was now sometime in April and he was within a few days of his Fifteenth birthday.

86

Spring Thaw
Martinez Canyon

With the cessation of the wind, the deep cold of winter broke. Snowstorms came less frequently and seemed to have lost their spirit. The days and nights were warmer. Water dripped from the face of the rimrock during the day and froze into icicles at night. Climbing out over the top was very treacherous during this period and he didn't even try without the aid of the rope.

There was no need to go far, as he still had provisions, but he was restless.

Cliff carried the atlatl and spears whenever he went out. He covered the narrow range on top, but nothing seemed to be out among the piñon and cedar. He went down to the bottom of the canyon and examined tracks where game birds had scratched at the crust of ice and snow into brown grass next to the creek.

Movement in an oak grove on the north slope of the canyon drew him to attention and he discovered a turkey flock foraging on acorns. Snow on the north slope of the canyon had melted more rapidly after each snowstorm than on the shady bottom and shaded south slope.

A well-camouflaged Cliff soon sneaked up on the oak grove on his hands and knees. He focused on a young gobbler just inside the scrub oak. He slowly placed a spear in the atlatl and took aim as he rose to his knees. He didn't have as much power from a kneeling position, but if he stood, the flock would take off. He leaned back and then forward as he tossed. The dart flew true, and the impaled gobbler remained behind as the rest of the flock burst from the grove in a violent clatter of wings.

Cliff carried the bird back to the dwelling where he skinned and cleaned them. The meat would be a welcome change from pemmican. He would save all feathers and use all parts. Viscera would be fresh food for Moonbeam and Maggie. The tail and wing feathers of the turkey was prime fletching stock. He would weave softer feathers into the cloth as he sat at the loom.

~~~

Cliff had hated the chicken house and gathering eggs because of tiny red mites. They crawled over his skin and although he didn't know if they actually bit or not, the thought and feel of them crawling on his skin repulsed him. He had spent as little time as possible in the chicken house when it came time to gather eggs.

He checked the turkey and grouse feathers and skin for mites before he entered the dwelling and found none.

To cut down the risk of mites and ticks he had followed a rigid routine
~~~

of hygiene since entering the cave to live. As soon as he had learned how to find and use yucca root for soap he had bathed, shampooed his hair and laundered his clothing daily. The spring in the back of the cave provided a constant unwavering supply of water.

He had begun shampooing Moonbeam as soon as the little skunk had become gentle and trusting enough to submit to it. After the first time or two, the animal seemed to enjoy having his coat lathered and groomed with the wooden comb that Cliff had carved. Maggie too submitted to the shampoo after his dust baths. All three friends had black glossy groomed hair and feathers. During the summer, he had aired his blanket and cottonwood seed fluff mattress in the sunshine to keep them fresh. During the winter, he had washed the saddle blanket and freeze-dried it. He regularly put the warming blanket out to air and hung it outside to freeze. Those times he relied on the fire and his clothes to keep him warm.

The routine had worked so far to keep the cave free of mites. When he roamed through the canyon in summer, especially through scrub oak, he checked his body carefully for ticks. Ticks, while not common on the Ridge, were common in the higher elevations where they went fishing. They especially were prevalent in the oak groves. They carried Rocky Mountain fever.

It had been nearly a year since his last haircut, and Cliff's hair hung past his shoulders. To keep it out of his eyes he had braided a headband from buckskin and tied it around his forehead with fringed ends hanging down the side of his face. He tied a small clump of iridescent bronze and gold breast turkey feathers to the fringe of the headband with a thin sinew thread. For additional embellishment, he strung bone beads among the fringe. It was very festive looking, he thought.

~~~

One night, when only small patches of snow remained on the mostly thawed ground, Moonbeam had a visitor. Cliff awoke to sounds of scrabbling around the floor of the dwelling. He rose from his sleeping mat and stirred the fire.

A second skunk the same size as moonbeam froze with its tail at attention at the sudden flickering light. Moonbeam nudged her visitor back into play and the two scampered toward the exit hole where the runoff from the spring flowed out under the wall.

"Oh, Moonbeam, have I seen the last of you?" he asked. "Of course it was inevitable, I presume. Well I hope you have a good time. He was certainly cute."

"Moonbeam, cute!" Mocked Maggie.

"Go back to sleep, Maggie," Cliff said.

"Go back to sleep, Maggie," Maggie said.
~~~

87

One-Year Anniversary
Martinez Canyon

Cliff guessed it had been about a year since he had moved into the dwelling.

The mud had dried up.

He had heard tractors running again. The ground was dry and warming. Farmers would be planting soon.

He picked fresh dandelion greens and had been drinking fresh dandelion blossom tea for several weeks. Willows were putting out new leaves. The cottonwood trees had suddenly leafed out.

He was 15, a year older, and he didn't know that he felt any differently. He had celebrated a birthday about the time Old Man Winter's back was broken and the spring thaw began.

He had seen some physical differences in the past year. The fuzz on his face was becoming more course and itchy. When he licked his upper lip, he could feel the beginning of a mustache growing. *I guess if I were home, I would begin to learn how to shave now. Will I have to use a straight razor like Dad's? I don't understand how he keeps from cutting his throat. And the way he pulls the skin tight by pulling on his nose. No wonder it's so big. I guess my nose will keep getting bigger too. I read that the Indians burned their whiskers off, pulled them or just let them grow. I wonder if they come back if you pull them. I'm sure not going to burn them off.*

He ran his arm above a flaming stick and it singed the hair down to his arm. It scared him a little and it smelled a lot. He wouldn't try that on his face. He pulled a whisker on his chin and it hurt. It was hard to grasp it between his fingernails. Pulling them all would require a somewhat better pinching tool than fingernails. It was easier to choose to let them go.

He had no mirror but he could see a dim reflection when he looked into the spring. He couldn't see any of the facial hair that he felt when he ran his hand over it.

He had run into some difficulty speaking during the fall and early part of winter. When he talked to Maggie his voice sometimes cracked and the whole word didn't come out just right. Now his voice was just fine, although it sounded a little different to him.

Actually, he liked it better. It was a little deeper, like his dad's. Maggie's imitation had changed too. She still used the old voice also, and it now sounded like she was holding a conversation between two different people.

~~~

When Cliff checked the sunrise that morning, it rose from just behind the left shoulder of Hesperus peak. When it got to the gap between Hesperus peak on the La Plata Mountains and Shark's Tooth, it would be summer again. That would be in about six weeks.

Spring always came suddenly to the Ridge. A week after the last frost all the trees had leaves. Fruit trees suddenly burst into bloom. He would go into the canyon that day and look for fresh asparagus shoots. He had already picked fresh cattail shoots. Green vegetables were once again breaking the monotony of his diet. The dried food along with potatoes and apples had sustained him well.

He had survived the winter. There had been a few sniffles, but nothing serious. Certainly, he had been healthier than usual. He had always had a healthy immune system. He had not had a migraine headache since the night he had fled the farm in shame because the neighbors were doing his job. Aside from a few headaches mostly from tired eyes while he worked in low light, he had come through the winter fine.

He had enough corn and beans left over to last until the new crop came on in the fall. He would not have to make any more visits to his dad's granary. He felt good about that. It made him feel more self-reliant.

To Cliff's utter delight, Moonbeam had returned alone to the dwelling and produced a healthy brood of furry black and white babies.
~~~

Book V

Monday June 1, 2000
Clifton Kelley's home after school

Clifton sat across the dinner table from his wife of 35 years. He filled her in on the day and with what he knew.

"And how are you doing?" Angelina asked.

Cliff's eyes were red and puffy from tears that seemed to come suddenly as he tried to talk.

"I think I'll be OK," he said. "But it seems like I keep seeing Emma laughing and talking last night. You were there. You saw how animated she was," he said and tears flowed again.

"I hate this," he said. "I can't seem to get out more than two or three words and I start crying again like a baby. It's been a hard day," Clifton said. He stared at his plate and she moved her chair closer and patted his hand.

"According to the radio, Zack will be on suicide watch tonight, she said.

"He is completely alone in the world. Emma told one of the teachers that she was so pleased that he was getting better. He had a lot of trouble with other boys harassing and bullying him in mid-school and even down into elementary school. This year things seemed to have gone away. He even tried out for the freshman football team," Clifton said.

"And then apparently it started up again. The counselors were working with him and trying to find those responsible, but it's hard. I can remember how well bullies cover their tracks."

"I can remember how cruel kids can be, and how cruel they were," Angelina said. "I took my share at Mesa Verde Grade School and Montezuma County High too. When you had naturally blond hair and blue eyes and a name like Martinez you didn't fit well with your own people and the Anglo kids assumed you dyed it and pretended you were something you were not, so they really poured it on."

"I remember," Clifton said.

"Today has been like déjà vu. I was devastated over Emma and the kids at North, but I also felt deeply for Zack. I've walked in his shoes. I've felt his rage and it has simmered under the surface all these years. I've seen it in the way I react to kids intimidating each other, politicians in their campaigning and sometimes people I've worked for. I remember those years of harassment and pain in grade school and kids refusing to talk to me. Even worse, today I remembered sitting down by the road there in Colorado, with a .22 on my lap waiting for Hector. That afternoon, if he had walked by while I was there, I swear, the mood I was in I would have killed him!

By God's grace, and every feeling of right and wrong that Dad and Mom taught me and from others who had influenced me, like meeting you at the lake and realizing everyone wasn't like the kids at East Lakeview, I came to my senses just long enough to run and keep on running away from that place and those kids. Within the next week, I came this close to stepping over a cliff in total despair and guilt over it. I hit total rock bottom, mentally and emotionally."

Angelina was speechless. She took him in her arms and held him tightly.

Over the years, he had confided in her and shared with her stories of his year in the canyon behind her family farm, but he had never told her exactly why he had gone there in the first place. He had told her about the bullying and about his dad and his boyhood fantasy of living like an aboriginal in the cliff dwelling. She had admired his actually having the guts to do it, even if it was a foolish thing to do. But, this was an entirely new slant that he had never revealed to her. Suddenly his reaction to the shooting and the emotion had new meaning.

"I was more fortunate than Zack. I had a place, the resources, and someone, or something, perhaps the spirits of my ancestors, looking over me. I had the time to heal in my own way, and on my own time, there in that wilderness. I reset my mind the way I have to occasionally reset my computer now, reload the operating system and download new software. I had to do all of that so that I could go on and make something of my life, and so that I could have a wonderful wife like you, children and friends.

"Zack almost made it, but he broke first. I think he was suffering from Post Traumatic Stress Disorder as surely as if were a veteran returning from war. Well, he has no one left now. He probably had no friend. Now he has no family. He took care of that!

"The courts will appoint someone from the public defender's office to take care of him. Who knows who that will be or whether they will even try to see that he is represented and taken care of.

"I loved Emma as a friend and colleague. She was so full of life and gave so much of herself to her students. She made the world a better place for everyone around her, but she couldn't make up for the hurt being dealt out to her own son even working within the system."

Angie held him close. "Beginning next week you are going to have a new life ahead of you. You won't have to worry about a career, working within a system. You finally have time for yourself. You have wanted to write. I think now it is time to tell your stories."

"Do you have any time off coming Angie? If you can find someone to cover for you at the clinic, why don't we get in the car Monday and drive back to see your folks? I'd like to walk the canyon again. I'd like to show you a world that was in your backyard when you grew up, that you might have been unaware of. And, I'd like to know if George is still alive. He'd be about 80 now."

"Actually, I already asked Dr. Adkins if she could handle things for the next few weeks and she said no problem."

"How....?"

"It was going to be a surprise for you before all this happened today.

Did you think I would be unaware of the travel books, cell phone literature, and so on you've been picking up lately? The veterinarian covering for me has expressed an interest in buying my share of the practice. This will give her and Dr. Adkins an opportunity to see if they can get along together."

Clifton kissed her and held her back enough to look into her face. "That's why we've clicked from the very first time we met there at Summit Lake when we were just kids. We were and are still in sync," he said. "I love you so much."

Near Martinez Canyon
The Kelley Farm
Summit Ridge Colorado
Spring 1955

88
Retribution
At the Pueblo Ruin

The door was uncovered to let in the spring night sounds, sounds no longer threatening but welcome. Frogs sang at the creek below. A few crickets called to each other. Owls hooted in the cedar tree answering calls from trees out on top, perhaps one on the snag above.

After the long winter, with the door closed to keep in the meager heat, he now left the door open even though the temperature got down toward freezing during the night. The fresh air circulating through the dwelling was welcome.

A faint sweet smell of tamarack was in the air. It had been a warm, pleasant spring day. Although it had cooled with sunset, it remained warm enough that he needed only his yucca shirt and breach cloth to keep warm. Cliff sat in the doorway looking out across the canyon. The three quarter moon cast enough light that he could see Mesa Verde clearly. The Milky Way seemed particularly bright that night.

He heard an unfamiliar sound. At first, he thought it was coyotes, and then he heard it again. It wasn't animal but human voices; loud raucous laughter carrying on the still night air. It was some distance away and the outbursts were brief. The sound seemed to come from above and from the same side of the canyon.

Cliff slipped into outdoor moccasins. He tied the headband around his forehead to keep his shoulder length hair out of his face, tied the belt carrying the hunting knife scabbard around his waist, draped the quiver with the atlatl and four short spears over his neck and stepped outside the dwelling. He climbed the cliff onto the rim and listened. He didn't hear the voices, but he smelled smoke. Someone had built a fire and left trash at the pueblo ruin the night before. They must be back.

By the light of the moon, he made his way through the woods toward the smoke. As he neared the ruin, he began to hear slurred male voices more distinctly. They were speaking Spanish.

Firelight flickered between the trees. Behind it loomed the mound of stones that perhaps had been the center for the Ancestral Puebloans. Minor vandalism had been occurring at the ruin recently. Cliff had picked up empty beer cans discarded by someone partying there since the arrival of warm weather, but he had not seen those responsible. He didn't know what he would do if he did see someone. It was government property. Whom would he notify? He couldn't do anything himself. Could he?

Cliff slipped from tree to tree until he was close enough to see each of the four individuals in the firelight. Three of the men he recognized as relatives of Hector Rodriguez. The youngest, but not necessarily the smallest of the group, was Hector Rodriguez himself. Hector was not old enough to drink, but he held a can of something in his hand.

Cliff watched as the four talked and laughed. He couldn't understand what they said, although he understood a few familiar Spanish words. He observed their body language and horseplay. The three older men seemed to be teasing Hector. He heard Angelina Martinez's name used repeatedly. He guessed they were teasing Hector about her.

Angelina was a pretty, fair-skinned girl with light brown/blond hair and blue eyes, unusual among the Mexican girls on the Ridge. She was slightly older than Hector putting her in the same grade Cliff would have been in had he gone to school the past year.

Hector protested a little too loudly, confirming Cliff's suspicion that he enjoyed being teased about Angelina.

Cliff's memory was still strong of the pleasant day he had spent with her once upon a time. It stirred his blood to hear them talking about her. She was the only girl he had met up to that time who had talked to him and seemed to have a good time with him. He knew from that short time that she was a nice girl and way too good for the likes of Hector.

Cliff focused on the laughing, beer drinking men around the fire. His dad didn't drink and neither did George. They both had a dim view of it and had expressed that to him frequently. He assumed the men in front of him were the ones trashing the ruin lately when they came there to party.

Finally Hector stood. "I'm going to take a piss," he said in English.

"Don't take too long," one of the men said.

"I think he will go see Angelina!" the second man laughed.

Obviously the four had been there for a while. Cliff guessed none of the men was much over twenty. They had each dropped several empty cans on the ground. *There are no empties where Hector sat. He's had only the one can he still carries. If I confront him, and he's still sober, he'll be much more dangerous than the others.*

I think that the moonlight, starlight, this old ruin and some good old-fashioned superstition might help me here. I'll bet I can make them afraid of more than just me out here, it sure use to work on me.

Cliff watched Hector climb up the side of the ruin. He didn't appear to be drunk.

Cliff slipped away from the tree. Keeping other trees between him, and the men at the fire, he circled around behind to the other side of the ruin.

Hector stood in full relief on the highest point of the ruin and began to unbuckle his belt and lower his trousers.

Cliff's blood boiled at the sight of Hector preparing to defecate there on the ruin. He removed a spear from the quiver. None of the spears had a dart with a point attached. Without a dart attached, the spear was blunt ended. The dart end of the spear was nearly an inch in diameter, wrapped in sinew, with a hole drilled in the center to accept the dart head.

Without the dart and its sharp bone point, the blunt spear wouldn't penetrate anything, but it would carry a punch. He loaded the spear onto the atlatl and aimed at Hector's exposed buttock, which gleamed white in the moonlight, and threw.

"Yiiieeee!" Hector yelled as the blunt spear struck his exposed buttock and bounced harmlessly down the north slope of the ruin. "What the Hell?" he yelped. Hector leaped to his feet, pulling up his trousers and looked down the slope at the spear that had come out of the darkness. The spear tumbled and lodged 20 feet below him against sagebrush at the bottom of the slope of the ruin. In the moonlight, he could see the feathers and decoration on the four foot shaft. He could not see Cliff who stood in the dark shadow of the trees.

Holding his trousers up with one hand, he turned and leaped over the edge of the ruin and scrambled down the south slope through the rock and brush back toward the fire. "Somebody threw a stick at me up there!" he yelled in Spanish.

His three companions had heard his scream and stood transfixed in the firelight watching him scramble down the slope, trying to hold his pants up with one hand. "Some *cabron* threw a stick at me!" Hector repeated. "It had feathers and decorations on it."

"A stick? You must be crazy Man! Who would do that?" his uncle demanded, also in Spanish.

"You want to see where it hit me?" Hector shouted dropping his pants and pointing to an inch round, lifesaver shaped, red welt. "Some crazy *Cabron* threw a stick at me. I saw it. I felt it. It's in the sagebrush on the other side of the ruin. I'll show you. Come on!" Hector said. He pulled up his pants, fastened his belt, and hobbled off toward the left end of the ruin.

"For a minute I thought he was going to show us his ass," his cousin laughed.

"I gotta see this!" Hector's cousin said derisively.

"I'm not sure about this," the second cousin and the more superstitious of the three said, holding back by the fire.

"Come on, let's see what Hector is seeing in the dark," their uncle said. The three followed Hector.

"What if the guy is still out there and has more?" The second cousin asked.

"You think he'd take on four of us? I don't think so. Come on!" Hector said.

The men spoke rapidly in Spanish that Cliff couldn't understand, but he knew by their excited voices that he had "kicked the hive."

Cliff retrieved the spear, returned it to the quiver, circled back around the right end of the ruin to the trees near the fire and watched the four as they began to pick their way around the ruin to search for the spear. As they disappeared out of sight, he picked up the remaining cans of beer, tossed them into the fire, moved back into the woods and waited.

As Hector searched for the bush where he had seen the spear drop, sounds like gunfire erupted on the other side of the ruin. "Son-of-a-bitch! Now the *cabron* is shooting at us," Hector yelled. "Hit the ground!"

The four men dropped to the ground. It took a moment to realize the shots had stopped and none of them was hit. Hector stood first. "I think the sound was from back at the fire," he said.

They rushed back to the bonfire where the remaining cans of beer had burst and were sizzling in the bonfire. From out of the dark, a blunt ended spear caught the last man in line in the buttock, causing him to scream and run into the man in front of him. He grabbed his buttock with both hands and danced around in pain. On the ground behind them was a four-foot long stick with feathers. It looked like a very long, heavy arrow with no point.

"Ghost!" yelled the cousin. "Get out of here!" he screamed. The four men began running back toward their pickup, parked a quarter of a mile back on the side of the county road.

They were not used to running through the woods at night. Even with the light of the three quarter moon, their progress was slow. Branches and bushes became the hands and arms of the ghosts of the Indians who were pursuing the superstitious quartet, and they dodged and turned and were even more disoriented.

Cliff helped their terror along by calling to them in a high quavering voice, suddenly appearing in front of them and then as quickly disappearing. He looked like an Indian ghost in buckskin breechcloth, and sleeveless shirt, his long hair held back with a headband with white bone beads. In one hand, he held the atlatl and in the other hand a spear.

He played cat and mouse with them as they dodged him and trees on their search for the road. Finally, Cliff managed to separate Hector from the group and let the older men charge headlong through the woods toward the pickup.

He herded Hector toward a small opening in the trees. When they reached the open moonlit glade, he commanded Hector to stop.

If Hector had been drinking beer, he was cold sober now. In front him stood a guy who Hector supposed was trying to pass himself off as an Indian. *This is obviously some crazy man living out here in the woods,* Hector thought. *He is smaller than me, and I'm wondering why I let this guy spook me? Why have I been running? I can take this carbon, Hector thought. The guy doesn't realize I've got a weapon of my own, and I know how to use it.*

Hector reached into his pocket and in the next instant moonlight flashed off the blade of the switchblade he held in his right hand. He crouched ready to strike with it extended in front of him.

Cliff eyed the boy who had bullied him for seven years in school. He felt amazingly relaxed. Hector obviously hadn't recognized him yet.

The vicious looking, razor sharp, six inch blade gleamed in the moonlight.

Would it make a difference if he knew who I am? Cliff wondered.

Hector had no time to react as the heavy end of the atlatl struck the thumb of the hand which grasped the switchblade knife.

The knife cartwheeled into the air toward Cliff. He caught it out of the air, and in a continuous motion, he sent it toward the nearest piñon where the point imbedded itself in the trunk.

"What the hell…?" cried Hector holding his painful right thumb.

Cliff smiled. Finally, Hector would know what it felt like to have an aching thumb for a few days.

"You really didn't need that knife did you?" Clifton asked.

Hector didn't recognize the voice. It was much deeper now than the high-pitched, breaking pre-pubescent voice that he was familiar with coming from the Clifton Kelley that he had beaten the year before at the school cistern. "You're armed," Hector said.

"I don't need to be armed to take on a bully like you!" Cliff said quietly.

"Oh, yea, Indio? Then get rid of them!" Hector said.

"Gladly," Cliff said. He slipped the quiver sash over his head, put the atlatl inside, and hung it from a branch on the piñon tree where Hector's knife blade glinted in the moonlight. He pulled the hunting knife from his belt, stuck it next to Hector's and returned to where Hector stood.

"So Indio, your puny stick is the reason my ass is sore?"

"You got it. You were crapping on my ruin. Would you like it if I took a dump on your house?"

"That old pile of rock and trash is nobody's house, Indio!"

"My spirit lives there! You think you can fight a spirit?"

"You are not a spirit, *Amigo*. And yes, I think I can take care of myself against you very well!" Hector raised his fists. The little finger on each hand curled a little tighter, making the knuckle point a little higher than the rest of his fist.

Cliff had seen those fists close up before with the knuckle raised. He had felt the effect of those raised knuckles and seen what they did to his face. Hector was even older and bigger now, more heavily muscled than the year before in the schoolyard. The hackles began to rise on his neck.

He visualized the bee tree with thousands of workers all with the ability to swarm out of the foot square hole he had cut, and sting him to death. Images of the charging coyote intent on tearing his throat out flashed through his mind. His heartbeat slowed and he breathed deeply. Cliff let his hands relax at his side, unlike almost exactly a yearly before. He said with a smile, "You want a piece of me, little brother!" To his own ears, it sounded remarkably like the teasing voice of his older brother Charlie.

Hector danced forward. He swung hard with his right fist and followed through immediately with his left, but he connected only with night air.

Cliff ducked and stepped aside sweeping his foot under the bigger boy, knocking him off balance. Hector fell to his knees hard but scrambled up. He was a large boy, but he was agile. He turned to face his opponent, who was suddenly not quite as sure as before.

He danced toward Cliff again with his fists in front of his face circling to his right as he did. Cliff swiveled in place never taking his eyes from the coal black spots in Hector's face. "Red Rover, Red Rover, send Hector over," he whispered.

"What did you say Indio?" asked Hector.

"I said, Red Rover, Red Rover, Send Hector Over," Cliff repeated, in a louder whisper.

"How do you know my name, *Cabron?*" Hector asked. Then he charged. "I'll come over all right!" Hector roared, swinging right and left.

Cliff stepped aside again at the last moment and at the same time grasped his own left fist in his right hand, as had Hector so many times on the playground, and blocked Hector's fist by bringing his own clenched fists down on Hector's right forearm with all his might. Hector grabbed his arm with his left hand and backed off glaring at his opponent a second as Cliff smiled.

"Annie Over," Cliff said in another loud whisper and he launched his own sudden, swift attack, catching Hector once in the ribs with his elbow where he himself had been hit so many times by Hector's hardball when they played the game of throwing the ball over the roof of the schoolhouse. As swiftly as he attacked, he whirled and was out of reach.

Hector gasped and clutched his side. He didn't cry out, but Cliff could tell he was hurting. It had been a solid hit.

Hector sneered and crouched, "You think this is a game *Cabron*? I have played long enough. I will finish you now. I will destroy you!" he cried angrily. A terrible, cold, mask of anger covered his face as he stared into the moon lit eyes of the apparition in front of him.

Who is this boy dressed up like an Indian who somehow is looking more familiar and bringing back memories of another time, another place? His arm ached. A sharp pain pierced his side where the kid had hit him in the ribs.

Six feet separated them as he charged, both arms spread out in front of him. He intended to tackle and destroy the figure in front of him.

Cliff felt calm. He no longer feared Hector. All those years, he had been defeated by fear as much as Hector's strength. During the three-week dust storm and the weeks following, he had distracted himself by visualizing this moment if the occasion ever arose again. He had re-constructed the mock wrestling play between Charlie and himself, the moves and holds that Charlie had used. He had practiced by the hour with no one else there to practice on.

It was finally just Hector and himself. There was no adoring crowd to egg either of them on. Neither one of them had to prove himself to anyone else.

Hector was big, strong and powerful and he knew how to fight. That was his strength. He had plenty of practice with real live opponents.

Cliff was thin, wiry and quick. In the past 12 months, he had developed more muscle and filled out some, although he was still slender. During the three-week dust storm, he had learned that his dad was right. He was much more powerful fighting with his mind than purely relying on his body. He had to make up with his lack of might, by fighting with his brains.

He had practiced every move and gone through it so many times in his mind that he was at last ready. That was his strength.

Cliff watched Hector's charge in slow motion, and at the last moment, he twisted to the side and dropped to the ground. He kicked out, catching his leg between Hector's, tripping him. Hector went down face first in the dirt, trying to catch himself with his hands before his chin hit the ground.

Cliff was on Hector's back in an instant with an arm threaded under Hector's right arm and back up over his neck extending Hector's shoulder in a painful stretch. If Hector moved, he could dislocate the shoulder.

"I thought about re-arranging your face for you, but I'm sure your family is proud of it the way it is," Cliff whispered in Hector's ear. "If I re-arrange your shoulder you can save your face, but I hear it is really painful."

Hector kicked and struggled to free himself, but the pressure on his arm increased each time he struggled, and the pain in his shoulder increased until he felt faint. Finally, he lay still.

"How do you like it when someone torments you and makes your life a living hell?" Cliff asked in a whisper and jerked the arm tighter, eliciting a loud moan from Hector.

"What do you want?" Hector asked.

"At one time I wanted to cause you the same fear and pain you caused others. I wanted to make you run and hide. I wanted to take you away from your family. I wanted to punish you permanently. I wanted to put you in the ground. That is what I really wanted, Hector. Now I don't want that any more. I just want you to know that I'm not afraid of you anymore," Cliff whispered.

"How do you know my name," Hector asked again with real fear in his voice this time.

"I know many things," the voice at his ear whispered menacingly. "And I can come for you any time I want, and I can make your life here on earth the same living hell you have made it for…for… others."

"When I get up from here, I will kill you!" Hector said. "Who are you?"

Unbelievable, Cliff thought. *He still doesn't know who I am. Should I tell him? He will fear a spirit more. I've beaten him, and he and I know it. That's all that counts, really. Let him think what he wants. The fear of the unknown is much stronger. Sooner or later, he'll figure it out. However, even in daylight and with no surprise, he'll never beat me again. He and his kind will never be a threat to me again!*

"What a stupid thing to say, Hector. I could dislocate your shoulder right now if I wished to do so. If I let you stand, it will be because I wish it! Do you think I have had no opportunity to take revenge? If I had wanted to, I could have put a point on that spear tonight and it would have gone clear through your butt. My aim is good enough to put a spear anywhere on your body that I want. With a point on it, it will go right through you!"

Cliff said.

"I want you to stay away from that pueblo. Take your parties somewhere else. Tell your cousins and uncles I will be waiting for them, if they come back here. This is sacred ground," Cliff whispered. He put more pressure on Hector's arm until it was near the dislocation point again. Hector screamed in pain and struggled, then became quiet.

Cliff suddenly released the arm and was off the boy's back. He dashed by the tree, collecting the switchblade, his hunting knife, and quiver and disappeared into the dark shadows of the trees.

Hector lay still for a moment before rising to his knees. "I promise to bring the Sheriff here! You don't scare me!" He screamed. His shoulder throbbed in pain as did his ribs, arm, and thumb. He wiped the dirt off his face and struggled to his feet.

The moon was lower in the sky and it was darker. Hector stumbled around looking for the road. Why had his uncle and cousins left him behind? He had never been afraid of the dark before, but suddenly every sound and shape in the dim light was menacing. He felt afraid for the first time. He half expected to, at any moment, be impaled with a spear.

He began to run and stumble through the trees. A tree branch brushed his face and he reflexively sprang backward, lost his balance and fell on his behind. He jumped up and ran through the trees and brush until mercifully he broke out of the timber at the Kelley fence line and knew where he was.

Hector stared out across moonlit shadows of the Kelley farm. The dim moonlit image of his tormentor came back to him as he stared across the open fields.

The gringo?

"Red Rover, Red Rover, Send Hector Over...." "Annie Over...." The voice was somehow familiar... "I just want you to know that I'm not afraid of you anymore...."

It couldn't be!

Hector followed the fence line to the county road. The cousin's pickup was gone. *Cabron's didn't wait for me.*

He walked the quarter of a mile home.

If his father was up, he would have some explaining to do.

89

Connection
At the Pueblo Ruin

County Sheriff Bill Kirkendall poked through the ashes of the smoldering fire near the Big Ruin as local residents called it. Scattered empty beer cans, some of them split open and charred, littered the area.

"What I want to know, Hector, is what you guys were doing partying out here anyway. Why was this ruin trashed this way? If you're going to come out here and party, can't you carry out your cans? It's on U.S. Government land. Why do you feel a need to come here and trash it?" the Sheriff asked.

"We were attacked by a wild man dressed up like an Indian, Sheriff," Hector said, ignoring the question. That's why we called you here. To catch a man who almost killed us last night," Hector said angrily.

"Were you drinking any of this beer, Hector? You aren't 21 are you?" the sheriff asked.

"No, of course not Sheriff. My uncle and cousins were drinking it. They are over 21. You can ask them. Right Dad? I was having a coke."

"Yes, they are over 21," Raul said. It was obvious that he was not pleased that his son had been there with his older relatives, but he was also concerned about his son's safety.

"So describe him to me again. What did your attacker look like?" Sheriff Kirkendall asked.

"It was dark except for the moonlight, so we couldn't see his face clearly. He was about five feet tall, maybe a hundred ten or twenty pounds. He wore a kind of leather skirt hanging down to here like in pictures of Geronimo and a brown shirt with no sleeves. His hair was long," Hector indicated to the sheriff by pointing low on his shoulder. "He wore a head band around his hair."

"Let me get this straight," the sheriff said. You describe him as about five feet tall and about a hundred pounds? You look to be about five feet eight or nine and what? About a hundred-fifty or a hundred-sixty?"

"Yes," Hector said proudly and stood straighter to show his full size, even though he winced from the pain in his side.

"So how did someone this size," he put his hand even with Hector's shoulder, "and someone about two thirds your weight do that much damage to someone your size without using a baseball bat on you?"

"He was very quick, and he could see in the dark!" Hector said angrily. "He caught me off guard. Each time I reached for him, he wasn't there. He knew how to wrestle. He took advantage of me! And he threatened to kill me!"

"I see. You said he had arrows or a spear?" the sheriff asked.

"They looked like long arrows. He hit me in the butt with one. It hurt really bad. He carried them on his back. But, we couldn't find them after he threw them," Hector said. "Do you want to see?"

"Did it draw blood?"

"No."

"Then I think we're OK. I'll take your word for it for now. Did he say anything to you? Was there anything strange he said that would help us identify him?" the sheriff asked.

"He threatened to kill me!"

"What exactly did he say?"

"He said he was thinking about 'rearranging my face.'" Hector paused. He seemed to be remembering something, but he seemed to reconsider and shook it off.

"What did you just think of Hector? You just remembered something there, didn't you?" The sheriff prodded.

"I remember the last time I saw the *gringo* Kelley boy who ran away last year. I was just joking with him a little bit before that, and I may have said something like that to him, just as a joke, you understand. But he thought I was serious."

"That was the fight the two of you had the day he ran away?"

"Maybe," he said insolently.

"Hector, do you think it's possible that the person who attacked you last night might have been the Kelley boy?"

"Oh, no Señor! The Kelley boy was such a coward, and he didn't know how to fight. The Indio last night knew how to fight, and he was no coward!"

"How big was he again?"

"The Indio?"

"I was thinking about Clifton Kelley."

"Well," Hector said uncomfortably. They were about the same size.... But that boy was such a coward. He thought he was so smart, reading all the time, but he couldn't fight."

"You showed him who the primo hombre at that school was whenever you wanted to didn't you? Wouldn't it be ironic if he came back here last night and showed you who the primo hombre on the plateau was now?"

"It wasn't him Sheriff! I tell you it wasn't him! Why are you asking me all this, and you're not going after that crazy man who threatened me last night?""So do you think you can find where he fought with you?"

"I don't know. We were running through the woods trying to find the road, and he kept confusing us in the dark. He separated us, and that is when he attacked me and threatened me," Hector said. "He was too much coward to attack me when my uncle and cousins were here."

"Oh, I see," laughed the sheriff. "Four-on-one makes better odds? Is that what you are saying?"

"No!" Hector said sullenly.

"And exactly what did he say when he threatened you?" The Sheriff asked.

"He warned me and my cousins and uncle to stay away from this Indian ruin. He said he lived here. He was trying to make me think he was some kind of spirit. But no kind of spirit could have nearly broken my arm like he did."

"Show him your arm and neck, Hector," Raul said.

Hector took off his shirt and showed the black and blue marks on the back of his neck and around his shoulder and the muscle of his bicep.

"Well, for what it's worth, I don't believe in ghosts much myself," Bill said. "I'll poke around here for awhile and see what I can find. You hear of any more odd things going on in the neighborhood, you let me know. Hector, I'd stay away from here. Obviously, whoever this was doesn't want you messing around this ruin. I think I have all the information I need for now Mr. Rodriguez. You can take Hector home. I'll keep you informed on what I find."

From the shadow of a cedar, Cliff observed the sheriff, Hector and Raul poking about the burned out campfire and exploded beer cans. He had come to the clearing to clean it up only to discover the sheriff, Hector, and Raul examining the bonfire site. He had lingered out of sight to watch and listen in amusement. He had extinguished the fire the night before, but by then it was too dark to find all the cans.

Cliff grinned as Hector began limping away with his father. Hector was obviously exaggerating his injuries. He hadn't touched Hector's legs. Hector was mostly suffering from injured pride. Cliff had put pressure on Hector's shoulder, and it should be sore this morning, but Hector was strong.

The ribs? Cliff hoped they really hurt. It would serve him right. He wondered what his own rib cage would look like under an x-ray. The film would probably show a spider web of healed cracks from being hit in the ribs repeatedly with a hard ball thrown by Hector when they had played the mandatory 'Annie Over' game.

Hector and Raul had gone only a few paces toward Raul's pickup before Clifton impulsively stepped from behind the cedar and called, "Red Rover, Red Rover, let Hector come over!"

Sheriff Kirkendall, Hector and Raul turned as one and stared as the slim sun tanned figure approached. He fit the description that Hector had given of the attacker from the night before, slight of build, wearing breechcloth, headband, moccasins and quiver from which protruded four short spears.

On his belt, he wore a hunting knife, several pouches and a two-foot long straight stick.

Cliff approached the sheriff who extended his hand. "Good morning Sheriff."

"Mr. Kelley?"

"Clifton. I think I met you before in town a couple of years ago with my family," Cliff said.

"We looked high and low for you last summer young man. It would be an understatement to say that a lot of good people, including your parents, are very worried about you. Were you around here all that time?"

"Maybe something like that," Cliff said quietly.

"This young man tells me you tried to kill him last night. Is that right Mr. Kelley?"

"He was the one carrying this," Cliff said. He pulled the illegal switchblade knife from the pouch on his belt and handed it to the sheriff. "He and his friends were vandalizing the ruin there. I tried to get them to stop."

"He nearly killed us with those spears!" Hector said vehemently. He pointed to the quiver on Cliff's back.

"Oh, if I'd wanted to kill him with one of these, rest assured, he wouldn't be standing there now!" Cliff said.

He pulled a spear from the quiver and a six-inch long dart with a bone point attached from a pouch on his belt. The end of the spear was blunt with a hole drilled in it to accept the dart.

"I was using a spear like this without a point. It couldn't hurt anyone without the point. It could leave a bruise maybe, and it might hurt. I just wanted to scare them away from the ruin. If I had wanted to hurt them, I would have put a dart on the end of the spear." He demonstrated by inserting the tapered end of a dart into the hole in the end of the spear. "Without a dart I can stun a cottontail if I hit it in the head, with the dart I can bring down a deer. All Hector and his friends got last night were sore butts."

The darts were safely stored away back at my home.

"So what do you do with these? Why are you carrying them?" the sheriff asked.

"I hunt rabbits. I use their meat for food and their hides for clothing and all kinds of things."

The sheriff pointed to the buckskin quiver. "Where did that buckskin come from?"

"This piece came from a deer that got hit by a car over on the county road below the Stone's house. I got to it before the coyotes and the road crew."

"Hector here says you didn't know how to fight the last time he saw you, but last night he couldn't get a hand on you. Where did you learn to fight all of a sudden?"

"I had plenty of time to think this winter. During the winter, I remembered when my brother and I use to wrestle. He would get me in those neck holds all the time and make me cry and say 'uncle'. I realized that since I'm smaller and quicker, if I had been calm enough and not so afraid, I could probably have stood up to Hector last spring. Instead, when Hector came after me, I let him take me on his own terms. Last spring I let my own fears defeat me, as much as Hector."

The sheriff turned to Raul. "It seems to me like Hector and Clifton got into a fight last night, and Hector came out on the rough end of it. It sounds like turnabout is fair play, if you know what I mean. Do you still want to come into town and swear out an assault complaint after what you've heard here?"

"Yes!" Hector said emphatically.

"I don't think so!" Raul said just as emphatically. "Let's go Hector; we have some things to discuss."

Hector glared at Cliff and stood his ground. Raul swung around and caught Hector off guard, as the side of his boot connected with Hector's rear end. Then he grabbed his by the scruff of the neck and pushed him toward the pickup truck.

From the look of shock and disbelief on Hector's face, it was obvious he wasn't use to this kind of treatment from his father

Sheriff Kirkendall smiled as he watched the pickup drive off, then he asked Cliff to join him as he turned toward the County pickup. "You know Clifton, it would make your parents feel a whole lot better if they knew you were alive and well," the sheriff said.

"I gave them a sign at Christmas time and sent a warning through George that coyotes were a threat to the livestock when the snow got so deep there in mid winter."

"Yea, they told me. Moreover, they haven't heard anything since, and we still had a lot of winter in between. Signs are one thing. Your presence is something else. How about you and me driving over there and saying 'hey' to them?"

"My mom might be glad to see me, but my dad will probably just want to take the razor strop to me, and I can't allow that to happen now. I might hurt him if he tries to whip me!" Cliff said. "I can't take that chance. I'm not the same kid who left a year ago. I'm not afraid of him now, just as I wasn't afraid of Hector last night," Cliff said quietly. *I guess I don't have much choice now. The sheriff knows I'm here. If I don't go with him, he'll soon find the ruin and me.*

Sheriff Kirkendall studied the self-assured boy who stood in front of him. He vaguely remembered the small sad eyed boy he had met outside the county extension office in town two years before when he had visited with Ed and Etta Mae. That boy had stood slump shouldered and with eyes downcast as he fidgeted by his mother.

"Clifton, I'll be right there with you, and as far as I'm concerned you aren't obliged to stay if you don't want to. I'll bring you back here if that's your wish. That's a promise."

"What will happen if I don't go with you?" Cliff asked.

"I'm going to visit with your parents regardless. They deserve to know where you are and that you are well. I'm obligated to do this. You are under age and your parents are in charge. It will be up to Ed and Etta Mae as to what happens next," the sheriff replied.

"And if they say put out another search party?"

"Then we'll put out a search."

"I will have to come back here, because I have animals to care for," Cliff said. "Do you think you could wait for me here for a few minutes so

I can get a couple of things for Mom and Dad?" he asked.

"You take all the time you need."

Cliff took off at a lope through the trees heading east parallel to the canyon until he was out of the sheriff's sight before cutting back south to the bare rimrock a quarter of a mile from the dwelling. He left no tracks on the bare rock all the way back to the snag and the toe hold access where he descended over the lip of the rim down to the ledge.

Cliff had saved a four-inch square comb of tamarack honey from the first bee tree robbing. He transferred it from a quart jar to a small rectangular pitch lined basket, one of the finest that he had made to date. He covered it with a matching lid and tied it with thin yucca cord. He was certain that his dad had never tasted tamarack honey before. It would be a special treat.

Next, he selected a red cedar carving of a coyote, his favorite carving from all those he had produced all winter. The winter's work filled several built in nooks in the wall. He wrapped the carving in woven yucca fiber and tied it with a buckskin lace.

He placed the two gifts in the knapsack and put the knapsack on his back.

Moonbeam curled up asleep in the corner with her brood. They would be ready to wean soon. Maggie flew down to Cliff's shoulder and accepted a sunflower seed. "See you later Maggie. Take care of things."

"See you later," Maggie mimicked.

Cliff climbed back out over the rim and retraced his route to where the sheriff awaited. He was very nervous and excited all at the same time.

"I radioed my office while I waited," Sheriff Kirkendall said. "They have phoned your parents that we are coming. That way they will be prepared. It might be a shock if you suddenly got out of the car after all this time."

"Thank you sir."

~~~

"He's coming home Papa!" Etta Mae cried. That was the sheriff's office. Clifton is with the sheriff now!"

"Was he arrested for something?" Ed asked worriedly.

They stood in the kitchen by the phone. Each time the phone had rung over the past year, they had picked it up, eager for a call from the Sheriff, yet dreading a call with bad news.

They had known since the arrival of Cliff's Christmas gift that he was alive, and George had confessed that he had seen Cliff the one time he had observed him in the fall and that he had left clothing for him. The last report of any kind had been a cryptic message left at George's barn warning of possible coyote trouble. It had caused more worry than hope.

"I think we should call George. He should be here, Papa," Etta Mae said.

"I think so too," Ed agreed.

"You'll have to make the call Ed. I don't think I can talk anymore right now."
~~~

90
Reunion
Kelley Farm

Sheriff Kirkendall, Ed Kelley, Etta Mae Kelley, Clifton Kelley and George Williamson sat around the kitchen table at the Kelley farm.

"Do you think I could have one more glass of milk," Cliff asked.

Etta Mae laughed. "What is this? Glass three or four?"

"So, who's counting?" Ed said happily. Help yourself to all you want."

Etta Mae removed mostly empty serving dishes to the kitchen counter and replaced them with a large mincemeat pie and the basket containing the new comb of honey Cliff had presented to his dad that morning.

His mother's gift, the coyote woodcarving, stood in the center of the table. The coyote figure stood with one front paw lifted, his head lowered, lips curled into a snarl. The animal was advancing on prey or warning off others.

Cliff did not share with them where he had seen that snarling face before.

Ed cut a square of the comb and savored the slightly crystallized honey in the comb contentedly. He smacked his lips and licked the spoon. "That's got to be about the most delicate tasting honey I've ever tasted," he said. "What do you think they were gathering Cliff?" he asked.

"About the only thing blooming at that time was tamarack," Cliff said. He didn't elaborate. The only place on the Ridge where tamarack grew was in the canyon bottoms. To be specific would too closely pinpoint where he had been living. The fact that the encounter that morning had been very close to Martinez Canyon seemed to pretty well point to which Canyon.

"Where did you get fresh honey this early in the season?" George asked.

"I robbed a bee tree," Cliff said, "last summer, early."

"That explains why it is a little crystallized," George observed.

"You robbed a bee tree. Just like that?" Bill laughed.

"I'm not surprised," Ed said. "It wasn't the first. Your hives here have been really busy too."

"I've seen bees on the tamarack, but I never tried to isolate the honey," George said. "This is really good."

Etta Mae lifted the delicately carved figure as her husband, son, and George discussed the honey. Cliff couldn't have pleased Ed more than with comb honey. To Ed, honey in the comb was better than any dessert she could make. She studied her son. The call from Bill's office had caught her unprepared. For months after Cliff's disappearance, she had clung to the hope Bill would call with news of Cliff, only to be disappointed. Then the gift had appeared shortly after Christmas. It was the first sign of hope that he was alive and well.

Then George had reported seeing him and that he was nearby and safe. He and Ed had gone back to the point where George had observed their son, but they had not seen him again.

Ed had reported to Sheriff Kirkendall. There was no active search by that time, although Bill still watched the wire and followed up on reports from any of the surrounding jurisdictions when there were reports of any kind of activity that included a boy Clifton's age.

Etta Mae had read and read the note that he had enclosed with the gift. *Merry Christmas. I am fine. Please don't worry about me. I am getting well in spirit and I am healthy. I will come home to stay one day when you can be proud of me. Please accept these Christmas gifts for now.* He seemed to have been telling them not to look for him, but how could they not. When the searches stopped again, she finally stopped jumping at each call. Nevertheless, she had never given up waiting for his return.

The framed note hung on the kitchen wall over the counter where she saw it every day when she prepared breakfast, dinner and supper. She had never given up. The winter had been brutal. It was the most severe winter they experienced during their time on the Ridge. George said it was a record for him too. She couldn't help worry that he might be found frozen to death.

Today she had blindly prepared the noon meal. She could hardly see through tear-swollen eyes. Her practiced hands had busily prepared her son's favorite foods while she listened to the conversation coming from the table where the men sat. She couldn't believe how he had changed. His voice had deepened. He sounded like Charlie. Were those fine whiskers on his face? What was that shirt made of and was that a loincloth? Didn't he wear underwear anymore? What would he say if she asked him to go into the bedroom, change into overalls and put on some underwear?

Cliff had come to her several times and interrupted her with hugs, and she had shooed him back to the table out of her way. She could hardly keep her eyes off him. He had grown. He had changed. He seemed so grown up. It was as if she suddenly had twin Charlie's in the house. Her heart ached, she had missed him so much and now he was here at last.

Would he stay?

Ed had changed too and for the better. He had become more patient and considerate with her. He seemed to be learning to keep his temper in check. She had heard him praying for Cliff's return. "Dear God make this all last," she had silently prayed.

Cliff finished his piece of mincemeat pie, pushed his chair back and sighed contentedly. He certainly would have a hard time climbing over the rim and down the rock face right at that moment after eating as much as he had. Etta Mae had kept putting more and more food in front of him.

Over the past year, he had fallen into the habit of foraging all day long rather than eating a big meal. His biggest meal was in the evening, when he settled in for the night, rather than a big dinner meal at noon. Even then, he usually wasn't that hungry and he didn't eat a large amount at a time. When he was out of the cave foraging during the spring, summer and fall, he ate whatever he came across as he gathered. Food gathering took a great deal of time each day. He ate as he gathered, and what he gathered went mostly into storage against those days when he couldn't be out or for the always-approaching winter.

Cliff had nearly forgotten the taste of fried chicken, baked bread, butter and dessert. Of all his mother's desserts, mincemeat was his favorite. He had missed it so much. She used it in pies, turnovers, and even put it between slices of bread for special sandwiches.

"Dad, after I delivered your Christmas gift, you could have come after me. It must have been obvious that I was nearby."

"That was our impulse. However, your note said you would come home when we could be proud of you. What did you mean by that?" Ed asked.

"Dad, when I left, I was very angry at everyone. I had to get away and figure out how to control that. I also needed time to figure out just who I was and how I wanted to live my life," Cliff said.

"Cliff you have to believe me when I say that your mother and I have always been very proud of you. We may have been hard on you, but that had nothing to do with how proud of you we were and still are," Ed said.

Cliff felt tears welling to his eyes, but he fought them back. "I think I figured that out, but it is nice to hear it said," Cliff said. "I came to realize something else while I was gone from here. You both have taught me so much. I couldn't have survived out there without the skill and knowledge you have both given me," Cliff said.

Ed started to speak but Cliff held up his hand, palm facing his dad to indicate he wasn't done. "I have to admit I was angry at you when I left. I counted you in with Mr. Johnson and Hector. I was finally able to sort those things out." He paused, a lump in his throat. "The conclusion I came to? I'm proud to be your son. You were spot on about many things I was doing that needed correcting. Maybe if I'd done that, you would have helped me more. I hope we can work together now instead of against each other."

Ed and Etta Mae sat staring at their son. They were speechless.

"So what is your plan now Clifton?" Sheriff Kirkendall finally asked.

"I don't know," Cliff said and looked at first his mom and then his dad.

"I hope you will come back here with us," Ed said and took his son's hand in his. "We would really like for you to consider that son."

"I think I'd like that Dad, but there would be some conditions," he said.

"What kind of conditions would that be?" Ed asked.

"If I foul up, which I know I will, you and I will sit down and talk about it. You won't get mad and start yelling and come after me with the razor strop or belt."

"I couldn't do that anymore son," Ed said. "I've had a year to think about things too."

"You have to know that if you lose your temper with me, I'll be gone again," Cliff said.

Ed wiped a tear from his eye, "I can't guarantee I'll never lose my temper again son. But I'll tell you one thing I've learned to do this past year. I've learned to walk away for a while when I begin to feel frustrated. I walk away and cool down. I've found it helps a lot. I know you are serious. I can promise you that I'll try my very best. I don't want to lose you again."

"I think that's fair enough. I will try too. I realized that I wasn't trying very hard myself either Dad. I have some loose ends to tie up. I can't just walk away from them. I have a place to close down and put back the way I found it. He smiled, "That's another thing I learned how to do while I was away. I learned how to finish what I start."

"Can I help you?" Ed asked.

"No, I have to do it myself. But thanks for offering."

"Clifton, I have a friend who I think would like to meet you," Sheriff Kirkendall said. "Would you consider that?"

"Why would your friend want to meet me?"

"I thought of him when I saw your hunting weapon this morning. He is kind of an expert on the Ancestral Puebloans who lived around here and that kind of thing. If you don't mind I'd like to give him a call and tell him about you and get the two of you together."

"Sure, Sheriff, if you want to do that. It would be OK," Clifton agreed. "But for the next few weeks I think we will be pretty busy around here."

"Can you sleep here tonight, Honey?" Etta Mae asked hopefully.

"I think I need to stay back at my place tonight, Mom. But soon, I promise, OK?" He pointed to the two figures he had given to them at Christmas time. "You see these two figures, Moonbeam and Maggie? They are real, Mom, and they are waiting for me back at my place. Moonbeam is a mom too now. She has six little ones. They are ready to wean. I need to see if she has enough food for them or if she needs anything else. When she weans them and they are out on their own, I'll see if she wants to stay with me. If so, I'll bring her back here with me.

Maggie is my other best friend. I'll have to try to convince him to move back here with me. Maggie imprinted with me when he was a baby. He may not be able to survive without me. I can't just abandon him."He's never met another human before. I'm the only human either of them has ever known, and although they are capable of getting along in the wild, they have been my companions. They have been with me since they were babies.

"I understand son," Etta Mae said.

"There is something I think you'd like to see outside, Cliff," Ed said. He led them all outside and around the house to the shaded corner where the last snow had melted only a few days before and already Cliff's mountain flower garden was lush with new green growth. Strawberry vine runners snaked among the fresh bright green clusters of columbine leaves and thin blades of mountain iris. Not a blade of grass or weeds mingled with the flowers.

"Wow! Dad. They should be spectacular this summer!" Cliff exclaimed. "I wondered what would happen to this little flower garden while I was gone. This means a lot to me Dad." He looked up at his dad who was studying his son's face.

Ed looked at George who smiled and nodded.

"All the time I tended to this garden last summer, I thought about us and what I wanted to do differently, if I had a chance, Cliff. I thought about this garden of wild flowers, how these columbines wilted and seemed to die when you planted them the first time. Then they came back stronger and more beautiful the second time. They seemed to be a symbol for us. I came out here and prayed every day last summer while I kept the weeds out and watered them. I prayed that you would come back and our wounds could be healed and we could start all over again."

Cliff grasped his dad's hand and then threw his arms around his dad and felt strong arms holding him close. "You have every right to not trust me, son, but I am asking for a chance to build your trust," Ed said softly to Cliff.

The sheriff dismissed himself with an offer to return Cliff to the spot where they had met, but Cliff declined.

"I'd like to spend the afternoon here. I'll be able to find my way back. Thank you for everything. I really appreciate it. If I owe you for the cost of the searching, I'll find a way to pay you back," he offered.

"We'll talk about that later," the sheriff laughed, "Right now enjoy your folks' company and don't worry about it."

"I have to be going too, George said. "It's good to have you home. I've missed our visits."

Cliff stayed through the afternoon visiting and catching up with his parents.

When it was time to do the afternoon water set, he didn't wait for his dad to ask, but he found his shovel and together they changed and set the water in the alfalfa in half the time it would have taken Ed alone. Ed told Cliff that Raul had required Hector to work in the Kelley fields in Cliff's place to make Hector understand the consequences of his action. He told Cliff that Raul had been unaware of his son's actions and that he had been angry with Hector and had punished him by making him work with Ed rather than in the mountains where he had dreamed of spending the summer. It explained things and corrected the perception that Ed had replaced Cliff with Hector out of anger.

When they got back to the house, he and Ed milked the cows and fed the livestock while Etta Mae stayed in the house preparing supper. Etta Mae couldn't remember the last time she had been able to prepare supper without having to do the outside chores first.

Cliff turned the cream separator. It seemed easy to get the separator core up to speed. He remembered it to be more difficult and the task more tedious than it now seemed.

Supper was congenial and laughter came often and quickly as Cliff related incidents with Maggie and Moonbeam. He revealed nothing about the ruin he had been living in and his parents had no reason to suspect he had been living in a cave. He was very vague about his living conditions, although he enthusiastically extolled the virtues of yucca soap and described making the fiber and weaving the cloth he had used to make the shirt he wore.

Etta Mae was eager to hear about his diet. She wanted to know about the various recipes he had concocted and what he had used for tea. She listened as he described cooking bread on the stone. He told her about grinding seeds and mixing them for bread and adding them to stews. She was concerned about his headaches and pleased that he had not suffered from any over the time of his absence. He did not tell her about the episode the Sunday night of the planting party.

Ed probed him about the buckskin. Cliff admitted that he had killed a deer with the atlatl and spear and about hide tanning.

Although he revealed much, he held much in reserve. He had heard the expression, "If it seems too good to be true, it probably is." The afternoon and evening with his parents went fast and were the best he had ever had with them. He hoped with all his heart that the "too good to be true" expression was just a cynical expression and nothing more. Only time would tell. He would give them every chance, but he had to keep his options open and an escape route safely at hand.

"You know that you have a percentage of Indian blood in you, don't you?" Ed said over dessert after supper.

"I remember you talking about it," Cliff said.

"Your great grandmother on my side was an Indian woman. We don't know what her name was but she was a full-blooded Choctaw. They lived in Arkansas. The census just listed her as an Indian maiden. I've seen a photograph of her. She was a tall handsome woman. You could see her in my sister's face. Your great grandmother on your mother's side was a Comanche Indian from down in West Texas. So maybe that is where your interest in the Indian ways come from."

"That's an interesting thought. It could explain quite a few things that happened to me this last year. Sometimes when calves were born, you commented that they were throwbacks. Does that work with people?"

"Maybe so son. Maybe so."

Etta Mae looked out the window at the falling darkness. "You are going to have to stay here tonight son. It's getting dark out there."

"Oh, that's OK, I can find my way."

"But, you have always been so afraid of the dark!"

"That is all behind me now Mom. It was one of those childish things. I have gotten over many things. I kind of like the night now. Sometimes

Moonbeam and I go out and look at the Milky Way and enjoy the quiet and the smell of the night."

"I'll be glad to drive you to where you need to go," Ed offered.

"Thanks Dad, but I'm OK, Really."

"When will we see you again?"

"Well it is about time to get crops in the ground isn't it?"

"I just brought home seed last week. Mama has finished most of the plowing. There is a little disking to do, and then I can get to the planting."

"You still working in town?"

"Yea, I'll probably never be able to quit that job."

"How come you were home today?"

"It's Saturday."

"I haven't seen a calendar since last May. So tomorrow is Sunday. Why don't I come back tomorrow morning? We can draw up a plan for getting the crops in the ground. Maybe I can get the disking finished on Monday. We should be able to have everything planted by the end of the week.

Ed stood looking at his son. He had bit his tongue several times that afternoon about cutting Cliff's hair and getting some new clothes to replace the buckskins and moccasins if he was going to come home and go to work. But, what difference did it make? If he accepted his son on his own terms, maybe he'd come back and be a willing partner. What difference did it make what clothes he wore? The choice was Cliff's, and he couldn't afford to let anything get in the way now.

Ed extended his hand. "Sounds like a plan Son."

"By the way Dad, do you still have those clippers? I haven't had much way to get to a barber shop or any money to pay one if I got there," he laughed. "And maybe you could loan me a shirt and a pair of pants, and I could catch a ride to Church with you and Mom tomorrow. Over the winter I came up with a lot of questions."

"That would be just fine son," he said with a big grin.

"See you tomorrow then, Dad."

"Night Mom. Love you both." He grabbed Etta Mae and squeezed her tightly before turning to go.

Cliff walked out the door and disappeared into the night. In the moonlight he strolled south down the lane in the center of the farm. The same time the night before, he had been engaged in a struggle that could have gone either way with Hector. Now suddenly his future had taken a hundred eighty degree turn.

91

Friends?
Kelley Farm

Cliff saw a figure climb over the fence next to the County road and walk across the freshly disked field. He shifted the Ford tractor into neutral, powered down and killed the engine as he recognized Hector approaching. He tilted the straw hat back on his head, wiped the sweat from his brow, lifted the water bag from the fender and stepped down to the freshly disked soil. Cliff uncapped the heavy canvass bag and slacked his thirst as he eyed his long time foe stop in front of him.

Neither young man spoke. A meadowlark sang in the distance. A flock of jays cackled noisily in a newly leafed cottonwood nearby.

It was nearing noon. The May sunshine was unusually warm for that early in the spring. Etta Mae would soon step out on the porch and wave her white dish rag to summon him to dinner.

Cliff slowly held the water bag out toward Hector as a gesture of good will.

Hector looked at the wet, weeping bag. He had walked from his home a half mile in the hot sun. He reached out for the bag and raised it to his lips with a nod of thanks.

He lowered the bag, wiped his lips with his sleeve and replaced the cork before handing it back to Cliff. "*Muchos gracias*. That was good Clifton."

"*De nada,* Hector. It's good to see you. About the other night..."

"Clifton, that's why I came here..." Hector said. "...I wanted to talk to you about the other night," he said quietly and looked away and then down. He looked up and into Cliff's eyes. "No hard feelings?..."

"I can handle that..."

"Let me say this please...," Hector said. "I am sorry about some things. I guess you and I could have been friends, maybe, during the years we were in school. But, I was mean to you and let the others make me feel big for it. The other night you showed me you don't have to be so big. You have to be smart too. I finally realized what my father has been telling me about your father. The size or shape of a man means nothing, it's the mind of the man that counts and how he uses it. In my mind you will be a big man too, Clifton. Maybe it is too late to be your friend, but I want to earn your respect some day."

Hector's comments and apparent sincerity left Cliff speechless. He had expected bitterness, not this. He stepped forward and clasped Hector's hand. He shook it firmly and looked Hector in the eye. "You have already earned my respect," he said. "Dad told me about your working here all last summer. You did a good job. You must have resented working here when you wanted to be working in the mountains."

"It was my own fault. As my dad said, 'I had it coming.'"

"Hector, I had to find a way to respect myself. That's why I withdrew, to learn to respect myself," Cliff said.

"I am sorry I caused you so much trouble for so long, Hector said. "I am ashamed."

"I permitted it, Hector. I should have ignored my father and waded into you the first time you looked cross eyed at me back in third grade," Cliff said. "We were a lot closer in size then too," he chuckled.

"Well that might have been a good idea, but then there were quite a few of us to take on too," Hector laughed. "But the sad thing is we would all have been so much better off to have had each other as friends."

"Thank you Hector for saying that. I would have liked having friends too."

"I think this last year you and I both learned a few things about ourselves," Hector said.

They chatted for a bit. It was not the same as two old friends visiting, but it was a beginning. There was a pause in the conversation and Hector took a deep breath and turned to face Cliff directly.

"I also came today to ask you for a favor?" Hector said.

"You came to ask me a favor?" For an instant, Cliff felt resentment rise at the thought that this boy who had caused him so much trouble for so long was there with an agenda, but he calmed himself.

"Yes, a favor. But, I will understand if you tell me to just go to hell for the way I've treated you," Hector said quickly.

"Please Hector," Cliff said. "Go ahead, ask your favor. If it is something I am able to do…"

"I came to ask if you will tutor me. I have difficulty in reading. You were always a good reader. Maybe I secretly hated you for it. It was so easy for you. Maybe that was one reason why I was mean to you. This fall you and I enter high school together. Now that you have returned, you do plan to go to high school this fall don't you?"

"Yes, I do. I'm a year behind now, but I do plan to get started."

"My father wants me to go to college when I graduate. I can't do that when I know I will fail in high school. I have shamed him enough. I don't want to fail him again. If you tutor me, maybe I won't fail high school. If you will tutor me in reading and maybe some other studies, I will help you here on the farm to pay for it."

Hector can't read? He fell through the cracks too. Possibly, I'm going to fail because of math. If I hadn't been able to read and research, I would not have survived the past year. No wonder he was frustrated.

"Hector, I'll be glad to tutor you, but I don't have the slightest idea how to go about it. I'll be glad to try. But, what about your work in the mountains?"

"I've already talked to my Uncle and my father. They said if you will do this, it is more important," Hector said.

"Then consider it done. I really could use some help this summer. If this heat continues, it could be a difficult one. When do you want to start?" Cliff asked.

"I am ready to begin."

"Tomorrow?" Cliff asked.

"Let's do it," Hector said.

"I begin irrigating at six o'clock."

"I'll be here," Hector said. "I have experience now," he laughed.

"One other thing Hector. The thing that made me mad was the teasing about Angelina Marinez. She's a nice girl and I couldn't understand what your uncle's were saying out there..."

"Don't worry about it. She's older than me and won't have anything to do with me, unfortunately. If you can get her attention, go for it. You won't have any trouble from me. I've been talking to Alicia Guzman lately," he laughed. "But you don't need to mention it to my Papa. *No la dega cabron,*" he laughed.

"Don't worry *cabron,*" Cliff said.

"I'll work out a study time for us with my dad. Next week I will begin studying with a math tutor."

They shook hands again. Hector turned and literally ran across the field back to the fence toward home as Cliff climbed back aboard the tractor and started the motor.

Cliff put the Ford into second gear and pulled the throttle lever down into the wide-open notch. As he let up on the clutch, the four-cylinder engine settled into an unwavering high-pitched monotonous droning whine as it slowly circled the field in an ever-narrowing circle.

Wow! Could Hector and me become friends? How do I feel about that? Dad and Raul have been the best of friends for as long as I can remember. If this tutoring works this summer, maybe it could happen. We have more to gain than lose. That could give me three friends already. Moonbeam settled in as if she has been at the house all along. Mom and Dad love her already. We have to do something about the roaming all night. Maggie has stayed around. Dad thinks I should cage him, or he will leave. I can't do that. He is waiting for me every time I step out of the house. It's nesting time though. I think he'll find a cute little señorita magpie and start courting one of these days. Speaking of señorita, I'm glad Mom talked me into calling Angelina last night. I can hardly believe she invited me to come over Sunday afternoon. I wonder if she would teach me to play the guitar.

Cliff felt happy. By opening his mouth slightly and puffing his cheeks in and out Cliff could make the droning tractor whine change into what sounded to him like a chorus of voices in his head. He began patting his hands on the steering wheel in time to the chorus and his mind converted the sound to drum beats. A cloud of dust raised by the disk behind the tractor drifted over the field. Half the time he drove away from it, the other half of the time, he drove through it and the dust enveloped the tractor and driver. Through clinched eyes Cliff thought he caught faint glimpses of the Indian hunter friend of his dreams slowly stepping, dipping his shoulder, turning, stepping, dipping his other shoulder, and turning the other way as he chanted in Ancient Puebloan… *"You used the time wisely. Well done …"* The tractor passed out of the dust cloud into the sunshine once again. Cliff looked back over his shoulder. A dust devil began to form and the dust cloud began to condense into a tall undulating lazily twirling mass. Cliff stepped on the clutch and moved the gearshift into neutral. He left the engine running wide open and watched the twirling mass as it slowly snaked its way across the field. In the center of the mass, he seemed to see his friend slowly stepping, dipping, turning, stepping, dipping, and turning the other way until the dust devil dissipated…

Acknowledgements

Two groups of writers encouraged this project over several years. It began with a group who met on Monday afternoons at Silver Lakes RV Resort at Naples Florida in 2004. A friendly group of us met to share under the heading of Writing for Fun. This novel began as a series of short stories shared there.

A similar weekly seminar at the Senior Center in Bend, Oregon produced more short stories about the ruin. With encouragement from the group, short stories became chapters and then a rough draft.

That group of friends, a cadre of well educated, well travelled individuals, several old enough to be my parents paused in their quest to write their family histories to give suggestions, and ask questions, and make sage comments. Their push was instrumental in keeping the project on track to the finish.

A good friend, Colleague and mentor for most of my teaching career at Springfield High School, Conrad Roemer, Social Studies Teacher, read the manuscript the year before the last major rewrite. He offered insightful observations and suggestions throughout that helped to either keep me on track or offer a "what if?"

I would like to acknowledge my brother Darrel, the painter and geographer, for the description of the awesome view of the Four Corners as seen through Clifton's eyes.

~~~

I acknowledge my wife and soul mate Lora. I grew up in a family where "spare the rod and spoil the child" was a common utterance. Lora was a product of a different philosophy. She recognized that the chain of child abuse in the name of discipline must be broken.

My wife knew there was a better way, and I knew she meant it when she said our children would not be ruled by "the rod."

Because of her, the chain was broken. Our children were "spared the rod" and we have been pleased to observe the loving, appropriate, discipline in their homes. Theirs are loving children, who are playful, respectful, artistic, have exemplary academic records are eager athletes and budding young writers and musicians.

~~~

I am indebted to Stephan Zacharias who at the time I observed him tanning deer hides was a Living History-Dramatic Performer and Interpreter at the High Desert Museum in Bend Oregon. He is now, at the time of this writing, an actor/performer at Colonial Williamsburg, Williamsburg, Virginia. I volunteered at the Museum between 2006-2008 while Stephan worked there. During that time Stephan tanned deer hides, played the roles of many of our western pioneers and mountain men. He answered my questions, and I observed him and the others when there were fur trader encampments, fire starting, hide scraping, weapons demonstrations, and Dutch oven cooking competitions. Many of the wilderness skills that Cliff uses in this book came from the information imparted from Stephan and his friends at the High Desert Museum during those two years.

I also am indebted to Shey Hyatt Collections Registrar of the High Desert Museum and Tracy Johnson the head of the Collections at the High Desert Museum for giving me access to the basket collection, letting me photograph many of the baskets in the collection and explaining the fibers used in their construction. In addition, I am indebted to Pat Courtney Gold, Fiber Artist in basketry for her workshops at the museum and the knowledge she shared there. For insight into basketry, I am particularly indebted to Jean Stark of Sisters, Oregon who term after term at Central Oregon Community College greets those adult education students who would turn pine needles into works of arts. Her gentle teaching leads them through the basic steps, concepts, materials and simple techniques. Seven hours later a shape has evolved into various degrees of basket around the table. In the middle of the table are examples of Jean's work showing possibilities after one has mastered the craft: beautiful works of art from clusters of ponderosa pine needles. The day ebbs and flows. Questions are asked and answered accompanied by patient demonstration. The group falls into quiet meditation as fingers pull artificial sinew through the bundles of needles with steel darning needles, building row upon row. During those lulls, Jean, the storyteller begins commenting on the role of baskets in Native American culture and how the members of the tribe sat around the campfire during the winter, just as her group are in late January, using the materials gathered in the summer, to make either trade goods, or household goods needed for everyday living. I have to admit my basket didn't resemble much of a basket, but it did give me insight into what Cliff would have faced in the daunting task of learning a craft like basket making on his own, that he would need to survive, with only the rude sketches in his journal to go by.

~~~

The area between Cortez and Summit Lake where this story takes place is much changed since 1954. The 160 are farms are now smaller parcels providing housing for a growing population in Montezuma County. It is no longer a "wilderness area" where a boy Like Clifton can roam at will. Fences and lanes now sport "no tresspassing" signs throughout the area where he roamed and hunted. The rim of the canyon that was the basis for the fictional Martinez Canyon now provides scenic vistas for homesites.

Since then, organizations such as Outward Bound, a Non-profit organization with five locations in the United States have stepped in to provide supervised programs however. Their 28 day programs emphasize personal growth through experience and challenge in the wilderness. On
~~~

a more long term basis is the Big Brother Big Sister program where a boy or girl Cliff's age can bond with an adult like George and receive guidance and friendship that is adjunct to the parental guidance.

Fortunately, for young men and women Cliff's age, contemporary progressive school systems have a no tolerance system in place for dealing with bullying. Children are supervised and at the first signs of bullying, an adult steps in. Comments from parents that "boys will be boys" are not tolerated, period! The victims are not at fault because they are of a body shape that doesn't match the stereotype in advertising, or if they are intellectually challenged. A quiet girl or boy has the right to be quiet. A scholarly student has the same right to excel in the classroom as the athlete has the right to excel on the playing field. Children of every racial and religious background have a right to be left alone, to make friends, and to be at peace.

According to Geno Dusan, Assistant Principal at LaPine Middle School, LaPine, Oregon a part of the Bend-LaPine School District, a guiding principal in the fight against bullying and harassment in schools is to teach students to be "Respectful, Safe, Responsible".

Corporal punishment was a common disciplinary practice in 1954 at the time of this story. A paddle resided in most teachers' desks. Some forward-looking schools required the paddling be done in the Principal's office. Other schools encouraged the individual classroom teacher to take whatever means to maintain order. In the many one or two room rural schools of the time how discipline was carried out was up the teacher.

Corporal punishment administered at school was re-enforced at home.

In 2008 corporal punishment was still practiced in some form in public schools in 20 states. Thirty states have banned it. Of those Utah and Ohio permit paddling with restrictions depending on parental approval. Most of the corporal punishment bans began in the mid 1980s through the early 1990s. Massachusetts led the way by banning corporal punishment in public schools in 1971.

Bullying is perhaps as old as the human race. Barnyard animals practice it. Chickens will for no apparent reason begin picking at one of their flock, frequently picking it to death once blood is drawn.

Bullying is a problem in schools, public and private, rich and poor, large and small suburban and urban.

There are many tragic consequences for the victim of bullying from loss of self-esteem to the extreme; suicide or taking the life/lives of the bully/bullies frequently with collateral damage.

~~~

This is a work of fiction.

The geography of the southwest corner of Colorado is real. Summit Ridge, Mesa Verde, Ute Mountain, The La Plata Mountains, Cortez, Mancos, Dolores, the farm on Summit Ridge, Lakeview School, Martinez Can-
~~~

yon, The Big Ancient Puebloan Ruin, the bee tree next to it, all existed in the world of 1954 and are in the geographic positions as described in the story.

The Ancestral Puebloans in this story are now commonly called the Anasazi. I never heard the term Anasazi in all those boyhood visits to Mesa Verde. The rangers referred to the Cliff Dwelling people as the Ancestral Puebloans and mostly still do in their literature.

The families and characters are fictitious and are not meant to represent any one who lived on the Ridge at that time.

The events described in 1954 are fictitious, but could have happened. The bullying and corporal punishment was real. If anything the amount of real conflict existing at the one room school, is downplayed in this story. After I graduated, my brother then a fifth grader and sister in third grade, lasted until midyear. My bullies joined theirs and our parents removed them from the school and drove them to the two room school in the Valley. The next year I was old enough to drive and could provide them transportation.

The contemporary portion of this book is based on the hours and days of memories burned into my mind the morning of May 21, 1998. I have tried to recreate what my students and I and the school where I taught went through during the first few hours of that morning.

A good friend and colleague Faith Kinkel attended my retirement party on May 20, 1998 in Springfield, Oregon. The next morning, during first period classes at Springfield High School, we received word that an unknown gunman had walked into the cafeteria at Thurston High School, our sister school, and opened fire on his classmates, killing two and wounding 25.

Faith Kinkel had not reported to school that morning. When the assailant was identified as Kip Kinkel, police were immediately dispatched to the Kinkel home where they found both Faith and Bill her retired teacher husband murdered.

Kip had been in counseling before the shooting, but his parents had thought he was improving. Although it wasn't reported in the media at the time, Faith had complained to friends at school that Kip had been bullied by classmates in middle school. It had been better when he started high school, but during the winter, it had started up again.

Kip did not stand trial, but plead guilty three days before jury selection so, details of his mental condition and possible abuse at school never came out in court.

A year later Eric Harris and Dylan Klebold walked into Columbine High School in Jefferson County Colorado and shot 12 students and one teacher and wounded 24 others. In investigations following that massacre bullying immediately rose to the forefront.

In the two years leading up to the Thurston High School shooting there were three other school shootings, two of those involved students who had been "relentlessly" or "frequently" bullied.

In 1996 Barry Loukaitis who claimed to have been the victim of "relentless bullying" killed a teacher, two students and wounded one other student at Frontier Junior High School in Moses Lake, Washington.

In 1997 Michael Carneal killed three students and wounded five more at Heath High School, West Paducah, Kentucky. He was said to have been a "B" student with no discipline problems who was "frequently bullied".

A compilation of recent school shootings list bullying as a contributing factor.

Seung-Hui Cho claimed bullying because of his diction as one of the reasons for his actions April 16, 2007 at Virginia Tech, Blacksburg, Virginia where he killed 32 and wounded 25.

More frequently, bullied students commit suicide.

Dan Barry, March 27, 2008, chronicled a typical situation in The New York Times news story Why do they bully young Billy Wolfe. Billy was a student at Fayetteville, Arkansas who became a target of bullies at age 12 and continued to suffer at age 16. More often than not, he rather than his tormentors, was punished by school officials for being bullied. In March of 2008 his parents finally, as an act of desperation, sued one of the bullies and were considering other lawsuits and a suit against the school district. They were not after money but to make the point that "School children deserve to feel safe."

Mental health expert Dr. Charles Ralston Psychiatrist, Emory University Medical School reported on CNNhealth.com March 31, 2009 that schoolyard bullying can cause victims to display the same behaviors as those suffering from PTSD (Post-traumatic stress disorder).

Kenneth Fenter, January 2010